MIDST TOIL
AND
TRIBULATION

MIDST TOIL AND TRIBULATION

✦

DAVID WEBER

TOR®

A TOM DOHERTY ASSOCIATES BOOK
NEW YORK

MIDST TOIL AND TRIBULATION

Copyright © 2012 by David Weber

A Tor Book
Published by Tom Doherty Associates, LLC
175 Fifth Avenue
New York, NY 10010

www.tor-forge.com

Tor® is a registered trademark of Tom Doherty Associates, LLC.

Library of Congress Cataloging-in-Publication Data

Weber, David, 1952–
    Midst toil and tribulation / David Weber. — 1st ed.
        p. cm.
    "A Tom Doherty Associates book."
    ISBN 978-0-7653-2155-8 (hardcover)
    ISBN 978-1-4299-4468-7 (e-book)
    I. Title.
    PS3573.E217M53 2012
    813'.54—dc23
                                                2012024401

First Edition: September 2012

Printed in the United States of America

0 9 8 7 6 5 4 3 2 1

As always, for Sharon, just for being you.
I love you, babe.

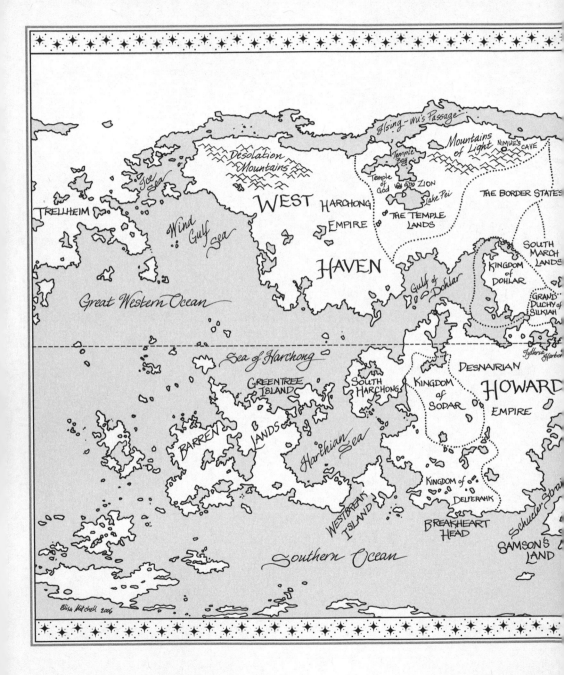

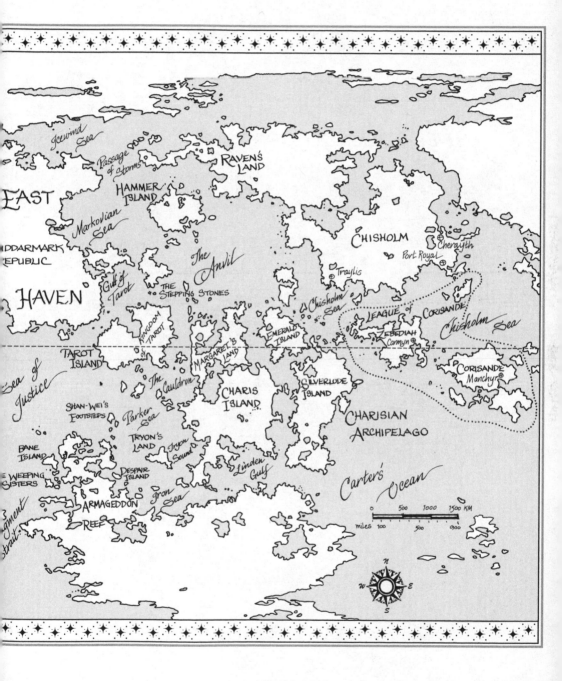

Icewind Sea

Passage of Storms

IRON
CAPE

ROLLINGS
HEAD

SELEKAR
POINT

Markovian Sea

WHEIRSTROM
MOUNTAIN

BLACK HILL MOUNTAINS

Rollings
Province

Province

ORTHLAND GAP

Midhold Province

vince

HAMMER IS.

Grayback
Lake

Old
Province

Chykag

CRAGNOR
POINT

Siddar
City

North Bedard Bay

CAPE
LANGHORNE

iddar
City

Bedard Bay

Forshym

	Held for the Protector
	Temple Loyalist
	Disputed

Dytrohm

Myrloh

Markan Province

Transhur Province

Province

Fallos Channel

Duchy of
Fallos

STAL LAKE
OUNTAINS

Detrych

Mantorah
Bay

Transhar Bay

Mantorah

Southguard
Province

Four Square

Green Plain

Windmoor
Sound

Gulf of Tarot

Prohspyr

Windmoor Province

Beltyr

NORTH
HEAD

Windtyn

Duchy of Holme

Malitar
Province

Tarot
Sound

Clahnyr

Thol
Bay

Malitar
Sound

KINGDOM OF TAROT

Clanhyr Bay

Tarot Channel

nce

Eralth Bay

Duchy of Thol

Duchy
of Tranjyr

SEKYR IS.

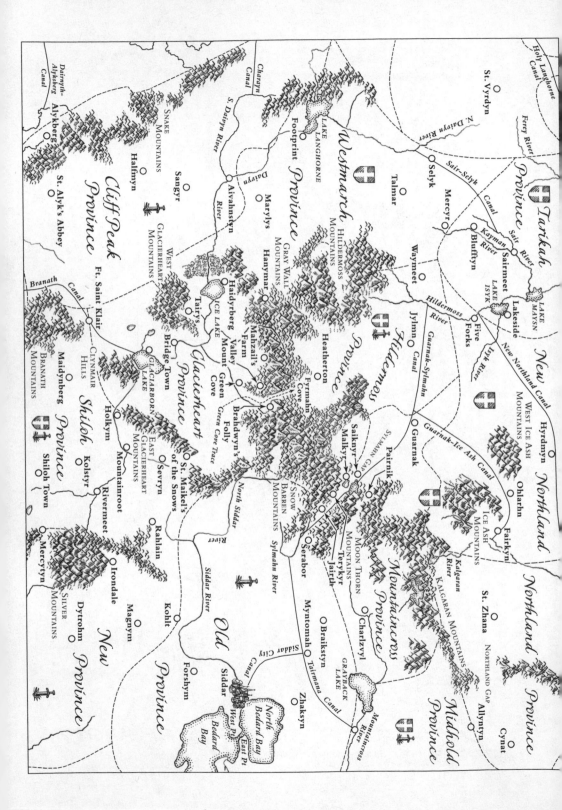

MARCH
YEAR OF GOD 896

Snow veils hung in the clear, icy air, dancing on the knife-edged wind that swirled across the snowpack, and the highest peaks, towering as much as a mile higher than his present position, cast blue shadows across the snow.

It looked firm and inviting to the unwary eye, that snowpack, but Wahlys Mahkhom had been born and raised in the Gray Walls. He knew better, and his eyes were hard and full of hate behind his smoked-glass snow goggles as his belly snarled resentfully. Accustomed as he was to winter weather even here in the Gray Walls, and despite his fur-trimmed parka and heavy mittens, he felt the ice settling into his bones and muscles. It needed only a momentary carelessness for a man to freeze to death in these mountains in winter, even at the best of times, and these were far from the best of times. The Glacierheart winter burned energy like one of Shan-wei's own demons, and food was scarcer than Mahkhom could ever remember. Glacierheart's high, stony mountainsides and rocky fields had never yielded bountiful crops, yet there'd always been at least something in the storehouses to be eked out by hunters like Mahkhom. But not this year. This year the storehouses had been burned—first by one side, then by the other in retaliation—and the fields, such as they were, were buried beneath the deepest, bitterest snow anyone could remember. It was as if God Himself was determined to punish innocent and guilty alike, and there were times—more times than he liked to admit—when Wahlys Mahkhom wondered if there would be anyone left alive to plant the next year's crops.

His teeth wanted to chatter like some lowland dancer's castanets, and he dragged the thick scarf his mother had knitted years ago higher. He laid the extra layer of insulation across the snow mask covering his face, and the hatred in his eyes turned harder and far, far colder than the winter about him as he touched that scarf and with it the memory of why his mother would never knit another.

He raised his head cautiously, looking critically about himself once more. But his companions were as mountain-wise as he was. They were just as well hidden under the white canopies of the sheets they'd brought with them, and he bared those edge-of-chattering teeth in hard, vengeful satisfaction. The snowshoe trek to their positions had been exhausting, especially for men who'd cut themselves dangerously short on rations for the trip. They knew better than that, of course, but how did a man take the food he really needed with him when he looked into the eyes of the starving child who would have to go without if he did? That was a question Wahlys Mahkhom couldn't answer—not yet, at any rate—and he never wanted to be able to.

He settled back down, nestling into his hole in the snow, using the snow itself for insulation, watching the trail that crept through the mountains below him like a broken-backed serpent. They'd waited patiently for an entire day and a half, but if the target they anticipated failed to arrive soon, they'd be forced to abandon the mission. The thought woke a slow, savage furnace of fury within him to counterpoint the mountains' icy cold, yet he made himself face it. He'd seen hate-fired determination and obstinacy kill too many men this bitter winter, and he refused to die stupidly. Not when he had so many men still to kill.

He didn't know exactly what the temperature was, although Safehold had remarkably accurate thermometers, a gift of the archangels who'd created Mahkhom's world. He didn't have to know exactly. Nor did he have to know he was nine thousand feet above sea level on a planet with an axial inclination eleven degrees greater and an average temperature seven degrees lower than a world called Earth, of which he had never heard. All he had to know was that a few moments' carelessness would be enough to—

His thoughts froze as a flicker of movement caught his eye. He watched, scarcely daring to breathe, as the flicker repeated itself. It was far away, hard to make out in the dimness of the steep-walled pass, but all the fury and anger within him had distilled itself suddenly into a still, calm watchfulness, focused and far colder than the mountains about him.

The movement drew closer, resolving itself into a long line of white-clad men, slogging along the trail on snowshoes like the ones buried beside Mahkhom's hole in the snow. Half of them were bowed under heavy packs, and no less than six sleds drawn by snow lizards accompanied them. Mahkhom's eyes glittered with satisfaction as he saw those sleds and realized their information had been accurate after all.

He didn't bother to look around for the other men buried in the snow about him, or for the other men hidden in the dense stands of evergreens half a mile farther down that icy trail from his icy perch. He knew where they were, knew they were as ready and watchful as he himself. The careless ones, the rash ones, were already dead; those who remained had added hard-learned lessons to the hunter's and trapper's skills they'd already possessed. And like Mahkhom himself, his companions had too much killing to do to let themselves die foolishly.

No Glacierheart miner or trapper could afford one of the expensive

Lowlander firearms. Even if they could have afforded the weapons themselves, powder and ball came dear. For that matter, even a steel-bowed arbalest was hideously expensive, over two full months' income for a master coal
miner, but a properly maintained arbalest lasted for generations. Mahkhom
had inherited his from his father, and his father from his father, and a man
could always make the ammunition he needed. Now he rolled over onto his
back under his concealing sheet. He removed his over-mittens and braced
the steel bow stave against his feet while his gloved hands cranked the windlass. He took his time, for there was no rush. It would take those men and
those snow lizards the better part of a quarter hour to reach the designated
point, and the mountain air was crystal clear. Better to take the time to span
the weapon this way, however awkward it might be, then to risk skylining
himself and warning his enemies of their peril.

He finished cranking, made sure the string was securely latched over
the pawl, and detached the windlass. Then he rolled back over, setting a
square-headed quarrel on the string. He brought the arbalest into position,
gazing through the ring sight, watching and waiting, his heart as cold as the
wind, while those marching figures crept closer and closer.

For a moment, far below the surface of his thoughts, a bit of the man
he'd been only three or four months earlier stared aghast at what was about
to happen here on this high, icy mountain trail. That tiny fragment of the
Wahlys Mahkhom who still had a family knew that many of those men had
families, as well. It knew those families were as desperate for the food on
those lizard-drawn sleds as the families he'd left huddling around fires in
the crudely built cabins and huts where they'd taken shelter when their villages were burned about their ears. It knew about the starvation, and the sickness, and the death that would stalk other women and other children when
this day's work was done. But none of the rest of him listened to that tiny,
lost fragment, for it had work to do.

The center of that marching column of men reached the base of the
single pine, standing alone and isolated as a perfect landmark, and under the
ice- and frost-clotted snow mask protecting his face, Mahkhom's smile was
the snarl of a hunting slash lizard. He waited a single heartbeat longer, and
then his hands squeezed the trigger and his arbalest spat a sunlight-gilded
sliver of death through that crystal mountain air.

Merlin Athrawes sat silently in his darkened chamber, eyes closed as he contemplated images only he could see. He really ought to have been "asleep," taking the nightly downtime Emperor Cayleb had mandated, but he'd been following Wahlys Mahkhom's group of guerrillas through Owl's SNARCs for over a five-day, and the distant AI had been instructed to wake him when the moment came.

Now he watched bleakly as the arbalests sent their deadly quarrels hissing into the totally surprised supply convoy.

They should've been more cautious, he thought grimly. *It's not like both sides haven't had plenty of experience murdering each other by now.*

But they hadn't been, and now the men struggling to deliver the food their families needed to survive screamed as steel-headed shafts ripped into them. Steaming scarlet stained the snow, voices shouted frantic orders and useless warnings, the men trapped on the trail tried to find some shred of shelter, tried to muster some sort of defense, and another volley of bolts ripped into them from the other side of the narrow valley. They tried desperately to turn the sleds, tried to break back the way they'd come, but a trio of quarrels slammed into the rearmost snow lizard. It collapsed, screaming and snarling and snapping at its wounds, and the trail was too narrow. No one could get past the thrashing, wounded creature, and even as they discovered that, the other jaw of the ambush—the men hidden in the evergreens where the valley floor widened, armed with swords and axes and miner's picks—flung themselves upon the stunned and decimated convoy.

It didn't last long. That was the sole mercy. No one was taking prisoners any longer—not in Glacierheart, not on its frontier with Hildermoss. Caring properly for one's own wounded was close enough to impossible under the brutal, broken-backed circumstances; no one had the resources to waste on the enemy's wounded . . . even if anyone had been willing to spare an enemy's life. But at least Mahkhom's band wasn't as far gone as some of the guerrillas stalking one another through the nightmare which had once been the Republic of Siddarmark. They spared no one, but the death they meted out was clean and quick, without the torture and mutilation which had become the norm for all too many on both sides of the bitter hatred which had ripped the Republic apart.

Only three of the attackers were wounded, just one of them seriously, and they stripped the dead with quick, callous efficiency. The wounded snow lizard was dispatched with a cut throat, and half a dozen raiders harnessed themselves to the heavy sled. Others shouldered packs taken from the dead men whose naked corpses littered the snow, and then they were gone, slogging off down the trail to the point at which they could break away towards their own heavily guarded mountain fastness.

The bodies behind them were already beginning to freeze in the bitter cold.

As he watched the attackers hurrying off, Merlin felt unclean as he realized he didn't feel the horror those freezing bodies ought to have evoked in him. He felt bitter, helpless regret as he thought about the women and children who would never see fathers or sons or brothers again, and who would succumb, quickly or slowly, to malnutrition and the icy cold of the winter mountains. And he felt a blazing anger at the man who was truly responsible for what had happened not just here in this single mountain valley but throughout the entire Republic in the months since Zhaspahr Clyntahn's Sword of Schueler had been launched at Siddarmark's throat. Yet as he gazed down through the SNARCs at the corpses stiffening in the snow, he could not forget, try as he might, that they were the corpses of Temple Loyalists. The bodies of men who had reaped the savage harvest of their own sowing.

And buried within the rage he felt at the religious fanatics who'd let themselves be used as Clyntahn's weapon—who'd torched food supplies, burned villages, massacred families on the mere suspicion they might harbor Reformist sympathies—was his fury at himself. Cayleb and Sharleyan might regret all too many of the things they'd been called upon to do to resist the Group of Four's tyranny, but they weren't the ones who'd touched off the cataclysm of religious war on a planetary scale. No, that had been the doing of Merlin Athrawes, who wasn't even human. Who was the cybernetic avatar of the memories of a young woman almost a thousand years dead. Someone without a single drop of real blood in his veins, immune to the starvation and the cold claiming so many lives in the Siddarmarkian mountains this terrible winter.

And worst of all, it had been the doing of someone who'd known exactly how ugly, how horrible, religious warfare—the most dreadful, all-consuming warfare—could be. As he looked at those bodies, Merlin knew he could never pretend he hadn't known this was exactly where any religious war must lead. That hating, intolerant men would find in religion and the name of God the excuse to commit the most brutal, barbaric acts they could imagine and congratulate themselves upon their saintliness even as they did. And that when that happened, men like Wahlys Mahkhom, who'd come home from a mountain hunting expedition to find his village burned to the ground by Clyntahn's followers and his entire family dead, would find the counter-hatred to be just as brutal, just as merciless, and call their vengeance justice. And perhaps the most hellish thing of all was that it was impossible to blame Mahkhom for reacting just that way. What else could any sane person expect from a man who'd found his mother hacked to death? Who'd buried his three children, the eldest of them less than six years old, and held his wife's raped and mutilated body in his arms while he sobbed out the wreckage of a heart which would never heal? Indeed, it was a miracle he and his followers had given their enemies clean deaths, and all too many other Reformists wouldn't have. They would have given their foes exactly what their foes had given them, and if along the way they caught some innocent who was simply trying to survive in the chaos and the cruelty and despair, that was just the way it was.

It's feeding on itself, he thought, shutting away the image of those naked bodies at last. *Atrocity leads to counter-atrocity, and men who can't avenge themselves on the ones who murdered their loves avenge themselves on anyone they can catch. And that creates still more hatred, still more thirst for vengeance, and the cycle goes right on building.*

Merlin Athrawes was a PICA, a creature of alloys and mollycircs, of fiber optics and electrons, not flesh and blood. He was no longer subject to the biochemistry of humanity, no longer captive to adrenaline and the other physiological manifestations of anger and fight-or-flight evolutionary programming. And none of that mattered one whit as he confronted the hatred burning inside him and his inability to penetrate the far-off temple in the city of Zion.

If I could only see what's happening there, he thought with an edge of despair. *If I could only know what they're doing, what they're thinking . . . planning. None of us saw this coming in time to warn Stohnar—not about anything he hadn't already picked up on his own, at any rate. But we should've seen it coming. We ought to've known what someone like Clyntahn would be thinking, and God knows we've had proof enough of the lengths to which he's willing to go!*

In many ways, his ability—his and his allies'—to see so much only intensified and honed his frustration at being denied access to Zion. They had more information than they could possibly use, especially when they couldn't let anyone else suspect how that information had come into their possession, yet they couldn't peer into the one spot on the entire planet where they most urgently needed to see.

But it wasn't *visions* of Zion Merlin Athrawes truly wanted, and he knew it. What he wanted was to bring Zhaspahr Clyntahn and his fellows into his own reach for one, fleeting moment, and he wanted it with an intensity he knew had come to border all too nearly upon madness. He'd found himself thinking about Commodore Pei more and more frequently as the brutal winter of western Siddarmark grew steadily more and more savage. The Commodore had walked into Eric Langhorne's headquarters with a vest-pocket nuke; Merlin Athrawes could easily have carried a multimegaton city-burner into Zion and destroyed not simply the Group of Four but the entire Temple in a single cataclysmic blast. The death toll would have been hideous, but could it possibly be worse than what he was watching happen inch by agonizing inch in Siddarmark? Than the deaths this war had already cost Charis and its allies? Than the deaths it would cost in the months and years ahead?

And would it not be worth it to cleanse himself of the blood guilt for starting it by ending his life—if life it truly was—like the biblical Samson, bringing down his enemies in his own destruction?

Oh, stop it! he told himself harshly. *You know it was only a matter of time before that lunatic Clyntahn would've unleashed the Inquisition on Charis even without your intervention. And do you really think for a moment he would ever have stopped again, once he'd tasted that much blood? Of course he wouldn't have! You may be partly—even largely—to blame for where and when the bloodletting started, but you aren't responsible for what was already driving it. And without your interference, Clyntahn would already've won.*

It was true, and in his saner moments—the moments when he didn't sit in a darkened room watching the carnage, tasting the hate behind it—he knew it was true. Just as he knew the Church had to be destroyed if humanity was going to survive its inevitable second meeting with the genocidal Gbaba. But truth . . . truth was cold and bitter bread, laced with arsenic and poisoned with guilt, at times like this.

That's enough, a voice which sounded remarkably like Sharleyan Ahrmahk's said in the back of his electronic brain. *That's enough. You've seen what you told Owl to show you. Don't sit here and beat yourself to death over things you can't change, anyway. Besides, Cayleb's just likely to check with Owl and find out you stayed up late . . . again.*

Despite himself, his lips twitched and a spurt of gentle amusement flowed through his rage, blunting the sharp edges of his self-hatred, as he pictured Cayleb Ahrmahk's reaction if he did discover Merlin's infraction. It wasn't as if Cayleb or Sharleyan thought for a moment that even an emperor's wrath could make any impression on Merlin Athrawes if he chose to ignore it, but that wasn't the reason Cayleb had issued his edict, nor was it the reason he would have pitched a truly imperial tantrum over its violation. No, he would have berated Merlin with every . . . colorful phrase he could come up with because he knew how much Merlin needed that. How much the PICA "*seijin* warrior" of myth and legend needed to be treated as if he truly were still a human being.

And perhaps—who knew?—Merlin truly was still human on some elemental level that went beyond fleshly envelopes and heartbeats and blood. Perhaps he wasn't, too. Perhaps in the end it didn't matter how much blood guilt he took upon his soul because perhaps Maikel Staynair was wrong. Perhaps Nimue Alban truly was as dead as the Terran Federation—perhaps Merlin Athrawes truly was no more than an electronic echo with no soul to lose.

There were times he hoped that wasn't so, and other times—when he thought of blood and pain, of thin-faced, starving children shivering in mountain snow—when he prayed it was.

My, you are feeling morbid tonight, aren't you? he asked himself tartly. *Maybe Cayleb's even righter than you thought to insist you get that downtime of his. And maybe you need to get up in the morning and drop by the imperial nursery to hug that goddaughter of yours and remember what this is all really about.*

He smiled more naturally, dreams of guilt and bloodshed softened by the memory of that laughing, wiggling small body in his arms like God's own promise the future would, indeed, somehow be worth its cost in the fullness of time.

And it will, he thought softly, prepping the commands which would switch him to standby mode. *When you look down at that little girl and realize why you're doing all this—realize how much you love her—you know it will.*

.III.
The Temple,
City of Zion,
The Temple Lands

I hope you still think this was worth it, Zhaspahr," Vicar Rhobair Duchairn said grimly, looking across the conference table at the jowly Grand Inquisitor.

Zhaspahr Clyntahn looked back with a face of bland, expressionless iron, and the Church of God Awaiting's treasurer managed—somehow—not to snarl. It wasn't easy, given the reports pouring in from Siddarmark, and he knew as surely as he was sitting there that the reports they were receiving *understated* the destruction and death.

"I don't understand why you seem to think all this is somehow my fault," Clyntahn said in a flat voice. "I'm not the one who decided when and where it was going to happen—you can thank that bastard Stohnar for that!"

Duchairn's lips parted but he stopped the fatal words before they emerged. He couldn't do much about the contempt and anger in his eyes, but at least he managed to refrain from what he truly wanted to say.

"Forgive me if I seem a bit obtuse," he said instead, "but all the reports I've seen—including Archbishop Wyllym's—seem to indicate the Inquisition is leading the . . . resistance to the Lord Protector. And"—his eyes swiveled to Allayn Maigwair, the Temple's captain general—"that somehow quite a few Temple Guard 'advisors' wound up assigned to the men who launched this 'spontaneous uprising.' Under the circumstances, I'm sure you can understand why it might seem to me you were a bit more directly involved in events there than anyone else in this council chamber."

"Of course I was." Clyntahn's lip curled disdainfully. "I'm Mother Church's Grand Inquisitor, Rhobair! As such, I'm personally answerable to the Archangels and to God Himself for her safety. I didn't want to create this situation in Siddarmark. You and Zhasyn made your . . . reasoning for keeping the traitorous bastards' economy intact amply clear, and however little I liked your logic, I couldn't really dispute it. But that didn't absolve me from my responsibility—mine and my inquisitors'—to watch Stohnar and his cronies. If it came down to a choice between making sure marks continued to flow into the Treasury and letting the entire Republic fall into the hands of Shan-wei and those fucking Charisian heretics, there was only one decision I could make, and I'm not about to apologize for having made it when my hand was forced!"

"Forced?" Zahmsyn Trynair, the Church's chancellor was obviously unhappy to be siding even partially with Duchairn, but he arched his eyebrows at Clyntahn. "Forgive me, Zhaspahr, but while you may not have intended for events to take the course they did, there seems little doubt that your 'Sword of Schueler' got out of hand and initiated the violent confrontation."

"I've told you and told you," Clyntahn shot back with an air of dangerous, put-upon patience. "If I was going to have a weapon ready to hand when I needed it, I could hardly wait to start sharpening the blade until after Stohnar had already struck, could I? Obviously a certain degree of preparation was necessary if the true sons of Mother Church were to be organized and ready to move when they were most sorely required. Yes, it's entirely possible a few of my inquisitors honed the Sword to a keener edge than I'd intended. And I won't pretend I wasn't more than a little taken aback by the . . . enthusiasm with which Mother Church's children sprang to her defense. But the truth is that it's a good thing Wyllym and I *had* started making preparations, and the proof is right there in the reports before you."

He jabbed a thick forefinger at the folders on the conference table. Duchairn had already forced himself to read the contents fully and completely, and he wondered what would have happened to Mother Church long since if his Treasury reports had borne so little resemblance to the truth. There were mountains of facts in those reports—facts which he had no doubt at all were true. But the very best way to lie was to assemble carefully chosen "truths" into the mask you wanted reality to wear, and Wyllym Rayno, the Archbishop of Chiang-wu, was a master at doing just that.

It's to be hoped he does at least a little better job of telling Zhaspahr *the truth,* Duchairn thought bitterly. *Or is it? For that matter, could Zhaspahr even* recognize *the truth if someone dared to tell it to him these days?!*

"You've got the figures, Zhasyn," Clyntahn went on sharply. "Those bastards in Siddar City were buying three times as many rifles as they told us they were! Just who in Shan-wei d'you think they were stockpiling them against? Could it possibly have been the people—us, Mother Church—Stohnar was *lying* to about the numbers he was buying? I don't know about you, but I can't think of any other reason for him to hide them from us!"

The Grand Inquisitor glared at Trynair, and the chancellor glanced uneasily at the treasurer from the corner of one eye. Duchairn could see what little backbone Trynair might still possess oozing out of him, but there wasn't a great deal he could do about that. Especially not when he strongly suspected that even though Rayno had inflated the figures grossly, Stohnar *had* been stockpiling weapons as quietly and secretly as he could.

God knows I would've been stockpiling them like mad if I'd known Zhaspahr Clyntahn had decided it was only a matter of when—not if—he was going to bring my entire Republic down in fire and blood!

"And when you add that to the way Stohnar, Maidyn, and Parkair've been coddling and protecting the Shan-wei-damned 'Reformists'—not to mention entire communities of Charisians!—throughout the Republic, it's obvious what they had in mind. As soon as they thought they had enough rifles for their immediate security, they were going to openly invite Charis into an alliance. Can you imagine what kind of reward they might've demanded from Cayleb and Sharleyan for giving them a foothold here on the mainland itself? Not to mention selling the entire Siddarmarkian army into their possession? Langhorne, Zahmsyn! We'd have had Charisian armies pouring across the Border States and into the Temple Lands themselves by summer, and you know it!"

The Grand Inquisitor's fire was directed at Trynair, but no one doubted its true target was Duchairn. The chancellor wilted visibly, and Duchairn knew the image of Siddarmarkian armies sweeping across the Border States had been one of Trynair's darkest nightmares—however little chance there'd been of its ever actually happening—for years. The thought of those same armies equipped with Charisian weapons, allied to the monarchs who'd sworn to destroy the Group of Four forever, had to be the most terrifying thing the chancellor could imagine . . . short of finding himself face-to-face with the Inquisition as Clyntahn's *other* enemies had, at any rate.

"Father Zohannes and Father Saimyn had reports from reliable sources that the army was supposed to conduct an 'exercise' closing the frontier with the Border States as soon as the first snows fell," Clyntahn continued. "An '*exercise!*'" He sneered and curled his lip. "One that would've just happened to put all of those rifles he wasn't telling us he had on the frontier right across the shortest path from Zion to Siddar City . . . or from Siddar City to *Zion*. Obviously they had no choice but to act when they did, whether it was what any of us wanted or not!"

Duchairn's jaws ached from the pressure it took to keep his teeth closed on what he really wanted to say. Of course Zohannes Pahtkovair and Saimyn Airnhart had reported Stohnar intended to seal his borders! They were Clyntahn's creatures, and they'd report whatever he needed them to!

"No one could regret the loss of life more than I do," Clyntahn said piously. "It's not the fault of Mother Church, however—it's the fault of her enemies. We had no choice but to act. If we'd hesitated for so much as five-day or two, Langhorne only knows how much worse it could've been! And if you expect me to shed any tears over what happened to heretics, blasphemers, and traitors or their lackeys, you'll be a long time waiting, Zhasyn!" He slammed one beefy hand on the tabletop. "They brought whatever happened to them on themselves, and however bad that might have been in this world, it was only a foretaste of what awaits them in the next!"

He glared around the chamber, nostrils flared, eyes flashing, and Duchairn marveled once again at the man's ability to believe whatever he needed to believe at any given moment. Yet surely he had to realize he was lying this time . . . didn't he? How could someone manipulate, twist, and pervert the truth that thoroughly if he didn't know, somewhere deep inside, what the truth actually was? Or did he simply rely on his subordinates to tell him whatever "truth" he needed to know to suit his requirements?

The treasurer's stomach twisted with familiar nausea as he thought about the other reports, the ones Clyntahn hadn't had time to "adjust." The ones about the atrocities, the rapes, the murders not simply in the Republic's communities of expatriate Charisians, but across its length and breadth. The churches burned with priests—even entire congregations—inside them because they carried the taint of "Reformism." The food stores deliberately burned or contaminated—or outright poisoned—in the teeth of winter. The sabotage of canal locks, despite the *Book of Langhorne*'s specific prohibitions, to prevent the western harvests from being transported to the eastern cities. Clyntahn could pass all those off as "unfortunate excesses," unintended but unhappily inevitable in the face of Mother Church's loyal sons' fully justified and understandable rage, but it had happened too broadly—and far too efficiently—not to have been carefully orchestrated by the same people who'd given the order for the uprisings in the first place.

And just what does Zhaspahr think is going to happen now? the treasurer asked himself bitterly. *Siddarmarkian armies on the Border States' frontier? A Charisian foothold on the mainland? Charisian weapons and gold pouring into Stohnar's hands now that those hands have become Mother Church's mortal enemy? He's* guaranteed *all those things will happen unless, somehow, we can crush the Republic before Charis can come to its rescue! If he had to do this—if he simply* had *to unleash this bloodshed and barbarity—couldn't he at least have done it* effectively?

And then there was the devastating financial consequence of the effective destruction of one of the only three mainland realms which had actually been managing to pay their tithes. How did Clyntahn expect the Treasury to magically conjure the needed funds out of thin air when the Inquisition was systematically destroying them at the source?

But I can't say that, can I? Not with Zahmsyn folding up like a pricked bladder and Allayn nodding in what has to be at least half-genuine agreement. And even if I said it, it wouldn't make one damned bit of difference, because the blood's already been spilled and the damage's already been done. The best I can hope for is to find some way to mitigate at least the worst of the consequences. And maybe, just maybe, if this works out the way it could, then—

He chopped that thought off, scarcely daring to voice it even to himself, and made himself admit the gall-bitter truth. However disastrous this might prove in the long term, in the short term it actually bolstered Clyntahn's power. The dispatches coming in from Desnair, the Border States, the Temple Lands, even—especially!—the Harchong Empire made that clear. The vision of Siddarmark collapsing into ruin was terrifying enough to any mainland ruler; the mere possibility of Siddarmark becoming a portal for Charisian invasion was even worse. Those rulers didn't care at this point whether Stohnar had truly been planning to betray them, as Clyntahn claimed. Not anymore. What mattered now was that Stohnar had no choice *but* to betray them if he wanted his nation to survive . . . and that every one of them scented the chance to scavenge his own pound or two of flesh from the Republic's ravaged carcass. And with the hysteria in Siddarmark—the atrocities against Mother Church which *Clyntahn's* atrocities were bound to provoke—the schism would be driven even deeper into the Church's heart, which was exactly what Clyntahn wanted. He *wanted* the polarization, the fear, the hatred, because that was what would give him the power to destroy his enemies forever and make Mother Church over into his own image of what she was supposed to be.

"I have to agree with Zhaspahr," Maigwair said. Duchairn eyed him with cold contempt, and the captain general flushed. "I'm not in a position to comment on or second-guess the Inquisition's reports," he went on defensively, "but the reports coming to me from Guardsmen in the Republic confirm that there really were a lot more muskets—almost certainly rifled muskets—in Siddar City than there ought to've been. *Somebody* was obviously stockpiling them. And it's certainly fortunate"—his eyes cut sideways towards the Grand Inquisitor for just a moment—"that we'll have had time to get the Guard fully recruited up to strength and equipped with more of the new muskets by the time the snow melts. At least half of them will be rifled, as well, and I understand"—this time he looked squarely at Clyntahn—"that your agents have managed to ferret out some of the information we most desperately need."

"The Inquisition has come into possession of quite a bit of information on the heretics' weapons," Clyntahn acknowledged. "We're still in the process of determining what portions of that knowledge we may safely use without encroaching upon the Proscriptions, but I believe we've found ways to duplicate many of their weapons without dabbling in the demonic inspiration which led the blasphemers to them."

He looked admirably grave, Duchairn thought bitterly. Every inch the thoughtful Inquisitor General truly finding ways to guard Mother Church against contamination rather than planning how he would justify anything that needed justifying.

"We've discovered how they make their round shot explode," he continued, "and I have a pair of trusted ironmasters devising a way to duplicate the effect. It's not simply a matter of making them hollow, and finding a way to accomplish it without resorting to proscribed knowledge has been tricky. There's also the matter of how you detonate the 'shells,' as the heretics call them. It requires a carefully compounded form of gunpowder to make the 'fuses' function reliably. Fortunately, one of Mother Church's most loyal sons managed to obtain that information for her—obtain it at the cost of his own life, I might add—and we should be able to begin making our own fuses within a month or two. By spring, you should have field artillery with its own exploding shells, Allayn."

The Inquisitor smiled benignly as Maigwair's eyes lit, and Duchairn closed his own eyes in despair. Maigwair had been in an understandable state of near panic ever since the Charisians had unveiled the existence of their exploding round shot. The possibility that he'd finally be able to put the same weapons into the hands of his own far more numerous troops had to come like a reprieve from a death sentence. He'd gladly overlook the deaths of a few hundred thousand—or even a few million—innocent

Siddarmarkians if the outcome offered him an opportunity to equalize the difference between Mother Church's combat capabilities and those of her enemies.

Especially when the possibility of a military success in the field will probably keep him out of the Inquisition's sights, as well, Duchairn thought bitterly.

He drew a deep, deep breath, then straightened and opened his eyes once more. It was his turn to look across the table at Clyntahn, and he saw something cold and pleased glittering in the other man's eyes.

"I can't argue with you or Allayn about where we are now, however we got there, Zhaspahr," he made himself say. "I agree it's profoundly regrettable the situation should've erupted so suddenly and uncontrollably. I'm deeply concerned, however, about reports of starvation—starvation among Mother Church's loyal children, as well as the heretics. I think it will be essential for us to give priority to moving food supplies into the areas controlled by her faithful sons. I realize there will probably be some conflict between purely military and humanitarian transport needs, but we'll have until the snow melts to make plans. I fear"—he met Clyntahn's gaze levelly—"that we'll lose far too many lives to starvation, cold, disease, and privation before spring, but it's essential Mother Church show her concern for those faithful to her. That's no more than her children deserve . . . and the very least they will expect out of us as her vicars."

Their gazes locked, and Duchairn knew it was there between them. Knew Clyntahn recognized that this was a point from which he would not retreat. He saw the familiar contempt for his own weakness, his own softness, in the Grand Inquisitor's eyes, saw the disdain in the twist of Clyntahn's lips at how cheaply he could buy Duchairn's compliance—his assumption of complicity, for that was what it would amount to. Yet it was the best bargain the treasurer could hope for at this table, in this conference room, and both of them knew that, too.

Silence hovered for a moment, and then Clyntahn nodded.

"Of course they'll expect it from us, Rhobair." He smiled thinly. "And you're the perfect choice to organize it for us."

"Thank you, Zhaspahr," Duchairn said as Trynair and Maigwair murmured their agreement. "I'll try to cause the least dislocation possible in purely military movements."

He returned Clyntahn's smile with one of his own while black murder boiled in his heart. But more than simple hatred simmered at his core. He sat back in his chair, listening to Clyntahn and Maigwair discussing the new weapons in greater detail, and his eyes were cold as he contemplated the future. It was astounding, really. Zhaspahr Clyntahn understood plots, cabals, treachery, and treason. He understood lies and threats, recognized the power of terror and the sweet taste of destroying his enemies. He knew all about the iron rod, how to break the bones of his foes. Yet for all his power and his ambition and ruthless drive, he was utterly blind to the deadly power of gentleness.

Not yet, Zhaspahr, he thought softly. *Not yet. But one of these days, you may just discover that the hard way. And if God is good, He'll let me live at least long enough to see you do it.*

.IV.
Gorath Cathedral,
City of Gorath,
Kingdom of Dohlar

Therefore, with angels and the Archangels, and with all the company of heaven, we glorify your glorious Name, evermore praising You and saying, holy, holy, holy, Lord God of hosts, creator of all the world, heaven and earth are full of Your glory. Glory be to You, O Lord, our maker. Amen."

Lywys Gardynyr, Earl of Thirsk, signed himself with Langhorne's scepter, rose from the kneeler, and seated himself in the richly upholstered pew with a suppressed grimace for the soft depth of that upholstery.

He'd been raised on his family's estates, far from the Kingdom of Dohlar's capital city and its cathedral, and he really preferred the plain, wooden pews of his youth to the glittering luxury of Gorath Cathedral. Of course, he preferred a rather plainer and less ostentatious lifestyle in general than that to which the wealthy and powerful of Gorath treated themselves. He'd found that distaste for ostentation becoming steadily more pronounced where religion was concerned, and he felt it now, even though he had no choice but to acknowledge the magnificence of the cathedral's architecture, statuary, and stained glass. There was no denying the glitter of its altar service, the smoothly gleaming perfection of its floor, paved in the golden stone for which Dohlar was famed and set with the Archangels' personal sigils, the majesty of its twin scepter-crowned steeples. He'd made his obligatory visit to the Temple in far-off Zion, and he knew Gorath Cathedral was but a smudged copy of the very home of God on earth, yet despite its smudges, it towered high into the heavens to the glory of God and the archangels. And despite his cross-grained preferences, its beauty was almost enough to help him forget, at least momentarily, the war being waged for the heart and soul of Mother Church.

Almost.

Now he watched Bishop Executor Wylsynn Lainyr lower his hands from the upraised position of supplication and turn from the altar to face the sparsely occupied cathedral. He crossed to the pulpit and stood behind it and its gold and gem-encrusted copy of the *Holy Writ*. But instead of opening the splendidly illuminated volume, he simply folded his hands upon it.

Thirsk looked back at the bishop executor stonily, face carefully expressionless. He didn't like Lainyr. He hadn't especially liked Ahrain Mahrlow, Lainyr's predecessor, either, but he'd found himself deeply regretting Mahrlow's heart attack, especially when he'd found himself increasingly at odds with Lainyr's policies and the way the bishop executor had insisted upon treating the Charisian prisoners who'd surrendered to him. He'd heard the details of what had happened to those same prisoners after he'd been ordered to surrender them to the Inquisition, as well, and those details had filled him with a cold and bitter self-loathing. He'd had no choice. It had been his duty, and triply so: as a noble of the Kingdom of Dohlar, charged to obey his king's commands; as the commander of the Royal Dohlaran Navy, charged to obey his lawfully appointed superiors; and as a son of Mother Church, bound to obey her commands in all things. And then there'd been his duty as father and grandfather to do nothing that might give Ahbsahlahn Kharmych, the Archbishopric of Gorath's Schuelerite intendant, an excuse to cast his family to the same Inquisition which had butchered those prisoners of war.

He knew all of that, and none of it made him feel any less unclean. Nor did he expect what was about to happen here in this glittering cathedral to change that.

He glanced to his right, where Bishop Staiphan Maik, the navy's special intendant, sat between the Duke of Fern, King Rahnyld IV's first councilor, and the Duke of Thorast, Thirsk's immediate superior. Maik's face wore as little expression as his own, and he remembered the auxiliary bishop's advice to him the day the peremptory order to surrender his prisoners had arrived. It hadn't been the advice he would have anticipated out of a Schuelerite, but it had been good.

Better than I realized at the time, the earl thought grimly. *Especially since I hadn't realized—then—just how closely the girls and their families are being watched. Purely for their own protection against crazed Charisian assassins, given my role in handing the Charisian Navy the only defeat—modest though it may've been—it's ever suffered. Of course.*

He felt his jaw muscles ache and forced himself to relax them. And the truth was, he didn't know which infuriated him more—the discovery that the Inquisition and the Royal Guard had decided to "protect" his family to make sure they remained hostages for his own obedience or the fact that he couldn't truly decide even now whether or not he would have continued to obey if his family *hadn't* been held hostage to ensure he did.

It's supposed to be clear-cut. Black and white—right and wrong, obedience or disobedience, honor or dishonor, godly action or service to Shan-wei. I'm supposed to know where my duty lies, and I'm supposed to do it without fear of any consequences I may suffer for doing what I know is right. And in any other war, it would be almost that clear-cut, almost that simple. When one side tortures prisoners to death and the other treats its prisoners decently, without abuse or starvation or the denial of healers, it should be easy to know where honor and justice—yes, and God and the archangels!—stand. But this is Mother Church, *the keeper of men's souls. She speaks with Langhorne's own authority in our mortal world. How dare I—how dare* anyone—*set his merely mortal, fallible judgment in opposition to hers?*

That was a question too many people had been forced to confront in the last five years, and the sheer courage—or arrogance—it had taken for so many of them to decide *against* Mother Church filled Lywys Gardynyr with mingled horror and awe. A horror and awe made only deeper by the growing hunger he felt to make the same decision.

No, he told himself harshly. *Not against* Mother Church. *Against that sick, murderous son-of-a-bitch Clyntahn and the rest of the "Group of Four." Yet how much of that anger of mine, that hatred, is Shan-wei's own snare, set before me and all those many others to seduce us into her service by perverting our own sense of justice? The* Writ *doesn't call her "the seducer of innocence" and "the corrupter of goodness" for nothing. And—*

"Brothers in God." The bishop executor's voice interrupted the earl's thoughts. All eyes focused upon him, and he shook his head, his expression grim. "I have received directions from Archbishop Trumahn, sent from Zion over the semaphore, to speak to you about fearful tidings. It's for that reason I requested all of you to join me here in the cathedral this afternoon. Partly because this is by far the best place for me to give you this news, and partly so that we might join in prayer and supplication for the archangels' intervention to protect and comfort two innocent victims of Shan-wei's spite and the machinations of sinful men who have given themselves to her service."

Thirsk felt his jaw tighten once more. So he'd been right about the reasons for this unexpected gathering of the kingdom's—or, at least, the capital's—highest nobility . . . and the senior officers of the Dohlaran army and navy.

"I'm sure that by now all of you, given your duties and your sources of information, have heard the wild tales coming out of Delferahk," Lainyr continued harshly. "Unfortunately, while there may have been little truth in much of what we've heard, there has, indeed, been a basis for it. Princess Irys and Prince Daivyn have been kidnapped by Charisian agents."

A rustling stir ran through the cathedral, and Thirsk snorted as he heard a handful of muttered comments. What is it actually possible some of these men *hadn't* heard the "rumors" Lainyr was talking about? If they were as poorly informed as *that*, the kingdom was in even more trouble than he'd thought it was!

"That is not the story you're going to hear from Shan-wei's slaves and servants." Lainyr told them. "Already Shan-wei's claim that the prince and princess were rescued rather than kidnapped has set its poisonous roots in the credulous soil of parts of Delferahk. In due time, no doubt, it will become the official lie spread by the so-called Charisian Empire and its eternally damned and accursed emperor and empress. Yet the truth is far different. The Earl of Coris, charged to protect the Prince and to guard his sister, instead sold them to the same Charisians who murdered their father in Corisande. Indeed, some evidence has emerged to suggest it was Coris who provided the blasphemer excommunicate Cayleb's assassins with the means to enter Manchyr without detection to commit that murder. The Inquisition and King Zhames' investigators have yet to determine how he communicated with Cayleb and Sharleyan *Delferahk*, yet the proof that he did is self-evident, for the 'guardsmen' King Zhames allowed him to recruit to protect the legitimate ruler of conquered, bleeding Corisande instead aided in his kidnapping.

"And lest anyone believe for even one instant that it was *not* a kidnapping, let him reflect upon this. The Charisian agent who led in this crime was Merlin Athrawes himself—the supposed *seijin* who serves as Cayleb Ahrmahk's personal armsman. The Charisian agent who, through the use of Shan-wei's foul arts, massacred an entire company of the Delferahkan Royal Guard who sought only to protect Daivyn and Irys. Guardsmen who were sent to protect those defenseless, orphaned children on the direct instructions of Bishop Mytchail, Delferahk's intendant, after he was forewarned of the threat by no less than the Grand Inquisitor himself. Father Gaisbyrt, one of Bishop Mytchail's most trusted aides, and another member of his order, sent to be certain of the Prince's safety, were murdered at the same time.

"At least two survivors of the Guardsmen heard Princess Irys herself crying out for rescue, begging them to save her brother from the same murderers who butchered her father, but Shan-wei has stepped more fully into our own world than ever since the Fall itself. We don't know what deviltry she armed her servant Athrawes with, but we know mortal men found it impossible to stand before it. Before he was done, Athrawes had burned half Talkyra Castle to the ground and blown up the other half. He stole the finest horses from King Zhames' royal stable, he and the traitor Coris bound Princess Irys—bound a helpless, desperately struggling young maiden—to the saddle, and he himself—Athrawes, 'Emperor Cayleb's' *personal* servant— took Prince Daivyn up before him despite the boy's cries for help, and they rode from the burning fortress where Prince Hektor's children had been protected into the night."

Lainyr turned his head slowly, sweeping the pews with bleak, cold eyes, and Thirsk wondered how much—if any—of the bishop executor's tale was true. And whether or not Lainyr himself believed a word of it. If he didn't, he'd missed a stellar career upon the stage.

"They rode east," the prelate continued in a cold, flat voice. "They rode east into the Duchy of Yarth until they reached the Sar River. And at that point, they met a party of several hundred Charisian Marines who had ascended the Sar in a flotilla of small craft while the Earl of Charlz' forces were distracted by the wanton rape and pillage—the total, vicious destruction—of the defenseless town of Sarmouth. A single platoon of Delferahkan dragoons intercepted the kidnappers, but they were in turn ambushed by the hundreds of Charisians hidden in the woods and massacred almost to the man. A handful of them escaped . . . and bore witness to the casual, callous murder of yet another consecrated priest of God who'd sought nothing but to rescue a captive girl and her helpless brother from their father's murderers.

"And then they escaped back down the Sar to Sarmouth, where they were taken aboard a Charisian warship which will undoubtedly deliver them to Cayleb and Sharleyan themselves in Tellesberg."

The bishop executor shook his head, his eyes like stone, and touched his pectoral scepter.

"It chills the heart to think—to imagine, even for a moment—what may befall those innocent victims in Charisian hands," he said quietly. "A boy of barely ten years? A girl not yet twenty? Alone, without protectors in the same bloody hands that butchered their father and older brother. The legitimate Prince of Corisande, in the grip of the godless empire which has conquered and pillaged that princedom and given Langhorne alone knows how many innocent children of God over into the grips of its own heretical, blasphemous 'church.' Who knows what pressure will be brought to bear upon them? What threats, what privations—what *torture*—would such as Cayleb and Sharleyan shrink from inflicting upon their victims to bend them to their will?" He shook his head again. "I tell you now, my sons—it's only a matter of time before those helpless children are compelled to repeat whatever lies their captors put into their mouths.

"And lest anyone believe this was anything other than the outcome of a long, carefully laid strategy, consider the timing. Daivyn and Irys were stolen away from their protectors at the very instant Greyghor Stohnar was plotting to sell Siddarmark to Shan-wei! Can you conceive of the consequences if he'd succeeded? Of how the credulous, the weak, among Mother Church's children might have reacted to the simultaneous rebellion and apostasy of one of Safehold's true great kingdoms and the 'spontaneous and voluntary' acceptance of the Charisians' savage conquest of Corisande by its rightful Prince? And what boy of such tender years would withhold that acceptance with not simply himself but his innocent sister—his only living relative—in the hands of heretics and torturers?

"No, my sons, this was a meticulously thought out, organized, and executed strategy, as monstrous as it was ambitious, and while it may have failed in Siddarmark, it succeeded in Delferahk. The future ramifications of Coris' treason and Charis' ruthlessness are yet for us to discover, but I tell you now that we must be wary. We must be on our guard. The Charisians have Daivyn and Irys, and they will force them to tell whatever lies best suit Charisian purposes. We have only the truth—only eyewitnesses to murder and kidnapping and arson, to rape and pillage—and Shan-wei, the Mother of Lies, knows how to defile the truth. That's a game she's played before, one which led to the destruction of Armageddon Reef and mankind's fall from grace into the captivity of a sinful nature, and we dare not permit it to succeed this time any more than Langhorne permitted it to succeed the first time. It's essential that the truth be known, far and wide, and that no one be permitted to spread Shan-wei's filth unchallenged. *That's* the message Archbishop Trumahn sends us in the Grand Inquisitor's name. As I stand here, the same message is being transmitted to every kingdom, every princedom, every cathedral, every intendant in all the world, and I call upon you as Mother Church's faithful sons, to do your part in protecting the truth against the foul fabrications of priest killers, regicides, blasphemers, and heretics."

Silence hovered, and Thirsk stared back at Lainyr, refusing to look away lest those sitting closest see the disbelief burning in his eyes. Unlike any of the rest of them, he'd *met* Cayleb of Charis. He'd been only a crown prince then, not a king or an emperor, yet some qualities went to the bone, unchanging as stone and less yielding than steel. Ruthless with his enemies when he felt it necessary Cayleb might be—Thirsk knew *that* from personal experience, as well—but someone who could dishonor himself the way Lainyr was describing? Someone who would abuse or torture children helpless in his hands? No, not *that* king. Not that *man*, whatever the potential prize. That was what Zhaspahr Clyntahn did, and Cayleb Ahrmahk would never stoop to Clyntahn's level. Eternally damned heretic, apostate, and blasphemer he might indeed be, but always a man of honor . . . and never a torturer.

Lainyr gazed out across the cathedral's pews for at least another full minute, then his nostrils flared as he inhaled deeply.

"And now, my sons," he said softly, "I ask and charge you to join with me in a mass of intercession. Let us beseech Langhorne and Chihiro to protect their servants Irys and Daivyn even in the very hand of the ungodly. And let us also beseech the Holy Bédard and all of the other archangels and angels to be with them and comfort them in this time of peril and trial. It is for us, their servants in this world, to free that brother and that sister—and all of God's children—from the power of heresy and evil, so let us rededicate ourselves to that holy purpose even as we commend Irys and Daivyn to their protection and comfort."

.V.

HMS *Destiny*, 54, Sea of Justice

O h, *my!*"
Princess Irys Zhorzhet Mahra Daykyn shook her head as the small, wiry, sunburned-but-tanning-quickly youngster squealed in delight. The ten-year-old stood at the back edge of HMS *Destiny*'s quarterdeck, leaning back sharply with bare feet braced hard against the taffrail, while he clung to the wildly bent rod with both hands. He wore no shoes, only a pair of cutoff shorts enormously too big for him, but a canvas harness—the type the Imperial Charisian Navy used with deckside safety lines during hurricanes—was fastened about his bare torso. The harness was firmly anchored to the binnacle beside the ship's double wheel, and two burly, seasoned-looking petty officers (either of whom weighed four or five times as much as the boy in question) stood alertly to one side, grinning hugely as they watched him.

"*It's a kraken!* It's a kraken, Irys!" the youngster shouted, managing to hang onto the rod somehow.

One of the watching petty officers reached out as if to lend a hand, but he visibly thought better of it. The boy never noticed; he was too busy having the time of his life.

"It's not really a kraken, you know, Your Highness," a voice said quietly, and Irys turned her head quickly. Lieutenant Hector Aplyn-Ahrmahk (known on social occasions as His Grace, Duke Hektor of Darcos) smiled at her. "A kraken would've already snatched the rod out of his hands," he said reassuringly. "He's probably got a forktail or a small neartuna. Either of which," he added with a reminiscent smile, "will be more than enough of a challenge at his age. I remember *my* first neartuna." He shook his head. "I was only a year or so older than His Highness is now, and it took me over an hour to land it. And I might as well admit I needed help. The damned thing—pardon my language—weighed more than *I* did!"

"Really?" Irys gazed at him for a moment, then gave him a smile of thanks. "I know he won't really go overboard, not with that harness. But I still can't help worrying," she acknowledged, her smile fading slightly. "And I can't say I was very happy about the thought of his actually landing a kraken with all those teeth and tentacles!"

"Well, even if I'm wrong and he has hooked a kraken—and he and the petty officers manage to land it, which they probably wouldn't without a *lot* heavier line—someone's going to hit it smartly between the eyes with an ax before it's allowed on deck." He shrugged. "The kraken may be the emblem of the House of Ahrmahk, Your Highness, but nobody wants to feed a hand or an arm to a *real* one."

"I suppose not," she said in a suddenly softer tone, looking away, and his sun-bronzed face turned darker as he realized what he'd just said.

"Your Highness, I—" he began, but she reached out and touched his forearm lightly before he could finish.

"It isn't your fault . . . Lieutenant. My father should've thought about that. And I've been forced to . . . adjust my thinking where the blame for his death is concerned." She turned to face him fully. "I don't doubt Emperor Cayleb would have killed him willingly in combat, but, then, Father would just as willingly have killed Cayleb. And after what Phylyp's learned, there's no longer any doubt in my mind that it was Zhaspahr Clyntahn who had Father and Hektor murdered. I won't pretend I'm reconciled to Corisande's conquest, because I'm not. But as for Daivyn's safety and my own, I'm far safer swimming with a Charisian kraken than waiting for an offal lizard like Clyntahn to have us both murdered at the time that suits his purposes."

"You are, you know," he said quietly, laying one sword-calloused hand over the slender, long-fingered one on his forearm. "I don't know how this will all work out, but I know Cayleb and Sharleyan, and I know Archbishop Maikel. Nothing— *nothing*—will happen to your brother under their protection. Anyone who wishes to harm either of you will have to fight his way through the entire Imperial Army, Marine Corps, and Guard. And"— he smiled suddenly, wryly—"past *Seijin* Merlin, which would probably be harder than all the rest put together, now that I think about it."

"I'm sure you're right about that!" Irys laughed, squeezing his arm gently. "I may still worry about whether or not he got away safely, but when it comes down to it, I think Daivyn's right. I've come to the conclusion there are very few things *Seijin* Merlin couldn't do if he put his mind to it. And I might as well admit that knowing a man like him serves Cayleb and Sharleyan did almost as much as Phylyp to convince me how wrong I'd been about them. Good men can serve bad rulers, but . . . not a man like him."

"You're right about that, Your Highness." Aplyn-Ahrmahk pressed down on her hand for a moment, then blinked and took his own hand quickly away. For a moment, he seemed remarkably awkward about finding somewhere else for that hand to go, especially for a young man who was so perpetually poised and composed, and the tiniest trace of a smile flickered across Irys' lips.

Her brother's fresh squeal of delight drew her eyes, and she released the lieutenant's forearm and reached up to adjust her wide-brimmed sun hat. The brisk wind of the Sea of Justice grasped at it with playful hands, flexing and pulling, bending all its cunning towards snatching it away, and her eyes gleamed in pure, sensual pleasure. It was summer in Safehold's Southern Hemisphere, but the Sea of Justice was a brisk place any time, and the wind had a crisp edge, despite her brother's eagerness to shed his shirt at a moment's notice. But there was a sense of freedom, of life, in that wind. Intellectually, she knew the ship was bearing her to another sort of captivity—one she had no doubt would be genteel, kind, and as unobtrusive as possible, yet captivity nonetheless. Somehow, though, that didn't really matter at the moment. After the endless, dreary months confined in King Zhames of Delferahk's castle above the waters of Lake Erdan, the blustering wind, the sunlight, the smell of salt water, the play of light on canvas and rigging, the endless rushing sound of water, and the creak of timbers and cordage all swirled about her like life itself. For the first time in far too long she admitted to herself how bitterly she'd missed the rough, feathery hand of the wind, the kiss of rain, the smell of Corisandian grass as she galloped across the open fields.

She felt the lieutenant at her side, her assigned escort here on *Destiny*'s deck. She was the single female human being aboard the entire, crowded galleon, whose tightly packed confines offered precious little privacy for anyone. Captain Lathyk had given up his cabin to her in order to give her something as close to privacy as conditions allowed, but that couldn't change the fact that she was the only woman on board, and she wondered how the Charisians had come to overlook that minor fact. In a way, it was comforting to know they *could* overlook things, and she was no shrinking violet. It was . . . an unusual experience to find herself without a single maid, female body servant, or chaperone, and she had no doubt three-quarters of the court back in Manchyr would have been horrified by the very thought or her suffering such an insult. Or as horrified as they could have been over mere insult to her station, given how much of their horror quotient would have been used up by the notion of any nobly born maiden of tender years, sister of the rightful Prince of Corisande or not, finding herself with her safety and virtue alike unprotected aboard a Charisian warship!

Yet not a single one of those Charisians—not a seaman, not a Marine, not an officer: not *one* of them—had offered even the slightest discourtesy. True, men who'd been at sea for months on end, some of them even longer, without sight or smell of a woman, watched with almost reverent eyes whenever she came on deck. Despite that, she was convinced that even without knowing what their officers would have done to anyone who'd dared to lay so much as a finger upon her, they wouldn't have anyway. Oh, some of them might have; they were human beings, and they were men, not saints. But the instant anyone tried, his own fellows would have torn him limb from limb. Which didn't even count what Tobys Raimair or the rest of her own armsmen would have done.

No, she'd never been safer in her father's palace than here on this warship of a hostile, heretical empire, and that was the true reason for the lightness in her heart. For the first time in far, far too long, she knew she and, ever so much more importantly, her brother were *safe*. And the wiry young man beside her in the sky blue tunic and dark blue trousers of the Imperial Charisian Navy was one of the reasons she was.

She glanced up at him from the corner of one eye, but he wasn't looking at her. He was watching Daivyn and grinning hugely. It made him look absurdly young, but then he *was* young, over two years younger even than she herself. Only that was hard to remember when she recalled his voice out of the darkness, leading his men in a charge against the Delferahkan dragoons who'd outnumbered them better than two to one to rescue her and her brother. When she recalled merciless brown eyes in the moonlight and the flash of the pistol as he put a bullet through the brain of the inquisitor who'd done his best to trick those dragoons into massacring her and Daivyn. When she remembered his competence and certainty on the long boat trip downriver to Sarmouth and safety. Or, for that matter, when she watched him and his easy assurance giving commands to men three times his own age here aboard *Destiny*.

He would never be a handsome man, she thought. Pleasant looking, perhaps, but not remarkably so. It was the energy that was so much a part of him, the quick decision and the agile brain, that struck any observer. And the confidence. She remembered that moonlit night again, then remembered the lecture Admiral Yairley had given him when they finally reached the Sarmouth and came aboard *Destiny*. She had a suspicion Yairley had lectured him more for *her* benefit than for his own, but she was a princess herself. She understood how the game was played, and she'd been grateful to the admiral for making it clear to her that Aplyn-Ahrmahk had proceeded entirely on his own to complete his mission—and just incidentally save her own life—when any reasonable man would have turned for home. She'd suspected that was the case from one or two remarks the seaman under his command had made during the trip down the river, but the lieutenant had simply brushed the entire notion aside. Now she knew better, and she wondered with a wisdom beyond her years, hard-earned as a prince's daughter, how many young men his age, with that accomplishment to their credit, could have refrained from attempting to bask in a young woman's admiration.

"That fish is going to have him into the water, safety harness or not!" she said now, as Daivyn was dragged bodily forward despite his braced feet.

"Nonsense!" Aplyn-Ahrmahk laughed. "He's not strong enough to hang onto the rod if the safety line comes taut!"

"Easy for *you* to say!" she said accusingly.

"Your Highness, you see that fellow standing to His Highness' right—the one with all the tattoos?" Irys glanced up at him and nodded. "That's Zhorj Shairwyd. In addition to being one of the best petty officers in the ship, he's also the squadron's champion wrestler and one of the strongest, quickest men I know. If it even *looks* like your brother's headed over the taffrail, Shairwyd will have him, the fishing rod, and whatever's on the other end of it, dragged up onto this deck faster than a cat lizard jumping on a spider rat. I didn't—I mean, Captain Lathyk didn't pick him at random to keep an eye on His Highness."

"I see." Irys carefully took no note of his quick self-correction. Now that she thought about it, though, Aplyn-Ahrmahk always seemed to be in the vicinity when *Daivyn* was on deck as well. It was obvious the prince liked him, and Aplyn-Ahrmahk had a much more comfortable, easy way with the boy than most of the other officers aboard Yairley's flagship.

"Tell me, Lieutenant," she said, "do you have brothers or sisters of your own?"

"Oh, Langhorne, yes!" He rolled his eyes. "I'm the middle one, actually—three older brothers, an older sister, a younger sister, and two younger brothers." Irys' eyes widened at the formidable list, and he chuckled. "Two of the older brothers and both of the younger ones are twins, Your Highness, so it's not *quite* as bad as it might sound. Mother used to tell me she'd thought four would be quite enough, though she'd been willing to entertain the thought of five, but she never would've agreed to eight! Unfortunately, Father didn't tell her twins run in his family. Or that's her story, at any rate, and she's sticking to it. Since they've known each other since they were children and Father has twin brothers, though, I've never really believed she didn't know that perfectly well, you understand. Still, I have to admit it was a relief when they were able to pack me and two of my brothers off to sea."

"I expect so," Irys murmured, trying to imagine what it would have been like to have seven siblings. Or, for that matter, *any* immediate family beyond Daivyn at this point. She envied the lieutenant, she realized. Envied him deeply. But that stack of brothers and sisters undoubtedly did help explain his comfortable approach to Daivyn. And so, she thought suddenly, must the peculiar circumstances of his ennoblement. He was a duke, a member—if only by adoption—of the House of Ahrmahk itself. She wasn't as familiar with the Charisian peerage as she wished, especially in her current circumstances, yet she was fairly sure no more than a handful of the

Empire's nobles could take precedence over him. Yet he'd been born a commoner, one more child in a brawling, sprawling, obviously happy family who'd never dreamed of the heights to which one of their sons would rise. And so he was neither a commoner dealing with a prince, afraid of overstepping his place, nor a noble by birth, trained to understand that one simply couldn't casually ruffle a young boy's sun-bleached hair if it should happen the young boy in question was the rightful ruler of an entire realm and must be safely fortified within the towering buttresses of the respect due his exalted birth.

It was all quite unacceptable, of course. Daivyn had no business dashing barefoot about a warship's deck wearing nothing but a pair of shorts, watched over by common seamen and tattooed petty officers. He had no business shrieking with laughter as he fought whatever fish was at the other end of his line or when he was allowed—in calm weather, under close supervision—swarming up to the maintop with half a dozen midshipmen, many of them no more than a year or so his elders. She should be horrified, should insist he be kept safely on deck—or, even better, *below* decks— where he would be sheltered from all threat or harm. And she certainly shouldn't allow Lieutenant Aplyn-Ahrmahk to *encourage* him to run wild! She knew that, just as she knew the consequences if something *did* happen to Daivyn Daykyn while in Charisian custody could be catastrophic beyond imagining.

But it didn't matter. Not to her, and not any longer. Daivyn was her Prince, her rightful ruler, a life far too important for anyone to risk, or to allow to risk itself. And that didn't matter, either. Because he was also her baby brother, and he was *alive* when he wasn't supposed to be, and he was happy for the first time she could remember since they'd fled Corisande. He'd rediscovered the boyhood Zhaspahr Clyntahn and the world had stolen from him far too early, and her heart rejoiced to watch him embrace it.

And none of it would have happened without the humbly born duke standing at her side.

"Thank you," she said suddenly.

"I beg your pardon, Your Highness?" He looked down quickly, and she smiled.

"That wasn't meant just for you, Lieutenant," she reassured him, wondering even as she did if she was being truthful. "It was for all of you— *Destiny's* entire crew. I haven't seen Daivyn laughing like this in over two years. And no one's allowed him to simply run wild and be a little boy again in all that time. So," she patted him on the forearm again, her eyes misty and her voice just the slightest bit unreliable, "thank you all for giving him that. Giving me the chance to *see* him like that again." She cleared her throat. "And, if it won't embarrass an emperor's officer such as yourself to pass that thanks along to Sir Dunkyn, I'd appreciate it."

"I'll try to bear up under the humiliation of passing on your message, Your Highness," he told her with a slightly crooked smile. "I'm sure it will be hard, but I'll try."

.VI.
The Siddar River,
Shiloh Province,
Republic of Siddarmark

W ill you *please* go back inside, Your Eminence?"

Archbishop Zhasyn Cahnyr looked over his shoulder at the much younger man who stood in the inn courtyard, hands on hips, glaring at him. The younger man's breath flowed out in a cloud of steam as he sighed in exasperation at his superior's deliberately blank expression. The icy wind whipping across the flat, gray ice of the Siddar River snatched the cloud into fragments almost instantly, something else of which Cahnyr deliberately took no notice.

"I simply wanted a breath of fresh air, Gharth," he said mildly.

"*Fresh air*, is it?" Father Gharth Gorjah, Cahnyr's personal secretary and aide, took his hands from his hips so that he could throw them up in the air properly. "If this air were any fresher, it'd turn you into an icicle the instant you inhaled, Your Eminence! And don't think I'm the one who's going to go home and discuss your foolishness with Madam Pahrsahn when it happens, either. She *told* me to take care of you, and standing around out here until you catch your death of cold isn't exactly what she had in mind!"

Cahnyr smiled faintly, wondering exactly when the last vestiges of control over his own household had slipped from his fingers. It was kind of all of them to pretend (to others, at least) they still deferred to him over such minor matters as whether or not he had the wit to come in out of the rain—or the cold—but they weren't really fooling anyone.

"I'm not going to 'catch my death of cold,' Gharth," he said patiently. "And even if I were, Madam Pahrsahn's a fair-minded woman. She could hardly hold my stubbornness against you. Especially with so many witnesses prepared to testify you nagged me absolutely unremittingly to behave better."

"I do *not* 'nag,' Your Eminence." Father Gharth crunched through the crusty snow of the inn yard towards him, trying not to grin. "I simply reason with you. Sometimes forcefully, I'll admit, but always with the utmost respect. Now, would you please get your venerable, highly respected, consecrated and ordained arse inside where it's warm?"

"Can I at least walk as far as the stable first?" Cahnyr cocked his head. "I want to see how they're coming on the repair of that runner."

"I just talked to them myself, Your Eminence. They say it should be done by suppertime. Which means we'll be able to get back on the trail after breakfast tomorrow. I have to admit it doesn't break my heart to think we're going to be able to sit you down by a fire this afternoon, keep you under a roof tonight, and wrap you around a hot meal in the morning before we set back out." He stepped up onto the veranda with the archbishop and folded his arms. "And now that you've had that reassurance, *please*—I'm serious—go back inside where it's *warm*, Your Eminence. Sahmantha isn't happy about the way you were coughing yesterday, and you know you promised to listen to her before Madam Pahrsahn, the Lord Protector, and Archbishop Dahnyld gave you permission to come along."

Cahnyr cocked his head quizzically at that particularly underhanded blow. Sahmantha Gorjah had left her infant son Zhasyn in Siddar City to accompany her husband—and Cahnyr—back to Glacierheart. True, Zhasyn was in the personal care of Aivah Pahrsahn, one of the wealthiest women on all of Safehold, who could be trusted to guard him like a catamount with a single cub, but she'd still left him behind. And she'd done that because she and her husband regarded themselves as the children Cahnyr had never had. They'd flatly refused to let him make the journey without them . . . and especially without Sahmantha's training as a healer. She'd never taken vows as a Pasqualate sister, but she'd been intensively trained by the order, and she had every intention of using that training to keep the undeniably frail archbishop she loved alive.

Of course, under the circumstances, she was only too likely to find *other* uses for those skills. Ugly ones he would not for the world have exposed her to, and his expression darkened at the thought. Not that it had been his idea, or even Gharth's in this case. No, it had been Sahmantha's, and there'd been no dissuading her. She'd always been stubborn as the day was long, even when her sainted mother had been plain old Father Zhasyn's housekeeper. He'd *never* been able to make her do anything she didn't choose to do, and this time she'd had help. Lots of help, given the way the Lord Protector and Aivah Pahrsahn—*and* that young whippersnapper Fardhyn!—had made the inclusion of a personal healer a nonnegotiable condition of their agreement to allow him to make the trip.

If the truth be known, he was considerably senior to Archbishop Dahnyld Fardhym, the newly created Archbishop of Siddarmark. The previous archbishop—the only *legitimate* archbishop, as far as the official hierarchy of the Church of God Awaiting was concerned—was Praidwyn Laicharn, but

Laicharn had enjoyed the misfortune of being trapped inside Siddar City when Clyntahn's "Sword of Schueler" failed to take the capital. He was a polished, distinguished-looking, silver-haired man, every inch the perfect archbishop, but he was an absolutely fanatic Temple Loyalist—less, in Cahnyr's opinion, because of the strength of his belief than because of his terror of Zhaspahr Clyntahn. He'd refused to have anything to do with Stohnar's "apostate and traitorous government" following his capture, and he'd denounced any member of the clergy who *did* as a faithless, treacherous servant of Shan-wei.

Cahnyr had known Laicharn for over twenty years. That was one reason he was convinced it was terror, not personal faith, which made the other archbishop such an ardent Temple Loyalist. And another reason for that ardency was that Laicharn understood perfectly that unlike Zhaspahr Clyntahn, Stohnar and the Reformists were unlikely to torture their opponents or burn them alive over doctrinal disagreements, which made it much safer to defy *them*.

Nor was Laicharn's attitude unique. The entire Siddarmarkian ecclesiastic hierarchy was in what could only be called acute disorder. Personally, Cahnyr thought "utter chaos" probably hit closer to the mark.

At least a third—and quite possibly closer to half—of the Church's clerics had fled to the Temple Loyalists. Losses were substantially higher among the more senior clergy, with a far higher percentage of younger priests, upper-priests, and very junior bishops openly embracing the Reformist position. That left all too many holes in very senior positions, which accounted for much of the disarray. Stohnar, Fardhym, and other prelates and senior priests in the provinces which had remained loyal to the Republic were laboring ferociously to restore at least some order; unfortunately, they had quite a few other pressing concerns at the same time. Even more unfortunately, there was a great deal of uncertainty as to just how far towards Reformism the Siddarmarkian church as a whole was prepared to go. There'd been a lot of Reformist sentiment in the Republic even before the Sword of Schueler, and the excesses of the Temple Loyalists who'd planned and executed Clyntahn's attack had hardened attitudes and strengthened that Reformist sentiment quite remarkably. Atrocities did tend to have a . . . clarifying effect when it came to choosing sides. Yet even some of the most enthusiastic Reformists hesitated to actively embrace the schismatic Church of Charis. That was going a step too far for many, even now, and they were trying desperately to find some halfway house between the Temple and Tellesberg Cathedral.

Lots of luck with that, Cahnyr thought dryly. It was a matter to which he'd given quite a lot of thought—and devoted much of his effort—during his own exile in Siddar City. *Whatever they may want, in the end they're going to have to choose between finding a way home to Zion or accepting the unavoidable conclusion of the steps they've already taken. And the truth is that the Charisians've been right from the very beginning. The Group of Four may be the ones twisting and perverting Mother Church at this particular moment, but if she isn't reformed—reformed in a way that prevents any future Group of Four from hijacking her—they'll only be replaced by someone else altogether too soon. More to the point, if the hesitators don't make up their mind to embrace Charis, they'll inevitably fall to the Temple, and there won't be any way "home" for any of them as long as Zhaspahr Clyntahn is alive.*

He'd reached that conclusion long ago, even before Clyntahn butchered all of his friends and fellow members of Samyl Wylsynn's circle of Reformist-minded vicars and bishops. Nothing he'd seen since had shaken it, and he'd spent much of his time during his exile from Glacierheart working to bolster the pro-Charis wing of the Reformist communities in and around Old Province and the capital. Fardhym had been one of the churchmen who'd very cautiously worked with him in that endeavor, which was a big part of his acceptability in Stohnar's eyes.

And it doesn't hurt that he had "Aivah's" recommendation, as well, Cahnyr thought, smiling faintly at the thought of the redoubtable woman who'd once been known as Ahnzhelyk Phonda . . . among other things. *At the moment, she probably has more influence with Stohnar than virtually any native-born Siddarmarkian. After all, without her he'd be dead!*

"You know, Gharth," he said out loud, "technically, Archbishop Dahnyld has no authority over me whatsoever without the confirmation of his elevation to Primate of all Siddarmark by the Council of Vicars, which I don't think, somehow, he's going to be receiving anytime soon. Even if, by some miracle, that should happen, though, no one short of the Grand Vicar himself has the authority needed to strip an archbishop of his see or order him not to return to his archbishopric. And with all due respect to the Lord Protector, no layman, regardless of his civil office, has that authority, either."

"Well, unless memory fails me, Your Eminence, the Grand Vicar named your *replacement* in Glacierheart quite some time ago," his undutiful secretary shot back. "So if we're going to concern ourselves about deferring to his authority rather than Archbishop Dahnyld's, we should probably turn around and head home right now."

"I was simply pointing out that what we confront here is something in the nature of a power vacuum," Cahnyr said with the utmost dignity. "A situation in which the lines of authority have become . . . confused and blurred, requiring me to proceed as my own faith and understanding direct me."

"Oh, of course it does, Your Eminence." Gorjah frowned thoughtfully for a moment, then slowly and deliberately removed one glove so he could properly snap his thumb and second finger. "I know! We can ask *Madam Pahrsahn's* opinion!"

"Oh, a low blow, Gharth. A low blow!" Cahnyr laughed, and Gorjah smiled. He hadn't heard that infectious laugh out of his archbishop very often in the last year or so. Now Cahnyr shook a finger under his nose. "A dutiful, respectful secretary would *not* bring up the one human being in the entire world of whom his archbishop is terrified."

" 'Terrified' isn't the word I'd choose, Your Eminence. I have observed, however, a distinct tendency on your part to . . . accept Madam Pahrsahn's firmly urged advice, shall we say."

"Diplomatically put," Cahnyr said, then sighed. "You really are going to be stubborn about this, aren't you?"

"Yes, Your Eminence, I am," Gorjah said in a softer, much more serious tone. He reached out and laid his bare hand affectionately on his superior's shoulder. "I know you don't want to hear this, but you truly aren't as young as you used to be. You've got to start taking at least some cognizance of that fact, because there are so many things you have to do. So many things *only* you can do. And because there are so many people who love you. You owe them a willingness to at least try to take care of yourself, especially when so many of their hopes are riding on your shoulders."

Cahnyr gazed across into the taller, younger man's eyes. Then he reached up and patted the hand on his shoulder.

"All right, Gharth. You win. *This* time, at least!"

"I'll settle for any victories I can get, Your Eminence," Gorjah assured him. Then he opened the inn's front door and ushered the archbishop through it with a flourishing bow. Cahnyr chuckled, shook his head, and stepped back inside resignedly.

"Sent *you* to the rightabout, didn't he just, Your Eminence?" Fraidmyn Tohmys, Cahnyr's valet for over forty years, since his seminary days, remarked dryly from where he'd been waiting just inside that door. "Told you he would."

"Did I ever mention to you that that I-told-you-so attitude of yours is very unbecoming?"

"Now that I think about it, you may have—once or twice, Your Eminence."

Thomys followed the archbishop into the small, rustic, simply furnished side parlor which had been reserved for his personal use. The fire crackled and hissed, and the valet divested Cahnyr of his coat, gloves, scarf, and fur hat with the ease of long practice. Somehow, Cahnyr found himself seated in a comfortable chair, stocking feet towards the fire while his boots sat on a corner of the hearth and he sipped a cup of hot, strong tea.

The tea filtered down into him, filling him with a welcome heat, yet even as he sipped, he was aware of the flaws in the picture of warmth and comfort. The fire, for example, had been fed with lengths of split nearoak and logs of mountain pine, not coal, and under other circumstances, the cup of tea would have been a cup of hot chocolate or (more likely, in such a humble inn) a thick, rich soup. But the coal that would normally have been shipped down the river from Glacierheart hadn't been shipped this year, chocolate had become an only half-remembered dream of better times, and with so little food in anyone's larder, the innkeeper was reserving all he had for formal meals.

And even the formal meals are altogether too skimpy, Cahnyr thought grimly as he sipped his tea. He'd always practiced a degree of personal austerity rare among the Church's senior clergy—one reason so many of that senior clergy had persistently underestimated him as they played the Temple's power games—yet he'd also always had a weakness for a savory, well-prepared meal. He preferred simple dishes, without the course after course extravaganzas in which a sensualist like Zhaspahr Clyntahn routinely indulged, but he had had that appreciation for food.

Now his stomach growled as if to punctuate his thoughts, and his face tightened as he thought about all the other people—the thousands upon thousands in his own archbishopric—whose stomachs were far emptier than his. Even as he sat here sipping tea—as Clyntahn was undoubtedly gorging himself once more upon the finest delicacies and wines—somewhere in Glacierheart, a child was slipping away into the stillness of death because her parents simply couldn't feed her. He closed his eyes, clasping the teacup in both hands, whispering a prayer for that child he would never meet, never know, and wondered how many others would join her before this bitter winter ended.

"You're doing what you can, Your Eminence," a voice said very quietly from behind him, and he opened his eyes and turned his head to meet Thomys' gaze. The valet's smile was lopsided, and he shook his own head. "We've been together a while now, Your Eminence. I can usually tell what you're thinking."

"I know you can. They say the shepherd and his dog grow alike, so why shouldn't my keeper be able to read my mind?" Cahnyr smiled. "And I know we're doing what we can. It isn't making me feel any better about what we *can't* do, though, Fraid."

"'Course 'tisn't," Thomys agreed. "Could hardly be any other way, now could it? It's true enough, though. And you'd best be concentrating on what it is we *can* do, not brooding over what we can't. There's a mortal lot of folk in Tairys—aye, and in a lot of other places in Glacierheart—as are waiting for you, and they'll be *looking* to you once we're there, too. You're not so very wrong calling yourself a shepherd, Your Eminence, and there's sheep depending on you. So just you see to it you've the strength and the health to be there when they need you, because if you don't, you'll fail them. In all the years I've known you, I've not seen you do that a single time, and Father Gharth, and Mistress Sahmantha and I—we're not about to let you do it this time, either."

Cahnyr's eyes burned, and he nodded silently, then turned back to the fire. He heard Thomys puttering about behind him for a few more moments. Then—

"You bide by the fire, Your Eminence. I'll fetch you when it's supper-time."

The door closed behind the valet, and Cahnyr gazed deep into the fire, watching the slow, steady spill of coals, feeling the heat, thinking about the journey which still lay before him. At the moment, he and his companions were near the town of Sevryn, crossing through the northernmost rim of Shiloh, one of the provinces where neither the Republic nor Clyntahn's Temple Loyalists held clear-cut control. The Loyalists had seized its south-western portions in a grip of iron, but the northern—and especially north-eastern portions—were just as firmly under the Republic's control. The middle was a wasteland, dotted with the ruins of what had once been towns and farms where hating, embittered men hunted one another with savage intent and a cruelty no slash lizard could have equaled. This particular por-tion of Shiloh had missed—so far, at least—the wave of bloodshed sweeping through so much of the rest of the province, but the destruction of food-stuffs (and the interruption in their delivery) had made itself felt even here. As many Shilohans as could, especially women and children, had fled down the Siddar to Old Province and New Province, where the army still prom-ised security and there was at least some hope food would somehow make it up the river to them from the coast. They'd fled by barge, by boat, by canoe and even raft before the river froze; now, with the river ice four inches thick, they pulled sleds loaded with pitiful handfuls of household goods and their silent, wide-eyed children down its broad, steel gray ribbon, trudging with gaunt, starvation-thinned faces towards what they hoped—prayed—might be salvation.

Cahnyr was using that same icy road, but in the opposite direction, into the very heart of the savagery Zhaspahr Clyntahn had loosed. The ice was thick enough already to support cavalry, even light wagons, much less dog-sleds and snow lizard sleighs. They'd come as far west by barge as they could before the ice forced them to put ashore and shift to the sleds, with the loads carefully dispersed to spread the weight, and the river ice had allowed them to make far better time than they would have made by road, at least until they'd broken a runner. Unfortunately, they were still almost five hundred miles from Mountain Lake, and that assumed Glacierborn Lake had frozen over as well. It might well not have, but there would certainly be enough ice about to prevent them from crossing the lake by boat. That would increase the distance by a hundred and forty more miles by forcing them to circle around the lake's north end, and it was another four hundred and thirty miles from Mountain Lake to Tairys. Nine hundred miles—possibly over a thousand—before he could reach his destination, and Langhorne only knew what he'd find when he finally got there.

He thought about what was on those sleds, about the food he'd begged, pleaded for, even stolen in some cases. It wasn't that Lord Protector Greyghor hadn't wanted to give him all he could have asked for; it was simply that there'd been so little *to* give, especially with so many refugees pouring into the capital. The Lord Protector hadn't been able to provide him with an army escort, either, because every soldier remaining to the Republic was desperately needed elsewhere, like in the Sylmahn Gap, with its direct threat to Old Province's frontiers. Yet Stohnar also recognized the vital importance of succoring the people of Glacierheart who'd risen against their own archbishop, the man the Group of Four had named to replace Cahnyr, and beaten back the "Sword of Schueler." It wasn't just a matter of the province's critical strategic location, either, although that would have been more than enough reason to support its citizens. Any people who'd paid the price Glacierheart's had, in defiance not simply of rebels but of the Grand Inquisitor himself, had *earned* the support they desperately needed. And so Stohnar had given Cahnyr everything he possibly could, and Aivah Pahrsahn had collected still more in voluntary contributions from the capital's Charisian Quarter and refugees who themselves couldn't be certain where their next five-day's meals were coming from. Aivah had provided medicines, bandages, and healer's supplies of every description, as well.

And, Cahnyr thought harshly, she'd provided the escort Stohnar couldn't: two hundred trained riflemen, under the command of a grim, determined young man named Byrk Raimahn. There were another three hundred rifles distributed between the caravan's sleds, and Stohnar—whose armories at the moment held more weapons than he had soldiers to wield—had offered a thousand pikes, as well. There were bullets and powder in plenty, and bullet molds, as well. Zhasyn Cahnyr was a man of peace, but men of peace were in scant demand just now, and those weapons might well—probably would—prove just as vital to Glacierheart's survival as the food coming with them. But even more important was what they—and Cahnyr's return—would represent to the men and women of his archbishopric.

They had kept the faith. Now it was up to him to keep faith with them. To join them, be with them—to be their unifying force and, if necessary, to die with them. He owed them that, and he would see to it that they had it.

Thank you for coming so promptly, Kynt," Ruhsyl Thairis, the Duke of Eastshare and commander of the Imperial Charisian Army, said as his aide withdrew.

"Your message indicated it was important, Your Grace," General Sir Kynt Clareyk, the Baron of Green Valley, replied. He grimaced down at the snow melting on his boots, then looked back up at his superior. "Under the circumstances, even a Charisian boy's going to hustle out into the snow when he hears that."

"So I see." Eastshare smiled and pointed at one of the chairs in front of his desk.

Green Valley nodded his thanks and settled into the chair, watching Eastshare's face intently. The duke's expression seldom gave away much, and at the moment, Green Valley's gave away even less. It would never do for Eastshare to realize the baron already knew exactly why he'd been summoned.

A cast-iron stove from Ehdwyrd Howsmyn's foundries radiated welcome heat from a corner of the office—a heat that felt more welcome still as the rattling sleet battered its windows. It was going to turn to snow before much longer, Green Valley thought, but not before the sleet inserted a nasty sheet of ice between the layers of snow and made Maikelberg's sidewalks and pavements even more interesting to walk upon. He'd decided he really, really disliked Chisholmian winters, and the fact that he was one of the handful of people who knew the truth about Merlin Athrawes and an artificial intelligence named Owl meant he got to watch far more detailed weather forecasts than anyone else in Maikelberg.

Which is how I know it's going to be another howling blizzard by Thursday, he thought glumly. Although, to be honest, the snowfall and high winds which would soon pummel Maikelberg would scarcely count as a "blizzard" somewhere like Glacierheart or Hildermoss. It would be more than severe enough for *him*, however, and the nature of the weather currently battering Safehold's northern hemisphere was going to have quite a bearing on the reason Eastshare had sent for him.

"I've received a dispatch," Eastshare said abruptly. "One I have to take seriously, if it's really from the man it claims to be from. And"—he grimaced—"it does have all the right code words and phrases. It's just . . . hard to believe it could be accurate."

"I beg your pardon?" Green Valley sat straighter, cocking his head, and Eastshare snorted.

"If it said anything but what it does, I'm sure I would've accepted it without turning a hair. But we haven't heard a word about this from Their Majesties, and if it's accurate, the entire strategic situation's just changed out of all recognition."

"I hope you'll forgive me for saying this, Your Grace, but you're making me nervous."

Green Valley's tone was just a bit tarter than most of Eastshare's officers would have adopted, but Green Valley wasn't just any officer. He was one of Cayleb and Sharleyan Ahrmahk's trusted troubleshooters, not to mention the man who'd first worked out practical tactics for rifles and modern field artillery, and one of the very few Charisian ex-Marines who'd turned out to have far more to teach the Chisholmian army than he had to learn from it. Over the last couple of years, he'd also become one of Eastshare's favored sounding boards, and the two men had developed a personal friendship to go with their professional relationship.

"Sorry," Eastshare said now. "It's just that the courier who carried it for the last third of its trip was half dead when he got here, and even he couldn't vouch for its accuracy. According to the dispatch, though, Clyntahn's finally run completely mad."

"With all respect, Your Grace, he did *that* quite some time ago." Green Valley's voice was suddenly harsh, and Eastshare nodded.

"Agreed, but this time he's done something I wouldn't've believed even *he* was stupid enough to do. He's instigated an open revolt against Lord Protector Greyghor and tried to overthrow the entire Republic."

"He's *what*?!" Green Valley was rather proud of the genuine note of astonishment he managed to put into the question, and he stared at the duke in obvious consternation.

"That's what the dispatch says." Eastshare shrugged. "Bad enough to infuriate a kingdom half the world away like Charis, but this time they've pissed off a nation right across the Border States from the Temple Lands—and with the biggest, best disciplined army on the mainland, to boot! If Stohnar makes it through the winter . . . ."

"You do have a way with words," Green Valley said as Eastshare let his voice trail off. "Does your dispatch indicate Stohnar's *likely* to survive the winter?"

"It doesn't offer an opinion either way." Eastshare grimaced. "It only tells us what the man who sent it knew when he sent it off, although I have to admit he seems to've been fiendishly well informed. Assuming, of course, he's telling us only things he knows to be true and not relying on rumor and hearsay. It doesn't read like it's from someone who'd do that, though, and it's signed by someone named Ahbraim Zhevons. His name's on the list of completely reliable agents, too, verified by Prince Nahrmahn, Baron Wave Thunder, and Sir Ahlber. And it *does* have the right code phrases to go with the name, so I have to take it seriously. But if he's right, everything you and I have been talking about in terms of the army for the next year just got stood on its head."

"It certainly sounds that way so far," Green Valley said slowly, sitting back in his chair once more.

Unlike Duke Eastshare, he knew exactly how that message had gotten here. Although he was a bit surprised it had arrived this quickly, given the state of the icy roads (if the term "road" could be applied to narrow, rocky tracks through dense forest and heavy woods) over which it had traveled. Merlin Athrawes, in his Zhevons persona, had personally launched it from Iron Cape, the westernmost headland of Raven's Land, across the Passage of Storms from the Republic's Rollings Province. An overland message could reach Chisholm much more quickly than the same word could come from Charis by sea, despite the atrocious winter going and the collapse of the Church's semaphore chain across Raven's Land since the beginning of the Jihad.

And, of course, the word would've had to officially reach Charis before anyone could send a dispatch boat to Cherayth, he thought.

"The message may be several five-days old," Eastshare continued, "but whoever this Zhevons is, he obviously knew the sorts of information we'd need. And there's a note that he's sending a copy of the same dispatch to Tellesberg, as well."

"Did he say exactly why he sent it to you, Your Grace?"

"Not in so many words, but I think it's pretty evident *he* thinks we're going to be shifting our priorities in light of the new situation, and if he does, he's damned well right. That's why I wanted you in here this afternoon. You're going to be point man on a lot of the planning, and you need to be brought into the loop as quickly as possible."

"I appreciate that . . . I think, Your Grace," Green Valley said wryly.

"You'll get your own copy of the entire dispatch as soon as my clerks have finished copying it out for you." Eastshare tipped back in his own chair, laying his forearms along the armrests. "For now, let me just hit the highlights. Then I want you to sit down with your own staff and start making a list of what we could send into Siddarmark if the Lord Protector requests assistance."

"This Zhevons thinks he's likely to go *that* far?" Green Valley raised both eyebrows, and Eastshare shrugged.

"I don't think he's going to have much choice, if this is accurate. It sounds as if Clyntahn did his level best to plant a dagger squarely in Stohnar's back, and he damned near succeeded. I don't know where else Stohnar and the Republic can look for an ally willing to stand up beside them against Mother Church and the Inquisition. Do you?"

"Not when you put it that way," Green Valley admitted.

"Well, in that case I think we need to take it as a given that if he does manage to survive the winter, he's going to want as much help as he can possibly get as early in the year as we can get it to him. From Zhevons' note, he's probably going to be more concerned with food shipments than troops for the next couple of months, but he's got all that border with the Border States. And with Desnair and Dohlar, now that I think about it. By late spring—early summer, at the latest—his western provinces are going to be swarming with troops from the Temple Lands, from the Border States, from Desnair. Shan-wei! By *late* summer, he'll probably have *Harchongian* troops closing in for a piece of him! I'd say the odds are against him pretty heavily at the moment, but if he can hang on, and if we can figure out a way to get worthwhile numbers of our own troops into the Republic, we've got at least a fighting chance of carving out the foothold we needed on the mainland. If Stohnar goes down, it's going to be a disaster for any hope that anyone else on the mainland is going to be willing to defy Clyntahn. But if he *doesn't* go down, if he manages to survive, we just may have found the ally we needed to go after the Group of Four on their own ground."

There was nothing wrong with Eastshare's strategic instincts, Green Valley thought. The duke couldn't have had "Zhevons'" dispatch for more than an hour or two, but he'd already cut directly to the heart of the matter. And he was clearly prepared to begin planning for active intervention in the Republic even without any instructions from Cayleb or Sharleyan. That was exactly the initiative Cayleb and Merlin had hoped for when they'd sent the message, and Green Valley felt a glow of pride in his superior as he watched Eastshare responding to the challenge.

"All right," the duke said, "according to Zhevons, the whole thing must've started months ago in Zion. Apparently, what Clyntahn did was to—"

APRIL
YEAR OF GOD 896

Tellesberg Palace,
City of Tellesberg,
Kingdom of Old Charis,
Empire of Charis

I hope they don't get hammered too hard crossing The Anvil," Cayleb Ahrmahk said somberly.

The Charisian Emperor stood looking out across Howell Bay from the tower window with one arm wrapped around his Empress. His right hand rested on the point of her hip, holding her close, and her head nestled against the side of his chest. Her eyes were as dark and somber as his, but she shook her head.

"They're all experienced captains," she said, watching the thicket of sails head away from the Tellesberg wharves. There were over sixty merchant galleons in that convoy, escorted by two full squadrons of war galleons and screened by a dozen of the Imperial Charisian Navy's fleet, well armed schooners, and twenty-five more galleons from Eraystor would join it as it passed through the Sea of Charis. It was the third convoy to sail from Tellesberg already—the sixth, overall, counting those which had sailed from Emerald and Tarot, as well—and it was unlikely they were going to be able to assemble yet another in time to be much help. Besides, there simply weren't enough foodstuffs in storage in Charis, Emerald, or Tarot to fill another convoy's holds. It was a miracle they'd found as much as they had; counting this convoy, they'd sent well over five hundred galleons, carrying a hundred and forty thousand tons of food and over a quarter million tons of fodder and animal feed. It was, frankly, an almost inconceivable effort for a technology limited to sail power and small, wooden-hulled vessels, but it still hadn't been enough, for there'd been a limit to how much preserved and fresh food was available. Indeed, prices in the three huge islands had skyrocketed as the Crown and Church poured every mark they could into buying up every scrap of available food and sent it off to starving Siddarmark. The cost had been staggering, but they'd paid it without even wincing, for they had no choice. Not when she, Cayleb, and their allies could actually see the hundreds of thousands of people starving in northern Siddarmark.

"They're all experienced," she repeated. "They know what the weather's like this time of year. And your sailing instructions made it clear they were to assume the worst."

"There's a difference between knowing what the weather's like and knowing you're headed directly into one of the worst gales in the last twenty years." Cayleb's voice was as grim as his expression. "I'll lay you whatever odds you ask that we're going to lose at least some of those ships, Sharley."

"I think you may be being overly pessimistic," a voice said over the transparent plug each of them wore in one ear. "I understand why, but let's not borrow any guilt until it's actually time to feel it, Cayleb."

"I should've delayed their sailing. Just three or four days—maybe a full five-day. Just long enough for The Anvil to clear."

"And explain it how, Cayleb?" Sharleyan asked softly. "*We* can track weather fronts—do you want to explain to anyone else how we manage that? And without some sort of explanation, how could we justify delaying that food when everyone in the Empire—this side of Chisholm, anyway—knows how desperately it's needed?"

"For that matter, Cayleb," Merlin Athrawes said over the com plugs, "it *is* desperately needed. I hate to say it, but any lives we lose to wind and weather are going to be enormously outweighed by the lives we save from starvation. And"—his deep voice turned gentle—"are the lives of Charisian seamen worth more than the lives of starving Siddarmarkian children? Especially when some of the children in question are Charisians themselves? You may be Emperor, but you're not God. Do you have the right to order them *not* to sail? Not to risk their lives? What do you think the crews of those galleons would've said if you'd asked them whether they wanted to sail, even if they'd known they were going to encounter the worst storm The Anvil has to offer, knowing how badly the food they're carrying is needed at the other end? Human beings have faced far worse dangers for far worse reasons."

"But they didn't *get* to choose. They—"

Cayleb cut himself off and waved his left hand in an abrupt chopping gesture. Sharleyan sighed and turned to press her face against his tunic, wrapping both of her own arms around him, and they stood that way for several seconds. Then it was his turn to inhale deeply and turn resolutely away from the window and those slowly shrinking rectangles and pyramids of canvas.

The turn brought him face-to-face with a tall silver-haired man, with a magnificent beard and large, sinewy hands, wearing an orange-trimmed white cassock. The dovetailed ribbon at the back of his priest's cap was also orange, and a ruby ring of office glittered on his left hand.

"I notice *you* didn't have anything to say about my little moodiness," the emperor told him, and he smiled faintly.

"I've known you since you were a boy, Cayleb," Archbishop Maikel Staynair replied. "Unlike Sharley and Merlin, I learned long ago that the only way to deal with these self-flagellating humors of yours is to wait you out. Eventually even *you* figure out you're being harder on yourself than you would've been on anyone else and we can get on to more profitable uses of our time."

"You always have such a compassionate and supportive way of dealing with me in my hour of need, Your Eminence," Cayleb said sardonically, and Staynair chuckled.

"Would you really prefer for me to get all weepy-eyed instead of kicking you—respectfully, of course—in the arse?"

"It would at least have the virtue of novelty," Cayleb replied, his tone dry, and the archbishop chuckled again. Then he cocked one eyebrow at the imperial couple and gestured at the small conference table waiting under one of the skylights set into the tower chamber's sloping roof.

"I suppose so." Cayleb sighed, and escorted Sharleyan across to it. He pulled out her chair for her, then waited until Staynair had seated himself before taking his own place.

"It'll be nice when you get home, Merlin. I can't throttle you properly when you're so far away," he remarked to the empty air as he sat, and it was Merlin's turn to chuckle.

"I'll see you tomorrow," he promised, "and you can throttle away to your heart's content. Or try to, anyway. And the trip's been worth it. We're never going to get over the hole Mahndrayn's left, but Captain Rahzwail's turning out to be pretty impressive himself. Even more impressive than I'd expected, really. In fact, I wouldn't be too surprised if he turns out to be a candidate for the inner circle in the not too distant."

"Rushing it a bit, aren't you?" Cayleb asked quizzically, and Merlin—perched like a cross-legged tailor atop one of King's Harbor Citadel's merlons—shrugged.

"I didn't suggest telling him tomorrow, Cayleb," he pointed out mildly. "I'm simply saying I think he has the . . . resiliency and flexibility to take it in stride. And given his new post, it would certainly be useful."

"Not as useful as telling *Ahlfryd* would be." Sharleyan's voice was unwontedly sharp, and Cayleb looked at her. "I understand all the reasons for not telling him," the empress went on in that same edged tone, "but we've told others who even the Brethren agreed were greater risks than he'd ever be, and there's not a more trustworthy man in the entire Empire!"

"Besides which, he's your friend," Staynair said gently. Her head whipped around, anger flickering in her eyes, but Staynair met them with his normal calm, unflurried gaze.

"That has nothing to do with my estimate of how useful it would be to have him fully integrated into the inner circle, Maikel," she said, her tone flat.

"No, but it has quite a bit to do with how guilty you feel for not having told him." Staynair gave his head a slight shake. "And how disloyal you feel for not having managed to convince the Brethren to trust him with the information."

The empress' eyes bored hotly into his for another handful of seconds before they fell. She looked down at her own slender, shapely hands, so tightly folded on the table before her that their knuckles had whitened, and the archbishop reached out to lay one of his own far larger hands atop them.

"I understand, Sharley," he told her softly. "But don't forget, Bryahn was his friend, too, and it was Bryahn who recommended *against* telling him. And you know why, too, don't you?"

Sharleyan never looked up, but, after a moment, she nodded ever so slightly, and Staynair smiled sadly at the crown of her head.

Sir Ahlfryd Hyndryk, Baron Seamount, was quite possibly the most brilliant Charisian naval officer of his generation, and he'd become one of Sharleyan's favorite people during her original visit to Charis. In fact, virtually everyone in the slowly growing circle of Charisians who knew the truth about the Terran Federation and the monumental lie which underlay the entire Church of God Awaiting knew him and held him in deep affection, although he was closer to Sharleyan than to anyone except, perhaps, Staynair's brother, Domynyk. No member of the inner circle questioned his loyalty or his intelligence. But Bryahn Lock Island had been right to fear his integrity . . . and his outrage.

In another time and another place, Ahlfryd Hyndryk would have been called a geek, and he had all of that breed's impatience with subterfuge and dissimulation. Sheer love of knowledge and impatience to rebuild the technology the Proscriptions of Jwo-jeng had denied to Safehold so long would have been bad enough, driving him to press the limits of what was being introduced, perhaps too hard and too fast. But his wrath at the way the entire population of the last surviving world of humanity had been lied to, been robbed of the stars themselves, would have been even worse. Lock Island had feared that the combination of impatience and fury—and the awareness of how desperately Charis needed every advantage it could find— would have pushed their brilliant, adaptive problem solver into too openly challenging the Proscriptions, defying the doctrine of the Church of God Awaiting, even denouncing the Church itself as the monstrous lie it was. And if that happened in the midst of the Charisian Empire's war against the Group of Four . . . .

Merlin gazed out over the blue water of King's Harbor, at the swarm of ships covering the surface, the hive of activity, so much of which had resulted directly from Seamount's fertile imagination and compulsive energy, and his sapphire eyes were cold. They dared not risk revealing the truth about the archangels, the Church, Langhorne's Rakurai and Armageddon Reef. Not yet. Not when such revelations would play directly into the Group of Four's denunciation of them all as lying, blasphemous servants of corruption. And so, if it had turned out Seamount was a threat to the secret they all guarded, that threat would have to be removed . . . permanently.

"I swear to you, Sharleyan," he said now over the com, softly, "the instant I'm certain it would be safe to tell him, I will." He smiled crookedly. "It won't be the first time I've, ah, *overridden* the Brethren, if you'll recall. And if I do it and it turns out I was wrong about the safety factor, I'll drag him off to Nimue's Cave and pop him into one of the cryo units until it *is* safe to turn him loose again." He watched through the SNARC remote perched on the ceiling above the conference table as the empress looked up with a sudden, astounded smile, and he chuckled softly. "I don't have room for many people," he told her, "but Ahlfryd's one of the special ones. If we end up telling him and it turns out we shouldn't have, he deserves space in the cave. Besides, that way we'll know he's still going to be around when we're able to begin rebuilding our tech base *openly!*"

"I hadn't thought of that." Cayleb sounded more than a bit chagrined.

"Well, you didn't exactly grow up with technology, now, did you?" Merlin shrugged. "On the other hand, I'd really hate to do that, because he's so damned useful where he is. You do realize he's come up with more original departures, even without access to Owl, than Ehdwyrd?"

"Fair's fair, Merlin," Staynair pointed out. "Ehdwyrd's deliberately picking his spots carefully—and giving someone else credit for them whenever he can."

"Oh, I know that, Maikel. I'm just saying Ahlfryd's a mighty impressive fellow to've come up with so many ideas, and inspired so many of his assistants—like Mahndrayn—to come up with ideas of their own. He's taken even the ones I've 'steered' him into and run with them, generally to places I didn't expect him to get to without at least another few nudges. The truth is, Bryahn was right about that, too. He's doing exactly what we need done even without Owl, and he's teaching an entire generation of navy officers and the civilians working with them to use their brains, push the envelope, and explore the possibilities."

"So now that we've all made me feel better," Sharleyan said in a tart tone much closer to normal, "perhaps we should go ahead and deal with the original agenda for our little get-together?"

"As always, your wish is our command, love." Cayleb smiled at her across the table, and she kicked him gently in the knee under it.

"Such a brutal, physically abusive sort," he mourned, and she stuck out her tongue.

"However," he continued more briskly, "you have a point. Especially since the rest of you have also made *me* feel better—sort of, anyway—about sailing the convoy despite the weather. So, Maikel. Your impressions?"

"I think . . . I think Stohnar is going to make it through the winter," Staynair said slowly, his expression far more somber. "For several five-days I was afraid he wasn't, especially when the Temple Loyalists in Mountaincross tried to push through the Sylmahn Gap." He shook his head. "It didn't seem possible he could stop them."

"He wouldn't have without 'Aivah.'" Merlin's own expression was as grim as his voice. "Those extra rifles—and the men trained to use them—are what made the difference. That and the food we were able to ship in."

"The food he didn't know was coming," Sharleyan said softly. "I think he's aged ten years since this started."

"Probably," Merlin acknowledged. "And I think he's going to be a long time forgiving himself for some of the calls he's made, but thank God for that military background of his. Without it, he *wouldn't*'ve made them, and in that case, Maikel's right—the Temple Loyalists would've come through the Gap into Old Province."

Heads nodded around the table. Greyghor Stohnar had recognized the absolute necessity of keeping his enemies locked up behind the Moon Thorn and Snow Barren Mountains at any cost. If the Group of Four's adherents had broken out of Mountaincross Province, they would have opened a direct invasion pathway from the Temple Lands into the most densely populated province of the entire Republic . . . and to its capital. He'd *had* to hold that mountain barrier, and so he had . . . even at the expense of sending desperately needed food from the starving families of Siddar City to the troops fighting in the snow and freezing cold of the Sylmahn Gap.

Eastern Siddarmark was far more densely populated than its western provinces, and the *south*eastern provinces were even more heavily populated than the more northern ones, thank God. Still, there were well over seventy million people in the portion of the Republic which remained under his control, and the timing of Clyntahn's uprising—and its deliberate attacks on food supplies and the transport system—had been catastrophic. Westmarch, Tarikah, New Northland, northern Hildermoss, western Mountaincross, and the South March were major centers of the Republic's agricultural production, and all of them had been taken by the rebels or were (at best) disputed battlefields where no one was worrying much about farming. Crop-burning rebels had done major damage to the harvests in Southguard, Trokhanos, Cliff Peak, and Northland as well, before they'd been subdued in those provinces. The lord protector had lost over a third of the Republic's best cropland and twenty-five or thirty percent of its normal winter food supply, and the disruption of the revolt had sent enormous numbers of refugees streaming into areas which wouldn't have been able to feed even themselves adequately. Starvation and disease—disease brought on by the breakdown of sanitation in the refugee camps, despite the *Book of Pasquale*'s stern injunctions, and the weakened resistance of human beings getting perhaps half the calories they actually needed—had stalked the Republic like demons, and that was the background against which he'd had to choose whether or not to reinforce and supply the field army driving into eastern Mountaincross, slogging ahead through snow and ice to reach the outnumbered, starving troops somehow clinging to the crucial mountain gap.

It was a decision he'd had to make long before any response to his frantic pleas for help could possibly come back from Tellesberg. He'd had no idea how soon—or even if—the first relief convoy from Charis could reach him, yet he'd made it anyway, sending every man he could spare, and the precious food to feed them, under his own first cousin's command. And Sharleyan was right: it *had* aged him overnight. It had engraved deep lines into his face, streaked his dark hair with thick swathes of iron gray, and turned his cheekbones hard and gaunt. Not by itself, but in conjunction with all the other decisions he'd had to make and the knowledge of what was happening to the Republic's citizens where he couldn't reach them at all, couldn't do one single thing about the privation and terror being visited upon them.

Greyghor Stohnar was a strong man, but he'd sat in his pew in Siddar Cathedral with his face buried in his hands, shoulders heaving, as he listened to the joyously tolling bells and wept in gratitude when that first convoy sailed into Bedard Bay. The schooner sent ahead to tell him it was coming, delayed by The Anvil's quixotic headwinds, had arrived less than twelve hours before the convoy itself, and the Charisian seamen aboard those galleons had labored until they collapsed, unloading sack after sack of Charisian and Emeraldian rice and yams and corn, Tarotisian potatoes, carrots, and apples. Swaying cask after cask of preserved fish, pork, beef, and dragon out of their ships' holds and into the lighters alongside or the wagons waiting in endless lines along Siddar City's wharves. Lightering ashore the milk cows sent to replace those which had been slaughtered in desperation as the fodder ran out and the people starved, and the fodder to keep at least some of the surviving farm animals alive.

Foods like rice and yams were virtually unknown in the Republic, but mothers with pinched, gaunt faces had stood for hours in biting wind and cold, soaking rain to take home a few pounds of the exotic Charisian foods which would make the difference between their children's lives and death. And as any galleon was emptied, it turned, setting sail back towards Charis, more often than not with a cargo of orphans or the sick to be delivered to Charisian orphanages, hospitals, and monasteries.

It was the largest relief effort in Safehold's history, tying up almost a quarter of the Empire's total merchant fleet. The repercussions of that on trade and military logistics scarcely bore thinking upon, yet it had sent enough food to feed over a million and a half people at least a thousand calories a day and keep almost a half-million desperately needed farm animals alive for three months. Three months in which Charis, Tarot, and Emerald would double the land they had under cultivation and labor gangs throughout eastern Siddarmark would put seed into the ground anywhere it wasn't too frozen to plow.

Too many had died anyway, and more would die still, but Siddar City wasn't the only place Charisian convoys had landed lifesaving supplies. Trokhanos Province, Malitar, Windmoor, Rollings . . . Charisian ships had been everywhere, landing their cargos wherever they could find a few fathoms of seawater.

There were those who wondered how even monarchs as legendary for their foresight as Cayleb and Sharleyan Ahrmahk could have known to begin organizing that relief effort five-days before the first messenger from Siddarmark ever reached them. Most accepted Maikel Staynair's explanation—totally honest, as far as it went—that Charisian agents had begun to suspect Clyntahn's intentions well before the Sword of Schueler struck. For the die-hard Temple Loyalists, there was a simpler, more acceptable explanation, of course—one supplied and endorsed by the Inquisition. They'd long since decided that in addition to all the blasphemies and heresies the world knew about, Cayleb and Sharleyan had sold themselves to Shan-wei—Cayleb in return for his demon familiar, Merlin Athrawes, and the sorceress Sharleyan in return for the power to steal the hearts and minds of even the godliest men and seduce them into Shan-wei's evil—so *of course* they could foresee the future as well.

Frankly, there was more truth in that explanation (in Safeholdian terms, at least) than Merlin really cared for, but the vast majority of Siddarmarkians didn't care how Cayleb and Sharleyan had known. No, what *they* cared about was that the House of Ahrmahk had begun assembling those convoys of food and medical supplies long before they'd been asked to, and that they'd sent them to the Republic with no strings attached. No demand for payment, for alliances. No political conditions or stipulations. The Empire and Church of Charis had simply sent everything it had the hulls to move, and that was why a strong man had sat in a cathedral and wept as his capital's church bells rang out the news that even in a world gone mad, there was a realm and a church which simply sent what it had to those who needed it so desperately.

There was an edge of realpolitik to it, of course. No one in Charis could be blind to the gratitude and goodwill that the relief effort had bought the Empire. Yet that truly hadn't been the primary reason Cayleb and Sharleyan had mounted it. A highly desirable second wyvern to hit with the same stone, yes, but Merlin knew that food would have moved north across Safehold's stormy seas even if they'd known no alliance, no treaties of mutual aid, would ever come of it.

Not that anyone was going to complain—assuming Staynair was right and Stohnar and the Republic survived the winter—over what *had* come of it.

"There's no question in my mind that Stohnar's going to agree to the draft treaty terms when they get to Dragoner," he said now. "There's not a thing in them that doesn't track exactly with his own offer of alliance, and frankly, without us, he doesn't have a chance of holding off the Group of Four."

"Especially not with that army Rahnyld's about to send over the border into the South March," Cayleb said grimly. "Oh, and let's not forget that 'voluntary' free passage for *Desnairian* troops Trynair's about to extort out of Silkiah, either."

"Agreed." Merlin nodded, his eyes watching as a trio of war galleons made sail, standing slowly out of King's Harbor into the broader, darker waters of Howell Bay for gunnery practice. "Clyntahn and Maigwair are at least smart enough to know they have to go for a quick knockout, before *we* can intervene effectively."

"How long do you think?" Cayleb asked. "Another month?"

"Probably." Merlin's expression was thoughtful. "It might be a little longer—thank God Rahnyld's army doesn't have its own equivalent of *Thirsk*! They're getting themselves organized faster than I could wish, though, even without that. Desnair's going to be at least another four or five five-days behind that, unless they do go ahead and ferry a Desnairian invasion force across Salthar Bay to support the Dohlarans."

"Not going to happen." There was no doubt at all in Cayleb's tone. "Rahnyld trusts Mahrys about as far as Clyntahn trusts *me*. Even if the Group of Four gives him a direct order to pass Mahrys through his kingdom, he'll drag his heels harder than Sharley ever did when the Knights of the Temple Lands ordered her to help Hektor burn Charis to the ground! He'll argue—and with some justification, really—that he doesn't have the bottoms to move that many men, or the logistic capability to support them all through Dohlar. And he'll spin it out long enough that by the time he's done, Mahrys will have his invasion route through Silkiah cleared, instead. At which point, it'll still take *another* month to actually get any Desnarian troops into Siddarmark."

It was possible Cayleb was being a bit overly optimistic, Merlin thought, but overall he agreed with the emperor's analysis, and Sharleyan was nodding firmly.

"That's good," Staynair said. "Unfortunately, unless I'm mistaken, that still means Emperor Mahrys is likely to be invading the Republic before Duke Eastshare can get anywhere near enough of the Army into Siddarmark to stop him. And then there's King Rahnyld, of course."

"True," Cayleb said in a harsher, darker tone. "That suggestion we send a message from Zhevons was a good one, Merlin. But even with Kynt to do the planning and prodding, the thought of marching an army through Raven's Land to the Passage of Storms obviously doesn't really appeal to Eastshare. And I'm not surprised it doesn't, to be fair. Even if the Raven Lords decide to actively cooperate rather than harassing him every step of the way, any army he force-marches across those so-called roads is going to be more than a little ragged by the time it finally gets to Siddarmark. At which point, I might add, it's going to be at the wrong end of the Republic to stop Dohlar or Desnair."

"I know, but it would still get them there faster than we could move them the full distance by sea. This time at least. And every mile he marches them west is one less mile a transport will have to cross. Even if he only gets them as far as Marisahl before we can start getting transports to him, it'll cut his arrival time a lot. And if he gets as far as, say, Malphyra Bay, we can cut the number of transports he needs in half because of the reduced turnaround time for the round trip. *Especially* if he keeps on marching west with the second echelon of his army while the first one's en route aboard ship. He can be in Marisahl forty days after he crosses The Fence, if he pushes hard, and in Malphyra in another twenty. And we wouldn't *have* to send him across to Rollings Province once we got him aboard ship, you know. There'd be time to pick another destination if it seemed like a good idea."

Cayleb grunted unhappily. The instinctive understanding of the huge logistical advantages conferred by oceanic transport was bred into the blood and bone of any Charisian monarch. The notion of sending an army or large amounts of freight overland instead of by sea was as foreign and unnatural to them as trying to breathe water, and all of those Ahrmahk instincts were insisting that it *had* to make far more sense to send any expeditionary force from Chisholm to Siddarmark aboard ship. They were persistent and clamorous, those instincts, and usually they would have been right. Unfortunately, the situation wasn't exactly usual.

A well-conditioned infantry army could make perhaps forty miles a day marching overland, assuming it didn't have to stop for niggling little details like, oh, foraging for food or allowing its draft animals to graze. Of course, grazing in Chisholm or Raven's Land in winter wouldn't have been very practical, even if it wouldn't have subtracted several hours a day from the army's marching time. Since grazing wouldn't be practical, an army with an overland supply route could count on adding its draft animals' starvation to all the other minor inconveniences it confronted. A transport galleon, on the other hand, under average conditions, could make between two hundred and three hundred miles a day, up to seven times the distance that army could cover on its own feet, and without losing the dragons and horses and mules its transport would depend upon once it reached its objective to starvation and sickness.

But Eastshare had very few transports available in Chisholm. In fact, he couldn't have squeezed more than a very few thousand men aboard the ships he had, and he couldn't put even that many of them aboard ship until he collected those ships in one spot. And that spot would have to be on the *east coast* of Chisholm, so even after he put the troops aboard, he'd still be over twelve thousand miles—and forty-seven days—from Siddar City.

He could probably commandeer a few more transports from Corisande, but not very many. Certainly not enough to make any real difference. The only place he could get the amount of troop lift he required would be to request it from Old Charis, and even with the most favorable winds imaginable, it would take a dispatch vessel over a month to reach Tellesberg from Maikelberg. Even after it did, it would take Cayleb and Sharleyan several five-days just to divert ships from the Siddarmarkian relief efforts and get them gathered together. Given how dire conditions in the Republic were, they couldn't possibly justify pulling galleons out of the relief convoys until the ships had been officially asked for, since there was no way even monarchs with their reputation for foresight could know Eastshare was going to need them. And, on top of all that, it would take at least a month and a half—more probably two months—for those galleons to reach Chisholm once they'd been collected and ordered to sail.

Those unpalatable facts had left Eastshare and Green Valley with very few options for moving troops rapidly into Siddarmark, and it was the duke, not the baron, who'd come up with the most radical solution. Green Valley had been prepared to suggest it if necessary, but that hadn't been required, which said some truly remarkable things about Eastshare's mental flexibility.

He didn't have the troop lift to move a worthwhile number of men, but he *did* have enough sealift to move quite a lot of supplies, especially food and fodder, and those two commodities were the Achilles' heel of preindustrial armies. An army which had to forage for food—and fodder—as it went (even assuming the season and agricultural productivity made that possible) did well to make ten miles a day, and it wreaked havoc on any civilian population in its path simply because it stripped the land bare as it went. But without that requirement, and with the ability to feed draft animals on grain and prepared fodder rather than requiring them to graze on grass, an army was limited only by the hours of daylight it had in which to march and the quality of the roads before it.

So Eastshare had sent off his dispatches to Tellesberg and begun concentrating the garrisons stationed throughout western Chisholm on Ahlysberg, the military city which had been built to support The Fence, the fortified frontier between the Western Crown Demesne and Raven's Land. It was the westernmost of Chisholm's true seaports, and its magazines and storehouses were well stocked with food, boots, winter clothing, and fodder. The galleons he'd been able to lay hands on in Cherayth and Port Royal were already loading additional food and supplies in Chisholm's eastern ports; within no more than another five-day or so, they'd be setting sail for Ahlys Bay. And from there, theoretically, at least, they would be available to leapfrog along the southern coast of Raven's Land, supplying a fast-moving army as it marched west overland.

The Chisholmian Royal Army had always emphasized physical conditioning and training in every sort of weather. It wasn't unusual for an army battalion to find itself ordered, with no previous warning, to fall in with full field packs and two days' iron rations for a sixty-mile march through February snows—or, conversely, June heat—and the Imperial Charisian Army hadn't changed in that respect. Assuming the Raven Lords were as amenable as usual to subsidies (it would never do to call them "bribes"), and that Bishop Trahvys Shulmyn couldn't convince them otherwise, Eastshare and Green Valley could theoretically have marched clear to Iron Cape, probably making good their forty miles per day, despite the narrow, snowy roads. Of course, it would have taken them several months, given the distances involved, but it was only forty days' march from The Fence to the city of Marisahl (the nearest thing the Raven Lords had to a capital), on Ramsgate Bay, while another twenty days' march would take them to Malphyra Bay, eight hundred miles farther west. That was still a long way from the Republic, but the voyage time from Tellesberg to Marisahl was less than half that of the time from Tellesberg to Maikelberg, and from Marisahl to Rollings Province by sea was only fifteen days. From Malphyra to Rollings was under ten days.

So if Eastshare was truly prepared to put his troops into motion as soon as possible, without direct orders from Sharleyan and Cayleb, and when he had no way to be certain his request for transports to be dispatched to Raven's Land despite winter storms and ice floes would be honored by the monarchs with whom he hadn't even discussed moving troops to invade a sovereign realm in the middle of winter, he could cut a minimum of two months from the transit loop. He'd have enough shipping to keep his men supplied as they marched along the coastal roads, but he wouldn't have enough troop lift to move them across the Passage of Storms. On the other hand, by reducing the total length of the sea passage by how far west his men could come on their own feet, he'd effectively reduce the number of transports needed for the voyage simply because they could make the round trip with half his men, then return for the other half, far more quickly than they could make the voyage clear from Chisholm.

If Eastshare was willing to take that gamble, the Imperial Charisian Army could have upwards of sixty thousand men—possibly as many as seventy-five thousand—in Siddarmark long before Clyntahn or Maigwair would have believed was possible. Perhaps not soon enough to stymie the general assault everyone knew was coming, but certainly earlier than anyone on the other side could have anticipated.

"Ruhsyl will do it," Sharleyan said almost serenely, her eyes as confident as Cayleb's had been when he was analyzing Rahnyld of Dohlar's motives and actions.

"Are you sure?" Cayleb's tone wasn't a challenge, only a question. "I know he's sent his message to Marisahl and he's already got the first divisions on the march, but he hasn't said a word to any of his generals about moving anywhere beyond Ahlysberg. I'd say it's pretty clear he's still thinking at least as much in terms of making the entire trip by sea."

"Only because he hasn't heard back from the Raven Lords yet," Sharleyan replied, and shrugged slightly. "He's hedging his bets, and you're right that he'd much rather have a guarantee of free passage from Shairncross and the Council. I think that's one reason he'd just as soon not start moving towards The Fence until he does hear back from Shairncross, actually. God knows the Raven Lords are a prickly, stubborn bunch, even without the religious aspect of it all! The last thing he'd want would be to look as if he were massing troops on their border to cow them into meeting his demands. Even if the Council agreed to grant him passage, those stiff-necked clansmen would consider it their sacred duty—in more ways than one!—to delay him any way they could if they thought the Council had caved in to threats. And he doesn't trust Lord Theralt as far as he can spit, either. But he'd be staging through Ahlysberg and its stores magazines no matter what, and I'm sure he's at least keeping the possibility of taking them all the way from Ahlys Bay to the Republic by sea in the back of his head, if something untoward happens. After all, the thought of marching through Raven's Land, in the winter, against guerrilla opposition would be enough to give anyone pause! But in the end, he'll do it anyway, if it comes down to it."

Cayleb couldn't quite expunge the doubt from his expression, but Sharleyan only looked back at him with a small, crooked smile.

"There's not a man alive whose loyalty and judgment I trust more than Ruhsyl Thairis'. It's obvious he understands how important it is to get troops into Siddarmark as quickly as possible, and he knows you and I will never leave his men hanging at the end of an unsupported supply route. He won't worry about whether or not we'll approve or disapprove; he'll only worry about whether or not it really is the fastest way to get those men where they have to be."

Cayleb gazed at her for a moment longer, then nodded in acceptance and agreement.

"That still leaves what's going to be going on in the western Republic before he can possibly get there, though," he pointed out after a moment.

"All we can do is all we can do," Merlin said, his tone more composed than he actually felt. "Paitryk Hywyt's going to land over five thousand Marines in Siddar City next five-day, and Domynyk's combing out every additional Marine he can find." He grimaced. "Admittedly, there aren't as many of them as there were before we transferred so many to the Army after the Corisande campaign, but if he drafts them from every galleon in Home Fleet and scours Helen Island down to the bedrock, he can probably turn up another six thousand or so. And he's prepared to draft seamen, as well."

It was Cayleb's turn to grimace, and Merlin chuckled.

"All right, I'll admit they're going to be out of their natural element. But you may have noticed it's a bit hard to find a coward amongst them even when you need one, and I'll take our seamen over most people's trained soldiers any day. Even if we can't stop Rahnyld dead, I expect we'll be able to slow him down. And with a little luck, his troops are going to react . . . poorly, shall we say, the first time they meet shrapnel shells."

"And at least most of the Marines will have Mahndrayns," Cayleb agreed, his grimace segueing into a thin smile, edged with sad memory, as he used the term. The decision to name the Charisian Empire's new breech-loading rifles after Urvyn Mahndrayn, the brilliant, murdered naval officer who'd come up with the design, had made itself without anyone quite knowing how. It was as fitting as it was inevitable, though, and even though the new rifles weren't available in the numbers anyone would really have preferred, they were going to come as a nasty surprise to the Group of Four and their allies.

At the moment, however, the Imperial Charisian Marines actually had more of them than the army. Virtually all of the conversions had been made here in Charis, in the newly completed Urvyn Mahndrayn Armory Ehdwyrd Howsmyn had constructed at the Delthak Works, his massive foundry complex on the shore of Lake Ithmyn, where the tooling existed and security could be maintained. The army troops who—hopefully—would soon be marching through Raven's Land, would be equipped almost exclusively with the old-style muzzle-loaders, whereas the Marines (the majority of whom were based either in Old Charis, Tarot, or Emerald) had been close enough to Howsmyn's facility to be reequipped with Mahndrayns as they left the workshop floor. There were several thousand more of them already crated for shipment as well, however, and Howsmyn's workers were laboring with fiercely focused energy to convert still more of them. More thousands were leaving the workshop floors as new build weapons, although that was slower than conversion of existing stocks. Hopefully, by the time Eastshare's column could reach Iron Cape, enough of the new rifles would have been completed to be shipped to him and exchanged for his muzzle-loaders, which could then be returned to Charis and converted in turn.

Or, more probably, simply handed over to the Siddarmarkian Army, whose troopers wouldn't give a damn that they were "old-fashioned." *Any* rifle was one hell of a lot better than *no* rifle. That was what the vast majority of the Republic's troops had at the moment, and the sudden appearance of forty or fifty thousand Siddarmarkian riflemen would come as a nasty and unwelcome surprise to Zhaspahr Clyntahn.

"I really don't like doing all our logistic reorganization on the fly this way." Cayleb's unhappy tone spoke for all of them. "There's too much chance we're going to drop a stitch somewhere, even with Kynt tied into the com net. Simply running into more bad weather could throw everything out of gear at exactly the wrong moment."

"That's been true of everything we've done so far, love," Sharleyan pointed out.

"Not to *this* extent," Cayleb replied with an off-center grin. "I realize I have a reputation for impetuosity, but I actually have tried to make sure I had—What was that expression of yours, Merlin? 'All my pigs and chickens in a row,' was it?—before I leapt headlong into yet another reckless adventure."

"I used the phrase *once*, Cayleb," Merlin said with a certain asperity. "One time. It just slipped out that single time, and I've never used it again."

"You can't fool me, Merlin. It's not just 'a phrase' at all, is it? Not really. It's a *cliché*—that's what it is. One that no one on Safehold ever heard of until you resurrected it out of the ash heap of history, where any decent soul would've left it."

"*I'm* not the one using it; *you* are!" Merlin shot back while Staynair and Sharleyan looked at each other in amusement.

"But only because you inserted that accursed string of words into my innocent and untrammeled brain. It's like . . . like one of those childhood songs you can't get out of your mind. Like that stupid jingle you taught me back in the carefree days of my bachelorhood, the one about bottles of beer on the wall. I'm doomed—*doomed*, I tell you! Within five-days, a month at the outside, that same fatal phrase will slip out of my mouth in a formal audience, and everyone will think *I* coined it. Every hanger-on, every flatterer and sycophant, will start using it when he thinks I'll hear about it. Before you know it, it'll creep into common usage throughout the entire Empire, and future historians will blame it on *me*, Merlin—not you, where the guilt truly belongs—when it's wormed its way inextricably into the very sinews of our language." The emperor shook his head sadly. "To think that I'll be remembered for that rather than for my prowess in battle."

"Given the penalties for regicide, I feel very fortunate to be here on the island instead of there in Tellesberg at this moment," Merlin said meditatively, and Cayleb laughed. Then the emperor's expression sobered once more.

"Even if it does sound incredibly silly, the concept's still valid," he said. "And I'd feel a lot better if our chickens really were neatly in line behind our pigs before we started on all this."

"We all would, Cayleb," Staynair said serenely. "On the other hand, Sharley does have a point. This isn't going to be any more of a scramble than the Armageddon Reef campaign was, and you're in a much stronger relative position than you were then. Not to mention having acquired quite a lot of well-trained subordinates since then, all of whom know exactly what you and Sharley are going to expect them to do. It's not given to mortal men and women to simply command success with the wave of a hand or a magic wand, and it's always possible we simply aren't going to be able to get enough troops into Siddarmark quickly enough to stem the tide. But if we don't, it won't be because we didn't try, and that's what God expects of us." The archbishop smiled slightly. "He's done pretty well by us so far, and I don't see any reason to expect Him to do any differently now."

"Neither do I, Maikel," Merlin said from Helen Island. "You do remember that other cliché, though, don't you? The one about God helping those who help themselves?"

"Indeed I do."

"Then in that case, I think Cayleb and Sharleyan and I would like you to do the heavy lifting with God while we see about doing as much of that more mundane helping as we can."

"I think that's an entirely equitable division of labor, Merlin," Staynair said with another, broader smile. "In fact, I've already started."

W
ell, *this* would've been a nasty business, even if we'd won at Darcos Sound," Phylyp Ahzgood, Earl of Coris, said.

The earl sat on the breech ring of *Destiny*'s number three quarterdeck carronade as he gazed across the sunlit blue and green water of The Throat, the long, narrow strait which connected Howell Bay to the Charisian Sea, at the tall walls and imposing battlements of the centuries-old fortress which guarded the island the Charisians had named simply The Lock. That island sat almost directly in the center of The Throat, and it was flanked by even larger fortresses on either shore of the strait, overlooking the ship channels which passed on opposite sides of Lock Island.

Those channels were too broad to be entirely covered by the fortresses' guns, but the Charisians had dealt with that. Floating batteries—little more than enormous barges with five-foot-thick bulwarks . . . and two complete gundecks each—had been anchored to sweep the narrowest portions of the channels. Coris was pretty sure the batteries he was looking at were replacements for the ones whose construction King Haarahld had rushed through to cover The Throat prior to the Battle of Darcos Sound. These actually had recognizable prows, rudders, bowsprits, and stumpy masts, indicating they were designed to move (clumsily, perhaps, but move) under their own power rather than simply being towed into position. And each of them mounted at least forty guns—very *heavy* guns—in each broadside. Some showed as many as fifty, giving them twice the firepower of any galleon ever built, even by the Charisian Navy. The possibility of any conceivable fleet forcing The Throat against that sort of firepower simply didn't exist.

"You *might*'ve gotten through against the original batteries, My Lord." Lieutenant Aplyn-Ahrmahk stood on the other side of the carronade, his arms crossed, his hat lowered on his forehead to shield his eyes against the sunlight, and his expression was somber. "They weren't this powerful," he continued, confirming Coris' own thoughts, "and they were armed completely with carronades, not krakens. But, yes, it would've been a 'nasty business,' My Lord. Almost as nasty as Darcos Sound."

Coris looked quickly at the younger man.

"I didn't mean to bring up unpleasant memories, Your Grace."

"Not your fault, My Lord." Aplyn-Ahrmahk smiled briefly. "And there are a lot of good ones to go with them. He was a *man*, King Haarahld. A good man, and a good king, and I was luckier than I ever deserved to have known him."

"It may be hard for a Charisian to believe," Coris said, "but a lot of Corisandians would've said the same thing about Prince Hektor." He shook his head. "He had his faults—enormous ones, in fact—but I'm sure even King Haarahld had at least *some* faults, and Hektor's subjects by and large thought well of him. Very well, in fact. And he was my friend as well as my prince."

"I know that, My Lord." Aplyn-Ahrmahk looked back across at Lock Island and grimaced. "And it's not hard for a Charisian—*this* Charisian, at least—to realize different men are different people *to* different people. For the most part, though, you'd be hard put to find a Charisian who didn't take a certain satisfaction in Prince Hektor's death." He shrugged, never looking away from the island as *Destiny* sailed slowly past it. "When everyone thought the Emperor had ordered his assassination, the main reaction was that it was a fitting punishment. And feelings ran even higher than that in Chisholm. In fact," the lieutenant smiled a crooked smile, "I think the Empress Mother is still a bit disappointed that Cayleb *wasn't* the one who had him assassinated."

"I can't say I'm surprised." Coris watched the young duke's profile. "For that matter, I'd probably feel the same in their position. But attitudes, even—or perhaps especially, *emotional* attitudes—can influence thinking in ways the people doing the thinking never realize they have."

"Oh, I know," Aplyn-Ahrmahk snorted. "I suppose the trick's to get past it, and I'd think reminding yourself it can happen even to you would have to be the first step. It's hard though, sometimes."

His eyes strayed from Lock Island to where Princess Irys and Prince Daivyn stood in the shade of the canvas awning stretched across the quarterdeck, watching the same island.

"Yes, it is," Coris agreed, following the lieutenant's gaze. "And it was especially hard for Irys. She loved her father a great deal, and he was her father first and her prince second. I think she'd probably be one of the first to admit she shared his ambitions, at least at secondhand, but that was because they were *his* ambitions, not because they were hers."

"No?" Aplyn-Ahrmahk turned to look directly at Coris.

"He was her *father*, Your Grace." Coris smiled sadly. "It's hard for anyone to admit the father they love isn't perfect or that anyone could legitimately see him as a villain. I think that's even harder for a daughter than it is for a son, sometimes. But you may've noticed my princess has a very, very sharp brain, and she never willingly lies to herself. She still loves him, and she always will, but that doesn't mean her eyes haven't been opened to the reasons other people might *not* have loved him. And she's a princess, the only sister of the rightful Prince of Corisande. She knows how politics and diplomacy work . . . and however little she may like to admit it even to herself, she knows who actually started the war between Corisande and Charis."

"I've never discussed any of that with her." It was Aplyn-Ahrmahk's turn to smile ever so slightly. "Mostly because I'm pretty sure we wouldn't agree."

"She might surprise you." The earl shrugged. "She and I *have* discussed it, which gives me a bit of an unfair advantage when it comes to predicting how she'd react. The fact that I've known her since she was born is an even bigger one, of course, but she's changed a lot over the last few years. A lot."

His eyes darkened as he repeated the last two words softly, and he, too, turned his head to gaze at the princess standing beside her tallish, golden-haired companion. Irys was smiling at something the other woman had said, and Daivyn was tugging impatiently at his sister's sleeve while he pointed to something on the island.

"There's been a lot of that going around, My Lord," Aplyn-Ahrmahk replied. "And I imagine it's only going to get worse before it gets better."

"Just because part of it's getting worse doesn't mean other parts can't start getting better," Coris pointed out. "That's what I've been telling Irys, and I think she's actually beginning to believe it."

"I hope so," Aplyn-Ahrmahk said quietly. "She and Daivyn have lost enough already. I don't want to see them lose any more."

Coris nodded slowly. He never looked away from his prince and princess, but he heard the lieutenant's tone, and he treasured it. Of course, duke or no duke, Aplyn-Ahrmahk wasn't even seventeen yet, hardly a gray-bearded and astute political advisor to his emperor. But he was a very *mature* sixteen-year-old, one who'd seen and done things that would have terrified a man three times his age. And however common his birth might have been, he was the adopted son of the Emperor and Empress of Charis. Although, Coris thought, there were times—many of them—when the youngster seemed unaware of all the implications of that relationship.

"I don't want to see them lose any more, either, Your Grace," he said after a moment, then smiled quirkily. "On the other hand, I *am* their legal guardian and chief political adviser. I don't doubt, somehow, that my notion of 'any more' probably won't be exactly the same as the Empire of Charis' notion."

"Neither do I, My Lord," Aplyn-Ahrmahk acknowledged with a grunt of laughter. "Neither do I."

▼   ▼   ▼

"I don't *know* how big those guns are, Daivyn," Irys Daykyn said as patiently as she could. "Why don't you go ask Hektor—I mean Lieutenant Aplyn-Ahrmahk? I'm sure *he* knows."

"Can I?" Daivyn looked at her, then shifted his gaze to the blonde-haired, gray-eyed woman beside his sister. "I promise not to get tar all over my pants, Lady Mairah—*really* I do!"

"Your Highness, you're a ten-year-old on a sailing ship," Lady Mairah Breygart, the Countess of Hanth, pointed out with a smile. "One *ounce* of encouragement and you'll be swarming up the ratlines like a spider monkey, and you and I both know it, don't we?" She shook her head. "You really shouldn't go around making promises you can't keep."

"But I promise to *try* really hard!" he shot back with a smile of his own. "That should count for *something*!"

"Miscreant!" Countess Hanth smacked him on top of his head with a chuckle, then threw up both hands. "A charming miscreant, though. Go ahead—pester the lieutenant. Maybe he'll toss you overboard and your sister and I will get some rest."

"I'm a really good swimmer, you know!" the prince assured her over his shoulder, his smile turning into a triumphant grin as he trotted quickly away.

"Is he really?" Lady Hanth asked, cocking an eyebrow at Irys.

"Not as good as he thinks he is . . . but probably a better one than I'm willing to admit, My Lady." Irys shrugged, watching him slide to a halt by Aplyn-Ahrmahk, grab the lieutenant by the sleeve, and start gesticulating enthusiastically in the direction of the fortress. "He'd be perfectly willing to jump off the ship and *swim* to that island for a closer look at the artillery."

"I shudder to think what's going to happen when we finally get around to introducing him to young Haarahld," Lady Hanth said, watching the same tableau. "Tell me, has Daivyn discovered marsh wyvern or duck hunting yet?"

"King Zhames wouldn't've dreamed of letting him out with a firearm in his hands," Irys replied with much less amusement. "And he was too small for anything like that before we left Corisande, of course."

"Of course." Lady Hanth agreed. If she was aware of Irys' changing mood, she gave no sign of it. "I wonder if I'll be able to convince Cayleb and Sharleyan to let the two of you spend some time with us at Breygart House? Young Haarahld's only about a year older than he is, and Trumyn just turned nine. The three of them would have a wonderful time tearing around the countryside together, and Haarahld and his brother Styvyn—Styvyn's only a year or two younger than you are, Your Highness—are both already accomplished hunters. Well, *enthusiastic* ones, in Haarahld's case, anyway. I'm sure we'd have to take along an entire Guard company as bodyguards, but Hauwerd swears by the marsh wyvern hunting around Lake Zhym. I understand it's a great deal of fun, and while I've never quite grasped the reasoning behind that myself, *he* seems delighted by it for some reason." She rolled her gray eyes expressively. "I know he—*and* the boys—always come home covered in mud with all sorts of explanations for why the really *big* marsh wyverns got away from them . . . this time, at any rate."

Irys chuckled, the shadows retreating from her eyes.

"I imagine Daivyn would enjoy that a lot, My Lady. Assuming the Emperor and the Empress really would let him."

"Oh, I imagine I could talk Her Majesty into it if I put my mind to it. I've known her a long time, you know."

Irys nodded. If anything, "a long time" was a gross understatement, for Lady Mairah Lywkys had been Queen Sharleyan of Chisholm's senior lady-in-waiting. A much younger cousin of Baron Green Mountain, Mairah was a decade senior to Sharleyan, and in many ways she'd been the older sister the youthful queen had never had. Mairah had accompanied Sharleyan to Charis to meet her betrothed husband, Cayleb Ahrmahk, and she walked with a slight but permanent limp from the "riding accident" which had prevented her from accompanying Sharleyan to Saint Agtha's for the visit which had almost ended in the empress' death.

Since that episode, Sharleyan had decided to dispense with formal ladies-in-waiting entirely. Charisian practice had never involved the crowds of nobly born attendants the mainland realms enshrined, and the Empress had become a firm proponent of Charisian traditions in that regard. Chisholm had been closer to the mainland in that respect, but she'd never really liked surrounding herself with ladies-in-waiting—an attitude which had hardened into steely determination since her unexpected ascent to the throne, when she'd been forced to fend off the sort of fluttery attendants most courtiers would have considered suitable for a twelve-year-old queen.

As part of that campaign, she'd fought hard to convince Green Mountain to make Mairah her chief lady-in-waiting. The baron had resisted the idea, fearing the possible political repercussions if it had seemed he was deliberately surrounding Sharleyan with his own adherents and supporters. But Sharleyan had insisted, and Mairah had served as the child-queen's buttress against all those other attendants, which explained why Sharleyan had insisted upon bringing her to Tellesberg with her when she'd gleefully left every other lady-in-waiting home in Chisholm. She hadn't had any of those ladies shipped to Tellesberg since, either. Nor had she selected any

Old Charisian ladies to add to Mairah. In fact, Irys suspected, the empress' deep affection for Lady Hanth was the only reason Sharleyan had waited until two years after her wedding—until Mairah's own wedding to the Earl of Hanth—before formally abolishing the post entirely.

Lady Hanth hadn't explained any of that to Irys, but Phylyp Ahzgood hadn't been her father's spymaster for so many years without learning a great deal about the Kingdom of Chisholm's internal dynamics. It hadn't taken him long to update his information on her, and Irys agreed with his analysis. Having Mairah Lywkys Breygart named as Irys' official "companion" (since the term "lady-in-waiting" had been so . . . enthusiastically eliminated by Empress Sharleyan) was almost certainly a good sign.

I hope it is, anyway, she thought, gazing across the water at the slowly passing island. *Phylyp's right about this being the best option open to us, but "best" doesn't necessarily mean "good." And Hektor's a good man, like Seijin Merlin, and he obviously trusts Cayleb and Sharleyan. But still, they're both Charisians and—*

"Sharleyan used to have an expression just like that when she was worried," Mairah said thoughtfully. Irys glanced quickly sideways, but all she saw was Lady Hanth's profile, for the older woman's eyes were fixed on Lock Island. "About half the time," she continued in that same considering tone, "if anyone could convince her discussing what worried her wasn't a sign of weakness, she'd find out it wasn't *quite* as bad as she'd thought it was while she was wrestling with it on her own. Not always, of course. But sometimes."

Irys smiled faintly.

"I'm sure it did . . . sometimes, My Lady. But as you say, not always."

"No," Mairah agreed. "The thing is, though," she turned her head to look into Irys' hazel eyes with a gentle smile of her own, "that until she did try talking to someone about it, she could never really know whether *this* was one of the times it would help."

Their eyes held for a moment, and then Mairah's smile faded.

"You're still worried about how she felt about your father, Your Highness." She shook her head ever so slightly when Irys opened her mouth. "Of course you are." She shrugged, never looking away from the princess. "When there's been so much hatred for so long, so much bloodshed—when two families have stored up so many mutual wrongs—it has to be that way. And, if I'm going to be honest, I'd have to admit I believe Sharley—Her Majesty, I mean—had much more cause to hate your father than he ever had to hate her. For that matter, I won't pretend that if your father had come into her power, she wouldn't have found it very, very difficult not to take his head and call it justice, not vengeance."

"And would you have agreed with her, My Lady?" Irys asked, so quietly her voice was scarcely audible through the sounds of wind and wave.

"I'm a Chisholmian, Your Highness. King Sailys was my King, not just my cousin's friend. And I was over twenty when he died. I knew him—knew him personally, not just as a king—as well as how he came to be where he was and die the way he did. So, yes." She met Irys' gaze very levelly. "Yes, I would've called it justice. Perhaps it would've been vengeance, as well, but it would've been just, wouldn't it?"

Their eyes held for a long, still moment, and then Irys' lips trembled and her gaze fell.

"Sometimes justice seems to solve so very little," she half whispered, and Mairah touched her shoulder gently. She looked up again, and the older woman's eyes were as gentle as her touch had been.

"Sometimes justice solves nothing at all," she said. "And vengeance solves even less. Have you heard how Sharleyan addressed your brother's subjects after one of them attempted to assassinate her on her very throne?"

"No." Irys shook her head, her folded hands tightening on one another. She hadn't learned of that assassination attempt until after she'd reached *Destiny*, and a part of her dreaded the way that experience must have hardened Sharleyan Ahrmahk's hatred for the princedom of her birth.

"I wasn't there myself," Mairah said, "but the clerks took down a transcript of every one of her sessions sitting in judgment . . . including that one. She'd just pardoned four convicted traitors, and when she looked at the body of the man who'd tried to kill her, she said, 'Surely God weeps to see such violence loosed among His children.' And then she said, 'Despite anything the Group of Four may say, God does *not* call us to exult in the blood and agony of our enemies!'"

"She did?" Irys' eyes widened, and Mairah nodded.

"She did. And she meant it. Empress Sharleyan is a good hater, Your Highness, but it's hard to make her hate in the first place. If that's what you truly want, then you harm someone she loves or victimize the weak, but I doubt you'll enjoy the experience in the end. She hated your father because he'd hurt someone she loved and because—much as I realize you loved him—he victimized a great many people weaker than he was. But she hated *him*, and because of what *he'd* done, not you or your brother, and she isn't one to visit vengeance upon someone's children or family. Neither is Emperor Cayleb—if for no other reason because neither of them would stoop so low as to take vengeance upon an innocent for someone else's crime. But it goes deeper than that, as well, especially with Sharleyan."

"Why?" Irys asked simply, and Mairah smiled sadly.

"Because you and she are so much alike. Because she lost *her* father early, and she knows the pain that brings. Because she knows who was truly behind his murder, and who planned your brother's murder, as well, and she *is* a good hater when it comes to the viciousness of a man who could kill a little boy out of cold, calculating ambition. Because people have tried to murder Cayleb, the man she loves, and she's seen the cost of that, as well. And because people've tried to murder *her*, not just once, but four times—twice in the last five years, plus the two assassination attempts her Guard defeated before she was fifteen years old. Your Highness, her own uncle tried to have her murdered—or, at least, aided those who wanted her dead, whether that was his own intention or not—and the only reason *I'm* alive, most probably, is because her uncle was also my cousin's friend and he 'arranged' the riding accident that left me with a broken leg when Sharleyan made her trip to Saint Agtha's. But the stories you may've heard about Saint Agtha's—the stories about how she picked up her dead armsmen's muskets and killed at least a dozen of the assassins herself . . . they're true, Your Highness. She *knows* what you've felt about your father, and she knows how terrified you've been, how desperate to protect your brother. She's felt those things herself, and I promise you this—no matter what may lie between the House of Daykyn and the House of Tayt or the House of Ahrmahk, *my* Empress will never allow harm to come to you or to Daivyn. If the need were to arise, she would pick up a musket—or a *rock*, if that was the only weapon she could find—and defend both of you just as she and her armsmen defended one another at Saint Agtha's. She couldn't do anything else and still be who she is."

Irys gazed at her, tasting the iron certainty in her words. Lady Hanth might be mistaken; she wasn't lying, and Irys smiled a bit tremulously as she reached up to cover the hand on her shoulder with her own palm. She started to say something, but then she stopped, gave her head a little shake, and inhaled deeply. She squeezed the older woman's hand, and then turned back to gaze at the passing fortress once more.

"I wonder if Daivyn's finished pestering Lieutenant Aplyn-Ahrmahk out of all patience yet?" she said instead.

.III.
Brahdwyn's Folly,
Green Cove Trace,
Glacierheart Province,
Republic of Siddarmark

*D*amn it's cold!"

Sailys Trahskhat cupped his hands and breathed into them as if he actually thought he could warm them through his thick gloves. Byrk Raimahn looked at him quizzically across the fire, and Trahskhat grimaced.

"Sorry about that, Sir. Guess it *was* pretty obvious without my saying, wasn't it?"

"I believe you could probably say that, yes," Raimahn agreed.

They were three days into the month of April and, technically, the season had tipped over from winter into spring ten days ago, but "spring" was a purely notional concept in northern Siddarmark, and especially among the high peaks of the Gray Wall Mountains, at the best of times. This winter had been particularly harsh, and the locals assured them they still had at least three or four more five-days of cold and ice before the thaw set in. He believed them. It was hard not to, given that at the moment the temperature was well below zero on the Fahrenheit scale Eric Langhorne had reinstituted here on Safehold.

That would have been more than cold enough for a couple of Charisian boys, even without the cutting wind; *with* the wind, it was as close an approximation to hell as he ever hoped to see. He remembered how cold he'd thought Siddar City was in the winter, and found himself longing for that balmy climate as that Glacierheart wind sang hungrily about him. He shivered, despite his thick, putatively warm parka and lifted the battered tin teapot out of its nest of embers. He poured himself a cup, cradling it in his own gloved palms, holding it so the steam could provide at least a momentary illusion of warmth to his face and cheeks. Then he sipped and tried not to grimace. Calling such an anemic brew "tea" was a gross libel, but at least it was hot, and that was something he told himself as it glowed its way down his throat into his hollow belly.

He wouldn't feel so frozen if he didn't also feel so constantly hungry. Unfortunately, even with the food Archbishop Zhasyn had brought with them, there was nowhere near enough to go around. Half of the relief expedition's draft animals had already been slaughtered for the precious protein they represented, and it was unlikely the others were going to survive more than another couple of five-days.

If that long, he told himself grimly with another sip of the hot water masquerading as tea. *Welcome to "spring," Byrk. I wonder how many of the ones who've made it this far are going to starve before the snow melts?*

He and Sailys were a long, long way from home, and he turned away from the fire to contemplate the Gray Walls' frozen, merciless beauty. There were mountains in Charis as well, of course. Some of them even had snow on their summits year-round, despite the climate. But Charisian mountains also had green, furry flanks, with trees that tended to stay that way year-round and snow that stayed decently on the highest peaks, where it belonged. *These* mountains were far less civilized, with steep, sheer sides carved out of vertical faces of stone and earth, thrusting raw, rocky heads above the tree line to look down on narrow valleys lashed by snow and wind. Beautiful, yes, and indomitable, but without the sense of warmth and life Charisian mountains radiated. Not in winter, at least. People had lived here in Glacierheart for centuries before anyone really tried to explore Charis' mountains, yet these valleys, precipices, and peaks had a primal, unsubdued ferocity that laughed at the notion humanity might ever tame *them*. He felt . . . out of place among them, and he knew Sailys felt the same.

He gazed out over the long, narrow valley known as the Green Cove Trace and hoped none of his sentries were going to lose fingers or toes—or noses—to frostbite this time. Or, for that matter, that none of them had become as numbed in mind and alertness as they no doubt felt in body. None of them had the opportunity for a fire like this one, not where the smoke might be seen, and he tried not to feel guilty about that.

The Trace faded into the blueness of mountain morning shadows as it snaked its way north towards Hildermoss Province, and if their information was as accurate as usual, there were men headed down that valley at this very moment. Men who were just as grim of purpose—and just as filled with hate—as Byrk Raimahn's men.

He lowered his gaze to the charred ruins of Brahdwyn's Folly and understood that hatred entirely too well. The blackened timbers and cracked foundations of what had once been a prosperous, if not overly large, mountain town thrust up out of the snowdrifts, like tombstones for all the people who'd died here. Died in the original attack and fire, or died of starvation and privation afterward. The actual graves were hidden beneath the snow, overflowing the modest, rocky cemetery surrounding the equally charred ruins of the town's church. Brahdwyn's Folly's priest and a dozen members of his congregation had been locked inside that church before it was fired, and as he looked out across the wreckage, Raimahn wondered how that barbarity had become so routine that it seemed almost inevitable.

"You reckon they're still coming, Sir?" Trahskhat asked after a moment, and Raimahn shrugged. He still wasn't certain how he'd become the commander of a double-strength company of riflemen, but there wasn't much question about how the solid, reliable Trahskhat had become his second in command.

Trakskhat's loyalty to the Church of God Awaiting, his faith in the vicarate as the archangels' stewards on earth, had carried him into exile in a foreign land where he and his family were insulted and harassed on a daily basis by bigots who hated *all* Charisians, regardless of their faith. It also had reduced the star third baseman of the Tellesberg Krakens to the harsh labor, meager salary, and penury of a longshoreman on Siddar City's waterfront, and he'd accepted that—accepted *all* of it—because the faith which had made him a Temple Loyalist had required it of him. Because he'd been unable to accept the schism splintering God's Church, despite the tolerance and legal protection the Crown and Church of Charis had guaranteed to the Empire's Temple Loyalists. His stubborn integrity and his belief in God had left him no other choice but to turn his back upon his native land and live in exile from all he and his family had ever known.

Until the "Sword of Schueler." Until he'd seen the rapes, the murders, the atrocities committed in Siddar City by mobs harangued, armed, and all too often led by men in the vestments of Mother Church's Inquisition. His own family had been swept up in that carnage, his children threatened with murder, his wife with rape, as well. He'd fought back, then, and as the mob closed in on their fleeing families, he and Raimahn had resigned themselves to death in the frail hope that by standing to die in the streets of Siddarmark's burning capital they might buy the people they loved the time to reach safety. And the two of them—and their families—had been saved from that mob only by the arrival of armed Charisians led by a Siddarmark-born Reformist.

A lot of attitudes had gotten . . . clarified that day, including those of Byrk Raimahn and his grandfather. That was why Claitahn and Sahmantha Raimahn had taken Sailys' family under their protection in Siddar City and promised to get them safely back to Charis as soon as they could find room aboard ship for all of them. It was also why Sailys Trahskhat was no longer a Temple Loyalist, and for someone with his integrity, the outcome of that change had been inevitable.

"No reason to think they're *not* coming, Sailys," Raimahn replied after another sip of so-called tea, and shrugged. "The information we fed Fyrmahn should've been convincing, and he's a determined son-of-a-bitch. Don't forget the Trace is the only real way through the Gray Walls east of Hanymar. If they're coming through from Hildermoss, this is where they have to do it. Then there's Father Gharth's report that he's been reinforced. The Father's sources could be wrong, but I don't think they are, and if he *has* been reinforced, he has more mouths to feed." The young man smiled bleakly. "I'm pretty sure that last raid of Wahlys' will've pissed him off enough–and *hurt* him enough—to send him straight at a prize like this one. If he's smart enough to see the hook he could still pass it up, but given his track record?" He shook his head. "I don't see him doing that, Sailys. I really don't."

Trahskhat nodded and glanced up the valley himself. His eyes were harder than Raimahn's, and his expression was as bleak as the mountains around them.

"Can't say that disappoints me, Sir," he said, those stony eyes dropping to the ruins of Brahdwyn's Folly. "Can't say that disappoints me at all."

Raimahn nodded, although he wasn't really certain he shared the older man's feelings about that. Or that he *wanted* to share them, at any rate.

He'd seen more than enough of Zhan Fyrmahn's handiwork to know the man would have to be high on anyone's list of people the world would be better off without. He wouldn't be quite at the top—that spot was re-served for Zhaspahr Clyntahn—but he couldn't have been more than a half-dozen names down. It had been Fyrmahn's band, along with that of his cousin, Mahrak Lohgyn, who'd burned Brahdwyn's Folly and butchered its inhabitants. Ostensibly, because they'd all been Reformists, hateful in the eyes of God, and there'd actually been three or four families in town of whom that was probably true. But Zhan Fyrmahn had had reasons of his own, even before the Grand Inquisitor's agents had stoked the Republic's maelstrom, and there was a reason he'd taken such special care to extermi-nate Wahlys Mahkhom's family.

Mountaineers tended to be as hard and self-reliant as the rocky slopes that bred them. From everything Raimahn had seen so far, Glacierheart's coal miners took that tendency to extremes, but the trappers and hunters like Mahkhom and Fyrmahn were harder still. They had to be, given their solitary pursuits, the long hours they spent alone in the wilderness, with no one to look out for them or go for help if something went wrong. They asked nothing of anyone, they paid their own debts, and they met whatever came their way on their own two feet, unflinchingly. Raimahn had to re-spect that, yet that hardness had its darker side, as well, for it left them dis-inclined towards forgiving their enemies, whatever the Archangel Bédard or the *Writ* might say on the subject. Too many of them were feudists at heart, ready to pursue a quarrel to the bittermost end, however many gen-erations it took and despite anything Mother Church might say about the virtues of compassion and forgiveness.

Raimahn had no idea what had actually started the bad blood between the Mahkhom and Fyrmahn clans. On balance, he was inclined to believe the survivors of Brahdwyn's Folly, that the first casualty had been Wahlys' grandfather and that the "accident" which had befallen him had been no accident at all. He was willing to admit he was prejudiced in Mahkhom's favor, however, and no doubt the Fyrmahns remembered it very differently. And whatever had *started* the savage hatred, there'd been enough incidents up and down the Green Cove Trace since to provide either side with plenty of pretexts for seeking "justice" in the other family's blood.

That was Zhan Fyrmahn's view, at any rate, and he'd seized on the ex-hortations of the inquisitors who'd organized the Sword of Schueler as a chance—a license—to settle the quarrel once and for all. If it hadn't been that, it would have been something else; there was always something haters could appeal to, something bigots could use. But when the hate and bigotry came from men who wore the vestments of the Inquisition, they carried the imprimatur of Mother Church herself. It wasn't simply "all right" for some-one like Fyrmahn to give himself up to the service of hate and anger, it was his *duty*, the thing God *expected* him to do. And if two or three hundred people in a remote village died along the way, why, that was God's will, too, and it served the bastards right.

Especially if their last name happened to be Mahkhom.

I wonder how many times Fyrmahn's reflected on the consequences of his own actions? Raimahn had wondered that more than once, and not about Fyrmahn alone. *Does he realize he turned every survivor of Brahdwyn's Folly into a dyed-in-the-wool Reformist, whatever they were before? If he does, does he care? And does he even realize he and the men like him are the ones who started all of this? Or does he blame Wahlys for all of it?*

He probably *did* blame Mahkhom, and his only regret was probably the fact that Wahlys hadn't been home when he and his raiders massacred Brahdwyn's Folly. It would have worked out so much better from Fyrmahn's perspective, especially since it would have prevented Mahkhom from becoming the center of the Reformist resistance in this ice-girt chunk of frozen hell. Raimahn had no idea if Mahkhom had truly embraced the Reformist cause, or if, like Fyrmahn himself, it was simply what empowered and sanctified his own savagery and violence. He hoped it was more than simple hatred, because under that icy shell of hate and loss, he sensed a good and decent man, one who deserved better than to give his own soul to Shan-wei because of the atrocities he was willing to wreak under the pretext of doing God's will. But whatever the depth of his belief, whatever truly drove Wahlys Mahkhom, by this time every Temple Loyalist within fifty miles must curse his name each night before lying down to sleep.

Archbishop Zhasyn's right; we do lay up our own harvests the instant we put the seed into the ground. And I can't blame Wahlys for the way he feels, even if I do see the hatred setting deeper and deeper into these mountains' bones with every raid, every body. It doesn't matter anymore who shed the first blood, burned the first barn, and how in God's name is even someone like Archbishop Zhasyn going to heal those wounds? For that matter, who's going to be left alive to be healed?

Byrk Raimahn had no answers to those questions, and he wished he did, because deep inside, he knew he was more like Wahlys Mahkhom—and possibly even Zhan Fyrmahn—then he wanted to admit. That was why he was out here in this ice and snow, sipping this watery tea, waiting—hoping—for the men he wanted to kill to come to him. Men he could kill without qualm or hesitation because they *deserved* to die. Because in avenging what had happened to Brahdwyn's Folly he could also avenge the arson and the rape and the torture and the murder he'd seen at Sailys Trahskhat's side in Siddar City's Charisian Quarter the day the Temple Loyalists drove the Sword of Schueler into the Republic's back. Perhaps he couldn't track down *those* Temple Loyalists, but he could track down their brothers in blood here in Glacierheart.

In the still, small hours of the night, when he faced his own soul with bleak honesty, he knew what he most feared in all the world: that if he'd stayed in Siddar City, he would have become the very thing he hated, a man so obsessed with the need for vengeance that he would have attacked any Temple Loyalist he encountered with his bare hands. Not because of anything that Temple Loyalist might actually have done, but simply because he *was* a Temple Loyalist. But here—here in the Gray Walls—the lines were clear, drawn in blood and the corpses of burned villages by men who branded themselves clearly by their own acts. Here he could identify his enemies by what they *did*, not simply by what they believed, and tell himself his own actions, the things *he* did, were more than mere vengeance, that what drove him was more than just an excuse to slake his own searing need for retribution. That he was preventing still more Brahdwyn's Follies, stopping at least some of the rape and murder. He could loose his inner demons without fearing they would consume the innocent along with the guilty and perhaps—just perhaps—without the man his grandparents had raised destroying *himself* along with them.

▼　▼　▼

"Well?" Zhan Fyrmahn growled.

"Looks right, at least," Samyl Ghadwyn replied. The burly, thick-shouldered mountaineer shrugged. "Plenty of footprints. Counted the marks from at least a half-dozen sets of sleds, too, and nobody took a shot at me. This time, anyway."

He shrugged again, and Fyrmahn scowled, rubbing his frost-burned cheeks while he stared along the Trace. The trail snaked along its western side, climbing steadily for the next mile or so, and the small Silver Rock River was a solid, gray-green line of merciless ice four hundred feet below his present perch. The river's ice was no harder than his eyes, though, and no more merciless, as he considered the other man's report.

Every member of his band was related to him, one way or another—that was the way it was with mountain clans—but Ghadwyn was only a fourth cousin, and there were times Fyrmahn suspected his heart wasn't fully in God's work. He didn't have the fire, the zeal, Mother Church's sons were supposed to have, and Fyrmahn didn't care for his habitual, take-it-or-leave-it attitude.

Despite which, he was one of their best scouts, almost as good a tracker as Fyrmahn himself and more patient than most of the others.

"I don't like it, Zhan," Mahrak Lohgyn muttered, his voice almost lost in the moan of the wind. "The bastards have to know we'll be coming for them."

"You've got *that* right." Fyrmahn's cracked and blistered lips drew up in a snarl, and the icy fire in his eyes mirrored the black murder in his heart.

Mahkhom and his heretic-loving cutthroats had stolen the food Fyrmahn's own family needed to survive the last bitter five-days of winter. Yes, and they'd massacred that food's entire escort in the process. Not one of the guards had survived, and it was obvious at least seven or eight of them had been taken alive by their enemies only to have their throats cut like animals. What else could anyone expect out of heretics? And what else could anyone expect out of Mahkhoms?

We should've killed the lot of them a generation ago! Cowards—cowards and backstabbers, every one of them!

The glare in his eyes turned bleak with bitter satisfaction as he remembered the way Mahkhom's woman had begged his men to spare her children's lives even as they ripped away her clothing and dragged her into the barn. The bitch hadn't even known they were already dead. If only he could have been there to see Mahkhom's face when he came home to Fyrmahn's handiwork!

Nits may make lice, he thought coldly, *but not when somebody burns them out first. Father Failyx's right about that!*

"They may've decided we *can't* come after them," he said after a moment. "Schueler knows they killed enough of us when they stole the food in the first place! If they don't know about Father Failyx and his men, they may figure they hurt us too badly for us to do anything but crawl off into a hole and die for them."

Lohgyn's jaw tightened, and Fyrmahn cursed himself. Lohgyn's brother Styvyn had been one of the murdered guards, and Father Failyx had said the words over the pitiful, emaciated body of his youngest daughter just before they set out for this attack

"Sorry, Mahrak," he said gruffly, reaching out to touch his cousin's shoulder. Lohgyn didn't respond in words, but Fyrmahn could almost hear the creak of the other man's jaw muscles. After two or three heartbeats, Lohgyn gave a curt, jerky nod.

"You may be right," he said, ignoring both the apology and the pain that evoked it. "But it makes me nervous. No offense, Samyl, but somebody should've spotted you."

Ghadwyn only shrugged again. There might have been a little spark down in his eyes at the implication that anyone could have seen *him* coming, but whatever his other faults, the man was a realist. There were bastards on the other side who were just as skilled at the tracker's trade as he was . . . and who knew the penalty for a moment's carelessness as well as he did, too.

"If they'd seen him, he wouldn't be standing here now," Fyrmahn pointed out. "He'd be lying out there somewhere with an arbalest bolt in his chest or a knife in his back." He bared his teeth in an ugly grimace. "You think any of those bastards would pass up the chance to do for one of us?"

Lohgyn frowned. Fyrmahn had a point, and Wahlys Mahkhom's men had proven how good they were when it came to killing any of the Faithful who entered their sights. They were no more likely to pass up the opportunity to kill one of Fyrmahn's men than Fyrmahn's men were to let one of *them* live. Yet even so . . . .

"I just can't help wondering if they're trying to be sneaky," he said finally. "What if they saw Samyl just fine? What if they just want us to *think* they've pulled back to Valley Mount?"

"Set a trap for us, you mean?"

"Something like that." Lohgyn nodded. "If they're sitting up there in the hills with those damned arbalests waiting for us, they might just have chosen not to take a shot at Samyl until they could get more of us out in the open."

It was Fyrmahn's turn to nod, however grudgingly.

"Might be you've got a point. But unless you're suggesting we just turn tail and crawl back to camp empty-handed, we've got it to do if we're going to find out."

Lohgyn's eyes flickered again at the words "empty-handed." He seemed about to say something sharp, but then he drew a deep breath and shrugged instead.

Fyrmahn turned and glowered up the steeply climbing trail, thinking hard. There *was* another way to the ruins which had once been Brahdwyn's Folly without using the Trace, but Khanklyn's Trail was long and roundabout. It would take them at least three days—more probably four, given the weather conditions and the effect of so many five-days of bad food (and too little of it) upon their stamina—to go that way. If the reports that Mahkhom was retreating to the protection of the larger town of Valley Mount, taking the stolen food with him, were accurate, he'd be three-quarters of the way there, even allowing for the anchor of his surviving women and children, before Fyrmahn's band could hope to overtake them. Besides, Khanklyn's Trail was too narrow and tortuous for them to get sleds through. If they were fortunate enough to catch Mahkhom and recover the food, all they'd be able to take back with them would be what they could backpack out. And their lowland allies couldn't possibly get through it with them, either.

But if Lohgyn's fears were justified, if it *was* a trap . . . .

Well, Father Failyx is right about that, too, he told himself grimly. *Sometimes serving God means taking a few chances, and at least any man who dies doing God's will can be sure of where his soul's spending eternity.*

"All right," he said. "Mahrak, Lieutenant Tailyr's about a thousand yards back down the Trace. Send one of your boys down to get him."

Lohgyn waved to one of his men, who disappeared quickly around one of the twisty trail's bends, and Fyrmahn turned back to his two cousins.

"This is why Father Failyx sent Tailyr along in the first place," he said grimly, "so here's how we're going to do this."

▼ ▼ ▼

"Seems you were right, Sir," Sailys Trahskhat said, peering through the Charisian-manufactured folding spyglass as he lay in the snow at Raimahn's side. They'd climbed the knife-backed ridge from the burned-out town's limited shelter when the first sentry reports came in. "That's Fyrmahn down there, sure as I'm lying here."

The younger man nodded. He'd never seen Zhan Fyrmahn before today, but the man had been described to him often enough. That tangled, bright red beard and the patch over his left eye could belong to no one else, and he felt a bright tingle of eagerness dance down his nerves.

Gently, Byrk. Remember what Grandfather always said.

"I think you're right," he said out loud, a bit surprised by how calm he sounded. "But my grandfather hunted a pirate or two in his day, you know. And he always told me the worst thing that could happen to somebody who'd set an ambush was to find out the other fellow had known it was an ambush all along."

"See your point," Trahskhat replied after a moment, lowering the glass and looking down with his unaided eyes at the black dots on the trail so far below them. "And they aren't pushing forward the way we'd like, are they?"

"Not as quickly as we'd like, anyway," Raimahn agreed. "That"—he gestured with his chin at what had to be between sixty and seventy men inching their way up the trail—"looks like an advanced guard. And one that's better organized than anything Wahlys and his lads've seen out of Fyrmahn before. It's showing better tactics, too, sending out a patrol to clear trail for the rest of it, and that other bunch back there isn't moving at all. I don't think it's going to, either—not until Fyrmahn gets word back from the leaders that the coast is clear. In fact, I think those might be some of those reinforcements we've been hearing rumors about. They're acting a lot more disciplined, anyway. Almost as good as our own boys."

"Um." Trahskhat grimaced and rested his chin on his folded forearms. "Not so good, then, is it, Sir?"

"Could be worse." Raimahn shrugged. "They could've decided to send everybody around the long way, instead."

"There's that," Trahskhat acknowledged. "And at least it doesn't look like the powder's going to be a complete waste, anyway."

"No, it isn't. I wish we had Fyrmahn further up the trail, but we never expected to get all of them. Besides, we need someone to take our message back to our good friend Father Failyx, don't we?"

"Aye, that we do, Sir." Trahskhat's voice was as grimly satisfied as his eyes. "That we do."

▼   ▼   ▼

Zhan Fyrmahn watched the force he'd sent ahead make its cautious way up the trail.

He didn't much like Lieutenant Zhak Tailyr. The man had all of a typical Lowlander's contempt for someone like Fyrmahn and his fellow clansmen, and his finicky Border States accent grated on a man's nerves. Fyrmahn was a loyal son of Mother Church, and he hated the heretical bastards who'd sold themselves to Shan-wei even more than the next man, but whenever he heard that accent, it was hard to forget the generations of mutual antagonism between Siddarmark and the Border States.

Despite that, Fyrmahn had been glad to see him when he arrived. Not because of any fondness he felt for Tailyr himself, but because the lieutenant was part of the three-hundred-man force of volunteers who'd struggled forward from Westmarch to join Father Failyx. It would have been nice if they'd brought more food with them instead of becoming yet more hungry mouths who had to be fed somehow, but they'd complained much less about their short rations than he would have expected of soft, citified Lowlanders, and Tailyr was an experienced officer of the Temple Guard. The sort of drill-field tactics the Guard trained for had little place in the fluid, small-scale warfare of these rugged, heavily forested mountains, but they'd been a visible sign of Mother Church's support. And they'd offered him a core of disciplined, well-armed infantry.

He'd brought fifty of them along just in case he needed them to break the resistance he'd anticipated at Brahdwyn's Folly. Now he'd found another use for them, and they moved steadily upward along the trail behind the advanced patrol of twenty more of his clansmen.

Ghadwyn had taken point again, fifty yards in front of his companions. That was close enough they could provide covering fire with their arbalests but far enough ahead to trip any traps before they could close on the entire patrol and the rest of his men. He didn't like sending them ahead that way, but his mountaineers were obviously better than Tailyr's Lowlanders at this sort of thing. *Someone* had to do it, and even if he'd—

CRAAAACCCCCKKKK!

Samyl Ghadwyn never heard the sound that went racketing and echoing about the valley, startling birds and wyverns into the sky with cries of alarm. The big, soft-nosed .48 caliber bullet was a bit smaller than the standard Charisian rifle round, but it slammed into the back of his neck with sufficient energy to half decapitate him. It struck like a mushrooming hammer, from behind and above, hurling his corpse forward to land with one arm dangling over the dizzy drop to the frozen river below.

Fyrmahn jerked at the sharp, ear-splitting blast of sound. He'd been watching Ghadwyn, seen the way his cousin went down, recognized instant death when he saw it, even from this far away, and his head whipped up, eyes wide as they darted about, seeking the shot's origin. None of his own men were armed with matchlocks, and he'd never fired one of the lowland weapons himself, but he recognized the sound of a shot when he heard one. Yet how could anyone have gotten close enough to score a kill shot like that?! Fyrmahn might never actually have fired one, but he knew the things were notoriously inaccurate. He'd never heard of anyone hitting a man-sized target with one of them at more than a hundred yards or so, especially with *that* sort of pinpoint accuracy, and no one could have gotten *that* close to the trail without being spotted, could they? It was ridic—

"*Shan-wei!*"

He swore savagely as the man who'd fired stood up, skylining himself without a qualm as he began reloading his weapon. He was at least four hundred yards higher up the mountainside above Ghadwyn's corpse, and he moved unhurriedly, with the arrogant contempt of someone who knew he was far beyond any range at which his enemies could have returned fire.

Fyrmahn was too far away to make out any details, but the other man's musket seemed too slender—and too long—for any matchlock. Yet it couldn't be anything *else*, could it? He'd heard rumors, tall tales, stories about the heretics' new, long-ranged muskets—"rifles," they called them—and Father Failyx and Tailyr had admitted there might be some truth to those rumors. But the Schuelerite had promised all of them the heretics couldn't have many of the new weapons, and any they might possess must all be back in Siddar City! That apostate traitor Stohnar would never have sent any of them off to the backwoods of Glacierheart when he knew he'd need every weapon he could lay hands on come the spring. And even if he'd been willing to send them, surely they couldn't have gotten here this quickly through the iron heart of winter!

Yet even as he told himself that, he heard another thunderous crack from the snow and boulder fields above the Trace. Smoke spurted from the hidden rifleman's position, twenty or thirty yards from the first shooter, and the rearmost of Fyrmahn's clansmen stumbled forward, dropping his arbalest, as the heavy bullet smashed into his shoulder blades. He went down, writhing in the suddenly bloody snow, and then more rifles opened fire. *Dozens* of them, the sound of their thunder like fists through the thin air, even at this distance. He watched helplessly, teeth grinding in rage, as his entire patrol was massacred. Four of his kinsmen lived long enough to run, but they were easy targets on that narrow, icy trail. One of them got as much as thirty yards back down the path before a bullet found him, as well. None of the others got more than twenty feet.

Fyrmahn swore savagely, his fists clenched at his sides, watching the merely wounded twist in anguish or turn and begin crawling brokenly towards safety. He couldn't hear the screams from here, and he was glad, but he didn't *have* to hear them. He could *see* their agony . . . and the bullets those unseen rifles continued to fire, seeking them out one by one until all of them lay as still as Ghadwyn himself.

Tailyr's detachment had frozen when the rifles opened fire. It was clear they'd been as stunned as Fyrmahn, but they reacted quickly, and they were wise enough to know pikemen and arbalesters had no business charging riflemen along a narrow, slippery ribbon of ice and snow. They turned, instead, moving swiftly back down the trail, and Fyrmahn drew a deep, bitter breath of relief as they turned a bend, putting a solid shoulder of earth and stone between themselves and those accursed rifles.

At least they weren't going to lose any more of their men, and he made himself a burning, hate-filled promise to repay Mahkhom and his Shan-wei-worshiping bastards with interest for this day's bloody work. They couldn't have enough damned rifles to stand off the forces of God for long, and when the day finally came, Zhan Fyrmahn would take the time to teach them the cost of apostasy properly. Until then, though—

The end of the world cut him off in mid-thought.

He stumbled backward, flinging himself to the ground in shocked terror, as the ear-shattering explosion roared. No, not *the* explosion—it was an entire series of explosions, a chain of them roaring high up on the mountainside above the Trace, and he heard the high, distant screams of Tailyr's men as they looked up into the maw of destruction.

It was a trap, Fyrmahn thought numbly, watching the entire side of a mountain erupt in red-and-black flowers of flying rock and snow. A long, cacophonous line of them, fifteen hundred yards and more in length. None of the charges were all that large individually, but there were a great many of them and they'd been placed very, very carefully. The sharp, echoing explosions folded together into a single, rolling clap of thunder . . . and then even the thunder disappeared into a far more terrifying sound as uncountable tons of snow and rock hammered down like Langhorne's own Rakurai.

The avalanche devoured over a mile of mountain trail . . . and forty-eight more of Zhan Fyrmahn's clansmen. Neither they, nor Lieutenant Zhak Tailyr, nor the body of a single one of his volunteers was ever found.

▼   ▼   ▼

"Think they got the message, Sir?" Trahskhat asked, watching the long, dark pall of windblown snow, rock, and dirt rising like a curtain above the Trace.

"Oh, I think they may have, Sailys," Byrk Raimahn said softly. "I think they may have."

Sharleyan Ahrmahk stood beside her husband in the bright sunlight. A warm breeze danced and curtsied around the terrace, rustling and chattering in the broad-bladed palmettos, spike-thorn, and tropical flowers which surrounded it. A pair of spider monkeys chased one another through the swordlike canopy of nearpalms high overhead, scolding and screeching at one another, their voices clear but distant through the wind's voice. Closer at hand, a brilliantly colored parrot sat on one limb of the ornamental sugar apple tree in the tree well at the center of the terrace, ignoring the human intrusion into its domain, hooked beak burrowing as it preened, and the same breeze brought them the whistles and songs of more distant wyverns and birds.

Crown Princess Alahnah lay in the hammock-like canvas cradle, embroidered with her house's coat of arms, which had been a gift from the crew of HMS *Dawn Star* the year before. The stitchery of the ship's sailmaker and his mates would have done any professional seamstress proud, and their gift had touched Sharleyan to the heart as the entire crew manned the yards with huge, beaming grins and watched Captain Kahbryllo present it to her on the infant princess' behalf. An empress had countless finer cradles for her child, many of them exquisite treasures of the woodworker's art, but not one of them meant as much to her as that simple length of canvas. Alahnah was too young to worry about things like that, but she, too, had loved that cradle from the very first day the ship's motion had lulled her to sleep in it, and they'd made it with plenty of room for growth. It fitted her just fine at fourteen months, and now she lay making happy, sleepy sounds while Hairyet Saltair, one of her nannies, substituted for the ship's motion and kept it gently moving.

A single blue-eyed armsman—a major of the Imperial Guard—stood at the feet of the shallow steps leading up to the terrace from the garden proper. Another, more grizzled armsman, this one a sergeant, stood beside the princess' cradle, but somehow their armed presence only emphasized the peacefulness of the moment. Because of the only other person on that terrace, perhaps—a white-haired man in an orange-trimmed cassock who seemed to carry peacefulness around with him like a personal possession.

"I guarantee you plenty of people will insist—after the fact, of course, and only when they can pretend they think we can't overhear them—that we ought to've done this in the throne room," Cayleb said now, one arm around Sharleyan's waist while he kept his eyes on the path winding its way between the banks of landscaped greenery. "And they're going to come up with all kinds of 'reasons of state' we ought to've done it, too. You know they will."

"Of course they will," Sharleyan replied. "On the other hand, most of those 'reasons' are going to be—what was that delightful phrase of Zhan's yesterday? 'Kraken-shit,' I believe?—manufactured by people whose *real* objection is that their own highly aristocratic selves weren't present. We really shouldn't encourage him to use language like that, I suppose, but the description does fit, doesn't it?"

"I know that. And you know that. Hell, *they* know that! Not going to shut them up, though. In fact, it's only going to make it worse than if they'd had some *substantive* complaint!"

"Now, now," Maikel Staynair soothed. "I'm sure you're worrying unduly. And even if you're not, I'm confident we'll manage to weather the tempest of their disappointment. If it will make you feel better, I'll even admonish them for it from the pulpit next Wednesday."

"Oh, I'm sure *that* will make it all better!" Cayleb rolled his eyes. "I think we'd make out better dropping hints about headsmen, actually."

"Such bloody-handed tyranny is not the best way to endear yourselves to your subjects, Your Majesty," Staynair pointed out.

"Who said I wanted to endear myself to them? I'll settle for shutting them up!"

Staynair chuckled, and Cayleb practiced a theatrical scowl on him.

"Don't encourage him, Maikel," Sharleyan said severely.

"Me? *Encourage* him?" Staynair eyed her reproachfully. "Nonsense!"

"No, it isn't." Sharleyan smacked him on a still-muscular shoulder. "You enjoy it as much as he does. Which, you might note, is my diplomatic way of saying you're just as bad as he is."

"He is *not* just as bad as I am," Cayleb said with immense dignity. "How can you, of all people, say such a thing? I'm *far* worse than he is, and I work harder at it, too."

It was Sharleyan's turn to roll her eyes, but they were interrupted before she could respond properly.

"*Seijin* Merlin!"

The voice came around the bend in the path before the boy who owned it did, but not by much. The youngster hurled himself around the turn, running hard, and left the ground several feet in front of the blue-eyed armsman. He launched himself with the fearless, absolute assurance that he would be caught, and the armsman laughed as he snatched the small, wiry body out of midair.

"I'm glad to see you, too, Your Highness," he replied in a deep voice. "It would appear your voyage hasn't imbued you with enhanced dignity, though, I see."

"I *think* that's your way of saying I'm not behaving." The youngster braced his hands on the armsman's shoulders so he could lean back against Merlin Athrawes' mailed, supporting arms and look into those sapphire eyes. "And, if it is, I don't care." He elevated his nose and sniffed. "Lady Mairah says I'm perfectly well behaved compared to her stepsons, and I'm a prince. So I get to choose to do what I want sometimes."

"Somehow I don't think that's *exactly* what Lady Hanth said, Your Highness," Merlin replied, shifting Prince Daivyn to sit on his left forearm as the rest of the prince's party followed him more sedately around the bend.

"Allowing for a certain liberality of interpretation, it's not all that far off, *Seijin* Merlin," Lady Hanth said as she arrived on Daivyn's heels. "I do think it wouldn't hurt His Highness' dignity for you to go ahead and set him back down, though."

"As you wish, My Lady." Merlin smiled, half bowed to her, and set the boy on his feet. Daivyn grinned up at him, and the armsman ruffled his hair with an answering smile, then looked up at Princess Irys and the Earl of Coris.

"I see you made it safe and sound after all, Your Highness," he greeted Irys.

"As did you, *Major* Athrawes." She smiled almost as warmly as Daivyn as she took note of his new rank. "I'll admit now that I was less confident than I could have wished that we'd see you again. But now that we do, thank you." She laid a hand on his forearm, her expression turning very serious. "Thank you very much. For my life, and for his."

She laid her other hand on Daivyn's shoulder, and Merlin gazed into her hazel eyes for a moment, then bowed again, more deeply.

"It was my honor to have been of service," he said softly. "And seeing the two of you here—and observing that someone"—he glanced down at Daivyn's tanned face—"seems to've grown at least three inches is all the reward I could ask."

"At the moment, it's also all the reward we can give you," Irys said. "In time, I hope that will change."

"That won't be necessary, Your Highness."

"I know." Irys smiled, recognizing the sincerity in his voice and, even more importantly, in his eyes as he gazed down at Daivyn's beaming expression. "But it's important to me—and to Daivyn—that we show the rest of the world we recognize our debt."

Merlin merely bowed again, then turned towards the terrace, and Irys followed the turn gracefully.

She found herself at last face-to-face with what were arguably the most powerful monarchs in the world, even if they seemed remarkably unaware of it at the moment.

They were both several years older than she was, although they still struck her as absurdly young to have accomplished as much—and acquired as many enemies—as they had. Cayleb Ahrmahk was taller than she'd expected, and a bit broader of shoulder, although still shorter than Merlin Athrawes, and the emerald-set golden chain which marked a king of Charis winked green and golden glory on his chest. The crown of Sharleyan Ahrmahk's head barely topped his shoulder, and her slender, not quite petite figure showed no sign she'd ever borne a child. The silken hair confined by the simple golden circlet of her light presence crown was so black the sunlight seemed to strike green highlights from it; her eyes were as brown as Cayleb's, and her strong, determined nose was ever so slightly hooked. There was very little of classic beauty about her, but she didn't need it, Irys thought—not with the character and intelligence sparkling in those eyes as they rested in turn upon Irys and her brother.

They gazed at one another for several seconds, and then Irys drew a deep breath, squeezed Daivyn's shoulder gently with the hand still resting on it. He turned and accompanied her obediently as she walked steadily towards the terrace. The boy's eyes darkened and she felt his shoulder tighten under her fingers, but her own expression was composed, almost serene, and only someone who knew her well could have recognized the tension swirling in her hazel eyes. Phylyp Ahzgood, Earl of Coris, followed the two of them, half a step back and to her left, his expression as serene as her own, and Cayleb and Sharleyan watched them come.

They reached the terrace and climbed the steps, and Coris and a suddenly very sober-faced Daivyn bowed deeply, while Irys curtsied. Then all three Corisandians straightened and stood gazing at the Emperor and Empress of Charis.

"Welcome to Tellesberg, Prince Daivyn," Cayleb said after a moment, meeting the boy's gaze. "Sharleyan and I are well aware that you and your sister have to be deeply anxious." He smiled slightly. "That's one reason we arranged to greet you here, rather than under more . . . formal circumstances." He looked up briefly, his eyes meeting Irys' and Coris', then looked back down at Daivyn. "The situation's very . . . complicated, Daivyn, and I know your life's been turned upside down, that frightening things have happened to you—and to your sister. You're very young to've had all of this happening to you. But my cousin Rayjhis was very young for some of the things that happened to him, too. It's one of the tragedies of the world that things like this *can* happen to people far too young to deserve any of it.

"My father and I were your father's enemies," Cayleb continued unflinchingly, and the boy found the courage to look back at him unwaveringly. "I don't know what would have happened if he and I had met across the peace table the way we were supposed to. It might've turned out almost as badly as it actually did. But I tell you now, on my own honor, and on the honor of the House of Ahrmahk, and under the eyes of God, I did *not* order, or authorize, or buy your father's and your older brother's murders. I think you know by now who actually did." He looked up again, meeting Irys' and Coris' eyes once more before he turned back to the boy. "I can't prove what actually happened in the past, but Sharleyan and I can and intend to prove our fidelity in the future. And that's why, now, before your sister and Earl Coris, your guardian and your protector, we formally acknowledge you as the rightful Prince of Corisande."

Irys inhaled sharply, astonished despite herself that Cayleb would say such a thing before he'd even begun laying out the conditions under which Daivyn *might* be permitted to claim his father's crown. For a moment, her mind insisted it had to be no more than a ploy, something to set the two of them at ease until the actual demands could be deployed. But then she looked away from Cayleb, her eyes met Sharleyan's, and she knew. Knew Cayleb truly meant what he'd just said.

"I don't know how this will all work out in the end, Daivyn," Cayleb went on. "The world's a messy place, and bad things can happen. You've already had too much proof of that, and I can't guarantee what will happen in Corisande, or how soon you'll be able to go home, or what will happen when you get there. But Sharleyan and I can promise you this: you're safe here in Tellesberg or anywhere else in our realm. No one will harm you, no one will threaten you, and no one will try to force you to do anything you don't *choose* to do. Except," he added with a sudden grin, "for the sorts of things grown-ups are constantly insisting that kids do. I'm afraid you don't get a free pass on brushing your teeth and washing behind your ears, Your Highness."

Irys felt her lips twitch, and Daivyn actually laughed. Then Cayleb turned directly to Irys and Coris.

"I'm sure we'll all have a great deal to discuss over the next few days and five-days. In the meantime, all of you are welcome guests in the Palace, but Sharleyan and I feel it would be better from a great many perspectives for you to be Archbishop Maikel's houseguests rather than quartered here. In your place, we'd feel more secure there, and we have complete faith in

Maikel's ability to keep you safe. We will ask you to follow his armsmen's instructions fully in light of the terrorist attacks and assassination attempts Clyntahn and his butchers have launched here in Tellesberg, but you are most emphatically *not* prisoners. You're free to come and go as you please, assuming you take adequate security with you. For obvious reasons, it won't be possible for any of you to leave Old Charis without our having made careful arrangements, but we understand Lady Hanth has invited Daivyn and you to visit her at Breygart House. We have no objection at all to that, nor to any other travel here in the Kingdom. Indeed, we'd be delighted for you to see more of our Empire and our people than you possibly could locked up in a palace somewhere.

"It's our hope that you—that *all* of you—will recognize in time where your true enemies lie, and that those enemies are *our* enemies as well. Neither of us will try to pretend we don't have all the pragmatic, calculating reasons in the world to want you to come to that conclusion. You and the Earl have both been too close to a throne for too long not to realize that has to be the case, and I'm sure both of you already see how advantageous that would be for us. But that doesn't change the truth, and it doesn't mean we or anyone else have the right to dictate to your conscience. We'll do all we can to convince you; we will *not* compel you. What you decide may determine what choices and decisions we have to make in regards to you and to Corisande. We can't change that, and we won't pretend we can. Yet we also believe it would be far more foolish of us, and far more dangerous, in the fullness of time, to attempt to force you to do our bidding. Not only would you inevitably become a weapon that would turn in our hand at the first opportunity, but you'd have every right to do just that, and the truth is that we have too many foes already to add such potentially formidable ones to them. We'd prefer to have you as friends; we *definitely* don't want you as enemies. I believe King Zhames and certain members of the Inquisition have already learned what having you as foes can cost."

He smiled very faintly, then stepped back beside Sharleyan and waved at the rattan chairs scattered comfortably about the terrace.

"And now, having said all of that depressing, formal stuff, would the lot of you please join us? We thought we'd have lunch out here on the terrace—assuming we can keep Zhanayt's damned parrot from swooping down and stealing everything!—and Zhan and Zhanayt will be joining us shortly. Before they descend upon us, however, we have quite a lot we'd like to discuss with you. For example, we've had Merlin's report on your escape from Talkyra, but the *seijin* has a tendency to . . . underplay his own role in that sort of derring-do. We'd like to have your version of it, and we'd like the opportunity to answer as many of your questions as we can in a suitably informal atmosphere as well. I'm afraid we *are* going to have to have a formal reception, and eventually we're going to have to have ministers and members of Parliament in to talk to both of you—and to you, My Lord," he added, glancing at Coris again. "But there's no need to dive into that immediately. We thought we'd give you at least a five-day or so to get settled with the Archbishop before anyone starts dragging you around like some sort of trophies. Would that be satisfactory to you?"

Recognized as rightful ruling Prince of Corisande or not, Daivyn looked up quickly at Irys, who smiled just a bit crookedly.

"I think that's not just satisfactory but quite a bit more graceful than we'd—than I'd—expected, Your Majesty. Or Your *Majesties*, I suppose I should say."

"It does get complicated sometimes," Sharleyan told her, speaking for the first time, and smiled back at her. "Actually, here in Old Charis, Cayleb is 'Your Majesty' and I'm 'Your Grace.' In Chisholm, we flip." The empress shrugged with an infectious chuckle. "It helps us keep track of who's talking to whom, at least!"

"I see . . . Your Grace." Irys dropped another curtsy. "I'll try to keep the distinction in mind."

"I'm sure you will," Sharleyan said. Then her smile faded and she cocked her head. "And before we get to all of that informal conversation, let me say formally that everything Cayleb just said he truly did say in both our names. I know—I *know*, Irys—what you felt when your father was murdered. And I know all the hatred which lay between me and him had to play a part in your thinking. But that hatred was between me and *him*, not between you and me or Daivyn and me. You aren't him, and imperfect as I am in many ways, I do try to remember the *Writ's* injunctions. I have no intention of holding a father's actions against his children, and you truly are as safe here in Tellesberg as you could ever be in Manchyr. I've lost my father; Cayleb's lost his; you and Daivyn have lost yours, and a brother as well. I think it would be well for all of us to learn from those losses, to try and find a way to create a world in which children don't have to worry about losing the ones they love so early. I can't speak for God, but I think it would make Him smile if we managed to accomplish a little good out of so much pain and loss."

Irys looked into those huge brown eyes and something—some last, cold residue of fear and distrust—melted as she saw nothing but truth looking back at her. That recognition didn't magically fill her with confidence for the future, nor did she think all the goodwill in the world, however sincere, could guarantee what the future might bring. Any ruler's daughter learned those realities early, for the world was a hard instructor, and her lessons had been harsher than most. Only time could tell what political demands she and Daivyn would face, what decisions might yet force them into fresh conflict with the House of Ahrmahk, and she knew it. But unlike Zhaspahr Clyntahn, Cayleb and Sharleyan Ahrmahk were neither monsters nor liars. Enemies they might yet be, or become once more, but honorable ones. They *meant* what they'd just said, and they would stand by it in the teeth of hell itself.

"I'd like that, Your Grace," she heard herself say, and her own lips trembled just a bit. "We've made Him weep more than enough," she went on, and saw recognition of her deliberate choice of words flicker in Sharleyan's eyes. "Surely it's time we made Him smile a bit, instead."

.V.
The Delthak Works,
Barony of High Rock,
Kingdom of Old Charis,
Empire of Charis

Well, it certainly *looks* impressive, Ehdwyrd," Father Paityr Wylsynn said dryly. "Now if it just doesn't blow up and kill us all."

"I'm crushed, Father," Ehdwyrd Howsmyn told the Charisian Empire's intendant in a composed tone. "I've shared all of Doctor Mahklyn's calculations with you, and Master Huntyr and Master Tairham do excellent work. Besides, we've had the smaller model running for over two months now."

They stood side by side under the canopy of smoke rising from what had become known as the Delthak Works in order to differentiate it from the additional complexes Howsmyn had under construction on Lake Lymahn in the Barony of Green Field. Or, for that matter, the two he was expanding near Tellesberg and the entirely new complex going up outside Maikelberg in Chisholm's Duchy of Eastshare. No other man had ever owned that much raw iron-making capacity, but the Delthak Works remained the biggest and most productive of them all. Indeed, no one before Ehdwyrd Howsmyn had ever even dreamed of such a huge, sprawling facility, and its output dwarfed that of any other ironworks in the history of the world.

Howsmyn didn't really look the part of a world-shaking innovator. In fact, he looked remarkably ordinary and preposterously young for someone who'd accomplished so much, but there was something in his eyes—something like a bright, searching fire that glowed far back in their depths even when he smiled. It was always there, Wylsynn thought, but it glowed even brighter than usual today as he waved one hand at two of the men standing behind them.

The men in question smiled, although an unbiased observer might have noted that they looked rather more nervous than their employer. Not because they doubted the quality of their handiwork, but because for all of his open-mindedness and obviously friendly relationship with Howsmyn, Paityr Wylsynn *was* the Empire's intendant, the man charged with ensuring that no incautious innovation transgressed the Proscriptions of Jwo-jeng. He'd signed the attestation for the device they were there to observe, yet that could always be subject to change, and blame (like certain other substances) flowed downhill. If the intendant should change his mind, or if the Church of Charis overruled him, the consequences for the artisans and mechanics who'd constructed the device they were there to test might be . . . unpleasant.

"I'm well aware of the quality of their craftsmanship, Ehdwyrd," Wylsynn said now. "For that matter, I've already ridden in your infernal contraption of a boat. And I have considerable faith in Doctor Mahklyn's numbers. But 'considerable' isn't quite the same thing as *absolute* faith, especially when I can't pretend I understand how all those equations and formulas actually work, and *this* 'engine' is an awful lot bigger than the one in your boat. If *it* should decide to explode, I expect the damage to be considerably more severe."

"I suppose that's not unreasonable, Father. I won't pretend *I* really understand Rahzhyr's numbers—or Doctor Vyrnyr's, for that matter. But I do have faith in them, or I'd be standing far, far away at this moment. For that matter, the model tests for this one have worked just as well as for the single expansion engines, you know."

"And weren't you the one who told me once that the best scale for any test was twelve inches to the foot?" Wylsynn asked, arching one eyebrow and carefully avoiding words like "experiment," which weren't well thought of by the Inquisition.

"Which is exactly why you're here today, Father."

Wylsynn smiled at the man known as the "Ironmaster of Charis," acknowledging his point, and both of them turned back towards the hulking mass of iron and steel they'd come to observe. It was certainly impressive-looking. The open triangular frame of massive iron beams—at least twice Howsmyn's height and almost as long as it was tall—was surmounted by a rectangular, boxlike casing. Three steel rods, each thick as a man's palm, descended from the overhead structure at staggered intervals. Each of them was actually composed of *two* rods, joined at a cross bearing, and their lower ends were connected to a crankshaft four inches in diameter. The entire affair was festooned with control rods, valves, and other esoteric bits and pieces which meant very little to the uninitiated.

Its very existence was enough to make anyone nervous. Before the Group of Four's attempt to destroy the Kingdom of Charis, no one would ever have dreamed of testing the limits of the Proscriptions in such a way.

Not that there was anything prohibited about it, of course. Father Paityr would never have been here if there'd been any chance of that! But every one of those watching men knew how unlikely the Grand Inquisitor in far-off Zion was to agree about that. All of them also had a very clear notion of what would happen to them if they ever fell into the Inquisition's hands, and that was enough to make anyone nervous, even if he'd had no qualms at all about the work to which he'd set his hands and mind. And, of course, there was always the possibility that even Father Paityr could be wrong about those potentially demonic bits and pieces. So it wasn't surprising, perhaps, that most of the onlookers looked just a bit anxious.

The man standing directly beside it, however, seemed remarkably impervious to any qualms anyone else might be feeling. He'd never taken his eye off the bizarre structure for a moment—or not off a sealed glass tube on one side of it, at any rate.

Stahlman Praigyr was a small, tough, weathered man with extraordinarily long arms and a nose which had obviously been broken more than once. When he smiled, he revealed two missing front teeth, as well, but he wasn't smiling today. He stood mechanically wiping his hands again and again with an oily cloth, his cap pulled down over his eyes as he stared at the slowly climbing column of liquid in that tube, watching it like a cat lizard poised outside a spider rat burrow.

Now he straightened abruptly and looked over his shoulder.

"Pressure's up, Sir," he told Howsmyn, and the foundry owner looked at Zosh Huntyr, his master artificer.

"Ready?"

"Aye, Sir," Huntyr replied. "Nahrmahn?"

Nahrmahn Tidewater, Huntyr's senior assistant, nodded and raised his right hand, waving the flag in it in a rapid circular movement. A bell clanged loudly, warning everyone in the vicinity—and especially the crew clustered around the base of the nearest blast furnace—that the test was about to begin.

"Any time, Master Howsmyn," Huntyr said then, and Howsmyn nodded to Praigyr.

"This is your special baby, Stahlman. Open her up."

"Yes, *Sir*!" Praigyr's huge grin displayed the gap where teeth once had been, and he reached for the gleaming brass wheel mounted on the end of a long, steel shaft. He spun it, still watching the gauge, and steam hissed as the throttle valve opened.

For a moment, nothing happened, but then—slowly, at first—the piston rods from the huge cylinders hidden in the rectangular box at the top of the frame began to move. They pivoted on the cross head bearings where they joined the connecting rods, whose lower ends were connected to the cranks, the offset portions of the crankshaft. And as they moved, they turned the massive crankshaft itself, much as a man might have turned a brace-and-bit to bore a hole through a ship's timber. But this was no man turning a drill; this was the first full-scale, triple-expansion steam engine ever built on the planet of Safehold.

The piston rods moved faster as steam flowed from the high-pressure cylinder into the mid-pressure cylinder, expanding as it went. The mid-pressure cylinder's piston head was much broader than the high-pressure cylinder's, because the lower-pressure steam needed a greater surface area to impart its energy. And once the mid-pressure cylinder had completed its stroke, it vented in turn to the low-pressure cylinder, the largest of them all. It was a noisy proposition, but the crankshaft turned faster and faster, and one of the workmen by the base of the blast furnace began waving a flag of his own in energetic circles.

"All right!" Huntyr exclaimed, then clamped his mouth shut, blushing, but no one seemed to care, really. They were all too busy listening to the sound coming from the blast furnace—a sound of rushing air, growing louder and louder, challenging even the noise of the steam engine so close at hand. The steam-powered blowers of the forced-draft system were bigger and more powerful than anything the Delthak Works had built yet, even for the furnaces driven by the hydro-accumulators, and Howsmyn beamed as Tairham slapped Huntyr on the back while they blew steadily harder and harder in time with the engine's gathering speed.

"Well," Wylsynn said loudly over the sound of the engine and the blowers, "it hasn't blown up *yet*, at any rate."

"I suppose there's still time," Howsmyn replied, still beaming. "But what say you and I retreat to the comfort of my office while we wait for the inevitable disaster?"

"I think that's an excellent idea, Master Howsmyn. Especially since I understand you've recently received a shipment from Her Majesty's favorite distillery back in Chisholm."

"Why, I believe I have," Howsmyn agreed. He looked at his employees. "Zosh, I want you and Kahlvyn to keep an eye on it for another—oh, half an hour. Then I want you, Nahrmahn, and Brahd to join me and the Father in my office. I think we'll all have quite a few things to discuss at that point." He flashed another smile. "After all, now that he's let us get *this* toy up and running, it's time to tell him about all of our other ideas, isn't it?"

"Yes, Sir," Huntyr agreed with just a shade less enthusiasm than his employer, and Howsmyn bowed to Wylsynn.

"After you, Father."

▼   ▼   ▼

"I must confess I really did feel a moment or two of . . . anxiety," Paityr Wylsynn admitted ten minutes later, standing at Howsmyn's office windows and gazing out across the incredible, frenetic activity. "I know the design was approved by Owl, and I know his remotes were actually monitoring quality control all the way through, but all joking aside, it would've been a disaster if that thing had blown up! Too many people would've seen it as proof of Jwo-jeng's judgment, no matter who'd attested it. I hate to think how far back that would've set the entire project, not to mention undermining my own authority as Intendant."

"I know." Howsmyn stepped up beside him and handed him a glass half filled with amber liquid. "And, to be honest, I'd've felt better myself if I'd simply been able to hand Zosh a set of plans and tell him to build the damned thing. But we really needed him to work it out for himself based on the 'hints' Rahzhyr and I were able to give him." He shrugged. "And he did. In fact, he and Nahrmahn did us proud. That single-cylinder initial design of theirs worked almost perfectly, and the two-cylinder is actually a lot more powerful than I expected—or, rather, it's turned out to be a lot more efficient at moving a canal boat. Propeller design's more complicated than I'd anticipated, but with Owl to help me slip in the occasional suggestion, they've managed to overcome each problem as it made itself known.

"But the really important thing—the *critical* thing—is that I've got a whole layer of management now, here and at the other foundries, who're actually coming up with suggestions I haven't even so much as whispered about yet. And best of all, we've documented every step of the process in which Zosh and Nahrmahn—oh, and let's not forget Master Praigyr— came up with *this* design. We've got sketches, diagrams, office memos, everything. Nobody's going to be able to claim one of Shan-wei's demons just appeared in a cloud of smoke and brimstone and left the thing behind him!"

"Oh, don't be silly, Ehdwyrd! Of *course* they are." Wylsynn shook his head. "Zhaspahr Clyntahn's never let the truth get in his way before—what makes you think he's going let it happen now? Besides, when you come down to it, that's almost exactly what did happen. I mean, wouldn't *you* call Merlin one of Shan-wei's 'demons'? I use the term in the most approving possible fashion, you understand. And while I'd never want to sound as if I'm complaining, just breathing out there does put one firmly in mind of 'smoke and brimstone,' you know."

"Yes, I *do* know," Howsmyn sighed, his expression suddenly less cheerful as he gazed out at the pall of coal smoke which hung perpetually over the Delthak Works. It was visible for miles, he knew, just as he knew about the pollution working its way into Ithmyn's Lake despite all he could do to contain it. "In fact, I hate it. We're doing everything we can to minimize the consequences, and I'm making *damned* sure my people's drinking water is piped down from upriver from the works, but all this smoke isn't doing a thing for their lungs. Or for their *kids'* lungs, either." He grimaced and took a quick, angry sip from his glass. "God, I wish we could go to electricity!"

"At least you've given them decent housing, as far from the foundry as you can put it," Wylsynn said after a moment, resting his left hand on the other man's shoulder. He didn't mention the schools or the hospitals that went with that housing, but he didn't need to. "And I wish we could go to electricity, too, but even assuming the bombardment system didn't decide to wipe us all out, daring to profane the Rakurai would be the proof of our apostasy."

"I know. I know!"

Howsmyn took another, less hasty sip, savoring the Chisholmian whiskey as it deserved to be savored . . . or closer to it, at any rate. Then he half turned from the window to face Wylsynn fully.

"But I'm not thinking just about health reasons, either. I've done a lot to increase productivity per man-hour, which is why we're so far in front of anything the Temple Loyalists have, but I haven't been able to set up a true assembly line, and you know it."

Wylsynn nodded, although the truth was that his own admission to the inner circle was recent enough he was still only starting to really explore the data stored in Owl's memory. The AI was an incredibly patient librarian, but he wasn't very intuitive, which hampered his ability to help guide Wylsynn's research, and there was a limit to the number of hours Wylsynn could spend reading through several thousand years of history and information, no matter how addictive it might be. Or perhaps *especially* because of how addictive it was.

"I know you and Merlin've been talking about that—about 'assembly lines,' I mean—for a while," he said, "but I confess I'm still more than a little hazy on what you're getting at. It seems to me you're *already* doing a lot more efficient job of assembling things than I can imagine anyone else doing!"

"Not surprising, really," Howsmyn replied, looking back out the window. "I've been thinking about this a lot longer than you have, after all. But the truth is that all I've really managed so far is to go to a sort of intermediate system, one in which workmen make individual, interchangeable parts that can be assembled rather than one in which a group of artisans is responsible for making the entire machine or rifle or pair of scissors or disk harrow or reaping machine from the ground up. My craftsmen produce parts from templates and jigs, to far closer tolerances than anyone ever achieved before, and we're using stamping processes and powered machinery to make parts it used to take dozens of highly skilled artisans to make by hand. They can produce the components far more rapidly, and I can put more of them to work making the parts I need in larger numbers, or making the parts that take longer to make, so that I'm turning out the optimum *number* of parts to keep the actual assembly moving smoothly, without bottlenecks. But each of those fabricating processes is separate from all the others, and then all the pieces have to be taken to wherever the final product's being put together and assembled in one place. It's not bad for something fairly small and simple, like a rifle or a pistol, but the bigger and more complex the final product, the more cumbersome it gets."

"And it still makes your workforce many times more efficient than anything the Church has going for it," Wylsynn pointed out.

"Yes, it does, and more and more of my fellow ironmasters are starting to use the same techniques. Some of them are clearly infringing on my patents, of course." Howsmyn grinned at the intendant, who was also the head of the Imperial Patent Office. "I'm sure several of them—like that bastard Showail—wonder why I haven't already taken legal action. Wouldn't do to tell them how *happy* I am about it, now would it?" He shook his head. "Eventually, I'm going to have to take some action to defend the patents, if we don't want them asking questions about why a mark-grubbing manufactory owner such as myself *isn't* complaining about people robbing him blind. But even with the new techniques spreading, we're still a long way from where we could be. And frankly, we need to crank our efficiency an awful lot higher if we're going to compensate for the sheer manpower, however inefficient it may be, the Temple can throw at the same sorts of problems now that it's finally starting to get itself organized. According to Owl's SNARCs, Desnair and the Temple Lands are beginning to build new water-powered blast furnaces and rolling mills, for example, with Clyntahn's blessings and Duchairn's financial backing. It won't be long before they start improving their drop hammers, too, and however good that may be for Merlin's overall plans, it's not the kind of news the Empire needs. We've got to stay as far ahead as we can, and that's especially true for *me*, since my foundries and manufactories are the Empire's cutting edge. That's where a real assembly line would come in, if we could only make it work."

"How does that differ from what you're already doing?"

"In a proper assembly line, whatever's being built—assembled—moves down a line of workstations on a conveyor belt or a moving crane—or, if it's a vehicle of some sort, on its own wheels, perhaps, once they've been attached. What matters is that *it* goes to the workmen, rather than the *workmen* coming to it. As it passes each station, the workman or workmen at that station perform their portion of the assembly process. They connect a specific part or group of parts, and that's all they do. Whatever they're building is brought to *them*. The workforce is sized so there's enough manpower at each station to let that part of the assembly be done in as close to the same amount of time as every other part so that the line keeps moving at a steady pace. And because each group of workers performs exactly the same function on each new assembly, they can do their part of the task far more efficiently . . . and a hell of a lot more quickly."

"I see." Wylsynn sipped from his own glass, frowning, and rubbed one eyebrow. "I hope this doesn't sound too obtuse, but why *can't* you do that?"

"I *can* do something like that with relatively small items, like pistols and rifles. I have runners on the shop floor who wheel cartloads from one workstation to another. But to do that on a true industrial scale, I need to be able to locate machine tools—*powered* machine tools—at the proper places in the assembly process. Before Merlin, we really didn't have 'machine tools,' although I'd been applying water power to as many processes as I could before he ever came along. Now my artisans've invented a whole generation of powered tools, everything from lathes to drill presses to powered looms and spinning machines for Rhaiyan's textile manufactories. In fact, they've leapfrogged a hundred years or more of Earth's industrial history—largely because of the hints Merlin and I have been able to give them. But all of them are still limited by the types of power available—they're tied to waterwheels or the hydro-accumulators by shafting and drive belts. They aren't . . . flexible, and they *are* dangerous, no matter how careful my managers and I try to be. The steam engines are going to help, but we still can't simply locate machinery where we need it located; we have to locate it where we can provide power to it, instead. Electricity, and electric motors, would give us a distributed power network that would let us do that. Steam and water power don't."

"Um."

Wylsynn nodded slowly, thinking about all of the patent applications he'd approved over the last four years. Probably two-thirds of them had come from Howsmyn or his artisans, although an increasing number were coming from Charisians who'd never heard of the Terran Federation. That was a good sign, but he hadn't really considered the problem Howsmyn had just described. Probably, he reflected, because he'd been so busy being impressed by what the ironmaster had already accomplished.

Like the steam engine they'd just observed. Thanks to Owl—and Merlin, of course—Howsmyn had completely bypassed the first hundred or hundred and fifty years of the steam engine's development back on longdead Earth. He'd gone directly to water-tube boilers and compound expansion engines, with steam pressures of almost three hundred pounds per square inch, something Earth hadn't approached until the beginning of its twentieth century. Oh, his initial engine had been a single-cylinder design, but that had been as much a test of the concept as anything else. He'd moved on to double-cylinder expansion engines for his first canal boat trials, but no canal boat offered anything like enough room for that monster they'd just watched in action. Still, the boat engines had been a valuable learning exercise . . . and even they operated at a far higher pressure—and efficiency—than anything attainable before the very end of Old Earth's nineteenth century!

The advances he'd already made in metallurgy, riveting and welding, and quality control had helped to make those pressures and temperatures possible, but Safehold had always had a working empirical understanding of hydraulics. That was one reason Howsmyn's hydro-accumulators had been relatively easy for Wylsynn to approve even before he'd been admitted to the inner circle; they'd simply been one more application—admittedly, an ingenious one—of concepts which had been used in the waterworks the "archangels" had made part of Safehold's infrastructure from the Day of Creation. But the compact efficiency of the engines Howsmyn was about to introduce would dwarf even the hydro-accumulator's impact on what Merlin called his "power budget." So perhaps it wasn't surprising Wylsynn had been more focused on that increase than on the even greater potentials of the electricity he still understood so poorly himself.

Especially since electricity's one thing we can be pretty certain would attract the "Rakurai" if the bombardment platform detected it, he thought grimly. *We're lucky it doesn't seem to worry about steam, but I don't think it would miss a generating plant!*

He shuddered internally at the thought of turning Charis into another Armageddon Reef, yet even as he did, another, very different thought occurred to him. He started to shake it off, since it was so obviously foolish. Even if it had offered any useful potential, surely Merlin and Howsmyn would already have thought of it! But it wouldn't shake, and he frowned down into his whiskey glass.

"How's the development coming on that 'hydro-pneumatic recoil system' you've been working on with Captain Rahzwail and Commander Malkaihy?" he asked.

"Pretty well," Houseman replied. "We had a little trouble with the gaskets and seals initially, and the machining tolerances are awfully tight. We have to do more of it with hand tools, handheld gauges, and individually fitted pieces than I'd really like—the templates in the different manufactories aren't as consistent as I could wish, even now—but I suppose that's inevitable, given how recently we got around to truly standardizing measurements. Amazing how much difference there was between *my* 'inch' and, say, Rhaiyan's! That didn't matter as long as we were only worried about what *we* were making, and not about how well parts from our shops would fit anyone else's needs. And those machine tools people like Zosh and Nahrmahn have been putting together still aren't quite up to the tolerances I'd prefer. They're getting there, and quickly, but we've still got a ways to go. Why?"

"But your fittings and steam lines and air lines are holding up? Meeting the pressure levels you were describing to me last month?"

"Yes." Howsmyn eyed the cleric narrowly. "It's still more of a brute-force approach than I'd really like in some cases, but they're working just fine. Again, why? You're headed somewhere with this, Paityr."

"Well, I know you and Merlin deliberately steered Master Huntyr and Master Tidewater towards reciprocating engines because you want them for ships, and I don't really disagree with your logic—or with what I under-stand of it, anyway. But I've been thinking about how they'd actually work. The turbines, I mean. About the way steam pressure would drive the vanes to provide power."

"And?" Howsmyn prompted when Wylsynn paused.

"Well, what if instead of steam, you used air? And what if instead of turning the turbine to produce power, you used air power to turn something like a turbine to do work?" Wylsynn grimaced, clearly trying to wrap the words around a thought still in the process of forming. "What I mean is that the machines you'd run with electric motors if you could . . . couldn't you power them with compressed air, instead? If you built air lines to the work-stations you're talking about, couldn't you use air compressed by steam engines—like the way you're powering the forced draft on your blast fur-naces—to drive the 'machine tools' your 'assembly line' would require?"

Howsmyn stared at him, his expression completely blank. He stayed that way for several seconds, then shook himself and sucked in a huge breath of air.

"Yes," he said, almost prayerfully. "Yes, I could. And without all that damned shafting and all those damned drive belts that keep crushing hands and arms no matter how careful we are! My God, Paityr." He shook his head. "I've been so focused on other aspects that this never even occurred to me! And it would be a perfect place to develop turbines after all, too. Running compressors, high RPMs would actually be *good*!"

His dazed expression was fading rapidly into a huge grin, and he punched Wylsynn on the shoulder, hard enough to stagger the priest.

"You can't run a turbine efficiently at low RPMs, and you can't run a propeller efficiently at *high* RPMs. That's why Domynyk and I went for re-ciprocating engines. They run a lot more efficiently at those lower RPMs, and trying to cut the reduction gears we'd need to make turbines work for the Navy would've put an impossible bottleneck into the process. Either that or we'd have to run them at such poor levels of efficiency fuel con-sumption would skyrocket. We'd be lucky to get half as many miles out of a ton of coal. But for a central compressor to power a manufactory full of air-powered *machine tools*, the higher the RPMs the better! I wasn't worried about that when we were talking about powering the blast furnaces or pumping water out of the mines. I was too busy thinking about the need to get the *Navy's* engines up and running, so of course we concentrated on reciprocating machinery first! After all, turbines were mostly the way to power those electrical generating stations we can't build anyway—it never occurred to me to use them to power *compressors*! That's brilliant!"

"I'm glad you approve," Wylsynn said, rotating his punched shoulder with a cautious air.

"Damned right I do!" Howsmyn shook his head, eyes filled with a distant fire as he considered opportunities, priorities, and difficulties. "It'll take—what? another five or six months?—to get Zosh and Nahrmahn headed in the right direction to put it all together, but by this time next year—maybe sooner than that—I'm going to have a genuine assembly line running out there, and I'll be able to put it in from the very *beginning* at Mai-kelberg and Lake Lymahn!" His eyes refocused on the priest. "Our efficiency will go up *enormously*, Paityr, and it'll be thanks to you."

"No, it'll be thanks to you and Master Huntyr and Master Tidewater," Wylsynn disagreed. "Oh, I'll gracefully accept credit for pointing you in the right direction, but what Merlin calls the nuts and bolts of it, those are going to have to come from you and your greasy, oily, wonderfully creative henchmen."

"I don't think they'll disappoint you," Howsmyn told him with another grin. "Did I tell you what Brahd suggested to me last Tuesday?"

"No, I don't believe you did," Wylsynn said a bit cautiously, wondering what he was going to have to bend the Proscriptions out of shape to permit *this* time.

Brahd Stylmyn was Howsmyn's senior engineering expert, the man who'd designed and overseen the construction of the canals for the barges freighting the thousands upon thousands of tons of coal and iron ore Howsmyn's foundries required down the Delthak River. His brain was just as sharp as Zosh Huntyr's, but it was also possessed of a bulldog tenacity that had a tendency to batter its way straight through obstacles instead of finding ways around them. The term "brute-force approach" fitted Stylmyn altogether too well sometimes, although there were also times, to be fair, when he was capable of subtlety. It just didn't come naturally to him.

"Well, you know he was the one who laid out the railways here in the works," Howsmyn said, and Wylsynn nodded. Like many of Howsmyn's innovations, the dragon-drawn railcars he used to transport coal, coke, iron ore, and half a hundred other heavy loads were more of a vast refinement of something which had been around for centuries but never used on the sort of scale he'd envisioned than a totally new concept.

"He did a good job," Howsmyn continued now, "and last five-day he asked me what I thought about laying a railway all the way from here up to the mines. I told him I thought it was an interesting idea, but to be honest— given how much we were already moving with the canals open, especially now that we're able to get steam into the barges, we were unlikely to be able to move enough additional tonnage, even with dragon traction, to jus- tify the diversion of that much iron and steel from our other projects. That was when he asked me why it wouldn't be possible to take one of our new steam engines, squeeze it down, and use it to pull an entire *caravan* of railcars."

"He came up with that all on his own?"

"You just called my henchmen 'wonderfully creative,' Paityr," Hows- myn replied with a broad, proud smile. "And you were right. I thought I might have to prod one of them with the suggestion, but Brahd beat me to it. In fact, he was practically dancing from foot to foot like a little boy who needed to go when he asked me if we couldn't *please* divert some of our priorities to let him build his steam-powered railway."

"Oh, my." Wylsynn shook his head. Then he took another long sip of whiskey, lowered the glass, and his gray eyes gleamed at the industrialist. "Clyntahn's going to burst a blood vessel when he hears about this one, you know. I guarantee it, this time, and I really wish we could have the oppor- tunity to watch him froth when he does."

"We won't be able to watch," Howsmyn agreed, "but I'm willing to bet we'll be able to *hear* him when he finds out." The ironmaster raised his glass in salute to the intendant. "Maybe not directly, but I can already hear the anathematization crackling down the line towards us. Makes a nice sizzling sound, doesn't it?"

.VI.
Shairncross House,
Marisahl,
Ramsgate Bay,
Raven's Land

Weslai Parkair glowered out the window at the gray sky. He regarded the handful of soggy snowflakes oozing down it towards the equally gray steel of Ramsgate Bay through the chill, damp stillness of a thoroughly dreary morning with glum disapproval, not to say loathing.

Not that it did any good.

The reflection did not improve his sour mood, although the weather was scarcely the only reason for it. He knew that, but the weather was an old, familiar annoyance—almost an old friend, one might say. It was less . . . worrying than other, more recent sources of anxiety, and he *was* a High-lander, accustomed to the craggy elevations of his clan's mountainous terri-tory. That was why he hated the winter climate here in Marisahl. He neither knew nor cared about the warm current which ameliorated the cli-mate along the southern coast of Raven's Land and the northwest coast of the Kingdom of Chisholm. What he did care about was that winter here was far damper, without the proper ice and snow to freeze the wet out of the air. He'd never liked the raw edge winter took on here in Marisahl, where the drizzling cold bit to the bone, and as he'd grown older, his bones and joints had become increasingly less fond of it.

For the last dozen years or so, unfortunately, he'd had no choice but to winter here. It went with the office of the Speaker of the Lords, just one more of the numerous negatives attached to it, and as his rheumatism twinged, he considered yet again the many attractions of resigning. Unfortunately, the clan lords had to be here as well, since winter was when they could sit down to actually make decisions rather than dealing with day-to-day sur-vival in their cold, beautiful clan holdings. It wasn't that life got *easier* in the winter highlands, only that there was nothing much anyone could do about it until spring, which made winter the logical time to deal with other prob-lems . . . like the Council of Clan Lords' business. So all resigning would really do would be to relegate him to one of the unupholstered, backless, deliberately spartan benches the other clan lords sat in, thereby proving their hardihood and natural austerity.

Might as well keep my arse in that nice padded chair for as long as I can, he thought grumpily, and then smiled almost unwillingly. *Clearly I have the high-minded, selfless qualities the job requires, don't I?*

"It looks like it may actually stick this time, dear," the petite woman across the table said, cradling her teacup between her hands. Zhain Parkair, Lady Shairncross, was eight years younger than her husband, and although his auburn hair had turned iron gray and receded noticeably, her brown hair was only lightly threaded with silver. Twenty-five northern summers and as many winters had put crow's-feet at the corners of her eyes, he thought, but the beauty of the nineteen-year-old maiden he'd married all those years ago was still there for any man with eyes to see, and those same years had added depth and quiet, unyielding strength to the personality behind it.

"*Umpf!*" he snorted now. "If it does, the entire town will shut down and huddle round the fires till it melts." He snorted again, with supreme con-tempt for such effete Lowlanders. "People wouldn't know what to do with a *real* snowfall, and you know it, Zhain!"

"Yes, dear. Of course, dear. Whatever you say, dear." Lady Zhain smiled sweetly and sipped tea. He glowered back at her, but his lips twitched, despite his sour mood. Then his wife lowered her cup, and her expression had turned far more serious.

"So the Council's reached a decision?" Her tone made the question a statement, and her eyes watched him carefully.

"What makes you think that?" he asked, reaching for his fork and studiously concentrating on the omelette before him.

"Your smiling, cheerful mood, for one thing," his wife said serenely. "Not to mention the fact that you're meeting this morning with Suwail, whom I know you despise, and Zhaksyn, whom I know you like quite a lot."

"You, woman, are entirely too bright, d'you know that?" Parkair forked up another bite of omelette and chewed. The ham, onion, and melted cheese were delicious, and he took the time to give them the appreciation they deserved before he looked back up at Lady Zhain. "And you've known me too long, too. Might's well be a damned *book* where you're concerned!"

"Oh, no, Father! Never anything so decadent as a *book*!" The young man sitting at the table with them shook his head, his expression pained. "Mother would never insult you that way, I promise!"

"You have three younger brothers, Adym," Parkair pointed out. "That means at least two of you are spares. I'd remember that, if I were you."

"Mother will protect me." Adym Parkair smiled, but the smile was fleeting, and he cocked his head in a mannerism he'd inherited from Lady Zhain. "She's right, though, isn't she? The Council has made a decision."

"Yes, it has." Parkair looked back down at his omelette, then grimaced and laid aside his fork to reach for his teacup once more. "And, to be honest, it's the one I expected."

Zhain and Adym Parkair glanced at one another. Most Raven Lord clan heads tended to be more than a little on the dour side—enough to give teeth to the rest of the world's stereotypical view of them and their people. Weslai Parkair wasn't like that. Despite his only half-joking distaste for anything smacking of "book learning," he was not only warm and humorous but pragmatic and wise as well, which had a great deal to do with how long he'd been Lord Speaker. Yet that humor was in abeyance today, despite his best effort to lighten the mood, for he was also a devout man, and the question which had occupied the Council of Clan Lords for the last five-day had been a difficult one for him.

"So the Council's going to grant them passage?" his son asked quietly after a moment, and Parkair grimaced.

"As your mother just observed, nothing else could possibly constrain me to spend a morning talking to that ass Suwail," he pointed out. "The thought doesn't precisely fill me with joyous anticipation."

Adym smiled again, very faintly. Although he was barely twenty years old, his father had initiated him into the clan's political realities years ago. No one was immortal, Lord Shairncross had pointed out to his thirteen-year-old son, and having to learn all those realities from a standing start *after* the responsibility landed on him was scarcely the most auspicious beginning to a clan lord's tenure. As part of that initiation process, he'd systematically dissected the character, strengths, and weaknesses of every other major clan lord for Adym. Fortunately, Raven's Land was so sparsely populated there weren't all that many clan lords to worry about. *Un*fortunately, one of those clan lords was Barjwail Suwail, Lord Theralt.

Suwail had never been one of his father's favorite people. Partly because the burly, dark-haired Lord of Clan Theralt had competed strongly for the hand of Zhain Byrns twenty-five years or so earlier, but most of it had to do with Suwail's personality. Lord Theralt had always seen himself in the tradition of the corsair lords of Trellheim, despite the fact that the Raven Lords had never been a particularly nautical people. Aside from a fairly profitable fishing fleet, there simply hadn't been any Raven Lord mariners to provide him with the "corsairs" he needed, but he'd proposed to overcome that minor problem by making Theralt Bay available to freelance pirates of other lands in return for a modest piece of their profits.

Suwail's activities had been . . . irritating to King Haarahld of Charis, who'd sent a squadron of his navy to make that point to Lord Theralt some twelve years ago by burning Theralt's waterfront, which had made a quite spectacular bonfire. He'd made it to the rest of the Raven Lords by sending the same squadron to Ramsgate Bay and *not* burning *Marisahl's* waterfront.

That time, at least.

Adym's father, who'd just been elected Lord Speaker, had been the recipient of that visit's warning, and some of the other clan lords had been in favor of sending a defiant reply back to Tellesberg. Not because any of them had been fond of Suwail, but because they were Raven Lords, and all the world knew no one could threaten *Raven Lords!* Besides, they weren't a maritime people. Charisian warships might burn the coastal towns to the ground, but not even Charisian Marines were going to advance inland to tackle the clans in their valleys and dense forests. Lord Shairncross had managed to talk them out of anything quite that invincibly stupid, pointing out that the only Raven Lord who'd actually been chastised was Lord Theralt, who'd obviously brought it upon himself. In fact, he'd argued, the Charisian response had been remarkably restrained, under the circumstances.

Suwail hadn't cared for his position, or for his own certainty that Shairncross had been privately delighted by what had happened to him, but he hadn't been particularly popular with his fellow clan lords even before he angered Charis. The Council had accepted its new Lord Speaker's advice, which hadn't done anything to improve relations between Clan Shairncross and Clan Theralt. Still, all of that had been eleven whole years ago, so *of course* all the bad blood had been given plenty of time to dissipate, Adym thought sardonically.

"I thought Suwail was opposed to the idea, Father," he said out loud, and Parkair laughed harshly.

"Suwail's been opposed to anything coming out of Charis ever since he got his fingers burnt along with his waterfront. Say what you will about the man, he *does* know how to hold a grudge. Probably because there's nothing else in his head to drive it out. But, give Shan-wei her due, he's greedy enough to set even a grudge aside for enough marks. In his case, at least, it was never about anything remotely approaching a principle, at any rate!"

Lady Zhain made a soft noise which sounded remarkably like someone trying not to laugh into her teacup. Her husband glanced at her, then looked back at his son.

"I'm sure he's going to hold out for as handsome a bribe as we can screw out of the Charisians, but once he's paid off, he'll be fine with the idea. And Zhaksyn's been in favor of it from the beginning. He's the logical one to serve as our liaison with Eastshare. As long as he doesn't end up letting the Charisians buy us too cheaply, anyway."

Adym nodded, but his eyes were thoughtful as he reflected upon what his father *hadn't* just said. He knew Lord Shairncross had been badly torn by the request the exhausted Chisholmian messenger had carried to Marisahl, and he respected his father's position, even if it wasn't quite the same as his own.

Weslai Parkair was a loyal son of Mother Church, and he'd raised his heir to be the same. The thought of openly permitting a Charisian army to march across Raven's Land to enter the Republic of Siddarmark for the express purpose of aiding Lord Protector Greyghor against a Temple Loyalist uprising had caused him immense pain. A Lord Speaker was traditionally neutral in any matter brought before the Council of Clan Lords, and he'd observed that neutrality this time, as always. Yet no one who knew him could have doubted how difficult he found the decision.

Poor Father, Adym thought. *Such a good man, and so loyal to such a bad cause. And the real hell of it, from his perspective, is that he knows it's a bad cause.*

They'd talked about it, just as Adym had discussed it with his mother, and his father knew they didn't see eye to eye on this particular topic. But Lord Shairncross was too astute a student of human nature not to understand the very thing his faith and loyalty to Mother Church insisted he deny.

And it helps that Bishop Trahvys knows it, too, Adym thought. *Of course, he's more like a clansman than a mainlander these days himself!*

Despite its impressive size, Raven's Land's tiny population was too miniscule to support an archbishopric. Instead, it had been organized into a single bishopric, and its climate, combined with its relative poverty and lack of people, meant it had never been considered any prize by Mother Church's great dynasties. Trahvys Shulmyn was the scion of a minor noble in the small Border State duchy of Ernhart, who'd never had the patrons or the ambition to seek a more lucrative post.

And he was also a very good man, one Adym suspected was much more in sympathy with the Reformists than his masters in fardistant Zion realized.

"I know this is a hard decision for you, Weslai," Lady Zhain said now, setting down her cup and looking into her husband's eyes across the table. "Are you going to be all right with it? I know you too well to expect you to be *comfortable* with it, no matter what the Council says. But are you going to be able to live with it?"

The dining room was silent for several seconds. Then, finally, Parkair inhaled deeply and nodded.

"Yes," he said. "You're right that I'm never going to be comfortable with it, but these aren't 'comfortable' times."

He smiled faintly. It was a fleeting expression, and it vanished as he looked back out at the slowly thickening snowfall.

"I never thought I'd see a day when the sons and daughters of God had to choose between two totally separate groups of men claiming to speak for Him and the archangels," he said softly. "I never *wanted* to see that day. But it's here, and we have to deal with it as best we can."

He turned away from the window and his eyes refocused as he looked first at his wife and then at his son.

"I know both of you have been . . . impatient with me over this issue." Adym started to speak, but Parkair's raised hand stopped him. "I said 'impatient,' Adym, and that was all I meant. And, to be honest, I've been impatient with *myself*. A man ought to know what he believes, where he stands, what God demands of him, and he ought to have the courage to *take* that stand. But I've been wrestling with myself almost since this war began, and especially since the Ferayd Incident and what happened in Zion last winter. What should be clear's been nothing of the sort, and even if it had been as simple and clear-cut as I wanted it to be, a clan lord has obligations and responsibilities. A man can take whatever position God and his conscience require of him and accept the consequences of his actions, but a clan lord, responsible for all the folk who look to him for leadership—*his* decisions have consequences for far too many people for him to make any decision this important impulsively. And in the quiet of his own thoughts, he has to ask himself whether or not he has a right to take all of those other folk with him to wherever he ultimately decides to go."

It was very quiet in the dining chamber, and his eyes were dark as he looked back and forth between the two most important people in his own life.

"Mother Church was ordained by Langhorne himself on God's own command. We owe her obedience, not simply because Langhorne created her, but because of the *reason* he created her—to be the keeper of men and women's souls, the guardian of God's world and all of His children's hope of immortality. And yet . . . and yet. . . ." He shook his head, his expression sad. "Mother Church speaks now with Zhaspahr Clyntahn's voice, and what she says has driven a wedge into her own heart. Bishop Trahvys has done his best to mitigate that here in Raven's Land, but not even a man as good as he is can *hide* the harshness of that voice. Or the fact that he finds himself in disagreement with so much of what it says."

He shook his head, his expression sad.

"I don't know how it started, or why Clyntahn and the others"—even here, even now, he avoided the term "Group of Four," Adym noted— "sought Charis' destruction. But I do know that if I'd been Haarahld Ahrmahk, I would've responded exactly the way he did. And there's no question in my heart or mind that it's Vicar Zhaspahr who's truly driving this schism. Maybe he's right to do that, and Langhorne knows a true servant of Shanwei *must* be dealt with severely, as Schueler commanded. Yet the doctrine he's announced and the policies he's set are only widening the schism. They're *justifying* this 'Church of Charis' defiance of the Temple, and I understand how someone like Maikel Staynair or Sharleyan of Chisholm or Cayleb Ahrmahk can see only the hand of Shan-wei herself in the Inquisition's actions. None of which changes the fact that by defying the Grand Vicar's authority, they threaten to completely splinter Mother Church.

"And that's why things have been so far from clear-cut for me. But clear-cut or not, we're called to make decisions, and the Council's decided. I can't pretend I find myself in wholehearted agreement with that decision, yet neither can I ignore or deny the arguments of those who pushed for it . . . or that Bishop Trahvys 'happened' to find himself called away from Marisahl Cathedral on urgent business the five-day he knew we'd be debating it."

He touched his plate, with its half-eaten omelette, and his expression was cold, his eyes as hard as Adym could remember ever having seen them.

"It can't be God's will for His servants to deliberately starve women and children in the middle of winter. Not *children*." He looked up to meet his wife's gaze, and those hard eyes were haunted now. "Not babes in arms, not children who never had the chance to choose. That much I do know, even if I know nothing else in the entire world." His voice was deep, with the pain of a clan lord who'd seen malnutrition in his own lands in far too many winters. "And the instructions to destroy that food came from Zion itself.

There are enough of our own people in the Republic for me to know East-share and the Charisians've told nothing but the truth about that, and what-ever else may be true, *Mother Church* would never have given that order. It came from the Grand Inquisitor, and so, in the end, we have to choose—to decide—whether or not Zhaspahr Clyntahn speaks for *God* as well as His Church.

"I don't know what will happen to the Church in the fullness of time, and no matter what, I'll never be able to draw my own sword against her. But if someone doesn't prevent this from continuing, if someone doesn't *stop* it, this schism can only become permanent. Mother Church will be broken forever, beyond any hope of healing, because the Reformists will have no choice but to break with Zion and the Grand Vicar completely and permanently. And whatever the Grand Inquisitor may think, he'll never be able to crush the hatred he's fanning."

He shook his head sadly.

"I may not be the theologian he is, but I've spent fifty years watching human beings. We clansmen are stubborner than most, and we pride our-selves on it, yet we're not all that different from others when it comes to it, and not even Vicar Zhaspahr can kill *everyone* who disagrees with him. He seems determined to try, though, and if he persists, if no one stops him, the wounds Mother Church has already suffered can only become eternal. Only Shan-wei can profit from that, and I fear, fear to the bottom of my heart and soul, that the only power on Safehold that can stop him now lies in Tellesberg . . . and that it can stop him only by the sword I can never draw against her myself. That . . . fills me with shame, in far too many ways, yet all of my grief and all of my shame can't change the truth into something else."

Adym Parkair looked at his father, hearing the pain and recognizing the honesty, and he reached across the table to touch Lord Shairncross' forearm.

"I think you're right, Father," he said quietly. "I wish you weren't, but I think you are."

"Of course I am." His father patted the hand on his arm gently as he tried to inject some lightness into his tone. He didn't succeed in that, but he managed a smile, anyway. "Of course I am. I'm a wise and experienced student of men, aren't I?"

"That's what you've always *told* me, at any rate," Adym responded in kind, and Lord Shairncross chuckled.

"You should always trust your father," he assured his son, then straight-ened his shoulders and reached for his teacup once more.

"On a more pragmatic note," he continued, "telling Duke Eastshare he *couldn't* march through Raven's Land would've been . . . ill-advised, I think. Our clansmen are almost as stubborn and bloody-minded as they like to think they are, but there aren't very many of us. Not enough to stop a

Chisholmian army, much less a *Charisian* one, with all those newfangled weapons, from marching pretty much wherever it chooses. And the Charisian Navy doesn't really need our permission to sail into places like Theralt Bay and land supplies for that army, either. That idiot Suwail discovered that a few years back, if I recall correctly."

His smile was tart, but this time it held some real humor, Adym noted.

"We could make their march unpleasant, and we could slow them down, and we could bleed them, but in the process we'd take far heavier losses. And"—his expression hardened once more—"we'd turn Raven's Land into what's happening in places like Glacierheart and Shiloh Province, as well. I'm not surprised the Council's declined to do that when we couldn't stop them anyway. And whatever my own doubts about this Church of Charis, I won't be party to that, either.

"So," he inhaled deeply, "if we can't deny them passage, we might as well make the best terms we can and find a way to profit from it."

"Profit?" Lady Zhain frowned distastefully, and he chuckled, this time with more than a little genuine amusement.

"Love, I realize we Highlanders have nothing but contempt for the soft, decadent luxuries that come with money, but even for us, money can be a useful thing to have. That's certainly what someone like Suwail's going to be thinking, at any rate. But there's more than one sort of profit, you know."

"You're thinking about Charisian goodwill, aren't you, Father?"

"In a manner of speaking," Parkair acknowledged, turning back to his son with an approving nod. "I've come to the conclusion that whatever else may happen, this Charisian Empire isn't going away. And if we align ourselves with the Charisians' enemies, it would have to be tempting for them to simply occupy us, the same way they've occupied Zebediah and Corisande. I think they'd prefer not to, but there's no point pretending it wouldn't be a lot easier for them to seize control of Raven's Land—especially when all they have to do is march right across The Fence to get to us—than it ever was for them to conquer a princedom as far away, across so much ocean, and with as many people and as much money as Corisande. They might find themselves faced with one revolt after another—clansmen being clansmen—but they could do it. Frankly, they'd be stupid *not* to do it, if we made ourselves their enemy, and one thing Sharleyan of Chisholm never was is stupid. I haven't seen much evidence that this new husband of hers is any slower than she is, either."

He paused, one eyebrow arched, and Adym nodded emphatically.

"So, given all that, it makes far more sense to welcome them in and do everything we can to speed them on their way, minimizing the opportunity for the sorts of unfortunate incidents marching armies frequently encounter, especially passing through hostile territory. And if in the process we get on their good side where things like trade opportunities are concerned while simultaneously staying off their *bad* side where things like invasions and occupations are concerned, I'll not complain."

He shrugged and sipped tea, looking back out the window.

"I wish it had never come to this, and I wish I'd never seen the day I had to help make this sort of decision," he told his wife and his son. "But we don't always get what we wish, and the Council knows that as well as I do. That's why we've made the decision we've made, and I'm as close to 'all right' with it as I suppose anyone could ever be, Zhain. Not happy, not enthusiastic, but definitely all right under the circumstances."

His eyes dropped back to that half-eaten omelette, and he smiled sadly, eyes darkened by the specter of starving children in Siddarmark.

"All right," he repeated again, softly. "All right."

.VII.
Royal College,
Tellesberg Palace,
City of Tellesberg,
and
The Citadel,
King's Harbor,
Helen Island,
Kingdom of Old Charis,
Empire of Charis

Doctor Sahndrah Lywys stepped into what would have been called her laboratory on a planet named Old Earth a thousand years or so ago. On Safehold, it was simply called her study, although the "studies" she carried on here had very little to do with the libraries and quiet reading rooms most Safeholdians meant by that term. In fact, she strongly suspected that if the Inquisition—at least the Inquisition as administered by Zhaspahr Clyntahn—had had any notion of exactly what she studied here, and how, the consequences would have been drastic and extremely unpleasant.

Of course Clyntahn and his agents probably do have a pretty good idea of what we're up to here at the College, she reflected as she used one of the Shan-wei's candles which had resulted from those same studies to light the lamps in the room's corners. *If they don't, it's not because they haven't been* told, *anyway! And if they do know, all of us better hope to Langhorne the Group of Four does lose this damned war in the end.*

Sahndrah Lywys was a Charisian to her toenails, and she had enormous confidence in her emperor and empress and in her homeland, but that didn't mean Charis *couldn't* lose, and she grimaced at that thought as she replaced the last lamp's chimney and adjusted the reflector behind it. It wasn't as good as sunlight, but no interior light source was, and her study here in Tellesberg Palace was still far better lit than her original one in the old Royal College. The original College had seldom been able to afford the quality of the lamp oil (refined from first-grade kraken oil) available to it now. The oil burned with a bright, clear flame, far better (and far easier on her eyes) than the tallow candles and poor-quality oil she'd had to use altogether too often then. And she could have literally as much of it as she needed, which was an almost sinful luxury after so many years of pinching every tenth-mark until it squealed.

Her new study was also bigger, far better equipped, and much safer. Lywys knew Rahzhyr Mahklyn had been very much in two minds about accepting Emperor Cayleb's (only he'd simply been *King* Cayleb at the time, of course) offer of a new home here in the palace immediately after the Battle of Darcos Sound. The official distinction between the College and the Kingdom of Charis had always been carefully maintained, despite its name, precisely because its quest for knowledge had been enough to make any conservative churchman uncomfortable. That had been true even before the schism; since the Church of Charis had declared its independence, it had grown only worse, as the act of arson which had destroyed the original College—and all its records—had made abundantly clear.

Cayleb had been pressing Mahklyn to move to larger, safer, and more efficient quarters for over eight months before the arsonists struck. After the attack, the king had been through arguing; he'd *commanded*, and Mahklyn had seen no choice but to acquiesce. Lywys had been in favor of the move even before someone started playing with lit lanterns, and nothing since had changed her mind. On a personal level, living on the palace grounds made her feel enormously safer. On a scholarship level—which was far more important to her, if the truth be known—the advantages were even greater. There was no comparison between the College's current funding levels, with open Crown sponsorship. And even more significant to someone like Lywys, the Church of Charis' full-fledged support of the faculty's research as a critical component in the Empire's and the Church's survival had let all of them step out of the shadowy, semi-condemned twilight of near-heresy to which their love of knowledge had once condemned them.

Not that there weren't some downsides to the move, she reflected more grimly, thinking about the decades of research and notes which had burned along with the old College. She extinguished the stub of the Shan-wei's candle carefully, testing the wooden sliver between her fingers to be certain it was out before she discarded it. There wasn't much to burn here in her study, but she was pretty sure all of the College's faculty had become almost as paranoid as she was where fires were concerned.

She smiled at that thought, given how much of her own studies of late had been dedicated towards finding better ways to *make* things burn. The Shan-wei's candle was a case in point, although a part of her *did* wish people could have found a less . . . pointed name for it. Personally, she'd held out for "instant match," or even just "match," since in many ways it was only a better development of the old slow match and quick match which had been used to light candles and fires and set off matchlocks—and artillery—forever. She still hadn't given up hope of eventually getting the name changed, but it was going to be an uphill battle, at best.

She chuckled and crossed to the cabinet in the study's corner. Her assistants would be coming in soon, and it was a point of honor for her to be already here, already working when her first student arrived. She knew she wasn't fooling any of them into thinking she'd really been here working all night—at her age all-night sessions had become a thing of the past—yet there were still appearances to maintain and, if she was going to be honest, she thought as she opened the cabinet door, it was a game she and they both enjoyed playing.

She removed her cotton apron from the cabinet, put it on, and turned to the stone-topped worktable to resume her current project. One of her students had obviously spent at least a little time here after she'd gone home, she noted, and reached out to move the bottles of acid whoever it was had left behind. Schueler's tears and vitriol distillate, she noted. Now what had whoever it had been—

"Oh, Shan-wei!"

She snatched her hand back, scowling, as she knocked over the bottle of Schueler's tears, which, in turn, tipped over the other bottle. Fortunately, whoever had left them out had secured the stoppers properly, but the impact of their fall was enough to loosen both of them. Quite a bit of both acids leaked, flowing together in an acrid-smelling puddle, before she could snatch them up once again.

She scowled, castigating herself for her carelessness, and carried both bottles carefully across to one of the lead-lined sinks. She rinsed them both thoroughly, one at a time, then dried them and set them back into the storage rack before she returned to the worktable.

The puddle of combined acids was bigger than she'd thought, and she looked around for something to clean it up with. Unfortunately, there was nothing handy, and she shrugged. Her lab apron was getting worn, anyway. If the acids ate holes in it, it would give her an excuse to replace it. She smiled at the thought, took it off, and wiped the table cautiously, careful to keep her hands out of contact with the acid. Then she crossed to one of the lamps with the sodden apron.

She spread the wet portion of fabric over the heat rising from the lamp chimney, holding the apron by its sides, moving it in slow circles to encourage drying. The fumes made her want to sneeze, but the study was well ventilated—she'd insisted on that!—and she'd certainly smelled far worse over the years. In fact—

"*Langhorne!*"

Lywys jumped two feet into the air as the center of her lab apron disappeared in a sudden, instantaneous burst of light, like the flash of Langhorne's own Rakurai.

▼　▼　▼

"So Sahndrah brought her new discovery straight to me," Rahzhyr Mahklyn said much later. He was tipped back in his swivel chair, gazing out the windows of his office, speaking—apparently—to the empty air. Now he grinned. "I don't know whether she was more pleased, startled, or upset with herself for having been so clumsy in the first place. But, being Sahndrah, she went through another half-dozen aprons and hand towels checking and duplicating before she came to tell me about it."

"Well, *this* will make Ahlfryd happy," Merlin Athrawes replied over the plug in Mahklyn's ear. At the moment, he was standing atop the citadel at King's Harbor, overlooking the anchorage. "I know it makes *me* happy. I never expected anyone to discover *guncotton* this soon."

"It sounds to me as if she discovered it pretty much exactly the same way Schönbein did," Mahklyn replied. Then he paused, his eyes narrowing. "Owl's remotes didn't happen to've anything to do with her spilling that acid, did they?"

"How could you possibly suggest such a thing?" Merlin responded in tones of profound innocence.

"Because King Haarahld was right when he called you Master Traynyr! *Were* you pulling puppet strings in this case?"

"Much as it pains me to disabuse you of your faith in my diabolical Machiavellianism, in this particular instance, I am as innocent as the new fallen snow. I had nothing—*nothing* at all—to do with it."

Mahklyn frowned suspiciously. It wasn't that he didn't trust Merlin's veracity . . . exactly. Still . . . .

"Well, I suppose I'll just have to take your word," he said after a moment. "And however it happened, she's jumped on it like a slash lizard on a prong buck." He shook his head. "She spent fifteen minutes telling me all about the additional research she'll need to do before she's prepared to make any definitive statements about the process or how it works. Then she spent the next two hours pointing out possible applications, especially where explosives in general—and artillery in particular—are concerned."

"I can't say I'm really surprised." Merlin shook his head. "She's been working too closely with Ahlfryd for too long for the possibilities not to hit her right in the eye."

"But are we going to be able to actually use it?" Mahklyn climbed out of his chair and walked across to the window, looking out over the courtyards of Tellesberg Palace. "I checked Owl's library before I commed you—that's how I knew about Schönbein. Chemistry isn't my discipline, and we don't really have anyone inside the circle who *is* a chemist. But according to what I skimmed out of the library, it took decades back on Old Earth to actually develop a reliable nitro-based propellant that didn't have a tendency to explode on its own at highly inconvenient moments."

"Yes, it did. Almost fifty years, in fact. But Safehold's got everything we'd really need to duplicate Veille's formulation. We'd have to drastically increase the scale of production for some of what we'd need, and the quality control involved in washing the guncotton would have to be worked on, but none of that's beyond the reach of what we have right now. It's only a matter of . . . steering the development."

"That sounds at least moderately Machiavellian to me," Mahklyn pointed out, and Merlin chuckled as he leaned his elbows on the battlements.

"Not *that* Machiavellian. Only a *little* Machiavellian. And a good thing, too. I'm going to have to reserve most of my Machiavellian wiles for application to the Brethren to really make this work."

"Oh?"

"You're right. We need a chemist in the circle, and to be honest, I can't think of a better candidate than Doctor Lywys. She strikes me as mentally flexible enough, and I'm pretty sure she could handle the shock better than most."

"Don't expect me to disagree with you. *I* nominated her for membership over five months ago."

"I know you did. And it hasn't taken them this long to make a decision in her case because they don't think it would be a good idea. They've had some other things on their minds."

"I know." Mahklyn closed his eyes briefly. "I knew Father Zhon's health was deteriorating, but I hadn't realized how sick he actually was."

"Not so much sick as simply old." Merlin's blue eyes darkened. "But there's no use pretending his final illness didn't distract the Brethren badly. And there were a lot of nominations in the pipeline in front of her as well. Which doesn't mean you and I can't push them—gently, of course—where Doctor Lywys is concerned. For that matter, I'd like to add Zhansyn Wyllys, as well."

"Ah?" Mahklyn crooked an eyebrow. "Oh! You want him because of his distillation work?"

"Especially since he's started experimenting with coal tar," Merlin agreed.

Distillation had been a part of Safehold's allowed technology since the Creation, but like all the rest of that technology, it had been applied on a rote basis, following the directions laid down in the *Holy Writ*, with no more theoretical understanding of the principles involved than the "archangels" had been able to avoid. Zhansyn Wyllys intended to change that. He was far younger (and more junior) than Mahklyn or Lywys—in fact, he'd joined the College only a year or so earlier—and unlike some of his fellow faculty, he made no bones about the fact that he fully intended to find out *why* the archangels, instructions produced the effects they did. He hadn't quite said so in so many words, but Mahklyn was pretty sure he meant to figure that out even if his inquiries brought him into direct conflict with the Proscriptions.

He hadn't joined the College without strenuous opposition from his father—a devout man who also happened to be one of Old Charis' wealthier lamp oil producers. Unfortunately for Styvyn Wyllys, his son was an obstinate, determined young man, and it was his family's trade which had first gotten him interested in reinventing the heretical scientific method as he worked on ways to improve the distillation and purification of the oil they produced.

For the most part, in Charis, that oil was now harvested from sea dragons, the Safeholdian equivalent of terrestrial whales, although it was still graded in terms of the older kraken oil. Sea dragon oil had begun to replace kraken oil only in the last forty years or so, as the dragoning industry—for food, as well as oil—grew with the steady increase in the seaworthiness of galleons, but by now sea dragon oil represented over two-thirds of the total Charisian oil industry. The green sea dragon was the most prized of all, not simply because it was the largest and provided the greatest yield per dragon, up to four hundred gallons from a fully mature creature, but because it produced what had been called spermaceti back on Old Earth.

The oil tree, a native Safeholdian species Pei Shan-wei's teams had genetically modified as part of their terraforming efforts, was a much commoner source of oils for the mainland realms. The trees grew to around thirty feet in height and produced large, hairy pods whose dozens of smaller seeds contained over sixty percent oil by weight, and Shan-wei's geneticists had modified the oil tree to make its oil safe for humans and other terrestrial animal species to consume. Unlike the imported olive tree, neither the fruit nor the seeds of the oil tree were particularly edible, although the seeds were sometimes ground into a form of flour and used in cooking.

The fire vine was another major source of plant oils, but it was also possessed of major drawbacks. It was a large, fast-growing vine—runners could measure as much as two inches in diameter—whose stems, leaves, and seeds were all extremely rich in a highly flammable oil. The oil was actually easier to extract than oil tree oil, but unlike the oil tree, fire vine hadn't been genetically modified, and its oil was extremely poisonous to humans and terrestrial animals. Worse, it was highly flammable, as its name implied, which posed a significant threat, especially in regions which experienced hot or especially arid summers. It wasn't very satisfactory as a lamp oil, either, since it burned with an extremely smoky flame and an unpleasant odor, but it was commercially cultivated in some regions—especially in the Harchong Empire—as a source of lubricating and heating oil.

Neither oil tree oil nor fire vine oil was very popular in Charis or Emerald—or in Corisande, for that matter—because kraken oil and sea dragon oil burned with a brighter, cleaner flame. The fact that sea dragons were also a major source of meat protein gave further impetus to sea dragoning, but the steady increase in the productivity of Charisian manufactories had been an even bigger factor in the industry's growth. Sea dragon oil was simply more flexible than oil tree oil, and unlike fire vine oil, it didn't tend to poison people, pets, and food animals. Even with the steady growth of the dragoning fleet, supply never managed to keep up with demand, however, and it was a far riskier trade on Safehold than whaling had ever been on Old Earth. Sea dragon oil might be less toxic and less dangerous to human beings in general than fire vine oil, but Captain Ahab's quest for vengeance would have ended much sooner (and just as badly) on Safehold, given the existence of doomwhales. The top of the oceanic food chain, the doomwhale had been known on occasion to attack—and sink—small galleons, and the dragoning ships sometimes attracted one or more of them, at which point things got decidedly lively. It wasn't unheard of for doomwhales to sink a half-dozen or more dragoning ships in a single season, although that was usually an accidental byproduct of the huge creatures' feeding on the sea dragons the ships in question had taken.

Personally, although Merlin understood the economics involved, he found it a little difficult not to side with the doomwhales. Sea dragons reproduced more rapidly than most species of whale, and commercial dragoning was new enough that it would be decades yet, even at the current rate of growth, before it started significantly reducing sea dragon stocks. None of which prevented Merlin from seeing the inevitable parallels between dragoning and commercial whaling, and he intended to do everything he could to encourage the move from sea dragon oil to other sources of fuel and lubricant.

At the moment, he had more pressing things on his mind, but that was one reason he'd been keeping an eye on Zhansyn Wyllys. Wyllys' family had grown wealthy harvesting and distributing sea dragon oil, and the dragoning industry had applied distillation to the process with quite a degree of sophistication. All of it was purely empirical, however, and the drive to understand and improve the existing methods was what had sparked young Zhansyn's initial interest in his own branch of proto-chemistry. As his interest and experiments had progressed, however, he'd moved from an interest in simply improving the existing processes to a desire to find alternative—and hopefully more abundant—oil sources, as well.

Conservatives (like his father) nursed significant reservations about his quest, and not all of them because of religious concerns. Styvyn Wyllys' wealth and his family's fortune depended on sea dragoning; he was none too pleased by his rebellious offspring's effort to find *other* sources of oil, despite Zhansyn's argument that if he could find them, Wyllys' Sea Dragon Oil could simply drop the "Sea Dragon" part of its name and get in on the ground floor in the *new* oil industry.

Whatever Styvyn Wyllys might think, Charisians in general, always more enthusiastic about innovation than mainlanders, had become even more enthusiastic over the past several years, and the College, prompted by the members of the inner circle, had supported Zhansyn's efforts strongly. He'd started out looking at conventional plant oil sources—oil wood, fire vine, nearpalm, and imported terrestrial soybeans, peanuts, and jojoba—and he'd already made some significant contributions to production and refining. Even better in many ways, unless Merlin was sadly mistaken, one of his projects was going to lead to the production of kerosene from coal tar in the not too distant future. And that, given the extensive oilfields in southern Charis and Emerald Island—and the fact that Safeholdian techniques for drilling and pumping from *water* wells were well developed and, with Howsmyn's new steam engines, about to get even better developed—was likely to lead to an entirely new industry. One that opened all sorts of interesting possibilities, given that the caloric energy of oil was fifty percent greater than that of coal.

But what Merlin was particularly interested in at the moment was the possibility of producing petroleum jelly in useful quantities. Quantities, for example, sufficient to use as a stabilizer in nitrocellulose-based propellants and explosives. With just a little nudging . . . .

"I don't know if anyone's even considered Wyllys," Mahklyn said after several thoughtful moments. "I see a lot of potential in the work he's doing, but I don't know anything about his attitude towards the Group of Four and the Reformists. Do you?"

"Not as much as I'd like. What I do know looks hopeful, though, including the fact that he and his father clearly don't see eye to eye. The fact that he's as much of a knowledge seeker as any of the rest of you 'eggheads' doesn't necessarily make him a Reformist, and even if it did, Reformism isn't necessarily the same thing as being prepared to completely jettison the *Writ* and the archangels. But we could put a couple of Owl's remotes on him, take a good look at him, before we ever actually suggested him to anyone. You're right that we need to get Sahndrah vetted and admitted to the circle first—that should've been a higher priority all along, and now that she's stumbled across guncotton, we really need her working with Owl to get chemistry properly launched as a science. Especially given what I have to tell Ahlfryd and Captain Rahzwail about my latest 'visions' tomorrow."

"It *would* be nice to be able to give them some good news with the bad, wouldn't it?" Mahklyn said almost wistfully, and Merlin shrugged philosophically.

"They're going to give Domynyk and me some good news to go with the bad, first, and it's not the end of the world. What bothers me more is where and how Clyntahn and Maigwair got their hands on the information, and without remotes in Zion, I don't think there's a chance in hell we'll ever be able to answer that question definitively. From examining the drawings they've actually sent out to the foundries and the formulas they're sending out to their powder mills, it looks to me like it had to come out of the Hairatha Mill—probably from the same son-of-a-bitch who diverted the gunpowder for Clyntahn's Rakurai. Unfortunately, that suggests whoever it was had complete access, at least at the time, and at this point we can't know what else he may have passed along."

"Not a good situation," Mahklyn acknowledged. "On the other hand, their powder mills' quality control is still way behind ours. For that matter, their *foundries* are in the same boat. The quality of their iron's a lot more problematical than ours, even from lot to lot in the same blast furnace, much less from foundry to foundry. That's a major handicap over and beyond the piss-poor—you should pardon the expression; I've been talking to Cayleb again—per-man-hour productivity of their manufactories. And without Ahlfryd and Ehdwyrd—among others—to push the support structure that's not going to change anytime soon, which means they're still going to be producing the new hardware in tenth-mark packets."

"And if you add ten tenth-marks together, you get a *whole* mark," Merlin pointed out acidly. Then he pushed back from the battlements and gave himself a shake. "Still, you're right. We've got a running start and our industrial plant *is* one hell of a lot more productive. Besides," he produced a crooked smile, "I'm the one who told Cayleb we needed the mainlanders and the Group of Four to adopt the new technology if we really wanted to topple the Church. It's still true, too. I think I've just become too much of a Charisian myself to be comfortable with the idea."

"Speaking as a *native* Charisian, I'm not really brokenhearted to hear that, you know," Mahklyn said dryly, and Merlin chuckled.

"Neither am I, Rahzhyr," he said, gazing out across the forest of masts in the harbor so far below. "Neither am I."

.VIII.
The Citadel,
King's Harbor,
Helen Island,
Kingdom of Old Charis,
Empire of Charis

I'm sorry I wasn't here yesterday, Sir," Sir Ahlfryd Hyndryk, Baron Seamount, said to High Admiral Rock Point. "The firing test ran over." He shrugged wryly. "I'm afraid one of the recuperators failed fairly drastically. It was, ah, quite lively there for a few moments."

"Was anyone hurt?" Sir Domynyk Staynair, Baron Rock Point and High Admiral of the Imperial Charisian Navy, asked sharply, although the truth was that he knew the answer to his question before he asked. He'd been watching the tests through Owl's SNARCs.

"Two of Captain Byrk's seamen were injured," Seamount acknowledged unhappily. "I think one of them may lose three or four fingers." He held up his own maimed left hand and wiggled its remaining fingers. "Unfortunately, it's his right hand and he's right-handed. The other fellow should be fine, though." He lowered his hand and grimaced. "I blame myself for it."

"Really?" Maikel Staynair's younger brother tipped back in his chair. "You personally built all the components of the recuperator that failed, I take it?"

"Well, no." Seamount shrugged. "I did have more than a little to do with its design, though. And I was supervising the test in person."

"And I'll wager no one could've prevented whatever happened from happening. Am I right about that?"

"Well . . . ."

"As a matter of fact, High Admiral, you are right," Captain Ahldahs Rahzwail said. He glanced at Seamount, then looked back at Rock Point. "It was a fault in the casting, My Lord. That's my initial analysis of why the cylinder wall split when the pressure spiked, at any rate. And there was no way anyone could've known it was there until the gun was fired."

"That's pretty much what I expected. So if you'll stop kicking yourself over that, Ahlfryd, what say we get down to the reason *Seijin* Merlin and I are here? I have to get back to the fleet, and he has to get back to Their Majesties, and I'll give you one guess how impatient Their Majesties are to hear about your latest developments."

"Yes, Sir," Seamount said, and opened the leather folder lying in front of him on the conference table.

Seamount's office seemed smaller than it had been, with the conference table and a complete additional desk crammed into it, but its slate-lined walls were still covered with smeared notations, Merlin observed. He was tempted to smile, but the temptation faded, because those half-smeared notes were all in Seamount's handwriting, or Ahldahs Rahzwail's. Urvyn Mahndrayn, who'd been Seamount's assistant for years, would never chalk another cryptic memorandum to himself on those slate walls again.

He settled into his own chair, across the table from Rahzwail. The burly, dark-haired captain reminded him of a shorter version of Rahzhyr Mahklyn's son-in-law, Aizak Kahnklyn, with blunt, hard features and a heavy forehead which did their best to disguise the quick brain behind them. He might not be another Urvyn Mahndrayn, but very few people were. Rahzwail couldn't multitask the way Mahndrayn had, and he lacked Mahndrayn's ability to intuitively leap across obstacles. Yet he was an immensely experienced officer, the ex-commander of the bombardment ship *Volcano*, and what he lacked in intuition he compensated for with relentless, methodical determination. In some ways, he was actually a better foil for Seamount then Mahndrayn had been, because of how differently their minds worked, but no one recognized what a disaster Mahndrayn's loss had been more clearly than Rahzwail himself.

Merlin glanced at Seamount as the short, portly baron gazed down at his own notes. Seamount had finally made admiral's rank, despite the fact that he hadn't commanded a ship at sea in decades. There were undoubtedly at least a handful of diehard old salts who might be tempted to denigrate Seamount's admiral's streamer because of that lack of seagoing experience, but if there were, they would be well advised to keep their opinions to themselves. Most of the Imperial Charisian Navy recognized how much it owed to Seamount's fertile brain, and Domynyk Staynair had finally taken the first concrete steps towards completing the naval reorganization Bryahn Lock Island had mapped out but never had time to implement.

Seamount was now the commanding officer of the Bureau of Ordnance, with authority over all weapons-related development for the navy and with Rahzwail as his executive officer and senior assistant. Rahzwail's primary focus was on artillery and its development, while Commander Frahnklyn Hainai, Seamount's liaison with Ehdwyrd Howsmyn's engineers and artificers, was focusing on the development of new and better alloys of steel and the new steam engines coming out of the Delthak Works. It was a comment on just how severe Mahndrayn's loss had been that it took both of them to fulfill all of the functions *he'd* fulfilled, although Merlin suspected Rahzwail and Hainai might each actually be better at their part of Mahndrayn's old workload than he himself had been, if only because they had to juggle so many fewer projects simultaneously. He also knew Rock Point had earmarked Hainai to take over the Bureau of Engineering once it was formally established (in about another two or three months, at the outside), just as Captain Tompsyn Saigyl (yet another Seamount assistant, who'd also worked closely with Rock Point and Sir Dustyn Olyvyr) would be assuming command of the equally soon-to-be-established Bureau of Ships. Captain Dynnys Braisyn was already settling in as the CO of the Bureau of Supply, and Captain Styvyn Brahnahr had been named to head the Bureau of Navigation just last five-day.

There were those who found all the reorganization disturbing, and others who questioned the newfangled notions—*especially* the newfangled notion of a shore-based naval academy—and whether or not the middle of a desperate war was the best time to be mucking about with problematic innovations. Most, however, realized it was the energetic adoption of new ideas which had permitted the Royal Charisian Navy and, now, the Imperial Charisian Navy to sweep all opposition from the face of Safehold's seas, and it struck them as a very good idea to continue to innovate if they wanted to keep things that way. As for those who *didn't* feel that way, the vast majority of them were at least wise enough to keep their opinions to themselves rather than carelessly scattering them about where they might come to High Admiral Rock Point's ears.

"For the most part, Sir," Seamount said finally, looking up from his notes to meet Rock Point's eyes, "we're essentially where we expected to be as of our last conference. Ahldahs and I just returned from the artillery tests, and Fhranklyn's headed up to the Delthak Works to confer with Master Howsmyn. The recuperators worked *fairly* well, but not perfectly. There's still too much fluid leakage, and I'm not as comfortable in my own mind about how well they'll stand up to really heavy guns. So far, we haven't tried them with anything heavier than a thirty-pounder or a six-inch rifle."

Rock Point nodded gravely. The thirty-pounder and the six-inch rifle had approximately the same bore, but the ICN had found itself facing much the same problem which had been faced back on Old Earth during the transition from smoothbores to rifled artillery. Smoothbores fired round shot; rifled guns fired elongated, cylindrical shot, which were considerably heavier than the shot from a smoothbore of equal caliber. Given the differences in performance—and bore pressures—that caused, it was a non-trivial distinction. The increase in bore pressures to which rifled guns' heavier projectiles (and tighter windages) contributed had turned out to be even greater than Seamount and Urvyn Mahndrayn had predicted, yet the advantages would be well worth the headaches. They *were* going into service, probably sooner than even Merlin had anticipated, and that made figuring out what to call them a rather more pressing concern than some people might have anticipated.

Seamount had initially proposed designating rifled guns by the weight of their solid shot while changing the designations for smoothbores to the diameter of their bores, since it was primarily the increase in projectile weight which presented the technical challenges he had to solve. In the end, however, he'd decided it would cause too much confusion. Every officer of the Imperial Charisian Navy knew exactly what a "thirty-pounder" meant right now, so he'd chosen to label the new guns using the new nomenclature rather than confuse the issue by making everyone learn yet another new one. Besides, the guns were all going to be firing more than one weight of projectile in the very near future, anyway. The thirty-pounder's solid shot actually weighed almost thirty-two pounds, but its shell—with fifty-five cubic inches less iron and a roughly two-pound bursting charge—weighed less than eighteen. The six-inch *rifle's* solid shot, on the other hand, weighed over a hundred pounds, and the standard shell carried an eleven-pound bursting charge and weighed sixty-seven pounds. And at the moment, Merlin knew, Seamount and Rahzwail were working on heavy shells for attacking armor and masonry. The thicker walls of the new shell's central cavity would reduce the bursting charge to no more than three or four pounds but increase overall shell weight by thirty-five percent, which would give it much greater striking power and penetration.

It would also increase the bore pressures and recoil forces still further, of course. Still, the same basic design for a recuperator—effectively, a hydro-pneumatic recoil system—ought to work equally well for the thirty-pounder and the six-inch, although he understood Seamount's reservations about applying their current design to the much heavier eight- and ten-inch rifles Edwyrd Howsmyn was currently designing. It *ought* to work, but until they positively proved it *would*, they couldn't approve a final design for the new guns' mounts.

The original concept had been Mahndrayn's, although Rahzwail had taken the dead commander's original rough sketches and, along with Hainai, turned them into a practical proposition. Essentially, it was simply a pair of large, sealed cylinders, one filled with oil and the other with compressed air. The gun was rigidly attached to a piston inside the oil-filled cylinder; when it fired, recoil pulled the piston towards the rear, forcing the oil through a small opening into the second cylinder. The second cylinder's free-floating piston separated the oil from a confined volume of compressed air, and as the floating piston was pressed forward, it compressed the air even further. The result was to absorb the recoil progressively, braking it smoothly as the internal air pressure rose, and at the end of recoil, that increased air pressure generated a back pressure that returned the gun forward to its original position.

It was only one of several approaches from Mahndrayn's fertile imagination, including the pivoting slide carriage the navy had adopted while it waited for the hydro-pneumatic system to be worked out. The current carriage, just being introduced, would have been called a "Marsilly carriage" back on Old Earth, and it was a major improvement on even the "new model" carriages Merlin Athrawes had introduced only five years earlier. There had been some resistance to it, since it required iron or steel slides, but its advantages had quickly become evident. Pivoted at the front end of the carriage, it could be quickly moved to new angles of train. Two men with roller-ended handspikes could train it quite easily on its eccentric axles, and since it used the friction between the metal slide and the transom of the piece to damp recoil, its recoil path was much shorter, which meant it could be loaded and fired much more rapidly. It had already been tested satisfactorily with thirty-pounders, and it could be fitted with compressor screws to increase the friction for still heavier guns, if needed.

The Mahndrayn carriage was more practical than some of his other ideas, although his spring-driven recoil mechanism would probably work for lighter pieces. (Another design, for coastal artillery, using counterweights in a deep pit under the gun platform had proved practical even for the heaviest cannon, although the system would have been totally unworkable for a naval mounting.) As far as the recuperator was concerned, however, Rahzwail had profited in his development of Mahndrayn's original sketches by consulting with the Royal College. Doctor Mahklyn had been able to nudge him gently past a couple of obstacles, but the vast majority of the work was his and Hainai's original work, with substantial contributions from the College's Doctor Vyrnyr. Merlin had found himself tempted to step in and push the project more than once, but Rahzwail and Hainai were doing exactly what he needed Safeholdians to learn to do, and so he'd let them run with it.

Still, he thought now, *we do have a few advantages Ahlfryd and the others don't know about. For example, I feel strangely confident that Ehdwyrd's artificers will solve that leakage problem before too much longer. I believe "Doctor Owl" will have a little something to say about that!*

"If—or, rather, when—we get the leak problem licked, we'll have an effective recoil absorbing system," Seamount continued, "and if we can manage that, I feel confident we'll be able to produce the 'pedestal mounts' at least for lighter pieces." He glanced at Merlin with a half smile as he used the term Merlin had coined. "For the heavier pieces, we're still going to need something more massive, but I think the pivot mounts Fhranklyn and Master Howsmyn have been working on should prove practical. Frankly, one of the things that's bothered me the most has been the need to integrate some sort of capture mechanism to latch the gun in the fully recoiled position for loading. It works fine with Urvyn's counterweight system for the shore batteries, but I'm less comfortable with it for the recuperator. It's an added complication and another potential failure point in the entire system, not to mention significantly increasing strain—or, at least, the period of maximum stress—on the pneumatic cylinder. But we have to bring the muzzle back inboard and keep it there if we're going to reload it. Or"—he looked back up from his notes suddenly, his eyes sharp—"that's been our working assumption from the time Urvyn and I started on the project. Now, however, Ahldahs and Fhranklyn have come up with a completely new suggestion."

"New suggestion?" Rock Point cocked his head at Seamount and Rahzwail. "They do seem to come rather fast and furious around your lot, Ahlfryd. Is this another one I'd rather not get too close to on the proving ground?"

"It should work fine, Sir," Seamount said reassuringly. "In theory, at least."

"I could've gone all month without that little qualifier," Rock Point said dryly. "I seem to remember a few other qualifiers which led to loud, noisy explosions."

"But most of them've worked out in the end, Sir."

"Including that flamethrower notion of yours? Or the liquid incendiary shell fillings?" Rock Point inquired just a bit tartly.

"I did say *most*, not all, Sir."

Rock Point eyed him coldly for a moment, then snorted.

"Yes, you did. And, yes, most of them have worked out . . . so far. So what has Captain Rahzwail come up with this time?"

"Ahldahs?" Seamount looked across the table at his assistant, and Captain Rahzwail squared his shoulders.

"The idea actually came to me from another of Commander Mahndrayn's sketches, My Lord. When he was looking at ways to seal the breech of his rifle, he considered the possibility of using a threaded plug, one that would screw in and out and produce a tight seal that way. He adopted the solution he finally chose because it would take much longer to screw a breech plug all the way in and out, and also because he was concerned fouling would cement the plug in place. But the notion of a threaded breech plug or block stuck in my brain, and it occurred to me that the plug didn't have to be completely threaded."

"I beg your pardon?" Rock Point frowned, his expression intent.

"If we were to cut away a part of the threads, My Lord, so that the plug could slide all the way into position, then rotate through a half–turn or so and lock solidly into place, it would greatly reduce the time between shots."

"I can see where that would be true," Rock Point said slowly. "But with part of the threads cut away, it would be impossible to seal the breech, wouldn't it? Especially with the sort of pressures a large caliber piece generates."

"I agree entirely, My Lord, but the idea intrigued me, so I discussed it with Captain Saigyl and with Admiral Seamount. We were throwing the idea back and forth last month, when Captain Saigyl pointed out the way in which Commander Mahndrayn used the felt bases of his cartridges to seal the breech of his rifle. Obviously, the pressures are much lower in a rifle, but Captain Saigyl wondered what would happen if we substituted a ring—a washer, if you will—of something else."

Rahzwail looked expectantly at Rock Point, who nodded thoughtfully. Safeholdian plumbing had developed sealing washers and gaskets made out of several materials, including rubber, many of which were suitable for working with remarkably heavy pressures, so it was scarcely surprising that the concept should have suggested itself to Saigyl. Or scarcely surprising in *Charis*, at any rate.

"And just what sort of material did Captain Saigyl have in mind for his washer?" Rock Point asked after a moment.

"Stone wool, My Lord."

"I see."

Rock Point glanced down the length of the table to meet Merlin's eyes. Stone wool was the Safeholdian term for asbestos, whose insulating properties and resistance to heat had been known since the Creation. Its use had been ringed around with warnings in the *Book of Bédard* and the *Book of Pasquale*, but it hadn't been outright prohibited. Pasquale *had* declared an anathema against any form of asbestos other than chrysotile, hence the term "stone wool" from the whiteness of the material. Merlin wasn't certain why he hadn't banned it, as well. Admittedly, chrysotile was far less dangerous than the others, especially with the handling restrictions Pasquale had imposed, but long-term exposure to its fibers were scarcely beneficial to one's health. Probably, he'd decided, it was because the archangels had managed to convince themselves the Proscriptions of Jwo-jeng had permanently eliminated the possibility of industrialization on Safehold. The material was undeniably useful—it had been used for thousands of years, long before Old Earth's industrial revolution—and Langhorne and his followers had apparently consoled themselves with the thought that the quantities a *preindustrial* society would use would be relatively benign.

Unfortunately for what they might have thought eight or nine centuries ago, however, Safehold in general and Charis in particular had been using more and more of it over the past hundred years or so . . . and especially in the last decade. There simply was no choice. Industrial works like Ehdwyrd Howsmyn's *needed* a material with asbestos' properties and didn't have the capacity to produce any of the synthetics which had eventually replaced it on Old Earth. As a result, "stone wool" output was climbing by leaps and bounds, and despite all Howsmyn, the Crown, and the Church of Charis could do to enforce Pasquale's handling restrictions, exposure to it was climbing as well. It wasn't the only health hazard Charis' innovators had been forced to embrace—the mercury being used in percussion primers was a case in point, as were the shafting and exposed drive belts involved in applying water power directly to machinery—but somehow asbestos bothered Merlin more than many of the others.

Which didn't mean Rahzwail and Saigyl weren't on to something. After all, "stone wool" was exactly the same material Charles de Bange, the father of practical breech-loading artillery designs on Old Earth, had used in his "obturator pad."

"Have you conducted any actual trials yet, Captain?" Rock Point inquired.

"Only with a modified Mahndrayn rifle, My Lord. So far, it appears a greased stone wool washer or pad should do the job, assuming enough pressure on the screw threads. I've asked Doctor Mahklyn and Doctor Vyrnyr to help us determine a way to calculate how long a breech plug would be required and how much of the threads we could safely cut away. Doctor Mahklyn's of the opinion that he and Doctor Vyrnyr should be able to give us some rough working formulas within the next several five-days. In the meantime, Captain Saigyl's consulting with Master Howsmyn about the feasibility of fabricating breech blocks to the necessary tolerances. We won't know for certain whether or not it's practical even to consider the approach until he's had a chance to discuss it with Master Howsmyn's artificers."

Rock Point nodded again. High-pressure dynamics was an entirely new branch of study here on Safehold, but it was making considerable strides. Dahnel Vyrnyr at the Royal College had begun formulating the rules of pressure and gasses, but it was one of Ehdwyrd Howsmyn's artificers who'd really started the process of examining pressure levels in artillery a year and a half ago when he proposed what had been called a "crush gauge" back on Old Earth. Essentially, it was a hollow-based device, consisting of a tube which contained a small, very strong piston and an open frame which contained a small cylinder of pure copper. The bottom of the gauge was threaded, and a hole was bored through the wall of a gun tube and tapped with matching threads. The gauge was then screwed into the hole to form an airtight seal, and when the gun was fired, the pressure entering the gauge through a tiny port in its hollow stem drove the piston upward. A strong steel screw at the top of the gauge prevented the copper cylinder from moving, which caused the piston to deform—"crush"—the hapless cylinder. By removing the cylinder and measuring it very precisely, then comparing the measurements to those of similar cylinders which had been deformed by known pressures, the pressure inside the gun tube could be determined within very close tolerances.

No one outside the Charisian Empire had ever even heard of the technique, and Howsmyn had cheated slightly. The numbers from the cubes which had been crushed to establish the original base index were derived from cubes Owl had crushed under far more precise and uniform pressures than Howsmyn's own machinery was yet capable of producing. Not even his own artificers knew that, since Owl's remotes had sneaked in and replaced the ones *they'd* crushed when no one was looking.

And it had been Urvyn Mahndrayn who'd invented the ballistic pendulum, the high admiral reminded himself sadly, suppressing a fresh stab of grief. He'd sketched out the basic concept for it on the back of an envelope one afternoon while waiting for a meeting at the Royal College, and Mahklyn and the rest of the faculty had been working out the details—and the math—to make it work by the next morning. Between the crush gauge's ability to accurately measure bore pressures and the ballistic pendulum's ability to accurately and consistently measure projectile velocities, the science of ballistics was off to a rousing, brawling start, he told himself with a deep, warm sense of satisfaction, and he suspected Mahndrayn would have been just as fiercely pleased by the knowledge as he was.

"In the meantime, however," Seamount put in, "Ahldahs has come up with a fallback position in case it turns out Master Howsmyn *can't* promise us the necessary precision in manufacturing the screw blocks. It's not as satisfactory a breech closure in a lot of ways, but it should work. Essentially, it's a completely separate breech plug fitted with a copper washer lapped over a compressible layer of stone wool. An external screw clamps it in place with enough force to give a seal which has proven gas-tight in all of our small-arms tests. I don't like it as much as I do this 'interrupted screw' approach, mostly because it will impose a much slower rate of fire, but also because I suspect it would be more fragile, more subject to external damage and breakage. Between the two, however, I think I can feel confident in proposing the adoption of breech-loading for our new generation of rifled artillery."

"I see," Rock Point repeated, and glanced at Merlin again. The *seijin* looked back steadily, then nodded ever so imperceptibly. "All right, Ahl-fryd," the high admiral said then. "It sounds to me like you and your pet geniuses are onto something yet again. And I'm sure that between you and Master Howsmyn, you will be able to make it work."

Merlin's expression was admirably grave. He, too, was sure they'd be able to make it work, especially since Howsmyn had access to detailed plans of de Bange's original design, including the "mushroom," the rounded "nose cone" at the head of the breech block. It was actually the most ingenious part of the entire concept in many ways, because when the gun fired, the mushroom was driven to the rear, compressing the asbestos "washer," squeezing it so that it expanded outward to seal the breech completely. And because the mushroom was driven by the firing chamber pressure, the tightness of the seal automatically adjusted to different weights of charge. Merlin had no doubt that when Howsmyn sat down with Saigyl to look at his drawings, the industrialist would experience another of those intuitive inspirations for which he had become known and start enthusiastically sketching in ideas of his own.

"All right, now that that's out of the way, what about this other problem you wanted to discuss?" the high admiral continued. "Something about bore pressures and combustion rates?"

"Yes, Sir," Seamount replied in a distinctly less cheerful tone. "I'm afraid we won't be able to get as much benefit out of some of the new advances as I'd hoped."

"Why not?"

"Well, Ahldahs and Commander Malkaihy and I have been going back over the results of Urvyn's artillery tests. We've repeated several of his firings using the new crush gauges to measure bore pressures and the pendulum to measure velocities, and they've confirmed something we already suspected. We'd hoped we could increase shot velocities by increasing barrel length, but it turns out we can't."

"Why not?" Rock Point repeated.

"Essentially, My Lord, the powder burns too quickly," Rahzwail said. "It gives all its propulsive power in a single, sharp kick the instant that the charge fires; with a longer barrel, we actually start losing some of that initial velocity due to friction between the projectile and the inside of the gun tube. Looking at the pressure gauges, we've concluded that a great deal of the powder is transformed into smoke—solid particles and soot—rather than the combustion gases that actually drive the projectile. Corning the powder clearly helps in that regard, given how the particulate mass is reduced and how much more of the powder is actually burned before it's ejected from the muzzle, but there are still limits, and we seem to've reached them . . . for the moment, at least.

"Of course, that's only part of the problem. The rifled pieces' shells are much tighter fitting, which means they rub against the walls of the bore more than round shot do. That increases friction still further, which costs us even more velocity, and the rifling studs only make it worse. Frankly, I suspect the new 'driving bands' Master Howsmyn's experimenting with will be even worse than the studded shells in that respect. I still think the advantages outweigh the problems, mind you, but there's no denying there'll be more than enough problems to keep us busy."

"And that's not the only difficulty we're experiencing," Seamount put in. "Among other things, Master Howsmyn's new steels, especially now that he's tried adding nickel to them, are even tougher and stronger than we expected. That's wonderful news in most ways, but, unfortunately, it also means we can't produce satisfactory armor- and stone-piercing shells out of them, after all. The shell walls will be too strong for gunpowder bursting charges to shatter properly if we make them out his new steels. At the moment, it looks like it'll be wiser to restrict ourselves to cast-iron shells for the smoothbores and the wrought-iron shells he's already developed for the rifled pieces."

"They seem to've worked quite well in the Gulf of Tarot and at Iythria," Rock Point said dryly.

"That they did, Sir. And they should still be quite effective against wooden ships and light shore structures. But it's only going to be a matter of time—and probably not a lot of it—before people begin designing shell-proof magazines for their fortresses, for example. Ten or twelve feet of earth, reinforced by a few feet of solid masonry, would most probably stop any of our present shells from penetrating, even from the angle-guns, and overhead protection for the batteries is also going to be high on fortress designers' list of priorities once they begin to recognize the threat's parameters. That's why we've been concentrating on producing shells heavy enough to do what the bombardment ships did at Iythria to the *next* generation of forts. Or even, eventually, to penetrate someone else's ironclad. Wrought iron isn't going to be as effective for those uses, and it's more likely to break up or shatter on impact than Master Howsmyn's steel, especially with the quenching processes he's been developing to harden the new shells' noses. But if we can't find some way to improve our gunpowder, there won't be any point putting a bursting charge inside those shells. Basically, we'd be restricted to essentially the same solid shot we've always used—heavier, with better penetration qualities, but still a solid projectile rather than an exploding shell."

"And have you and Captain Rahzwail had any thoughts about how that might be accomplished?" Rock Point asked.

"At the moment, all we've really come up with is the idea that we should find a way to increase the uniformity of the powder grains, My

Lord," Rahzwail replied. "It seems to me that if we could . . . compress the powder, make the individual grains denser, and possibly produce it in shapes that would increase the surface area, we ought to be able to retard the burning rate at least somewhat. That would mean combustion would take longer, and the projectile would be *accelerated* for a longer period, rather than beginning to lose velocity from friction. For that matter, if the grains were all a uniform size, we ought to get a more uniform *burn* rate from powder lot to powder lot, which would make for much more consistent ranges and trajectories for a given charge of powder. I suspect that pelletizing the powder we're using in the new Mahndrayns would improve their muzzle velocity measurably, as well. And Commander Malkaihy's also suggested we might find some ingredient or adulterant that could slow the combustion rate for artillery propellants still further. Since it's the charcoal in the gunpowder that provides the actual fuel, we're considering alternative types of charcoal that would burn more slowly, but we haven't found one that would do the job yet."

Merlin managed to keep his expression blank, but it was harder than usual. Admittedly, Rahzwail had certain advantages, given the significant boost one Merlin Athrawes and his friend Owl had provided to the Safeholdian science of pyrotechnics. And the resources of the archangels' allowable technology gave Safeholdians a much broader base of capabilities to build upon than their pre-Merlin artillery and explosives might have led most people to expect. Still, the captain's summary had been almost breathtaking, carrying him—conceptually, at least—all the way from the corned powder of the seventeenth century through Thomas Rodman's prismatic powder in mid-nineteenth century to the German "cocoa powder" of the 1890s in no more than a handful of sentences.

And he doesn't even know about Sahndrah's little discovery yet! Dear Lord, what are these people going to come up with next?

He didn't have a clue, but as he sat at that conference table, looking back and forth between Sir Ahlfryd Hyndryk and Ahldahs Rahzwail, he suddenly felt far less concerned about how they were going to react when he had to get around to telling them about the information the traitor in Hairatha had sent to Zhaspahr Clyntahn.

The bastard can steal whatever "secrets" he wants, and he's still going to fall further and further behind, Merlin thought with grim, harsh satisfaction. *He can't begin to match what our people can come up with, even without me standing in the corner handing out ideas. And that's why the son-of-a-bitch is going to lose. I don't care how many men he can put into the field, our people— my people—are going to kick their sorry arses all the way back to the Temple, and then that bastard is going to pay the price for Gwylym Manthyr and everybody else his sick, sadistic butchers have tortured and killed.*

"That sounds like a very interesting idea, Captain," he said out loud, his voice calm, his expression intent. "Have you given any thought to how you might do that? It occurs to me, that if you were to manufacture a form—a nozzle, perhaps—of the right shape, then force a gunpowder paste through it under heavy pressure using one of Master Howsmyn's hydraulic presses, what you'd get would be—"

.IX.
Archbishop's Palace,
City of Tellesberg,
Kingdom of Old Charis,
Empire of Charis

It was strange how alike and yet unalike Manchyr and the city of Tellesberg were, she thought, standing on the balcony and looking out across the Charisian capital. Tellesberg was cooler, without the fiercer heat of the city of her birth, but it was also twice as far from the equator. The flowers and trees were very different here, as well, yet equally bright, and Lady Hanth was a botanist. She'd spent much of her time here, especially since her marriage, cataloging the countless differences between Chisholm's northern plant life and her new home's. She'd been making that knowledge available to Irys and enthusiastically expanding her own store of knowledge by adding everything Irys could tell her about Corisandian botany to it. And the two of them had made several visits to Emperor Cayleb's Royal College, to discuss the subject with Doctor Fyl Brahnsyn, the College's senior botanist.

Irys' hands tightened on the balcony railing as she thought about those visits. She remembered her father's comments on the College, the way he'd recognized—and envied—the advantages it bestowed upon King Haarahld and yet simultaneously seen it as one of Haarahld's great vulnerabilities. He'd been right about both those points, she thought now. He usually had been right about things like that, and she knew he'd been tempted to emulate the Charisian king. But in the end, he'd decided the advantages the College had given to Charis had been outweighed by the vulnerability it created. Instead of copying Haarahld, he'd been careful to avoid any policies which might have suggested to Mother Church that he was tempted to follow in Charisian footsteps where questionable knowledge was concerned. And he'd been equally careful—and invested enormous bribes—when it came to pointing out to the Inquisition just how "questionable" the Royal College of Charis' knowledge truly was. In fact, she admitted, he and Phylyp Ahzgood had been quite . . . creative when it came to carefully crafted rumors about the way in which the College was secretly transgressing against the Proscriptions, despite all its public professions to the contrary.

Actually, she thought, they hadn't been so much creative as *inventive*. She rolled the word over her mental tongue, tasting its implications, for it represented the biggest single difference between Manchyr and Tellesberg. In Corisande, "inventive" remained the pejorative it had always been under Mother Church; in Charis, the same word had become a proudly worn badge of men—and women—who deliberately and aggressively probed the limits of what man might and might not properly know.

It made her skin crawl, sometimes, to realize how hard and how far people like Rahzhyr Mahklyn and his colleagues were pushing those limits. The proof of her father's appreciation of the College's value to the House of Ahrmahk was all around her, in the forest of sails and rigging she saw in the harbor, the huge, sleek, low-slung warships lying to anchor or heading out into Howell Bay, the enormous stacks of crates, boxes, and barrels waiting to be swayed aboard merchant ships and ferried off to every corner of Safehold. It was that same "inventiveness" which had allowed those warships to defeat every foe who'd sailed against Charis, and in many ways, it was also that inventiveness which was allowing Safehold's newest empire to blunt the starvation the Sword of Schueler's fanatics had wreaked upon the Republic of Siddarmark. Yet, what if that butcher Clyntahn was right? Not about his bloody persecutions, or his amoral policies of assassination and terror, or his gluttonous, sensual lifestyle, but about the taint which clung to all this Charisian innovation? What if the Royal College of Charis truly *was* Shan-wei's foothold in the world God and the archangels had made?

And why did the possibility he was right *bother* her so much? Fill her with such a confusing mix of trepidation, apprehension, foreboding, and . . . regret.

Because you *want it, too*, she told herself now, finally admitting the point, remembering the hours she'd spent talking to Brahnsyn, the gleam of delight in his eyes as he'd jotted down note after note from her recollection of Corisande's botany. The questions he'd asked had elicited more details than she would have dreamed she could have provided, too. He'd known exactly which to ask, actually assembled the information he'd already gotten from her in ways that let him shape and focus his follow-on questions almost as if he'd physically examined the plants she could describe to him only in frustratingly incomplete ways. The sheer depth of his knowledge had been astonishing, yet he'd been only one of the scholars she'd spoken with, all of whom had willingly taken time from their own studies to answer her questions and ask questions of their own.

She hadn't understood a great deal of what Doctor Mahklyn had had to say about the new mathematics. She'd been forced to acknowledge that after the first five minutes—or, perhaps she'd actually managed to stay in shouting distance for the first *nine* minutes, although she was certain she'd been completely lost by the time he got to ten. But even the limited amount she'd been able to follow had filled her with wonder and a sense of half-terrified delight. There'd been nothing in what he'd said that actually violated any aspect of the Proscriptions, so far as she could tell, yet the *implications* of his new "calculus" and the other, frankly brilliant, mathematical operations and theories he'd proclaimed, would affect *everything*. She knew very little about scholarship in general, compared to the minds assembled in the College, but she knew enough to recognize the way in which Mahklyn's new math must provide those minds with new, immensely potent tools. She'd seen proof of that already in the pages of diagrams Doctor Dahnel Vyrnyr, another of those scholars had enthusiastically displayed to her.

Vyrnyr was the College's leading expert in the field of pressures, which wasn't something Irys would have thought of as a field of study in its own right. The *Writ* explained why the Archangel Truscott had arranged for the boiling point of water to increase in a tightly sealed vessel, after all, and taught mankind how to construct pressure cookers to take advantage of his foresight in seeing to it that it was so. The benefits for food preparation and preservation were well known to anyone who'd read the *Book of Truscott* and the *Book of Pasquale*, yet Vyrnyr wanted to understand *how* the Holy Truscott had arranged for it to work, and she'd been using her own observations and Mahklyn's new mathematical tools to pursue that understanding. She'd shared some of what she'd discovered with Irys on one of the princess' visits to the College with Lady Hanth, and the scholar's eyes had glowed with pleasure as she displayed the elegant rules and processes Truscott had imposed on the seemingly simple act of lighting a fire under a sealed pressure cooker.

There was a beauty to those rules, those processes, Irys thought now, leaning on the balcony rail, gazing out over the sun-soaked roofs of Tellesberg, listening to the voice of the city that never slept, seeing the new construction sweeping up over the hills around the city as the Charisian Empire's southern capital grew yet larger and watching gulls and sea wyverns of every description and hue swirl in raucous crowds above the flotsam-rich harbor. The meticulous way in which the archangels had fitted the universe together had never been more obvious than when Doctor Vyrnyr explained about pressures, or Doctor Mahklyn attempted to explain the magnificent inevitability of mathematics, or Doctor Lywys demonstrated the ways in which separate, dissimilar materials combined into new and unique compounds, or Doctor Hahlcahm talked about his efforts in conjunction with Doctor Vyrnyr's studies of heat and pressure to determine how Pasqualization purified milk and food. *Surely* God couldn't object to His children trying to understand and appreciate the majestic beauty and intricate detail with which His and His archangels' gifts had imbued His universe?

Yet there'd been another side to Doctor Vyrnyr's studies and revelations, for it was obvious they provided a basis for the systematic expansion and improvement of processes which already pressed far too closely for the Inquisition's taste on the bounds of the Proscriptions. The College had even proposed new names for the practical applications of Vyrnyr's studies. "Hydraulic" and "pneumatic" fell strangely on Irys' ear, and the fact that the College had seen a need to coin those words—indeed, had set up a committee chaired by Doctor Mahklyn himself, for the express purpose of naming new fields of study—was a chilling reflection on how its faculty's determination to expand and quantify human knowledge drove them inevitably towards the Proscriptions' limits.

And you want to join that quest, don't you? she asked herself, hazel eyes dark as Tellesberg's morning breeze teased tendrils of silk loose from her braided hair. *That's what truly frightens you, isn't it? You see that beauty, want to understand that intricacy, and you're afraid the Inquisition is right after all, that it truly is exactly the same lure Shan-wei and Proctor used to seduce men into damnation when they first rebelled. That's what Clyntahn's saying, after all, and he's not the only one. You want the people who say that to be wrong, but inside you're afraid they aren't. That Shan-wei and Proctor are still using that temptation, that hunger to get just a glimpse of the mind of God, to entice men away from the God they think their quest honors.*

"Good morning, Your Highness," a voice said behind her. "May I join you?"

"Of course you may, Your Eminence." A smile replaced her brooding frown, and she turned from the railing to greet the speaker. "It's your balcony, after all."

"True, in a manner of speaking," Maikel Staynair replied with an answering, gentle smile. "For the moment, anyway. Personally, I prefer to think I'm simply holding it in trust for my eventual successor. Although, actually, you know, I really miss my rather more spartan little palace over there." The ruby ring on his hand glittered in the sunlight as he indicated the building on the far side of Tellesberg Cathedral which was home to the Bishop of Tellesberg. It was, indeed, smaller than Archbishop's Palace . . . and still bigger than any other structure in sight. "A humble little hovel, I know, but the truth is that I really don't need the extra seventeen bedchambers, the second ballroom, or the state dining room," the Archbishop of Charis continued, his smile turning almost impish. "Fourteen bedrooms and a single dining room—on the large size, admittedly, but only one—were quite sufficient for my needs when I was a simple bishop, and I'm sure I could get along under such straitened conditions even now if I truly had to."

Irys' lips quivered at Staynair's tone, and that, too, was something she wouldn't have believed was possible as little as two months ago. The archbishop was the very heart of heresy and voice of apostasy, after all. That was what the Inquisition taught, and Staynair's ability to seduce the faithful away from Mother Church, even from among her own priesthood, was legendary. She'd read Earl Coris' reports about Staynair's visit to Corisande, about the way he'd drawn her father's subjects towards him, and she hadn't understood how it could have happened. What sinister gift had Shan-wei bestowed upon him to allow him to so easily beguile the faithful into accepting his words? To bewitch Mother Church's own bishops and priests into accepting *his* authority over that of the Grand Vicar himself? Whatever might have been true about Cayleb Ahrmahk's reaction to the assault upon his kingdom, his father's death in battle, Maikel Staynair, the fallen bishop and betrayer of Mother Church, bore the true guilt for the schism, for it was he who had led the revolt against the Temple and the Vicarate from *inside* Mother Church, splitting all the world into warring camps for the first time since Shan-wei's Rebellion.

Yet she'd discovered it was impossible to see that monster in the heretical archbishop's gentle, compassionate eyes . . . or to spend ten minutes in his presence without feeling the way he reached out almost unconsciously to those about him.

Cayleb and Sharleyan had been meticulous about not requiring Daivyn and her to attend mass in Tellesberg Cathedral. They'd even guaranteed them regular access to Father Davys Tyrnyr, an upper-priest who'd fearlessly maintained his loyalty to the Temple and the Grand Vicar. They'd allowed him to celebrate mass privately for them in one of Archbishop Palace's numerous small chapels, and the sanctity of the confessional had been rigorously observed. It was amazing enough, and totally contrary to the Grand Inquisitor's version of events in Charis, that Temple Loyalists were actually allowed to practice their faith—their adherence to the Grand Vicar and the Group of Four—openly in the very heart of Tellesberg, without fear of suppression from Crown or Church. She knew only too well what had happened to anyone who openly professed Reformism—far less any suggestion of support for the Church of Charis!—in Delferahk or any other mainland realm. How could it possibly be that here, in the very capital of an empire which had no hope of victory, or even survival, without Mother Church's defeat, those who remained loyal to her were *protected* by the Crown even while Reformists were savagely persecuted in other lands? It made no sense—none at all—yet the evidence of her own eyes and ears had forced her to recognize that it was true, and Father Davys himself had acknowledged as much.

Yet it had taken Irys over three five-days to discover that the person who'd actually made certain she and Daivyn had access to Father Davys had been Maikel Staynair himself. She had no doubt—now—that Cayleb and Sharleyan would have granted that access anyway, but it was Staynair who'd made it explicit, ordered his personal Guardsmen to admit a known Temple Loyalist and his acolytes to Archbishop's Palace without even having them searched for weapons, despite at least two Temple Loyalist attempts, one on the floor of his own cathedral, to assassinate him. And he'd insisted upon that because he truly did believe human beings had both the right and the responsibility to decide for themselves where their spiritual loyalties lay. That the human soul was too precious for anyone but its owner to endanger or constrain it, and that no political purpose, however vital, could be allowed to trump that fundamental, essential article of faith.

She'd been stunned by that discovery. She'd grown up a princess. She *knew* how political reality sometimes had no choice but to transgress even against the letter of the *Writ*. Mother Church herself acknowledged that, made provision for rulers to confess their transgressions, do penance for the times they'd been forced by necessity to compromise the *Writ*'s full rigor. Her own father had paid thousands of marks to Mother Church and the Office of Inquisition for dispensations and absolution under exactly those provisions, and Irys Daykyn knew every other ruler, upon occasion, had found himself or herself forced to do the same.

Yet where personal faith and obedience to God were concerned, Maikel Staynair flatly rejected that concept. He would not compromise his own faith, and he refused to force anyone else to compromise his, and *that,* Irys had realized, almost against her will, was the true secret of his ability to "seduce" the faithful. The reason even many of the Temple Loyalists here in Old Charis respected him as a true son of God, however mistaken he might be in what he believed God and his own faith required of him.

She'd attended mass in the cathedral three times now, although she'd insisted Daivyn not do so, and she'd heard Staynair preach. And as she'd listened to him speaking from the pulpit, seen the joy bright in his eyes, heard it in his voice, she'd recognized the proof of what she'd already come to suspect. He was, quite simply, the gentlest, most devout, most compassionate and loving man she'd ever met. It might be true, as the Temple Loyalists insisted, that he was doing Shan-wei's work in the world, but if he was, it was never because he'd knowingly given his allegiance to the Dark.

"I'm sure you could survive even under such atrocious conditions, Your Eminence," she said now. "Personally, however, I'm much more comfortable here in the ostentatious luxury of your current domicile. I suspect the same is true of Daivyn, as well, although it's hard to be certain what he thinks when I so seldom have a chance to speak to him. I'm afraid he spends too much time playing basketball on your private court with Haarahld Breygart and Prince Zhan for any long and meaningful conversations with a mere sister. When he's not swimming with them in the Royal Palace's pool, that is. Or running madly about the baseball diamond in Queen Mairah's Court with them, for that matter."

"It does the boy—I mean, His Highness—good, Your Highness." Staynair's smile broadened, then softened. "Forgive me, but it seems to me your brother's had very little opportunity to simply *be* a boy since your exile from Corisande. I think it's important we give some of that boyhood back to him, don't you?"

"Yes," Irys replied softly. But then she gave herself a mental shake and tilted her head, hazel eyes taking on an edge of challenge. "Yes," she repeated, "and it doesn't hurt Charis' position with him one bit for him to play baseball and basketball with the boy who's still second in line to the Charisian Crown, does it, Your Eminence?"

"Of course it doesn't. And I won't pretend that consideration isn't a part of Their Majesties'. . . calculations where you and your brother are concerned. But do you truly believe they wouldn't have done the same thing anyway?"

Irys locked gazes with him for a moment. Then she shook her head.

"No," she admitted. "I think they would've done *exactly* the same thing. And"— she confessed—"they've given him a degree of freedom here in Tellesberg he never would've had in Manchyr."

"But not without seeing to his security very carefully, Your Highness."

"No, not without that," she agreed, and her lips quirked almost against her will. "Seeing three boys, the oldest barely fourteen, playing baseball with two complete teams of Marines and Imperial Guardsmen in full uniform— including the Guardsmen's *armor*—is . . . not something I would've seen back in Manchyr. And it's amazing how good Colonel Falkhan is at losing after absolutely playing as hard as he possibly could."

"Ah, well, Your Highness, he *was* Emperor Cayleb's chief bodyguard when Cayleb was crown prince himself, you know. And the truth is that I suspect Zhan would be having rather a harder time of it if it weren't for the younger boys. Colonel Falkhan had quite a lot of practice doing the same thing with Cayleb, but it began to change somehow when Cayleb turned fourteen or fifteen." The archbishop smiled in memory. "At that point, Cayleb suddenly discovered it was far more difficult to beat his armsmen than it used to be. He's one of the brighter fellows I know, and it didn't take him long to realize they'd been—I believe the term is 'throwing'—the games when he'd been younger. Which only made him even more determined to beat them fairly now that he was older. Not a bad lesson for a future monarch to learn early, I think."

"Probably not," Irys said thoughtfully. "Especially the bit about people letting him win because he was a prince. People get—or *some* of them get, at any rate—more subtle about it as they get older, but there are always plenty of flatterers and toadies around. Learning to watch for that sort of thing would be a useful lesson for any ruler."

"Actually, Your Highness, you're missing the point," Staynair corrected gently. She looked a question at him, and the archbishop shrugged. "*Every* child is allowed to win, at least sometimes, by adults who truly love him. It gives him the confidence to try again, to become steadily better, to master challenges. It's important that he not realize the adults in his life are deliberately losing to him, because he needs that sense of accomplishment. And it's important for them to challenge him even when they let him win, so that he truly does gain in proficiency and capability. But for someone destined to wear a crown, it's even more important for him to realize those who truly care for him are willing to *beat* him, to *force* him to stretch to the very limit of his capabilities, and to show him the difference between glib-tongued sycophants and those he can trust to be honest with him. That's a valuable lesson for anyone, Your Highness, but especially for someone destined to rule. And one reason it's especially valuable for a ruler is because it also teaches him to cherish those who are honest with him, to *encourage* them to tell him when they disagree with him or when he's making a mistake. And to listen to them when they tell him that." He shook his head. "That's the lesson young Crown Prince Cayleb learned from Lieutenant Falkhan all those years ago, and it's stood him—and the Kingdom and Empire of Charis—in very good stead since King Haarahld's death."

Irys' eyes had narrowed while the archbishop was speaking. When he finished, she stood for a moment, still gazing up at him, and then, slowly, she nodded.

"I hadn't thought of it exactly that way, Your Eminence," she confessed, and a shadow touched her expressive eyes. "And I wish my father had had the opportunity to have this conversation with you years ago," she went on very softly. "I think . . . I think it might have served *him* in good stead where my brother Hektor was concerned."

"Perhaps."

Staynair captured her right hand in his, tucking it into the bend of his left elbow as he stood beside her and they both turned to look out over the city once more.

"Perhaps," he repeated. "But perhaps not, too."

He turned his head, gazing at her profile as the breeze cracked the banners flying from the cathedral's façade like whips.

"I can't speak to your father's relationship with your brother, of course," he continued. "But I can say that looking at you and Daivyn, who you are and who you've become despite everything that's happened, gives me a far better opinion of Prince Hektor than I ever had before." She twitched in surprise at the admission, and he smiled. "I still have . . . significant reservations about him as a ruler, you understand, Your Highness. But he—or he and your mother, perhaps—obviously did something right as parents where you and your *younger* brother are concerned."

"Flattery won't win you anything with me, you know, Your Eminence," she said lightly, trying to mask how deeply his last sentence had touched her. "Father may not've allowed my armsmen to beat me at baseball, but he did make sure I understood how dangerous honeyed words can be!"

"I'm sure he did, and if he hadn't, Earl Coris would've repaired the deficiency long since," the archbishop said, so dryly she chuckled. Then he turned to face her more fully, and his expression turned more serious.

"I must confess, Your Highness, that I didn't follow you out onto the balcony this morning simply to enjoy the sunlight and the breeze with you. I've just received word from the Palace, and it concerns you and Daivyn."

"It does?" Irys felt a quick stab of anxiety, but it didn't touch her tone, and her eyes were level as she gazed up at him.

"It does," he replied. "I'm sure you're aware that the marriage treaty between Cayleb and Sharleyan not only established a joint Imperial Parliament but requires that the government spend half of each year, minus travel time, in Tellesberg and the other half in Chisholm?"

He crooked an eyebrow, and she nodded.

"Well, I'm afraid they're off schedule." He grimaced. "What with that affair in the Gulf of Tarot, and the need to get you and Daivyn—and Earl Coris, of course—safely out of Delferahk, and now this business in Siddarmark, Cayleb's been here in Tellesberg for almost an entire year, and Sharleyan's been here for the better part of eight months. They should've departed for Chisholm four months ago, and even though everyone in Cherayth understands why they haven't, they really can't justify putting it off any longer. Or, rather, Sharleyan can't. She's going to be returning to Chisholm in the next few five-days, whereas Cayleb is going to be sailing for . . . well, to coordinate with Duke Eastshare and, possibly, for a personal meeting with Lord Protector Greyghor. In any case, neither of them is going to be here in Tellesberg very much longer, and you and young Daivyn will be accompanying Empress Sharleyan when she leaves."

Irys' eyes widened.

"But—forgive me, Your Eminence, but I thought Daivyn and I had been placed in *your* custody."

"As you have been." He patted the hand tucked into his elbow. "I'll also be accompanying the Empress. One of the ways in which the Church of Charis differs from the Group of Four's Church is that the archbishop travels to the constituent states of the Empire rather than reigning imperially here in Tellesberg and requiring all those other prelates to come pay homage to him. We haven't yet established a firm schedule for my pastoral visits, however, and I'm rather behind. So I'm taking this opportunity to sail with you and Daivyn at least as far as Cherayth. From there, I'll continue to Zebediah and Corisande, before I return home, possibly by way of Tarot. I imagine I'll be gone for the better part of a year myself, but you and your brother will still be under my protection."

Irys' heart leapt when he mentioned Corisande, but she tried—almost successfully—to keep that response from showing in her expression or her eyes. Was it possible she and Daivyn would be permitted—

Don't be silly, she told herself. *Yes, the Archbishop—and Cayleb and Sharleyan—have treated both of you far more gently than you expected. But they aren't going to let you return home without first making* damned *sure you won't do anything to . . . destabilize their control. Archbishop Maikel may travel to Manchyr, but* you *won't.*

She knew it was true, and she knew the logic which made it so was irrefutable. That she would have made exactly the same decision, no matter how kind she might have wanted to be. She even knew Daivyn would be far happier to be allowed to remain a boy a few months longer, rather than be trapped in the role of a child monarch in the hands of a Regency Council over which he had no control. But it still hurt.

Maybe it does, but at least you'll still be together, you'll both still be alive, and Chisholm's much closer to home. Maybe it won't feel quite as lonely there as it did in Delferahk.

"Thank you for telling me, Your Eminence," she said finally. "I appreciate the warning. Can you tell me when we'll be departing?"

"Not for certain, Your Highness. There are several details that still need arranging. Lady Hanth's travel plans, for example."

"Lady Hanth's? Lady Mairah is coming with us?" Irys heard the happiness and relief in her own voice, and Staynair smiled.

"Yes, or that's the plan right now, at any rate. Emperor Cayleb's recalled Earl Hanth to active duty—you knew he was a Marine before he became Earl, I believe?" He paused until she nodded, then shrugged. "Well, it seems Their Majesties have decided his services could be very useful in Siddarmark, and to be brutally honest, the Empire's going to need every experienced Marine it can lay hands on for the summer campaign. So, since he's going to be out of the Old Kingdom anyway, Lady Hanth is taking her stepsons to meet her parents and her cousin, Baron Green Mountain." His expression saddened. "She may not have another opportunity for them to meet the Baron, I'm afraid."

Irys nodded in understanding. Mahrak Sahndyrs, Empress Sharleyan's first councilor in Chisholm, had been savagely wounded in one of the terrorist attacks which had swept through the Empire. He'd been too badly injured to continue as first councilor, and he'd been replaced by Braisyn Byrns, the Earl of White Crag, who'd been Sharleyan's Lord Justice. White Crag had been replaced in turn as Lord Justice by Sylvyst Mhardyr, the Baron of Stoneheart, and although she and Phylyp Ahzgood had enjoyed a quiet chuckle over a kingdom's chief magistrate being known as "Lord Justice Stoneheart," he was actually an excellent choice, an intelligent and humane man with a strong legal background and over twenty years' experience on the Queen's Bench.

"I didn't realize Baron Green Mountain had been injured quite that severely," she said now.

"Well, reports at this distance tend to get garbled or exaggerated. It's quite possible we're being overly pessimistic. But I won't deny that the Baron's health is one reason the Empress is determined to set out for Chisholm as soon as possible." Staynair smiled again, with a sort of wry sadness. "I doubt she'd be leaving, despite that, if Cayleb weren't going to be called away from Tellesberg, as well. The amount of time they have to spend apart from one another to make the Empire work is hard—very hard—on both of them. It's not often a marriage of state turns into the kind of love match that litters so many children's tales, but in this case, it truly has."

Irys nodded again. She'd seen enough of the emperor and empress to know what Staynair had just said was no more than the simple truth. And everyone in Charis seemed to know it as well as the archbishop did. In fact, Irys had come to the conclusion that the deep and obvious love between them—and the fact that they were so willing to let that love show—was a huge part of the magic which bound their subjects to them like iron. And the fact that Sharleyan had willingly come from distant Chisholm to stand beside their youthful king in the teeth of the Inquisition and hell itself had forged a fierce, fiery devotion to her in the hearts of Old Charisians of every kind, clergy, commoners, and peers alike.

They really are the kind of characters you only meet in legend, aren't they? Larger than life, beautiful, fearless, determined, beloved by their subjects . . . no wonder so many of their people are ready to walk straight into the fire at their heels, face even the Inquisition and the Punishment of Schueler at their side! Father's subjects loved him, too, but not the same way. They respected him, they trusted him—in Corisande itself, at least—but they didn't love him the way Charisians love Cayleb and Sharleyan. And whatever the Inquisition says, it's not sorcery, it's not some malign influence from Shan-wei or any of the other Fallen. It's just who they are— what they are. And I wish . . . I wish some of that same magic would touch me.

Her eyes widened as she realized what she'd just thought, yet it was true. She envied them—envied them their love and their obvious courage, the depth of their faith and the strength of their combined will. The love of their subjects, the loyalty of their followers . . . and the certainty of their purpose. Their steadfast, unflinching commitment to all they believed and held dear. They might yet prove wrong, might yet discover that whatever they thought, they truly had served Shan-wei and not Langhorne. But mistaken or not, they served their beliefs with a bright, ardent intensity Irys Daykyn could only envy in a world in which so much certainty had disappeared into confusion and hatred and bloodshed.

No wonder she wanted some of that magic, that flame of reflected legend and bright honor, to touch her. It was, she realized wonderingly, what bound *all* their followers to them—that aspiration to be worthy of them as they had proven *they* were worthy of their crowns. The intensity of that awareness shook her to the bone, like some silent whirlwind, and in that moment, she recognized its seduction. To seize upon something, *anything*, that gave purpose and certainty and honor to a life in the midst of all the bewilderment and doubt—who could not crave that? How could anyone not long to say as Cayleb Ahrmahk had said into the teeth of the Grand Inquisitor himself, with scorching, fearless honesty "Here I stand; I can do no other"?

Back away, Irys, she told herself. Back away. Yes, you want it, but you need to think about why. You need to understand what's driving that hunger. It's too seductive, too strong. Father Davys would tell you you're succumbing to all the undeniable goodness within Cayleb and Sharleyan, just as they themselves have been seduced into Shan-wei's service through their very love of their people. It isn't through the darkness in our hearts that Shan-wei takes us; it's the light within us that she twists and perverts and uses against us.

"I hope the reports about Baron Green Mountain are wrong, Your Eminence," she heard herself saying out loud. "Father had very few good words to say about him, I'm afraid, but even he admitted there'd never been a more capable or loyal first councilor in the entire world."

"No, there hasn't. And it's particularly sad that Cayleb and Sharleyan have both lost the services of first councilors of whom that could've been said. But it's even worse in her case, I think. She hasn't completely lost him yet, of course, but he was effectively her second father after her own father's death."

"I can see that," Irys said, her heart twisting as she thought of Phylyp Ahzgood and all he'd come to mean to her, and touched the archbishop's forearm again, impulsively. "I can see that. And would you tell Her Majesty for me, please, that I'll be remembering the Baron in my prayers?"

"I'm sure she'll be grateful to hear that, Your Highness." Staynair patted her hand briefly, then looked back across the crowded harbor.

"There are several other questions which need to be considered, of course," he said. "For example, Father Davys has many commitments among the Loyalist congregations here in Tellesberg. I think it would be difficult for him to leave the Old Kingdom, that he'd feel he was abandoning those who depend upon him. Neither Their Majesties nor I wish to deprive you of clergy of your choice, however. Would you wish for me to ask Father Davys to nominate a Loyalist chaplain to accompany you on the voyage? I'm sure he'd be able to come up with several possibilities."

"That . . . would probably be a good idea, Your Eminence," Irys replied slowly, her eyes hooded. "I think, if you'll forgive me for saying it, that it's important Daivyn not be faced with . . . competing orthodoxies at this time in his life."

"It's never a good idea to confuse children," Staynair agreed. "At the same time, however, if you'll forgive *me* for saying it, they're capable of grasping differences of view with rather more acuity than adults give them credit for. Your brother is going to have to decide what he himself believes in the fullness of time, and I'm afraid he'll probably have to make that choice earlier in his life than most, simply because of who he is. I agree that this is no time for him to be trapped between men of God who both claim to know the truth yet persist in telling him different things, but I think you owe it to him—and to yourself, perhaps, if you'll forgive the observation—to see both sides of the issues which are currently wounding Mother Church so severely."

"I can't disagree with you about that," Irys said, meeting his gaze levelly, "but neither am I prepared at this moment to lend myself to undermining my brother's beliefs. The truth is that he's more concerned about winning at baseball or basketball—or telling me about that marsh-wyvern hunt Earl Hanth took him on—than he is about the state of his immortal soul. I think it's called being a ten-year-old." Despite herself, her lips twitched into a brief smile, but it disappeared quickly. "Yet I think that makes it even more important for me and for the adults in his life not to confuse him. Give him a little longer, Your Eminence, please. You yourself say in your sermons that a child of God has to *choose* what he or she believes, and whether or not I can agree with you about Mother Church and the Grand Vicar, I do agree with you about that. But no one can make an informed choice when they don't understand what it is they're choosing between, and Daivyn doesn't. Not yet. For that matter," her nostrils flared as she made the admission, "*I* don't understand yet, not fully, what I have to choose between."

"Of course you don't," he said simply. "I think, perhaps, you've come closer to that understanding than you yet realize, but you're absolutely right that it isn't something you rush into. Not if you're going to give it the amount of thought and prayer a decision that important deserves. And we're also right about the need to give Daivyn as much time as we can before he's pushed to decide. I'll send Father Davys a note this afternoon asking him to nominate a chaplain for both of you. And for Earl Coris, of course."

"Thank you, Your Eminence," she said with quiet sincerity.

"I do have to wonder where Captain Lathyk's going to put everyone, though," the archbishop said with a faint smile.

"Captain Lathyk?" Irys asked just a bit more quickly than she'd really intended to, and the archbishop's smile grew a little broader.

"Admiral Yairley—I'm sorry, I mean Baron Sarmouth, of course—is being sent out to Chisholm, and he's retaining *Destiny* as his flagship. Their Majesties thought that since he and Captain Lathyk seem to've done a reasonably adequate job of plucking you and your brother out of captivity and delivering safe and sound to Tellesberg, the Empress might as well avail herself of their services for delivering her—and you—safe and sound to Cherayth, as well."

"Daivyn will be delighted to hear that, Your Eminence!" Irys felt her own eyes sparkling. "He had *so* much fun aboard *Destiny*! Of course, with Haarahld Breygart to help him get into trouble, it's going to take the entire crew to keep the two of them from burning the ship to the waterline."

"Oh, I doubt it will be quite *that* bad, Your Highness." Staynair's eyes twinkled back at her. "Not with you and Lady Hanth there to keep an eye on things, at least. For that matter, it takes a very brave person to cross Empress Sharleyan as well, now that I think about it. And although I'm afraid *Seijin* Merlin won't be able to join you for the voyage, I understand your brother has become almost as fond of Lieutenant Aplyn-Ahrmahk. I imagine he'll serve as a . . . restraining influence on the two of them."

"I'm sure you're right about that," Irys agreed, uncomfortably aware her cheeks had grown ever so slightly warm for some reason. "The truth is that Daivyn adores Hektor—I mean, Lieutenant Aplyn-Ahrmahk—almost as much as he does *Seijin* Merlin. He'll be so happy to make another voyage with him."

"I'm glad to hear that." The twinkle was still in Staynair's eyes, and Irys felt her face turn a little hotter, but he only smiled. "I'm rather attached to young Hektor myself," he said, "and I'm sure Her Majesty will look forward to spending some time with him as well. When he can be spared from his duties and from riding herd on Daivyn and Haarahld, of course."

"Of course, Your Eminence," Irys agreed, and turned quickly back towards the panoramic view of the harbor. "Is that *Destiny*?" she asked just a bit hurriedly, pointing at a galleon making its way into the outer roadstead.

"No, Your Highness," the archbishop said gravely. "No, I believe *Destiny*'s currently at King's Harbor, refitting for the voyage to Cherayth, although that's obviously one of her sister ships."

"I see," she said, keeping her eyes resolutely on the ship's sails until she could be sure that inexplicable heat had faded from her face.

"Of course, Your Highness." She sensed rather than saw the archbishop's small, possibly slightly ironic half-bow. "But now, I'm afraid, I have to return to my office. There are a great many details I have to deal with before our departure as well, I fear."

"Of course, Your Eminence," she replied, still gazing at the nameless galleon making its slow, steady way closer to Tellesberg. "Thank you for taking the time out of your schedule to tell me about all this in person. I appreciate it."

"It was my honor, Your Highness," Staynair murmured, and she heard the glass-fronted door open and close as he left her to the view, in sole possession of the balcony once more.

.X.
The Fence,
Western Crown Demesne,
Kingdom of Chisholm,
Empire of Charis

At least it's a nice day for it," Ruhsyl Thairis said dryly.

The Duke of Eastshare stood on the parapet of one of the interval forts of the fortified line known as The Fence. The population of Raven's Land was tiny by the standards of any major Safeholdian realm. In fact, all the Raven Lords and their clansmen together would not have equaled the population of his own duchy. Unfortunately, they were a fractious lot and among the finest—if not simply *the* finest—horse thieves, dragon thieves, and sheep stealers in the entire world. That was why The Fence had been built in the first place. The line of observation posts, with interval forts every twenty miles, ran almost a hundred and fifty miles east to west across the single neck of land connecting the Western Crown Demesne and Raven's

Land. The observation posts were placed on high ground where sentries could keep an eye on the countryside between the interval forts. They also ran patrols, during anything resembling survivable weather, and the forts' relatively small garrisons were big enough to deal with any typical Raven Lord incursion the observation posts reported. They didn't catch all of them, by any means, but any raid large enough to carry back significant amounts of booty was generally large enough for the observation posts to spot, and the forts' garrisons consisted primarily of cavalry and dragoons, who tended to be a bit speedier than clansmen driving recalcitrant sheep into captivity.

They could still send skin boats and fishing boats across the Chisholm Bight (or cross the ice in midwinter), but neither of those avenues were likely to accomplish much beyond irritating the local landlords. And what with the navy's light units in summer and the tendency of ice rifts to appear in inconvenient spots, crossing the bight was always a risky proposition. Risky enough that even the hardiest of wing warriors (the title awarded to blooded Raven Lord warriors) preferred to take their chances with The Fence, instead.

And if we don't catch them all when they do *try The Fence, it's still good training for both sides,* he reflected wryly. *Besides, we've been doing it for so long now that I think we'd all be* disappointed *if the tradition came to an end.*

At the moment, however, the small party of horsemen making its way through the steady rattle of sleet towards the fort on whose parapet he stood, wasn't trying to be particularly unobtrusive.

"I wonder what the Council's decided?" he asked out loud.

"Oh, I imagine they've agreed, Your Grace." Kynt Clareyk smiled tartly. "I doubt any of the Raven Lords can really picture just how large a force the one you're talking about marching through their territory really is, but I'm pretty sure they can at least figure out they can't actually *stop* it, whatever they might try to do. Doesn't mean they couldn't make us thoroughly miserable, though, so unless I miss my guess, the real sticking point for them was calculating how much we'd be prepared to pay to avoid the nuisance value of their harassment."

"That's such a *Charisian* attitude," Eastshare complained with a twinkle.

"Marks make the world move, Your Grace. I will acknowledge that wind, weather, and tide can also generate movement, but when it comes to *human* activity, well—"

Green Valley shrugged, and Eastshare chuckled. Not, he reflected, that the baron didn't have a valid point.

"Then I suppose it's a good thing the Empire has more marks than almost anyone else at this particular time," he said. "Of course, there's the small matter of how many of them I can obligate to the Raven Lords without Their Majesties' approval or knowledge."

"I don't know Her Majesty as well as you do, Your Grace, but I've worked with both of Their Majesties quite a bit over the last few years. I'm reasonably certain they'll stand by any agreement you might make with Shairncross and the rest of the Council."

"And if they don't, they can always take it out of our pay."

"I suppose. Although, to be perfectly frank, Your Grace, given the disparity in our pay levels, I believe it would only be fair for you to pay the slash lizard's share"

"I *thought* you seemed remarkably complacent about the possibility."

Eastshare gazed at the oncoming horsemen for another several seconds, then shrugged.

"There's no point our standing out in this crappy weather until they get here. For that matter, we're going to have the opportunity to march in weather a lot worse than this soon enough, assuming this brilliant inspiration comes to fruition. So what say you and I make sure the tea and chocolate are both hot before our guests arrive?"

"An excellent notion, Your Grace." Green Valley smiled approvingly. "And, of course, the only way we can be positively certain they're hot enough is by personally sampling them to assure ourselves of their quality."

"Exactly what I was thinking," Eastshare agreed, one gloved hand brushing at the layer of sleet gathered on the shoulders of his thick coat. The other hand waved at the heavy wooden door behind them. "After you, General Green Valley. After you."

▼　▼　▼

Flahn Tobys wrapped his hands gratefully around the outsized mug of hot, steaming tea. Any Raven Lord wing warrior was a tough, skilled fighting man, inured to the worst of weather, trained by his high northern homeland's bitter winters to laugh at snows which would seem like the end of the world to any effete Lowlander.

Of course *we are.* He inhaled the steam appreciatively, then took a satisfying sip of the almost-scalding liquid. *And when we're especially young and stupid, we actually think that way. Fortunately, I'm no longer young. I suppose the verdict's still out on the other quality.*

"Thank you, Your Grace," he said in the slow, harsh accent of a Raven's Land Highlander as he lowered the cup and gazed across it at the Duke of Eastshare. "It's a rare nasty day out there, to be sure."

"Yes, it is," Eastshare agreed, leaning back in his own chair on the other side of the hearth as he considered his guest.

Tobys was a weathered-looking man of about forty-five, with dark hair and eyes. Some people might have allowed his backwoods appearance to deceive them into missing the intelligence in those dark eyes, but Eastshare knew his Raven Lords better than that. He recognized the gold rings and the red tip of the single raven's feather in Tobys' warrior's braid. They indicated he'd won his wing warrior status on more than one field of battle, and he was the senior wing—and close kinsman—of Phylyp Zhaksyn, Lord Tairwald, who'd been chosen by the Council of Clan Lords to speak for them in any discussions with Chisholm. The fact that Tairwald had sent Tobys was proof the Council had reached a decision.

Tobys looked back, studying the duke with equal care. He'd heard lots of stories about Eastshare, and no one who'd ever tangled with the Royal Chisholmian Army was likely to take its commander lightly. Still, he liked what he saw in the duke's level regard. There was no sign of the scorn he'd seen in other Lowlanders' expressions, at any rate, and he allowed himself a mental nod of satisfaction before he turned his attention back to his surroundings, waiting for the duke to finish his own appraisals and get to the matter in hand.

The interval fort housed its garrison in relative comfort, but it was plainly furnished, without frills or anything smacking of luxury. The massive wooden beams overhead were darkened by decades of wood and peat fires, and as the wind drove thickening curtains of sleet and snow across the chimney tops, an occasional tendril of fresh smoke crept from the fire currently radiating heat into the fort commander's commandeered office to add its mite to that patina. The northern daylight had already faded, the heavy overcast turning the evening into something more akin to midnight than late afternoon, and the whiskey bottles and glasses on a small side table gleamed in the lamplight, throwing back stronger flickers of light every so often as the fire on the hearth crackled higher. Tobys was acutely aware of those bottles, but Raven Lord etiquette required whiskey not be offered until the serious business was discharged.

After all, the wing reflected, *wouldn't do for us to get all liquored up and give away the keys to the clan lord's castle, now would it? And, clansmen being clansmen, wouldn't we just?*

His fellow Raven Lords, alas, took their drinking seriously.

"Speaking of the weather," the duke continued after several seconds, crossing his booted ankles as he stretched his legs out before him, "I'm sure my men are going to spend quite a lot of time over the next several five-days cursing my name. Assuming, of course, that the Council of Clan Lords has seen fit to agree with my . . . suggestion."

To the point, Tobys thought. *More like a Raven Lord than a Lowlander, in fact. Man knows us better than most, or else*—the clansman's eyes considered the tall, dark-haired young general sitting to Eastshare's left—*he's had good advisors.*

"Well, as to that, Your Grace, and bearing in mind the quality of good Chisholmian whiskey, I'd sooner not beat about the bush myself. And it's no fancy diplomat I am, either. So, to get right to the heart of it, Lord Tairwald's told me to be telling you Lord Shairncross and the Council are minded to agree to let your army pass. Of course, while it's well known the Royal Army's better disciplined than most, there's no way in the world that many men could be passing through without doing at least a wee bit of damage. With the best of goodwill, you just can't send that many men down our roads—the most of which pass right through the heart of our towns and villages, you know—without the odd bit of breakage. And it's well known that sometimes small possessions stray from where you thought you'd left them into the pockets and knapsacks of visiting soldiers."

"Yes, I've observed that myself, here in the Crown Demesne, when armies—or warriors, at least—come calling." Eastshare's smile held genuine humor, Tobys observed. "Should I, ah, assume the Councilors were able to determine a sum which they felt would . . . indemnify their clansmen against any such completely unintentional harm?"

"Well, in fact they have," Tobys admitted. "It was in the Council's mind to set a number based on the number of troops you're thinking of passing through. Say, ten Charisian marks for an infantryman and fifteen for a cavalry trooper—those horses eat a sight of fodder every day, you know, and we've the thatched roofs to be thinking of. Not to mention the haystacks. And they were thinking perhaps, say, seven marks five for each wagon. But they'd be passing your artillery through free and clear."

"That seems a bit high, Wing Tobys." Eastshare sipped his tea thoughtfully and glanced at the younger officer at his side. "We quite understand the clan lords' concerns, of course. But still."

"It's just that we've had bad experiences in the past, Your Grace." Tobys shrugged apologetically. "With armies passing through, I mean."

"While I'd never want to be tactless or bring up past unpleasantnesses, Wing Tobys," the other officer—Green Valley, his name was—put in, in an accent which definitely wasn't Chisholmian, "unless I'm mistaken, those other armies passing through Raven's Land were, for want of a better word, *invading* your land, weren't they?"

"We prefer to think of it as responding to someone else's provocations, My Lord," Eastshare chided. " 'Invade' has so many unpleasant connotations."

"Oh, I see, Your Grace." Green Valley nodded.

"Nonetheless, the Baron does have a certain point, Wing Tobys," Eastshare said, turning back to the Raven Lord envoy. "Not that anyone is implying that this particular proposed journey would have anything in common with an invasion, of course. But troops who are there for the specific purpose of . . . delivering a message do tend to do far more damage than ones just marching past, smiling at the pretty girls as they go."

"True, Your Grace. Very true." Tobys sipped more tea, his expression thoughtful, then shrugged. "Can I take it, then, you've another set of numbers in mind?"

"Well, actually, it seems to me—speaking off the cuff, you understand—that something closer to two Charisian marks per infantryman and five per cavalry trooper would be far more reasonable. And perhaps three marks five, rather than seven and a half, per wagon. Trust me," Eastshare's eyes hardened ever so slightly, "given the number of men I'm planning on taking with me, that will still come to a *very* tidy sum."

Tobys raised his teacup again. Clansmen were a hardy lot, less impressed by birth and more by ability than the folk of many another land, and Lord Tairwald and the Council of Clan Lords had chosen him as their envoy because they trusted both his wit and his judgment. He actually had more authority to adjust prices than might have been expected in someone of his outwardly lowly rank, and he'd known before he set out that Eastshare would never accept the Council's initial offer. The Raven Lords' current estimate was that he'd be moving at least forty thousand men, perhaps a quarter of them cavalry, through their territory. Leaving aside the freight wagons which would certainly have to accompany them, how ever much of their total supplies might be carried by water along the coast, that would have come to three hundred thousand marks, enough to buy one of the new Charisian-style war galleons with all the trimmings. It would also have been more cold, hard cash than the Council normally saw in an entire year. Eastshare's counter offer, however, would drop it to only a hundred and twenty thousand marks. Still, as Duke Eastshare had just pointed out, a tidy sum, but . . . .

"I think we need a number somewhere out in the middle of that, Your Grace," he said now. "Suppose I were to suggest four marks per infantryman and horseman alike and accept your three-and-five for each wagon? And, of course, the artillery would still be passing through free of charge?"

"That might be acceptable," Eastshare said after a moment. "Assuming, of course, that my quartermasters don't find themselves being exorbitantly charged for landing supplies at any of your ports along the way."

"The Council thought you might be a wee bit bothered by that possibility." Tobys smiled slightly. He'd never liked Lord Theralt, anyway. "So, after debating it a bit, they thought it best to assure you you'll not be charged a tenth-mark more than the normal port fees per ton of cargo landed. And"—his eyes gleamed for a second—"the Council's also made it clear that the 'normal port fees' are the ones as were in force before ever the thought of your little jaunt along the coast was first suggested."

"I see."

Eastshare's lips twitched. He was quite well informed on the relations between Barjwail Suwail and the rest of the Council, and he didn't doubt for a moment that Lord Shairncross had taken a certain pleasure in ramming *that* proviso through. Not that Theralt and the other small harbors and fishing ports along Raven's Land's southern coast weren't going to receive an ample landfall, even at existing rates. And not that Eastshare had any objection to improving the local economies as he passed through, either. And, for that matter, he rather suspected the Raven Lords didn't realize how many troops he'd been able to concentrate in Ahlysberg. He'd be taking the next best thing to eighty thousand men through their territory, which would mean a greater profit than they'd probably anticipated, even at the lower rate Tobys was suggesting now.

And, frankly, it's as good as you've got any realistic prospect of getting out of them—especially with the Council sitting on Theralt and the others. Theralt, for one, would cheerfully double or triple his fees when we arrived . . . without ever mentioning ahead of time he was going to do it.

"Well," he said after a moment, setting his teacup aside and nodding to Green Valley. "Now that we've got that out of the way, I think it's time we opened one or two of those bottles, My Lord."

. XI.
King's Harbor,
Helen Island,
Kingdom of Old Charis,
Empire of Charis

There were too many of them to fit into Baron Seamount's office this time, so they'd met in Sir Dustyn Olyvyr's drafting office, instead. The drafting tables where the assistant designers of the Imperial Charisian Navy's Chief Naval Constructor normally labored had been moved back against the enormous room's walls and a conference table had been moved into the middle of the floor. The louvered skylights were open, allowing the harbor breeze to swirl through, and sunlight poured through the glass, flooding the room with the light the draftsman normally required. The smells of salt water, freshly sawn timbers, tar, and paint came with the breeze, and the cries of gulls and sea wyverns, mingled with the shouts of foremen and their work crews, floated through the opened windows over the racket of hammers and saws.

"Every time I get out here, it seems like you've figured out how to cram at least one more building into the waterfront, Sir Dustyn," Cayleb Ahrmahk said wryly.

"It's not really *that* bad, Your Majesty," Olyvyr said.

"No, not quite," Domynyk Staynair agreed. "Although, I *do* seem to recall having authorized you to demolish four of those warehouses associated with the old foundry in order to build new slips over there. Is my memory playing me false?"

"Well, no. It isn't."

"I thought not." Baron Rock Point nodded, standing behind his chair at the table and surveying the assembled group. Almost half were members of the inner circle, which was going to make the ensuing conversation interesting, since they'd have to remember the other half weren't.

"All right." Cayleb slid Sharleyan's chair up to the table after she was seated, then dropped into his own, "I know we're all short on time—especially with Sharleyan due to leave for Chisholm in only seven days." He grimaced. "She and I both have a lot of things we need to do before then, and all of you have just as many projects and responsibilities waiting for you. It's not often we get a chance to sit down in one place together, though, and before we scatter to our various roosts, I want to make sure we cover everything that needs to be covered. Ehdwyrd," he looked at Ehdwyrd Howsmyn, "I know you and Captain Rahskail and Commander Malkaihy need to spend at least a full day of your own discussing the new artillery designs. I want to sit in on that as well, if I can find time. At the moment, though," he returned his attention to Olyvyr, "I'm more interested in where we are on the new ship designs."

"Of course, Your Majesty." Olyvyr nodded and settled into his own chair, like all of the others—except *Seijin* Merlin, who stood comfortably beside the only door into the big room—after the emperor and empress had been seated. Then he folded the hands which bore the long-faded scars of chisel, saw, and adze on the table in front of him and nodded to the man at his right, Captain Tompsyn Saigyl. "Tompsyn and I have been working on that, and we're confident we've solved the last design problems—assuming Ehdwyrd and Commander Hainai's final drawings and performance estimates on the engines are accurate?"

He raised one eyebrow, and Howsmyn shrugged.

"The test engine's completed and running, Dustyn, and we're actually producing about ten more dragonpower than predicted."

Olyvyr nodded. One dragonpower, the unit Stahlman Praigyr had proposed to measure the energy output of his beloved engines, equated to about twenty-five Old Earth horsepower.

"Of course, at this point we haven't had a chance to see how well our projected propeller efficiency will stand up," Howsmyn continued, "but the rest of the numbers we've given you are sound. And the canal boat propellers we've tested so far have come out fairly close to the efficiencies we'd predicted. We'll be delivering the first harbor tug in about another three five-days, so you should be able to play with it yourself, if you like."

"And the plate production estimates?"

"There I can't be quite as confident," Howsmyn admitted. "Those depend on whether or not we're able to continue to increase capacity at the projected rate. And whether or not we have enough iron, for that matter. Nickel production's running a little ahead of our estimated requirements, but there's only so much iron ore to go around."

"That's why I authorized you to strip the iron guns off our Desnairian and Navy of God prizes," Rock Point said. "It's not like we've got the manpower to crew every ship we have anyway, and the workmanship on the Desnairian guns, especially, is less than reliable, so if we're going to find you scrap metal, better there than anywhere else I can think of." He glanced at Cayleb and Sharleyan and grimaced, his expression unhappy. "I don't like disarming that many galleons, but Ehdwyrd's already melted down everything else I could think of, and we can always move guns from some of our early emergency-build ships into the prize vessels later. We always knew using so much green timber was going to cost us in the end. God knows we're starting to have enough problems with dry rot, and it's only going to get worse over the next year or two."

Cayleb nodded, although he was actually hard put not to smile, and from the way Sharleyan was squeezing his hand under the table, she was as well. The idea had been hers, after all. They were going to need lots of transports to lift Eastshare's expeditionary force across to the Republic, once they officially found out about it, and Howsmyn and the rest of the Empire's foundries needed all the iron they could get. So, since war galleons were already fitted to carry large crews, which meant they had the berthing space and water and food stowage for feeding and transporting sizable numbers of men, why not kill two wyverns with one stone? Go ahead and begin stripping the artillery out now for Howsmyn and his fellow ironmasters, which would just *happen* to leave Rock Point with a significant number of galleons, berthed right here at Helen Island or Tellesberg, which could immediately be sent off to Chisholm.

"That's going to help a lot, obviously," Howsmyn said with admirable gravity. "And Brahd Stylmyn thinks he can increase output at the High Rock mines by perhaps another five, possibly even six percent once the new engines are fully available. I think he's underestimating a bit, but there's no way we're going to get an output increase of more than, say, ten percent in anything less than four or five years, no matter what we do. Those new deposits in the Hallecks are going to help, too, but it's going to take at least several months to get the mines operating, and transport's going to be a real problem even after we do. That's why we're putting so much effort into the Lake Lymahn Works right now, to decrease how far we'd have to ship it." It was his turn to grimace. "Which, of course, is diverting trained manpower at the moment we need it most to support your new project, Dustyn."

"So, bottom line, are we're going to be able to produce the necessary iron and steel or not?" Sharleyan asked.

"The answer is . . . probably, but not certainly. For the immediate future, that is," Howsmyn said, manifestly unhappily. "On the other hand, the answer for the entire program the High Admiral and I originally discussed is more likely going to be no, I'm afraid, at least in anything like our original time frame."

"Would that change if we pulled those workmen of yours home from Lake Lymahn and the other new works you're building?" Rock Point asked.

"Not hugely." Howsmyn leaned back and shook his head. "And if we pull them back, we lose the increased production we're going to need even worse down the road."

"I think you're entirely right about that," Cayleb said. "In fact, I think we probably need to make it a hard and fast rule that we're going to reserve at least, what, ten percent of your total capacity for expansion?"

"Your Majesty, I don't know if we can do that," Baron Ironhill, the Empire's treasurer, said. He looked back and forth between Howsmyn, Rock Point, and the emperor and empress. "Your Majesties know how bad the Treasury numbers look right now, especially with the loss of all the trade that was moving through Siddarmark to the rest of the mainland. I expect to see some recovery in the revenue numbers in the next year or so, but it's not going to make up for what we've lost. Frankly, I don't know if I'm going to be able to steal enough money to finance the Crown's projected share of the new works after all, and even if I can, we're going to be committed to supporting a major land war in Siddarmark. That means we're going to have to operate on a mainland scale, and we've never done that where the Army and the Marines are concerned. If we don't produce what they need *now*—and find the money to pay for it somehow—it won't matter what we may be able to produce in another three years' time. And right now, frankly, Ehdwyrd's running at full capacity just to meet current needs."

"Ahlvyno's right about what we're going to need, at least in the next year to fifteen months." Trahvys Ohlsyn, the Earl of Pine Hollow, who'd replaced the murdered Rayjhis Yowance as Cayleb's first councilor, didn't look happy to hear himself saying that. "We can't afford to cut back the Navy—the Empire's fundamental security won't let us do that—but we're going to find ourselves under huge pressure to support Stohnar and any troops we put ashore in Siddarmark. But you're right, as well, Your Majesty. We have to keep expanding output if we're going to meet our future needs."

"But—" Ironhill began, only to close his mouth again as Cayleb raised his hand.

"I understand both viewpoints, Ahlvyno, and I'm sympathetic to both. Unfortunately, the best we can manage in this case is a compromise no one's going to like. We'll talk about it—let Ehdwyrd, Ahlfryd, Domynyk, and Sir Dustyn discuss exactly how they need to balance expansion and present output—and do our very best to meet those numbers, but we *have* to continue to expand. I hate to say it, but even if we lose more—or all—of Siddarmark, we'll still survive and still have a chance to win in the end as long as we can maintain and increase our qualitative edge. But however good our quality, we have to be able to produce it in sufficient *quantity*, as well. So if it's a choice between cutting current production to the bone over the next year or so, whatever problems that causes in Siddarmark, and not having the capacity we need *two* years from now, we're going to have to opt for the future."

Ironhill looked worried, but he recognized an unpalatable reality—and a final decision—when he saw them, and he nodded in understanding.

"All right," Cayleb continued, turning back to Olyvyr and Howsmyn. "I think one place we're going to have to make some hard choices is by reducing the number of new ships." He shrugged his shoulders unhappily. "God knows we need as many as we can get, but at the moment we have effective superiority over every remaining ship the other side has, and we are going to have to shift emphasis to supporting land operations. So instead of a dozen, I want you to plan on only six, Sir Dustyn. At the same time, though, I want you and Captain Saigyl to begin thinking about ironclad riverboats." He showed his teeth. "With any luck at all, we're going to need them even more than we need the oceangoing variety."

"Of course, Your Majesty," Olyvyr replied. "No one saw Siddarmark coming, so we haven't really considered it yet, but we'll begin immediately. And while I hate postponing the full number of blue-water ships, the idea of building a smaller group first has a certain appeal. It might not hurt to see how well our first experiments work out before we commit to building vast numbers of seagoing ships."

"I'm glad you think so . . . even if I can't quite escape the feeling that you're searching hard for a bright side to look upon."

"If you have to do it anyway, Your Majesty, you might as well see the upside as well as the downside."

"That's true enough," Sharleyan agreed. "Although, personally, I think your 'first experiments' are going to turn out quite well, Sir Dustyn."

"I hope so, and I actually believe you're right, Your Grace . . . assuming Doctor Mahklyn's newfangled numbers work out as well as everyone keeps assuming they will." Olyvyr grimaced, and Sharleyan nodded gravely, although the truth was that Olyvyr had been initiated into the inner circle almost a year ago. He'd been using Rozhyr Mahklyn's new formulas to calculate displacement and sail area even before that, and he'd been like a little boy in a toy store ever since he got access to Owl and started calculating things like stability, metacentric heights, prismatic coefficients, and a hundred other things which had always been rule-of-thumb—at best—before. He still had to do quite a lot of those calculations himself (or have Owl do that for him) rather than allowing his assistants to perform them, since the formulas—and concepts—hadn't been officially "invented" yet, but he and Mahklyn were working hard to introduce the ideas. Within another year or so, at the outside, Charisian shipbuilders outside his own office would be starting to apply all those even more "newfangled" theories and rules, as well.

"In the end," he continued, looking around the table, "and even before we started worrying about Ehdwyrd's output numbers, it became obvious to Fhranklyn and me that we *were* going to have to go with composite construction, at least for the first blue-water class." He twitched his shoulders. "It would simplify things enormously to go directly to all-iron construction, but we simply don't have the output. So, we'll be using cast-iron framing and deck beams, wooden planking, and steel plate from the Delthak Works for armor. Iron frames will give us enormously better longitudinal strength than we've ever had before, which is critical for the weights incorporated into these designs, and there are several other foundries here in Old Charis which can produce them while we leave the more complex aspects to Ehdwyrd's artificers. Of course, I'm sure some of your captains are going to scream at the notion of ironwork, Domynyk," he said, looking across the table at Rock Point. "In fact, I'm positive at least one of them is going to point out that they can't repair an *iron* deck beam at sea the way they can one made out of wood."

"Oh, I'm sure your number's off, Dustyn." Rock Point waved one hand dismissively. "I'll be astonished if I hear that from less than a *dozen* of them!"

A laugh circled the table, and Olyvyr shook his head with a smile. Then he sobered.

"The river ironclads we can probably build with wooden frames if we have to, although it would help a lot to use iron framing for them, as well. They'd have to be a lot smaller, too, which is going to mean a lot of compromises. In particular, it'll probably mean thinner armor, but they should be facing primarily field artillery or light naval guns, which will help a lot.

"The blue-water ships, on the other hand, are going to be the largest vessels ever built," he said, looking around the table. "According to Doctor

Mahklyn's numbers, they're going to come out at over five thousand tons *displacement*, not burden—better than three times our biggest war galleon. They're going to be three hundred feet long, and they'll draw around twenty-eight feet at normal load, which is the main reason Fhranklyn and Commander Malkaihy are already working with Ehdwyrd's artificers on steam-powered dredges—we're going to need them for some of our more critical ship channels as soon as we build anything *bigger* than this. The sheer weight and size of a rudder for something that big is going to pose problems, too. I'm not at all sure it could be handled using raw muscle power, so we've put quite a bit of effort into coming up with a hydraulic-assistance system for it. It's going to require at least one small steam engine permanently on line to power it, but the fuel requirements for that engine will be very low, and there are other places where having steam available on that scale would be very useful. For one thing, in raising and lowering the screw. And we've designed the system so it can be disengaged in an emergency, although at that point you're going to need at least eight to ten men on the wheel. That's why the thing's going to have a triple wheel—so they can all find a place to get a grip."

Many of the heads around the table nodded at that. Even with the efficiency Howsmyn had been able to engineer into his "first-generation" steam engines, providing the internal fuel capacity for a steamship to obtain the kind of cruising distances required by the Imperial Charisian Navy would be difficult. It was over eight thousand miles from Tellesberg to Siddar City, for example, and that was far from the longest voyage a Charisian warship was likely to face, nor did it even consider the need to remain on station for extended periods, which was why the first generation of Charisian armored warships would be fully rigged for sail as well. The truth was that they probably *could* have designed solely for steam power, but only at the cost of establishing chains of coaling stations along critical shipping lanes and in forward deployment areas. That would be far from impossible for them to do on an internal basis, for the separated islands of the Charisian Empire itself, but it would certainly be expensive, and they couldn't afford to assume it would be equally feasible elsewhere.

"It would simplify things a great deal if we could leave the screw permanently in place," Olyvyr continued, "but the more efficient it is for moving water, the greater the drag when it isn't revolving. Fortunately, once Fhranklyn came up with a notion for indexing the shaft and locking it in place, it turned out to be a lot simpler than I expected to design a moving cradle to unlock the screw and raise it into the above water well." He snorted. "Mind you, it would've been a lot *harder* if we hadn't decided to go with hydraulic power for the rudder. Since we were doing that anyway, it only made sense to apply power to raising and lowering the screw as well." He shrugged, then grinned almost impishly. "I think we could still've done it, but I wouldn't be surprised if it had required three or four hundred seamen—probably complaining at the top of their lungs the entire time—to do the same thing by muscle power."

"Then I'd say it's a good thing you didn't do that, Sir Dustyn," Sharleyan said with a smile. "I gather from what you're saying that the amount of fuel required for this . . . auxiliary engine, I suppose we should call it, won't have any significant impact on the designed cruising radius?"

"We're allocating that fuel in addition to the coal for her normal steaming radius, Your Grace. Our calculations indicate that one of the new ships ought to be good for about five thousand miles at twelve knots under steam alone. Assuming average weather conditions, she'll probably be able to maintain sixteen knots under sail and steam combined at an economical rate of fuel consumption. With the propeller raised, she should still be able to maintain between six to ten knots under sail alone—possibly as much as fourteen or fifteen in blowing conditions, given her size and ability to carry more sail than anything smaller. Her maximum speed under steam is actually going to be almost twenty knots, but her endurance at that speed will drop catastrophically."

Several of the faces around that table looked stunned, perhaps even incredulous, at those numbers. Of course, twenty Safeholdian knots was also twenty miles per hour, not the twenty-*three* miles per hour twenty knots would have been back on a planet called Earth. Still, it was an unheard-of speed for any ship.

"In addition to being the biggest and the fastest ships in the world," Olyvyr continued, "they're going to be the toughest. We began our original plans for them before Ehdwyrd's artificers came up with steam engines, when we would've had to power them by sail alone. That also means we started on them before he began experimenting with nickel steel and hardening plate faces with his new quenching procedures as well. At that point, we'd estimated it would take at least twelve inches of cast-iron armor to stop one of Ahlfryd's projected ten-inch rifles firing solid wrought-iron shot at short range. Ehdwyrd's 'face-hardened' plate is much tougher than that. We should be able to use as little as eight inches, probably even less. Our current calculations are that three inches of Howsmynized nickel plate will stop anything the Navy of God has, even at point-blank range, but we're going to go ahead and design to defeat our own guns, so we'll use six inches and back it with twelve inches of teak to help damp the shock of impacting shot.

"For the riverine vessels, we'd probably go with something more like three-inch armor and backing of six inches. I'd prefer thicker, but that probably won't be practical on their displacement—we'll know better once we actually start looking at them—and we're already set up to produce three-inch plate, since Ehdwyrd chose that thickness to perfect his new techniques and he's actually got several hundred tons of it sitting at the Delthak Works right now. Actually, what I'm more worried about is the thinner backing. The new plate's nowhere near as brittle as iron, so we're not as concerned about its shattering under the impact, but the cushioning effect should help prevent the securing bolts from shearing.

"I assume any river vessels will be armed with existing guns, at least in the interim. Assuming the projected weights for the new guns hold up, the ocean ironclads should have twelve eight-inch in each broadside and a pair of ten-inch on pivot mounts, one each forward and aft, all of them behind armor. The masts and rigging will be vulnerable, of course, but these ships are designed to move and fight under steam, so the loss of a mast or two won't be a major handicap in battle. Since we don't have a design for the riverboats yet, I can't estimate building times on them, but I estimate we can launch the first blue-water ship between six months and a year from the day we lay her down. And under the circumstances," he sat back in his chair with an expression of profound satisfaction, "I don't think Zhaspahr Clyntahn will like her one bit."

"No, he won't," Cayleb agreed, and his expression had hardened. It was his turn to look around at the others, his brown eyes grim. "And just in case the bastard doesn't get the message on his own, Sharleyan and I have decided what we're going to name the first three ships." The others looked at him, and he smiled coldly. "We thought we'd begin with the *King Haarahld VII*, the *Gwylym Manthyr*, and the *Lainsair Svairsmahn*." The eyes around that table turned as hard as his own, glittering with approval. "If he doesn't quite grasp what we intend to do with them from the first three names," Cayleb continued, "I'm sure he'll get the point when we sail them and a dozen more just like them clear up Hsing-wu's Passage to Temple Bay and start putting the troops ashore."

▼ ▼ ▼

"Ehdwyrd?"

Ehdwyrd Howsmyn lowered his glass as the deep voice spoke in his ear plug. The ironmaster was alone in the study of his Tellesberg townhouse, the last of his daily correspondence spread across the desk before him, and it was very late. Rain battered the roof and cascaded in torrents from the eaves and wind and rain ruled the night outside his windows, lit by an occasional flash of lighting and rumble of thunder, but inside those windows was an oasis of comfort, so quiet between thunder grumbles he could hear the crisp ticking of the clock in one corner. The light of sea dragon oil lamps gleamed on the frames of paintings, polished the deep-toned leather of hundreds of book spines with a burnished glow, and pooled golden in the Chisholmian whiskey as he set the glass on his blotter beside one of the neat stacks of paper. There were quite a few of those stacks. He seldom had much time to spend in the luxurious townhouse these days, and even when he did, the correspondence followed him wherever he went.

"Merlin?" He cocked an eyebrow in mild surprise. He'd left the day's final conference with the *seijin* less than five hours ago. "Has something come up?"

"More a matter of something occurring to me that I should've thought of a five-day ago," Merlin replied, and Howsmyn heard a note of genuine chagrin in his voice.

"Which would be what, exactly?" the Charisian inquired.

"Ironclads. To be specific, *river* ironclads."

"What about them?"

"When you were all discussing them this morning as I stood ominously guarding the door, my brain was on autopilot. In fact, I was actually using the time to review some of the take from the SNARCs rather than concentrating on what all of you were saying."

"I'm crushed to learn our conversation was insufficiently scintillating to hold you riveted to our every word," Howsmyn said dryly, and Merlin chuckled over the com.

"I've discovered the lot of you are all grown up—or close enough I can trust you to talk things over without me, anyway. Besides, we'd already discussed everything I knew was going to come up, so I figured you could play without adult supervision this once."

"You have a true gift for flattering my ego, don't you?"

"If I told you and the others how good you really are, you'd all be impossible to live with. That wasn't the reason I commed, though."

"So what *was* the reason?"

"Exactly how much of that three-inch armor plate do you actually have?"

"Um. I'd have to check the inventories to be sure. A fair amount, though. Probably close to fourteen or fifteen hundred tons, I suppose. Might be a little more or a little less. Frankly, I haven't worried too much about the actual quantities, since there wasn't any rush. It's too thin for those five-thousand-tonners Dustyn's come up with, for one thing, and I know we don't have anywhere near enough to cover them even if we wanted to use multiple layers to build up the needed thickness. And Dustyn hasn't even started the design on the riverboats. For that matter, we won't be starting construction on any of them until one of the other foundries is ready to start casting the frame members. Why?"

"Because I've got another question for you, to go with the first one.

How much of it would be needed to armor one of your steam-powered river barges?"

Howsmyn blinked.

"I don't know," he said slowly. "I never thought about it."

"Neither had I until this evening," Merlin told him. "I've been thinking all along in terms of purpose-built ironclads, and going at it this way, we'd have all the wooden-hull worries Dustyn was talking about. But those barges are pretty damned heavily framed, given what you wanted them for in the first place. I'm willing to bet they'd hold up at least as well as the steamboats the Americans converted into ironclads on the Mississippi in the American Civil War—probably better. And unlike Dustyn's designs, they already exist. All we'd have to do would be slap the armor on them."

"I think it'd be a *little* more complicated than that," Howsmyn said dryly. "I don't really know about your 'Mississippi' conversions—I take it that was a river back on Old Earth?—but I'm willing to bet they hit the odd little problem along the way. On the other hand, you have a point about the fact that the barges already exist."

He pulled out a blank sheet of paper, slid his abacus in front of him, and began jotting numbers.

"They're a bit bigger than the standard mainland river barges, you know," he said as his pen scratched and abacus beads clicked busily. "We don't have anywhere near the dependency on barge traffic they do, and we haven't got anywhere near the same number of canals. A lot of their canals are over five or six hundred years old, though, and making any major changes in them would be an incredible pain, so they worry a lot more about barge interchangeability than we do. The newer canals mostly have bigger locks to let them use bigger barges for purely local traffic, but one of the really old trunk lines—like the Langhorne—can't accept outsized barges. Since barge owners never know when they're going to have to use one of the lines with smaller locks, they tend to build small unless it's for purely local use, like the wheat trade out of Tarikah via the Hildermoss and the New Northland Canal. That limits their really long-haul barges to about a hundred and twenty-five feet. We didn't have to worry about fitting through something like the Langhorne, though, so we just stole the plans for the New Northland's locks when we built the Delthak canal."

He grimaced and shook his head with a chuckle.

"If I'd known about the inner circle then, I might've thought about coming up with another design, but the truth is, the ones based on the *Writ* are about as good a fit to allowable technology as anything Owl could've come up with. And at least that way I didn't have to worry about getting anything past Paitryk. The *old* Paitryk, I mean."

He shrugged.

"Anyway, because of the lock size we chose, our barges are a hundred and forty feet long and forty-five feet in the beam with a draft of about six and a half feet and around fifteen or sixteen feet depth of hold, which lets them carry a hell of a lot more than your typical mainland boat. Within limits, of course. They're basically just big, square boxes with round ends, when you come down to it. We did slightly redesign the sterns for the powered barges, but not enough to change their volume so anyone would notice, so each of them can carry about ninety-five thousand cubic feet of cargo. That comes to around twenty-three hundred tons of coal per barge, which we figured was pretty much the ceiling for animal-drawn loads, even with tow roads as wide as the ones we used. Takes a four-dragon team to move the unpowered ones, and it also just about doubles their draft to twelve feet, which is as deep as you want to go in even one of *our* canals. The steam-powered boats are a little less than that because of the weight the engine and boilers and the fuel take up, but still . . . ."

His pen stopped scratching and he looked down at his notes.

"All right, here're the fast-and-dirty numbers. A cubic inch of armor steel weighs about a quarter of a pound. Figuring three-inch side armor over a length of a hundred and forty feet and a height of ten feet—we might need a little less height than that; that's the freeboard unladen, and by the time you put armor and guns aboard—oh, and you'd need to throw in a gun*deck* to mount the damned things on, too, you know—you're bound to deepen the draft a little, so—"

He cut himself off with another grimace.

"Sorry. The point is that you'd need about one-point-six million cubic inches to armor the sides and ends of a box that size. Call it four hundred thousand pounds or around two hundred tons."

"But that's only the sides and ends," Merlin pointed out. "You'd need to armor the top, too. They're bound to take plunging fire from a river bluff somewhere. For that matter, we know Thirsk is already starting to produce his own version of Alfryd's angle-guns."

"You don't want much, do you?" Howsmyn demanded sarcastically. "You do realize we can't armor the top as thickly as the sides, right? The roof of the box is going to be about twice the area of its sides. That'd be a *lot* of weight, especially that high up in the ship, where it's not going to do stability any favors."

"The roof would be more likely to take glancing hits or hits from fairly light shells," Merlin countered. "What if you dropped it to, say, one-inch thickness?"

"Great," Howsmyn grumbled, and started scribbling again. A short while later he sat back with a grunt.

"I'm assuming no taper in the casemate sides or ends here, which is probably wrong. I'm sure we'd want to slope at least the sides for a better ballistic coefficient and to improve stability, which should narrow the 'roof' quite a lot, but at this point I'd rather overestimate than underestimate. At any rate, using those numbers I come up with around a bit over another hundred and thirteen tons. Call it three hundred and fourteen for the entire armor weight, just to be on the safe side. And, of course, none of that allows for cutting out gunports. That would reduce the total armor requirement at least some . . . although I suppose you'd want shutters for the gunports?"

"I don't know," Merlin said in a thoughtful tone. "Probably. But, you know, the numbers are actually better than I thought they'd be. If you have fifteen hundred tons of three-inch armor already fabricated, you could armor four of them, couldn't you? Maybe even five, if you're right about the taper reducing the width of the casemate roof."

"Except that none of that *one*-inch armor exists yet, of course," Howsmyn observed in a pleasant but pointed tone, and Merlin chuckled.

"True, but I bet you could produce another four or five hundred tons of armor that thin pretty quickly, couldn't you?"

"Faster than three-inch, anyway," Howsmyn agreed. "The quenching process wouldn't take as long, for one thing. I don't know how much time we'd save total, but you could probably figure we'd be able to turn it out in—oh, I don't know, a month if we made it a category-one priority? Something like that, anyway."

"And how long would it take you to haul four of your barges out of the water and armor them?"

"Probably about a month . . ." Howsmyn said slowly.

"Then I think this might be very worth considering," Merlin said in a serious tone. "Especially given how critical water transport and river lines are going to be in Siddarmark."

"Maybe. But they're going to be pushing the limit on any mainland canal, Merlin. They can probably—*probably*—get through most of the newer ones, but they sure as hell won't get through *all* of them. And they were never designed for open water," Howsmyn protested.

"With that low a freeboard, they'd be useless in a seaway," Merlin agreed. "But we're talking about brown water, not blue. Ten feet would be plenty for inland work—or in most harbors, for that matter."

"Sure, but first you have to get them to the mainland in the first place." Howsmyn shook his head. "I'm not the sailor you or Cayleb are, but it occurs to me that something that small and shallow-draft would be a pain in the arse under typical ocean conditions!"

"Worse as a sailboat than a steamer," Merlin replied. "And there are ways we could work around a lot of the problems. Garboards or leeboards to give the hulls more effective depth, for example, like we used on the landing craft we took to Corisande and the ones Dustyn is running up for Siddarmark. As for size, they're not that much shorter or narrower than most war galleons. They *are* smaller, and they're a lot shallower draft, with only about half as much freeboard, which means the hulls are nowhere nearly as deep, so they've got a lower displacement. But, again, that's not a big problem for a steamer with leeboards. And since they were designed originally to carry coal, I'm pretty sure we could load them up with enough fuel for the voyage, especially if we wait to mount the guns till we get them to Siddarmark and only put a passage crew aboard them for the trip itself. And they're good for, what, twelve knots?"

"A little better than that, actually," Howsmyn said. "In fact, the operational boats are ridiculously overpowered for canal work—they were propulsion experiments, and we've had them up to over fourteen knots on the lake. The ones we're building now'll have a maximum speed of no more than *ten* knots. Even the operational ones probably wouldn't be able to make that kind of speed at sea, though. Not more than twelve or thirteen, tops, I'd think."

"Even twelve would let them make the trip to Siddar City in only about six or seven five-days, though. Still a lot better than a galleon can do. Especially since they wouldn't have to worry about calms or beating to windward."

"True," Howsmyn agreed. He sat rubbing his chin thoughtfully for several seconds, then sighed.

"All right. Much as I hate to do this, knowing what will happen if I do, I have to concede it's at least theoretically possible. So should I go ahead and start shredding my production schedules right now, or shall we wait and pretend you actually intend to leave the decision up to Cayleb and Sharleyan?"

"What a perfectly dreadful thing to say!" Merlin told him austerely. "I am deeply affronted by the very suggestion. Now that you and I have discussed the feasibility, I will, of course, present the *possibility* to the two of them. It would be most unbecoming for us to presume to reorder their established priorities without their having had due time to consider all of the pros and cons of the suggestion."

"But I should go ahead and start planning for it right now, right?" Howsmyn asked with a grin.

"Well, of course you should. Good manners are good manners, but we can't let them get in the way of *efficiency*, now can we?"

Y ou're joking!" Sir Taryl Lektor, the Earl of Tartarian, stared at Sir Rysel Gahrvai. "Tell me you're joking—*please!*"

"Is this my 'Oh, I'm so funny' face?" Sir Rysel, also known as the Earl of Anvil Rock and the head of Prince Daivyn Daykyn's Regency Council, shot back.

"Sweet Bédard." Tartarian dropped into his normal chair at the long, heavy council table, staring at Anvil Rock while his racing thoughts tried to process the information.

The earl was a strong-minded, unflappable individual. Anvil Rock had been given ample proof of that over the last tumultuous few years, especially since Prince Hektor's death had forced them into their present roles as his son's official regents in a princedom occupied by the empire most of Hektor's subjects were convinced had hired his murder. Tartarian was Corisande's senior admiral—or had been, when Corisande had possessed a navy—and he'd been Anvil Rock's closest ally in holding the princedom together. In many ways, Anvil Rock knew, his friend was actually more mentally flexible than he himself was, and he'd come to rely upon the other earl's resilience almost as much as he did upon his integrity.

Not that resilience was the very first word which would have occurred to anyone looking at his current expression. Despite the gravity of the news, a tiny part of Anvil Rock took a certain satisfaction in seeing Tartarian look just as flabbergasted as he had been when the message arrived.

"What in Langhorne's name was Phylyp *thinking?*" Tartarian demanded.

"Well, according to his message, he was mostly thinking about keeping the boy—and Irys—*alive*," Anvil Rock replied. Tartarian looked at him sharply, and Anvil Rock scowled, sliding into his own chair at the head of the table. "Oh, come on, Taryl! You and I both know—in fact, we've known from the beginning, however long it took us to admit it to one another— that Cayleb Ahrmahk never had Hektor murdered! Obviously, Phylyp's come to the same conclusion, and according to his message, Clyntahn was preparing to have Daivyn and Irys murdered as well. And for exactly the same reasons."

His voice turned hard, almost as cold as his expression, with the last six words, and his eyes held Tartarian's across the table. Tartarian looked back for a second or two, then nodded.

"I know," he said, explicitly admitting something the two of them had been taking for granted in the privacy of their own thoughts for a long, long time.

Emperor Cayleb's analysis of all of the reasons he'd had for not killing Hektor had been convincing, yet the suspicion had lingered that just perhaps Empress Sharleyan might have arranged it without ever mentioning it to her husband. That notion had been knocked firmly on the head for both of them during Sharleyan's own visit to Corisande the previous year, however, and it had been making steady headway through the rest of Hektor's subjects since then. Acceptance of Cayleb and Sharleyan's innocence was still far from universal, especially given the fact that the princedom remained under Charisian occupation, however lenient that occupation might attempt to make itself, but the change since the days immediately after Hektor's murder was dramatic. And quite a few other Corisandians had been drawing the same conclusion Tartarian and Anvil Rock had drawn about who else might have had their prince and his heir assassinated. It was producing an interesting quandary for the Temple Loyalists, who'd managed rather effectively to use resentment over Hektor's murder to bolster loyalty to "the Old Church" in the face of the Reformists' slowly but steadily growing numbers. What had helped them in the past was beginning to hurt them now, and if Coris had anything remotely like proof that Clyntahn had now ordered Irys and Daivyn's murders . . . .

"I assume he told you something more than simply that he was taking the children and running by Tellesberg for a friendly visit?" Tartarian said after a moment in a voice much closer to normal.

"As a matter of fact, he did." Anvil Rock leaned back, one hand toying with the hilt of his dagger. "I'll get you the entire dispatch to read for yourself, of course. The entire Council's going to need copies, as soon as I can get them made, but some of its information has more to do with how Phylyp came to his conclusions than I'd care for the rest of them to know at this time."

"What sort of information?" Tartarian's eyes narrowed, and Anvil Rock shrugged.

"Oh, the fact that he's had a double agent planted on Wyllym Rayno for years, for example. In fact, it was *Hektor* who planted the man on the Inquisition even before he inherited the throne himself. I think that's one tidbit we might keep to ourselves. I don't think it would bother North Coast too much, but I'm not so sure about Airyth, and I think Margo might still have some . . . issues about it."

Tartarian nodded. Sir Bairmon Chahlmair, the Duke of Margo, had been a political ally of the Earl of Craggy Hill, and as Prince Daivyn's distant cousin, he probably had a better claim to the throne than anyone else currently in Corisande. There was no evidence he'd been part of Craggy Hill's Northern Conspiracy, though, nor had he ever given any sign of cherishing designs upon the throne. That didn't mean the man responsible for protecting that throne could afford to assume he *didn't* cherish those designs, however, and Margo was clearly less than comfortable with Corisande's new Reformist church hierarchy. For that matter, so was Trumyn Sowthmyn, the Earl of Airyth. Neither Tartarian nor Anvil Rock doubted Airyth's loyalty to Prince Daivyn for a moment, but he was almost as uncomfortable as Margo where Reformism's steady spread was concerned. The thought that Earl Coris had been spying upon the Inquisition probably wouldn't sit as well with either of them as it might with others, no matter what his spy might have reported . . . or prevented.

"You may have a point," Tartarian conceded. "I agree there's no need to find out at this point, at any rate." He smiled thinly. "If Phylyp actually manages to get home, we can always let him explain it in person."

"Or *not* explain it," Anvil Rock agreed. "But the rest of his message is actually fairly straightforward. It reads like a really bad novel, you understand, but it *is* straightforward. When he found out Clyntahn was planning to have Daivyn and Irys killed—probably, he says, because there wasn't enough resistance to Charis here in Corisande to make the pig happy—there was only one place left to run." He grimaced. "I'm inclined to think he was right about Clyntahn's reasoning."

"I imagine he was." Tartarian nodded. "Not that we had a lot of choice about cooperating. On the other hand, no matter what we'd done, the same idea would've occurred to a man like Clyntahn eventually." He shrugged. "What possible drawback could there be to the murder of a ten-year-old boy and his sister, after all?"

"None that I can think of." Anvil Rock's expression was as disgusted as Tartarian's. "Phylyp couldn't see one from Clyntahn's perspective, either, and he's always been the sort of fellow who likes to lay out sheet anchors well ahead of time. Apparently he'd been in correspondence with Earl Gray Harbor well before he got confirmation Clyntahn had decided to act. And—you'll *love* this part, Taryl!—before those frigging fanatics murdered him, Gray Harbor sent one of *Seijin* Merlin's friends to . . . discuss the details of exactly how the heir to the Corisandian throne might 'escape' into the safety of Charisian custody. And then, Cayleb and Pine Hollow sent Merlin himself to orchestrate the escape!" He smiled at Tartarian's expression, but then his expression sobered. "From what Phylyp had to say, it was a damned good thing Merlin was there, too. Without him—and, I might add, without the assistance of the Imperial Charisian Navy and the personal services of the Duke of Darcos—none of them would've gotten out of Delferahk alive."

"It sounds like all that is going to make fascinating reading," Tartarian said. "And you're right, it's exactly like Phylyp, and it proves he hasn't lost his touch. Or his instincts. I doubt he was happy at the thought of asking Charis for help, but given the nature of the prize, he had to know Gray Harbor would jump at the chance. And pull out all the stops, too." It was his turn to smile with sardonic amusement. "I could point out that losing them after agreeing to help them 'escape' would've been absolutely disastrous from Cayleb and Sharleyan's viewpoint. If I were inclined to point out cynical, calculating political realities, that is."

"Of course you could. And the same thought occurred to me. None of which changes the fact that the only reasons either of them is still alive are *Seijin* Merlin, Cayleb, and Sharleyan. That gives them a certain degree of leverage with me, at least."

"And with me," Tartarian agreed. "Still, it does raise the question of exactly what Cayleb and Sharleyan will do with them now they're safely out of Delferahk, doesn't it?"

"Oh, indeed it does." Anvil Rock showed his teeth. "Thanks to Phylyp we have at least a bit of a head start, but I'll be very surprised if there's not a message—an *official* message, I mean—from Tellesberg arriving shortly. And I don't think someone like Cayleb or Sharleyan is likely to overlook just how much additional 'leverage' this is going to give them with the rest of Corisande, either."

"Well, if *they* should suddenly have turned into drooling idiots, I'm sure Pine Hollow hasn't. For that matter, Staynair's a pretty smart fellow—and one who understands mercy can be a much deadlier weapon than any amount of bloodthirsty terror. And then, let's not forget the redoubtable *Seijin* Merlin. 'Official' adviser or not, he's probably got more influence with them than all their official councilors combined! They go out of their way to hide it in public, but he's always there, and I couldn't help noticing the way both of them keep the corner of one eye on him no matter who else they're talking to. And then there's that *seijin* spy ring he seems to have going in every corner of the world." Tartarian shook his head. "They *listen* to that man, Rysel. He never seems to put himself forward, never seems to intrude, but they trust him to do one hell of a lot more than just keep them alive, and I don't blame them one damned bit, given the quality of advice he seems to offer."

"I noticed that myself," Anvil Rock agreed, then he straightened in the massive wooden chair and inhaled deeply. "I noticed that," he repeated, "and between you and me, I think it's a good thing they do. And, also between you and me," he met his friend's eyes levelly, "I've never been happier to hear anything in my life then the news that Daivyn and Irys are safely clapped into durance vile in Charisian hands instead of being honored guests of King Zhames."

"You and me both. Of course, it does lead to the interesting question of how the Regency Council goes about announcing this to the Princedom. And, of course, the minor matter of what our official position on requesting Daivyn's return to Corisande might happen to be."

"Both excellent points, and decisions which have to involve the Council as a whole."

"Oh, I *know* that. But don't you think it might be a good idea for the two of us to go ahead and decide what the 'Council as a whole' is going to decide after we get done explaining its choice—you did notice I said 'choice,' as in the singular form of the noun?—to it?"

"You're entirely too cynical sometimes, Taryl," Anvil Rock said severely, and Tartarian snorted.

"Not cynical, pragmatic," he shot back. "And you know this situation's far too tricky to let it bog down in too much debate."

"True." Anvil Rock pursed his lips thoughtfully for several seconds, then raised his eyebrows. "Since we're alone, there's no point pretending you're not the brains of the team. What do *you* think we should be doing?"

Tartarian chuckled and shook his head. There was some truth to Anvil Rock's statement—Tartarian did tend to be more mentally agile—but there was nothing at all wrong with Anvil Rock's brain. It was more a case of the tenacity with which he focused on the task at hand narrowing his vision until alternate possibilities could slip past him unnoted.

"Well, I think we should get Koryn and Charlz in here and listen to their advice before we make any hard and fast decisions," Tartarian said after a moment. Sir Koryn Gahrvai, Anvil Rock's son, commanded the new model Corisandian Army responsible for maintaining domestic order . . . under, of course, the supervision of General Sir Zhoel Zhanstyn, who'd replaced Hauwyl Chermyn as the Charisian viceroy in Corisande when Chermyn assumed the title of Grand Duke of Zebediah. And Sir Charlz Doyal, his chief of staff, doubled as the Regency Council's effective chief intelligence officer.

"If anyone has a feel for how the Princedom's likely to react to this, it's them," Anvil Rock agreed. "I think we need to bring in Archbishop Klairmant, too."

"Not until after we talk to Koryn and Charlz, though," Tartarian said quickly, then grimaced as Anvil Rock looked a question at him. "I trust Klairmant as much as I trust anyone in this world, Rysel, but he's already riding a restive horse. You know how much more ground the Reformists have been making ever since Staynair's visit and—especially!—Sharleyan's. I'd trust him to give us the best advice he has, but, frankly, this is more a political than a religious decision. Oh, it has enough religious *implications* to sink a galleon, but the actual decision belongs to the Council, and he's not on it. And the reason he's not was specifically to insulate the Church from these sorts of decisions. I suspect there's going to be a lot of uncertainty—and a lot of renewed questions—in most people's minds now that Daivyn's actually in Charisian custody, however he got there, and it's likely to have all sorts of impacts on that truce Klairmant's been maintaining between the Reformists and the Loyalists. I just think it would be a lot better if he can honestly say he wasn't consulted ahead of time about any *political* decisions we and the rest of the Council may take."

"You may have a point there," Anvil Rock conceded after a moment, his expression thoughtful. "In fact, I think you do. And I've already sent for Koryn and Charlz, but they're out supervising a field exercise. It'll take them a while to get here, and I'd still like to hear your current thinking while we wait."

"All right."

Tartarian got out of his chair, folded his hands behind him, and crossed to one of the council chamber's windows to look out over the sun-drenched landscaping of the palace courtyard. He stood that way for quite a few seconds before he turned back to his friend and fellow councilor.

"I think we have to be cautious," he said seriously. "If we don't seek Daivyn's return to Corisandian soil, we'll provide fresh fodder for the anti-Charis hotheads, and Langhorne knows there are still plenty of them left, even after Sharleyan's visit. On the other hand, she and Cayleb are going to be very cautious about letting the two of them come home, for a lot of reasons. And if they *do* let them return home, how much freedom of action will Daivyn—and his Regency Council—truly have? Turning him into their puppet here in Corisande could have all sorts of downsides from their perspective, including validating the anti-Charis element's suspicions, but they'd be fools to let him return without at least *some* binding restrictions. Yet by the same token, if they *refuse* to let him come home—especially if we press them on the issue—the consequences could be even worse. At that point, the people who're already inclined to distrust them and their lackeys—that would be *us*, Rysel—will declare that they didn't really rescue him and Irys at all, no matter what that corrupt, nefarious spymaster Coris or their other lackeys here in Manchyr may claim. Instead, the sinister *Seijin* Merlin and his agents *kidnapped* them, snatching them out of the safety of their kinsman's custody for the sole purpose of using him as a tool here in Corisande."

"Which is what *Clyntahn's* going to say, whatever we do," High Rock pointed out.

"I'm less concerned about that asshole than I am about people closer to home." Tartarian's tone was harsh and his eyes had gone cold. "When he sent his frigging Rakurai into Corisande and killed eight hundred people right here in Manchyr, I decided once and for all which side I'm on, as far as the Church is concerned, Rysel. And don't pretend you didn't do exactly the same thing! I know better, and Koryn's even further into the Reformist camp than you are!"

Anvil Rock looked back at him without speaking. Silence hovered for several heartbeats, and then Tartarian shrugged.

"At any rate," he continued in a lighter tone, "I'm more concerned about the effect on people close enough to make their . . . displeasure immediately evident. Trust in Clyntahn's veracity's taken a serious hit here in Corisande even among a lot of the Loyalists and even before we make Phylyp's letter public; as long as we can avoid doing anything that would tend to support Clyntahn's version of events, I don't really expect his fulminations from Zion to have much effect. The people who still trust him will take them as coming straight from the *Writ* no matter what we say, but they're already so firmly in the anti-Charis—and anti–Regency Council—column that it won't make any difference to the overall situation. It's the ones with open minds we have to worry about, and that means coming up with a way to help this whole hairy mess land as softly as possible."

"So you think we *shouldn't* press them for his return?"

"I think we should buy some time by sending messages asking about his and Irys' health, asking for assurances of their physical safety, and asking for the two of them to be allowed to communicate directly with us." Tartarian turned back to the window. "That would be the natural first step no matter what, and the sailing time between us and Tellesberg will work in our favor. We publish the glad news of their safety to the Princedom as a whole, and we also publish copies of our letters to them and to Cayleb and Sharleyan to show our concern and demonstrate we're pushing to regularize the situation. And I think we should also publish a copy of the Council's renewed oath of loyalty to Daivyn as rightful Prince of Corisande, witnessed by Klairmant for Mother Church. It would only be appropriate for us to renew the oaths we took in his name now that he's out of Church custody . . . and it would also be a way for us to demonstrate our loyalty is to *him*— which means to Corisande—first and foremost."

"All right." Anvil Rock nodded. "All of that makes sense. But after we send all that and, presumably, get a response?"

"A lot will depend on what Cayleb and Sharleyan indicate they're willing to consider. I'm sure they're both more than bright enough to realize how important it will be for us to have some guidance into what they're thinking before we start proclaiming any public positions of our own. At the moment, I'm inclined to think the next step for us would probably be to ask for Daivyn's return, though. The phrasing of both the peace treaty and our oaths as councilors gives Cayleb and Sharleyan a certain amount of wiggle room in this instance, but they have recognized him as Duke of Manchyr and as Hektor's legitimate heir to the crown. There are all sorts of stipulations in there about what he'll have to do to be allowed to *assume* the crown, but there's no question of his claim to it. So I think we can approach this with an air of calm, even courtesy, by couching our requests at least initially as a request for clarification on how Charis interprets those stipulations. If we work it right—and I think that's going to include being as public as we can in our messages, publishing our correspondence as broadly as possible, at least on this point—we can spend as much as two years in civil, rational discussion. We can make our loyalty to Daivyn crystal clear, and we can let Cayleb and Sharleyan demonstrate their own reasonableness in the form of their replies and willingness to discuss things with us. Assuming they're smart enough to see what we're doing, the process should give us quite a lot of time for temperatures to cool."

"And if, after we do all that, Daivyn and Irys refuse to cooperate with Charis—or, for that matter, if it appears to *us* that they're being constrained or that Cayleb and Sharleyan have decided to deny him the crown after all?" Anvil Rock asked softly.

"In that case, we're all in a hell of a mess," Tartarian replied, equally softly. "I doubt Daivyn and Irys would be in any *physical* danger, even then, but if it looks to our people here in Corisande like they might be—or if enough of our people decide Cayleb and Sharleyan *aren't* going to let Daivyn take the crown, no matter what they may've promised—I have no idea how they'll react. The one thing I am afraid of, though, is that in a situation like that one, what might happen could just make what Craggy Hill, Storm Keep, and the others tried look like a children's birthday party."

.XIII.
HMS *Chihiro*, 50,
Gorath Bay,
City of Gorath,
Kingdom of Dohlar

What do *you* think of the new weapons, Stywyrt?"

The Earl of Thirsk tipped back in his chair. The cabin skylight was open, and voices floated down from the quarterdeck as Haarahld Bradlai, *Chihiro*'s third lieutenant, put the topmen through sail drill. It was a familiar, homey sound for any seaman, Thirsk reflected, and the quarter windows were open as well. Combined with the wind scoop rigged to the skylight, they created a gentle breeze, and fresh air stirred throughout his cabin. It plucked at the corners of the notes paper-weighted down on his blotter, and he inhaled deeply, smelling the familiar scents of harbor water, tar, and timbers. Among those gently flapping notes were the diagrams of the newly approved artillery shells and fuses the Navy and Army of God were putting into production in the far-off Temple Lands. They'd be going into production quite soon in Dohlar, as well, and his index finger tapped one of the drawings as he looked across at his flag captain.

"I'm glad we'll have them, too, My Lord . . . I suppose," Captain Stywyrt Baiket replied after a moment. Then he made a face. "Mind you, I'd just as soon *nobody* had them, judging from the reports out of Iythria. Since we can't take them away from the damned Charisians, though, I'm a lot happier now that we can at least respond in kind."

Baiket, Thirsk had noticed, had fallen into his own bad habits. He seldom referred to Charisians as "heretics" any longer—probably because, like his admiral, *Chihiro's* commanding officer felt personally dirtied by what had happened to Gwylym Manthyr and the other Charisians who'd surrendered to the Royal Dohlaran Navy, trusting in its honor. Of course, his flag captain's rot could go deeper than that, as well. God knew it did among all too many of the navy's personnel, he thought sardonically. Reformism was dangerous to one's health in any of the mainland realms, yet it was making a sort of creeping progress anyway, and Dohlar was no exception. Personally, Thirsk thought that was largely a response to the Inquisition's brutality. The *Writ* might specify the Punishment of Schueler for heresy, but it was hard for good men and women to watch it happen, whatever God might demand of them.

And it's harder still when deep inside so many of them are beginning to wonder if perhaps, just perhaps, the Charisians've been right about Clyntahn all along, he thought. *Especially when the Church of Charis specifically renounces the Punishment and permits Temple Loyalists to maintain their own churches, even in the middle of Tellesberg itself. Not to mention when they listen to the difference between what Clyntahn and someone like Maikel Staynair has to say.*

He didn't know if Baiket was one of the Dohlarans beginning to read the printed broadsides which, despite the Inquisition's best efforts, continued to appear mysteriously on walls in most of Dohlar's major cities—the ones which regularly quoted sermons by the heretical archbishop—and he'd made it a point not to find out. He wouldn't have been too terribly surprised if the answer had been yes, however.

"I think I agree with you," he said now, running his finger across the diagram's neat lines and frowning. "It was bad enough when Charis introduced the new model artillery. Langhorne!" He shook his head, recalling the terror of thundering broadsides off the coast of Armageddon Reef. "I thought it couldn't get any worse. But now . . . ."

He allowed his voice to trail off and shook his head. The reports they'd received about Iythria had obviously been heavily edited, which struck him as a particularly foolish thing to be doing at a time like this. He understood all the arguments about preventing moral and spiritual corruption, but surely it was more important than ever that Mother Church's commanders knew the truth about the weapons they faced! If they didn't, how were they supposed to fight her enemies effectively? And how was any officer, be he ever so loyal, supposed to believe the information he *was* allowed to see was truthful and accurate when so much else obviously was not? And how was that same officer supposed to know what vital bit of information might have been left out in the editing process by clerics who simply weren't equipped by training or experience to recognize its importance? But they'd edited his own reports after the Battle of Armageddon Reef and Crag Hook, and they'd done the same thing after the Battle of the Gulf of Tarot, so it hadn't really surprised him when they did it again in Iythria's case.

He didn't for a minute believe the allegations of cowardice and treason leveled against Baron Jahras and Duke Kholman, however. They wouldn't have suffered the casualties they'd suffered if they'd just rolled over and supinely surrendered the way the official report insisted they had. And after they'd surrendered, "deserting" to Charis—and getting their families out of the Inquisition's reach—had been their only real option. Still, he expected most of the actual information about the Charisians' weapons was relatively accurate. That would certainly explain the casualties Jahras had suffered before his ships began surrendering, at any rate, and that part of the report made grim reading for the commander of the last battle-worthy fleet Mother Church possessed.

On the other hand, there's battle-worthy, and then there's battle-worthy, he thought with mordant humor. *Generally speaking, the term does normally connote an ability to meet the enemy in something like reasonably equal numbers with at least some chance of beating him, after all.*

"I think the one thing we can count on, My Lord, is that things are going to go right on getting worse." Baiket's tone was bleak. "That's what's happened for the last four or five years, and I don't see any sign of its slowing down anytime soon. And with this business in the Republic now, we're going to be even more hard-pressed to keep the Navy ready to fight. Or even *intact*, for that matter!"

"Duke Fern assures me our funding and manpower priorities won't be changed," Thirsk replied. Their gazes met, and Thirsk was hard-put not to snort as he recognized the matching skepticism in the flag captain's eyes.

"Nonetheless," he continued in an admirably steady tone, almost as if he actually believed a word of what he'd just said, "it would be ridiculous to assume there aren't going to be consequences where any *improvements* to the fleet are concerned."

And Thorast *sure as Shan-wei isn't going to try to stop it from happening, either,* he added in the privacy of his own thoughts.

Aibram Zaivyair, the Duke of Thorast, might officially be in charge of King Rahnyld's navy, but like the vast majority of that navy's senior officers—up until the Battle of Armageddon Reef, at least—he was actually an army officer. As such, he'd never really been sympathetic to the navy's claims whenever they seemed to conflict with those of the army. And given the fact that Thirsk had been right when Thorast's brother-in-law, Duke Malikai, had completely ignored Thirsk's advice and sailed the entire navy into disaster, the more *Thirsk* argued for a sane naval policy, the less likely Thorast was to listen. Only the Duke of Fern's unremitting pressure had forced Thorast to tolerate Thirsk's reforms at all, and not even the kingdom's first councilor could prevent him from dragging his feet every step of the way. Or from seizing any remotely plausible excuse for favoring any of Thirsk's rivals, whether in or out of the navy.

At the moment, Langhorne knew Thorast was in a position to find any number of excuses to do just that. Nor did it help that Shain Hauwyl, the Duke of Salthar, who commanded the Royal Army in Rahnyld VII's name, had picked Sir Rainos Ahlverez to command the army massing even now to invade the Republic. Ahlverez was the deceased Duke Malikai's first cousin, and while he was demonstrably smarter than his cousin had been, that wasn't really saying much. Malikai could have made *anyone* look smarter by simply opening his mouth in the same room with him. And, smarter or not, Rainos wasn't about to let anything as trivial as rationality get in the way of his hatred for his cousin's "betrayer." He could be expected to fight tooth and nail for every man, every musket, and every artillery piece he could get, not simply because he legitimately needed them, or despite the fact that it would take those same resources away from the navy, but *because* it would take them away from the navy . . . and its commander.

"I suppose that's inevitable, My Lord," Baiket agreed. "Have you heard anything more about when the Army's going to be ready to march?"

"Not officially, no. I imagine a lot of it depends on the weather, and judging from reports of how badly the Republic's food supplies've been hit, logistics are going to be a nightmare. I'm no general, but when the civilians along your route are already starving, it seems unlikely you'll be able to forage for much in the way of supplies, which means hauling everything your troops are going to eat along with you as you go, and there are only so many canals and rivers." Thirsk shrugged, his expression grim. "I know we're being told to plan to expect a major supply lift through the Gulf of Tanshar to Dairnyth, and the Army's already gathering galleons and coasters to carry it out. That's going to have its own implications for us, I'm sure. After all, if *I* were the Charisians and I found out about it, I'd probably try to make our lives difficult as soon as I could."

"Wonderful." Baiket shook his head. "Is there any chance we're going to have enough of these . . . 'shells'"—he used the new term carefully—"before that happens? Just in case the Charisians, who obviously *do* have them, should decide to be as difficult as you'd be in their place, My Lord, you understand."

"I think that's . . . unlikely," Thirsk replied.

In fact, the army had been promised priority on the new ammunition as soon as it became available. In theory, at least, the first shipments of shells would be arriving from the Temple Lands within the next month, and the foundries which had been producing naval artillery were already turning out the first new fieldpieces to make use of them. He couldn't deny that, in many ways, that was a sensible provision on someone's part, since the army was obviously going to need the new weapons in the next few months, whereas the navy was halfway around the world from the Charisians. Unfortunately, the Imperial Charisian Navy had already proven it was perfectly capable of—and willing to—operate halfway around the world. And, as it had proven in the Gulf of Jahras, its most recent improvements to its already fiendishly effective artillery meant it would be able to hit with devastating power if it should decide to extend the same treatment to Gorath Bay. Admittedly, the Gulf of Dohlar provided a far greater degree of defensive depth to Gorath than the Gulf of Jahras had provided for the city of Iythria, but Thirsk was grimly certain an adversary like Cayleb Ahrmahk would send his navy wherever he thought it *needed* to be sent, regardless of the difficulties involved.

Despite which, given King Rahnyld's unambiguous orders to support the Temple Loyalists in Siddarmark against the lord protector—and Rainos Ahlverez' and the Duke of Thorast's attitudes towards one Lywys Gardynyr—it wasn't just *unlikely* the navy would be seeing the new ammunition even after the army's needs had been met. The only good news was his confidence that he could rely on Bishop Staiphan Maik to support his efforts to get the output of shells from at least one of the navy's own foundries diverted to his fleet. It wouldn't be much, even if they succeeded, but at least it would offer *some* chance to get a trickle of the new projectiles into his men's hands so they could begin training with them. And to give his navy the opportunity to inflict at least some losses on the Imperial Charisian Navy if it should come calling during his efforts to supply the army through the Gulf of Transhar.

I'm sure even Thorast would approve of my managing that much, he thought grimly. *Or maybe not.* That *bastard would probably be perfectly* happy *to see the Army starve—and pillage the people it's supposed to be protecting just to survive—if he got to put my head on a stick for "failing to support" Ahlverez' needs properly!*

"I believe in miracles, My Lord," Baiket said, "but I hope His Majesty's ministers are remembering the archangels help those who help *themselves.*"

The flag captain's voice had taken on a dangerously pointed tone, and Thirsk gave him a cautioning glance. After a moment, Baiket inhaled deeply and sat back in his chair.

"Well, at least once we *do* get shells of our own, we'll be able to respond to the Charisians in kind." He grimaced. "It sounds like it's going to be a damned bloodbath no matter what we do, My Lord, so I suppose the best we can hope for is to make it just as bad a bloodbath for the other side."

"In some ways, that's how it's always been," Thirsk replied. "Not that I don't take your point, Stywyrt," he added, remembering a conversation of his own with Bishop Staiphan. "I don't really like to think about it this way," he went on, "but if we could count on exchanging losses on an equal basis with the Charisians, or even on a two-to-one basis in *their* favor, we'd win in the end simply because we've got more bodies to throw at them. Unfortunately, that's a formula that works better for armies on land than it does for navies at sea, because we've got to build the damned ships as well."

"I hope you won't mind me saying this, My Lord, but that's not the way you've been teaching us to win battles."

"No, but unless we can figure out some way to successfully protect a ship against these new explosive shells, sea battles are going to turn into mutual suicide pacts. Oh, I'm not going to give up on the theory that with proper tactics you can still mass fire and eliminate enemy units faster than they can eliminate yours, but it's going to be like fighting a duel at twenty paces with carronades loaded with grapeshot."

"*There's* a mental image I could've done without, My Lord," Baiket said dryly.

"I'm not enamored of it myself, Stywyrt. And I may be being overly pessimistic, but I don't really think so. Not judging by the reports from Iythria. I think it's going to be a matter of the fellow who fires first winning, since right at this moment I don't really see any way to *effectively* protect a galleon against shellfire."

"That idea of draping chains to protect the sides of the hull sounded to me as if it had some promise, My Lord."

"It probably does, but there's only so much anchor chain to go around. I've had Ahlvyn and Ahbail out canvassing every ship and every warehouse on the waterfront, and it seems a lot of *old* anchor chains've been melted down to make *guns* out of these days." The earl grimaced a smile at his flag captain. "And looking at these diagrams," he tapped the sketch on his desk again, "I'm less confident than I was about their stopping a shell with walls this thick at short ranges, anyway. It looks like it's going to be heavier and hit with more force than I'd expected when I came up with the notion. I still think it'll help, possibly a great deal, but we're still looking for a better option, too."

"I see, My Lord. Well—"

The sentry outside Thirsk's quarters thumped the butt of his musket on the deck.

"Commander Khapahr to see the Admiral!" he announced, and Paiair Sahbrahan, Thirsk's valet, emerged from his cubbyhole to scurry over and open the door.

"Forgive me for interrupting, My Lord," Commander Ahlvyn Khapahr said, following Sahbrahan into the day cabin and coming to attention with his hat clasped under his arm. He was about thirty, dark-haired and complexioned, with a luxurious mustache. He was also a very smart young officer, in Thirsk's opinion, which was how he'd come to hold the position which would have been called chief of staff back on Old Earth . . . or in the Imperial Charisian Navy. He was accompanied by another officer, one Thirsk had never seen before, in a lieutenant's uniform.

"I knew you were going to be speaking with the Captain about the new weapons," Khapahr continued, "and I thought I should bring Lieutenant Zhwaigair here to your attention while you're doing it."

"Indeed?" Thirsk sat back in his chair, resting his elbows on the chair arms, and regarded Zhwaigair thoughtfully.

Lieutenant Zhwaigair was even younger than Khapahr—indeed, he was probably younger than Sir Ahbail Bahrdailahn, Thirsk's flag lieutenant—with fair hair and eyes that hovered between hazel and brown. He was a well-muscled fellow, and quite tall; he had to stand with hunched shoulders and a bent neck to clear the deckhead without cracking his skull. Thirsk was a much shorter man, and he felt a pang of sympathy as he imagined how many self-inflicted headaches Zhwaigair must have enjoyed aboard ship.

"And why did you think you should bring the Lieutenant to my attention, Ahlvyn?" he asked mildly.

"Because he has an idea. It sounds pretty ridiculous at first, and I'll admit I wasn't particularly interested when he brought it to my attention this morning, In fact, I was distinctly *not* interested, but he's a persistent sort, and since you had me inventorying those elusive, vanishing anchor chains, I decided I was, ah, willing to lay aside my vital labors long enough to hear him out." The commander smiled at his superior, but then his expression sobered. "As it turns out, I'm glad I did. As I say, it sounded ridiculous when he started, but what he had to say actually began to make sense when I listened to it. A *lot* of sense, in fact, I think."

Zhwaigair looked distinctly nervous. Unless Thirsk was mistaken, though, most of that nervousness came from finding himself face-to-face with an admiral, not from any doubt over whatever bizarre idea he might have in mind. Those oddly colored eyes were too level and steady for a man who felt *uncertainty.*

"All right." The earl waved one hand in an inviting gesture. "Why don't you go ahead and tell me about this idea of yours, Lieutenant Zhwaigair?"

"I've actually taken the liberty of asking the Lieutenant to bring along some sketches of his proposal, My Lord," Khapahr put in, beckoning at the heavy envelope under Zhwaigair's right elbow.

"And I'll be delighted to look at them . . . probably," Thirsk said pleasantly. "First, however, let's hear the Lieutenant explain it to me. After all," he smiled, "if it turns out to be a good idea, *I'm* likely to find myself explaining it to quite a few people who aren't going to be interested in looking at sketches and diagrams. Perhaps I can pick up a few pointers from the Lieutenant that will help me impress them if that happens."

Zhwaigair flinched ever so slightly before the earl's smile, but his eyes met Thirsk's steadily, and the admiral noted that steadiness with approval.

"Very well, My Lord," Zhwaigair's voice was deeply resonant, despite his youth. "What I've actually been thinking about are the rumors about what happened at Iythria and what we might do, if it turned out they were accurate, to improve our own chances against the heretics. I haven't had access to any of the official reports, but from what I've heard it seems evident the heretics've found a way to make their round shot explode. I'm assuming that means they've found a way to put a charge of powder inside a hollowed-out shot and somehow convince it to explode after it hits its target, which strikes me as a bit more of a challenge than some people might think." He grimaced quickly. "My family's been foundry workers since my great-grandfather's day, My Lord," he explained, "and I spent five years apprenticed to my Uncle Thomys before I joined the Navy. In fact, that's why Admiral Tyrnyr assigned me to help develop the new gun carriages and mountings. So I suspect I have a better notion than most people would of some of the difficulties the heretics must've faced in making hollow, exploding shot work, especially when it came to making them explode reliably and consistently. At any rate, though, those are the stories I've heard, and I've heard some . . . additional rumors"—he seemed to be picking his words carefully, Thirsk noticed—"that it may be possible for *us* to . . . acquire the same sort of ammunition."

The last six words came out in a slight but clearly discernible questioning tone, and Thirsk regarded him thoughtfully. No one had expressly told him the information about the new ammunition was to be kept secret, and it was unlikely any Charisian spies were going to be able to run all the way to Tellesberg from Gorath Bay to tell Cayleb Ahrmahk about it before its existence was demonstrated in combat. Of the other hand, no one had told him he *could* start waving around the reports, either.

"I think, Lieutenant," he said after a moment, "that you should probably assume that if one set of rumors was accurate, there's probably also at least *some* accuracy to the other. Could I ask exactly how this relates to whatever this idea of yours is?"

"Well, My Lord, it occurred to me that if the rumors were true, each hit was going to become much more dangerous. Put another way, it's going to take a lot less hits to beat a ship into surrender—or even destroy it outright—which means it's going to be more important to shoot accurately and actually *hit* an opponent—consistently, I mean—than it is to simply line up a lot of guns and blaze away in hopes at least some of your shots will find the enemy."

"I'd say that's not unreasonable . . . with"—Thirsk's tone was desert-dry—"the minor caveat that my experience has been that the more rounds you fire, the greater your chance that you *will* score a hit."

"Agreed, My Lord. Certainly." Zhwaigair nodded, acknowledging the point yet clearly unfazed by the earl's irony. "But there are other factors than simply the number of guns. For example, how well trained your gunners are, how inherently accurate their weapons are, how big their target is, how steady your gun platform is, and perhaps most importantly of all, especially if both sides are using exploding shot, how readily you can maneuver your ship to give *your* gunners the best chance of hitting while giving the *other* fellow's gunners the worst possible chance of hitting you in return. Or, that would seem to be the case to me, at any rate."

"I can't argue with any of that, either," Thirsk agreed, steepling his fingers beneath his chin while he wondered where the lieutenant might be taking all this.

"Well, when I'd gotten that far, My Lord, it occurred to me there might be ways to make those other factors work for us. For example, I suspect that with a longer barrel, bored to tighter tolerances, we could considerably increase accuracy at extended ranges. With more time for the shot to accelerate before it leaves the muzzle, we'd probably get a flatter, more accurate trajectory even at closer ranges, but more importantly, the longer the range at which you can begin reliably hitting your opponent, the better, especially if he can't match the range with his own weapons. In fact, I've had another thought, based on the new rifled muskets. If it's truly possible to fire exploding shot out of a cannon, then it seems to me it would be worthwhile to consider whether or not it would be possible to rifle the *cannon* the same way we're rifling muskets now. That wouldn't simply increase accuracy, either; like lengthening the gun tube, it would probably extend the piece's maximum range well beyond what a smoothbore can achieve, since a rifled projectile would have to have less windage, which ought to mean more of the force of the gunpowder could be trapped behind it before it leaves the gun."

Thirsk's eyes widened, and he darted a quick look at Baiket, whose expression looked as surprised by the suggestion's audacity as the earl felt. And especially, Thirsk realized an instant later, by the realization that what Zhwaigair had just suggested *had* to be possible. Perhaps not simple, and not easy, but clearly if a *musket ball* could be rifled, then so could an exploding artillery shell. It was simply a matter of scale, after all. And if an exploding shell *could* be rifled—

"It also occurred to me," Zhwaigair went on, apparently oblivious to Thirsk's surprise, "that since one gun, firing exploding shot, will undoubtedly be able to do the work of *many* guns firing solid shot, it might be worthwhile to think about ways in which we could bring our guns to bear while presenting the enemy with the smallest possible target, even if that meant a reduction in the total number of guns we could bring to bear. I suppose what I'm trying to say is that what matters is the ratio of *hits*, not the ratio of *guns*, and that a bigger exploding shot is probably going to do much more damage than a smaller exploding shot, since the bigger shot can carry a bigger charge of power with it. So anything that made our ships harder to hit would be worthwhile as long as we still managed to hit *them* reliably and consistently, with the biggest guns possible. And when I thought about that for a bit longer, it fitted rather neatly with another thought I'd had a year or so ago."

"And what thought would *that* have been, Lieutenant?" Thirsk asked intently, watching Zhwaigair through narrowed eyes, half frightened of where this remarkable young man might be about to go next.

"An alternative to the galleon, at least in coastal waters, My Lord." Zhwaigair smiled for the first time, wryly. "At the time, it seemed best to keep any such notions to myself, since you appeared to be having difficulties enough convincing the Navy we needed galleons for blue water without someone coming along and proposing a new style of galley, instead. But it did seem to me the galley still retained several advantages over the galleon, especially in coastal waters or river defense. It was far more maneuverable, for one thing, and much less dependent on wind conditions. Obviously, with the new broadside artillery arrangements the *traditional* galley wasn't practical any longer, but it seemed to me it might be useful to find a way to hang onto its advantages, if we could find a way that let us offset or eliminate it's *dis*advantages. So I came up with an idea I think would let us do that."

"You came up with *what*?" Baiket asked, startled into interrupting. He looked quickly at Thirsk, but the earl only waved his hand and kept his gaze on Zhwaigair.

"I really do need to show you one of my sketches to make this make sense, My Lord," the lieutenant said apologetically.

"Then bring it out, Lieutenant. You're beginning to interest me."

"Thank you, My Lord."

Zhwaigair opened his envelope and drew out a folded sheet of paper. He unfolded it on Thirsk's desk, and the earl's eyes turned even more intent as he gazed at it.

"The galley's two biggest disadvantages are endurance, since it's dependent on the backs and arms of its rowers, and, obviously, the need to use its entire broadside length for banks of oars, instead of guns. I couldn't see any way to get around the advantages sail and wind power offer in terms of endurance, no matter what we might change about the way we apply muscle power to movement, but it did seem to me there was a way to move the galley without oars."

Baiket scowled skeptically, but Thirsk only cocked his head and looked down at Zhwaigair's drawing. It was neatly done, with labels and arrows pointing to different parts of it, and the lieutenant traced it with his finger.

"As I said earlier, My Lord, my Uncle Thomys is an ironmaster in Bess," he said, "and this is something he came up with some years ago to improve the draft on his forging hearths. It's called a 'crankshaft' because, as you can see, that's basically what it is, and it's been used to power small machines for as long as anyone can remember. A lot of the bigger, dragon-drawn fire engines use something like this, too, although a lever pump's more common on horse-drawn engines, since it can be smaller and lighter. But the crankshaft lets the larger engines build much greater water pressure, since you can put a lot more men on it at once. The practice for larger foundry machines has normally been to use horses, or possibly mules or even donkeys, on a sakia gear if the power's going to be required for a lengthy period and there's no convenient water source available for a waterwheel.

"What Uncle Thomys did was come up with a crankshaft a lot longer than the ones we usually use—long enough he could put more workmen on it and generate a lot more power. A dozen or so of his men stand side by side in two lines with the crankshaft between them. Then, when he needs to increase the draft, they turn it, using these offset grips here and here. Actually, to be completely accurate, they're the 'cranks,' and the shaft is this long bit, here, that actually rotates. You can think of it as a really big version of a carpenter's brace and bit, if you like."

The lieutenant tapped the drawing, looking up to meet Thirsk's eyes.

"It's actually a remarkably efficient way to transfer energy, when you come down to it, My Lord. And while I was thinking about ways to make galleys better, I realized that if it were possible to connect a crankshaft like this to the same sort of . . . impeller or fan blade he uses in his hearth, there's no reason those blades couldn't be submerged, where they could push *water* instead of air. When you come down to it, that's all oars really do—push water, I mean—and anyone who's ever used a hand fan knows how much more efficiently a rotary fan pushes *air*. I imagine the same thing would be true of water, and if you had enough men on the crank, and if your impeller was big enough, it could actually move the galley without oars. Better yet, to work effectively, the crankshaft would have to be in the middle of the ship, just above the keel, which would put it below any gun-decks. In fact, it would be below the waterline, which would protect it from enemy shot. You'd have to change out the men on the crank at frequent intervals because of fatigue, of course, which is the main reason animal power's always been preferred if it has to be provided for extended periods. But my calculations suggest you'd need fewer men on the crank, assuming my assumptions about the relative efficiency of impellers and oars are ac-curate, than you'd need on the oars of a regular galley. In fact, it's even possible—I haven't tried to work out the numbers on this, you understand, My Lord, since I don't have any way to demonstrate how accurate my as-sumptions about impeller efficiency actually are—that it might be possible to install *two* crankshafts and two impellers in a single vessel. If that turned out to be possible, you might be able to increase your galley's speed quite a bit, at least in relatively short bursts. Endurance would still be a factor, but I can't think of any reason why you couldn't put masts and sails on it for cruising between engagements. We did that for years and years with tradi-tional galleys, and they only went to oars for maneuvering purposes or to enter battle. And with crankshafts and impellers, we wouldn't need to stack oardecks on top of each other, so we could probably build a less lofty, more weatherly galley with the same propulsive power."

"Langhorne," Thirsk said softly, looking at the drawing, trying to think of some reason why it *wouldn't* work.

"I've built a model, My Lord," Zhwaigair continued. "It's only a fifteen-footer, and I can only get four men on the crank at once, but it does work. On that scale, at any rate."

"I'll want to see it, Lieutenant," Thirsk told him, and Zhwaigair nodded.

"Of course, My Lord. I'll be honored to show it to you."

"And you said something about reducing target size, as well, I believe?" the earl continued, looking at him very intently indeed now.

"Yes, My Lord. It seemed to me that if the . . . crank galley, for want of a better term, was practical at all, it might be possible to build ships half the size, or even a third the size, of our present galleons—something a lot closer in size to our prewar galleys, or even a bit smaller—that could still be effective warships. They wouldn't be remotely as useful as galleons off soundings, but in *coastal* waters they could be very useful indeed. They'd be fast, small, much more maneuverable, and shallower draft. And, especially now, with exploding shot, smaller size might actually be an advantage in combat. If we mounted three or four guns in the bow, to fire straight ahead, and protected them with the thickest possible wooden bulwarks—possibly faced with some kind of iron plate or something like that to break up incoming shot, or at least keep them from penetrating—a handful of the heaviest possible guns would be capable of sinking the biggest galleon the heretics have with only a handful of hits. The idea would be to outmaneuver the heretics' galleons, staying out of their broadside firing arcs as much as possible, and present only the protected bow and the crank galley's own artillery to them." He shrugged, looking up from the drawing to meet Thirsk's eyes. "We wouldn't have as much total firepower on any given crank galley as they'd have on one of their galleons, My Lord, but a squadron of crank galleys—or even an entire *fleet* of them—could be quite a different story. And with no oars to get in the way, they could probably mount a moderately heavy broadside of carronades for close action if somebody managed to get around them and maneuver out of their own firing arcs."

"Assuming it's possible, I think you might very well have a point, Lieutenant," Thirsk said slowly. He stood looking down at the crankshaft drawing for several seconds, then inhaled deeply and nodded.

"Ahlvyn," he looked at the commander, "I'll want to see the Lieutenant's boat as soon as possible. Arrange that—for this afternoon, if we can manage it. And please ask Ahbail and Mahrtyn to make themselves available afterward. If the Lieutenant's demonstration is as successful as he seems to think it will be, I imagine I'll have quite a few letters to write. Oh, and send a messenger immediately to Bishop Staiphan. Ask him to repair aboard *Chihiro* at his earliest convenience. I'd like him to see the Lieutenant's boat at the same time I do."

"Of course, My Lord." Khapahr smiled, stroking his mustache with a pleased—one might almost have said complacent—expression, and Thirsk shook his head at him.

"All right, Ahlvyn, I'll go ahead and say it. You were right to bring the lieutenant to see me directly . . . even if you did use it mainly as an excuse to abandon the anchor chain hunt. Now go and do something else virtuous.

And, Lieutenant," he turned back to Zhwaigair, "do me the favor of keeping yourself available aboard *Chihiro* for the rest of the day, if you please."

"My Lord, I'm expected back aboard *Wave Lord*. I have the afternoon watch."

"Commander Khapahr will see to that, Lieutenant."

"In that case, My Lord, I'm at your service."

Zhwaigair bowed slightly, and Thirsk nodded back. Then he watched Khapahr and the lieutenant withdraw from his day cabin, taking Zhwaigair's envelope with them.

"Shan-wei, My Lord," Baiket said quietly as the door closed behind them. "I thought he was out of his mind, but if he really *can* make all this work, or even just *half* of it . . . ."

"I know, Stywyrt." Thirsk nodded again, then crossed to brace his hands on the quarter window, leaning his weight on its sill as he looked out across the anchorage. "I know. Of course," he smiled mirthlessly, "if young Zhwaigair really *is* onto something, it's going to cost Shan-wei's own pile of marks to do anything with it. I'm sure you can imagine how well *that's* going to please certain of our superiors, especially with the situation in the Republic. And none of this is going to be available in the next five-day, whatever we do. But the possibilities . . . the *possibilities*, Stywyrt." He shook his head, his eyes bright with wonder. "For the first time—"

He broke off and straightened with a shrug, and Baiket frowned as he looked at his admiral's back, wondering what Thirsk had just stopped himself from saying.

Thirsk couldn't see the flag captain's expression, but it wouldn't have surprised him. Not that he had any intention of completing his thought where Baiket or anyone else was likely to overhear it.

But it's true, he thought. *For the first time—the very first time since this rolling disaster began—we may actually have the opportunity to introduce something the* Charisians *won't see coming!*

He was vaguely amazed by the fierceness of his satisfaction at the thought. It didn't magically change any of his other concerns or worries, didn't suddenly fill him with confidence Clyntahn and the Group of Four were truly on God and the archangels' side, after all. Nor did it make him feel any cleaner about what had happened to Gwylym Manthyr's men. But Lywys Gardynyr was a fighting man, one who'd had his fill and more than his fill of leading his seamen into battle against someone whose weapons and ships were always superior to anything he could give them.

That could be about to change, he told himself. *But before I start sending letters to anyone like Thorast or Fern, I'd better have a word or two—or possibly three—with Bishop Staiphan. We* need *someone like Zhwaigair—in fact, we need as many of him as we can get!—but that doesn't mean some fool of an Inquisitor won't decide he's dabbling in the forbidden, especially if they realize just how many new ideas he has. I'm not going to offer him up to the Inquisition until I'm sure someone with enough seniority—and enough deeper into the Inquisition's favor than I am—is in a position to protect him.*

He looked out over the harbor, and his expression tightened at the thought. How had the world become this insane? What kind of madness required an admiral to worry about protecting a man who wanted only to serve Mother Church—to find better ways to *defend* Mother Church—from Mother Church's own inquisitors? What could the archangels be thinking to let it happen?

Lywys Gardynyr had no answer for any of those questions, but he did know Dynnys Zhwaigair was far too valuable to lose . . . no matter *what* he had to do to protect him from that murderous idiot in Zion.

.XIV.
Imperial Palace,
City of Tellesberg
Kingdom of Old Charis,
Charisian Empire

I think our priorities just got simplified." Cayleb Ahrmahk laid his palm on the thick, many-paged dispatch lying on the council table in front of him. "Sharleyan and I are both delighted by Duke Eastshare's initiative, but there's no use pretending it won't require us to rethink a lot of our earlier planning."

"That's true, Your Majesty," Domynyk Staynair replied gravely. "Fortunately, though, we've got all those Navy of God galleons whose guns we've already landed and turned over to Ehdwyrd for scrap. I think our best solution for transporting the Duke's troops the rest of the way to Siddarmark will be to use them. They're already fitted out to transport and mess large crews, so they'll be the most effective way to move *people*. Horses and other draft animals are going to be more problematic, but I think we've got enough shipping either already here in Tellesberg or on its way back from Siddarmark to handle that. That's assuming his projected numbers for his advance guard are accurate, at any rate. We'll have to scare up some additional horse and dragon transports for his main body, but we ought to have time to do that before it gets to Ramsgate Bay."

"Assuming the weather cooperates," Cayleb pointed out.

"Assuming that, of course." Baron Rock Point smiled a crooked smile.

"That proviso always attaches to *anything* an admiral says, you know, Your Majesty."

"I most assuredly do," Cayleb said with a brief, answering smile. It fled quickly, however, and he turned his attention to Ahlvyno Pawalsyn.

"Even given that Domynyk can free up the transport, it's going to play hob with our original logistic schedule, Ahlvyno. Can we come up with enough rations to supply his troops as well as the Marines we've already deployed or put into the pipeline?"

"It's a case of needs must when Shan-wei drives, isn't it, Your Majesty?" Baron Ironhill looked undeniably harried, but he returned his emperor's level gaze with the smallest of shrugs. "I'll find the money somewhere, but it's going to be months yet before food prices stabilize after the relief effort. It's going to cost a pretty mark to do it."

"As you say, we don't have much of a choice," Sharleyan agreed. "On the other hand, given the reports out of Trokhanos, Malitar, and Windmoor, I think food prices might start stabilizing sooner than we'd feared. It sounds like they've at least doubled the amount of land under plow in those provinces. We're probably still going to lose more people to starvation—enough to give any of us nightmares for years to come—but by summer, we ought to be seeing much greater food production in the eastern Republic."

"That would take a lot of the strain off here in the Empire, Your Grace," Ironhill acknowledged. "On the other hand, when it happens, farmers who've invested in increased production here are suddenly going to find their markets glutted, which may drive the price of food down as catastrophically as it's been driven up at this point." His expression was unhappy. "The last thing we need is even more internal market instability at the very time our external markets've been cut off at the knees, but that's exactly what we're going to have to deal with, I'm afraid."

"Then we'll just have to deal with it." Sharleyan gave him a tight smile. "By which, of course, I mean *you'll* have to deal with it, with Cayleb and me pressing our entirely unreasonable demands that you do it even faster all the while."

A chorus of chuckles flowed around the conference table, and Ironhill smiled back at her much more naturally.

"At least you and His Majesty aren't in the habit of beheading those of us who fall short of your unreasonable standards, Your Grace. That's something, I suppose."

"I always said you had a level head on your shoulders . . . for now, at least," Cayleb observed, and the chuckles turned into laughter as Ironhill reached up and checked the back of his neck.

Cayleb was pleased to hear that laughter, but it couldn't change the reality they faced.

"Food aside," he said, returning their attention to the matters at hand, "there's also the question of what we do with Eastshare's rifles. Are we going to have enough Mahndrayns to swap them all out by the time he reaches Ramsgate?"

"Probably not immediately, Your Majesty," Ehdwyrd Howsmyn replied. "We're talking about almost eighty thousand men, better than three-quarters of them infantry. That's sixty thousand Mahndrayns, and we're not going to have that many ready to ship by the time the Domynyk's talking about sending off the first wave of transport ships."

"What about sending them straight to Siddarmark, instead?" Earl Pine Hollow asked. "It's going to take time for the transports to reach Raven's Land, then the Republic. Could we steal enough time to produce the number he'd need if we had them meet him in Siddarmark instead of sending them to him immediately?"

"I think we could definitely manage that," Howsmyn said after a moment.

"Then I suppose the next question is whether or not we ship his regular rifles home for conversion," Sharleyan said.

"I'd argue against that, at least for right now, Your Grace," Rock Point said. "Those rifles will be a lot more useful, muzzle-loaders or not, in Siddarmark, than sailing back and forth to Delthak."

"I think you're right about that," Cayleb said. He cocked an eyebrow at Sharleyan, who nodded, then turned back to Howsmyn and Ironhill. "We'll do it Domynyk's way."

"Of course, Your Majesty." Ironhill dipped his head in a small, seated bow and jotted a note on the pad at his elbow.

"The next question is where in Siddarmark we land them," Cayleb said.

"Given the Lord Protector's latest messages, I'd suggest landing them in Siddar City," Rock Point said. Cayleb gazed at him for a moment, then turned to look over his shoulder at the sapphire-eyed Imperial Guardsman just inside the council chamber's door.

"Merlin, I think you'd better come over here and find a seat," he said. Most of the people already sitting around the table were either members of the inner circle or at least cleared for the "the *seijin* has visions" version of the truth, and no one seemed surprised by the emperor's invitation.

"You spent enough time conferring with Duke Eastshare and Baron Green Valley for us in Chisholm that you're probably the closest thing to an informed expert on the Army we have at the moment," Cayleb continued as the *seijin* obeyed his command. "I want to hear anything you might have to say about where and how we could use his troops—and our Marines, for that matter—to best advantage."

"Of course, Your Majesty," Merlin murmured respectfully, slipping into a fortuitously empty chair between Rock Point and Seamount.

In many realms, the notion of sharing the imperial council table with a commoner would have been outrageous, but Charisian nobles were more inclined than most Safeholdian aristocrats to value capability over birthright to begin with, and all of *these* Charisian nobles knew how close their monarchs were to Merlin Athrawes. For that matter, they respected Merlin's judgment almost as much as Cayleb and Sharleyan did, if not for exactly the same reasons.

"So, do you agree with Domynyk?"

"I think I do, for the most part, Your Majesty." Merlin shrugged ever so slightly. "I know our reports indicate the Lord Protector already has the largest single portion of his remaining regulars concentrated in Old Province, but that's because of the threat coming out of Mountaincross and New Northland. Not to mention the need to relieve loyal forces in Midhold, as soon as he can spare the strength. If he can do that, hold the Sylmahn Gap, and secure control of the Northland Gap, he can seal off everything north of Shiloh against the Temple Loyalists and stop any immediate threat to the capital. I'm sure that's why he's concentrated his troops the way he has. I wish we had better information on exactly how much of the Army has remained loyal and intact, but given what we know so far, his deployments make a lot of sense."

In fact, of course, Merlin and the inner circle knew almost exactly—better than Stohnar himself, actually—what the lord protector's troop strength consisted of, and the knowledge was not enheartening

Owl's SNARCs had finally managed to come up with reasonably reliable population numbers for Safehold as a whole. Or, he reminded himself grimly, for what the population numbers of Safehold had been before Clyntahn had launched the Sword of Schueler.

At just over one billion, the overall human population of Safehold was roughly equivalent to that of Old Earth in the year 1800, and Safeholdian realms tended to be far, far larger than their Old Terran equivalents, thanks to the manner in which they'd formed and the Church's influence. Siddarmark's area, for example, was over nine million square miles, roughly the size of the entire Old Terran continent of North America, and Safeholdian agriculture and medical arts were better than anything on Old Terra in 1800. There were still huge areas for improvement, even within the constraints of animal traction and muscle power, but Safeholdians had draft dragons, practiced four-crop rotation, understood fertilizers, and had the advantage of genetically engineered, high-yield food crops, courtesy of Pei Shan-wei's terraforming crews. In addition, realms like Siddarmark had the better part of nine hundred years worth of *Writ*-enjoined canal and road building behind them. Where the old nation of Great Britain, with perhaps the best agricultural practices in the world in 1800, had been able to support about eight and a half human beings per square mile, Siddarmark's farmers could support over thirteen, which had given the Republic a pre–Sword of Schueler population of more than 129,500,000 citizens.

In theory, that permitted armies far larger than anything Old Earth had seen before its twentieth century, but there were countervailing factors. A huge one had been the way in which industrialization had been hobbled by the Proscriptions of Jwo-jeng. Farming might be more efficient than it had been in the early-nineteenth, but manufacturing was not, since everything still had to be done using only wind, water, or muscle power and production had been concentrated in the hands of skilled artisans who turned out high-quality goods but only in strictly limited quantities.

Charis had begun changing that even before Merlin's arrival, but that was the point; the change had only been *beginning*. It still had a long way to go, and even with Safeholdian roads and canals, Safeholdian armies were forced to rely on animal traction to move large quantities of supplies. Then there was the fact that traditional Safeholdian armies were far less well articulated—not simply tactically, but strategically—than post-Napoleonic Old Earth's. Tactically, pikemen required the support of missile troops, whether musketeers or bowmen, and infantry required cavalry support. There was no such thing as an infantryman who could march, deploy, and fight independent of his supports, which inevitably made for a cumbersome and clumsy army organization. And no one had ever heard of the notion of dividing an army *strategically* into divisions and corps. It marched as one huge force, usually down a single line of advance.

The Imperial Charisian Army was in the process of changing that, because a rifle-armed infantryman with a bayonet *could* march, deploy, and fight independent of his supports. The rest of Safehold remained a long, long way from realizing that, however, and none of them—yet—could match the Empire's ability to provide *all* of its infantry and dragoons with rifles. Until they could, they were stuck with all the traditional problems not simply of supplying but of *maneuvering* large field armies.

Besides, standing armies were expensive propositions, and they were only useful if one intended to go conquer someone else or expected someone else to attempt to conquer one's own realm. Given Mother Church's views on that subject, the creation of large standing armies prior to the current unpleasantness had been discouraged by the Council of Vicars.

Prior to the Sword of Schueler, Siddarmark's standing army, with a troop strength of 1,200,000, had represented just under one percent of the Republic's total population, which, given the size of the Republic and the sheer space its army had to defend, was a lot smaller than it might seem at first glance. On the other hand, that army had been highly professional and well equipped, especially its renowned and deadly pikemen, and it had been supported by an organized militia half again as strong, giving the Republic a theoretical troop strength of just over three million.

But then the Sword of Schueler had struck, and more than two-thirds of the Republican Army died, disintegrated, or went over to the rebels. At the moment, the army total strength stood at under four hundred thousand, supported by only nine hundred thousand militia . . . including militias still in the field against the Temple Loyalists in the disputed provinces and those still waging their own guerrilla resistance in places like Tarikah and Westmarch. Of that available troop strength, by far the largest single portion—roughly seventy thousand regulars and ninety-six thousand militia—were concentrated in Old Province, whose pre–Sword of Schueler population had been twenty-three million, almost twice that of New Province, the Republic's next most heavily populated province.

Given the population numbers, and the fact that Old Province and New Province had absorbed by far the largest proportion of refugees as well, it was little wonder Stohnar had concentrated his forces to protect them.

"At the same time," he continued aloud, "we can't ignore the threat coming out of Dohlar and Desnair. Stohnar had to hold the north to survive the immediate threat, but Glacierheart, Shiloh, and Trokhanos are just as critical to the Republic's *ultimate* survival as its northern half, and Rahnyld and Emperor Mahrys are going to be able to invade the South March no later than the early part of March. Our agents' reports"—he didn't mention that the best of the "agents" in question were Owl's SNARCs—"suggest that between them, they'll be able to commit around three hundred and sixty thousand regulars." More than one face blanched at that number, but he continued unflinchingly. "The Army of God and its contingents from the Border States will be able to commit at least that many troops, and probably more, although they'll be heading into Westmarch, Tarikah, New Northland, and Mountaincross, too far north to coordinate closely with Dohlar and Desnair. Then there are the Republic's own Temple Loyalists. Our best estimate at the moment is that there are somewhere around a half million of them already under arms and in the field. And, finally, it looks as if the Harchongian contribution to the invasion is going to come to somewhere over one and a half million all by itself."

"My God," someone murmured, and Merlin couldn't really blame him.

The Imperial Charisian Army's total strength, even after transferring the bulk of the Marine divisions which had been raised for the invasion of Corisande to it, was barely four hundred and fifty thousand, and the Imperial Charisian Navy's strength was roughly three hundred and twenty thousand, including everyone assigned to various shore stations. The remaining Imperial Charisian Marines added fifteen thousand more warm bodies, but the total of the Empire's military strength was barely over seven hundred and eighty thousand . . . little more than a quarter of the forces poised to crush the Republic. Even with every single man in the Imperial Army and Marines added to Stohnar's regulars and militiamen, they would be outnumbered by two to one, and there was no way the Empire could pull its garrisons out of Corisande or leave its own homeland completely unprotected, lest some mainland raiding force manage to somehow evade the navy.

"The good news," Merlin continued, his eyes focused on Cayleb and Sharleyan, pretending he wasn't actually telling the rest of the councilors things the emperor and empress already knew entirely too well, "is that Rahnyld and Mahrys detest each other. Even with the Church and the Inquisition getting behind and pushing, their field commanders are unlikely to cooperate very smoothly. And while the Harchong Army is huge, it's also very old-fashioned, not to mention ill-disciplined and worse-officered. The Harchongian contribution will have a lot of weight behind it, but it's going to be far clumsier than the Republican Army would've been, and a *lot* clumsier than Duke Eastshare's troops. They're also not going to be as well equipped as our troops, and as you and General Chermyn—I mean, Grand Duke Zebediah—demonstrated in Corisande, that's going to make an enormous difference."

He let that sink in, then raised his right hand, like a man releasing a wyvern.

"As I see it, based on my own observations of Duke Eastshare, Baron Green Valley, and the rest of the Army's officers, our people ought to be able to handle two or three times their own number of anything they're likely to meet. Our agents do report that at least half the Army of God's infantry and the bulk of Desnair and Dohlar's infantry will be equipped with rifles of their own, but they'll all be muzzle-loaders, which will be at a significant disadvantage against Mahndrayns. Our people's tactics and training are going to make the other side's disadvantages even more pronounced, and I'd expect Lord Protector Greyghor's troops will be at least the equal of their opponents, assuming we can get them equipped with rifles. The problem is going to be that the Group of Four's proxies have the initiative, and we're going to be forced to divide our available—and limited—strength to oppose threats along several different lines of approach.

"The Lord Protector's reserves are well placed to cover the northern and eastern Republic against internal Temple Loyalists, but he doesn't begin to have the troop strength to stop the Army of God. The state of its equipment, its training, and the fact that it's under a truly unified command, rather than two theoretically 'cooperating' armies which hate each other almost as cordially as they hate heretics, make it far more dangerous than the Dohlaran and Desnairian armies. That's why I believe we'd be best advised to send Duke Eastshare directly to Siddar City, where he can support the Lord Protector against that threat. At the same time, however, I'd strongly recommend landing as many Marines and armed seamen as we can in Trokhanos. I'd actually prefer to land them even farther west than that— possibly in Tabard Reach or even Thesmar Bay, if Thesmar's still holding— but that might be too risky. Eralth Bay's probably the safest place, at least for an immediate destination. From there, we'd be able to barge them up the Dragon Fish River faster than the Desnairians or Dohlarans can march overland, or we could use our sealift advantage to move them farther west if that ended up seeming like a good idea. And even if it turns out Thesmar's fallen by the time we could get there, there are probably somewhere around thirty or forty thousand militia in Trokhanos alone. If we send in our Marines to stiffen them and give them at least a small force with new model weapons, they'll fight hard to defend their homes and families."

He closed his raised hand into a fist.

"For the moment, Your Majesty, my recommendation would be to concentrate on covering the Lord Protector's southern flank, especially given the way our sea power will increase our mobility in the Gulf of Mathyas and along the coast. Let him—and Duke Eastshare—stabilize his *northern* flank against the more serious threat coming out of the Temple Lands. After they've done that, they can dispatch additional forces to our support."

He lowered his hand, and Cayleb looked around the table. Not everyone looking back at him seemed equally reassured by Merlin's analysis, yet while he saw more than a little anxiety, hesitation seemed to be in very short supply.

"All right," he said. "Assuming we follow the *seijin*'s advice, Domynyk, how many Marines could we sent to Eralth? And how soon could we send them?"

"That's a good question, Your Majesty." Rock Point frowned, rubbing his upper lip, his eyes thoughtful. He stayed that way for several seconds, then shrugged. "We've already sent the bulk of our available Marines to other points in the Republic, Your Majesty. I believe I could probably squeeze another seventy-five hundred men—two-thirds of them will be armed seamen, not Marines, I'm afraid—out of the ships here in Tellesberg and at Helen Island." He smiled crookedly. "After all, we've got the Marine contingents from those Navy of God galleons we're going to be using as transports, don't we? And I believe—I'll have to check with Captain Braisyn to be certain—that we could equip all of them with Mahndrayns out of the weapons we're crating up for shipment to Siddarmark. We won't have much in the way of field artillery to send with them, but I imagine we could scare up a few dozen naval guns for them. Have to cobble together field carriages for them, but if we load the wheels and ironwork for the carriages aboard ship, I imagine the ships' carpenters mates could run those up during the voyage."

"And how soon could we send them?" Cayleb pressed.

"I could have them ready to board ship in . . . two days," Rock Point replied. "But it's nine thousand miles from Tellesberg to Eralth. That's over a month's voyage, even with favorable winds."

"I see."

It was Cayleb's turn to frown. He turned to gaze out a window at the sun-drenched treetops for perhaps a minute, then looked back at Rock Point.

"What if we went overland to Uramyr?"

"That *would* cut the total travel, wouldn't it?" Sharleyan said, then grimaced. "Or would it? I should know the Old Charis maps better than I do, but wouldn't you lose several days in the mountains? And you'd still have to get transports there to meet you."

Uramyr, on the coast of the Barony of Crest Hallow on the southern edge of Westrock Reach, lay on the far side of the Styvyn Mountains, the narrow but very mountainous isthmus separating Howell Bay from The Cauldron.

"The roads through the mountains are a pain in the arse," Cayleb conceded. "But it'd cut the voyage to Eralth by more than half. And if we sent word to Admiral Shain immediately via semaphore, he could have galleons from Thol Bay there to meet us within—what, Domynyk?—a couple of five-days?"

"No, Your Majesty." Rock Point shook his head. "It's over four thousand miles from Thol Bay to Uramyr. You'd lose most of the time you're trying to save. But"—he continued, raising his index finger to punctuate his own point as the emperor's expression fell—"we're not talking about an enormous force. We've got a small squadron in Brankyr Bay under Commodore Sarforth. I'll bet there are enough galleons in the bay, if we authorize Sarforth to impress them for the Crown's service, and Brankyr's less than fourteen hundred miles from Uramyr and the wind would favor him. He could make the trip in only a five-day, which would get those ships there about the time you could arrive overland, I imagine. From there, it would be another three five-days or so to Eralth. Overall, you'd cut your transit time almost in half. With a little luck, you could be in Eralth by the first five-day in May."

"No, *you* couldn't, Cayleb," Sharleyan said in a firm, no-nonsense tone. The emperor—and his councilors—looked at her, and she shook her head.

"One of us has to go to Siddar City to deal with *this*." She tapped the message from Greyghor Stohnar pointedly. "You remember, that little matter of the formal treaty we need to sign? And since *I'm* leaving for Chisholm in three days, that leaves it up to you."

No one around that table doubted for a moment that Sharleyan Ahrmahk was hugely relieved to be able to point out why her husband wouldn't be leading an outnumbered force of Marines into combat any time soon. At the same time, that didn't make her wrong.

"All right," Cayleb conceded. "I'll go as far as Uramyr with the Marines, and then Commodore Sarforth can put me aboard one of his galleons and send me off to Siddar City. Will that work?"

He sounded the tiniest bit snippy, but Sharleyan only nodded with the air of a woman who knew when to accept victory without rubbing it in.

"In that case," Cayleb returned his attention to the others, "I suppose we should look at the details of how we're going to get our reinforcements on the road to Uramyr as quickly as we can. And while we're thinking about movements, I think we'll also want to consider ordering Admiral Shain to move a heavy squadron to Eralth immediately. If he bases on Eralth Bay, he'll be much closer to the Gulf of Mathyas, and I think we should take Merlin's suggestion and commence raiding operations in the Gulf of Jahras as quickly as possible. Let's make that bastard Mahrys go overland the whole way instead of ferrying his troops across the gulf."

Heads nodded, and Cayleb pointed at Rock Point.

"You're the High Admiral around here, Domynyk, so why don't you start?"

"Of course, Your Majesty." If Rock Point was perturbed by being put on the spot, he showed no sign of it. "The first thing—and I think we should probably call in a messenger and do this right now—is to get the movement orders off to Shain and Sarforth. I think Admiral Hywyt's at Thol Bay now, so I'd recommend his squadron for the Eralth detachment."

Cayleb nodded and made a summoning gesture at the footman in the black and gold of the House of Ahrmahk seated beside the council chamber door. The footman rose, bowed, and vanished silently. He returned an instant later with Lieutenant Haarlahm Mahzyngail, Rock Point's flag lieutenant.

"Yes, Your Majesty?" the fair-haired, blue-eyed Chisholmian inquired, bowing gracefully to both of his monarchs.

"High Admiral Rock Point has an errand for you," Cayleb replied with a smile while Rock Point scribbled a pair of short, concise dispatches on his own notepad. It didn't take long, and he spent another moment glancing over them to be sure they said what he needed them to say. Then he handed them over to Mahzyngail.

"The semaphore station, Haarlahm," he said. "I want them dispatched within the quarter hour."

"At once, My Lord!" Mahzyngail saluted sharply, bowed again to Cay-leb and Sharleyan, and disappeared as quickly as he'd come. More quickly, in fact: he was half-trotting by the time the door closed behind him.

"Now," Rock Point continued, "with that taken care of, the next point of business will be to get a dispatch boat off to Helen Island and then make sure my memory's not playing me false about which ships are here in Telles-berg. After that—"

.XV.
Green Cove Trace,
Gray Wall Mountains,
Province of Glacierheart,
Republic of Siddarmark

Your Eminence, you shouldn't be *up* here!" Byrk Raimahn glared at Zhasyn Cahnyr. "That bastard Fyrmahn has small parties creeping all over these mountains. Can you think of a *single* person they'd rather kill more than they would you? I only ask because *I* can't, and what *they* may do doesn't even count broken necks on miserable trails! With all due respect, Your Eminence, what the Shan-wei were you *thinking*?"

Archbishop Zhasyn only leaned on his staff, returning the younger man's glare with mild eyes. Cahnyr was much frailer than he'd been when he set out from Siddar City, mostly because he'd refused a ration any more nourishing than they could feed anyone else, but his thin face was calm and the constant shivering of his starvation-gaunt body was scarcely noticeable under his thick coat and gloves. It was as if the power of his spirit was sub-stituting for the flagging energy of his flesh, and Raimahn's obvious anger glanced off the armor of his serenity without so much as a scuff mark.

"You're not saying a single thing Father Frahnklyn and I haven't al-ready told him, Captain Raimahn." Sahmantha crossed her arms and turned her own glare upon the recalcitrant prelate. She, too, had lost weight. It was readily apparent, despite her fur-lined parka, but her face wasn't as gaunt as the archbishop's. Partly that was because she was less than half Cahnyr's age, but the archbishop and her husband had also managed to bully her into ac-cepting a slightly larger ration in recognition of the endless hours she spent hiking from one refugee tent or jury-rigged hut to another, caring for the sick and dying.

"No, you aren't, Captain," Cahnyr agreed. His voice remained stronger than his body, and he tilted his head to one side, considering Raimahn much as a bird might have considered a particularly tasty worm. "And since it didn't do Sahmantha any good, and she's known me a great many years longer than you have, young Byrk, perhaps you might save your energy and spare both of us a great deal of wear and tear."

"*Your Eminence!*" Raimahn began, then threw up both hands.

"I give up," he told the mountainside. "The man's obviously a dangerous lunatic!"

"I assure you, I pose no threat to anyone," Cahnyr replied with a small smile, clenching his teeth to prevent them from chattering in the sharp-edged, icy breeze.

"You mean you don't pose a threat to anyone *else*," Raimahn said grimly. "And the truth is, Your Eminence, that you *do*. Pose a threat to someone else, I mean." He jabbed an index finger at the archbishop. "As long as you're up here, I'm going to have to assign an escort to you, and you know perfectly well that if *anything* looks like happening to you, whoever that escort is, he's going to jump straight between it and you. I hope you'll still think this trip was worth it if that happens, Your Eminence!"

Cahnyr winced at the underhanded blow, and Raimahn noted his reaction with a certain satisfaction. He didn't really think he could convince the archbishop to take himself back to a safer position, but it would seem he'd found an argument which might make the crazy old man exercise at least a trace of caution while he was up here!

"I assure you, I'll be as careful as humanly possible," Cahnyr said after a moment. "And I'll even promise to obey any orders my escort might choose to give me."

"And you'll take Madam Gorjah with you, just in case."

"No, I won't," Cahnyr said firmly. "There's no point and no reason in allowing Sahmantha to endanger herself up here. Quite aside from any other factor, she's far too valuable for that, especially considering Father Fhranklyn's immobility."

Father Fhranklyn Haine had suffered massive frostbite to both feet struggling through what everyone hoped had been one of the winter's last blizzards in a vain effort to save a half-starved young mother from appendicitis. He'd lost most of his toes and half of his left foot, which had hurt him far less than losing his patient had. Nonetheless, the injury had confined him to the "hospital" in Green Cove, a hundred miles south of the ruins of Brahdwyn's Folly. He *really* should have been two hundred and fifty miles farther back, at the hospital in Tairys, the provincial capital . . . but, then, so should Cahnyr. And as the Pasqualate had pointed out, there was nothing wrong with his *hands*. All he really needed was someone to wheel him from patient to patient, and half the time he had some orphaned waif tucked in his lap, making the huge-eyed child laugh at least briefly as they raced down the Green Cove clinic's crowded hallways shouting for people to get out of the way.

"Speaking as the military commander the Lord Protector and Madam Pahrsahn sent out here to hold this pass, I respectfully disagree, Your Eminence," Raimahn said flatly. "You don't quite seem to grasp how central you are to our defense of this province. Fortunately, some of the rest of us do, and we're not taking any chances we can avoid with you. In other words," he looked the archbishop squarely in the eye, "when we can't stop you from doing foolish things"—it was obvious from his tone that he really wanted to use a word considerably stronger than "foolish"—"we'll just have to do our best to minimize the consequences. And *that*, Your Eminence, means sending a trained healer to keep an eye on you. At the moment, we only have one of those available. So either you take Madam Gorjah with you or else you admit *neither* of you has any business up here and go back at least as far as Green Cove."

Cahnyr opened his mouth, then closed it again as he recognized the unyielding light in Byrk Raimahn's normally mild eyes. The archbishop fumed, but the truth was that however little he wanted to admit it, he knew Raimahn was right. His presence, his return to Glacierheart, had been met by the starving people of his archbishopric with cheers, and not simply because of the food he'd brought. They'd cheered him as the living proof they hadn't been abandoned, that the lord protector and the rest of the Republic knew about the stand they'd made—were making—and that if they could just hold on long enough, help would come. And he was also the focal point of every Reformist hope in Glacierheart, the archbishop who'd been outlawed by the Group of Four for his stance against their corruption yet returned, despite the condemnation to the Punishment of Schueler which hung over his head, to lead their fight to return Mother Church to what she was *supposed* to be.

No one had to know how unworthy of all that hope and faith and trust he truly felt, yet he couldn't pretend the people of Glacierheart didn't feel it. And because it was his responsibility to live up to that hope and faith, somehow he'd do it. He didn't know how, yet he knew he would, that God would show him the way to do it. But he couldn't ignore his pastoral responsibilities in the doing. He was God's priest before he was anything else, and his heart wept when he read Raimahn's messages, realized the grim brutality of the struggle raging back and forth across the hundred-mile stretch of narrow, icy roads and even more treacherous mountain paths between Brahdwyn's Folly and Fyrmahn's Cove on the Hildermoss side of the Gray Walls. These were his people, too, the ones dying up here in the snow—the ones *killing* up here in the snow . . . and sacrificing bloody bits and pieces of their own souls in the process.

The truth was, although he would never have admitted it to a living soul, he had to make this trip *now*. His strength, his stamina, was fading more quickly than he thought even Sahmantha realized, and if he'd waited as little as another five-day, he would have been physically unable to make the arduous climb even this far. A part of him had almost been seduced by Sahmantha's cajolery—and threats—into coming no farther than Green Cove, or even returning to Tairys. After all, young Raimahn was probably right about the effect his death would have, not just on the fighting men resisting the unremitting pressure from Hildermoss but on everyone else in Glacierheart as well. But he was an old man, and if he was going to die this winter, he would do it among the people fighting to protect their families and their beliefs and their faith, not under a pile of comforters in the archbishop's palace in Tairys.

He wondered again if his determination was some bizarre form of penance, an act of contrition for having survived the slaughter of Samyl Wylsynn's Reformists. Was he trying to expiate some self-guilt? Or was he actively seeking the release of death to escape his heartsick grief at the ghastly deathtoll Glacierheart had suffered through this bitter, bitter winter of starvation and privation?

Oh, don't be foolish! he scolded himself. *Do you really imagine all of this revolves around you, whatever young Byrk or anyone else may believe? You're one man, Zhasyn Cahnyr, one archbishop. One servant of God and the archangels. If you should happen to die up here, God will find someone else to take up your burden. And as for owing Samyl and the others some kind of death debt, or being personally responsible for all the suffering of Glacierheart, just how big an ego do you have? It's your job to do something about it, not to find some reason to justify feeling responsible for every bit of it!*

"Very well," he said, his testy tone and the glitter in his usually mild eye an admission Raimahn had found an argument that would actually make him exercise caution. "Since you intend to be unreasonable about it and I'm merely an old and feeble man who no longer possesses the strength and intestinal fortitude to resist your autocracy, Sahmantha may accompany me. I trust that will be satisfactory?"

" 'Satisfactory' would be me standing here looking at your backside headed down the trail to Green Cove," Raimahn said inflexibly. "Under the circumstances, however, and bearing in mind what an 'old and feeble man' you are when it comes to having your own way, I'll settle for what I can get." He looked over his shoulder and whistled sharply. "Sailys!"

"Yes, Sir?"

A shaggy, brown-haired fellow in a hard-used parka materialized out of the straggly evergreens which provided the illusion of a windbreak for Raimahn's small fire. It took Cahnyr a moment to recognize Sailys Trahskhat behind the thick beard blowing on the wind. The Charisian's right cheek was badly mottled by frostbite, making him even harder to recognize, but he smiled in welcome as he saw the archbishop.

"Don't smile," Raimahn told him sternly. "The last thing we need is to be encouraging this . . . this *old gentleman* to be wandering around up here amongst the mountain peaks!"

"As you say, Sir." Trahskhat banished the expression instantly.

"That's better. Now, I'm putting you in charge of making certain he and Madam Gorjah don't get into any unpleasantness while they're here. Take one of the ready duty squads with you, and be sure you keep an eye peeled. That bastard Fyrmahn's out there somewhere—I can *smell* him—and I *don't* want him getting a shot at His Eminence. Is there any part of that which isn't clear to you?"

He kept one eye on Cahnyr as Trahskhat shook his head firmly.

"No, Sir. I think I've got it."

"Good. Because—I don't want you to take this wrongly, Sailys—but if *he* doesn't come back, *you'd* better not come back. I don't think either one of us would like to explain to the rest of Glacierheart how we came to mislay him."

▼   ▼   ▼

Zhan Fyrmahn lay very still under the white canopy which had once been a bedsheet. The cold wind billowed the sheet, whispering knife-edged secrets, and its bitter kiss sank deep into his bone and flesh.

There wasn't much of that flesh left, and his belly had stopped snarling and retreated into sullen, aching silence five-days ago. Without the food Wahlys Mahkhom and his men had stolen, over half his own women and children had perished. They'd finally gotten the surviving gaunt-faced mothers and hollow-eyed children out of Fyrmahn's Cove, passing them up the high road through Heatherton towards safety under Mother Church's protection in Tarikah. Fyrmahn wouldn't be surprised if they lost half the remaining survivors before they ever reached Tarikah, and it was all that bastard Mahkhom's fault. His and all those other heretical, Shan-wei-worshiping traitors who'd betrayed Mother Church in her hour of need.

He'd tried, for a time, not to think about the empty cottages in the village his great-great-grandfather had established over a hundred years ago. About snow blowing in under doors and lying in herringbone patterns across floors where no hearth fire would melt it, drifting ever higher against doors and shutters no hand would open with the coming of spring.

About the bodies hidden under that canopy of white because the ground was too frozen to bury them, or because no one even knew where they'd died.

Oh, yes. He'd tried not to think about it, but he'd failed. And a part of him was glad, for the rage gave him strength when the food ran out. It burned at the heart of him, like a furnace, and he raised the edge of his canopy to peer down the long, steep mountain flank at the trail below him.

He couldn't see the four men who'd accompanied him, no matter how hard he looked, but he knew they were out there . . . unless the cold had claimed them. That could happen too easily to men weakened by starvation, and the journey to get here would have been grueling even if they'd all been well fed and in good health. The mountain snowpack was even deeper than usual this year, though the smell of an eventual thaw was in the air. That air was still so cold it squeaked in a man's lungs, yet he sensed a damp edge behind it, like the breath of that thaw sighing in his ear. When it hit, the snowpack would turn treacherous and mountain streams would become rivers while rivers became torrents. Travel would be almost impossible for several five-days, and he wondered if it would be possible for any of them to return the way they'd come.

We won't be "returning" anywhere if we don't capture at least some food, he reminded himself harshly.

The thought held curiously little terror, although he'd insisted to his companions that they planned on returning—that this wasn't some sort of suicide mission. Yet deep inside he'd always known better, whatever he'd told them. Just as they'd known, whatever they'd told themselves. None of them had anything to return to.

He thought again about Father Failyx. The Schuelerite was a hard man, he thought approvingly, a good hater. Lowlander he might've been born, but he had a Highland heart when it came to vengeance. He'd known what Fyrmahn intended when he set off into the mountains, and he'd only gripped the mountaineer's hand tightly and squeezed his shoulder in silent blessing. One or two of Fyrmahn's men had muttered that there might have been food enough—if only barely—to have made it through the winter after all, if not for Father Failyx and the lowland troops he'd brought forward. Perhaps they were even right. But without those trained troops, the bastard Reformists with their rifles and bayonets might well have driven Mother Church's loyal sons completely back out of the Gray Walls. As it was, despite months of bitter fighting which had dyed the snow crimson, the line between Hildermoss and Glacierheart had moved barely thirty miles north.

And even with the food they stole, the heretic scum's rations are almost as short as ours, he comforted himself bitterly. *We've whittled them down to the bone, too. If there's any truth to the rumors about what'll be moving south when the snow melts, Mahkhom's and "Archbishop Zhasyn's" remaining men will never be able to stop it.*

The thought gave him bleak, bitter satisfaction, even if he wasn't likely to see it happen. And in the meantime—

His thoughts broke off and his single eye narrowed as he saw movement.

▼   ▼   ▼

Cahnyr considered asking for a halt to catch his breath. Accustomed as he was to Glacierheart's altitude, he'd seldom been *this* high, and the thin air was a scalpel in his lungs, despite the muffler wrapped across his mouth and nose. His legs ached, the pernicious weakness which had become an inescapable part of him turned his knees to rubber, and he knew the unsteadiness of his footing came from more than just the ice and snow underfoot.

If you ask them to stop, they'll turn around and head back, even if they have to bind you hand and foot and drag you behind, he told himself. *And the fact that you know as well as they do that it would be the smart thing for them to do only indicates what a sound point young Byrk had about the state of your so-called sanity.*

He grimaced at his own perversity behind the muffler, but they had only one more stop before they all turned around and headed back to the ruins of Brahdwyn's Folly. The outpost ahead of them—the support camp for the advanced pickets covering the approaches from Fyrmahn's Cove—consisted of barely sixty men, but according to the senior man at their last stop, at least a quarter of them were ill. Even a minor sickness could be deadly dangerous to men whose resistance had been undermined by hunger and cold, and he'd known from Sahmantha's expression that the healer in her needed to do what she could for them. He'd seen that need warring with her concern for him, and he'd felt the same need himself. Not to heal their bodies, for that skill wasn't his, but the need to minister to them, to hear their confessions, grant them absolution and blessing . . . that was even more his duty than healing was hers.

He started to ask how much farther they had to go, but asking that would be as good as asking for a halt. And unless he missed his guests, Sailys Trahskhat would be calling another rest break soon. The man was watching Cahnyr like a hawk; it couldn't be much longer before he insisted on resting the archbishop's aged legs.

Of course, the problem is that if we stop to rest them, they're likely to freeze solid, Cahnyr thought wryly. *Either that or just fall off. Maybe it would be better that way. I could sit on my episcopal arse and let them tow me like a sled.*

His mouth twitched in an exhausted smile and he tightened his grip on his mountaineer's staff while he concentrated on putting one foot in front of the other.

▼   ▼   ▼

Fyrmahn studied the moving figures. This far south, any man he saw was a legitimate target, but there was something about them . . . .

His jaw clenched as he made out the rifles slung over their shoulders. There were ten of them with the weapons—six carrying them slung, and four with rifles at the ready. Three of the ready quartet broke trail ahead of the main body, while the fourth tagged along behind, watching their rear. They were obviously alert, and their wariness—and their weapons—would make things tricky.

He chewed on his thoughts, watching them come closer. He hadn't really planned on locking horns with so many men, and especially not so many *riflemen*. The object had been to creep around behind the heretics' line, pick off couriers and messengers, wring any information they could out of anyone they managed to take alive, and—hopefully—live off their enemies' captured food while they spread panic and confusion. But ten of them, in one party, all armed with those infernal rifles . . . that was more than he and his companions had counted on tackling.

Yet even as he considered, he was watching, wondering what they were doing out here. And as he wondered, his eye was drawn to the two figures at the center of the riflemen.

Neither of them was armed, as far as he could see. And one of them . . . the shorter one . . . . That was a woman, he realized abruptly, and what in Shan-wei's name was a *woman* doing this deep into the Gray Walls at this time of year?

He scowled, but then, suddenly, his eye widened as he saw the bag slung over her shoulder—the one he was suddenly certain bore the caduceus of Pasquale—and remembered the reports. Could it really be . . . ?

His gaze went back to the taller but bent figure in front of her, the one slogging through the snow wearily yet with a sort of granite determination, leaning heavily on his staff. If one was a woman, the one in front of her was old, it showed in the way he moved, and only one old man would drive himself along such a bitter trail accompanied by a woman healer. And if they were who Fyrmahn thought they were, no wonder they were escorted by an entire squad of riflemen!

His hollow eye glittered with sudden, burning determination, and he pursed his chapped and bleeding lips. His whistle was barely audible above the sigh of the wind, but he heard it repeated back a handful of seconds later, and he bared his teeth.

Then he slid his already cocked arbalest into position and checked the quarrel with loving care before he set it to the string.

▼　▼　▼

All right, Cahnyr thought. *You win, Sahmantha. I've got to take a break, no matter what opportunity it gives you to browbeat me for my foolishness. But at least we're probably close enough to camp for me to convince you to drag me the rest of the way there instead of turning around and heading back down the mountainside to—*

The arbalest bolt came out of nowhere. He never even saw it before it drove into the great muscle group on the front of his left thigh. Agony ripped through him and blood sprayed as the quarrel drove clear through and out the other side. He went down with a cry of pain, and even as he fell, three more quarrels ripped into their party.

One of Trahskhat's riflemen collapsed without a sound, his body pitching silently over the steep edge of the trail, plummeting into the shadowed depths below. Another staggered, stumbled, and went to one knee, swearing viciously as a quarrel slammed into his right shoulder joint, staining his parka with a sudden flood of crimson.

And Zhasyn Cahnyr's heart seemed to stop as he heard a sound like a line drive in a shortstop's glove and saw Sahmantha Gorjah go down.

▼   ▼   ▼

Fyrmahn cursed aloud as the man who had to be the heretical archbishop Cahnyr went down. The range had been less than a hundred and fifty yards, and the quarrel should have gone straight into Cahnyr's belly. But however fiery the spirit might be, it couldn't simply ignore hunger and cold, and his convulsive shivering had thrown the shot off. Almost worse, there'd been only three other quarrels to accompany his own, which meant the cold had claimed at least one of the others while they waited. He wondered who they'd lost, but the question was distant, unimportant under the lava of his rage and the frustration of having missed his mark at such short range.

It might still do the job. If he'd managed to sever the artery the apostate bastard would bleed out in minutes. Even if he hadn't, out here in the middle of ice and snow on a narrow, slippery trail, Langhorne knew they were likely to kill him simply trying to get him back down . . . especially with the Shan-wei-damned healer already down. But if that truly was Cahnyr, this was no time to settle for "might." If there was one man in all Glacierheart who needed killing even worse than Wahlys Mahkhom, it had to be Zhasyn Cahnyr, the heart and soul of the heresy.

He unfolded the crank from the side of his arbalest and began respanning the steel bow. It wasn't easy in a prone position, even with the built-in crank's mechanical advantage, and he swore again, quietly, as the clicking sound of the cocking pawl taunted him. He was well hidden, but the heretics on the trail were survivors, graduates of a hard school. They'd dropped prone themselves, and their heads were up, the rifles ready, as their eyes searched the slope above them. If one of them—

A rifle cracked viciously, and Fyrmahn heard a shrill, ululating scream from his left. He didn't know how Dahrand had drawn the heretic's attention, and he clenched his teeth, trying to ignore his cousin's agonized sounds as they slowly, slowly faded. He turned the crank harder, faster, keeping his own head down under his sheet, and cursed savagely as another rifle cracked.

There was no answering scream, but the rifleman wouldn't have fired if he hadn't thought he had a target. He might have been wrong, but the heretics weren't in the habit of wasting powder and shot on targets they weren't certain of. And—

A third shot cracked and echoed, and this time there was a scream—a choked off, chopped short scream that told him he'd just lost a second kinsman.

▼   ▼   ▼

Cahnyr rolled over onto his belly, teeth clenched in anguish, dragging himself through the snow towards Sahmantha. There was blood on the hood of her parka, and his soul froze within him at the thought of facing Gharth. Then he shook his head, fiercely, banishing the thought and forced himself to crawl faster.

"Lie *still*, Your Eminence!" Sailys Trahskhat shouted. "Mahrtyn, get a tourniquet on the Archbishop's thigh and then get him the hell out of here!"

"Aye, Sailys!" another voice responded, and the corner of Cahnyr's eye saw one of Trahskhat's men crawling towards him.

The archbishop ignored him, just as he ignored Trahskhat's repeated order to lie still. He had other things on his mind, and he struggled towards Sahmantha, lips moving in prayer.

▼   ▼   ▼

Fyrmahn's arbalest string clicked over the roller nut, and he yanked the crank out of the spanning gear and shoved it flat once more. He groped in his quiver for another quarrel, fitting it to the string, and even as he did, he heard two more rifle shots. He didn't know if they'd hit anything, but if they'd actually seen a target before they fired, his last companion was undoubtedly pinned down, if not worse.

It was up to him, and he set his jaw, glaring down the steep, white slope. His target was dragging himself grimly towards the fallen healer, leaving a trail of red in the snow as proof of his own wound. Fyrmahn could almost taste the traitor archbishop's anguish, but the man wasn't slowing down, and his progress had carried him out of Fyrmahn's line of fire. The arbalest was a long, heavy weapon, with a two-hundred-pound pull and a twelve-inch draw; under the right conditions, he could make a killing shot at six hundred yards. But along with that length and power came clumsiness, and he couldn't lower his point of aim enough to hit the crawling archbishop.

Or not from a prone position, at any rate.

His nostrils flared, but the decision was remarkably easy to make. After all, his family was already dead; he might as well join them, especially if he could send that bastard Cahnyr to hell along the way.

He drew a deep breath, settled himself for just a moment, then pushed up onto one knee in a single, flowing motion, and the arbalest's butt pressed his shoulder.

▼   ▼   ▼

Sailys Trahskhat saw the sudden motion, saw the red-haired, red-bearded figure throw aside the white fabric under which it had lain hidden. He saw the arbalest coming up, and he knew—*knew*—who that hard, hating man was.

He twisted around, bringing his rifle sights to bear, but not quickly enough. The arbalest rose to Fyrmahn's shoulder even as his own finger tightened on the trigger, and the roar of his rifle and the snap of the arbalest string were a single sound.

▼   ▼   ▼

A hammer pounded a fiery spike into Zhan Fyrmahn's chest. The rifle bullet shredded its way through his right lung, missing his heart by less than an inch, mushrooming and ripping and tearing as it went. The impact drove him back, slammed him into the snow, and he felt his life soaking into his parka on the scalding tide of his own blood.

His left hand groped towards the anguish, already feeble, his strength already failing. He didn't know what he hoped to do. It was simply instinct, the body's futile effort to somehow stanch the blood. If his brain had still been functioning, he would have known it was useless, but it wasn't working—not well, not clearly enough to understand.

Yet there *was* room in his fading mind for one last, clear thought.

I got the bastard. I got him.

It wasn't much, there at the end of all things, but for Zhan Fyrmahn, it was enough.

▼   ▼   ▼

"Shan-wei *damn* it, Your Eminence! If you don't lie still, I *swear* I'm going to—!"

Sailys Trahskhat made himself close his mouth, clenching his teeth against quite a few rather disrespectful and irreligious but undeniably pithy comments.

Archbishop Zhasyn ignored him, continuing to struggle towards Sahmantha.

"*Damn* it, Your Eminence! Let me at least get a dressing on your thigh before you bleed to death!"

"Don't worry about *me*," Cahnyr panted. "*Sahmantha!* Take care of Sahmantha!"

"I'll do that if you just settle down and let me bandage that thigh first," Trahskhat grated. Cahnyr turned his head, glaring at him, and the Charisian glared right back. "Your Eminence, it glanced off her skull!" He shook his head as Cahnyr's eyes widened. "You think I haven't seen enough head wounds by now to know when someone's just been grazed?! I'm not saying she couldn't have a concussion, even a serious one, and arbalest bolts are nasty, so she could have a skull fracture as well. But it's still only a grazing hit, and we can't do anything about it except put a dressing on it out here on this damned trail. And I can't put a dressing on *her* until you let me put one on the wound that's bleeding like a stuck pig in *your* thigh. Or are you somehow of the opinion that she wouldn't skin me alive and salt me down if I were to let you bleed to death while I was tying a bandage around her head?"

Cahnyr looked back up at him for a moment, then slumped back.

"All right," he managed. "I see you aren't going to give me a moment's peace if I don't let you do what you want. So go ahead."

"Are all archbishops as *stubborn* as you are?" Trahskhat demanded, stooping over the older man.

He reached down and gripped the arbalest bolt standing out of the archbishop's parka and yanked. It came free with a tearing sound, and he checked the knife-sharp head carefully. There was no blood, and he sighed in relief. The old man had lost enough weight over the long grueling winter that his coat hung upon him, loose enough —thank Langhorne!—for the quarrel to have punched right into it and never even grazed him.

The thigh wound was another matter, although for all the archbishop's bleeding, there was no arterial spurt. That was a good sign, as long as they could keep him from going into shock out here on the mountainside, at any rate.

He drew his belt knife, cutting open Cahnyr's quilted breeches to get at the wound, and pursed his lips as he saw the ugly entry point and even uglier exit wound. Assuming they didn't lose the archbishop after all, the old man was going to have one hell of a scar, he thought.

He reached for Sahmantha Gorjah's shoulder bag. He was no trained healer, but after this brutal winter, he'd learned more about dressing wounds than he'd ever wanted to know. He knew how to apply Fleming moss, at any rate, although he wasn't about to fool around with any of the healer's painkillers. Still—

Sahmantha stirred. Her eyelids fluttered, and she moaned softly, raising one hand to the blood-oozing furrow the arbalest bolt had gouged across the right side of her head. Her eyes blinked open. For a moment, they were vague, unfocused. Then they narrowed abruptly.

"*His Eminence!*" She braced herself on her hands, ready to shove herself upright, and Trahskhat put a heavy hand on her shoulder and pushed her back down.

"Langhorne, not *you*, too!"

"His Eminence," she repeated hoarsely. "I saw—"

"You saw him go down, lassie," Trahskhat said more gently, "but it's no more than a leg wound. Now, if you'll just bide for a moment, long enough for me to get his bleeding stopped, then I'll see to you. And if you can keep your eyes uncrossed long enough to play seamstress and stitch him up, and maybe see to Vyktyr's shoulder," he twitched his head to where another of his men was applying a compress to the shoulder of his wounded rifleman, "then maybe—just maybe—I'll be managing to get all three of you off this damned mountain and back to Captain Raimahn still breathing. And as for *you*, Your Eminence," he glowered down at the archbishop even as he began tightening a dressing over the ugly wounds, "the *next* time the Captain tells you you've no business doing something, you'd best listen! Damn it, what d'you think I'm going to tell him if I have to come back and admit I lost you! He'd never forgive me—*never!* Of all the stubborn, *stiff*-necked, obstinate, *pigheaded* old—!"

He broke off, blinking on tears, and Cahnyr reached up to pat his forearm.

"Oh, hush, Sailys!" he said gently. "You haven't lost me yet, and if Sahmantha's still her usual efficient self, you aren't going to. In fact, she needs to see to Vyktyr first—his wound's obviously far worse than mine."

"But—" Trahskhat looked down at him, and the archbishop shook his head.

"I'll be fine, my son. And if I'm not, I've no one but myself to blame for not having listened to you—and, yes, Captain Raimahn. So let's see to Vyktyr and to Sahmantha, and then let's drag my preeminent, ordained, *stubborn* episcopal arse back down this mountain so all three of you can abuse me properly."

. XVI .
HMS *Destiny*, 56,
Howell Bay,
Kingdom of Old Charis,
Charisian Empire

I imagine you wish you'd been home longer."

Irys Daykyn stood at the after rail of HMS *Destiny*, watching as the steeples and rooftops of the city of Tellesberg disappear into the distance. She wasn't quite certain how she'd found herself standing there. It wasn't as if Tellesberg was *her* home town, after all! Yet somehow it had . . . just happened, and she was a little surprised by how comfortable it felt.

"Seamen get used to it, Your Highness," Hektor Aplyn-Ahrmahk replied, his own eyes on the brilliantly gilded scepter flashing back the sun in golden glory from atop Tellesberg Cathedral's highest steeple. He shrugged. "Merchant sailors only get short visits between voyages, and those of us in the Crown's service spend a lot longer at sea between them than most." He turned his head to look at her and smiled slightly. "I think that makes us appreciate it more when we do get home, but at the same time, we don't quite . . . fit ashore anymore. This"—the wave of the hand took in the masts, sails, rush of water, and croon of wind—"is where we fit. To be completely honest, this has been my 'home' since before I was Daivyn's age. When I visit my parents, my brothers and sisters, I'm visiting in *their* home now, not mine."

"Really?" A shadow touched her eyes. "That's sad."

"Oh, no, Your Highness!" He shook his head quickly. "Or not any sadder than for anyone when they grow up. Mother and Father will always be what I think of when I . . . reach back for where I came from, but every child has to become an adult someday, doesn't he? Or she? And when that happens, they have to find their own places in the world. That's something a life at sea teaches early, too."

She studied his face and expression, and then, slowly, she nodded.

"I suppose that's true. But at the same time, isn't home what makes us who we are? The place we're constantly comparing other places and other times to?"

"Maybe." He cocked his head, considering. "Maybe," he repeated, "but we outgrow it, too. We have to learn and change."

He snorted suddenly and grinned. There was at least a hint of remembered pain in that grin, she thought, yet that only seemed to make him appreciate whatever had prompted it even more strongly.

"What?" she asked.

"Oh, I was just thinking how *much* my life's changed, Your Highness!" He twitched his head in Countess Hanth's direction. "I remember the day Earl Hanth returned to his earldom. We delivered him to Hanth Town on this very ship, you know."

"No." She shook her head, turning to look in the countess' direction herself, and her own lips quirked. "No, I hadn't realized Sir Dunkyn's made such a habit of delivering people places."

"He's an interesting man, Sir Dunkyn," Aplyn-Ahrmahk said. "And so is Earl Hanth. I was only a midshipman then, of course, and His Majesty had only just hung this ridiculous title on me. I was feeling . . . overwhelmed's probably a pretty good word, I guess. And Earl Hanth felt the same, given what an incredible mess that bastard—" He grimaced. "I'm sorry. I shouldn't use that kind of language speaking to you, Your Highness. But I can't think of a better word for Tahdayo Mahntayl, and he left Shan-wei's own mess for the Earl to clean up. I think he would've given just about anything to stay plain old Colonel Breygart, but he couldn't run away any more than I could, so he gave me some good advice, instead. None of which makes it seem any less crazy sometimes, when I think about it."

"Would you like to go back to being someone else?" She wondered why she'd asked the question almost before it was out of her mouth, yet she watched his face intently.

"Sometimes," he said. "Or maybe I just *think* I'd like to. As Archbishop Maikel says, we are who we are, and all anyone can ask of anyone else is that we *be* who we are to the very best of our ability. And who I am now, ridiculous as it may seem, is His Grace the Duke of Darcos, so that's who I have to be. I can't go back to being plain old Hektor Aplyn any more than a chicken or wyvern can crawl back into the egg. And it'd be pretty stupid to pretend there aren't some nice advantages to the change." He gave her another quick grin. "Mother and Father tried to tell me not to waste money on them when I first suggested it, but I don't think they really *mind* living in Darcos Manor, now that they've gotten used to it. I *did* have to point out to them that it came with the title and it would just stand empty the entire time I was at sea if they didn't, so they'd actually be doing me a favor by living there. I'm not sure Father bought my argument, of course, but Cayleb—I mean, His Majesty—was pretty insistent when he tried to talk his way out of it." His grin turned into a smile. "And having the money to get the younger ones proper educations . . . that was a wonderful change, Your Highness. Did I tell you my brother Chestyr's just been accepted at the Royal College?"

"No, you didn't. Let's see . . . Chestyr is the left-handed twin, is that right?"

"I see I've bored you with too many details about my family, Your Highness," he acknowledged. "But, yes. Father's proud enough of him to burst his buttons, although I think Mother's a little more concerned about where exposure to all that 'dangerous knowledge' is likely to lead."

Irys smiled and nodded, yet a part of her couldn't help agreeing with Sailmah Aplyn. She was still very much in two minds about exactly what the Royal College represented, and her own temptation to embrace its knowledge only made that mental ambiguity murkier. And she knew not even Aplyn-Ahrmahk's title would have won his brother admission if he hadn't earned it. From its inception, the Royal College had admitted students solely on the basis of competitive examination, without favor or exception.

Still, from a practical, secular viewpoint, it didn't matter one bit whether or not Chestyr Aplyn became a student there. If Charis lost its war, Zhaspahr

Clyntahn would never allow a single member of the House of Ahrmahk—however remote, or however indirect the connection—to survive. He wouldn't need Chestyr's exposure to heretical or tainted knowledge for that, although the butcher would probably cloak his pogrom in the Inquisition's responsibility to stamp out such blasphemous teachings.

Her smile faded at the thought, and she wondered why it disturbed her so, why it troubled her on such a . . . personal level. She'd only met Chestyr once, and despite his obviously keen intellect, he was still a scrubby schoolboy, all knees and elbows, with hair that stubbornly resisted the hardiest comb. His admiration for his magnificent older brother had been only too evident as well, and it had seemed as if there were far more than three years between him and Hektor.

That's because he is a schoolboy, she realized, *and Hektor—the Lieutenant, I mean—isn't a boy . . . and hasn't been since the battle of Darcos Sound, I imagine.*

She laid a hand on his forearm, without realizing she had, as that thought went through her mind. Hector Aplyn-Ahrmahk was as much younger than her as Chestyr was younger than him, but only in years. He'd seen and done things she could only imagine—only *try* to imagine, because she was far too intelligent to think anyone could truly conceive of them without having actually experienced them. He'd won his title the hard way, and he'd become a member of what had become the most powerful ruling house in all of Safehold's history, and what was his first thought? Was he *proud* of his honors? Did he reflect on how he'd been elevated to the most rarefied heights? No. He was grateful his new position let him move his parents into a comfortable home, pay for his brothers' and sisters' education. He was proud not of his honors but of the fact that his younger brother had been admitted to the Royal College. She tried to think of anyone she'd known in Corisande as her father's daughter who would have felt the same way and wondered why she felt obscurely satisfied when she couldn't.

"I understand why your mother might be a little concerned," she said out loud, "but I'm happy for Chestyr. And for you. I can see how proud of him you are."

"He always was the needle-witted one," Aplyn-Ahrmahk agreed with a grin. "I expect he'll rise to faculty level like one of the new rockets, and we'll all walk around in awe of his erudition and fame." His grin broadened. "That's my new word for the day, you know—'erudition.' Has a fine ring to it, doesn't it?"

"Oh, indeed it does!" she agreed with a laugh. "And a rich, rolling cadence, too!"

"Try to help me remember to use it casually in conversation this evening, if you would, Your Highness," he said, his expression earnest. "Sir Dunkyn still requires me to learn one new word a day as part of my ongoing education."

"I'm sure I can find a way to generate an opening over dinner," she promised, and it was his turn to laugh.

▼　▼　▼

Sharleyan Ahrmahk looked up from her daughter's smiling face at the sound of laughter. She lifted Alahnah, holding her against her shoulder, and looked past her to where Irys Daykyn stood with one hand on Hektor's forearm, smiling up into his face as they both laughed.

There was no sign of Prince Daivyn just at the moment, but she'd seen him and the two younger Breygart boys disappearing with a properly conspiratorial air. No doubt they were about to get into thoroughly satisfying amounts of mischief, which would undoubtedly end in the not too distant future with all three of them being hailed in front of their older sister and their stepmother in disgrace. The thought made her smile, despite the ache inside as *Destiny* and her accompanying squadron carried her and her daughter farther and farther away from Cayleb.

"Well," Mairah Hanth said softly, "*that* seems to be going well."

"I beg your pardon?" Sharleyan looked up at her taller, oldest friend, one eyebrow arched, her eyes innocent.

"Oh, don't look so demure and guileless at *me*, Your Majesty! Or should I still be calling you 'Your Grace' until we clear The Throat?" Mairah shook her head. "I know it hasn't crossed Hektor's mind yet—I rather suspect he's thinking with a rather less . . . cerebral portion, assuming he's actually *thinking* at all—but I'll guarantee you it's flickered across *her* mental landscape a time or two. Not that she hasn't probably jumped up to beat it to death with a shovel whenever it does."

"I think you're probably doing both of them a bit of a disservice," Sharleyan replied with a much more serious expression. "Hektor's a deeper pool than most people realize. I'm very satisfied with him, as a matter of fact, even if I can't really claim any of the credit as his official stepmother. I got hold of him rather later in the process than you've managed with Hauwerd's children. I'll happily acknowledge that what he's feeling is far from platonic, but it goes a lot deeper than that, too, and he's not the sort to be impressed by glamour or birth. Not that Irys has made any attempt to impress him with either of those," she added in the tone of someone giving another her just due. "Still, there's still a lot of plain Hektor Aplyn in him, too—thank God!—and whether he lets it *impress* him or not, I guarantee you he's never forgotten for a moment that unlike him, she was *born* into about the highest rank of the nobility imaginable. I'm not at all certain Hektor Aplyn is allowing himself to even consider acting on those . . .

nonplatonic feelings of Hektor Aplyn-*Ahrmahk's*, but I promise you, he's aware of them."

"And Irys?" Mairah asked, her own eyes more intent.

"*She's* the one who just happened to gravitate across the deck, away from you and me, and without even trying to keep an eye on her brother, towards *him*, Mairah," Sharleyan pointed out a bit tartly. "I'm certain she must be deeply conflicted where anything she might be feeling about him is concerned, though. In fact, I wouldn't be a bit surprised if *she's* the one who hasn't realized what she's not thinking about at the moment. I could be wrong, and God knows her situation's complicated enough to make anyone think three or four or five—or a hundred—times about *anything* that could affect her position, or her brother's. Maybe she has thought about it and figured out how she wants to deal with it, but I don't think so."

"Do you want me to *encourage* her to think about it?" Mairah asked quietly. Sharleyan looked at her sharply, and the countess shrugged. "I'm not about to push her into anything she doesn't want to do, Sharley. For one thing, I'm not that stupid. In her situation, even an idiot—and Irys is *far* from an idiot!—would have to be suspicious if anyone started trying to shove her into Hektor's arms. And if that 'anyone' happened to be someone she knows is as close to you as I am, she'd instantly leap to the perfectly correct conclusion that you'd put me up to it. By the same token, she has to be as aware of the potential advantages—for the Empire, at any rate—as you and I are, and she has to be nervous about her brother."

"You're thinking about how quite a few rulers—her father comes to mind—might encourage her to marry a member of their own family and then quietly . . . remove Daivyn in some unpleasantly permanent fashion so they could claim the throne through her children?" Sharleyan's huge eyes had turned grim, and Mairah nodded.

"It has to cross her mind, Sharley," she said softly. "She loves him. No, let's be more accurate about it—she *dotes* on that boy, even if she is smart enough to try her damnedest not to spoil or indulge him. From a thing or two she's said, I think she worries about the way her *older* brother was turning out before he was killed. She's determined Daivyn isn't going to do that, and Coris is backing her all the way. It helps that Tobys is in her corner, too," the countess added, her eyes twinkling suddenly as Tobys Raimair emerged from the amidships hatch hauling his vociferously arguing liege lord by the scruff of a tunic which had magically gone from pristine to ruined in less than thirty minutes.

Sharleyan turned her head to follow her gaze as two more of Irys' armsmen followed Raimair with Haarahld and Trumyn Breygart in tow. If anything, Haarahld looked even more disheveled than Daivyn, and his expression turned suddenly anxious as he beheld his stepmother.

Daivyn's protests increased in vigor, not to say desperation, as his sworn guardsman marched him towards his sister. The other two armsmen followed him, and it was apparent Haarahld, at least, was vastly relieved by the prospect of being dragged before a mere princess rather than haled before his stepmother.

So far, at least.

Sharleyan and Mairah watched Irys turning from her conversation with Aplyn-Ahrmahk to fold her arms and glower down at the filthy, still loudly expostulating Prince of Corisande, and Mairah laughed.

"No wonder she loves the scamp! And"—her voice turned more serious—"I know she's more relieved than she could ever admit to anyone about how he's responded to getting out of Delferahk. But that's my point. No matter what she may want—or *think* she wants—that girl will never do *anything* that might hurt or threaten her brother. So the trick, if you do want to encourage her, would be to reassure her that it *wouldn't* threaten him."

"Maybe." Sharleyan used her free hand to cup the back of Alahnah's head and leaned closer to press a kiss on the little girl's cheek. Then she looked back at Mairah. "No, not 'maybe'—not in that regard, at least. But the last thing we'd want to do, assuming we did want to encourage things between her and Hektor, would be to turn it into some sort of quid pro quo. If she thought we were offering to spare Daivyn if she'd marry Hektor, she might well do it, but she'd never forget she'd been pressured into it. Worse, she'd always wonder if we *wouldn't* have spared Daivyn if she hadn't agreed."

"Something to think about," Mairah agreed, her expression thoughtful as she watched Daivyn doing his very best to explain the state of his apparel and person to his sister. "Definitely something to think about. But it would be ever so useful in ever so many ways, wouldn't it?"

"Ever the mistress of understatement, Mairah," Sharleyan said dryly. "Of course, Clyntahn and the others—probably quite a few diehards in Corisande, for that matter—would scream we'd forced her into marrying our base-born henchman and that we were planning on having Daivyn killed any time now. But for anyone with a working brain in Corisande—?" She snorted. "As Merlin would say, hard to see the downside of that one."

"Besides which," Mairah said softly, "you think it would truly make them happy."

"Besides which I *hope* it would make them truly happy," Sharleyan corrected, hugging her daughter with both arms. "You know how seldom it's given to people like Irys to be allowed to marry for happiness and not for reasons of state, Mairah. Cayleb and I have been more blessed than anyone could possibly deserve to take such joy in one another. I'd love to see Irys—and Hektor—find the same sort of joy. Is that so much to ask, given all the pain and horror that's been loosed upon the world?"

"Of course it isn't." Mairah Breygart touched the side of Empress Shar-leyan's face the way Mairah Lywkys had once touched a much younger Queen Sharleyan's face when the world's demands beat in upon her. "Of course it isn't, and I hope they do. But they aren't just anyone, you know—any more than you and Cayleb were. So, do I get behind and gently push or do I stand back and let nature take its course?"

"For now, we let nature have its way," Sharleyan replied. "We've got five-days before we ever get to Chisholm. Let's see how things shape up."

"But you're definitely not *opposed* to the notion?"

"Do I *look* like an idiot?"

"No, not very much, now that I think about it," Mairah replied with a smile. Then she turned her head as Irys started across the deck towards them, followed by a somewhat woebegone Daivyn and the two younger Brothers Breygart, with three armsmen and a navy lieutenant (who was obviously having a very hard time not laughing out loud) in her wake.

"For the moment, though, I think I've got something else to deal with," she said from the corner of her mouth, eyes dancing as she took in Irys' expression. "It looks like this ought to be good, too. But I'll bear our conversation in mind."

Her eyes came back to Sharleyan's for a moment, and the empress nodded. Then it was the empress' turn to regard the procession of culprits sternly.

"Yes, Your Highness?" Lady Hanth asked pleasantly.

"It would appear my little brother has been leading your sons astray, Lady Mairah."

"I did *not*!" Daivyn protested. "I was—*we were*—only going down to the orlop deck, Lady Mairah. We would've stopped there—*really* we would have!—but . . . but the hatch was *open*, and no one said we *couldn't*—"

"Daivyn!" Irys interrupted the torrent and he looked at her quickly. "Let me finish giving Lady Mairah *my* version of events. I'm sure I have it all entirely wrong, and you'll have your opportunity to explain it all to her when I'm done."

Daivyn looked rebellious when she started speaking, but his expression relaxed in obvious relief at the offer of the opportunity to explain all the manifold reasons none of it was *his* fault. His sister looked back down at him for a moment, then shook her head.

"You *do* remember she has three sons of her own, don't you?" she asked her brother. "How many times have you seen Haarahld or Trumyn put one over on her?"

Daivyn abruptly looked much more thoughtful, and she nodded.

"That's what *I* thought, too," she told him, and turned back to Lady Hanth. "As I was saying, Lady Mairah, my little brother here convinced

Haarahld and Trumyn to go below decks and 'explore.' Exactly how they got away from Tobys is something he and I will be discussing later." The bald, fiercely mustachioed armsman behind her rolled his eyes in philosophical resignation. "At any rate, it would appear that when no one was looking, they found the cable tier. Now, anyone with any sense—I realize we're talking about *my* brother here, but still—would've realized that since we set sail less than an hour ago, the cable would still be just a little wet. However—"

. XVII .
The Temple,
City of Zion,
The Temple Lands

Spring always came late to the city of Zion.

Rhobair Duchairn stood gazing out through the crystal window whose frame never leaked drafts and whose inner surface was always exactly the same pleasant-to-the-touch temperature at the wind-driven snow slashing almost horizontally across the Temple's precincts. It turned everything a fresh, innocent white, mercifully concealing the huge scorched marks in the Plaza of Martyrs. Yet it was a cruel innocence, one which claimed too many lives every year, and the fact that it would claim fewer this year did very little to make him feel better. He and Father Zytan Kwill had built additional shelters for the poor, and he'd ordered a dozen of the Church's underutilized warehouses cleared to shelter still more of them. Despite that, and despite the additional funding he'd poured into the project, they were beginning to run short of fuel as the winter dragged on and on, thanks in no small part to the interruption in coal shipments from Glacierheart.

He'd often wondered why the archangels had decreed this location for Mother Church's greatest city. In summer, Zion was a place of cool breezes when Lake Pei was dotted with pleasure craft and children ran barefoot in the streets and parks. In winter, it was a bitter desert of ice and snow, where heat became almost more precious than air itself, where exposure all too easily meant death and frostbite became a fact of life. So why here? Had it been to demonstrate their God-gifted powers by rearing the Temple here, of all places? Had it been because they'd sought a place fortified by nature against Shan-wei's rebellious servants during the war which had raged even after the destruction of Armageddon Reef? Or had it simply been that, as archangels, cold and snow had bothered them not at all? That unlike mortals, they'd been able to enjoy the undeniable beauty of winter without experiencing its brutality? Perhaps they'd never considered the fact that with their withdrawal from the world they'd created under God's direction, stubborn men would insist on building an entire city around the Temple they'd left to God's glory? Shan-wei's ability to suborn so many mortal followers was proof even archangels—even Langhorne himself—had fallen short of God's omniscience, His ability to know what man might do under all circumstances. Would they have left a prohibition against building an imperial city in such an inhospitable place if it had occurred to them that might happen? And Zion *was* an imperial city; any effort to pretend otherwise would have been ludicrous, although there were still those who argued Mother Church's power in the world was limited.

Well, there may not be that many of them anymore, he thought grimly. *After the way the entire world's run mad—thanks to our doing—Mother Church clearly has plenty of power in the world. Too much, I think sometimes.*

It was a thought which had come to him increasingly often, although he'd been careful not to share it with any of his colleagues. But he'd been studying the "heretic" Staynair's policies for the Church of Charis, and he'd been impressed by the fashion in which Staynair had steadily and systematically reduced the secular power of *his* Church. He'd yielded not an inch in the Church's responsibility to proclaim right and wrong, to lend moral and spiritual guidance to every member of her flock, yet he'd made it clear war and justice was the business of the Charisian Crown, not the Empire's Church. That it was the business of Emperor and Empress and Parliament to govern and enact laws. And he'd counseled, again and again—from the very beginning—against treasuring up hatred against those who simply and honestly disagreed with one's own beliefs.

But that's the point, isn't it, Rhobair? He folded his arms, watching the torrent of snow surging past his window. *He's telling the members of his Church men have the right, the* responsibility, *to decide for themselves. To hear God's voice in their own hearts, as much as ever they hear it in the* Writ, *and to remember others have the same right and the same responsibility. Even if someone totally different sat in the Grand Inquisitor's chair, how could Mother Church stand by and see essential doctrines, the very word of the archangels, shredded and tossed aside on the basis that individual men can know God's will better than His divine messengers and servants knew it? Than Mother Church knows it now as their stewards and inheritors? How can she renounce her power in the world when the* souls *of the world are in her care and she's been expressly charged to prevent any from leading those souls astray?*

He sighed heavily, wishing he could see an answer. None had come to him, however hard he'd searched, yet if he couldn't answer those questions, there were others which he could. Perhaps if he gave himself to answering enough of those *other* questions the great, intractable ones might answer themselves in the fullness of time.

"Thinking about your shelters, Rhobair?"

It wasn't Clyntahn's fleering, contemptuous tone, and he turned his head calmly as Zahmsyn Trynair stopped beside him.

"Among other things," he said in a tranquil voice, turning to gaze back out the window once more.

Trynair studied the treasurer's profile for several seconds. Then he inhaled deeply and turned to stand at his shoulder, looking out into the beautiful, wind-lashed wildness of that deadly afternoon.

"I know there are a great many things we don't agree on these days," the chancellor said quietly, "but I want you to know, I truly admire what you've accomplished here in Zion. I don't spend the time out in the city that you do, and to be honest, I wouldn't want to. That doesn't mean I don't hear the reports, though. I know how you and Father Zytan reduced the death toll last year, and I'm sure you'll reduce it even further this winter."

"It's a pity Zhaspahr doesn't see things that way," Duchairn replied.

"Zhaspahr is a very . . . focused personality." Trynair's nostrils flared. "He sees what he wants to see—what he thinks he *needs* to see—very clearly, and his attention to detail in those instances is almost terrifying. Anything that doesn't fall into that category is unimportant. Or at least not important enough for him to allow it to distract him from that narrow, focused viewpoint of his."

"That's an interesting way to put it," Duchairn observed. "Not quite the one *I'd* choose, although I'll grant you it has its points. But it would be far better for everyone, not just the people freezing to death out there, if Zhaspahr could at least consider the *pragmatic* advantages of appealing to men's hearts as well as to their terror."

Trynair's wordless sound neither agreed nor disagreed. Perhaps he was afraid one of Clyntahn's eyes was watching them, listening to them, even now. Keeping tabs on his fellow vicars, knowing what they were thinking, was the sort of "focused" vision and attention to detail that clearly qualified as important to the Grand Inquisitor.

As Samyl and Hauwerd Wylsynn discovered, the treasurer thought with a familiar, bitter tang of guilt.

"I was on my way to your office, actually," Trynair said, after a moment. "I have letters from Dohlar and Desnair—even Sodar—that all ask basically the same thing, and I'm going to need your input replying to them."

"*My* input?" Duchairn turned from the window, eyebrows arching, but Trynair continued to look out into the snow.

"You're the one I usually have to talk to when it comes to money." The chancellor shrugged. "It seems to come to that quite a bit these days."

"Why am I not surprised?" Duchairn chuckled mirthlessly. "I assume they want to know how much we can increase their subsidies for the coming year?"

"Something like that, yes." Trynair grimaced at the window. "Hard to blame them. When we set the subsidies, none of us anticipated we'd be asking them to put armies into the field this year."

"None of us but Zhaspahr, you mean," Duchairn said grimly, and Trynair shrugged again, perhaps a little irritably this time.

"I think Allayn should've seen it coming as well."

"Allayn *did see* the need for armies coming; he simply had no idea it would be coming this quickly and on this scale. You do recall that it wasn't so very long ago we were all in agreement that the Charisians couldn't possibly field an army of their own big enough to invade the mainland? Even after the Gulf of Tarot all of us—including Zhaspahr, if I remember correctly—were of that opinion. That's why Allayn was still working with me to find a way to balance the cost of rebuilding the Navy while putting the new rifles and field guns into production. Of course, none of us anticipated they'd be *invited* in by one of the mainland realms, now did we?" The treasurer showed his teeth for just a moment. "I don't think it's very fair to blame him for what's going on in the Republic when Zhaspahr hadn't bothered to mention his plans there to any of us."

"He told you he had to act more quickly than he'd anticipated," Trynair pointed out. "If he wasn't expecting to move yet, it's hard to blame him for not warning Allayn."

"Not if he truly wasn't expecting to," Duchairn said softly.

The chancellor turned his head to dart a quick look at him, then returned his gaze resolutely to the snow-covered Plaza of Martyrs.

"I see no reason not to take his word for that."

Now that's *an interesting choice of words, Zahmsyn,* Duchairn thought dryly. *I suppose it depends on how you view your responsibilities, doesn't it? Would there be no reason to doubt Zhaspahr's word because there's no "doubt" involved, given that we're both completely certain he's lying? Or would there be a reason to go out of our way* not *to doubt Zhaspahr's word because challenging him on it might be a good way to get killed, given that we're both completely certain he's lying?*

"Well, I suppose it's the practical consequences that matter, isn't it?" he said out loud. "And the practical consequences are that Allayn was no closer to having the Army of God—or any other formed troops—ready to advance into the Republic before snowfall than he was to invade Charis itself. For that matter, he had less than eighty thousand men anywhere near the frontier."

"A point, I assure you, I'm well aware of," Trynair said a bit tartly. "And one of the primary causes for my correspondence with Desnair and Dohlar, for that matter."

Duchairn nodded. The road and canal network in East Haven was well developed, especially between Siddarmark and the Border States, the band of smaller, independent realms between the Temple Lands and the Republic, which helped explain the quantity of goods—the bulk of Charisian manufacture—which had passed through Siddarmark into the continental interior in the last half century or so. Yet there were limits in all things, and one of those limits in *northern* East Haven was the snow driving down outside the Temple at this very moment. By the time Allayn Maigwair had discovered what was happening in the Republic, it had been literally impossible for him to move and supply large bodies of troops. Oh, he'd been moving them anyway all winter long, in smaller formations, despite the weather, and he'd have quite a sizable force along the Siddarmarkian frontier by the end of this month or the middle of the next. But it was taking far longer than it would have if Clyntahn had warned him last summer, when he could have marched them in clear weather, with ice-free canals to transport the food, fodder, and ammunition those troops would have required.

At least the southern weather had at least allowed Desnair and Dohlar to begin moving troops sooner. On the other hand, the Imperial Desnairian Army was less well organized than the Army of God. Its supply arrangements struck Duchairn, as the man responsible for the Army of God's logistics, as ramshackle—or perhaps the word he wanted was improvisational—and it seemed to him that Desnair remained too committed to the primacy of cavalry, without making sufficient allowance for the new infantry weapons. The Royal Dohlaran Army had a much higher percentage of infantry—and all reports indicated the Dohlaran foundries had managed to equip a higher percentage of that infantry with rifles and bayonets than even the Army of God—but it was also much smaller than its Desnarian counterpart.

And then there were the Border States and the Army of God.

Half the Border States' armies were either hopelessly obsolete, with virtually none of the new model weapons, or little better than rabble; the other half were mostly well equipped, well organized . . . and very small. In theory, they could cross into the Republic as soon as the snow melted—or, at least, as soon as the canals did. In fact, most of them would contribute little to Mother Church's combat power if and when they did.

Which left the Army of God, the largest of any of the armies currently at Maigwair's command. In some ways, the winter-imposed hiatus had actually helped the army, and Maigwair, frankly, had worked miracles. The foundries in the southern Temple Lands and the Harchongian works closest to the Temple Lands border had labored frantically to churn out additional rifles, shifted from naval artillery to fieldpieces, and—in the last month and a half or so begun putting the new exploding artillery shells into production. It would take some time after the weather improved to get the new weapons transported to the front in quantity, and Maigwair still had a higher ratio of pikes to rifles than he would have preferred, but output was climbing steadily. He'd be able to start improving the ratio by mid- or late summer.

Always assuming we can find a way to continue paying *for it,* he reflected.

"I've been working closely with Allayn since the 'unanticipated' and 'spontaneous' popular uprising in the Republic changed all our calculations," he said after a moment. "We've had to essentially shelve plans for rebuilding the Navy, of course." He grimaced. "Harchong's continuing to work to arm the ships they've already got built, but between you and me, that's mostly because there's so much graft tied up in them. If they don't get finished, certain people don't get paid."

Trynair grunted in acknowledgment. Harchong's immense population and monolithic loyalty were crucial, and the Empire's bureaucracy was actually capable of accomplishing things quite efficiently. That wasn't the same thing as *economically,* however. In fact, in Harchong, "efficiently" and "economically" were contradictions in terms, since *nothing* happened—efficiently or not—until the proper palms were greased.

"Their eastern foundries, in Maddox and Stene, have effectively become extensions of our own, though," Duchairn continued. "We've been able to exert much more direct control over them—I have to admit Zhaspahr's decision to assign individual inquisitors to each of them helped a lot in that respect—and we've shifted all their naval orders over to additional rifles and field artillery. But there's no point pretending the marks haven't been running like water while we've done it, and the money we've had to shift into orders for army weapons is money we aren't able to continue paying for the ships we were working on, so we've actually produced a significant unemployment problem in all those shipbuilding centers we've created." The treasurer grimaced. "And while I really know everyone's tired of hearing it, when people can't earn a living, they can't pay their tithes, either."

"I know," Trynair sighed. "I know! And what's happening in Siddarmark isn't helping, is it?"

"That's a little bit like asking whether or not Hsing-wu's Passage is wet, actually. Of course it's not helping! Siddarmark and Silkiah were the only two realms which were actually managing to pay *more* than their pre-Jihad tithes. Up until October, at least. Now the Republic's fighting a civil war, Silkiah's economy is in almost as much chaos as Siddarmark's, and the Border States' economy—whose relative prosperity *depended* on Siddarmark's—has gone straight into the crapper, too, to use one of Zhaspahr's delightfully pithy phrases. Effectively, Mother Church's current income amounts to the percentage of the tithe that manages to get past the various . . . hurdles, let's say, in Harchong, plus what Dohlar can continue to pay and what's coming from Desnair. Delferahk was never a major revenue source in the first place, and Sodar—the one realm whose tithe level has remained almost unchanged—was also the poorest of the mainland realms to begin with."

The treasurer turned away from the window and tapped the taller Trynair's chest none too lightly with his index finger.

"I've put together the new taxation policy for the Temple Lands," he said. "And I've drawn up plans to dispose of a full half of Mother Church's less critical real estate. I'm also preparing a letter to Emperor Waisu which you'll have the indescribable pleasure of redrafting into properly diplomatic language."

"What sort of letter?" Trynair's expression was unhappy, and Duchairn smiled thinly.

"The one telling him his tithes are going up to twenty-five percent . . . and that Mother Church will require the imperial treasury to make good any shortfall."

"We can't tell Waisu that!" The chancellor's expression had gone from unhappy to horrified.

"First of all, we both know we'll actually be telling his *councilors* that, since I doubt he's allowed to make policy in anything more significant than deciding whether to have rice or noodles for supper. Second, we don't have a choice—we *need* the cash, Zahmsyn, and Harchong's economy's the least damaged of any of the major mainland realms. Partly that's because its economy is so damned backwards compared to all the others that disturbances in trade patterns haven't affected it all that much, but it's still true. And third, you and I both know the Harchongian bureaucracy and aristocracy have been filching from Mother Church for generations!" Duchairn stopped tapping the Chancellor's chest and waved his hand. "Oh, we both know why we've permitted that to *continue*, as well, Zahmsyn; I'm not saying I'm unaware of the reasoning. But we can't allow it any longer, and if the imperial treasury is on the hook for the thirty percent or so of the tithe various powerful Harchongese've been pocketing for as long as anyone can remember, I'm pretty sure they'll pay up."

"But . . . but we need—I mean, you know how loyal Harchong's always been! If we start making unreasonable demands, we—"

"It's not an unreasonable demand." Duchairn's voice was flat. "And Zhaspahr can't have it both ways. He's the one who kicked off this 'spontaneous uprising' without warning any of us. And his 'spontaneous uprising'"—the treasurer's irony was withering—"is what's created so much starvation in western Siddarmark a damned *wyvern* would have to carry its own rations to cross it." Fury crackled in Duchairn's normally mild eyes. "You've seen the reports, Zahmsyn. You know how many people are starving to death, how ugly the fighting's been, and now we expect Allayn to take entire armies through the same area? Just how in the names of Sondheim and Truscott d'you expect him to *feed* those troops when the people who live there are already starving? He's going to need every scrap of food we can beg, borrow, or steal, and then he's going to need every river barge, every wagon, every draft dragon we can find to ship it to him! And all of that's going to cost money that has to come from somewhere. So either Zhaspahr can agree with my . . . unpalatable prescription for Waisu and the rest of Harchong, or *he* can damned well figure out how Allayn's supposed to march across the wilderness *he* frigging well created!"

Trynair shrank visibly from Duchairn's ferocity. He swallowed hard, but the treasurer never looked away from him. Finally, the chancellor drew a deep breath.

"All right, Rhobair," he said quietly. "All right, I'll support you. But for Langhorne's sake, don't . . . explode at Zhaspahr that way. Please." He waved both hands. "I accept that you're right, but you know Zhaspahr as well as I do! You know how he feels about Harchong, too. If you turn this into a confrontation, and especially if you make it sound like an *attack* on Harchong, he'll just dig in his heels and get stubborner and stubborner. And if that happens . . . well, let's just say it won't work out well."

Duchairn snorted harshly, a sound that mingled understanding, resignation, and contempt in equal measure, but he also nodded.

"Of course I understand that, but I've already talked to Allayn. He's prepared to support me, because he's looked at the numbers along with me. He knows we're going to need the marks and need them damned soon. The two of us need *your* support, as well. If all three of us confront Zhaspahr on this, present a united front, with Allayn explaining why he needs the money, and you explaining why Desnair and Dohlar and—Langhorne save us all!—even Sodar need money, and me explaining the only places where we can *get* money, maybe even Zhaspahr will see reason."

"And if he doesn't?" Trynair asked very quietly.

"Zahmsyn, I'm already issuing drafts on money we don't have," Duchairn said equally quietly, and Trynair's eyes widened. "This Jihad's hammered our cash flow from the beginning, both because of the tithe base we've lost and because of how damned much it's cost," the treasurer continued. "In order to pay for it, Mother Church is running a deficit for the first time in her history, and we started doing that more than *three years ago.* Worse, *we're* the ones *other* people usually borrow money from—the entire banking system was never set up for us to borrow large sums of money from secular sources. Which doesn't even consider the fact that the primary mainland banking houses are all in eastern Siddarmark and happen to be . . . unavailable to us. We're not going to be able to borrow our way out of this, even if the interest on the money wouldn't eat us alive. Oh, Zhaspahr saved us some of our debt, since we've just pretty effectively repudiated payments we hadn't already accounted to Siddarmark, but that's less than a drop in the bucket compared to the revenue we've *lost* from the same source. We actually saved more—and lost less—when Corisande surrendered to Cayleb and we repudiated all of that debt. Neither of those paper transactions changes the fact that, at this point in time, what we actually have in the Treasury's accounts is almost eighteen percent less than our current obligations without any consideration at all of future interest on what we've already borrowed. Worse, other people know we're issuing notes we can't cover, even if they don't know exactly how bad the situation actually is, and that means our drafts are trading below their face value. No one wants to be too open about it, but anyone but an idiot is taking hard currency over our paper any time he possibly can get it, and my Treasury agents are hearing more and more reports about clipped, underweight coins or even outright counterfeits. For that matter," he met Trynair's eyes levelly, "one of my senior assistants has actually suggested—very quietly, you understand—that we begin . . . reducing the bullion content of our coinage."

Trynair's nostrils flared, and Duchairn smiled thinly. The *Book of Langhorne* made the archangels' position on debasing or adulterating coinages very plain. Or that was the way Mother Church had always interpreted Langhorne 14:72 where *secular* coinage was concerned. "You will give honest measure and honest weight in any transaction, for he who would cheat his brother in smaller matters is but teaching himself to cheat in larger ones, and treachery to a brother in God will surely beget treachery to God Himself." The Inquisition had used that passage to crush any secular ruler's temptation to debase his coinage for the better part of seven centuries, and if *Mother Church* now began to violate it . . . .

"From our perspective, though," the treasurer continued, "what matters is even without that sort of, ah, *questionable* approach, we're effectively putting money that doesn't exist into the economy, and everyone knows it. Put another way, we're about to see an explosive . . . *inflation*, for want of a better word, in the cost of everything we buy because a Temple mark is going to be worth less and, with Charis now completely excluded from mainland markets, there are going to be fewer goods available for those less valuable marks to purchase in the first place. We were already losing ground on the Charisian mark before this entire war began, but it was a slow gradual process at that point. Now it's accelerating like an avalanche. Before the Jihad, a Temple mark was worth roughly fourteen percent more than a Charisian mark; now it's worth eleven percent *less*, and I don't think it's going to get any better anytime soon. Ultimately, our income depends on the size and wealth of the economies from which the tithe is drawn. We literally can't squeeze out money that doesn't exist, although Zhaspahr seems to have difficulty grasping that minor point from time to time. I've almost given up on making him understand *that*, but what he'd damned well *better* understand, at least in the short term, is even simpler. We no longer have the reserves to back our debt, and if people realize that—which they assuredly will if the situation continues heading in its present direction—everything I've just described will only get worse. We'll literally be unable to pay Mother Church's bills, and our ability to support the war will collapse. We have to increase our revenue flows, or the Jihad fails. It's that simple."

Trynair winced as the other vicar used the verb "fails," but Duchairn's steely eyes never flinched.

"But we *can* put Allayn's armies into the field this year?" the chancellor pressed.

"We can *put* them into the field, but without an agreement to increase revenue significantly—which is going to mean the provisions I've already mentioned *at a minimum*—we can't *keep* them there. That's the bottom line, if you'll forgive me for using the term, and we damned well better make sure Zhaspahr understands that before we send a couple of hundred thousand men we won't be able to feed—or pay—into a wasteland where food supplies are already exhausted or destroyed. Somehow I don't think having hordes of hungry soldiers nominally in the service of Mother Church pillaging—and undoubtedly raping and looting, once they start stealing food—the provinces which revolted against the Lord Protector in *her* name will have a very salutary effect on their future loyalty to her. Do you?"

Zahmsyn Trynair stared at Mother Church's treasurer, and the snow roaring outside the window was no colder than his own heart.

. XVIII .
Bargetown,
Barony of High Rock,
Kingdom of Old Charis,
Empire of Charis

Well, Zosh?"

Ehdwyrd Howsmyn stood beside his master artificer in the hot, late-morning sunlight, staring up at the beached sea dragon looming above them. The empty river barge seemed enormous, despite its squat appearance, as it crouched on the massive timbers of its supporting skidwork. Getting it out of the water had been significantly harder than getting it *into* the water when it was first launched. The gravity which had slid it down the ways then had worked against the four hill dragons who'd been harnessed in tandem to get it back out again. Fortunately, Howsmyn's minions had acquired a remarkable degree of experience in moving massive weights and coming up with ways to use blocks and tackle to get the job done.

Now Zosh Huntyr scratched his short brown beard and grimaced.

"It'd've been a hell of a lot easier to haul the bitch back out if we'd had time to do it Nahrmahn's way, Sir. I know we didn't, but steel rails and proper wheels would've moved her a lot more efficiently"—he grinned as he used Howsmyn's favorite word to his employer—"than rollers did."

"No doubt," Howsmyn said dryly. "Unfortunately, Their Majesties were rather firm about wanting us to get this done *this* year. Speaking of which—?"

"I think we can do it, Sir—and meet Their Majesties' schedule . . . more or less. I can't promise, but barring something none of us've thought of to worry about yet, we should do it."

"Including the re-engining?" Howsmyn turned to look at his master artificer, rather than the unlovely functionality of the barge's design, and his expression showed a certain degree of worry.

"Stahlman says we can do it, Sir. Not without pulling more work crews from other assignments than either of us is going to like, but we can do it. The original engine room was only a box in the hold, with the boilers in the open out front. So all we're really looking at doing's just a question of building new foundations, moving the thing, putting in a second engine and the second set of boilers—and balancing them to maintain stability properly, of course—then pulling the original propeller shaft, moving it, stealing another shaft from one of the incomplete boats, building the boxing around both of them, plugging the hole in the hull where the original shaft went, stealing a second propeller and thrust bearing from the same barge we stole the second *shaft* from, installing it as well, and then building the gundeck across the whole length of the ship. Oh, and the cabins, bunkers, and such, of course." He shrugged. "What could be simpler than that, Sir?"

"Well, put that way, I don't understand why you needed anyone else to help you with it at all!" Howsmyn said. "I'll get right back to the office and tell all those other work crews you're going to handle it personally."

He and the master artificer grinned at each other, but then Huntyr shrugged.

"The truth is, Sir," he said in a less ironic tone, "right now that's just a big empty box. We can arrange its innards any way we need to, and doing it before we build the gundeck's going to make that a lot simpler." He shrugged. "It's going to take a lot of sweat, but we'll get it done. And we'll be going right ahead armoring the casemate while we do it. As long as the armor mill can turn out the one-inch plate in time and keep the supply of bolts ahead of requirements, we'll meet the schedule."

"Good, Zosh. In fact, very good." Howsmyn patted his master artificer on the shoulder. "I knew you could do it all along. Honestly—I did!"

Huntyr gave him a moderately skeptical look, and Howsmyn chuckled.

"Well, I *hoped* you could, anyway, when I was making my promises to Their Majesties."

"None of the lads're any more wishful of disappointing Their Majesties than I am, Sir. We'll get it done," Huntyr repeated, and Howsmyn nodded in satisfaction.

"Then I'll get out from underfoot and leave you to it."

He gave Huntyr's shoulder one more pat, then turned and headed purposefully towards his waiting conveyance.

The introduction of the deceptively simple bicycle was another of those small things with profound consequences, he reflected as he swung his leg over the frame. He would have been a lot happier with pneumatic tires, but that wasn't going to be possible for quite some time, so he'd settled for providing the saddles with the best springs he could contrive. No spring could turn a tooth-rattling ride over cobblestones into an enjoyable experience, but the ability of human beings to move themselves at average speeds of ten to fifteen miles per hour over a *smooth* surface was nothing short of revolutionary, and the wonderful thing about this particular innovation was that no one could possibly suggest it came even close to infringing the Proscriptions.

And it doesn't do us sedentary, paper-pushing, ruthless robber-baron capitalists one bit of harm to burn off a few pounds getting back and forth to work, either, he told himself dryly as he stepped down on the raised pedal and moved off in a smooth rattle of bicycle chain. *Although I do have to admit that falling on my arse when I first tried to master the damned contraption didn't do a thing for my sense of dignity!*

The current model remained fairly crude, a coaster-brake design without gearing and far heavier than the lightweight versions a more sophisticated industrial plant could have produced, but it was still the most efficient mode of human transport Safehold had ever seen. Eventually, it would have military implications as well. For now, however, Howsmyn had discovered his bike was a faster and more convenient way to get back and forth between his Delthak Works office and the waterfront/freight terminal on the roughly four mile by six mile, thimble-shaped spit of land between Lake Ithmyn and the channel from the Delthak River which fed his hydro-accumulators and waterwheels. Dubbed—inevitably, he supposed, but unimaginatively—"Bargetown" by the men who worked there, it was his own private shipyard, with barge building ways lining both sides of the channel from the river.

As he pedaled back towards the main works' pall of smoke, passing pedestrians headed both ways and a handful of other bicycles headed in the opposite direction, he reflected on his conference with Huntyr.

The master artificer was right about how badly the ironclads were going to disorder other projects in his carefully organized queue. On the other hand, that "carefully organized queue" of his had been pulled apart and put back together so often over the last few years that it had acquired a certain . . . flexibility. And Huntyr was also right about the priority they'd been assigned.

The good news was that the project was doable, always allowing for the provisos Huntyr had just registered. In fact, his rough calculations when Merlin first suggested the possibility had, as he'd anticipated, been heavy. The supply of three-inch plate on hand would actually be enough to convert four of them and leave several hundred tons to spare, which had allowed for things he hadn't counted on, like properly armored pilothouses placed where the helmsman could actually see where he was going.

The bad news, which had contributed significantly to the labor and resource costs, was that Sir Dustyn Olyvyr had flatly refused to send converted river barges with a single propeller and shaft across several thousand miles of salt water. Despite his faith in Howsmyn's artificers, and despite his own inclusion in the inner circle, with the information access and vast reservoir of technical knowledge that bestowed, the navy's chief constructor was a firm believer in the Demon Murphee. And however good the workmanship, and however reliably the engines in question had run during their brief operational experience on the Delthak River and the Delthak River Canal, they'd never been run continuously for five-days on end. Had it been possible to accompany them with galleons to assist in the event of a breakdown, Olyvyr probably wouldn't have complained, but that *wasn't* going to be possible, given that the ironclad's sustainable speed was so much greater than that of a wind-dependent galleon.

Somewhat to Howsmyn's surprise, Stahlman Praigyr had firmly supported Olyvyr's position. Much as the artificer loved the new steam engines, he was a practical man, and love hadn't blinded him to the teething problems of his beloved offspring. Cayleb had come down firmly on Olyvyr's side as well, so Praigyr and Olyvyr had put their heads together. Both had been determined to make the project work, and the solution they'd come up with was simple: just install a second engine and propeller in each barge for redundancy's sake. With two engines and twin propeller shafts, immobilizing breakdowns would become far less likely, and with four ironclads traveling in company, a tow should always be available even if that were to happen to one of them. Nor would it hurt anything to have that same redundancy in the face of possible combat damage . . . or the additional power, if it came to that. Fortunately the engines and propellers had been available from barges still under construction, so Howsmyn hadn't had to sacrifice four more operational boats, thank God. The hole taking *these* four out of service had already made in his materials transport chain was painful enough.

"See?" a voice said in his ear as he pedaled onward. "I told you we could do it!"

Howsmyn glanced around, making sure no one was close enough to hear him, then snorted.

"Who's this 'we' you're talking about, Merlin? Correct me if I'm wrong, but I don't seem to recall seeing *you* turning any wrenches or swinging any hammers on this little project of yours."

"That's because I'm a concept sort. A big-picture person," Merlin returned airily. "I come up with ideas, then delegate. You should try learning to do that yourself."

"How badly will it hurt my toe to kick a PICA in the arse the next time I see one?"

"Alas, the fate of great minds is always to be resented."

"Yes, sure." Howsmyn shook his head, grinning. Then his expression sobered. "It really is making a big hole in the rest of our production schedules, though, Merlin," he said, voicing his earlier thought. "And even when we're finished, we're only going to have four of them. I'm willing to admit they'll be able to handle just about anything they run into, but they'll still only be able to be in four places at once, and that's if we're willing to operate them in singletons."

"Agreed." Merlin's voice was more serious than it had been. "And I hate throwing improvisations at you. One of your greatest strengths is your ability to coordinate—to envision the parts of a task and organize the best way to accomplish it—and I know how far the ripple effect of upsetting that organization of yours can flow. In this case, I really don't think we have much of a choice, though."

"I agree they're going to be good to have," Howsmyn said. "At the same time, and fully acknowledging how important rivers and canals are going to be to our operations, I'm afraid I don't see any way just four of them could hope to be anything like decisive. Not given how badly outnumbered we're going to be. It's not just the *size* of their armies, Merlin; it's how *many* of them they have."

"I don't know that they are going to be decisive," Merlin acknowledged. "I do think they're going to be extraordinarily useful in the Gulf of Mathyas, though, and I've got a couple of other notions noodling around in the back of my brain. Having them available can't hurt, and the resources we're diverting to them aren't going to directly impinge on your production of small arms or artillery." Howsmyn had the sense of an unseen shrug at the other end of the com link. "They give us options—or I hope they will, anyway—and as you've just pointed out, we're outnumbered enough we're going to need every bit of flexibility we can scrounge up."

"Can't argue with that," Howsmyn sighed.

He pedaled in silence for another minute or so, then snorted.

"I've been looking at what Thirsk is up to, again. This whole conversion project got me to thinking about him, because when he hears about it, he's going to use it to hammer Fern and that idiot Thorast where his own ironclad project's concerned. You do realize it's likely to guarantee him a higher priority for all of those other projects his Lieutenant Zhwaigair's come up with, don't you?"

"Can't be helped," Merlin said philosophically. "They're not going to start building steam plants next five-day, whatever they do, and they aren't going to be able to match the quality of your Howsmynized armor, either."

"No, but they *are* going to be able to build quite a few of them, given the yard capacity the Church built up building its galleon fleet. In some ways, I'd like to see them do that, since every pound of iron they divert to armor is a pound they won't have to use for artillery or rifles. But for the foreseeable future, even with me operating at full stretch, the majority of our fleet's still going to be wooden-hulled and sail-powered, and I'll be damned if that 'screw-galley' approach doesn't look like working, at least in short, tactical bursts. It's going to give our galleon skippers fits. And God only *knows* what Zhwaigair's going to come up with next!" Howsmyn shook his head. "The inventive little bastard reminds me entirely too much of a much more junior Ahlfryd!"

"He does, doesn't he?" Merlin said, and Howsmyn's eyebrow rose at the oddly approving edge in the *seijin's* tone.

He started to reply, but he was coming up on a work crew trudging towards Bargetown. It would probably be a bad idea for his employees to decide he was beginning to talk to himself, he reflected, and waited until he'd passed them.

"You say that like you think it's a good thing," he observed then.

"I do . . . in a way," Merlin replied. "Oh, I'm not blind to how much more difficult someone like Zhwaigair's likely to make our job in the long term, but he's not going to have any *immediate* effect in Siddarmark, as far as I can see. And, let's face it, no matter how smart he is, unlike Ahlfryd, he doesn't have even indirect access to Owl or the Royal College. Or to *you*, for that matter. But he represents what I've been looking for all along, when you come down to it. Once the mainlanders get into the habit of coming up with innovations, the genie's out of the bottle, Ehdwyrd. Clyntahn's not going to be able to cram it back inside once it gets its feet under it. And the beauty of it from our perspective is that he doesn't have any choice but to *let* the genie out if he's going to try to beat us militarily. If it weren't for the little problem of the 'archangels' promised millennial return to check on things, all we'd have to do would be survive long enough for that genie to cut the ground out from under his feet. Unfortunately, we're on a shorter time limit than I'd ever expected."

The "genie in a bottle" was a concept all the inner circle had become accustomed to, although the ancient Old Earth story had no exact parallel in Safehold's literature. The idea behind it was far from alien to Safehold, but it traditionally took the form of fiercely denunciatory religious parables and *Writ* passages designed to demonstrate the dark consequences of challenging the Proscriptions. "Shan-wei out of her prison" was the way *Safehold* told the story. And, unfortunately, there were moments when, as a Charisian, he found his own appreciation for genies popping out of *other* people's bottles was somewhat less pronounced than Merlin Athrawes'.

"So you're not even tempted to nip down to Gorath and arrange an accident for him?" he asked.

"No more than I am to arrange one for Thirsk." Merlin's voice was flatter than it had been. "I don't plan on getting into the assassination business, Ehdwyrd. Not unless it's absolutely critical, anyway. Besides, if the history of assassination demonstrates one thing, it's the law of unintended consequences. Sometimes it works exactly the way you hoped it would, but even then you can't predict what the repercussions are going to be. And other times, it works out the way Nahrmahn's attempt to assassinate Hektor would've worked out if he'd succeeded. You may've observed that *Clyntahn's* order to have him killed caused us just a few little problems? And that we got blamed for it, despite the fact that we'd had nothing to do with it? There are a few people on the other side I'd take great pleasure in eliminating, Ehdwyrd, but I'm not going to go after even them unless I have no other choice."

Howsmyn nodded. He was getting close to the main works, and foot traffic was picking up, so he wasn't going to have much more time for this conversation en route. And he knew he wasn't going to change Merlin's mind on this particular point. For that matter, he wasn't at all certain he truly *wanted* to change it. There was a lot of weight to Merlin's logic . . . and that didn't even consider the fact that he knew how morally repugnant Merlin would find the sort of godlike role of chooser of the slain which would undoubtedly have appealed to someone like Langhorne or Chihiro.

Or the potential nightmare consequences for Safehold if Merlin had turned into someone like Langhorne or Chihiro, for that matter.

"I noticed Thirsk and Bishop Staiphan went to considerable lengths to protect Zhwaigair when Thirsk started talking about his ideas," he said instead.

"I noticed that, too," Merlin agreed in a satisfied tone. "More proof that even people in the Church, like Maik, are beginning to think for themselves . . . and recognize the need to protect not just themselves but others from Clyntahn."

"I do wish Thirsk had the moral courage to face the implications of what he's supporting, though," Howsmyn said more grimly. "I realize he's in a hell of a position to do anything about it, and I recognize the risk he took doing what little anyone could for Gwylym and the others. But I can't help thinking about how Coris responded to the situation, or the way Irys seems to be reacting."

"Actually, I feel incredibly sorry for Thirsk," Merlin said softly. "I think he's a good, honorable man trapped between duty, religious belief, his own morality, and fear. And I don't think the fear's for himself. At this point, I don't think it's even for his country."

"Fear that if the 'heresy' succeeds we'll give all our souls to Shan-wei?" Howsmyn asked, just a bit skeptically.

"There probably *is* some of that wrapped up inside it. You should know as well as anyone how hard it is to confront an entire lifetime of programming, Ehdwyrd—and unlike Thirsk, you had the advantage of . . . call me a guide, if you like. He doesn't have that, and his faith goes to the bone. But I think that whether he knows it or not himself, he's pretty much crossed the Rubicon."

" 'Crossed the Rubicon?' "

"Sorry—one of those Old Earth clichés. It's a reference to crossing a river, but what it really describes is taking an irrevocable action or decision. What I meant is that I think Thirsk—and possibly even Maik, to an extent— both realize the Reformists are right. Neither of them are in positions to do much about it at the moment, but they're self-honest enough to recognize the evil they're being forced to compromise with. It's not really fair to compare Thirsk to Coris, though. Much though I've come to respect and even like Coris, he didn't have any choice when Clyntahn decided to murder Daivyn. We were the only port available at that point, no matter what terms we might exact in return, and he knew it. Thirsk has an entire family, and every member of it's been 'invited' by Rahnyld and Archbishop Trumahn to come live close to him in Gorath."

"You think it's only the threat to his family holding him back?"

"I didn't say that. He has a very complicated moral equation to solve, and there's still a part of him that hates Charis for what we did to his navy off Armageddon Reef. But thinking back over a conversation he had once with Bishop Staiphan, I think the threat to his daughters and his grandchildren is probably the biggest single factor."

"He's never said or done a single thing that I'm aware of to indicate he might even consider turning against Rahnyld and the Church," Howsmyn pointed out. "I don't try to keep track of all Owl's reports about him. That's not my area of expertise and never will be. But I haven't heard anything from Bynzhamyn—or from you, for that matter—to suggest he's said or done anything."

"Because he hasn't, but don't forget how smart he is. He's not going to say or do anything that could implicate or involve one of his subordinates, because he knows the Inquisition has ears everywhere. I wouldn't be surprised to find he's very, very careful about what he commits to writing as well, especially given the sort of 'collective responsibility' Clyntahn's embraced by targeting the families of those who disappoint him. But that doesn't mean something isn't cooking away inside the man, and the more he alienates the Inquisition hardliners, the more pressure it's going to be cooking under. I actually nourish some hopes—modest ones—where the good earl's concerned."

"Well," Howsmyn said, approaching the main works gateway, "Mother always told me it wasn't polite to call someone crazy, so I'll tactfully refrain from doing so. Besides," he smiled, braking slightly to delay his arrival at the gateway and the waiting ears ahead, "you've conjured some fairly amazing miracles out of thin air so far. I'm not going to say you can't produce another one, no matter how unlikely it seems."

.XIX.
HMS *Empress of Charis*, 58,
The Cauldron,
and
HMS *Destiny*, 56,
Dolphin Reach

I know we're lucky to be able to do this, but I still hate it," Emperor Cayleb Ahrmahk remarked to the swirling wake stretching away behind HMS *Empress of Charis*.

He stood on his favorite flagship's stern walk, leaning on the rail while he looked out across the unwontedly calm waters of The Cauldron and *Empress of Charis* sailed steadily northwest, close-hauled on the starboard tack in the fading light. The galleon was no longer as heavily armed as once she'd been, but Sir Dustyn Olyvyr had learned a great deal from the design of her class. Among other things, he'd learned the limit of the number of heavy cannon he could cram into the length of a wooden-framed ship without its keel hogging under the weight. Despite the reduction in armament that had required in *Empress of Charis'* case, the ship Cayleb continued to insist he hadn't really named after his wife remained one of the most heavily armed vessels on the face of Safehold.

"I don't like it a lot, either, you know," Empress Sharleyan Ahrmahk replied.

It was considerably darker aboard HMS *Destiny* as she sailed equally steadily north*east* across Dolphin Reach, already two thousand miles (and three hours) east of *Empress of Charis*. She, too, occupied her ship's stern walk, but she wasn't quite alone. Crown Princess Alahnah drowsed in the hammock cradle beside her, and Sergeant Edwyrd Seahamper stood watch to insure no one disturbed her and her daughter.

"I don't like it," she continued, "but you know you *are* right about how much luckier we are than a lot of people. Mairah, for example. She won't admit it, but I know how dreadfully she's missing Hauwerd right now."

"If it's any consolation, I think he's missing her just as badly," Cayleb assured her with a wry smile. Hauwerd Breygart would be leaving *Empress of Charis* in the next day or so to continue to Eralth Bay with the Marine expeditionary force, but he'd been Cayleb's dinner guest every night since they'd left Old Charis. "Big, tough, competent—God, he'd already served, what? Twenty years in the Marines before he ever became Earl?—and all he can talk about over the dinner table is her and the kids."

"That's because he's a good man," his wife scolded. "Good enough he actually *deserves* Mairah!"

"I didn't say he doesn't," Cayleb replied mildly. "For that matter, I don't recall saying my dinner conversation was a lot more varied than his." His smile turned into a grimace. "We spend enough time talking about things like strategies and tactics during the day, Sharley. Over dinner, we can just be husbands and fathers."

Sharleyan's expression softened as she heard the yearning in his voice, and she reached down to lay one hand very gently on Alahnah's chest, feeling the slow, steady breathing and the heartbeat so precious to her and Cayleb alike.

"I think what irks me the most," Cayleb continued, "is that we have such a brief window to talk to each other every night. I know—I know! We both just agreed on how lucky we are to be able to do it at all, but having to wait all day, then have so little time together, is . . . hard."

"I know."

Sharleyan moved her hand to Alahnah's cheek, smiling down at the little girl, then leaned back in her canvas-backed chair. The last time she and Cayleb had been at sea simultaneously—in different ships, that was—their communications schedule had been more flexible. HMS *Dawn Star*, the galleon which had borne her from Chisholm to Corisande and then, finally, to Tellesberg, was no larger than *Destiny*, but she'd been far less crowded. Sir

Dunkyn Yairley's flagship—escorted by no less than six other galleons, given her cargo—had surrendered eight main deck guns to free space that could be turned into temporary cabins, but she was still packed tight as a jar of sardines. Sharleyan could no longer rely upon the privacy of her cabin to be certain no one would hear her talking apparently to thin air, and so she and Cayleb could speak only at moments like this, when each of them was alone on the stern walk of his or her galleon.

Fortunately, they'd established the custom, on the occasions when they were aboard ship together, of retiring to the privacy of the stern walk to watch the sun set. They maintained the habit when they sailed separately as well, and their subjects were pleased to be able to give them that small bubble of privacy in which to think about the spouse they missed so badly. Of course, her lips quirked briefly, very few of those subjects and retainers could possibly have guessed just how . . . *closely* they thought about one another during those moments.

"Well," she said more briskly, "I assume you've kept up on the SNARC reports? I don't mean those unimportant ones about things in Siddarmark and Dohlar and Delferahk. I'm talking about the *important* ones!"

"Would those be the ones about Daivyn and Haaralhd getting themselves confined belowdecks all day by Mairah and Captain Yairley for that race up the rigging? Or the ones about Sairaih's quarrel with Glahdys over who gets to take Alahnah up on deck for her afternoon sunbath every day? Or the ones about just how badly Maikel and Mairah trounced you and Sir Dunkyn at spades yesterday? Or the—"

"How about the ones about your stepson and a certain princess?" Sharleyan interrupted, and Cayleb chuckled.

"Oh, *those* reports!"

"You do realize how fortunate you are to be safely out of reach at this particular moment, don't you?"

"As a matter of fact, I do. Although," his voice deepened with a note she remembered well—*too* well, considering the distance between them, "letting you have your way with me after you beat me into surrender for my thoroughly misplaced levity doesn't sound so bad, now that I think about it."

"I have no idea what you're talking about," she said, her prim tone somewhat marred by the twinkle in her eye.

"Oh, of course you don't. On the other hand, it's probably better this way, given how crowded *Destiny* is, I mean. You are a little . . . noisy at moments like that."

"*Noisy?*" Sharleyan shook her head. "You are *so* going to pay for that one, Cayleb Ahrmahk!"

"I await the moment in cringing trepidation," he assured her, and she laughed.

"I promise it's going to be dreadful. But getting back to my original question, what *do* you think about Hektor and Irys?"

"I never really thought I'd say this, considering our . . . relationship with her father, but the more I look at it, the more I think they'd both be lucky. I don't know if they'd be as lucky as we've been, but she's even smarter than I thought, and there's more going on inside her brain—and heart, I think—than she's admitted even to Coris. And not just where our Hektor might be concerned, if you know what I mean."

"Of course I know what you mean." Sharleyan tugged the blanket more snugly over Alahnah as the evening grew chillier. "I haven't spent this long with her without realizing *that*. Or were you of the opinion *my* brain had ceased to function?"

"Certainly not," he said virtuously. "I think it's true, though. I just wish there was a way to peek through her skull and see what's actually going on inside it." He shook his head. "Rahzhyr agrees with us about how interested she was in everything she saw at the College, and I'd say she's refocused every bit of the hate she felt for you and me when she thought *we'd* had their father assassinated. For that matter, I think she's added interest to it! But she really is remarkably good at keeping her own counsel. I'd hate to play cards with her for serious money. I'll bet she could even take Maikel at spades!"

"I've noticed the same thing, maybe even more strongly than you have." Sharleyan shrugged. "I try not to be overly influenced by the similarities between her and me, but sometimes I think even you don't truly understand what it's like to be a girl—a young woman—who knows every step she takes is through the middle of a snake pit. It's not *herself* she's worried about, of course, but she's every bit as aware of how . . . precarious Daivyn's position is as I ever was about my own. I understand exactly why she's giving so little away."

"I do, too, and I don't blame her. In fact, I admire her. That doesn't change the fact that I'd like to know what she's really thinking, though, and not just because it would give us a better feel for whether or not we should be trying to encourage whatever may or may not be happening between her and Hektor. If she's leaning the way I *think* she's leaning, the advantages could be enormous. But is she really leaning that way, or do I only think she is because we want her to be so badly?"

"One of the reasons I try not to be influenced by those similarities. And even if she is, it doesn't help that she's so far below the Brethren's cutoff age."

"Sharley, I don't know if it would be a good idea to tell her the entire—" Cayleb began, but the empress shook her head.

"I'm not proposing to tell her the truth about Langhorne and the other lunatics over tea tomorrow, Cayleb," she said just a bit tartly. "In fact, I'm not proposing to tell her the truth about *any* of it without first discussing it with the rest of the circle in ample detail, first. But I will tell you this, Cayleb Ahrmahk—I don't care if she is ten years short of the official notification age, she'd be a lot better prepared to handle the truth than some of the other people we've considered telling. And," she added with an undeniable note of triumph, "I might point out that neither of *us* has yet attained that venerable old age of thirty, either. She's really not that much younger than we are, you know. In fact, unless I my memory fails, she's several months older than a certain crown prince was when *Seijin* Merlin first came into his life."

"As a matter of fact, I *do* know that. And you may be right about Irys—always assuming her thinking really does go where we think it's headed. It would give the Brethren fits, though, especially now that we don't have Father Zhon to knock heads together during one of their anxiety attacks!"

"Now that is *not* fair, Cayleb," Sharleyan half laughed. "They don't suffer 'anxiety attacks,' and you know it." Her humor faded. "Actually, I think a lot of their more recent hesitancy is because Father Zhon was their . . . touchstone, I suppose. Or maybe their compass. They'd gotten so accustomed to being advised by him, to trusting his judgment, that they're all second-guessing themselves to make sure they don't let their own judgment fail them now that they don't have his to fall back on anymore."

"You're probably right," he said thoughtfully, then snorted. "You and Merlin are both more likely to look at how the minds of people who aren't doing what I want or need them to do work and why. I'm afraid I have a pronounced tendency to regard them as nails that need to be hammered."

"Yes," she said gravely, "I've observed what a callous, tyrannical, insensitive sort you are, but I hadn't wanted to mention it."

"Oh, thank you."

"You're welcome. But since you've brought it up, has *Merlin* said anything about the possibility of admitting Irys to the inner circle?"

"No, he hasn't. Of course, it hadn't occurred to me to ask him until you brought it up just now. And"—a trace of asperity entered his tone—"at the moment, I can't."

"What?" Sharleyan's eyes widened. Merlin made it a habit to stay out of her private conversations with Cayleb unless one of them invited him in, but still . . . .

"I'm afraid the mysterious *Seijin* Merlin has retired to his cabin to spend the night in austere meditation," Cayleb said sourly.

"Oh, Lord!" Sharleyan rolled her eyes. "What's he really up to this time?"

"I'm afraid I can't tell you anything more about that than I could tell anyone else," Cayleb said even more sourly. "That's because he didn't tell *me*."

This time, Sharleyan's eyes didn't roll; they widened. It wasn't unheard of for Merlin to make decisions on his own, or even to undertake errands without discussing them with anyone else first. Sometimes, as in his reaction to Tymahn Hahskans' brutal murder in Manchyr, even when he expected his decisions might infuriate her and Cayleb. Whatever the rest of the world might think, the two of them—and the rest of the inner circle—knew Merlin's mission on Safehold went far deeper than obedience to the Crown and trumped even the survival of the Charisian Empire. No one doubted his dedication to Charis, or to his friends, but neither did they doubt Merlin Athrawes would do whatever *he* decided Nimue Alban's mission required, no matter the cost. Yet she couldn't recall a single time when he hadn't even explained what he was doing—not when there'd been time to explain, at any rate.

"He didn't tell you *anything?*"

"All he said was that he had 'a couple of errands' he had to run and that he'd tell me about them later, if he could."

Cayleb's tone was light, but Sharleyan heard the worry in its depths, anyway. Not because he distrusted Merlin, and certainly not because he was angry at having his authority flouted. No, he was worried for the same reason she was.

What are you up to, Merlin? she asked the silent night. *Where are you? And what could be so dangerous you can't tell anyone about it even now?*

A sudden thought struck her, and she started to speak. But she stopped herself in time, swallowing the words unspoken.

Surely not! He wouldn't—*however big the circle's grown!*

She bit her lip, remembering a conversation with Merlin after his return from Delferahk. Remembering what he'd said, the satisfaction in his voice, as he'd talked about the size the circle had attained. About how many native born Safeholdians knew the truth now . . . about how they could carry on if "something happened" to him.

Merlin. She sent the plea winging out into the gathering darkness. *Merlin, don't start taking chances you wouldn't've taken before just because you think we don't need you anymore! We do need you, and not just because you're our magical seijin! We don't need you as our guide—we need you as you, because we love you.*

"Well," she said serenely to her distant husband after a moment, "I'm sure he'll tell you all about it as soon as he gets back."

A Recon Skimmer,
Above the Tarot Channel

Merlin Athrawes turned the skimmer up on its side so he could activate the zoom function of his artificial eyes as he gazed down through the transparent canopy to the herringbone geometry of the waves sweeping endlessly across the waters of the Tarot Channel, the better part of four miles below his present altitude.

It wasn't often he saw Safehold's surface from so high above in daylight. There wasn't really any reason why he shouldn't. The skimmer's engines left no contrails, and its stealth systems had been designed to defeat sensors far more capable than the human eye. For that matter, darkness offered no protection from the one set of sensors he might actually have to fear. The sensor arrays serving the bombardment platform still patiently orbiting Safehold cared very little about the quantity of visible light.

No, the main reason for his nocturnal flight habits was simply that it was extraordinarily difficult for *Seijin* Merlin to simply disappear when human beings were up and about. It could be done—in fact, he'd done it several times, but almost always in emergencies when he had no choice. Partly because of the possibility someone might go looking for him and find him inexplicably not where he was supposed to be, but also because the moments when Owl sent the skimmer to fetch him were also the moments when they were most vulnerable to being spotted. Owl's SNARCs and the skimmer's own surveillance systems were good enough to make it *almost* impossible for them to fail to spot any potential, awkward witnesses, but almost wasn't the same thing as a certainty. And the odds that someone would stumble across them at an exceedingly inconvenient moment were considerably greater during daylight than in the middle of the night.

On the other hand, there were certain advantages (and quite a few *disadvantages*) to having Owl pick him up at sea. For one thing, boats and ships tended to stand out rather distinctly in the middle of vast, empty stretches of ocean, which made it even more unlikely Owl would miss any potential witnesses. For another, a PICA had no need to breathe, and Merlin was as much at home swimming below twenty or thirty feet of seawater as he was bobbing about on the surface, which turned Safehold's oceans into one, vast hiding place where he could remain comfortably out of sight, waiting until the ship he'd left disappeared in the distance before the skimmer picked him up. The main disadvantage, of course, was that ships were very small places packed with relatively large numbers of people. That made "dropping out of sight" more than a bit difficult.

Fortunately, *Seijin* Merlin's need for occasional periods of meditation had become an accepted part of his legend. Everyone understood why he'd been assigned his own cabin, even in the crowded precincts of *Empress of Charis*, and no one would dream of disturbing him for anything short of fire or shipwreck once he'd announced his need for privacy and retired to it. It scarcely eliminated the risk, but it clearly reduced it, and he'd had little choice but to get an earlier start than usual for this particular flight.

You really should've told Cayleb and Sharleyan about this little project, he told himself, watching water give way to the coast of Malitar Province far below him. *They're probably going to be pissed when they find out you didn't, and it's going to be hard to blame them. Of course, if it doesn't work, they won't be finding out about it after all, will they?*

"Pissed" could turn out to be an understatement, he reflected, although he expected they'd *probably* understand why he hadn't told them once they'd had a chance to think it over. And the bottom line was that it had been his decision to make—if it was anyone's—not theirs. And if it worked out as well as he hoped it might . . . .

He looked down at the green, deceptively peaceful Malitar coast, thinking about the brutality of the fighting and hatred and starvation he was about to fly so swiftly across, and a fresh flicker of guilt washed through him. He wasn't the one who'd orchestrated the uprising in Siddarmark, and certainly not the one who'd ordered his agents to destroy and sabotage food sources. He knew who to blame for instigating that barbarity, yet he couldn't really absolve himself of responsibility for the Church of God Awaiting's jihad. The Group of Four might be the ones who'd instigated the actual fighting, who'd attempted to casually crush a problem which was merely potential when they unleashed their initial attack on the Kingdom of Charis without so much as a moment's hesitation. And there was no question that Zhaspahr Clyntahn and the Inquisition must bear the blood guilt for the atrocities being committed in God's name. Yet there was equally no question that Nimue Alban's mission had made the jihad inevitable. It was the only way to destroy the Church's death grip on human innovation and freedom, and that death grip *had* to be broken. So in the end, Group of Four or no Group of Four, Merlin Athrawes would have brought religious war and all its brutality and savagery to Safehold in the fullness of time, for he would have had no other choice.

He grimaced and gave himself a shake, pushing the familiar thought back into its mental cupboard and locking the door behind it. If Maikel Staynair was correct and he still had a soul, the time would come when he had to render an accounting for everything he'd done—and had still to do—but that time wasn't yet. And if the judgment was against him in the end, so be it. He couldn't—and wouldn't—pretend he hadn't known exactly what he was doing, and that mission was worth any sentence a rational deity might impose.

But for now, there were other things to think about, and he checked the time display racing downward towards his ETA in the Mountains of Light.

.XXI.
Nimue's Cave,
The Mountains of Light

He woke up.

He lay there for a moment, trying to understand why that surprised him, but he couldn't. It was as if there was something he couldn't quite remember, which was a most unusual experience. He pursed his lips, frowning in thought as he hung a moment longer on the lip of wakefulness, yet nothing would come to him, and he shrugged the question away and opened his eyes. He looked up at a familiar ceiling, hearing the distant sound of waves and the whistles of the palace's song wyverns through the open window, and a sense of delicious well-being banished his momentary sense of confusion. It was early morning, past dawn but still cool, the sun still low on the eastern horizon. That wasn't going to last, since the city of Eraystor sat almost directly upon the equator, but this was where he'd grown up. He knew the pulse and pattern of the days, which was why morning had been his favorite time of day since childhood. The world was quiet, still in the process of waking up, and the morning air was like a clear, cool wine or a lover's caress. He treasured that sensual, caressing freshness almost as much as he did the star-strewn clarity of the breezy night, and he stretched luxuriously before he sat up. He inhaled deeply, filling his lungs to the aching point before he exhaled once more, and climbed out of bed.

He pulled on a robe without summoning any of the servants and opened the glass doors to his private balcony. He stepped out into the morning breeze, feeling it pluck at his hair, and smiled as he saw the tray of melon balls, strawberries, and grapes beside the carafe filled with his favorite blend of apple and grape juice. He stood for several moments, leaning on the rail, looking out over the palace grounds and, beyond them, to the roofs and steeples of Eraystor. He could hear the city beginning to rouse—the sound of voices, the rattle of wagon wheels, the cadence of a Guard sergeant marching his detail off to relieve the night watch. He listened to it, absorbing it, feeling the world coming awake, before he turned to the table and poured himself a glass of juice.

He drank slowly, savoring the taste, then dropped into the rattan chair and reached for the first melon ball. He popped it into his mouth, chewing slowly, and his brow furrowed as he tried again to pin down whatever it was that was, not *disturbing*, yet somehow . . . wrong. There was something he should be recalling. Something which would have explained why this restful, peaceful morning seemed . . . out of kilter somehow.

He swallowed the mouthful of melon and smiled as he recalled the first time he'd heard Merlin use that phrase—"out of kilter"—and asked what it meant. It was a very useful one, actually. A lot of the odd turns of phrase Merlin used with those who knew his secret were that way, and quite a few had started leaking out into the language. It was a gradual process, filtering down from the circle of Cayleb and Sharleyan's most trusted subordinates and advisors, but it also appeared to be inevitable. That was the way things usually worked, he'd observed. In fact, he reflected, reaching for another melon ball, he'd been discussing that very point only day before yesterday with Rayjhis Yowance. The First Councilor had said—

His eyes flared suddenly wide. No, that couldn't be right . . . could it? Rayjhis had said . . . but Rayjhis was *dead*. He'd been . . . been killed. In . . . in an explosion? But . . . but if that was *true*, then what—?

The melon ball crushed in his hand, juice running over his fingers, and he looked down at it, amazed to find his hand trembling. He inhaled deeply, not luxuriously this time, but in something too much like panic, trying to marshal the thoughts crashing around inside his brain. But his mind's habitual focus failed him. He couldn't make the jumble of thoughts and impressions make sense, couldn't hammer them into obedience while he—

"Hello, Nahrmahn," a voice said quietly, and he whirled in his chair.

He'd never before seen the tall, black-haired, extraordinarily attractive young woman in the bizarre black and gold uniform. He knew that. Yet there was something about those sapphire eyes . . . about that contralto voice he'd never heard before, almost like a lighter, sweeter echo of another voice . . . .

"Merlin?" He heard the confusion in his own voice and shook his head. "But . . . but—"

"I know this is all very confusing," the young woman who wasn't Merlin Athrawes said. She crossed the balcony and pulled out the other chair, sitting with the same graceful economy of motion he'd seen out of Merlin so many times. And yet it was indefinably different. Merlin was a man; this person definitely wasn't.

"You're . . . Nimue," he said slowly, and she nodded.

"Here I am, anyway." She smiled. It was exactly the same smile he'd seen from Merlin more times than he could count, he thought, but without the dagger beard and the fierce mustachios. And without the scarred cheek, either. "I'm afraid the interface wasn't loaded with Merlin, though. An oversight." The smile turned wry. "I forgot Owl isn't supplied with an overabundance of initiative or intuition. I simply assumed he would've adjusted it, and there wasn't time to fix it after I realized he hadn't."

"Here? Interface?" Nahrmahn shook his head. "I . . . I don't understand," he said, and yet even as he spoke, he had the strangest sensation he *did* understand . . . and simply didn't want to admit it to himself.

"Yes." Nimue/Merlin's smile faded, and she sat back, regarding him intently. Those blue eyes searched his face with an intensity that was almost unnerving, and her nostrils flared as if she'd drawn a deep breath, steeling herself for something.

"Nahrmahn," she said, "I owe you an apology. I didn't really have any right to do this—or even try to do it—without your permission. But there wasn't time for that, either, I'm afraid. And I didn't know whether or not it would even work. Or how *well* it would work, assuming it worked at all. For that matter, I still don't know."

"You're making me a bit nervous . . . Nimue," he said, and was relieved to hear it come out in something almost like his normal tone.

"Sorry." She smiled again, fleetingly. "It's just . . . well, the truth is, Nahrmahn, that you and I have something very much in common now."

"In common?" He cocked his head. "And what would that be?"

"The fact that we're both dead," she said quietly.

▼　　▼　　▼

"So let me get this straight," Nahrmahn Baytz said, a great many minutes later, sitting back and waving both hands at the balcony, the palace, the sunlight, the quickening noises of the city. "All of this—everything—is inside a computer? It's not real at all?"

"No, for certain values of 'real,' it's as real as it gets." Nimue popped one of the melon balls from the plate into her mouth, chewing appreciatively. "By every test you could give it, it's completely real, Nahrmahn. Too much of that sunlight up there will cause you to turn red as a boiled spider crab. Fall off this balcony, and you'll be lucky if you only break an ankle. Of course, that's because Owl's still in charge of the governors."

"The governors?" he repeated in a resigned tone.

"The software that controls the parameters. There are some restrictions on what anyone inside the reality can change, but there's actually quite a bit of elasticity. You can . . . readjust things in quite a few ways, once you get the hang of it."

"But for the purposes of this discussion," Nahrmahn leaned forward over the table, tapping it with an intent fingertip, "it's *not* real. It's a simulation. Obviously a very *convincing* simulation, but still a simulation?"

"It's called a virtual reality, Nahrmahn. And it's a construct, put together out of your own memories and the software's extrapolations of them, supplemented by data—a lot of it in near real-time—from Owl's SNARCs. In every sense that matters, it's just as 'real' as you or Merlin Athrawes. But just as 'Merlin' exists only in his PICA, what you can almost think of as a mobile virtual-reality module that happens to be capable of interacting with the physical world, you exist only inside *this* module."

"But . . . how?" Nahrmahn folded his arms. "I understand that Merlin is actually, well, *you*, or at least an electronic recording of you. But that recording was made long before you ever woke up here on Safehold. How did *I* end up"—he unfolded one arm to wave at the world about them—"here?"

"You remember the explosion?" she asked gently, and his mouth tightened.

"Yes," he said shortly. "I remember. And I remember holding Ohlyvya's hand." He swallowed and closed suddenly stinging eyes. "I remember her crying. And . . . and I remember *you*—or Merlin, anyway—turning up." His eyes opened once more and narrowed. "Turning up with that . . . whatever it was you put on my head. Is *that* what caused all this?"

"Yes," Nimue admitted. "And that's what I meant when I said I really didn't have any right to do this without your permission. In fact, I violated at least half a dozen Federation laws by doing it *at all*, much less without your informed consent. But I wasn't certain it would work, and . . . and I wasn't going to take away any of the time you had left with Ohlyvya trying to explain it."

"And if you weren't sure it would work," he said slowly, "you weren't about to mention it to her, were you?" Nimue looked back at him without speaking, her blue eyes very dark and still, and he nodded. "No, you weren't. You wouldn't've given her what might've turned out to be false hope."

"That . . . was part of it. And another part was that I didn't know if you'd have wanted me to tell her."

"Of course I would have!"

"Really?" She cocked her head. "I hoped you would—I hope you still will—but think about it first. Outside this VR module, you don't have a body anymore. In that sense, you're even more of a ghost than I am, and you know I've never been really certain whether I'm still *me* or just a pattern of electrons that only *thinks* it is. I love Ohlyvya, and I might as well admit—if it won't make you uncomfortable, remembering you only ever knew me as Merlin—that I love *you*, too. But I can't guarantee how she'd react if she started hearing your voice from the dead. She watched you die, Nahrmahn.

She held your hand, and she wept on your chest, and she buried you. I think she has the strength and heart to understand what's happened, but I can't guarantee that, and the human heart can be a very unpredictable thing. And before you rush into anything, you have to understand that Ohlyvya will never be able to visit you here the way I can."

"Why not?" Nahrmahn asked, watching her closely.

"Because she doesn't have the neural receptors to plug into the VR net."

"That doesn't make any sense." He shook his head. "I didn't have any neural receptors, either. In fact, now that I think about it, I distinctly remember your telling us it was the lack of receptors which meant we couldn't use any of the neural education units in your cave to give us all complete educations."

"That's right."

"But if that's true, then how in God's name did you . . . 'record' me in the first place?"

"You don't have—didn't have—the *receptors*, Nahrmahn. The NEATs are designed to impart information, not record it. They're transmitters, and the human doesn't come brain-equipped with a receiver. That has to be provided if the NEAT's going to connect. But the human brain *does* radiate, if a receiver's sensitive enough to pick up its transmissions, and that's one of the things—the most important thing, really, under the circumstances—that headset I used is specifically designed to do."

"But that's not *all* it was designed to do, is it?" Nahrmahn watched her expression even more closely than before. "I've had personal experience now to disprove that cliché about your entire life passing in front of your eyes, so pardon me if I find it unlikely I was spontaneously 'radiating' all those memories for you just then. And I've learned enough about your technology to be pretty sure data had to be flowing both ways if you were going to record something as complex as a human personality and its memories."

"Well, yes," Nimue admitted. She drew another deep breath. "You were dying, Nahrmahn. We couldn't stop that. So I overrode the programming on your bio nanotech and I enabled a tertiary function on the headset. I didn't have it made specifically for you, you know. I actually intended it for me, but when I ordered Owl to run it up on his fabricators in the cave, he simply duplicated a standard piece of hardware Terran EMT—emergency medical technician—units routinely carried with them. You do remember how I used it to block the pain you'd been feeling?"

"Yes," he said slowly.

"Well, that was what it was most often used for, its primary function. Its *secondary* function was to make recordings just like you and me." She smiled briefly at his expression. "Of course, it was designed to do that using the NEAT connections all Terrans were equipped with—nothing else would give it enough bandwidth to record something so complex under such adverse conditions—but that's where the nanotech I've injected all of you with comes in." Her smile vanished. "When I activated the headset, Owl used its tertiary function to reprogram the nannies' base parameters. He needed my authorization to do it, and he couldn't've done it without the headset's EMT functions, but, to be honest, if you hadn't already been dying, Nahrmahn, it almost certainly would've killed you anyway."

"Killed me?" Nahrmahn's nostrils flared. "You mean our nanotech could kill *any* of us?"

"Yes." Nimue met his gaze unflinchingly. "Under the right circumstances. As I said, however, Owl couldn't do it without the headset's interface *and* my personal and direct authorization as the nannies' originator. It's not some sort of 'kill switch,' Nahrmahn; it's part of the standard package I used as the basis for all of you. And what it's normally used for is targeted emergency repair of the nerves controlling your vital functions. It's an emergency medical intervention technique that bypasses destroyed or severely damaged nerves to keep things like a critically injured person's heart and lungs working until the medical teams can get him into a trauma center."

"That . . . sounds reasonable."

"It is. Unfortunately, it's a . . . brute-force approach. It's a quick-and-dirty, emergency-only technique to be used only in a last-ditch situation, because it requires pretty close to a complete regen afterwards."

"'Regen'?" he repeated the unfamiliar word carefully.

"Regeneration, Nahrmahn. In some cases, a complete body regen, which could take up to a couple of years, even with Federation medical tech. In other cases, a more limited regen, affecting only the specific nervous tissue that was, for want of a better term, scavenged to build the bypass."

"That sounds . . . unpleasant," Nahrmahn observed, and Nimue laughed briefly.

"I did mention that I only tried it because you were dying anyway."

"True. But what exactly does this have to do with how I ended up here?"

He pointed at the balcony's flagstones.

"The nannies built the receptors we needed," Nimue said in a flat tone. "And they found the material to build them by scavenging other parts of your brain. They had to do that anyway for me to block the pain, since you didn't have the receptors someone on Old Terra would've had, but it wasn't easy and they couldn't do it without inflicting a lot of additional damage. If by some miracle you hadn't died after all, Nahrmahn, you'd've been a complete paralytic afterwards. That's why I'd never have used it, despite the horrible pain I knew you were in, if there'd been the least chance of your surviving your wounds. But there wasn't, and I didn't want to lose you, and that meant Owl and I had to push the nannies even further, because we needed to reach more than just your brain's pain centers. What we did certainly *would*'ve killed you in the end, whatever else happened, and, frankly, I didn't think we'd be able to do it, anyway. Not really—not in the time we had left, and not with how badly the nannies had already burned themselves out keeping you alive until I got there."

"But obviously they worked after all," Nahrmahn said.

"Not . . . entirely," Nimue replied.

He stiffened, looking at her, and she sighed.

"The connection wasn't perfect, and we didn't have a lot of time. Under normal circumstances, there's a very complete data-checking function in the software and it's designed to do a thorough, methodical information search. There's a stupendous amount of storage capacity in a human brain, and especially with the jury-rigged receptors we had, there's only so much bandwidth. When you combine that with how little time we had, Owl had to disable some of the anticorruption protocols built into the software. He estimates we lost at least fifteen percent of your total memories. Probably a little more, to be honest."

Nahrmahn stared at her, then picked up his juice glass and drank deeply. Crystal clicked on polished stone as he set the glass back on the tabletop, and he looked down into it for a moment before he looked back up at Nimue.

"Fifteen percent doesn't sound all *that* bad," he observed with a whimsy he was far from feeling at the moment. "Pity I didn't get to pick the ones I discarded, though."

"We've managed to recover, or reconstruct, at least, quite a bit of it. In many cases, it was fairly straightforward for Owl to fill in the blanks, especially if he could locate a similar memory and borrow from it. But the truth is that there are holes, Nahrmahn, and we can't know exactly where they are until you hit one of them. According to Owl's analysis, they're concentrated in the earlier part of your life. Childhood memories and probably some extending into your adolescence. Some of them *are* from later, though. I'm sorry, but it was the best we could do."

"I see."

Nahrmahn sat back, breathing deeply, looking around the undeniably real world about him, then back at Nimue.

"I see," he repeated, "but what I don't see is how you just happened to have this available. Or is this where a PICA's stored memories live when it's offline?"

"No." Nimue rose and walked to the balcony railing, leaning one hip against it, her arms crossed as she looked out over the city Nahrmahn remembered so well. "No, this is more like the VR units the Federation used for R&D. AIs—even the big ones, not the more limited ones like Owl—don't have anywhere near human-level intuition, Nahrmahn. They're not very good at making leaps of the imagination. On the other hand, their computational speed is so fast that in many ways it seems as if they're capable of doing exactly that. But the Federation discovered that if it created virtual personalities of its best scientists or strategists and loaded them into the proper VR matrix, they got the best of both worlds: an AI's computational speed, since the matrix could be 'accelerated'—compressed, really—pretty much at will, plus human-grade intuition. They called it 'hyper-heuristic mode,' which I understand was a reference to some ancient Old Terran writer." She shrugged. "The only thing they couldn't do was carry out real-life experiments inside the matrix. Those had to handled outside the VR, which meant the virtual personalities had to slow down to interface with the world everyone else lived in. But by the same token, it offered a huge multiplication of the talent pool that meant the Federation could assemble a dozen teams, or a hundred, or even a thousand, all consisting of the same virtual personalities, and assign them separate problems to solve simultaneously. That's one reason we'd managed to close so much of the gap between our capabilities and the Gbaba's before they punched through and wiped us out."

"I see. Or, actually, I *don't* see, not yet. But I think I'm at least following the explanation."

"There were some pretty strict restrictions, even when the war was at its most desperate, on what could be done to—and with—virtual personalities. They were more than just programs floating around, and it was absolutely illegal to record anyone for a virtual environment without their permission and a court-certified permit. And the personalities had a legally protected existence, independent of the individuals from whom they were recorded. But the truth is that the entire technology was inherently vulnerable to all sorts of abuses. The Federation did its best to make sure none of those abuses happened, but I'd be lying if I didn't say I suspected some did. For that matter, I wouldn't be a bit surprised to find out the Federation itself was guilty of a violation or two as the situation against the Gbaba went further and further to hell."

"And do you think it's possible *this*"—his right hand made another of those all-encompassing waves—"is what's actually under the Temple?"

"I'm almost certain it isn't," Nimue replied, turning and putting her back against the railing to face him. "I could be wrong, but if there was a virtual personality of one of the archangels under the Temple, I can't believe it would've let things go this far without intervening. I'd like to think it would've intervened to prevent the Group of Four from becoming so powerful, abusing their positions so blatantly, in the first place. But even if it didn't care about that, it certainly would've recognized the implications of the Delthak Works and our new steam engines. I suppose it might've chosen not to use the Rakurai again as long as there's a chance the Church can defeat us and reestablish the full rigor of the Proscriptions, but I don't think so. That kind of . . . moderation doesn't seem to've been part of the 'archangels' thinking. And even if it were, I would've expected it to go ahead and strike Charis and probably Chisholm long ago, before the 'contamination' could spread to the rest of the planet and it had to kill even more people to burn out the poison.

"On the other hand, it's always possible there's a canned virtual personality under there. One that isn't currently active but can be awakened at need. That could be what Schueler was telling Paityr's family about in that holo he left them."

"Why shouldn't it be currently active?"

"Boredom, mostly." Nimue shrugged. "There are two ways a virtual personality can lose itself, Nahrmahn. One is by climbing deeper and deeper into its own private reality until it's not even remotely interested in interacting with the world its original donor lives in. That's one reason the software of most VR modules contains safeguards preventing the personalities inside them from taking control of all of the simulations' parameters. Think about it. The ability to completely control every facet of your existence? To reshape the entire world however you want it reshaped? To give yourself whatever superpowers you could conceive of? To satisfy *any* desire you may ever have felt? Can you imagine a more completely addictive drug?"

"No. No, I can't," Nahrmahn said with a small shiver.

"And the opposite side of that coin is boredom. Even immortality can turn into a curse. That's been a feature of every human culture's fairy tales and folklore, and it turns out it's actually true. And with the time compression effect of a VR world, you can get to immortal status awfully quick. That's one reason virtual personalities would tend to climb ever deeper into realities they could alter at will, to escape too much . . . sameness."

She paused, looking away from him for a moment, then turned back to him, her expression serious.

"It goes a little further than that for some people. Some virtual personalities simply can't handle the knowledge that they're only recordings of someone else—copies, not the original. So while some personalities become terminally bored, weary, of a 'pocket universe' that doesn't contain anybody else 'real' aside from whatever other virtual personalities've been loaded to it, others withdraw into themselves and eventually shut down completely. Effectively, they go catatonic and withdraw from the only reality they have because it isn't really reality at all, as far as they're concerned."

"You're making this all sound remarkably dismal for such a beautiful morning, Nimue," Nahrmahn pointed out.

"Well, I suspect most of the personalities likely to react that way are probably rather less . . . resilient than yours," she said with a small smile.

"I'll try to take that as a compliment."

"Good."

She gave him another smile, then straightened and unfolded her arms.

"I can't stay a lot longer, Nahrmahn," she told him. "With my high-speed data interface down, Owl can't adjust the data transmission speed to let me interface with you when you're operating on a compressed timescale. Which, by the way, is what you've been doing ever since you got here, even if you weren't awake at the time. Owl's spent quite a while locating, repairing, and reintegrating your memories. You've always been a . . . complex sort of fellow, and you didn't get any less complicated in the act of dying."

"I'm devastated by the thought of inconveniencing you and Owl," he said politely, and she laughed.

"I'm sure you are. But what that means is that for me to actually come visit you, first, I have to be physically here in the cave, where I can plug into the interface unit. And, secondly, every second I spend in here with you is just as long as a second in the 'real world.' Since I'm going to have to get back aboard *Empress of Charis* without anyone seeing me, I'd just as soon get back while it's still dark. Which means—"

"Which means you'll have to be going." Nahrmahn nodded, managing to keep his expression tranquil. It was harder than he would have expected as he contemplated being left alone in his own private little world.

"Yes."

Nimue looked at him for a long moment, then walked over and laid a slender hand on his shoulder.

"Yes," she repeated in a gentler voice, "but I don't think it's going to be quite as bad as you may be worried about. First, you'll have direct, continuous access to Owl. Second, now that you're 'awake,' you'll also have access to the SNARCs com network. I'd, ah, suggest not suddenly starting to communicate with people without giving me the opportunity to warn them about you, but you'll be able to talk to people. You just won't be able to . . . visit them."

"Or touch them," Nahrmahn said very, very softly.

"Or touch them," she agreed, equally softly. "I'm sorry, Nahrmahn. I wish that weren't the case, but it is. And that's one of the reasons I haven't told anyone else yet, even after Owl told me he'd reached a point at which he projected at least a ninety percent probability of our being able to success-fully reintegrate you. You have the right to decide your own fate. I violated your trust in a very real way by recording you at all, but if I hadn't, you wouldn't have a choice. You'd simply be gone. If that's what you choose— and, in some ways, I wouldn't blame you; believe me, if anyone in the universe understands what it's like to wonder if you're real or only someone else's memories, it's me—that's your right, too. No one has the moral right to make you stay with us, especially when you'll be trapped on the other side of an interface no one but me can cross, so if you want to go, all you have to do is tell Owl. And because you have that right, I'll never tell Ohlyvya or anyone else you exercised that option if that's what you decide to do. You won't hurt her a second time, Nahrmahn. Not that way, I promise."

"But if I tell her I'm still alive—or that this version of 'me' still exists . . . somewhere, anyway—and we can never actually touch one another again, am I going to hurt her anyway? Will *she* think it's me, or will I be some abomination, a reminder of the flesh-and-blood man who loved her, but not him? Only his ghost talking to her over a communications link?"

"I don't know," Nimue admitted. "I don't think she thinks of *Merlin* as someone's ghost, but the situation's not the same, and I know it. That has to be your decision, your call. I'll just say this. I did this, put you in this position and left you with those choices, because you're important to me. Because . . . because I've lost too many of the people here on Safehold already, and I was too damned selfish to lose another if there was any way at all I could prevent it. But that's not the only reason I did it. In fact, the *other* people who love you aren't the only reasons I did it, either. We still need you—*I* still need you. We need your insight, and your advice, and—frankly—your sneakiness."

She smiled faintly as he turned a laugh into a rather unconvincing cough.

"As I say, the choice is yours. Don't rush to make it, though." She looked around the morning, gazing out over Eraystor's rooftops again while the breeze stirred her black hair. "It's not so bad a world, your memories, and I think you'll probably find the odd amusement in it. And on the other side of that com link, there are still a lot of people who need you and who've come to love you quite a lot. I didn't ask your permission before I did all of this to you, so instead I'll ask your forgiveness now. But don't decide too quickly . . . either way. If you do decide to stay, decide to tell Ohlyvya you're here, take the time to think about it first. It will be your voice over the com, Nahrmahn. Be sure it says what you want her to hear."

"I will."

He stood, crossing the balcony, standing beside her as the sun rose higher and the breeze freshened.

"I will," he repeated, and reached out to lay a hand lightly on her arm.

"And whatever I decide, there's no need to ask my forgiveness," he said gently, and smiled when she looked down at him. "If you hadn't done what you did, there wouldn't be any decisions *to* make, now would there? And wouldn't *that* be boring?"

.XXII.
HMS *Destroyer*, 54,
Howell Bay,
Kingdom of Old Charis,
Empire of Charis,
and
Lord Protector's Palace,
Siddar City,
Republic of Siddarmark

Sir Domynyk Staynair stood on the stern walk of HMS *Destroyer*, leaning on the railing and watching as the confusion of galleons got underway and sorted itself out. The war galleons, which had been stripped of their armament, floated unnaturally high to his experienced eye, but that would change once they reached Raven's Land and weighted themselves down with their freight of soldiers. The dozen fully armed galleons who'd been detailed to escort them hovered protectively, awaiting them, and Baron Rock Point stifled an ignoble sense of envy as the transports forged slowly past his anchored flagship and headed out to do so something *useful*.

"We really do need you where you are, you know," a voice said over the plug in his ear. "And since we do, you might as well stop lashing your tail like a slash lizard with a sore tooth."

"I do *not* have a sore tooth, Kynt," the high admiral replied more than a bit tartly. "I will concede to lashing my tail," he admitted after a moment. "I hope that's not as obvious to everyone else as it appears to be to you, however. I do have a reputation for imperturbability to maintain among my admiring staff officers and subordinates."

"Oh, imperturbability is the very first thing *I'd* associate with you," the Baron of Green Valley assured him, smiling as the image projected on his contact lenses showed him his friend's expression. At the moment, Green Valley's horse was picking its way through a particularly wretched sleet storm on its way to yet another inspection and he was scarcely in a position to fully enjoy the imagery. While he trusted the horse, he *did* like to keep at least half an eye on his environs at moments like this. But Owl was adept at allowing for a recipient's current lighting conditions when projecting the visual take from his remotes. Rock Point was clearly visible, yet he was also translucent, and despite the brilliant sunlight beating down on Howell Bay, the imagery wasn't so bright as to inhibit Green Valley's ability to see his actual physical surroundings.

Just as well, too, he told himself, surveying the truly execrable weather. *It's so nice that we're officially into spring. Now if only someone would tell the weather that. Soon, I hope.*

From his most recent reports, he wasn't the only one who felt that way. The Imperial Charisian Army's brigades were almost ready to begin their undoubtedly miserable slog through Raven's Land, and the quartermaster's draft dragons seemed to have gotten wind of what was about to be demanded of them. They were being unusually ornery, at any rate, although Green Valley suspected some of that orneriness might be more apparent than real. Or, even more probably, a reflection of the drovers' attitude towards what was about to be demanded of *them.* Inspecting the dragons, their harness, and the wagons in question wasn't likely to change the draft animals' attitude, but he intended for it to have a pronounced salutary effect on the humans involved.

And my mood when I get there on the other side of all this crap, he thought, glowering about him at the rattling sleet, *should give my pithy observations on their state of readiness a certain added panache.*

"I guess I shouldn't complain too much," Rock Point acknowledged after a moment. "At least I don't have a saddle punishing my arse like *some* people do. And the weather's a lot nicer down here."

The last sentence came out in undeniably dulcet tones, and Green Valley grimaced at the low blow.

"For that matter," Rock Point continued more soberly, "it's not as if they're really going to need me along, either."

"No," Green Valley agreed, guiding his horse around a particularly treacherous looking icy spot, "but I'll admit I'm glad to see the escort squadron."

"Probably not necessary, but I've never been that happy about words like 'probably,'" Rock Point said. "Shailtyn should keep anybody from annoying you, though. And until we figure out a way to keep those damned privateers from sneaking by Tyrnyr, we don't have much choice."

Green Valley grunted in unhappy agreement, and it was Rock Point's turn to grimace. Captain Daivyn Shailtyn, promoted to acting commodore—or, to use the term Merlin had gotten introduced, "frocked" to that rank— while still serving as HMS *Thunderbolt*'s commanding officer, was an experienced seaman. Protecting a gaggle of transports from determined privateers wasn't as easy as a landsman might assume from the disparity of firepower between a ten- or twelve-gun schooner and a fifty-eight-gun galleon, but Shailtyn was up to the task. And it didn't hurt that the transports in question were all commanded by experienced naval officers . . . or that Rock Point had delayed their departure just long enough to put a half-dozen guns back aboard each of them for self-defense. They'd keep as tight a formation as sail-powered ships could expect, and they'd be able to look after themselves reasonably well. They'd *better* be, at any rate.

Especially, he thought, *given what the aforementioned damned privateers did to us last month. Seven galleons might not sound like all that much, but it's the first sign someone on the other side's finally tumbled to the one way they can still hurt us. Bad enough to lose the ships, but if the bastards really think about how badly the need to establish some sort of worldwide convoy system's going to hurt our flexibility, they'll really push it. And if Maigwair's actually smart enough to reflect on how providing those convoys with* escorts *is going to cut into the Navy's deployable hulls . . . .*

Commodore Ruhsail Tyrnyr, assigned to command the Imperial Charisian Navy's outpost on Howard Island in the mouth of Howard Passage, had a less enviable task than Shailtyn. Although the Imperial Desnairian Navy's presence in the Gulf of Jahras had been reduced to splinters after the assault on Iythria, Desnair hadn't abandoned the notion of making itself a pain in Rock Point's neck, among other portions of his anatomy. It appeared Mother Church had finally accepted that she wasn't going to be able to match the Charisian Navy for the foreseeable future, and her naval efforts had taken a different direction since the Battle of Iythria. The schooners and brigs being built by Desnarian carpenters in every bay, inlet, and puddle surrounding the gulf were far too small to challenge Charis' galleons, but they were going to be big enough to pose a very real threat to merchant shipping. They weren't being built in handy, centralized locations like Iythria, either, which made the task of just finding all of them, far less raiding in sufficient strength to actually destroy them before they got to sea, problematic at best. And despite Howard Island's strategic location, the passage it guarded was too broad to prevent small, agile, shoal draft vessels from sneaking past Tyrnyr's patrols in foul weather or darkness.

And we've had plenty of both of those this winter, the high admiral thought glumly. *Which doesn't even consider that the Desnairian Empire runs over four thousand miles from north to south . . . with better than* nine *thousand miles of actual coastline completely exclusive of the Gulf of Jahras. They can build privateers in just about any bay or creek, and we don't begin to have enough ships to watch an entire coast that extensive.*

"Pity Tyrnyr doesn't have access to the SNARCs," Green Valley remarked, clearly following Rock Point's own thoughts.

"Wouldn't help unless all his schooner and galleon captains had coms," Rock Point pointed out. "All the satellites would do for him in that case would be to make him as frustrated as *I* sometimes feel!"

"True." Green Valley nodded. "We do get spoiled by the ability to talk to each other, don't we?"

"That's one way to put it." Rock Point snorted. "I imagine it must be as frustrating to you as it is to me, though."

"Yes and no." Green Valley shrugged. "I don't usually have units scattered over several million square miles of seawater. And"—his tone darkened—"so far, at least, I haven't had to watch something like what happened to Gwylym Manthyr's squadron happen to one of my regiments while I was thousands of miles away and couldn't even warn them what was coming. Don't think I haven't thanked God for *that* a time or two, Domynyk! But 'frustrating' is probably putting it a bit too mildly when it comes to tactical situations. The truth is, I think exercising command's going to be more maddening in Siddarmark, now that I have access to the SNARCs, than it was in Corisande, when I couldn't be sure what was on the other side of the next hill." He shook his head. "Sometimes I wonder how Cayleb stood it when he knew exactly what our lead units were moving into and there was no way for him to *tell* anyone about it!"

"Get used to it," Rock Point advised harshly, then inhaled deeply. "You're right about how maddening it is, but it's a useful capability, too. You're right about how useless we all felt watching what happened to Gwylym, too, but it had a lot to do with what we managed to accomplish in the Gulf of Tarot, as well." His mouth tightened as he remembered that nighttime chaos and the loss of Bryahn Lock Island, but then he shrugged. "It's a hell of a lot more than anyone on the *other* side has, and it's likely to save our backsides more than once before this whole frigging mess is over. Just make the best use of it you can, Kynt. That's all any of us can do."

"I'll try to bear that in mind."

"Do. And now, it's time for me to get back on deck and do some more admiral things. Have fun floundering around in the snow and sleet."

"If there's any justice in the world, you will soon find yourself miserably seasick and half-frozen in the middle of a gale somewhere," Green Valley shot back.

"Probably," Rock Point conceded affably. "On the other hand, what could possibly lead you to believe justice has anything at all to do with what happens?"

▼   ▼   ▼

"If there were any justice in the world," Henrai Maidyn observed more than a little bitterly, "Zhaspahr Clyntahn's spine would be sprouting a dagger about now."

The Chancellor of the Exchequer, the Republic of Siddarmark's treasurer, and the man in charge of all of its spies, glowered down at the map on the huge table, his blue eyes hard. The chancellor had a full head of fair, silvering hair and a far less weathered face than Bynzhamyn Raice, his Charisian counterpart, but both of them took intelligence failures personally, and the unpalatable portrait painted by the tokens on that map depended on information which, all too often, was little better than a guess.

And then there was the fact that if anyone in an official position of authority here in the Republic might have been in charge of seeing that a dagger reached the Grand Inquisitor's back, it would have been him. The fact that he resented his inability to make that happen was rather obvious at the moment.

"We can only hope someone will get one there eventually, Henrai," Samyl Gahdarhd said. The Keeper of the Seal, roughly equivalent to the Republic's first councilor, wore an expression even sourer than Maidyn's.

"I don't suppose there's any prospect of that happening anytime soon, is there?" Daryus Parkair, the Republic's seneschal and the commanding officer of its army, raised his eyebrows as he looked at the sole woman present. She was a remarkably attractive woman, as it happened, but her eyes were almost as unhappy as Maidyn's and she made a small moue as she looked back at the seneschal.

"There are things I'd like to be able to accomplish but can't, My Lord. And getting through Clyntahn's security is one of them, unfortunately. For that matter," her expression hardened, "there are distinct limits on what anyone can accomplish in the Temple Lands right now."

"I know." Parkair shook his head. "And I apologize, Madam Pahrsahn. It's just—"

"It's just that the reward for having accomplished one miracle is to find people demanding still more of them," Greyghor Stohnar interrupted. The lord protector smiled briefly, although the expression looked strange and out of place on his worn, worried face. "Ungrateful of us, I know, but we're only human."

"Which is more than I'm inclined to say for that pig Clyntahn," Aivah Pahrsahn, who'd once been known as Ahnzhelyk Phonda (and before that as Nynian Rychtair), replied. She looked back at Parkair. "Clyntahn's 'sword' surprised me just as badly as it did anyone else, I'm afraid, My Lord. I knew how bad the Group of Four's revenue picture was getting, and I made the mistake of believing even he couldn't be stupid enough to kill the wyvern that fetched the golden rabbit this way. I didn't expect him to move against the Republic for at least another year or so, and my organization back home was still in the building phase. For that matter"—she showed her teeth in a brief smile—"quite a few rifles I intended to send into the Temple Lands have gone other places, instead."

"Thank God," Stohnar said quietly.

"I agree with the Lord Protector," Parkair said, looking back down at the map, "but I'm afraid we're still far too short of rifles—or men—for what's coming at us."

"We're lucky we've had the winter to build more of them, Daryus," Stohnar pointed out. The seneschal looked at him, and the lord protector shrugged. "For that matter, we're lucky we could still find the money to *pay* for the one's we've managed to build. I wish we'd been able to build a lot more of them than we have, but let's not turn up our noses at the ones we *have* managed to get into the troops' hands."

"I assure you, no one's going to do that." Parkair's tone was grim. "Unfortunately, it looks like the other side's got a hell of a lot more of them than we do."

"That's true, My Lord," Brigadier Mahrtyn Taisyn put in, his Charisian accent contrasting strongly with those of the others present. "But one thing we discovered in Corisande was that simply getting your hands on rifles doesn't necessarily mean you understand all the implications of having them."

The brown-haired, brown-eyed brigadier, the commanding officer of the Imperial Charisian Marines (and seamen) quartered in and around Siddar City, was a square-shouldered, square-faced man. In fact, he radiated a sense of squareness—of solid, unflappable dependability. Some might have gone so far as to call him stolid.

"We had a significant advantage when we went ashore in Corisande three years ago," he continued, "because Brigadier Clareyk—I mean, General Green Valley—had spent better than a year experimenting with them first. The Corisandians hadn't had that opportunity, and I'm not convinced the Army of God's had it, either. Or that Maigwair's even recognized the need to consider it systematically."

"What sort of implications are you thinking about, Brigadier?" Stohnar asked.

"My Lord," Taisyn looked up from the map, "some of the advantages rifles provide are easy enough to grasp. Skirmishers, for example—everybody's provided their advanced scouts with missile weapons to harass the other side's scouts forever. The accuracy and range of a rifle is a natural fit for that sort of mission, so I expect we'll see the Army of God doing that much, at least. But there's a natural tendency to think of rifles as simply longer-ranged matchlocks or arbalests, at least at first. Just how *much* longer ranged—and more effective—they actually are seems to take a little longer to grasp. And one of the things we saw in Corisande was that the other side tended to hang onto dense, shoulder-to-shoulder formations to mass and control their fire long after they should have figured out they were just providing riflemen with better targets. They went right on doing it once they had rifles of their own, despite the fact that *we'd* gone to open order and skirmishers using individual, aimed fire."

"Our own formations are pretty damned dense and shoulder-to-shoulder," Parkair pointed out a bit acidly, and Taisyn nodded.

"I realize that, My Lord," the Marine said unapologetically. "That's how it has to be with pikes. And to be honest, that's going to hurt us, especially if these reports about their having new model field artillery are accurate."

His listeners' faces tightened in understanding. The semaphore chain from Windmoor to Siddar City remained basically intact, although a handful of stations had required rebuilding after Zhaspahr Clyntahn's Temple Loyalists had burned them in the opening days of their rebellion. It had taken far longer than any of them liked to remember to find enough semaphore crews to man the chain, however, because so many of the Church's operators had remained loyal to the Temple. As a result, the semaphore had actually begun passing messages reliably once more only within the last couple of five-days. And one of the first messages they'd received had been a warning from Tellesberg that Charisian agents reported the Army of God had somehow acquired the secret of exploding artillery shells to go with its flintlock rifles.

Unfortunately, as Taisyn and Parkair had both admitted, the Republican Army was likely to provide a painfully good target for those shells and rifles. The professional, superbly disciplined and trained pikemen of Siddarmark had been the terror of the Republic's enemies for the better part of two centuries, ever since it had evolved a radically different doctrine for their employment.

It was a simple fact of life that horses, wiser and less imbued than their riders with a sense of martial glory, would not charge a wall of pikes. They, after all, were smart enough to recognize a barrier too big and too wide for them to jump across when they saw it. All those nasty, pointy pikeheads on the front of that barrier only added to their distaste for such silly goings-on.

Yet for all its effectiveness as an anti-cavalry and standoff infantry weapon, the pike was long, heavy, and clumsy, and most infantry armed with it were relatively immobile. That was why most Safeholdian armies had evolved tactics which used a two or three-deep line of pikes, supported by cavalry on the wings and screened by light, missile-armed infantry. The pikes held the center or (at best) advanced very slowly and directly ahead—the only direction a line *could* advance without disordering the troops in it—under the protection of its own missile troops, who did their best to keep the *other* side's missile troops from inflicting serious casualties upon it. Meanwhile, the cavalry sought first to disperse the other side's mounted troops and then to use their greater mobility to sweep around the opposing pike line's flank and take it from the rear, where its pikes offered no protection against them.

The introduction of the matchlock hadn't changed things greatly, because the matchlock fired little if anymore rapidly than the arbalest, nor had anyone introduced the longbow here on Safehold, and things had remained remarkably static for centuries.

Until Siddarmark changed them, at any rate.

A Siddarmarkian pike regiment was an *offensive* formation: a solid square of just under two thousand ruthlessly drilled infantry, not a line, supported by four hundred arbalesters or matchlock-armed musketeers, and capable of advancing rapidly across a field of battle. A square could march in any direction, simply by changing its facing; it offered no flanks for the cavalry to attack; and it moved as a column, not a line. As a result, it had far more tactical mobility, and the sheer shock power of such a formation was disastrous for any line it struck.

It took endless hours on the drill ground and in field maneuvers for pikemen to acquire and maintain that fluid mobility, and the army had lightened their armor, reducing it to simple breastplates and helmets over tunics of buff leather to let them move even more quickly. That made a regiment's individual soldiers more vulnerable to missile fire, yet the changes had proved amply worthwhile. A Siddarmarkian pike block could present a solid wall of pikes in every direction when it halted to defend itself, but it was its mobility which made it truly fearsome, and the Siddarmarkian army had evolved a sophisticated tactical doctrine to go with it. Deployed in a checkerboard pattern, the intervals between the pike blocks filled with their organic arbalesters musketeers during the approach to the melee, they were the next best thing to unstoppable as they came rumbling across the field.

But those formations required density, and that very density made them particularly vulnerable to massed missile fire. Against arbalests and matchlocks, that vulnerability was acceptable. Against a rifle-armed adversary—or exploding shells—the story was likely to be very different. Ironically, the armies which had never been able to match the Republic's pike squares, who'd been forced to employ the pike *line* with its lower level of training and drill, were actually better placed to profit from the introduction of the flintlock and bayonet. Their linear formations were simply better adapted to massed musket fire, and with the addition of the bayonet, every man became his own pikeman, as well.

"My point," Taisyn continued, "is that we can at least hope it's going to take the other side a while to truly grasp the capabilities of their weapons. To be honest, I think we're going to have to be . . . cautious about forming the pikes. The longer we can keep this an affair of ambushes and skirmishing and avoid head-on battle with the Army of God, the better. It will give us more time for Duke Eastshare to arrive, and for the extra Marines and rifles Their Majesties have promised to get here, for that matter. And the truth is, the other side's still scared to death of facing your people. Your pikes've been beating the snot out of everyone else for so long it could hardly be any other way. The longer we can keep them from realizing how the new model weapons have changed things, the better."

"I hope you won't be offended if I point out that you're basically reminding us our entire army's just become obsolete, Brigadier," Stohnar said a bit dryly, and Taisyn bobbed his head in acknowledgment.

"My Lord, three years ago—*two* years ago—the thought of facing one of your pike regiments would've scared me shi—ah, I mean *spit*less." Taisyn glanced quickly and apologetically in Aivah's direction. "You would've run over even Charisian Marines without rifles and bayonets like a hill dragon through a cornfield. Things've changed, but your pikes earned their reputation the hard way. I'm simply saying it's time for us to capitalize on that reputation for as long and as strongly as we can. If the other side knows your regiments are waiting to run over them as soon as they come out into the open, they're going to hesitant about doing that."

"Until they've seen one of our pike regiments shot to pieces," Parkair said grimly.

"We'll just have to try to see to it that that doesn't happen, My Lord. And it hasn't happened so far in the Sylmahn Gap," Taisyn pointed out.

"But so far that's been a case of our facing rebels, not Temple regulars," Gahdarhd observed, and Taisyn nodded.

The fighting in the Sylmahn Gap had been close, vicious, and prolonged. At least two small cities—Jairth and Serabor—had been reduced to depopulated ruins, and civilian casualties had been even higher than military ones. The rebels who'd seized control of western Mountaincross understood the importance of the Sylmahn Gap as well as anyone in Siddar City; indeed, their overriding drive to take and hold it was the reason they'd steadfastly refused appeals to send reinforcements to their fellows in Hildermoss. The Guarnak-Sylmahn Canal, which ran through the Gap, was Old Province's major link to northwestern Siddarmark and to the Border States, which also meant it was the Temple's most direct route to Siddar City.

The regular army units in western Mountaincross had disintegrated, died, or gone over to the rebels, and most of their unit organization had disappeared in the process. The provincial militia had remained closer to intact, however, and it had absorbed the majority of the regulars who'd joined the Temple Loyalists. The Sylmahn Gap was one of the very few places where pikeman had met pikeman over the bitter winter, and even though the regular army regiments Stohnar had dispatched from the capital were better disciplined and equipped than the majority of the militia units opposed to them, their losses had been heavy.

The tide of rebellious militia had pushed all the way down the Gap, far enough to repeatedly assault the city of Serabor at its extreme eastern end. Somehow Serabor's defenders had held, fighting from its flaming ruins and eating God only knew what, even when a second wave of Temple Loyalists from Charlztyn had assailed it from the *east* as well. They'd held Serabor under actual siege, completely cut off from the outside world, until General Stohnar's relief column reached it.

The attackers had been at the end of their own tether from starvation and winter weather when Stohnar's relatively fresh regulars smashed into them, and the Charlztyn force had simply disintegrated. The militia from western Mountaincross had held together, but even its stubborn retreat had turned almost into a rout at times as the vengeful regulars drove it back north as far as Terykyr, a small mountain town about halfway up the Gap from Serabor. But then the militia had been reinforced, and it had been the rebels' turn to hammer Stohnar's men back. The regulars had given ground only slowly and sullenly, but they'd been thinned by their own casualties, and the Gap was too wide for them to put together a continuous front across it without major reinforcements of their own. Unfortunately, no one had those reinforcements to send. The few hundred rifles the pike regiments' light companies had been issued had been invaluable in both the attack and the defense, and the flooding created by the spring thaw helped troops on the defensive far more than it helped those pressing the attack, yet Trumyn Stohnar's position could only be called "precarious."

And what was going to happen when the flooding eased and when, not *if*, the Army of God managed to reinforce the militia with riflemen was one of Greyghor Stohnar and Daryus Parkair's worst nightmares.

"So far, Trumyn's rifles—and the weather—have been able to fend off the worst they could do to us there," Stohnar said now. "And the reports out of Glacierheart say the same thing about the Gray Walls." He glanced at Aivah, whose lips had tightened at the reference to Glacierheart. The news of how close Zhasyn Cahnyr had come to death had reached Siddar City barely three days ago, and she hadn't taken it well. "We'll just have to hope it stays that way until we can reinforce."

"With all due respect, My Lord," Maidyn said, "how likely is that? Madam Pahrsahn's agents' reports have been damnably reliable so far. I don't see any reason to expect their reliability to change now."

"Probably not," Stohnar acknowledged. "I don't suppose you've heard anything since you and I last spoke, Aivah?"

He raised his eyebrows, and she shook her head.

"My best guess from what they're saying is that Maigwair's troops are still at least two months away from crossing the border and reaching the disputed provinces. We *might* have a little longer than that if the weather stays bad in Tarikah and Westmarch, but I wouldn't count on that. And when they do move, it's going to be in strength, despite their supply difficulties."

"And Rahnyld's going to be invading the South March by the end of May, at the latest," Maidyn observed grimly.

"About that," Parkair agreed. "Most probably, he's going to head into Shiloh when he does." He tapped the map with his finger. "They've already got a pretty firm grip on the western part of the province. Once he links up with the rebels, the logical thing for him to do would be to swing north, punch up into Glacierheart, and clear the Gray Walls from behind."

"And pincer Cliff Peak between him and whatever Maigwair sends south from Westmarch to meet him." Stohnar's voice was even grimmer than Maidyn's had been, and he shook his head. "We can't let him get away with that, Daryus."

"Agreed. Of course, exactly how we go about stopping him's another matter. Especially when that bastard Mahrys comes across Silkiah at us. If he and Rahnyld can forget how much they hate each other and join hands, we're really going to be up against the slash lizard."

"It seems to me," Aivah said, "that we have to reinforce Glacierheart. I'll admit I have personal reasons for feeling that way," she met Stohnar and Parkair's eyes levelly, "but that doesn't change the reality. If we lose Glacierheart, we lose Cliff Peak as well. And if they can put together a solid arc from South March up through Glacierheart to Mountaincross, you'll have that entire mountain barrier to fight your way across to kick them back out again."

"Which is exactly why I agree we have to hold Glacierheart," Stohnar said. "But Daryus is right. We can't lose Glacierheart, but we can't pull anyone out of the Sylmahn Gap at this point, either, Aivah."

"If I may, My Lord?" Taisyn said, and all of them looked at him.

"If you have something to add, Brigadier, by all means do so!" Stohnar invited.

"My Lord, I have about thirty-five hundred Marines and rifle-armed seamen here in the capital. I realize we've been regarding that as a reserve force, but since we know His Majesty and Duke Eastshare are both moving to support us as rapidly as possible, I'm prepared to take them to Glacierheart to reinforce Archbishop Zhasyn. It's not as much as I'd like, but we could probably 'borrow' some naval guns from the galleons in North Bay, and three thousand more rifles in the mountains . . . ."

He shrugged, and Parkair nodded.

"They'd have a major impact," he agreed, and his eyes narrowed in calculations of his own. They stayed that way for several seconds before he looked back at the lord protector.

"We need to send at least some additional strength into the Sylmahn Gap, My Lord," he said, "and we've got to send some additional support to hold the line against Midhold, as well. We won't need as much there, though, judging from current reports. I think we could probably cut loose another . . . five thousand and send them up the Siddar along with Brigadier Taisyn. Call it a total of nine thousand men, and somewhere between a third and a quarter of our contribution would be arbalesters."

"Will that be enough for Zhasyn—I mean, for Archbishop Zhasyn—to hold?" Aivah asked.

"Against what he's facing now, certainly." Taisyn's response came quickly, without hesitation. "Against what Rahnyld and possibly Emperor Mahrys can send against him, though, no." The Marine shook his head. "Not in a thousand years."

"Then we'll just have to plan on finding someone else to send him before Rahnyld and Mahrys get their thumbs out of their arses," Stohnar said, his eyes on the map.

The lord protector's tone was firm, but all of them heard the unspoken qualifier, and their eyes followed his back to the map, asking themselves the same question.

Not that any of them had any better idea than he did of where they might find the "someone else" they needed.

MAY

YEAR OF GOD 896

.I.

Lord Protector's Palace
and
The Charisian Embassy,
Siddar City,
Republic of Siddarmark

The voice of the trumpets was as lost and tiny as the thud of the fortresses' saluting guns under the roar of approval as the tall, brown-haired young man started down the gangway. That roar went up suddenly, as if an unseen hand had been waiting for his appearance to pull some metaphysical lever, and clouds of seabirds and wyverns were startled into the heavens by the unanticipated tempest of sound. They wheeled and gusted around the congested anchorage, darting in and out of thickets of masts, yards, and rigging in a flurry of wings, and the deep-throated cheer went on and on.

The crowd gathered on Siddar City's waterfront pressed in on the cordon of Siddarmarkian pikemen charged with safeguarding the area around the foot of the gangway. It would have been madness to assume every citizen of the imperial capital was delighted to see Cayleb Ahrmahk, but shouts of disapproval were few and far between, and the reason wasn't difficult to understand. The weather was warmer than it had been, yet many of those cheering, whistling faces were gaunt and thin. Even now a bite of chill lingered in the air, reminding everyone of the bitter winter barely past, and anchored beyond HMS *Empress of Charis* were the most recent Charisian merchant galleons to arrive here in North Bedard Bay. The people behind those welcoming shouts were only too well aware of how great a difference those galleons and their predecessors had made over the winter the Republic's capital had just survived.

Lord Protector Greyghor met Cayleb as he stepped onto the pier's solid stone. The lord protector began a deep bow of greeting to the younger man, but Cayleb stopped him with a hand on his shoulder. Neither could have heard himself speak, far less whatever the other might have said, but the emperor shook his head with a smile, and the cheers grew still louder. No one would have blamed Stohnar for bowing to the emperor, yet the Republic's tradition had always been that its lord protector bowed to no secular ruler. Everyone understood the reasons why he'd begun to bow anyway—those Charisian-flagged galleons out in the bay were answer enough—but that only made them appreciate Cayleb's response still more.

Instead of bowing, Stohnar inclined his head in a nod of greeting, which Cayleb returned, and then the lord protector stepped to one side, waving to indicate the carriages drawn up to await them. The emperor glanced at the tall, sapphire-eyed Imperial Guardsman at his shoulder, and the armsman inclined his own head in acknowledgment before he and a dozen other Guardsmen crossed to the carriages to examine them briefly but closely. The worst of Zhaspahr Clyntahn's wave of "Rakurai" had spent themselves—and killed all too many innocents in the spending—yet the habits they had engendered remained. One of those Guardsmen crawled entirely underneath each carriage, assuring himself no explosives had some-how gotten past the Siddarmarkian army. Then the blue-eyed armsman returned to his emperor and touched his fist to his blackened breastplate in salute and Stohnar, Cayleb, and the rest of the emperor's entourage climbed into the carriages that rolled off towards Lord Protector's Palace through streets lined with vigilant pikemen and the ongoing avalanche cheers.

▼   ▼   ▼

"Well, that was an impressive greeting, My Lord," Cayleb Ahrmahk said as he and Greyghor Stohnar walked side by side along the stone-flagged pas-sageway.

"No more than you deserved, I think, Your Majesty. A lot of those people would've been dead, or the next thing to it, by now if not for you and Empress Sharleyan. I won't embarrass either of us by thanking you again—particularly since your correspondence has made your own attitude on that so abundantly clear—but the people of this city are as aware of our debt to you as I am."

"There are debts, and then there are debts, My Lord," Cayleb said qui-etly. "Sharleyan and I would've had to do anything we could this winter, no matter what had caused a disaster such as the one you faced. But no one in Charis is blind to the fact that Zhaspahr Clyntahn's madness here has quite a lot to do with his quarrel with *us*. If his war with us hadn't reached the point it has, none of this"—he waved his hands, the gesture encompass-ing the entire city beyond the palace's walls—"would've happened."

"It might not have happened *yet*, Your Majesty. It would have eventually, though." Stohnar's expression was hard. "I lied to myself for years about that. I kept hoping something remotely like sanity where we were concerned might break out in Zion, but you might say my eyes have been opened over the last year or two. Given how not just Clyntahn but the entire vicarate has viewed the Republic for so long, something like this became inevitable the moment he took the Grand Inquisitor's chair. We made the mistake of growing too large, too powerful . . . and too tolerant. I suppose"—he smiled thinly—"at least part of that tolerance might be Charis' fault. We did, as Clyntahn put it before he ran completely mad, 'climb further into bed' with you than any of the other major mainland realms, so it's possible the 'Charisian contagion' was partly to blame for our . . . dangerous attitudes. I think it would be wrong for you to take all the credit for our waywardness, though." He shook his head. "We were quite capable of despising the Group of Four on our own. We simply didn't have the gumption—or courage, perhaps—to do anything about it."

"Trust me, My Lord," Cayleb replied dryly, "a few thousand miles of seawater, plus the fact that the idiots didn't leave us any choice, had a lot to do with Charisian 'gumption' and 'courage.'" It was his turn to shake his head. "My father saw this coming years ago, but that doesn't mean all of us wouldn't have preferred to avoid it."

"Some things *can't* be avoided, Your Majesty," Staynair said as one of the Siddarmarkian armsmen outside the conference chamber doors opened the hand-rubbed, brilliantly polished doors. "I've had quite a bit of experience with that over the last few months."

"You certainly have." Cayleb followed the lord protector into the chamber, Major Athrawes at his heels, and Stohnar's most trusted advisers bowed deeply.

"And I'm afraid none of us are done having that experience just yet, Your Majesty." Stohnar's nostrils flared. "You can't get armies through our mountains very well, but individual couriers are another matter. We've been receiving a lot of information from the occupied provinces, and none of it makes very happy hearing."

"I'm not surprised." Cayleb carefully didn't glance over his shoulder at his personal armsman. "We have spies and sources of our own, and I'm sure they're telling us essentially what yours are telling you. That's the reason I've sent Earl Hanth and our Marines to Eralth Bay. It seemed to us in Charis that you're actually most exposed on your southern flank at the moment, so it seemed best to shore it up while we wait for Duke Eastshare to arrive here in Siddar City . . . and to see which way the Army of God jumps in the north. But no matter what we do, I'm afraid we're likely to lose more of your territory before we can hope to start driving them back."

"But we *will* drive them back, Your Majesty," a burly, broad-shouldered man with traces of silver in his brown beard said flatly.

"Lord Daryus Parkair, the Republic's Seneschal, Your Majesty," Stohnar said. "I'm afraid Daryus is a bit bluntly spoken from time to time."

"In which case we should get along fine, My Lord." Cayleb quirked a smile. "I've been known to be just a tad blunt myself upon occasion. And Empress Sharleyan would suggest that it's even remotely possible I'm just a little on the stubborn side as well."

"Would she really?" Stohnar snorted in amusement. "I believe my wife occasionally said much the same about me. Certainly our elder daughter's continued to say it for her since we lost her."

"And, with all due respect, Your Majesty," another Siddarmarkian said, "in Her Majesty's case that might be a bit of the pot and the kettle. All the world's heard how . . . determined Sharleyan of Chisholm can be."

"Lord Henrai Maidyn," Stohnar said in introduction, and Cayleb nodded.

"And your spymaster, if my own sources are correct," the emperor acknowledged with a smile, then bowed to the only woman present. "And this must be the redoubtable Aivah Pahrsahn." She swept him a courtesy, and he kissed the back of her hand. "I've heard a great deal about you," he continued, "and I've looked forward to meeting you myself. A friend of Major Athrawes—an Ahbraim Zhevons—asked me to extend his greetings."

Every set of Siddarmarkian eyes narrowed at that, but she seemed unaware of their sharpened interest as she gave the visiting emperor a dimpled smile.

"Thank you, Your Majesty." She inclined her head again. "And, please, should you or *Seijin* Merlin be speaking to him again anytime soon, give him my greetings in return. I do trust you've made good use of all that . . . correspondence I sent you."

"As deep background and to help us understand what we think are the likely factions within the Temple, we certainly have," Cayleb told her. "We've hesitated to make open use of its more . . . sensitive aspects for several reasons. Our fear of the possibility of reprisals against anyone named in it who might still be in Zion is part of that, but the nature of the propaganda battle between us and the Group of Four is a factor as well."

"I can appreciate both those reasons, Your Majesty. But a weapon's only a weapon if the one who holds it is prepared to *use* it." She looked deep into his eyes. "There are some aspects of that information which could have serious repercussions for quite a few vicars I'm sure Clyntahn thinks are firmly in his pocket."

"Indeed there are. But there's also the matter of timing. My own advisors and I have been of the opinion that it might be better to make use of those aspects at a time when we'd be seen as speaking from strength, not the desperation of weakness."

"Definitely something worth keeping in mind," she acknowledged, and Cayleb gave her hand another squeeze before he turned to the two men who had not yet been introduced.

"Lord Samyl Gahdarhd," Stohnar said, "and this, Your Majesty," his voice deepened ever so slightly, "is Archbishop Dahnyld."

"Your Eminence." Cayleb bent to kiss Dahnyld Fardhym's ring.

"Your Majesty," the archbishop replied gravely, returning the emperor's bow.

"I bring you Archbishop Maikel's greetings," Cayleb said. "I regret that his pastoral duties prevented him from accompanying me. At the same time, I think we might all agree that welcoming a mere emperor is likely to cause repercussions enough without the Republic's extending a formal welcome—and recognition—to the head of the Church of Charis, as well."

"Not to mention the repercussions of the Archbishop of Siddarmark doing the same thing in *Mother Church's* name," Fharmyn observed.

"Well, of course, Your Eminence. That goes without saying. I *was* trying to be diplomatic, however." Cayleb shrugged apologetically. "I promised my wife I would."

"I see."

The archbishop was several inches shorter than Cayleb and twice the emperor's age, with a lined face, a stocky build, and dark hair going white at the temples. He smiled briefly at the emperor's last sentence, but his eyes, which Cayleb suspected were usually warm, were darker and harder than agate.

"I appreciate the effort, Your Majesty," he continued. "Under the circumstances, though, it's not really necessary. I might quibble with some points of Archbishop Maikel's doctrine, but compared to my differences with those monsters in Zion, those quibbles would be minor indeed."

"They would?" Cayleb raised his eyebrows, his tone mild, and Fharmyn snorted. It was a harsh, angry, explosive sound, and his eyes turned harder than ever.

"I'm a Bédardist, too, Your Majesty. Like the Pasqualates, we're charged to heal, not harm. That's the first and deepest obligation of our order, after faith in God Himself, and that's been an increasing problem for quite a lot of us. Indeed, I'll readily confess I was of a Reformist bent, like many of my order here in Siddarmark, even before Clyntahn loosed his Sword of Schueler on the Republic. Not as strongly as your archbishop, perhaps, and with a faith that burned less fiercely. Perhaps less fearlessly. But this past winter's changed that, because I've seen the same reports Lord Protector Greyghor's seen. I've visited the Charisian Quarter here in Siddar City. I've talked to the refugees, seen proof in scars and broken bodies of the atrocities committed in God's name, and I know who's truly responsible for all of them. It would give me the greatest pleasure imaginable to welcome Archbishop Maikel in Siddar Cathedral, and the only thing that could possibly flaw that pleasure would be my own knowledge of how much of it came from flinging that welcome in Zhaspahr Clyntahn's face rather than from the strength of my agreement with the Archbishop's doctrine. I do agree with it, you understand; it's simply that I'm still too fallible a mortal to deny how deeply and passionately I've come to hate the men who have chosen to pervert everything God stands for in the name of their own foul ambition."

Cayleb's eyes widened, and his head twitched as he suppressed the urge to look in Merlin's direction. Fardhym had never expressed himself that openly, that bluntly, to anyone. Their analysis of the take from the remotes deployed to keep watch upon him had noted the obvious sincerity of his own faith, yet they'd never dared to anticipate such a forthright declaration. Certainly none of the inner circle would have expected to hear it from him so soon, and from the expressions of the other Siddarmarkians, even they were a bit surprised to hear it now.

"Your Eminence, I won't pretend the prospect of having the Republic as a mainland ally didn't come as a gift from God from Charis' viewpoint," the emperor said after a moment. "Despite that, I can't tell you how deeply I regret the fact that you've been forced to observe such atrocities here. But I think what you've seen is simply part of what and who Zhaspahr Clyntahn truly is. God knows we've had enough experience in Charis, and those ghastly pogroms of his in the Temple Lands only underscore it. But the truth is that he'll never stop, never admit any limit on his own excesses, until someone *stops* him, and that's what the Empire of Charis has sworn to do. We *will* stop him, Your Eminence, and when we do, he'll pay in full for his crimes here in the Republic and everywhere else."

"In that case, Your Majesty, all I'll say is this—God send the day, and Langhorne send that it comes soon."

Iron was softer and far flimsier than that voice, and silence lingered in its wake until Stohnar cleared his throat.

"I think we can all agree with that sentiment, Your Eminence. And towards that end, Your Majesty," he turned to face Cayleb, "I believe you and I have a formal treaty to sign this afternoon. Before we do, though, I thought it would be a good idea for you to be fully briefed by Daryus and Henrai on just how bad your new ally's situation truly is."

"I doubt it's any worse than ours was before the Armageddon Reef campaign, My Lord. And, as you can see, we're still here." Cayleb smiled grimly. "I'm not concerned about my new ally's situation. Oh, tactically, perhaps," he waved one hand, "but in the end? The *Writ* says evil prepares its own downfall. It seems the Grand Inquisitor missed that passage, somehow, but I haven't, and I have boundless faith in it."

"As do I, Your Majesty. Which isn't to say I don't anticipate a few . . . anxious moments along the way."

"Of course you do." Cayleb actually chuckled. "The *Writ* also says God tests those worthy of His service. Given the service to which He's called us, it would be remarkable if the tests weren't severe enough to make anyone feel anxious. Occasionally, at least."

He smiled and turned to Parkair and Maidyn.

"I have no doubt you're about to make me feel more than anxious enough to be going on with, My Lords. So why don't we go ahead and get started?

▾   ▾   ▾

"Thank you for seeing me, Your Majesty."

"There's no need to thank me, Sir Rayjhis," Cayleb said quietly. "The service you've performed here in Siddarmark has been . . . extraordinary. Her Majesty and I are both deeply grateful for how faithfully and unsparingly you've served Charis."

The emperor sat in a massive wooden armchair that was vaguely throne-like, with Merlin Athrawes at his back, while morning sunlight streamed through the windows behind him. The office wasn't especially huge—rooms tended to be smaller and with lower ceilings in Siddar City, largely to make them easier to heat in the winter—but it was comfortably furnished and its walls were lined with floor-to-ceiling bookcases. It had, in fact, been Sir Rayjhis Dragoner's own office until the Charisian ambassador to the Republic moved elsewhere to free up space in the embassy for Cayleb's use. He appreciated the ambassador's willingness to move, although he hadn't looked forward at all to this morning's meeting. He knew why Dragoner had requested it.

Now he sat back, studying the worn, exhausted face and haunted eyes of the man who'd represented Charis' interests in Siddarmark so long and so well. He'd only met Dragoner a handful of times before King Haarahld dispatched the career diplomat to Siddar City, but since then, the man had aged far more than the simple passage of time could account for. His dark hair had turned almost completely white, his cheekbones stood out like eroded knobs of rock, his eyes were dark and sunken, and his fingers shook with a slight, almost imperceptible quiver whenever they weren't tightly clenched.

We should've recalled him, Cayleb thought remorsefully. *We should have. It wasn't fair to him.*

But they hadn't, because no one else could have matched Sir Rayjhis Dragoner's contacts in the highest circles of the Republic's government. No one else would have had his insights, his awareness of the pulse and pattern of Siddarmark's political life. And no one else could have represented Charis better, despite his own deep religious reservations.

The religious reservations and internal conflict which had aged him so visibly.

"Your Majesty," Dragoner began, but Cayleb raised one hand in gentle gesture which halted the ambassador instantly.

"Sir Rayjhis, I want you to know that no one could possibly be better aware than Empress Sharleyan and I of how faithfully you've served Charis. We know how long and hard you've labored since the Group of Four's original attack on Charis. We know how hard you've driven yourself, how unstintingly you've spent your strength in our service, how vigilant and honest you've been. And"—the emperor looked deeply into Dragoner's eyes—"we know how personally and painfully difficult it's been for you to discharge your duty to us so faithfully and so well."

Dragoner's lips trembled, and he started to open his mouth, but again that raised hand stopped him.

"I know why you requested this meeting," Cayleb said quietly. "I regret that you felt it necessary, but I regret even more that the extraordinary skill and unremitting diligence you've displayed prevented us from recalling you long ago. It was wrong of us. Sir Rayjhis, we knew—we *always* knew—that what we demanded of you as Charis' ambassador caused you immense pain as a son of Mother Church. That we were setting your loyalty to Charis at odds with your sense of what you owed to God Himself and to the archangels. And we knew that for all the pain we were causing you, you would never ask to be relieved—never desert your post—when Charis stood in danger. And because we knew that, we *used* you, Sir Rayjhis. We used you mercilessly and cruelly because we had no choice. Because we needed you so desperately."

Dragoner swallowed hard, and Cayleb shook his head.

"It shames me to admit that to you. As a king and an emperor I had no choice, but as a man, I am ashamed. As a king and emperor, I ought to've refused this meeting, because no man could possibly be more valuable to us here in Siddar City, even now, than you've proven yourself to be. I know that if I demand it of you, you'll continue that service even now, and an emperor, knowing that, can return only one answer to the request which brings you here. But I've discovered I'm not simply an emperor. Not in this. I understand why you're here, and there are times a man's duty as an emperor must take second place simply to his duty as a *man* . . . which is why the answer is yes."

The ambassador's eyes glistened with unshed tears, and Cayleb stood. He crossed to the older man and laid his hands on Dragoner's shoulders.

"I know that even now, despite all Zhaspahr Clyntahn's done, you could never draw your own sword against Mother Church," he said softly. "I think you're wrong about that. I believe the damage is too deep, the poison too deeply set, for there to be any resolution short of the sword. But I understand your reverence for Mother Church, your respect for all she may have been and accomplished in the past and your fear of the doors we may open if we settle our conflict with those who have twisted her teachings by raising our own hand in impious violence. I respect that difference of view between us, and knowing that difference exists, we've driven you too hard and too far in what we've already demanded of you.

"The time has come for us to stop. The treaty I signed with Lord Protector Greyghor yesterday is as much your work as ours, and it's work done well, despite the pain we know you felt in every sentence, every comma and period. We couldn't have expected more of any man and we cannot *demand* any more of *you*. So I release you from your office, Sir Rayjhis Dragoner, with my thanks and Sharleyan's, and with our most profound apologies for all we've done to you and taken from you. Return to your family, heal, and if you can find it in your heart to forgive us, we ask that last gift of you."

"Your Majesty," Dragoner said hoarsely, "there's nothing to forgive. I could have asked you to relieve me at any time. I chose not to. Perhaps that was the wrong decision, but it was *my* decision. Yet you're right. I can't . . . I can't serve you any longer, not in this." The tears in his eyes broke loose, and he shook his head as they trickled slowly down his cheeks. "I love Charis, and I always will. I could never—*would* never—do anything to harm her, or you, or your house. But I look at what I've already done in Charis' name and the consequences it may have for Mother Church, and I know I can do no more. I'm tired, Your Majesty—so tired. Perhaps it's a form of cowardice, but I need that chance to heal, and I thank you from the bottom of my heart for giving it to me with such understanding and compassion."

"You've been in a terrible place in our service, Sir Rayjhis. It's a place too many people have been forced into, but that only makes it more terrible, not less. No one can blame you for following your own faith and your own conscience. That's the reason Sharleyan and I have agreed with Archbishop Maikel from the beginning that Temple Loyalists in Charis must have the right to do precisely that. So how could we possibly deny *you* that right, when you've served us so long and so well? I know you fear the ultimate consequences of our actions to Mother Church, but I'll say this in the words of the *Book of Langhorne.* 'Well done, you good and faithful servant. Rejoice in the love and appreciation of your Lord and enter into the reward you have so well deserved.'" Cayleb shook the ambassador very, very gently. "Go home, Sir Rayjhis. Go home to those who love you, and know Sharleyan and I will never forget the debt we owe you."

Irys Daykyn had never particularly cared for needlework. In fact, given her choice between having a tooth pulled and spending an afternoon embroidering, she would have required several minutes to make up her mind. Nor would her final choice have been a foregone conclusion.

Nonetheless, she sat in a canvas sling chair on HMS *Destiny*'s stern walk between Empress Sharleyan of Charis and Lady Mairah Breygart, setting relatively neat stitches into a napkin, of all useless things, while water bubbled around the rudder and sea wyverns swirled and darted above the ship's wake. Those wyverns had come well over a hundred miles, from Wyvern Beak Head, the northwestern tip of the large island of Zebediah, and she heard a triumphant whistle from one of them as a ship's cook dumped a load of garbage over the side. Half a dozen wyverns swept down, plucking the choicest morsels with glee, then squawking in outrage as their greedier brethren decided it would be simpler to steal someone else's treasure than to go hunting for their own.

I suppose they're not so very different from men, after all, she thought wryly.

There was an edge of darkness to the reflection as thinking of those wyverns' origin reminded her of her father's conquest of Zebediah. His armies had occupied the island before she herself was out of diapers . . . and he'd mounted his last punitive expedition against Zebediahan rebels less than a year before the attack on Charis. Of course, the rebels in question had been aristocrats, not the common folk of Zebediah, but those common folk had felt no loyalty to their Corisandian conquerors, either.

And burning their towns and villages around their ears—and over their heads—because the local nobles had shown the poor judgment to rebel against Father didn't make them feel any more loyal, did it?

"Not even embroidery should cause that much unhappiness, Your Highness," Lady Mairah said with a chuckle, and Irys looked at the countess and felt her tanned cheeks darken as she realized she'd sighed more heavily than she'd realized.

"When you're as poor a hand at it as I am, embroidery's cause enough for a screaming tantrum, My Lady," she replied lightly. "Or to justify a fit of deep, dark depression, at least." She held up the embroidery ring, showing off the lopsided wyvern she'd been working on. It was colorful enough—she had to give it that—but she was pretty sure it would have been anatomically incapable of flight. "As you can see, it's not exactly my strong suit."

"You could always try knitting," Sharleyan offered, looking up from her busily clicking needles.

The empress' tone was light, but there was something in her eyes which made Irys wonder if Sharleyan had followed the thought she'd chosen not to voice more clearly than Irys might have wished. In the five-days they'd spent aboard *Destiny*, the princess had come to the conclusion that while there was obviously no truth in the Inquisition's claims of sorcery and fornication with demons on Sharleyan's part, she might very well be capable of reading minds after all.

"It's still a matter of manual dexterity, Your Majesty." She shook her head ruefully. "I'm afraid that would make knitting a . . . poor choice on my part. At least when I'm embroidering the interval between stitches is longer. It may not sound like much, but it slows the rate at which I can do damage."

Both the other women laughed, and Irys returned to her stitchery.

The odd thing was that as much as she hated embroidery, she found herself actively enjoying her afternoon sessions with Lady Mairah and Empress Sharleyan. She'd discovered she liked both of them far more than she really ought to, and for all her size and stability, *Destiny* was a small world, particularly given how many people had been packed aboard the galleon. It had been far too long since she'd been permitted to spend the long hours on horseback that she truly craved—not counting the grueling overland flight across Delferahk to safety—and the lack of scope for physical activity of any sort was the worst aspect of the trip. And while embroidery work might not exactly come under the heading of physical exercise, at least it gave her something to do. Something she could go on doing for a long, long time, as a matter of fact, if the object was to actually become proficient at it.

Even Daivyn and Haarahld Breygart had begun to run out of ways to get into trouble, and at Baron Sarmouth's suggestion, Captain Lathyk had incorporated all of the boys into the midshipmen's daily lessons. Daivyn—predictably—had whined and attempted to sulk when his regular expeditions down into the hold, or up the ratlines, or into the middle of the drilling gun crews—"just to get a *really* close look at the breeching tackle and the gunlocks, Irys, honest!"—had been preempted for something which smacked inescapably of *study*. But Lady Mairah and Irys had been implacable, especially after he'd come within inches of having his left foot crushed under a gun truck when the crew ran it inboard for practice. If Rahskho Mullygyn, Tobys Raimair's third in command, hadn't been hovering to snatch Daivyn—and Haarahld—out of the way in the nick of time, Corisande's rightful prince would undoubtedly have gone down in history as "Daivyn the Lame."

Rather to Daivyn's surprise (although astonishment might have been a better word) the lessons had proved be anything but boring. Irys had sat in on a few of them herself, and she'd been almost as surprised as he had as she watched his intent expression and saw him scratching numbers onto a slate right along with all the rest of *Destiny*'s midshipmen. She'd known Charis was in the process of revolutionizing arithmetic; they'd been doing that ever since they introduced the oddly named "arabic numerals" six years ago. What she hadn't realized was how much more than a simple new notation method they'd produced. The clicking beads of the abacuses—themselves an incredibly useful tool—had competed with the sound of wind and wave as the midshipmen labored to solve a problem in what the Charisians had christened "trigonometry," by which they'd actually been able to determine (more or less; as a group, their math skills still left something to be desired) the ship's latitude and longitude.

People had known since the Creation what latitude and longitude were; they were marked (in the cumbersome old-style numerals) on Archangel Hasting's master maps in the Temple. But actually managing to *calculate* them from observations of the sun and the stars . . . that was something entirely new. She could see where it would be useful, although Captain Lathyk made remarkably little use of it, except as an occasional check on his estimated position. He preferred the art of dead reckoning—steering headings calculated by compass, wind direction, time, and the ship's speed through the water referenced against the sailing directions Charisian seamen had spent decades assembling. The Royal College had played its part in that effort as well, compiling and filing the sailing directions as they came in. All the originals in their files had been destroyed when the original College burned, but virtually all of the sailing directions extracted from them had been broadly distributed first. In addition, most of the original effort had been the work of hundreds, if not thousands, of individual Charisian captains who'd painstakingly recorded their courses as they picked their way from point to point, and the majority of them had kept their original copies, which had helped insure that the precious knowledge wasn't lost in the fire.

A good navigator accustomed to using the directions—and so far as Irys could tell, *all* Charisian captains were good navigators—could make landfall within thirty miles of his intended destination even after a voyage of thousands of miles, relying upon nothing more than a compass, his measured speed, and the wind. That ability explained why Charisians had taken the lead in sailing beyond sight of land, why they were more proficient (and far more confident) navigators than anyone else . . . and why Charis had so heavily dominated Safehold's merchant traffic even before she'd systematically exterminated everyone else's after she found herself at war with all the world.

In the fullness of time, Irys suspected, the new ability to navigate free of charted routes would become more and more important. For now, experienced seamen like Captain Lathyk clearly regarded it as little more than a useful adjunct, but there were far more uses for the new arithmetic than simple navigation. And even if it had possessed no practical utility at all, Daivyn would have been fascinated by it. She could almost see the little gears and wheels turning in his brain as he discovered an entire world of numbers he'd never known existed. There were times he reminded her irresistibly of Hektor Aplyn-Ahrmahk's brother Chestyr.

She sighed again, much more circumspectly this time as that familiar thought ran through her brain. She'd come to the conclusion that there were far worse men her brother might have patterned himself upon than Lieutenant Aplyn-Ahrmahk, and the lieutenant was no dilettante where the new math was concerned, himself. But the thought of what the Inquisition and Corisande's Temple Loyalists might do with Prince Daivyn's interest in the "unholy, unclean, and blasphemous knowledge" of the Royal College if that interest ever became generally known was not one to gladden her heart.

Especially because you *feel the same temptation, Irys,* she told herself tartly. *You should've remembered that old warning to be wary of Charisians bearing gifts! Too bad not even Phylyp thought to warn you about the blandishments of learning to understand how God and the archangels set the world into operation.*

That was the true beauty of it. It had taken her less time than it probably ought to have to get past her own fear that the College truly was unholy and unclean. She'd realized that nothing Doctor Mahklyn or the College's other scholars were learning and discovering on a daily business subtracted one iota from the magnificent craftsmanship God and the archangels had lavished upon the creation of Safehold. The marvelous intricacy of the rules they'd established, the processes they'd set into motion, the miracles of subtlety and beauty, were enough to make anyone drunk with admiration and awe, and how could God, having given man the ability to reason and understand, *not* want him to explore all the beautiful marvels with which He'd surrounded him?

She looked down at the embroidery in her lap and realized her hands had stopped moving. She wondered how long she'd been sitting that way, and she sat staring at those motionless fingers, unwilling to look up and meet Sharleyan or Lady Mairah's eyes.

I think, a small, quiet voice said in the back of her brain, *that this is what they call an epiphany. Funny. I always wondered what one of those felt like. Now it's here, and I still don't know.*

Her hands tightened on the embroidery hoop, and her own, utterly familiar fingers looked different as if they belonged to a stranger. Or perhaps as if they were simply one small part of an entire world which had turned into something else between one breath and the next.

That's what it's all about, really, isn't it? She felt tears welling behind her eyes—tears of wonder, of terror and joy and a wild, strange elation. *Clyntahn and the Inquisition can claim Charis has fallen to the Temptation of Proctor, given themselves to the unclean and the forbidden, but it's a lie. There's nothing "unclean" about studying and seeking to understand all the glorious complexity of the world that encircles us, gives us life. That world is one huge, magnificent portrait, the mirror of God Himself, and all people like Doctor Mahklyn and Doctor Brahnsyn and Doctor Lywys want is to see that portrait more clearly. To look into the face of God and find Him looking back at them. How can that be evil? How can it be wrong? And if Charis and the Church of Charis are right about that, how can they be wrong about the dark, twisted thing men— men like Zhaspahr Clyntahn, not God!—have made of Mother Church? It's not death and evil and destruction they worship; it's life and love, understanding and acceptance, and the tolerance to defend even their enemies' right to believe whatever their consciences demand of them. Whatever Clyntahn may think, they celebrate the joy of God, not the darkness to which he's given himself. And if they have fallen prey to Proctor, or even to Shan-wei herself, I would rather stand with them in the darkest corner of the deepest pit of hell than stand with Zhaspahr Clyntahn at the right hand of any God who agreed with him.*

An icicle of terror ran through her as she realized what she'd just thought, yet it was true. The old proverb about knowing someone by the company he kept flowed through her mind, and she drew a deep, shuddering breath, wondering how something like this could have happened at such an unlikely moment. Wondering where her new realization would take her and what fate awaited her and her brother.

She raised her eyes, gazing across the water, watching those jeweled wings beat and sweep or hold rigid, riding the wind, and the beauty of God's handiwork looked back at her from them. The wind swirled about her, plucking at her hair, stirring the loose edges of the napkin, filling the space about her with life and movement and energy. It was a completely ordinary sight, something she'd seen virtually every day of the voyage. And yet it was the farthest thing from ordinary she'd ever seen in her entire life.

"Irys?" She turned her head, looking at the empress as Sharleyan spoke her name gently. "Are you all right?" Sharleyan asked quietly.

"I—"

Irys stopped, laid the embroidery ring aside, and used both hands to wipe the inexplicable tears she hadn't realized she'd shed. Her nostrils flared, and she shook her head.

"I . . . don't know, Your Majesty," she admitted after a moment. She drew another deep breath, then stood, feeling somehow awkward and off balance.

"It's not anything for you to worry about," she continued, wondering even as she spoke whether or not her own words were accurate. "I've just—" She shook her head. "I've just realized there's something I have to think about, Your Majesty. Something I have to think about very carefully. With your permission, I think I need a little time alone to grapple with it."

"There's no need to ask my permission for that," Sharleyan said, even more gently, and looked at Countess Hanth, who shared one of *Destiny's* small cabins with Irys. "Do you think Irys could have your cabin to herself for a while, Mairah?"

"Of course she can." Mairah nodded quickly and reached out to squeeze Irys' hand quickly. "Take as long as you need, Your Highness. Would you like me to send Father Bahn to you?"

"No, thank you," Irys said, and felt another of those strange shivers of elated terror as she realized she truly wanted to grapple with this herself, without the aid of her confessor and chaplain. What did *that* say about her . . . and about her sudden, overwhelming temptation—her need—to decide this question for *herself*?

"If I decide I need his counsel, I'll send for him, of course," she continued, knowing that whatever else happened, she would never do that. Not this time, not about this question.

"Of course," Mairah repeated. "Would you like me to . . . ah, *divert* Daivyn when he finishes his current smudgy excursion into the wonder of mathematics?"

"I'd appreciate that, actually."

Irys' lips quirked in a smile, and that smile was genuine, even though her amusement carried its own razor-sharp edge of uncertainty. The Inquisition would have denied she had the right to decide something like this even for herself, far less anyone else, so what right did she have to decide it for Daivyn? And there was no doubt in her mind that her decision would be pivotal for Daivyn. There was no question that the bright and shining wonder of the world he was discovering under the corrupting Charisian influence already drew him like an insect to a flame. If she surrendered herself to it, there'd be no stopping him from plunging into it right beside her, and what would the consequences of that be? Not simply for her baby brother's soul, but for the princedom he'd been born to rule and every other soul in it?

I'm not even twenty *yet,* a voice wailed somewhere deep inside. *I'm not supposed to have to make these kinds of decisions—not yet! It's not* fair. *It's not my* job*!*

Yet it *was* her job, however fair or unfair that might be, and she realized that was one reason this moment had been so long coming. She'd been frightened of it, sensed its irrevocable import, and no wonder. Was this what it had been like for Cayleb, for Sharleyan, when the same moment came for each of them? When they realized *they* had to decide where they stood, whatever anyone else might think or tell them or insist upon, in the full knowledge of what their decisions would mean for the people they ruled? And how in the name of God and all the archangels had they found the strength to face it with such unswerving courage? The question burned through her, for now it was her turn to need that courage, and she didn't know if she possessed it.

There's only one way to find out, she told herself, and then she felt herself blushing as another thought ran through her. *It's not Father Bahn you want to ask about this, lean on, is it, Irys? It's someone else entirely, and it's tempting, so tempting. He'd have every reason in God's creation to lie to you, to convince you to surrender to Proctor's seduction along with his brother and his monarchs . . . and himself. It would be his duty to do that, just as clearly as it's your duty to remember all the implications of whatever you decide today . . . and you know he'd never do it, anyway.*

It seemed to be a day for realizations. She looked back out across the wyverns, and the blue water of the Chisholm Sea and the sunlight, and wondered where the earthquake and tempest might be, the pillar of fire and the terrible flash of the Rakurai that were supposed to mark moments like this. But what she saw instead was only the severe beauty of wind and salt water, the white froth of the wake, the glassy crests of the waves . . . and the mental image of a smiling, dark, strong-nosed face.

"I think I'd better be going, Your Majesty," she told the woman who'd conquered her homeland. "I really do have a lot of thinking to do."

.III.
**North of Jairth,
The Sylmahn Gap,
Old Province,
Republic of Siddarmark**

At least we're not up to our arse in snow anymore, Sir," Sergeant Grovair Zhaksyn said philosophically. "That's something."

"Can't argue with that, Grovair," Major Zhorj Styvynsyn, the commanding officer of Second Company, Thirty-seventh Infantry Regiment, Army of the Republic, agreed.

After the winter just past, there wasn't much to tell any casual observer which of them was the officer and which the noncom as they lay on the high, stony bench, gazing northwest along the Sylmahn Gap's long, straight length. Both of them looked sadly tattered and more than a little starved, and their carefully maintained equipment harnesses and breastplates were badly worn.

"I might, however," Styvynsyn continued, eyes narrowed as he tried to make out details and wished his spyglass hadn't been broken in the desperate, hand-to-hand fight before the 2nd had been driven out of Terykyr at the end of last month, "observe that water and knee-deep mud aren't all *that* much of an improvement. And I'd settle for a howling blizzard if it kept those bastards home."

Not that blizzards had done a great deal to keep the rebels home, he admitted to himself. In fact, they'd made damned good use of snowfall to get close enough to punch his men out of Terykyr. He still didn't know what had happened to his pickets, but he suspected frostbite, starvation, and exhaustion had played a significant role.

I just hope the poor bastards were all dead before Baikyr's butchers got their hands on them, he thought bitterly.

"Can't kill 'em if they don't come out where we can get at them, Sir." Zhaksyn shrugged, his expression much harder than his light tone might have suggested. "And from the way those scouts're just ambling along down there, I'd say it's most likely they haven't figured out we're up here."

"Appearances can be deceiving," Styvynsyn replied.

He peered down into the deep valley for another handful of minutes, then puffed what someone from Old Earth would have called a walrus mustache and pulled a dog-eared notebook from his belt pouch. He sat up, careful to keep his head off the skyline despite the distance to the oncoming enemy scouts, and scribbled a quick but legible note. He ripped out the page and handed it to the private with the red brassard of a runner who'd accompanied Zhaksyn and him up to the rock bench.

"Take this to the heliograph and get it off to the Colonel immediately."

"Yes, Sir!"

The runner slapped his breastplate, turned away, and went half dashing and half slithering down the steep, muddy trail. Styvynsyn watched him go, then shook his head and looked back at Zhaksyn.

"Ah, to be young and agile." The gray-haired sergeant snorted, since Styvynsyn was barely out of his twenties himself. "I believe we can follow a little more sedately, in light of your advanced years and my own towering seniority," Styvynsyn continued.

"As the Major says," Zhaksyn replied with exquisite courtesy. "I'll try to make sure my ancient and decrepit bones don't slow you down *too* much, Sir."

"I appreciate that, Sergeant." The major patted him on the shoulder. "I appreciate that."

▼ ▼ ▼

Colonel Lywys Maiksyn growled as he removed his helmet and mopped his streaming forehead with a handkerchief which had once been white. That had been long ago, unfortunately. Almost as long ago as the days in which his militia uniform had presented a peacetime picture of neatness. Or in which he'd been a simple, reasonably prosperous merchant shipping grain, cattle, apples, slabnuts, and mountain ananas down the Canal to Siddar City. Today, he was neither of those things as he stood on the sodden spit of land leading down into a standing lake of cold water from which the crowns of neat rows of apple trees rose like the gravestones of yet another small, productive farm which had gotten in the Jihad's way.

Shan-wei take it! he thought resentfully. *First we spend the entire winter freezing to death. Now it's barely May, and it's like a frigging* oven *down here!*

He shoved the handkerchief back into his pocket with an irritated forcefulness made even worse by the fact that he knew the temperature was actually nothing of the sort. Warm, yes, down on the Gap's floor, but nothing remotely furnace-like. That, unfortunately, didn't keep it from *feeling* hotter than the hinges of hell, after the long, bitterly cold winter, and the insects starting to buzz above the sodden, muddy, flooded going on either side of the Saiknyr High Road's elevated bed didn't make him feel one bit better. Snowmelt, beginning to cascade off the lower peaks in earnest, gurgled and rushed through the high road's drainage culverts, pouring into the Guarnak-Sylmahn Canal. The northernmost tributary of the Sylmahn River, which ran back and forth through those culverts, snaking its way along the eastern face of the Snow Barrens, was filling steadily with water, just like all the creeks and small streams, and the level of the canal was rising dangerously. If those idiots at the far end of the Gap didn't open the Serabor Locks sometime soon, the entire damned valley was going to flood!

Which is what the bastards want, he thought, admitting the real reason for his irritation. *If we let them sit there, they'll back up the canal—and the damned river—all the way to Terykyr just to make sure nobody can come down the Gap before July. And* that's *why Baikyr's sending us down here, lucky souls that we are.*

Maiksyn wasn't fond of Colonel Pawal Baikyr—a regular who'd brought almost a quarter of his regiment across to the Faithful and who had a far higher opinion of regulars in general than of militiamen—yet he couldn't argue with the other man's decision. First, because Baikyr *was* a regular, which automatically made him senior to a mere militia colonel. Second, because Baikyr had been placed in command by Father Shainsail Edwair, and the Schuelerite upper-priest spoke with the voice of the Grand

Inquisitor himself. And third . . . third, because however big a pain in the arse Baikyr might be, he was also good at his job.

Not to mention being right about what's going to happen in about another five or six days—maybe seven—if we don't get our own hands on the Serabor Locks.

Knowing orders made sense didn't always make them any more pleasant to carry out, however. They hadn't managed to take Serabor even when their own regiments had been at full strength, and the going had been much easier then. The *weather* might be better now—at least they weren't likely to see more men freezing to death—but with his mobility choked by the canal's high water and the flooding coming to meet it from down-gap, the terrain was even worse. That might not matter if the scouts and Father Shainsail's spies were right about what the heretics were up to, but that was the point, wasn't it? There was only one way to find out how accurate those reports actually were, and the 3rd Saiknyr Infantry had been chosen to do the finding out.

One of the regiment's scouts came trotting back towards him on one of the few gaunt-sided horses who'd managed to survive the winter. Under normal conditions, the nag would probably have been put down five-days ago; under the conditions which actually obtained, it was worth its weight in gold. Or in silver, at least.

"Road's clear as far as Jairth, Sir. No sign of any of 'em."

"And *off* the road?"

"Can't say 'bout that, Sir."

The scout was one of Maiksyn's own militiamen, and any faint patina of military punctilio the 3rd Saiknyrs might once have possessed had disappeared over the winter. But however informal their survivors might have become, they'd also acquired a hard, dangerous competence.

"Water's spreading right nasty to the west, Sir," the corporal continued more than a bit gloomily. "Lot of crap's getting itself caught in the drains."

That wasn't much of a surprise. Much of the Gap's soil tended to be shallow and rocky, unlike the fertile tablelands to the north or the rolling plains south and east of the mountains. Most of the farms in the Gap itself had been one- or two-family affairs, with a heavy concentration on orchards of apples and mountain ananas as their cash crop. And most of them—like the small towns on either side of the high road—had been thoroughly destroyed during the earlier fighting. The handful of buildings which hadn't been burned had been abandoned; now the rising floodwaters were washing through the rubble and ruin which had been left behind, and quite a bit of it, inevitably, was being sucked into the culverts, which worried Maiksyn more than he cared to admit. Keeping those culverts clear of natural debris was a major maintenance task every year, and it made him . . . itchy to fail in the *Writ's* charge to do that maintenance. With all the added clutter, the

problem was even worse than usual, though, and the Gap had been de-
nuded of the manpower to deal with it. If the drainage waterways plugged
solid, they'd transform the high road's elevated bed into a dam two hundred
miles long, turning everything between it and the Snow Barren Mountains
into a treacherous lake that might take months to drain. The Sylmahn Gap
was already a bottlenecked nightmare for any attacking army; reducing its
frontage to just the high road would make it impossible.

But *Writ* or no *Writ*, neither of the contending armies was going to provide the manpower even to inspect the culverts properly, far less clear them,
when it knew the other side would pounce on its work crews the instant it
did. So the only way the Faithful could solve either of their problems was to
drive through to Serabor, one way or the other, and the sooner the better.

"Man's likely to break a leg wading out into that shit," the scout went
on. "Can't tell how deep it is, neither—not without swimming, leastways,
and water's a mite cold for that." He shrugged. "Getting almost as bad nor it
is to the east, even given how the canal's backing up. And even if we could
get across the water, that's a steep slope up into the Snow Barrens. Probably
couldn't get up there on my own feet, much less this thing." He patted the
horse's shoulder with a gentleness which belied his dismissive tone. "Figured
if there *was* anything up there, I'd end up with an arbalest bolt in my belly
'stead of being able to come back and tell you I couldn't get far enough up to
take a look, so I didn't try." He shrugged again. "Sergeant's got the rest of
the section keeping their eyes peeled, Sir, but we haven't seen anything yet."

"Good enough." Maiksyn nodded in satisfaction. He'd far rather have a
scout who admitted the limits of his knowledge than one who tried to pretend he'd done a more thorough job than he'd actually been able to. "Get
back to your sergeant and help him keep those eyes peeled."

"Aye, I'll do that thing, Sir."

The scout slapped the boiled-leather cuirass which served a militiaman
in place of a regular's steel breastplate, wheeled his horse, and headed back
down the Gap. Maiksyn watched him go, then turned and beckoned to
Major Hahlys Cahrtair, the commanding officer of the 3rd Saiknyrs' 3rd
Company.

Cahrtair was a very ordinary looking man and just as muddy and
ragged as anyone else, although like the majority of Maiksyn's officers he'd
managed to get his hands on one of the breastplates no longer required by
regulars who'd stayed loyal to the blasphemer Stohnar. Yet Maiksyn disliked the captain, for a lot of reasons. He always had, even before the Sword
of Schueler had risen against Stohnar's apostasy, and nothing since had
changed his mind. Behind that inoffensive, even pleasant-looking façade,
Cahrtair had a cold, calculating vicious streak. He'd kept it under control
during peacetime, although he'd been one of the militia's least popular of-

ficers because of his penchant for "rigorous discipline." If that discipline had made his company any more efficient than its sister companies, that would have been one thing, but most of his idea of "discipline" had amounted to petty fault-finding and capriciousness.

Still, he hadn't been any *less* efficient than most militia officers, and his popularity had increased markedly since the Rising. No doubt that had a lot to do with the nature of the fighting, because Cahrtair was a natural when it came to ruthlessness. That suited the bitterness of a great many of the men who'd rallied to Mother Church, and that sort of man seemed to migrate naturally to officers like Cahrtair. The 3rd Company had picked up more recruits from the . . . self-motivated scourges of apostasy than any of Maiksyn's other companies. Probably because his other commanders had found those sorts of recruits almost more of a liability than an asset, given their lack of discipline, training, and equipment. But Cahrtair welcomed them, and they responded with a fierce loyalty to a man who clearly shared so much of their own attitude. As far as Maiksyn could tell, he'd never even tried to take prisoners, and his men had been among the first to begin burning farms and villages. They hadn't wasted any time letting the owners of those farms and villages flee before firing their roofs over their heads, either, and there'd been ugly rumors about rape and torture.

Given Stohnar's corrupt alliance with Charis, Maiksyn wasn't going to waste any misplaced sympathy on anyone who'd chosen to set his allegiance to the lord protector ahead of God's own Church. But that didn't mean he approved of freelance torture or turning women and babes out into the snow without so much as a scrap of food. And there was nothing in the *Book of Schueler* about soldiers of God raping women who might or might not have been heretics, either.

He'd made that point to Cahrtair. Unfortunately, Father Shainsail's sermons clearly supported the severity the major and those like him advocated. The upper-priest was probably right about the attitude towards heresy Schueler had prescribed—he was God's priest, and Maiksyn was only a layman of the sort who left doctrinal matters in the hands of the Church, where they belonged—and there wasn't any *proof* of the rape and atrocity accusations. As a result, the colonel had been forced to let it pass—that time, at least—which hadn't done much for the 3rd Saiknyrs' discipline. Maiksyn found it ironic Baikyr had quietly supported him, not Father Shainsail, in the field regulations he'd issued shortly afterwards. The severe penalties they'd prescribed for *proven* cases of rape—or, for that matter, the torture and execution of anyone who hadn't been formally judged before the Inquisition—had at least mitigated the damage in Maiksyn's other companies. Yet the dislike between him and Cahrtair had grown both deeper and stronger as a consequence, and he was certain Cahrtair and the others like him continued to ignore the threat of Baikyr's regulations whenever it suited them. They'd grown more cautious about it, and their reports had assumed a certain bland lack of detail, but he knew it was still going on.

Yet however much he might detest the man, he had to admit the same vicious streak which sent women and children to freeze in the heart of winter made Cahrtair a man to fear in battle. If there was a timid bone anywhere in the major's body, Maiksyn had never seen it. In fact, if he had a fault on the battlefield, it was that he was overly aggressive.

That's what makes him the perfect man for this job. And if it's a choice between seeing him or Chermyn get chewed up, I know who I'd pick. In fact—Maiksyn's lips twitched with an inappropriate temptation to smile as he watched the captain leave the high road and slog across the mud towards him—*I already have picked, haven't I?*

"Sir?" Cahrtair even touched his breastplate; Baikyr had made it abundantly clear in a personal interview that he wasn't tolerating insubordination to any of his regimental commanders out of a mere militia major, even if he was one of Father Shainsail's favorites.

"The scouts say it's clear through Jairth," Maiksyn said briefly. "They weren't able to scout the flanks properly or get anyone up the slopes, though. Take your company along the road as far as the ruins. If you can get patrols as far forward as Ananasberg, do it, but hold your company at Jairth. I'll be sending First Company up to join you, and I don't want you bringing on a fight until we've got supports close enough to help out if you need them, especially if they have any of those damned rifles pushed forward."

"If the road's clear as far as Jairth, why not keep pushing towards Serabor . . . Sir?" The military courtesy was something of a second thought, Maiksyn noticed. "If they've fallen back the way we think they have, the farther down-gap we get before they're reinforced, the better."

"Unless I'm mistaken, *Major*," Maiksyn said a bit coldly, "we don't know if they've fallen back 'the way we think they have' at all. For that matter, Colonel Baikyr specifically reminded us all, I believe, that the reports to that effect are completely unconfirmed. Is my memory at fault?"

"No . . . Sir," Cahrtair said after a moment.

"And, if my memory of the map—not to mention of the countless times I've made the trip down-canal from Saiknyr—serves me, the terrain south of Jairth would be an excellent spot for an *ambush*, wouldn't it?"

He held the overzealous major's eyes until Cahrtair nodded unwillingly. Then he drew a deep breath and made himself step on his own temper.

"I appreciate your desire to drive the enemy as far south as possible, Major. And if the opportunity presents itself, that's exactly what we'll do. But we've lost too many good men already. We don't need any more widows and orphans, and I don't want your men getting into a crack before the rest of the regiment's in a position to pull you back out again."

"I understand, Sir." Cahrtair's voice and expression were at least marginally more respectful, and he nodded.

"Good. On your way, then," Maiksyn said briskly, and watched as 3rd Company moved on down the broad, paved high road.

.IV.
75 Miles North of Serabor,
Sylmahn Gap,
Mountaincross Province,
Republic of Siddarmark

W ell, I wish I could say it was a surprise," Colonel Wyllys said, looking down at Major Styvynsyn's note. "At least it doesn't look like they're moving in more than regimental strength . . . assuming Zhorj's right, anyway."

Lieutenant Charlz Dahnsyn, the colonel's senior aide, was an intelligent young man. As such, he kept his mouth firmly closed.

"I'm not going to bite you, Charlz," Wyllys half growled. "Mind you, I'd like to take a chunk out of *somebody*, and not just because I could use the meat."

"Yes, Sir."

"Oh, relax." Wyllys shook his head. "We knew it was only a matter of time. And at least the snow's melted. Besides, this is a splendid opportunity to see if Captain Klairynce's brilliant inspiration has a hope in Shan-wei of actually *working*. Not that I doubt its success for a single moment, you understand."

"Yes, Sir." Dahnsyn's tone and expression were considerably more relaxed this time, and Wyllys smiled sourly before he bent back over the map on the slightly charred kitchen table which had been hauled from some farmhouse's ruins to his command post.

The Sylmahn Gap stretched well over two hundred and fifty miles from north to south, as if some archangel's battleaxe had cloven the deep, narrow gash between the Snow Barrens and the Moon Thorns. For most of its length, it was little more than twenty or thirty miles wide, and it narrowed to considerably less than half that in places. The widest portion—its northwestern end, where it broke free of the mountains into the high, fertile tableland of western Mountaincross at the city of Malkyr—was almost a hundred miles wide, but that width was badly constricted by the deep, cold waters of Lake Wyvern.

The Gap's floor descended steadily as it made its way south, and the Guarnak-Sylmahn Canal ran right down its center. That canal connected the uppermost navigable reaches of the Sylmahn River to the Hildermoss River, six hundred and fifty miles to the northwest as a wyvern flew, and, via the Guarnak–Ice Ash Canal, to the Ice Ash River five hundred and thirty miles to the northeast. To the south, the Sylmahn connected to the Tairmana and Siddar City Canals, giving direct access to the capital, seven hundred and twenty miles to the southeast.

The next best thing to a hundred and fifty feet across and twenty-five feet deep, with tow roads for the hill dragons who, in more peaceful days, pulled barges along it, the canal was a formidable obstacle. The high road from Guarnak all the way to Siddar City ran down the west side of the canal, raised almost twenty feet above water level, on the far side of the forty-foot wide bed of the northbound tow road. The southbound tow road ran down the canal's *eastern* side, making the canal's entire cut the next best thing to a hundred yards across, and there was less clearance between the canal and the steep slopes of the Moon Thorns than to the west. Below Jairth, there wasn't much room on either side, since the entire Gap narrowed to no more than thirteen miles at that point. Thirteen miles was still a lot of ground to cover with only his own regiment, though, especially after the casualties the 37th had taken over the winter.

Still, he reminded himself, *it's not like there isn't some good news to go along with the bad. In fact, I'm sure Zhaksyn is pointing that out to Styvynsyn about now.*

He smiled with genuine humor at the thought, because he hadn't picked his lead company at random. Young Styvynsyn was a solid, steady commander, and Grovair Zhaksyn had served in the Republic's army longer than Styvynsyn had been alive. He wasn't especially worried about the 2nd getting overly frisky, and if things worked out the way they were supposed to, he'd have Ghavyn Sahlys' 5th Company to help keep a lid on things.

Of course, that assumes the other fellow doesn't have plans of his own you happen not to have thought of, Stahn, he reminded himself.

He ran his finger along the line of the high road. As the *Writ* stipulated, it was sixty feet across, with a fifteen-foot shoulder to either side, and raised above the surrounding terrain, with its hard, well-paved surface sloped to promote good drainage. Here in the mountains, the built-up roadbed was pierced at regular intervals by large, sturdy culverts to further promote drainage, especially where it crossed the upper Sylmahn's channel. The river was completely unnavigable, little more than a shallow, rapidly flowing creek, once it got above Serabor—that was why the canal ran into the artificial basin at the Serabor Locks—but it ran high, deep, and fast in the spring, filled with brown water and foam. By now, it was fretting and fuming as it backed up, spreading out as it overflowed its usual channels to send the extra water from all that melting snow through additional culverts. That happened every year, but *this* year at least half those culverts had been blocked with rubble and debris—some accidentally; more of them because he'd ordered his men to do exactly that as they retreated from Terykyr. There'd been some protests about that, at least until Father Ahlun, General Stohnar's chaplain, had pointed out in his sermons that the *rebels* had begun sabotaging the canals and high roads, despite the *Writ*'s prohibitions, on the direct authority of the Grand Inquisitor's own order. That hadn't completely ended the unhappiness, but it *had* stilled the protests.

Now the water between the Snow Barrens and the high road was spreading fast, turning the entire area into a treacherous sea of mud and swamp covered by anything from several inches to as much as ten or fifteen feet of extremely cold water. Given the number of stone walls, rail fences, barns, and farmhouses—not to mention gullies, granaries, wells, and a burned-out village or two—submerged in that water, wading through it would be as exhausting and dangerous as it was chilling. And if the roadway's canal side was still relatively clear for now, that wasn't going to last, either.

Normally, the Faithful's possession of the high ground around Terykyr would have allowed them to control the water level in the canal by closing the locks there. With the snowmelt beginning to pour down off the mountains, though, water was in copious supply, and the level in the canal's cut was already far above its banks. If things worked out as General Stohnar had planned, that was only going to become even more pronounced over the next several five-days, too. The Serabor Locks were too low to produce that effect by themselves, but the dam the engineers and civilian volunteers had built was considerably higher. Now water was backing steadily up in the cut, beginning to spill across the tow roads. Very shortly, only the high road itself would remain above water, like a causeway surrounded by ruin.

And neither side's going to get more than a single company down the high road at a time, he thought grimly. *That favors us, since all we really want at the moment is to keep them from coming any farther south. But I'd really prefer to do that without gutting Styvynsyn's company. And I don't think the General's going to complain if we manage to kill off a few hundred more of the treasonous bastards along the way.*

Actually, he knew, although General Trumyn Stohnar would have preferred to be considerably farther north than he was at the moment, they were lucky to be here at all. The Sylmahn Gap had been high on the list of the "Sword of Schueler's" initial operations in Mountaincross, and the rebels had flooded down it in overwhelming numbers during the early days of the uprising. Indeed, they'd driven the militia who'd tried to hold it all the way back to Serabor before the battered defenders managed to stop them. Most of the deep, narrow valley had been turned into wreckage and ruin in the process, and Serabor itself was little more than a charred and churned wasteland.

At one point, Serabor had been under attack from the east as well as the west, and the rebels had thrown incendiaries into the town during the month-long siege it had endured before Stohnar's column cut its way through to the defenders. Most of its wooden structures had burned before his arrival, and the majority of its stone houses and warehouses had been pulled apart by the defenders themselves. Unlike some realms, the Republic possessed few walled cities or fortified towns east of the border marches. It was the army's job to make sure they didn't *need* fortifications, and Serabor had been no exception to that unfortified norm. The desperately outnumbered militiamen, who'd joined the two badly understrength companies of regulars to hold it, had been forced to throw together whatever fieldworks they could.

The rebels had been at the end of their own tether when General Stohnar came on the scene, however. Half-frozen and half-starved, outnumbered by the relatively fresh, well-trained, and enraged regulars the lord protector had sent, and faced for the first time with rifles (if only in small numbers), the attackers from over-mountain had been driven in a rabble for over a hundred and seventy miles before they'd managed to dig in in turn and hold at Malkyr. But then it had been *their* turn to reinforce heavily, and Stohnar—short on supplies and with little hope of additional reinforcements of his own—had been driven one bloody step at a time back down the long, weary way his men had come. Now his front lay little more than halfway between the wreckage of Serabor and the ruins of Jairth, and he couldn't afford to be driven any farther south.

Well, the colonel thought now, *you knew the lull was too good to last, Stahn. They may be traitors and they may be butchers, but that doesn't necessarily make them blind, drooling idiots. They have to know we're going to turn the entire Gap into one huge swamp if they can't break through and destroy the dam, and at least they gave you almost two full five-days to catch your breath before they decided to do something about that. I guess it's time to see whether or not all that scheming you did while you were resting is going to do you any good in the end.*

He hoped it would. Not that he was looking forward to it, whatever Father Ahlun might have to say, but if they weren't going to be able to *hold* the high road . . . .

"Get a courier to Major Sahlys," he told Dahnsyn without looking up from the map. "I know he's already in position, but pass him Styvynsyn's message and tell him I expect first contact between the rebels and the Second in the next hour and a half."

"Yes, Sir!"

The lieutenant slapped his breastplate and disappeared in a rapid squelching of mud, and Wyllys smiled grimly.

I can't get more than one company onto the road at a time, he thought in the direction of the oncoming rebels. *But neither can you bastards, and you know the terrain a lot better than I do, so I'm not going to manage any surprise attacks, now am I? Of course I'm not! So you just keep on coming.*

His smile turned into something very much like a slash lizard's snarl, and his right index finger tapped the map. It was probably a good thing he'd shared his plans with General Stohnar ahead of time, he reflected, although, to be honest, the idea itself had come from Lieutenant Hainree Klairynce, 3rd Company's acting commander. Klairynce was the youngest of his company COs. Indeed, legally he was too young to command a company at all, even one as understrength as the 3rd. But he was as smart as he was young, and he'd been born and raised in Glacierheart. He knew mountains, he had plenty of initiative, he figured anything Clyntahn had authorized could be used against *him*, and his family had been coal miners and canal workers for generations.

And that, my fine Temple Loyalist friends, is going to be a very bad thing indeed from your perspective, Wyllys thought coldly. *After all, you're the ones trying to fight your way out of the Gap. All I have to do is keep you penned up inside it until the Lord Protector can reinforce us, and I intend to do just that.*

.V.
Jairth,
Sylmahn Gap,
Mountaincross Province,
Republic of Siddarmark

Hahlys Cahrtair's horse's hooves clattered on the high road's stony surface and his face was grim as he followed 2nd Platoon. At least one in ten of his pikemen was barefoot, without even boots, although Father Shainsail and Colonel Baikyr promised new boots would be forthcoming from Guarnak any day now. Personally, Cahrtair would believe that when he actually saw them.

At least the weather's turned, he reminded himself harshly. *We're not still losing the boys to frostbite. Not that we haven't lost more than enough of them already.*

The Siddarmarkian army had long been noted for its quartermaster's efficiency, but that had been before it was two-thirds destroyed in the Rising. Both sides had burned or destroyed the army's peacetime network of provincial magazines in order to keep them from falling into the *other* side's hands. That had inevitably increased civilian suffering, since those magazines had also been intended to feed civilians in times of disaster, and the devastation of the Republic's transportation system, especially the sabotage of so many canal locks, had turned a dire situation into catastrophe. Indeed, the chaos as vast numbers of refugees struggled through snow and ice, seeking some sort of security, amply demonstrated the reasons for Langhorne's charge to *protect* the canals on which so much depended. The fact that the Grand Inquisitor had been forced to suspend that rule, despite the consequences for so many civilians, had been equally ample proof of God's decision to punish Siddarmark for its leaders' sins, nor had that been the only scourge laid across the Republic's bleeding back.

The starving, ill-equipped troops in the field had been unable to comply fully with Pasquale's Law, and the inevitable upsurge of disease had cost the Faithful many more casualties than they'd suffered in battle. Unless Cahrtair missed his guess, they weren't done yet, either. His own company—made back up for this attack to something which actually approached its assigned strength with drafts from the reinforcements which had arrived three five-days ago—had lost over half its original strength. Most of those men were dead, and over fifty of those who hadn't died—yet—were too sick to march. And with their privation-weakened resistance, at least half of them would die in the end, even if fresh food miraculously arrived tomorrow. That was simply the way it was, and there wasn't one damned thing he could do about it.

And if those heretic bastards manage to flood the lower Gap completely, we'll be frigging well stuck here in the middle of a goddamned swamp until next *autumn. Pasquale only* knows *what kind of sickness levels we'll be looking at then!*

Hahlys Cahrtair didn't know, and he didn't want to find out, which was why he intended to push as far south as he possibly could, whatever Maiksyn might have to say.

He's not as much of an old woman as I thought he was before the Rising, the major admitted grudgingly. *Not quite. And I'd just as soon have some support handy when I run into the bastards, for that matter. But the high road runs too close to the west side of the Gap at Jairth. If the heretics get their damned riflemen up on our flank, especially with a couple of hundred yards of water between us and them, we'll play hell pushing farther down the road later.*

The truth was that those riflemen had proved far more effective than anyone had anticipated. Indeed, they'd played a major role in breaking the

Faithful's morale when Stohnar's attack drove them back from Serabor. Not because they'd killed all that many people; there hadn't been enough of them for that. No, it was the *range* at which they'd been able to kill. Nobody on the Temple Loyalist side—not even Colonel Baikyr and his regulars—had ever actually experienced rifle fire. They'd expected it to be more effective than matchlocks, but they'd never counted on a weapon that could hit specific man-sized targets at three hundred yards! It was only through the grace of Langhorne and Chihiro the heretics had so few of them, but those few had been more than enough to give Cahrtair and his men a profound respect for their capabilities. Indeed, in his opinion, Maiksyn had yet to fully appreciate the range at which rifle fire could dominate exposed terrain, and he was only glad Stohnar didn't have any artillery.

Yet. That we know of, anyway, he corrected himself. *Of course, we don't either, do we?*

That, too, was something they were promised, along with rifles of their own, but they hadn't seen either yet. And the unhappy truth was that it was going to take a lot of both to beat the damned heretics in the end. At the moment, though, the new weapons were still too thin on the ground, even among the heretics, to be decisive, and that meant the campaign for the Gap all came down to a race. In a head-on confrontation, a well-prepared defender always had the advantage, and in the confines of the Sylmahn Gap, the only attacks possible were going to be frontal. No one was going to manage to get men armed with eighteen-foot pikes through the lizard paths that snaked through the mountains above it, at any rate! The heretics clearly understood that as well as Cahrtair did, and their efforts to flood the valley until only the high road itself stood above water would make that even worse.

Langhorne only knows how many thousands of men we've already lost. But if we don't break through the Gap before the heretics dig in and build a frigging fortress all the way across it, we'll never get through at all, and all the men we've already lost will've died for nothing, Cahrtair reflected with cold, harsh pragmatism. *We have to drive through* now, *even if it costs another regiment or two. Father Shainsail understands that, and if he's behind me, I'll take my chances with Maiksyn and Baikyr.*

▼　　▼　　▼

"I think it's time to open the dance," Major Styvynsyn said, watching the column of rebel infantry march steadily down the high road towards him.

He and Sergeant Zhaksyn stood on the crest of a little hill, no more than a dozen feet high. It said a great deal about the flatness of the Sylmahn Gap's floor that such a small terrain feature could be considered a "hill" at all, and it would have offered very little in the way of concealment or tactical advantage if the rebels had scouted the towering slopes to either side properly. From such elevated perches, they would have been able to see for miles along the Gap, and they'd easily have spotted anything Styvynsyn had hidden behind the hill.

The rebels weren't doing that kind of scouting, though, the major reflected grimly. Even the relatively small number of rifles General Stohnar had brought with him were enough to allow his troops to dominate the narrow paths which snaked through the mountains to either side of the Gap. In this instance, though, they weren't sending patrols very far out in front even down here on the valley floor, and he wondered whether that was caution—they'd lost a lot of scouts to ambushes—or arrogance.

Not that it mattered at this point, since Styvynsyn had precious little to hide . . . and absolutely no intention of holding his position. On the other hand, a little uncertainty on an adversary's part never hurt.

Now he looked down to where Captain Dahn Lywkys, commanding his Second Platoon, stood watching him intently and waved his hand in a rapidly rotating circle. Then he pointed up the road towards the oncoming rebels, and Lywkys waved his own hand and nodded to his standard-bearer. 2nd Platoon's colors started forward, and a forest of upright pikes followed them as Lywkys' men moved up.

▼   ▼   ▼

Hahlys Cahrtair's stomach muscles tightened as the heretics moved into sight at last, but he was hardly surprised to see them. If he was surprised by anything, it was that he hadn't run into them sooner. Not that they hadn't chosen their position well when they finally decided to turn up, he conceded sourly.

He was several miles south of Jairth, between the charred ruins of the villages of Ananasberg and Harystn. It was a stretch he knew well from 3rd Company's operations last autumn, and it put him a good six miles past the point at which Maiksyn had expected him to halt. He was well aware of that minor fact, just as he was aware that the gap between him and Dahnel Chermyn's 1st Company had widened considerably . . . probably because Chermyn had obeyed orders and stopped where he'd been told to instead of exercising a spark of initiative. Well, that was fine for him, but 3rd Company had more gumption than that. Given the total absence of opposition, it would've been criminally stupid for Cahrtair to simply park his entire command on its collective arse and wait for Chermyn's dawdling, timid company to catch up—*if* it caught up! With his flanks secured by the swamp of steadily rising runoff to his right and the canal the heretics had so obligingly backed up on his left, the only way anyone could come at him was from the front, and the high road was only a hundred feet wide, including its shoulders. The encroaching flood on his right had reached almost to the roadbed itself, and even the northbound tow road, usually a good six feet above the canal's surface was less than two feet clear of its climbing water level now. Of course, the tow road was also fifteen feet lower than the high road, at the foot of a sharp, ballasted slope, and it added only another forty-five feet or so to the road's width.

The water to his right was shallow enough to allow men on foot to slog forward through it, at least in theory, but it would have been impossible even for regulars to maintain formation wading through that muddy, icy water, not to mention all the unseen dips and other obstacles lurking under its surface to trip anyone foolish enough to try. Even worse, a tangled mass of spiretree, slabnut, wild ananas, and hickory sprawled across the three thousand yards between the roadbed and the valley's western wall, stretching to within no more than a hundred yards of the road and rising out of the standing water like gloomy sentinels. Even the sharply pointed spiretrees seemed to droop dispiritedly, the tips of their spreading evergreen branches trailing in the brown water, and the seasonal trees were just beginning to throw out their spring foliage. The frail green leaves looked lost and forlorn against the mud and desolation, but Cahrtair, never an imaginative man, didn't care about their dismal, dejected appearance. What he *did* care about was the fact that no pike formation in the world could have moved through that tangled, sodden barrier. So his total effective frontage was no more than fifty yards, even after he accepted the need to deploy troops on the lower level of the tow road despite the awkward break in his lines the slope down to it would impose.

This is exactly why the motherless bastards are so busy flooding the goddamned valley. We know how badly we've hurt them since we kicked them back past Terykyr, so they've created a situation where we can't use our numbers effectively.

Normally, a Siddarmarkian pike regiment arrayed for battle had a frontage of sixty yards. Each of its four hundred and fifty-man companies was organized into seven platoons, each of two thirty-man sections, plus a fifteenth section attached directly to the company commander. Formed for battle, each section marched directly behind the one in front of it. Since each man required a yard of frontage but six feet of depth, a platoon formed a line thirty yards across and four yards deep, and a company column was thirty yards across and (counting the headquarters section) thirty yards deep. As a result, each company could form its own pike square at need, although that wasn't standard tactical doctrine. A regiment was supposed to form two companies abreast and two companies deep, with its fifth company of light infantry deployed to screen its front with arbalests or muskets as it approached the enemy. Alternatively, the light infantry could be pulled back into the gaps between pike blocks when multiple regiments were arrayed in the checkerboard pattern proper tactics required. In either case, once the pikes came into contact with the enemy, it was time for the light troops to get out of the way by flowing back between the advancing squares or peeling away to screen the main body's flanks. Sword-armed musketeers and arbalesters had no business confronting a solid wall of pikes in melee, and they knew it.

At the moment, thanks to the reinforcements he'd received, Cahrtair's company was at better than three-quarters of its official strength. That meant he was in much better condition than the heretics' tattered companies could claim, but it wasn't a great deal of help just at the moment. Even if the entire regiment had been behind him, and fully up to strength to boot, its frontage, allowing for the interruption of the slope down to the tow road, would have been limited to a single company . . . like his.

His column halted, obedient to the orders he'd issued before setting out as the heretics moved over the crest of the hill. The enemy's formation was better and tighter than his own men could have produced, and his jaw tightened as he recognized the standard of the 37th Infantry. He'd acquired a lot of information about the heretics' units and their troop strengths—it was amazing how talkative a heretic became with the proper . . . encouragement, and he had just the boys to supply it—and the 37th had been the core of the force which had snatched victory from the Faithful by driving them back from Serabor just as the town had been about to fall. In the process, they'd displayed the tighter unit organization and lethality imparted by the longer, more intensive drill possible for a full-time standing formation. His own militiamen, limited to part-time, periodic drill, fell short of that standard of training, and it had cost them dearly against Colonel Wyllys' regulars.

But the 37th had suffered disproportionate casualties of its own, since it had been called upon to lead the heretics' offensive and then pounded during the Faithful's counteroffensive. According to Father Shainsail's spies, the regiment was at scarcely half its paper strength, and General Stohnar's other units were in little better shape. Coupled with the failure of the heretics' supply chain—Stohnar's last convoy of supplies was almost two five-days overdue, and his hungry men were beginning to desert in small but steadily increasing numbers—they'd had no choice but to fall back under the Faithful's driving attacks. Stohnar was using Wyllys' regiment as his rearguard because it was the most effective formation he had left, with the best morale and cohesion. If they could break *it*, they'd be up against mostly militia who'd already been disheartened at being forced to give up all the ground they'd retaken since Stohnar's arrival.

Of course, he thought bleakly, *the problem is that heretics or not, they're tough bastards, and they're in a defensive position that's going to be a bitch to drive them out of. And it's not—*

His thoughts paused as a second standard appeared. He climbed down from the saddle and unslung the spyglass hanging over his shoulder. He would have preferred to be able to use it from the higher vantage point of his saddle, where he could see over the heads of the infantry halted in front of him, but the heavy tube was a two-handed proposition, and his horse would never have stood still enough. It didn't matter too much, since the heretics' higher position let him see them clearly, and he smiled thinly as the image swam into focus and confirmed what he thought he'd seen.

Each Siddarmarkian platoon had its own banner, although it was less than half the size of the company and regimental standards. That banner was the reference point the men of the platoon looked to when it came to keeping their formation aligned in the smoke and confusion of battle. That was no small task when it came to maneuvering something as inherently ponderous as a pike square, even for the ruthlessly drilled regulars, and when formation changes were ordered, the platoons' standard-bearers led the way through the evolution. They were less useful to the militia units, whose lower standards of training couldn't match the regulars' maneuvering ability anyway, but even for the militia, they were important to unit cohesion and morale.

They also made it easier to estimate the number of platoons in an opposing formation, however. That didn't much matter under normal circumstances, but it did this time. It should have required only fifty men to form a single line completely across the bed of the high road *and* the tow road. Allowing for casualties and routine sickness or injury, a platoon was usually closer to fifty men than sixty, so it shouldn't have been too difficult for the heretics to fit two platoons abreast, each formed into the standard double line, into that space. But there were *three* standards in those first two lines . . . and it didn't cover the entire width of the two roadbeds, anyway. More than that, he could see at least three more standards in the next two lines. He couldn't be certain about the lines farther back, since they were concealed by the crest of the hill, but he didn't have to. If it took the full remaining strength of six platoons to form a line no more than fifty yards wide and twenty-four deep, the regiment they belonged to must have taken more than fifty percent losses. *Substantially* more, in fact . . . unless he wanted to assume the opposing commander was an idiot who'd put his *weakest* units out in front to take the initial shock of combat.

And these are the same bastards who got their arses kicked at Terykr. I'll guarantee you the assholes're remembering that right this minute—yes, and that we're the ones who did the kicking! Their morale has to be at the bottom of the crapper right now, especially for the ones who've begun figuring out who's going to be waiting for their sorry souls after we get done with them! "Regulars" or not, they've got to be hanging by a thread over there. So if we kick them again quick, right in the teeth . . . .

He re-slung the spyglass, climbed back into the saddle, and looked around quickly. It didn't take him long to find what he was looking for, and he drove in his heels so hard his thin-fleshed horse jumped in surprise before it leapt forward.

"Yes, Sir?" Captain Mahrtyn Mahkhom, 2nd Platoon's commanding officer looked up from a hasty conference with his section commanders as Cahrtair reined the horse back in beside him.

"The bastards're even thinner on the ground than we thought, Mahrtyn," Cahrtair said, without dismounting. "They've got the leftovers of six entire platoons in a line less than fifty yards across and half that deep! If we hit 'em hard enough and fast enough, we'll punch through like shit through a wyvern! We may clear the route all the way to Serabor, and if we don't manage that, we've still got a chance to finally break these heretical sons of bitches once and for all! Get your men formed up!"

"Yes, Sir!" Mahkhom slapped his breastplate, turned to the section commanders, and smiled thinly. "You heard the Major, so why're you all still standing here?!"

Hungry smiles, most as hard and hating as his own, answered him, and his subordinates headed for their own commands at a run.

▼   ▼   ▼

"I hope the rest of the boys aren't too pissed off at me for taking their standards away from them," Major Styvynsyn remarked, watching the leading rebel platoon's pikes drop from a vertical moving forest into fighting position.

"'Spect they'll get over it, Sir," Sergeant Zhaksyn reassured him. "Long's they get 'em back, that is. And 'specially if this works out half as well as you expect it to."

There might, Styvynsyn reflected, steadfastly keeping his eyes on the rebels rather than giving his senior noncom a beady look, have been something less than total enthusiasm in Zhaksyn's tone. If so, the major was disinclined to argue with him, although he did think it was a bit unfair of the sergeant to call it *his* idea. The truth as Zhaksyn knew perfectly well, was that he'd been less than ecstatic over the battle plan when Colonel Wyllys described it to him, and he intended to have a few words with that overly innovative sprout Klairynce. On the other hand, it might just work. It was his job as the man charged to carry it out, to act as if he believed that, at any rate, and he was going to take immense satisfaction out of what happened if it did. Especially since he'd identified the banners of the rebels coming towards him.

According to our reports, the one good thing about that bastard Cahrtair is that he's got the guts to stay up close to the front. That's nice.

Hahlys Cahrtair's company had earned itself a large debt of hatred. At first, Styvynsyn had been disinclined to believe the stories, but not after he'd personally interviewed the handful of survivors who'd escaped—or survived—the 3rd Saiknyrs' attentions, most of whom had the scars to prove their stories. None of the rebel militia regiment's companies had been notable for their restraint, but 3rd Company had certainly distinguished itself for its *lack* of restraint.

Styvynsyn didn't like where this war was headed—or where it had already *gone*, for that matter—if only because he knew what it was going to do to discipline when—if—the time came for them to move into territory which had gone over to the rebels. If one thing was as certain as the fact that the sun rose in the east, it was that even the best troops in the world were going to retaliate for what they'd seen in the Sylmahn Gap. Some because every man had at least a bit of Shan-wei down inside somewhere, clamoring to get out, and that bit of the Fallen would seize the opportunity to sate itself in bloodlust with cackling delight. But more because they were so sickened and infuriated by what the rebels had done "in God's name" that they were going to visit retribution on anyone they could catch. It didn't take the sight of too many naked girls and women dead in the snow, often enough with babes beside them, to fill even a good man with hatred. Styvynsyn understood that perfectly, because he'd felt exactly the same thing when the 37th advanced through Harystn on its way north and found the half-stripped skeletons of the village mayor's entire family nailed to the wall of what had been the town hall. The youngest couldn't have been much more than ten or eleven years old and the spikes driven through his wrists and ankles had been thicker than one of his own finger bones. Zhorj Styvynsyn wasn't a man whose stomach turned easily, but it had then, and he'd lost the one hot meal he and his men had been able to wolf down that entire five-day.

He hoped the boy had been dead before that atrocity was visited upon him and his older brother and sister. Judging by the way the back of his skull had been crushed, he probably had, and wasn't it a sad, miserable thing to find himself *grateful* someone had smashed in a ten-year-old's skull? Styvynsyn had seen all too many other atrocities since that day, and whatever he might have wished, not all had been committed by rebels. Yet it was those animal-gnawed, half-demolished skeletons, still hanging against that charred, half-consumed wall, that stayed with him and visited him in his dreams. He didn't know—not for certain—that Hahlys Cahrtair's company had had anything to do with that particular massacre, but from the things he knew they *had* done, it seemed likely. And even if they hadn't, they had more than enough blood on their hands. So much as he might fear where the ever-building cycle of blood and hatred was going to end, he didn't really care right this moment.

It was time to inflict a little retribution of his own.

▼　▼　▼

The Siddarmarkian army didn't use bugles. It relied instead on drummers, who accompanied the company and regimental commanders. Now Cahrtair's drums snarled and rolled as Mahrtyn Mahkhom's 2nd Platoon assembled itself across the high road with Shawyn Mahlyk's 1st Platoon behind it.

There was almost enough space for Cahrtair to have formed the company with two platoons abreast, instead of the standard one, but not quite. He probably could have crowded that many into line if he'd packed them shoulder-to-shoulder, and it was tempting to get as many men as possible into action against the weakened 37th as quickly as possible. But even with all his subunits slightly understrength, he would have required a generous fifty yards to squeeze them in, and the slope down to the tow road took too big a bite out of the available level ground for that to work. Even if it hadn't, crowding them that tight would have grossly inhibited their mobility. A unit of regulars like the 37th might have made it work; Cahrtair was too smart—and had learned too many lessons the hard way—to try it with militia.

He'd also disbanded his 7th Platoon and his headquarters section to bring the remainder of his platoons back up almost to full strength. Captain Arystyn, the 7th's CO, had died with a pike in his guts in the attack on Terykyr, anyway, and he'd needed the men elsewhere. The redistribution had cost the company some depth, and none of its platoons was quite at full strength, despite the move, but no unit ever was, really.

He didn't like attacking on a thirty-man frontage, but it was the formation the men were most accustomed to, and he wasn't about to try introducing new wrinkles in the heat of combat, especially with no one close enough to support him if things went badly. Besides, if the heretics were as understrength as those crowded banners suggested, they had to have lost a lot of unit cohesion. Their line would be marginally wider than his, but they were going to be less resilient, without the staying power to resist the shock of four hundred charging men with the power of God upon them.

He did wish there was more room to deploy 8th Platoon's arbalesters, but in such constricted terrain, there was no way they could have fallen back to get clear of the melee when the pikes crossed. Besides, the 8th was at barely half strength, and the heretics didn't have any of their accursed riflemen deployed anywhere where he could see them, anyway.

Doesn't mean they don't have some on the backside of that hill, he reminded himself as his company settled into position and gathered itself. *But they can't shoot through their own men, and if they're trying something fancy, the boys'll have time to close with them while their pikes try to dodge out of the way.* His lips drew back from his teeth. *I'd love to see how their damned "bayonets" make out against proper pikes if we can get to them!*

The drums gave one last roll and then began the hard, hammering tattoo that sent the company rumbling down the high road towards the waiting heretics.

▼   ▼   ▼

"I don't think the boys are going to like this," Styvynsyn said as he watched the rebel advance begin.

"Well, I'm not so very fond of it myself, Sir, begging the Major's pardon," Zhaksyn said tartly. Styvynsyn looked at him, and the sergeant shrugged. "Oh, if it works it'll be a right fine sight, and no mistake. But if it *doesn't* . . . ."

Styvynsyn could have done without the eloquence of the sergeant's shrug . . . mostly because Zhaksyn had such an excellent point. The major wouldn't have dreamed of trying something like this with any of the militia units, but his men were regulars. They had the discipline to maneuver with machine-like precision even in the heat of battle . . . and to run away when they were told to without its turning into a *real* rout.

Or I hope *to hell they've got it, anyway,* he thought. *And we're going to find out just . . . about . . .* now!

▼   ▼   ▼

Major Cahrtair's eyes went wide.

The pikemen aligned to withstand his attack held their ranks with the rocklike steadiness of the veterans they were. Despite his numerical advantage, it was going to be ugly, and he expected to take at least as much damage as he inflicted. Then again, he had the strength to absorb the damage, and they didn't. Besides—

That was when it began.

It was almost imperceptible at first. A tiny stir, a slight wavering, like the branches of a tree at the first touch of a breeze. But it grew. That steady, unyielding wall of pikeheads began to move, and as he watched, he saw the unthinkable happen.

The 37th Infantry Regiment broke.

It didn't simply *break*—it shattered, before his own men had gotten within sixty yards of its line, At least a quarter of its men actually threw away their pikes, turned, and ran.

The 3rd Saiknyrs faltered, breaking step at the unbelievable sight of an entire Siddarmarkian pike company retreating in wild disorder before the mere threat of an attack. There was something so *wrong* about it, so contrary to the way the world worked, that they couldn't quite make sense of what their eyes were seeing. But then as the 37th's platoon standards disappeared into the swirl of fleeing bodies, a roar of delighted triumph—and contempt—went up from Hahlys Cahrtair's men.

"After them!" Cahrtair bellowed. "Stay on them! Don't let them rally! *Kill the fucking heretics!*"

The drums snarled, translating his commands, and the entire 3rd Company went forward at the quick-march in pursuit.

▼ ▼ ▼

Styvynsyn hated throwing away those pikes, but the sad truth was that they had more weapons than they had men these days, and all the world knew a Siddarmarkian pikeman died with his weapon in hand rather than discarding it. It was the one sure proof 2nd Company had actually broken, and Colonel Wyllys' orders had been clear.

His men headed down the high road, and if the rebels had been able to see past the hill on which Styvynsyn stood, they might have been astounded by the orderly way in which the rearmost sections of his "wildly fleeing" line funneled along the roadway. They were less concerned with maintaining meticulous formation than usual, but they were far from the bolting rabble the rebels thought they'd seen. And as Colonel Wyllys had prophesied—and as one Zhorj Styvynsyn had devoutly hoped—his regulars could march much more rapidly than the less well trained rebels. Unless the rebels chose to break ranks, of course, which he doubted they were stupid enough to do.

The one thing he'd actually worried about—aside from his minor concern about whether or not the entire plan was going to work—was that Cahrtair might bring his arbalesters forward. Unencumbered by pikes or the need to maintain a rigid formation, the light infantry *could* have overtaken him, and their arbalest bolts could have inflicted painful casualties. But as he'd hoped, Cahrtair had been too smart to let his missile troops get trapped between opposing pike walls, and he'd been too eager to halt the pikes and pass the arbalesters around them.

Hard to blame him, really, Styvynsyn thought, jogging along the shoulder of the high road with Zhaksyn at his side. *He's got to be thinking about breaking clean out of the Gap, but even if he doesn't manage that, the farther south he can get before he has to stop, the better. And on this kind of frontage, he can hold two or three times his numbers until his supports come up. So the last thing he's going to do is give a routed enemy the chance to catch his breath, turn around, and find a place to stand after all.*

Personally, he didn't much care for letting the rebels this far south himself, but Colonel Wyllys hadn't asked his opinion. And it wasn't as if they hadn't been likely to be pushed farther back over the next few five-days, anyway.

▼ ▼ ▼

Major Cahrtair swore with venomous passion as the gap between the fleeing regulars and his own company widened steadily. There wasn't anything he could do about it—cowards running away were always faster than the people chasing them; something about the fear of death seemed to give them an extra speed advantage—and at least they showed no signs of stopping.

He saw the half-flooded ruins of the town of Harystn drawing nearer on the right as the high road stretched across a vast expanse of flooded terrain. There was a broad, shallow valley here, he remembered, one the high road crossed like a wall, with a tributary of the Sylmahn River at its bottom. Under normal conditions, it was only a shallow, bubbling stream running through the trees which had grown even thicker to either side, but the culverts under the roadbed were more clogged than usual here. The water spread out to the west, and it wasn't much better to the east. The canal had overflowed into the same valley where the tow road had crossed it on a wooden bridge whose gaunt, blackened trestles stood up out of the water swirling about them, and the high road was a virtual causeway across the flood.

Third Company was beginning to slow. The quick march—a hundred and twenty paces per minute, as opposed to the normal marching rate of seventy-five paces per minute—was hard to sustain in formation even on a flat, paved surface and even for men whose endurance hadn't been undercut by starvation, and none of his men had been particularly well fed over the last several months. The heretics, however, actually seemed to be moving still faster, and he felt the opportunity to overhaul them and wipe them from the face of the earth slipping away from him. Sooner or later they were going to run into another heretic position, and if the fleeing 37th managed to escape past another blocking formation, the chance would be gone, probably forever.

On the other hand, panic's contagious, and they might just hit the next position hard enough to carry it with them. Or if it holds, they might not be able to get past it before my boys catch up with them. At any rate, the farther south we get before we have to stop, the better, and nobody's getting past us if we have to stop here!

He looked out over the watery waste of flooded trees stretching away to either hand with a sense of satisfaction. The entire Gap was less than ten miles wide at this point, and choked by the tangled forest crowding in on the high road and overshadowing the tow roads from either side. No open flanks here, no way for the regulars to use their greater mobility to slip a pike block around his position and force him to retreat. No, even if he had to stop right here, they wouldn't be moving him before that sluggard Chermyn came up in support, and then—

▼   ▼   ▼

Zhorj Styvynsyn peeled off from his "routed" column as its head passed the ruins of Harystn and headed into the denser woodland to the south. The canal bed was relatively clear aside from the flotsam and jetsam on its flooded surface, but the high road passed through a dense belt of mixed evergreens and seasonal trees just south of the burned, half-flooded village. The woods didn't actually constrict the roadway, but it felt as if they did as the rough-barked trunks rose from the water on either side of it like walls. He looked back and muttered a short, pungent phrase. Their pursuers were closer behind than he'd hoped. It was time to slow the bastards down and convince them to go back where he wanted them.

"Any time now would be good, Gahvyn," he said a bit sharply, looking at the officer who'd just materialized beside him, and Major Sahlys nodded.

"I believe you have a point," the commanding officer of 5th Company, 37th Infantry said calmly, and glanced once to each side of the road. Then he nodded again, this time in satisfaction.

"Fire!" he shouted, and the fifty-three men of Captain Ellys Sebahstean's 3rd Platoon braced their rifles on the carefully concealed rests they'd built hours earlier and squeezed their triggers.

▼　▼　▼

"Shan-wei fly away with their souls!" Major Cahrtair snarled as the woods ahead blossomed suddenly with puffs of smoke. The riflemen were still a good three hundred yards away, but his company made a solid, compact target. The bullets slammed into his men with a sound like fists punching a side of meat, and he heard the screams as half Mahkhom's front rank went down in a tangle of blood and broken bones.

▼　▼　▼

Sebahstean's riflemen stood and stepped back from their firing positions, biting the tops off paper cartridges, pouring powder down their rifle barrels. As they reloaded, Captain Zhon Trahlmyn's 1st Platoon took their places, and another deadly volley roared. Only two of 5th Company's seven platoons had been equipped with rifles, and neither was at full strength, but they still had just over a hundred men between them, and their bullets hammered Cahrtair's men mercilessly.

▼　▼　▼

Cahrtair mastered his temper.

It wasn't easy. He'd been able to taste his triumph, but now it had been snatched away. Yet there was no point lying to himself. He might—*might*—be able to drive forward through the rifle fire. It didn't sound like there could be more than eighty or ninety of the damned things, after all. But he'd lose half the company doing it, and with the trees crowding the road that way, bayoneted rifles would be at least as dangerous as his pikes. Ramming his head into a stone wall and losing men he couldn't afford to lose would be not simply stupid but pointless. Better to fall back to the more solid ground to the north and dig in behind proper earthworks, bring up his own arbalesters, and get Chermyn's lazy arse forward to support him after all. He still wouldn't be able to match the rifles' range, but with good solid parapets to cover his arbalesters until the heretics came to *him* he'd become a cork they wouldn't be pulling out of the bottle anytime soon.

"Pull back!" he commanded, and the drums began a different beat.

▼   ▼   ▼

Styvynsyn drew a deep breath as the rebel pike column stopped, then began pulling back. They'd lost no more than thirty or forty men, he estimated— not even rifles were truly magic, and the range was long—but Cahrtair was obviously just as smart as their reports suggested. He wasn't going to bloody his nose by coming any closer to riflemen dug in amongst such dense tree cover.

Which means he's doing exactly what we want, the major thought coldly. *Assuming, of course, Klairynce knew what he was doing.*

He shaded his eyes with one hand, once more wishing he still had his spyglass. But if his had been smashed, Sahlys' hadn't. The other major was peering through the glass, watching the rear of Cahrtair's formation, which had just become its front, falling rapidly back along the high road.

"About even with the marker," he said, and Styvynsyn frowned.

"They're a little more spread out than we'd hoped for," he replied, watching Bairaht Charlsyn's 1st Platoon forming up on the high road. It had reclaimed its standard from the men he'd taken north with him, and Charlsyn was almost quivering with anticipation. "Give them another few seconds."

"Going to lose a lot of their arbalesters," Sahlys warned.

"Assuming it works at all," Styvynsyn shot back, then shrugged. "I'd prefer to eliminate as many *pikes* as we can get, given who's going to be responsible for the cleanup and all."

"A point," Sailys agreed. His lips quirked at Styvynsyn's tone, but he never lowered his glass. He simply stood there peering through it, then inhaled deeply.

"Now," he said simply, and Captain Sebahstean personally lit the fuse.

▼   ▼   ▼

Hahlys Cahrtair never had the opportunity to discover how thoroughly misinformed he'd been.

It was quite true that Trumyn Stohnar's units were badly understrength; unfortunately, they weren't nearly so badly weakened as Father Shainsail's spies had informed him. But then, Father Shainsail hadn't realized several of "his" spies were actually loyal to the Republic or that General Stohnar had deliberately misled the civilians under his charge when he'd asked them to be on the lookout for all those deserters who hadn't actually deserted after all. Or when he'd complained about those serious delays in the arrival of his supply convoys. Not that he'd been *completely* mendacious. Food *did* remain in short supply, but somehow he'd neglected to mention the twenty-seven tons of gunpowder which had been delivered to Serabor by canal boat.

Eleven tons of that gunpowder had been carefully emplaced in culverts under the high road by soldiers working under Hainree Klairynce's direction. Waterproofing the charges had been a challenge, but the mayor of Serabor had remembered a canal warehouse full of pitch and turpentine which had escaped destruction during the siege. Enough pitch smeared on the outside of flour barrels had worked quite handily.

The trickiest part had been waterproofing the *fuse*, which had to run several hundred yards through soggy conditions. Fortunately, Klairynce had been up to the task, coating the quick match in pitch, as well. It slowed the combustion rate slightly, but it protected it from the wet—a trick he'd picked up from an uncle who'd learned it while working to extend the Branath Canal. He'd tucked it up along the side of the elevated roadbed, above water level, using the pitch's darkness to make it even harder to spot. One or two of Cahrtair's men might have seen the sputtering combustion racing up the black length of cord, but it was unlikely any of them had time to realize what they were seeing.

Cahrtair himself certainly didn't. He was still fuming over his lost opportunity when the eight hundred pounds of powder directly under him and his horse erupted like a crazed volcano.

▼   ▼   ▼

"Well, I'll be damned. It actually worked." Styvynsyn's tone was almost conversational, although he doubted Sahlys could have heard him through the thundering echo of the massive explosions even if he'd shouted at the top of his lungs.

No one else had heard him, either, he realized. In fact, no one was even looking in his direction. All eyes were locked on the enormous columns of dirt, water, mud, and pieces of men spewing into the heavens. Styvynsyn couldn't tell for certain, but it looked like the explosion had killed or maimed at least three-quarters of the rebels, and the others were undoubtedly too stunned and shocked to do more than stand there, trying to understand what had happened.

I never really believed it would work, but damn *if it didn't! I guess I owe Hainree that beer after all . . . as soon as there's any beer to buy him, anyway. Pity we couldn't've gotten the rest of Maiksyn's regiment into our sights, but let's not be greedy,*

Zhorj. So far, you haven't lost a man, and it's just possible even some of Cahrtair's butchers will be smart enough to surrender after this.

"Go!" he shouted. He could hardly hear his own voice through the ringing in his ears. Fortunately, it turned out at least one person *had* been watching him and not the explosions, after all. He didn't know whether or not Bairaht Charlsyn had heard him, but the captain obviously saw him waving vigorously and nodded.

"Advance!" he shouted, and 1st Platoon, followed by 3rd Platoon, rested and unwearied, swept out of the trees and bore down on the shattered, shaken survivors of Hahlys Cahrtair's company.

Well, that's *going to be a godawful mess,* Styvynsyn thought, watching the wreckage reach the top of its flight and begin plunging back towards earth. *Must've taken out a good thousand yards of the roadbed, and I wonder how much of the debris landed in the canal? Rebuilding the road's going to be a copper-plated bitch, but we were going to have to wreck it somewhere if we didn't want the bastards punching us out by sheer weight of numbers eventually. Hopefully, Langhorne'll forgive us, and this is a pretty damned good spot, actually. And taking out an entire company— especially that bastard Cahrtair's—* that's *a nice bonus.*

He watched Charlsyn's men closing with leveled pikes and smiled thinly.

I wonder if any of the bastards really will be smart enough to surrender? If they're really quick, dump their weapons in the canal, get their hands on their heads, and act very meek they might actually manage it without getting their throats cut.

He thought about that for another moment, then shrugged. Bairaht knew the rules about accepting surrenders, and it was out of his hands at this point, either way.

Still, he thought coldly, *I can always hope they're a little slow, can't I?*

.VI.
Siddar City,
Old Province,
Republic of Siddarmark

Merlin Athrawes sat in his small, neat, but comfortable chamber in the Charisian Embassy. It was rather cramped, but it was also one floor below Emperor Cayleb's suite and just happened to be located directly off the stairwell. No one could reach the emperor's level without passing Major Athrawes' door, which could be expected to have a . . . dissuading effect on any assassin familiar with the *seijin's* reputation.

Unfortunately, there were quite a few people in the Republic of Siddarmark, let alone right here in the capital city, who were unlikely to be dissuaded by anything. As someone had remarked many years ago on a planet called Old Earth, when someone actively *wanted* to die to accomplish his mission, the only way to stop him was to give him what he wanted. The sort of people who preferred to survive the attempt were easier to stop, but there were also more of them. So far, Henrai Maidyn's agents had uncovered and defeated two plots to assassinate Cayleb. Aivah Pahrsahn had quietly (and without mentioning it to anyone) defeated another and seen to it that the would-be assassins' well-weighted bodies had been equally quietly disposed of in North Bay, and Merlin and Owl's remotes were tracking five different groups of plotters who all at least aspired to striking down the heretical emperor in the name of God, the Holy Archangels . . . and Zhaspahr Clyntahn.

It wasn't much consolation that there were even more plots afoot to assassinate Greyghor Stohnar, and everyone was unhappily aware of how much easier it would be for Zhaspahr Clyntahn's "Rakurai" to trundle wagonloads of gunpowder around the mainland cities. Merlin had his own remotes seeded as thickly around Siddar City as he could, but even with Owl manufacturing more of them, there was a limit to the available supply. For that matter, even Owl's was reaching a point of diminishing returns simply trying to filter, far less process, all the data available to them. And a city the size of Siddar City was a huge, complex target. Even the best chemical tracers could be diverted or fooled by the complex brew of humanity, animals, processes, and—especially with the city's sewers overloaded by the influx of refugees—human and animal waste.

Had Merlin been a living, breathing human being, trying to keep track of threats to the emperor he'd come to love would have been more than enough to deprive him of sleep. As it was, no one would have been especially surprised, had they opened his chamber door, to see him sitting at the table with his already famous—or infamous—"revolvers" disassembled for cleaning. Ehdwyrd Howsmyn's Delthak Works had established a new wing to its pistol shop which was already turning out duplicates of the *seijin's* revolvers in quantity (although in a somewhat shorter-barreled, lighter version than he himself favored) and, as expected, the Inquisition was inveighing mightily against the new weapons. After all, had they not been instrumental in the abduction of the innocent Prince Daivyn and his sister by the heretic Cayleb's demon familiar? *Clearly* they must be the work of Shan-wei herself!

At the moment, however, even as Merlin's fingers smoothly and efficiently took the second revolver apart, his sapphire eyes were focused on something else entirely, and behind his neutral expression, he watched with a mixture of profound satisfaction and sorrow as Zhorj Styvynsyn's company closed in on the stunned remnants of Hahlys Cahrtair's pikemen. The imagery projected across his vision was hideously clear, and his lips tightened as keen-edged pikeheads drove into human flesh. It didn't look like many of Cahrtair's men were trying to surrender . . . and even less like any of Styvynsyn's men were inclined to let them.

"*As ye sow, so shall ye reap,*" he thought grimly. *Even the* Writ *says that, and if anyone ever deserved what they're getting, it's Cahrtair's butchers. None of which makes it any less ugly when it happens. And it's going to get worse—* much *worse.*

He picked up the stiff-bristled brush and began running it through one revolver's barrel.

We've been damned *lucky at home in Charis, and even in Corisande. We've avoided almost all this mutual butchery, partly because Reformist sentiment was so much stronger than I think even Maikel and the Brethren realized, and partly because Cayleb, Sharleyan, and Nahrmahn were all so popular with their own people. And it didn't hurt one bit that everyone from Hauwyl Chermin to Koryn Gahrvai jumped on it with both feet . . . and that no one has the intestinal fortitude to massacre anyone where Maikel Staynair can catch them at it! But an even bigger factor was Maikel, Cayleb, and Sharleyan's insistence on tolerance, not only in the Empire's integrated territory, but in Corisande, as well. It's hard to convince someone whose churches are actually protected by imperial troops that they're a threatened minority who needs to strike out in self-defense, especially without mass communication to pour propaganda into our homegrown Temple Loyalists' ears. I'm not real crazy about the Proscriptions in general, but right at the moment, thank God for the ban on electricity! The mere thought of what someone like Clyntahn would be doing with HD or even old-fashioned radio broadcasts would be enough to turn my stomach, if I still had one! And Rayno would probably make just a wonderful Goebbels.*

That sense of safety despite differences in belief, was not, unfortunately, the case in Siddarmark. In fact, both sides in the Republic had ample proof they *were* threatened, and they were still in the process of reckoning up how much blood had been shed over just the past three months. Given the assistance of the SNARCs, Merlin was grimly aware that all the current estimates were actually low. By his own estimation, somewhere over two and three-quarters million people had died . . . so far. Just under a quarter million had been Charisians—or foreigners, at any rate; the mob hadn't differentiated very clearly—who'd lived in Siddarmark's Charisian Quarters. The rest had been native Siddarmarkians, more than half of them children, and while more had perished of starvation, hypothermia, or disease than from any other cause, all too many of them had been deliberately massacred. That sort of violence was exactly what generated the ferocity which had made religious warfare so especially ugly, and it was only going to get worse as the fighting intensified.

And what's that going to do to our own troops? Merlin wondered, watching through the SNARC as the handful—the very *tiny* handful—of prisoners who'd survived were cuffed and kicked into a huddled group. *When our men see the same things Styvynsyn and his men've seen, how are they going to react? It's one thing to know what's been happening; it's another thing entirely to actually see it, smell it. And this is exactly what fills the very best of men with the very deepest of hatreds.*

So far, at least, the Marines and armed seamen who'd made it to Glacierheart, reinforcing Zhasyn Cahnyr's exhausted fighters barely in time, seemed to have avoided that particular toxin. On the other hand, Brigadier Taisyn's people were fighting from fixed defensive positions, and they'd arrived only after Byrk Raimahn and the Glacierheart militia had stabilized the lines. They'd missed the worst of the massacres and see-saw atrocities, and they'd escorted in enough food to ameliorate the worst of the starvation. They hadn't seen the monster yet, not in all its loathsome, carrion-breathing horror, whatever they might think.

And we're going to be sending more thousands of Charisians into the same maelstrom as soon as Eastshare's troops land. For that matter, Earl Hanth'll be taking his men up the coast from Eralth even sooner than that. That's going to put them right on the flank of that mess in South March.

He sighed and switched his vision to magnification as he withdrew the brush and inspected the pistol barrel to be sure the bore was clean. It was, and he ran an oiled patch through it before he began reassembling it with a loaded cylinder.

It's only a matter of time until what's going on over there spills onto Hanth, especially with Rahnyld's little surprise, and then—

"Merlin?"

The voice in his "ear" was clear, and his eyes narrowed as he heard it.

"Yes, Nahrmahn?" he subvocalized over his internal com.

"Sorry to disturb you, but it didn't look like you were excessively busy at the moment."

"Just thinking while I worked. And, to be honest, a distraction from the things I was thinking *about* wouldn't exactly be unwelcome at the moment."

"The Sylmahn Gap?" Nahrmahn's voice had darkened, and he sighed as Merlin nodded ever so slightly. "I've been watching through the SNARCs myself. It's going to be really bad, isn't it?"

"It's already bad enough for me." Merlin grimaced, then laid the reassembled and reloaded pistol aside, picked up its mate, and began running the brush through its barrel. "But you're right. There's still lots of room for it to get worse . . . and it will."

As he spoke, the imagery from the Sylmahn Gap faded, replaced by another image, this one of Nahrmahn sitting on the palace balcony looking out over a night cityscape of Eraystor under a black velvet sky sprinkled with stars. The portly little prince leaned back in one of the rattan chairs with a glass of wine, and someone was seated on the other side of the stone-topped table.

"I don't doubt you're right about how bad it's going to get," Nahrmahn said soberly. "I've seen enough of human hearts to know there's at least some of the beast in the best of us, and even if I hadn't, there's more than enough about this kind of thing in Owl's archives." He shook his head. "I've been spending a lot of time in that 'hyper heuristic mode' of yours. I haven't liked quite a bit of what I've been finding out while I was at it, but one thing about being dead is that it's finally given me a chance to catch up on my reading." He snorted suddenly, wryly, despite his obviously somber mood. "Of course, I've also discovered—being dead, you understand—that I've suddenly got a lot more reading to catch up *on*." He shook his head again, this time in wonder. "I thought I had some notion of what you meant when you talked about Owl's data storage, but I never imagined there could be *that* much knowledge in one place. It's downright scary!"

"Even that's only a fragment of everything we once had, you know. A big fragment, maybe, but only a fragment."

"I'm sure it is, but it's still going to be an enormous heritage on the day you can finally share it with everyone on this planet."

"I've been looking forward to that moment for quite a while now."

"I know, and . . . I've decided I want to be here to see it with you." Nahrmahn sipped wine, then lowered the glass and smiled crookedly. "I'm not sure about telling Ohlyvya yet. That's . . . a harder decision than I thought it would be. But I think I've come to understand Nimue Alban a bit better now, and I can't leave this particular task unfinished any more than she could. So if you want me around, and if you don't mind dead men's voices nattering away in the back of your brain, I'm here for the duration."

"I can't tell you how glad I am to hear that," Merlin said quietly, his hands pausing. "And not just because of how useful you'll be."

"I suppose there are worse things we could dedicate our afterlives to," Nahrmahn observed in a lighter tone. Merlin smiled, and the prince smiled back, lifting his glass in Merlin's direction. Then his expression sobered and he set the glass on the table and leaned forward.

"Before we go any farther, I'd like to introduce someone." He waved at the person sitting across the table from him. "Merlin, meet Owl."

Merlin's eyebrows rose. The person in the other chair was of no more than medium height, which made him considerably taller than Nahrmahn but shorter than Merlin, with dark hair, blue eyes, and a curiously androgynous face. There was, he realized after a moment, a strong "family resemblance" between that face and his own.

"Owl?" he said after a very long second or two.

"Yes, Lieutenant Commander Alban," the blue-eyed stranger replied in a very familiar tenor. Yet even as Merlin recognized it, he realized it had changed subtly. He couldn't put his mental finger on precisely what the change was, yet it was clear.

"This . . . is a surprise," he said.

"Prince Nahrmahn required a more comprehensive interface." Owl's avatar actually *shrugged*, Merlin observed. "It became apparent to both of us that a physical avatar within his VR environment would be the most effective way to provide it."

"What he means is that having someone besides empty air to talk to when we conversed made me feel a bit less like a lunatic," Nahrmahn amplified with something suspiciously like a chuckle. "And it's been good for him, too."

"Really?"

"Oh, absolutely!" Nahrmahn laughed out loud this time. "We've spent the equivalent of several months getting to know one another since your visit. I remember how difficult I found it to understand your complaints about the limitations of Owl's self-awareness. He always seemed so incredibly . . . human, for want of a better word, to me, given that he was actually a machine. I'm afraid that once I found myself dealing with him on a continual basis, I became unhappily aware of those limitations myself, though. He really *didn't* have much of an imagination, did he?"

"Well, that's hardly his fault," Merlin replied, slightly surprised by his own almost defensive tone. "He was designed as a fire control system, and the Navy didn't want its weapons systems to have *too* much imagination."

"I wasn't trying to insult him," Nahrmahn said mildly, although the gleam in his eye suggested he'd gotten exactly the response he'd wanted. "It was merely an observation—and an accurate one, I think you'd have to agree. For that matter, I think Owl would agree, wouldn't you?"

He looked back across the table, and the avatar nodded.

"I would be forced to acknowledge the validity of your point, Your Highness. 'Imagination,' as 'intuition,' is not, in fact, a truly valid or complete descriptor of the qualities you and Lieutenant Commander Alban are subsuming under them, yet the terms as used are clearly applicable."

Merlin suppressed a reflex to blink, and Nahrmahn chuckled again.

"Owl and I have been interacting on an almost continuous basis for quite a long time now, subjectively speaking. You said the manual indicated he'd become increasingly capable through use, and you were right. You'd already started the ball rolling by how continuously you'd had him online monitoring functions and analyzing data, but you'd never really had the time to sit down and, well . . . talk to him, I suppose."

"That's true," Merlin acknowledged slowly, feeling a stir of something rather like guilt. "I had so much to do, especially before I found out about the Brethren and we started bringing more people into the inner circle." He looked at the avatar's smooth, calmly attentive expression. "I'm sorry about that, Owl."

"There is no reason you should feel sorrow or guilt, Lieutenant Commander Alban. I was not, in fact, sufficiently self-aware to be concerned by the frequency or infrequency with which you communicated with me. It is, however, true that the combination of my heuristic programming and Prince Nahrmahn's more sustained level of communication has significantly advanced the development of an actual gestalt. As such, I am pleased to meet you, Lieutenant Commander Alban."

"And I'm pleased to meet you, Owl." Merlin nodded in response, then glanced back to Nahrmahn. "On the other hand, if he starts talking like this to anyone except Sharleyan, they're going to want to know why he's changed."

"One of the reasons I decided I should introduce the two of you," Nahrmahn agreed. "Owl's breakthrough occurred—oh, two or three five-days ago as far as we're concerned, but only about fifteen minutes ago the way you slowpokes count time. And, unfortunately, he can't lie to anyone unless his commanding officer instructs him to. So if anyone asks him what's changed, he'll cheerfully tell them all about me. Which I would very much prefer not happen until I'm able to make my mind up about whether or not to tell Ohlyvya I'm still more or less here."

"I can tell him to *lie?*" This time Merlin did blink in surprise.

"As nearly as I can determine, only military and very high security civilian AIs ever had that capability," Nahrmahn said. "Believe me, I've dedicated quite a bit of subjective time to researching the question since his 'gestalt' woke up, although information on this particular topic is scarce—not surprisingly, I suppose. As I understand it, it was part of the security function. It wouldn't have done for just anyone to be able to place a com call to, oh, one of the system defense command center AIs and ask it all sorts of embarrassing questions!"

"Access was just a bit more tightly controlled than that," Merlin replied rather repressively.

"But the example was so appropriate I couldn't resist," Nahrmahn replied with a smile. "At any rate, you're listed in Owl's core programming as his commanding officer. As such, you can instruct him to maintain a cover story. I can't."

"I see."

Merlin finished cleaning the second revolver and sat back, reassembling it rather more slowly while his attention focused on the avatar seated across from Nahrmahn.

"I think Nahrmahn's request is reasonable, Owl," he said after a moment. "Are you comfortable with the thought?"

"Prevarication is alien to my essential programming protocols and core value hierarchy, Lieutenant Commander Alban. I am, however, provided with the flexibility to exercise deceptive measures when circumstances require. I do not at this time possess sufficient comparative data to determine whether or not that equates to the human concept of 'comfort,' but practicing such measures will not compromise my functionality in any way."

"In that case, I formally instruct you to not reveal Prince Nahrmahn's existence without my—or his—express authorization. When the others remark on the expansion of your self-awareness, you will inform them that it's the result of your having crossed the interaction threshold necessary to produce it."

"Understood." The avatar seemed to smile slightly. "That explanation will, after all, be essentially accurate, Lieutenant Commander Alban."

"I'm glad you feel that way."

The AI didn't reply, but Nahrmahn cleared his throat, recapturing Merlin's attention.

"I didn't contact you just to introduce you to Owl," the Emeraldian said in a considerably darker tone.

"No?" Merlin finished reloading the second pistol and stood. He crossed the room, turning his back to the door and leaning on the windowsill, looking out over Siddar City and the blue waters of North Bedard Bay as the sun settled steadily into the west somewhere behind his vantage point. "What else did you have on your mind?"

"I've discovered that the ability to operate in hyper-heuristic mode lets me spend a lot more time, subjectively speaking, analyzing and correlating the take from the SNARCs. The truth, unfortunately, is that we've reached the point of using a very significant factor of Owl's total monitoring capacity, and even in hyper-heuristic, I can't take much of the *monitoring* function off his shoulders. I just don't have the multitasking ability to handle that kind of bandwidth. But I do have the ability now—or, rather, the *time* now—to look at things far more closely and to . . . redirect Owl's attention towards bits and pieces of information whose relationships to one another aren't as apparent to him as they are to me."

"I have to admit, that was one of the things I'd hoped might happen," Merlin admitted. "I hadn't even remotely considered the possibility of your 'waking up' Owl, but having our best analyst in a position to look at information in depth as it came in seemed to me to be something very much worth having."

"I can't promise that will be true in all ways, but I'm afraid I have figured out who the mole in the Hairatha powder mill was."

"You have?" Merlin's tone sharpened, and Nahrmahn nodded, his expression unhappy.

"I'm almost certain it was Captain Sahlavahn."

"Mahndrayn's *cousin?*"

"Yes," Nahrmahn confirmed sadly. "The evidence is all fragmentary, but once it's assembled in one place, it's pretty damning. As far as I can tell, looking at every scrap of recorded imagery of him—and there's quite a bit of it, given his position at Hairatha—he never said a single word to anyone about strong Temple Loyalist feelings, but he was always a devout man. I'm pretty sure that was what motivated him originally, and the chronology suggests it was something Commander Mahndrayn said or did on that last visit that pushed him into blowing up the powder mill . . . and himself."

"That's a serious charge, Nahrmahn. Do you have anything except the coincidence of Urvyn's visit to support it?"

"I think so." Nahrmahn's image didn't look much happier than he himself felt, Merlin reflected. "He spent a great deal of time writing, Merlin. Most of it was in a journal he was keeping, and from the little scraps of it the remotes captured, even in his journal he was remarkably circumspect. But there are still a few suggestions of his actual inclinations, and he spent a lot longer writing letters to his sister, Madam Thyrstyn, right there in the embassy in Siddar City, than he should have. I mean he spent way too much time on individual letters, given their final length . . . but it wasn't consistent. Some of them didn't take very long at all, but others took much longer. In fact, one of them took almost an entire five-day. One of the reasons we didn't notice it at the time was that they'd always exchanged acrostics and word puzzles, and obviously it takes time to create something like that. It made sense for him to use reference books while he was doing it, too." Nahrmahn shook his head. "He couldn't possibly have suspected he might be under observation, but even if he'd thought anything of the sort, he'd come up with almost the perfect way to avoid arousing our suspicions."

"Are you certain that wasn't exactly what he was doing? I mean, simply creating puzzles for his sister?"

"I wouldn't have been inclined to think anything else . . . if we hadn't caught her on a scrap of imagery passing two of those 'acrostics' on to her husband's relatives in the Temple Lands." Nahrmahn shrugged. "We obviously weren't looking at the right moment to see any drawings he might've slipped them, but I don't think Captain Sahlavahn was relaying 'simple puzzles' to the Temple Lands through his sister in the Charisian Embassy, Merlin. And because they were traveling to her with the diplomatic courier, we didn't worry about what might be in his letters. After all, we knew who they'd come from and where they were going, and only people in whom we had complete confidence had access to it . . . which just happened to make it the perfect conduit."

"So that makes her a traitor, too," Merlin said slowly, remembering the sad-eyed woman he'd seen here in the embassy.

"That depends on how you define treason," Nahrmahn pointed out quietly.

"That's been true for a lot of people lately," Merlin agreed heavily.

"I'm just as happy to leave any decisions about her up to you," Nahrmahn admitted. "But if I'm right about who the traitor in Hairatha was, and if that's where Clyntahn's information about the new artillery came from, he probably still doesn't know anything about the new Mahndrayns or about the percussion fuses, because Sahlavahn never had access to that information. On the other hand, it would explain how he and Rayno found out so much about the smoothbore shells and the time fuses. And it *might* mean they've got information on the rifled shells, as well. We haven't seen any sign of their putting those into production, but that could be because the information simply hasn't reached them yet. For that matter, we don't know his sister was his only conduit. In fact, I'm almost inclined to think he did have at least one secondary—I suspect he'd be worried about sending actual *drawings* to her, since no one who happened to see them could fail to recognize what he was looking at, including her. I wouldn't be surprised if he'd used her as a dead drop, actually—just a relay with no idea what was actually in the messages she was passing on. From everything I've been able to discover about him, he wouldn't have endangered her any more than he could help."

"No. No, he wouldn't have." Merlin inhaled deeply. He'd gotten to know Trai Sahlavahn fairly well during his work on the original artillery board. Not as well as he'd known Mahndrayn, but well enough. "And if you're right, it also means that particular leak is plugged."

"I think I am right, but I also think we'd better not operate on any blithe assumptions about my infallibility." Nahrmahn quirked a brief grin. "I'm beginning to understand your frustration at being unable to operate remotes inside Zion a lot better, by the way. I'd really love to be able to listen in on all of this at the source. Or, even better, to deposit a nice anti-personnel charge under Rayno's office chair. Something . . . slower and more lingering would be in order for Clyntahn, himself."

"I've considered the possibility myself, more than once." Merlin's smile was considerably grimmer than Nahrmahn's had been. "For that matter, I've considered simply nuking Zion and having done with it." His smile vanished completely, and his eyes turned bleak. "There are more than enough bastards in that city who need killing, and a 'Rakurai' strike on the Group of Four would be sort of hard for anyone to ignore. But I can't, Nahrmahn. I just can't. Even if I could bring myself to push the button, it would only destroy any chance I might have to convince people to listen to me afterwards. It's the largest city on the face of Safehold. How in hell could I justify destroying it just to get at the Temple? And the way that damned thing's built, it would *take* that kind of a strike to be sure I got whatever's sleeping underneath it."

"I agree that would be just a bit extreme," Nahrmahn said in a careful tone. "If there were some way to target a few, select individuals, though . . . ."

He let his voice trail off, and Merlin snorted in harsh agreement. But the *seijin*'s sapphire eyes remained cold, bleak.

"I know what you mean. At the same time, I think it's probably been a good thing I don't have the ability to simply strike down anyone I think should be dead. Trust me," he shivered, "killing so many people one by one is bad enough. If I had the ability to simply visit death on anyone I decided was an enemy or an obstacle, I'd start to do it. And I'm not at all sure that, in the end, that wouldn't turn me into another Schueler."

"I don't think you have to worry about that, Merlin," Nahrmahn told him quietly. "On the other hand, I have to admit it got easier for me to justify ordering assassinations as I got . . . more practice at it." He twitched a shrug. "I still think it was actually a less bloody way of dealing with problems, but it does have a tendency to make you stop thinking about your targets as anything *except* targets. And just between you, me, and Owl, I think we need you, especially, to go right on *not* doing that. It's a funny thing, I suppose, especially since both of us are technically dead, but it's your *humanity* that's brought us this far, Merlin. I know it's caused you to do some things no proper, calculating strategist ought to do. I've watched Owl's imagery of that incident with the krakens and the kids in King's Harbor, for example, and of that insane risk you ran at Saint Agtha's." He shook his head again. "Cayleb was right when he said you just plain aren't very good at hiding who you really are, and who you are—*what* you are—is all that's saved any of us. Hang onto it."

"I'll . . . try."

"Good." Nahrmahn smiled, reached for his wine glass, and raised it in a lazy toast. "And now," he continued more briskly as a chessboard materialized on the table between him and Owl's avatar, "since I've accomplished my mission and upset your own schedule for the day, Owl and I have a game to complete." The pieces for a game in progress set themselves as he spoke, and his smile grew broader. "I'm sure even a computer will get sufficiently tired of beating me to let me win a game . . . eventually."

D o you have time to discuss something with me, Your Eminence?"
Maikel Staynair looked up from his conversation with Father Bryahn Ushyr. Irys Daykyn stood in his cabin door, hazel eyes shadowed. There was no sign of Earl Coris or of any of her armsmen, which was un-usual. At least one of them was always unobtrusively in her vicinity, al-though the archbishop suspected that she wasn't fully aware of that minor fact. She knew they kept an attentive eye on her younger brother, yet she seemed not to have noticed they kept an equally close watch over her . . . except, for some odd reason, when Lieutenant Aplyn-Ahrmahk assumed that duty for them.

His lips twitched at the thought, but the incipient humor fled as the shadows in those eyes registered. He hadn't spent fifty years in God's service without learning to recognize a troubled soul when he saw one.

"Of course, my dear." He looked at Ushyr. "We'll finish that corre-spondence later, Bryahn. God knows we'll have plenty of time before we reach Cherayth!"

He rolled his eyes past the young under-priest at Irys, inviting her to share his amusement, but she only smiled briefly and obediently.

"Certainly, Your Eminence," Ushyr murmured, gathering up his notes. "Your Highness." He bowed to Irys and withdrew quietly.

"A very good secretary, young Bryahn." Staynair waved for Irys to take the bench seat under the quarter gallery window which was one of the prized features of his own small cabin. "Actually, he's a very good young *man.* I really ought to send him off to a parish somewhere for a few years, let him get the pastoral experience for the bishop's ring I see in his future. Unfortunately, I'm too selfish to let go of him now that I have him so nicely broken in. God forbid I should have to start all over training a re-placement!"

Irys smiled again, a bit more naturally, as she settled on the indicated seat. The windows were open, admitting a steady flow of crisp, clean air, and she turned her head slightly, taking the breeze on her cheek and gazing out at the water's bright sun sparkle. She sat that way for several seconds, and Staynair turned his chair to face her, then folded his hands in the sleeves of his cassock and simply waited.

Finally, she turned back to him.

"I seem to be taking longer than I expected to come to the point, Your Eminence."

Her tone was apologetic, and Staynair shook his head.

"Conversations are like seeds, Your Highness. They flower in their own good time."

"Is that a perspective of your faith, Your Eminence? Or of your . . . ah, maturity?"

"You mean of my ancient decrepitude?" he asked affably, and smiled as he was rewarded by a slight twinkle in those somber eyes. "I'm sure that to someone of your modest, not to say tender, years it seems the world takes forever to get anywhere. Since I'm somewhat better than three times your age—we won't talk about how *much* better, thank you very much—I probably have acquired a bit more patience. And"—his voice softened—"I've also discovered that quite often things that seem extraordinarily weighty turn out to be much less so when they're shared with another."

"I hope so," she said, looking back out the window and speaking so quietly the words were hard to hear. "Aside from Phylyp, I haven't had anyone to share my 'weighty things' with in . . . forever."

"Forgive me, my dear," he said gently, "but would you prefer to discuss this with Father Bahn?"

"No."

The word came out softly, but she shook her head almost violently, then turned back to face him.

"No," she repeated much more firmly. "I don't want to put him in the position of having to deal with what I need to discuss with you, Your Eminence."

"That sounds faintly ominous," he observed, watching her face closely, and she laughed with very little humor.

"Only if you're particularly concerned about your immortal soul, Your Eminence."

"Ah." He tipped back in his chair. "I must tell you, Your Highness, that I've seen very little sign that *your* immortal soul might be in any particular danger."

"Really? When I'm the daughter of Hektor of Corisande?"

"You're the daughter of a father who, whatever his other faults, loved you very much," Staynair replied in a tranquil tone. "And I believe, all things considered, that you're also quite an extraordinary young lady in your own right. If nothing else, I've seen you with your brother."

She looked at him through a few heartbeats of silence, then dipped her head in acknowledgment of his final sentence.

"I rather doubt your parentage or your brother is what brings you here this afternoon, however," he continued.

"No." She looked at him again, her fingers folding together with atypical tightness. "No, you're right. I've . . . I've experienced what I suppose I'd have to call a crisis of faith, Your Eminence. I need your advice."

"Your Highness—Irys." He let his chair come forward and leaned towards her. "Remember who I am, the office I hold."

"Are you a priest, Your Eminence?"

Those hazel eyes challenged him, and in that moment, they seemed older than his own. He looked back at her for a long, wordless moment, then inhaled deeply.

"Before I am anything else in this world," he told her softly.

"Then speak to me as a priest, Your Eminence. Not an archbishop, not a politician, not a statesman. As a *priest* . . . and as the man who's extended his protection to me and to my brother. I know where my own heart leads me, but I don't know if I have the right to follow it. I haven't discussed it even with Phylyp—not yet. I need to *deal* with this first. To understand— *truly* understand—what it is I'm being drawn to. And I need a true man of God to explain to me what really lies under the surface of all this killing and blood and hatred. Help me *understand* it, Your Eminence, because until I do, how can I truly choose?"

"Oh, Irys." He shook his head, eyes gentle. "That sounds so simple, yet the truth is, none of us truly understands until we complete our journey. We do our best, we listen for that small voice of God deep within us, and we do our best to hear it—to hear *Him*—and to obey. But there are so many other voices, so many other charges on who and what we are, that it's hard— sometimes terribly hard. Especially for someone like you, trapped by who you were born to be. I understand how you must yearn for an explanation, a map which won't fail you, yet all I can offer you is faith and prayer. I can explain my own feelings, my own understanding, limited though any mortal mind must be where the grandeur of God is concerned. I can share my own explorations, and the discoveries I've made with you. But in the end, neither I nor anyone else can make that journey *for* you. I can and will love and cherish you as a daughter of God . . . but I can't tell you what to think or decide, my dear. That final step must be yours and yours alone, and I cannot—*will* not—tell you what it must be."

Her eyes widened, and he shook his head again.

"That's the fallacy into which Mother Church has fallen. It's not just the Group of Four, Irys. They could never have done the damage they've done if Mother Church hadn't allowed them to, and she allowed them to because she insists so adamantly on *telling* God's children what to think—*ordering* them to think it and punishing them if they dare so much as question a single point of doctrine, however sincere their faith—rather than allowing them to listen to God themselves. The *Writ* gives her that authority, at least as she reads it, yet it's a terrible power, as well. One which has come to threaten not simply the mortal lives of God's children, but their souls, as well. That truth is evident even to many who love her most—men like Samyl and Hauwerd Wylsynn—and she murders them for their love, because she will *not* relent or relinquish that power, that control, even if it leads us to a Zhaspahr Clyntahn or something still worse."

Irys' tanned face had gone pale, and he laid one hand very gently on her knee.

"Don't mistake me, my daughter. What I'm saying to you is the true, fundamental difference between the Church of the Temple and the Church of Charis. It's been the truth from the very beginning, and those who've listened to us know it, even if for many that process of understanding is still just beginning. We are a hierarchical church, and we instruct those committed to our care, but what we teach them is to remember they have a deep, *personal* relationship with God. That it's *His* voice they must listen for, find in their own hearts. And if we succeed, if we survive this whirlwind of fire and blood, we won't overthrow simply the Group of Four. We will also overthrow the coercive power of the Inquisition, and that will change the lives of every living human being in ways those men sitting in Zion could never conceive, understand . . . or accept."

One of her hands had risen to her throat, and he smiled gently, compassionately . . . sadly.

"That's what *you* must understand," he told her with implacable gentleness, "and I must explain it to you clearly, as unambiguously as I possibly can, despite the pain I fear that explanation may bring you, because it's an explanation you *must* grasp. One you must understand before you make any choice, any decision, because of who and what you are, because of who and what your brother is. There is nothing on the face of this world I would more treasure than your decision to commit yourself to the cause to which I've committed *myself*, but I won't—I *can't*, Irys—counsel you without being as completely honest as I can. There are things I can't explain to you, that no one can explain to you, right now. That's true for everyone on Safehold. But before you commit your heart and your soul—that strong, *valiant* heart and soul—you must understand that in this much, at least, Zhaspahr Clyntahn has spoken the truth. He doesn't understand why, and he doesn't understand how, and there is nothing but foulness in that man's soul, yet in the midst of all the hatred and poison he spews out, there is this one slender fragment of truth. If the Church of Charis lives, we will change the Church of God Awaiting more profoundly than she has changed since the Creation itself. If you cannot give yourself—your strength, your courage, your hope, your passion, all you are or ever hope to be—to that goal, then as a priest of God, I cannot advise you to embrace the Church of Charis, for it will lead you only to heartbreak and sorrow."

Silence fell, enfolding them, perfected and made somehow absolute by the faint sound of voices from the deck above, of water rushing about wooden planking and the breeze blowing through the open window to play with the end of Irys' braid. She stared at him, looking into his eyes as if she could somehow see the truth in their depths. And then she drew a deep breath.

"And if I *can* give myself to that goal, Your Eminence?" she said very softly.

"Then you may still find heartbreak and sorrow," he told her unflinchingly, "but it won't be because you have acquiesced in evil in God's name, and it will never be the heartbreak of fear and uncertainty. We may yet fail, Irys. I don't believe God would have allowed us to come this far, achieve this much, if that was what we were destined to do, but I could be wrong. And if we do fail, Zhaspahr Clyntahn's vengeance on all we love or care for will be terrible beyond belief. Yet at least we will have this—that we chose knowingly. That we *decided* what we stood for and that as Cayleb himself said, we could do no other."

He looked back into her eyes, his gaze gentle and caring and as unyielding as steel.

"So I suppose the question, Irys, is what *you* believe God wants you to stand for."

▼　　▼　　▼

"Have you seen Irys, Mairah?"

"Irys?" Mairah Breygart looked up from the book she'd been reading to her seven-year-old stepdaughter as the Empress of Charis stepped into her cabin. "I thought she was with you."

"No." Sharleyan shook her head. "I thought she was still here, thinking."

"She left over an hour ago," Mairah said. Fhrancys tugged on her sleeve, pouting at the interruption, and Mairah wrapped her arms around the child and kissed the top of her head, but she never looked away from the empress. "It was closer to *two* hours, really. I thought she was going to talk to you about whatever it was she had on her mind."

"I haven't seen her." Sharleyan looked perplexed. "And it's not as if this were an especially *big* ship, but no one seems to've seen her, and I'm beginning to get a little—"

"Excuse me, Your Majesty," a voice said behind her. "Were you looking for me?"

Sharleyan turned quickly, her face showing her relief as she saw Irys standing in the cabin door behind her.

"Yes, I'm afraid I was. I didn't realize someone besides Merlin could just . . . disappear aboard a ship in the middle of the ocean!"

She smiled, and Irys smiled back, but there was something odd about the younger woman's expression.

"I didn't mean to cause you any alarm, Your Majesty. I just found myself in need of a conversation with His Eminence. And after that, I had a few things I needed to discuss with Phylyp—I mean, Earl Coris. I . . . didn't want to be disturbed while I was talking to either of them, and I'm afraid I asked Tobys to be creatively vague about my whereabouts."

"I see." Sharleyan's smile had faded into a thoughtful expression, and she cocked her head. "Or, more honestly, I *don't* see . . . yet."

"I'm not trying to be mysterious, Your Majesty. It's just that my life's been even more complicated than I'd realized myself. I needed . . . I needed a little clarity."

"And have you found it?" Sharleyan asked carefully.

"Clarity?" Irys' tone was wry. "Yes, I believe I've found that. Courage, though . . . *that* came a bit harder. I think it did come in the end, though. That's what I had to discuss with Phylyp." She snorted gently. "I suppose I shouldn't have been as surprised as I was to realize he'd already figured out what I was thinking."

"Which was . . . ?"

"Which was that I've been contaminated by the pernicious, heretical, blasphemous apostasy of the Church of Charis," Irys said softly. "And if that costs me my soul in the end, then at least I'll be in better company than Zhaspahr Clyntahn's at the Judgment."

.VIII.
Siddar City,
Republic of Siddarmark

I'm getting a bit tired of surprises," Greyghor Stohnar said grimly, looking down at the updated map on the enormous table.

"*Pleasant* surprises I could handle," Cayleb Ahrmahk told him from the other side of the table, studying the same map. "Unfortunately, those seem to be a little thin on the ground just now."

"There've been a few of them, Your Majesty." The lord protector looked up. "Like those food convoys of yours. But the bad do seem to have outnumbered the good, don't they?"

Cayleb nodded, his expression equally unhappy. And the truth was that although he wasn't actually surprised by the latest news, that very lack of surprise only made his mood worse. He'd decided he liked Greyghor Stohnar quite a lot, and that made his inability to share information even more irksome than usual. He reminded himself—again—that the Republic was so enormous there was time for most information to reach Siddar City by . . . more conventional means before it became critical.

Sure. Just like there was plenty *of time for Stohnar to react to the "Sword of Schueler," right?*

"We'd've found out sooner if we hadn't lost those semaphore stations in Cliff Peak," Daryus Parkair growled, and this time Stohnar and Cayleb both nodded.

The raid out of western Shiloh, across the Branath Canal through the gap between the Clynmair Hills and the Branath Mountains, had crossed the southern tip of Glacierheart, stabbed deep into Cliff Peak, and burned three semaphore stations—one a junction station for multiple chains. It had also massacred the entire crew of all those stations, and it might have done even more damage if it hadn't taken the time to make sure the massacres were done right. The Republic's military was primarily infantry, but it did have some cavalry, and a detachment of it had overtaken the raiders.

There hadn't been any prisoners.

"Well, we know now," Samyl Gahdarhd said gloomily. "Who would've thought Rahnyld of Dohlar, of all people, could actually move *faster* than someone expected?"

"I have to agree it's not what we would've expected out of him a few years ago," Cayleb replied.

He looked back up from the map and glanced over his shoulder at Merlin. Stohnar and his ministers had very little problem accepting Merlin's position as Cayleb's aide and one of his most trusted military advisors as well as "simply" his bodyguard.

"I'm not certain this can all be laid at Rahnyld's door, Your Majesty," Merlin said now. "All the same, I have to admit Rahnyld—or the Dohlarans, at least—have actually been Clyntahn's most effective minions so far. Certainly they have on a man-for-man basis, at any rate."

"What bothers me even more than the fact that he's moving at least three five-days sooner than we expected is that he seems to be moving faster, too," Parkair admitted, tapping a map token already over a hundred miles inside the South March border.

"The canal and road net out of Thorast and Reskar are good enough to explain a lot of that," Stohnar said. "And it looks like they must've hired a semi-competent quartermaster this time, too." His lips twitched humorlessly. "Who would've thought he could have found one of *those* in Dohlar?"

"I suspect that may be because we're looking at a supply organization managed by Mother Church, not Rahnyld, My Lord," Merlin murmured, and Stohnar looked at him sharply. Then, after a moment, he nodded.

"A very good point, *Seijin* Merlin. And one we should all bear in mind."

Other heads nodded around the map table, and a profound silence fell as all of them considered what had already been said.

Merlin was glad to see it. The Republic's leaders' disdain for the Royal Dohlaran Army was probably inevitable . . . but it was also dangerous as hell. These weren't stupid men. In fact, they were smart, competent, gutsy, and willing to actually exercise their brains, or they wouldn't have survived this far. But their estimates of Dohlaran capabilities were predicated on realities which had existed two or three years ago. Try though they might—and they were trying, conscientiously and hard—it was difficult to cast aside decades of hard-won experience when it came to evaluating their opponents.

The forces Rahnyld of Dohlar—or the Church of God Awaiting, at any rate—had sent marching out of the Duchy of Thorast into the South March consisted of forty-two thousand men, two-thirds of them cavalry, under General Sir Fahstyr Rychtyr (an unfortunately capable-seeming sort), but it was only his vanguard. Another fifty-five thousand men—three-quarters of them *infantry*, this time—would cross the border within the next five-day or so under Sir Rainos Ahlverez' personal command, and *they* were a very different breed of cat lizard from anything any Siddarmarkian general had ever before seen. Eighty percent of those infantry would have rifles or smoothbore muskets and bayonets, and the new-model artillery which would roll along behind them was equipped with at least a partial loadout of exploding shells, as well as round shot, grapeshot, and canister. The Church's—and Dohlar's—main field gun was a twelve-pounder copied directly from Charis (essentially an Old Earth twelve-pounder Napoleon), but Dohlar had added lighter horse guns and—at Earl Thirsk's insistence—it was actually developing its own howitzers, though none had yet been deployed, thank God. Any conventional pike block that went up against that army would be massacred, and he hoped Stohnar's field commanders had accepted that unpleasant truth as thoroughly as the lord protector and his personal staff seemed to have.

At the moment, most of that infantry was still only a threat on the horizon, but Rahnyld's vanguard was advancing at better than twenty miles a day—and could have doubled that rate if it hadn't been linking up with rebellious militia units as it came. The Dohlaran horsemen heading that column, unlike their infantry, would normally have been no match for organized Siddarmarkian pike blocks. That didn't much matter, though, since it *did* have six-pounder horse artillery. Worse, there *were* no organized bodies of pikes left in its path, aside from regiments still clinging to isolated forts here and there, and the Republic was already beginning to lose additional semaphore stations in the path of the advance. Many were being captured or destroyed well before the Dohlarans could have reached them, too, which suggested careful coordination between the invaders and the rebels under the Temple's control.

For that matter, the Royal Army itself was effectively under the Church's direct control, with "special intendants" attached to every major unit. They were careful to maintain the pretense that they were there simply as spiritual advisors, yet no one was under any illusions in that respect, and given the criteria by which Clyntahn and Rayno chose their agents, the atrocity quotient had probably just risen yet again.

"Given that the Church is managing Rahnyld's supplies," the lord protector said finally, "I think we're going to have to look carefully at the possibility Rahnyld and Mahrys may actually end up cooperating. After all," he showed his teeth briefly, "it won't really be *them* cooperating at all, will it? Just their inquisitor keepers."

"I think you're right about that, My Lord," Cayleb agreed. "Our own agents indicate Desnair's well behind Dohlar at this point, and I don't think they're going to be moving any sooner than we'd originally anticipated. But at Rahnyld's present rate of advance, he could be into Shiloh in no more than a month and a half, given that the rebels hold Fort Tairys and both ends of the Tairys Gap. Or, if he's willing to cut loose from the Sheryl-Seridahn Canal and head northeast, he could hit Saint Alyk's and punch through the gap between the Snakes and the Branath Mountains. And if Mahrys follows up through Silkiah, he can come in on Rahnyld's heels headed in either direction."

The emperor ran his finger across the Gulf of Mathyas and up the Silkiahan coast.

"We can flood the Gulf of Jahras with light cruisers, and we'll have a couple of squadrons off the grand duchy that can operate as far up as Sandfish or Thesmar Bay. That cuts Desnair's direct canal links to the South March, but we can't operate into Salthar Bay until we've dealt with the Dohlaran Navy and gained control of the Gulf of Dohlar, and I just don't think we've got the hulls to do that this summer. We've got to control eastern waters, protect Duke Eastshare's move to the Republic, interdict enemy ship movements, support army operations along the coasts and, probably, inland on the rivers as well, and deal with the fact that the idiots on the other side have finally started systematically attacking our commerce. Which means they'll also be doing their damnedest to attack any transports shipping food, munitions, and men into the Republic from the Empire."

"I understand," Stohnar said, "but as long as they're free to move supplies through Port Salthar and then up the Silk Town–Thesmar Canal, their supply line's going to be effectively secure at least to the South March border. It'll be slower than if they could ship directly across the Gulf of Mathyas, and staging overland through Hankey and Coastguard will entail a lot more wastage, but there won't be anything we can do to interfere with it."

"Trust me, I'm entirely too well aware of that, My Lord," Cayleb replied grimly. "But our agents report the Temple"—by common, unspoken consent, the Church of God Awaiting controlled by the Group of Four had become "the Temple," and not "Mother Church," here in Siddar City—"is getting its own exploding shells into production in greater quantity than we'd hoped. And Earl Thirsk isn't letting any grass grow under his feet." The emperor shook his head, his expression wry. "I don't know exactly how he pulled it off, but he's managed to get the entire shell output of one of Dohlar's larger foundries dedicated to his fleet, and he's seeing to it that they get allocated to their coastal fortifications as well. By the time we could redeploy enough of our galleons to go in after him, his defensive batteries will all be equipped with exploding shell, and I'm afraid galleons burn—and blow up—somewhat more readily than fortresses. Those river barge conversions we're working on ought to be able to reach Siddarmarkian waters, and they could probably operate effectively along your coasts in the Gulf of Mathyas. That ought to give us at least a little immunity from shell fire in those waters—until we've actually seen them in action we can't say how much for certain—but they could never reach Dohlaran waters. We're working on an answer to that problem, but it's going to take us at least through into the winter before we can have it ready to use."

"In that case, we're just going to have to do the best we can, and give thanks to Langhorne you can watch our own coast for us." Stohnar's nostrils flared, then he looked back up. "Don't mistake me, Your Majesty. I'd love for you to be able to get into their back garden, but the last thing I'm going to do is complain! Since Clyntahn and the other three wouldn't trust us with a navy of our own, we'd've been helpless against Desnair in the Gulf if you hadn't destroyed Mahrys' navy for him. They'd be sending in men and supplies literally by the shipload, and the fact that you're in a position to support us along the coast and they can't do a damned thing about it will be a huge advantage. Without it—"

He shook his head, his eyes cold.

"In the meantime, though," Cayleb said, "there's the question of what we want Earl Hanth to do. My thought is that I should join the Earl in Eralth as soon as possible. With Admiral Hywyt covering our flank, we could move up the Dragon Fish or even try a combined naval and land attack to retake Fort Darymahn. If we managed that, we could operate up the Taigyn towards the Shingle Mountains, and we could probably get there in time to block Rahnyld's advance further east. If we manage that, then—"

"No."

Stohnar's single word stopped Cayleb in midflight. The emperor looked at him, and the lord protector shook his head again.

"You are *not* going to lead less than eight thousand men, more than two-thirds of them sailors, off on an adventure in the South March against *at least* forty thousand Dohlarans, Your Majesty," he said flatly

"With all due respect, My Lord—" Cayleb began, then stopped himself as he saw the other expressions around that table. Including, he observed, Merlin Athrawes'.

"I don't like sending my people in harm's way without me," he said instead, very quietly, remembering the Gulf of Tarot and his sense of utter, wretched powerlessness as he watched the men he'd sent out to die, and Stohnar inhaled deeply.

"I realize that. And I sympathize—I've had the same experience, and never more than this past winter. But you're going to be far more valuable here in Siddar City when Duke Eastshare gets here, or even back in Telles-berg, making sure everything runs smoothly from that end, given how heavily we're all going to be depending on your manufactories, than you could ever be at the front. You're going to have to leave that part of it to someone else. Like your Earl Hanth."

Cayleb looked at him for several seconds, then nodded unhappily.

"Point taken, My Lord," he said heavily.

"Thank you, Your Majesty." Stohnar bowed slightly, then straightened and turned back to the map.

"And now," he said with very little humor, "let's see what—if anything—*besides* you we can scare up to put in Rahnyld's way."

.IX.
**Merlin Athrawes' Chamber,
Charisian Embassy,
Siddar City,
Republic of Siddarmark**

Merlin frowned as he sat in his darkened chamber and worried. If Cayleb realized he was "awake" in what was supposed to be one of his down periods, there'd be hell to pay, but at the moment, Merlin didn't really care. He was looking at the glowing schematic of a map only he could see, provided courtesy of Owl, and watching the projected movement of the scarlet troop icons moving out of Dohlar.

Stohnar and Parkair aren't the only ones who need to shake themselves loose from a few preconceptions where those bastards are concerned, he rebuked himself sourly. *You knew* better—*or you damned well* should *have*—*and you still underesti-mated how fast they could move once they got started. Which leads to the interesting question of how fast the* Army of God's *going to be able to move once* it *finally gets started. I think you're going to find out your "worst-case" estimate wasn't "worst" enough, Merlin.* He shook his head, expression grim. *That bastard Clyntahn may actually've known what the hell he was doing this time.*

He reminded himself that two-thirds of the advancing Dohlarans were mounted, but even so, twenty-plus miles per day would have been an astonishing sustained rate of advance for any pre-mechanized army out of Old Earth's history . . . especially one that was thirty percent infantry, taking the time to link up with the local Temple Loyalists as it came, *and* moving through an area which had been devastated during the autumn and winter fighting. There was precious little forage for man or beast in the South March, and that wasn't going to change before the end of the summer, which was probably why Rahnyld's advisors—or the Church—had been smart enough to split his initial invasion force into two separate waves. The real reason for the speed of his advance, though, was the combination of the canal and road network and the existence of draft dragons.

The mainland continents were home to the oldest, largest human populations on the planet, and those humans had been busy building things for the better part of a thousand years. They'd lacked the sort of construction aids—like dynamite, for example—an industrialized civilization took for granted, unfortunately, so they'd often had to detour around obstacles those more advanced civilizations would have bulled right through. But they'd had plenty of manpower and precise directions from the archangels about the value of transportation systems, which meant the roads connecting major mainland towns and cities were built to a standard laid down by the *Writ* itself, with a permanence to make an engineer of the Roman Empire green with envy, and that their maintenance was a *Writ*-mandated religious duty.

And along with those high roads—and much more important than them, in many ways—was the canal system. As Ehdwyrd Howsmyn had mentioned when he and Merlin first discussed the River-class ironclads, some of those canals were ancient. In fact, the very first of them—including the longest one of all, the Holy Langhorne Canal—had been dug by Pei Shan-wei's terraforming crews even before "the Day of Creation." The others had been built over the centuries since by dint of backbreaking toil and persistence, and they were the only reason the mainland realms had been able to transport the tonnages of materials they'd needed for Mother Church's military buildup after Charis closed the seas to her.

Even with Safeholdian high roads and draft dragons, the costs of land transport were extremely high, but a draft animal could pull roughly thirty times the same load in a canal boat as over a road. That was the reason canals had been so popular on Old Earth before the invention of railroads, although Old Earth's preindustrial canals had been far less ambitious than those the "archangels" had prescribed for Safehold, many of whose tow roads were designed to allow three- or even four-dragon draft teams. Given the Proscriptions of Jwo-jeng's stranglehold on anything like railroads, canals connecting navigable stretches of river had made an enormous amount of sense.

The northern Harchong Empire, in West Haven, was unfortunate in that its shallower, largely unnavigable rivers and less conveniently placed mountains had precluded the construction of canals on anything like the same scale as in *East* Haven. Merlin suspected that had had a great deal to do with why the Empire's primitive economy had reverted to a level well below that which the "archangels" had installed for the original colonists. No doubt the tendency of human beings to seek power and use it for their own benefit also had a great deal to do with it, but the lack of any adequate means to move large quantities of goods had to have factored into the equation as well.

And that same problem had probably a great deal to do with the introduction of gunpowder as well, because it was pressure from traditionally backwards, anti-innovation Harchong which had led the Church to decide in its favor. Merlin had been baffled at first as to why a society like Harchong, so thoroughly dedicated to—and dependent upon—a serf- and slave-based economy, had pressed for such a status quo disturbing decision, but the answer had dawned on him. Someone among the Harchong powerbrokers had realized what the Empire's lack of canals had done to it and wanted gunpowder's blasting ability to build his own canals. Unfortunately for Harchong and its people, that project—like many in the Empire—had come to naught in the end. That tended to happen in Harchong when whoever had made it his business to push a particular project (and pay the bureaucrats the necessary graft) died, and in this case, there might well have been active opposition as well, from members of the aristocracy who'd recognized an adequate canal system's potential to destabilize the stagnant and monolithic economy which granted them such absolute power.

The absence of *any* navigable rivers in Sodar certainly contributed to that kingdom's relative poverty, especially hemmed in between mountains to the south, South Harchong to the north, and the Desnairian Mountains and Empire to the west.

The best canal in the world was still inferior to oceanic transport in terms of cost and efficiency. With the delays imposed by passing through locks and the need to coordinate traffic and rest draft animals, loads normally moved no more than forty or so miles a day, as opposed to two hundred or even as much as two hundred and fifty-plus a day by sea, but they still gave Safehold a transportation system Old Earth had never dreamed of before its twentieth century. Indeed, it was almost like having an amazingly capital-intensive, glacially slow railroad system . . . of sorts, anyway. And "glacially slow" was probably an unfair way to describe it, actually, when the maximum sustained speed for land transportation was only about five miles per hour, even on Safeholdian roads.

Of course, then there were the dragons.

A fully adult male hill dragon weighed in at just under fifteen thousand pounds, about ten percent more than an African bull elephant, and its digestive processes were *far* more efficient than any elephant's had ever been. Of course, most of Old Earth's other ruminants' digestion had been fifty percent more efficient than an elephant's, as well, but the hill dragon's was over *seventy* percent more efficient. And the damned thing could eat just about any form of vegetable matter, which helped to explain how such massive creatures sustained themselves in the wild in large numbers without destroying their environment. (The carnivorous great dragon was another reason; unlike elephants, there was a Safeholdian predator which could— and did—pull down even adult hill dragons all by itself.) With their six limbs, as opposed to the elephant's four, they were also capable of higher sustained speeds in poor terrain and of carrying proportionately heavier loads. With a properly designed pack frame, a hill dragon could carry up to thirty percent of its body weight, which compared favorably to a horse's twenty percent, far less an elephant's capacity of barely ten percent.

Even more to the point, dragons were almost as efficient as oxen when it came to drawing weights. With a "burst" draft capacity of better than five times its own weight, a hill dragon's sustained load-pulling capacity was about eighty percent of that, which as a practical matter, meant a single fifteen-thousand-pound hill dragon could pull a thirty-ton load, and Safeholdian wagon design, like many aspects of the planet's technology, was considerably more advanced than one might have anticipated. With high wheels, broad wheel rims to distribute weight, leaf springs, and low-friction wheel bearings, a draft dragon could move a two-and-a-half-ton articulated wagon with a cargo load of twenty-seven tons at sustained speeds of four miles an hour along a decent surface (and Safeholdian high roads had very decent surfaces, indeed). Theoretically, even allowing for rest and feeding time, a dragon could have moved that load almost forty miles a day through relatively level terrain, although twenty-five to thirty would have been a more realistic estimate, at a "fuel cost" of under six hundred pounds per day. And even that cost could be reduced if it was possible to feed the creature wholly or in large part on grain, rather than relying on hay, grazing, and other roughage.

That conferred a degree of mobility on a Safeholdian army which pre-industrial Old Earth commanders couldn't even have imagined. Not only could they move much faster, but they could also operate farther from supply depots. A commander from the American Civil War back on Old Earth had been able to supply his troops, using animal-drawn transport, for distances of perhaps sixty miles from the closest railhead or riverboat landing. A *Safeholdian* commander who devoted a quarter of his tonnage to feeding his dragons could deliver the *rest* of that tonnage up to five hundred miles from the nearest canal. It would take those dragons sixteen of even Safehold's long, twenty-six-hour-plus days to cover that distance even one way—thirty-two for the round trip—but they could do it.

Eventually, even with dragon-drawn transport, the Dohlarans would overreach their logistics if they moved away from the canal system, especially in light of how badly the Republic's agricultural sector had been damaged. Spring was always the worst time for an animal-powered army to invade, because food stocks in the target area had been run down over the winter and its ability to subsist on the countryside was at its lowest. This spring in Siddarmark was far worse than usual, which meant the Dohlarans had to plan on transporting every pound of food their men and their animals needed, and food was a far greater logistical problem than ammunition for any field force. Forty thousand men and forty thousand horses would require four hundred and sixty tons of food a day—over eighty-five percent of it for the horses alone—which was a pretty convincing explanation of why water transport was so important when it came to keeping an army supplied. But all that food could be transported in a mere seventeen dragon-drawn wagons, and there were two hundred of them in the Dohlaran supply train moving out of Thorast with Rychtyr's vanguard. Worse, the canal system in Dohlar hadn't been damaged the way the Republic's canals had been. The east-west canal route gave them waterborne communications all the way from Sairhalik in the Duchy of Windborne across the Siddarmark border to within a hundred and fifty miles or so of the Seridahn River. The locks had been temporarily crippled at that point, but Rychtyr was bringing along the engineers to repair them, and from there he could cover the remaining distance to Ervytyn, on the Seridahn, in about eight days. From there he could go upstream to the fortified Siddarmarkian town of Alyksberg or downstream to the far more lucrative objective of Thesmar, and there wouldn't be much to dispute his passage.

And there's actually an upside, from their perspective, to how devastated the countryside is, Merlin reflected harshly. *Since they can't live off the countryside, anyway, there's no point sending out foraging parties, and that was the thing that really slowed preindustrial armies. When you have to go out and sweep up the food you need, you can only advance as fast as the people doing the sweeping can scour the farms in your path. But since there's no point even trying to do that, they can get their troops on the move early and keep them there late every day. If they had a clue about dividing into corps and using parallel routes of march, they could move even faster!*

He was beginning to realize why Stohnar and the other Siddarmarkian officers had been so much more pessimistic than the Charisian and Chisholmian commanders—*and me, damn it to hell!*— about the balance of troop strength in *central* Siddarmark. Cayleb's Safeholdian advisors had expected it to take far longer for massive armies to move overland, because they didn't have anything like as dense a road and canal net as the mainland did. *Their* expectations had been predicated on a lifetime of *knowing* no cargo—or army—could move as rapidly overland as they could move the same loads by sea. *His* estimate, on the other hand, had resulted from how damned much he "knew" from Old Earth's history.

And they'd all been wrong.

You can't afford to fuck up this way, he told himself bitterly. *Damn it, you've taken advantage of the way Safehold* doesn't *mirror-image preindustrial Earth over and over again. You should* know *better than to let preconceptions bite all of you on the ass!*

He sat in the darkness, drumming his fingers on the table before him, trying to visualize how the unanticipated rate of advance by the Church's armies was going to upset his own estimates. Only time would tell, he thought bleakly, but he already knew at least part of the answer.

The word he wanted, he thought, was badly. *Very* badly.

.X.
HMS *Destroyer*, 54,
Tellesberg Harbor,
Kingdom of Old Charis,
Empire of Charis
and
Charisian Embassy,
Siddar City,
Republic of Siddarmark

W ell, that's impressive," High Admiral Rock Point said, bracing his hands on the stern walk railing as he watched the galleons get underway.

"Less impressive than some of the food convoys," Merlin replied over the plug in his ear.

"I was talking about the *Mule*," Rock Point said, jutting his chin in the direction of the small, smoke-streaming vessel pushing a galleon clear of a fouled mooring buoy. Its bluff bows were liberally furnished with fenders, and water foamed white under its counter as it put those bows against the galleon's flank and thrust it around until it took the wind on its quarter.

"Oh." Merlin sounded a bit abashed, the high admiral thought. "How are people dealing with her?" he asked after a moment.

"So far, so good." Rock Point rapped his knuckles on the railing for luck. "A few people screamed and had conniptions when they saw her, but we'd warned everyone she was coming, and Paityr issued all the proper attestations." He chuckled. "I think half the people who saw her expected her to burst into flames any moment, and I'm *sure* at least a hundred people suffered a very embarrassing accident the first time she sounded her whistle! But they actually started adjusting to her faster than I'd expected. And God knows she does the work of four or five galley tugs, and does it one hell of a lot faster!"

"I can't say that surprises me."

"Nor me, even if I did have to take it all on faith until I actually saw it. And Dustyn and his shipwrights spent an entire day doing nothing but crawling around her gizzards. Then they took her into the Bay and played with her for twelve solid hours! I think some of them hadn't quite been able to convince themselves Ehdwyrd's riverboats—or the *King Haarahlds*—were really going to work until they actually saw her."

"Hard to blame them. But I still say the convoy's not as impressive as the food shipments. Not to me, anyway. Terrible as the situation was, there was still something . . . good about knowing we were loading ships with something that would *save* lives instead of taking them."

"I don't disagree," Rock Point said more grimly, straightening his back, "and I'm not trying to downplay how important that food was, Merlin. But this load's going to let us do something about the people responsible for Siddarmark's *needing* that food, and I've discovered I'm very much in favor of being more . . . proactive where those bastards are concerned."

"There is that, I suppose," Merlin conceded, watching with Rock Point through Owl's SNARCs as the convoy began shaking down into formation.

That precaution was scarcely necessary in the protected waters of Howell Bay, which—as it had been for centuries—was a Charisian lake. But he approved of their getting into the habit from the beginning, because the privateers leaking past Commodore Tyrnyr and beginning to sail from ports as far south as Desnair the City were becoming more than a mere nuisance. And any privateer or regular navy commerce raider who got his hands on one of *these* galleons would become a very wealthy man if he could only manage to get its cargo home.

Eighty-five thousand Mahndrayns; a hundred and fifty twelve-pounder smoothbores; forty four-inch muzzle-loading rifled cannon; a hundred and fifty infantry mortars; forty-two *million* rounds of rifle ammunition, fifty thousand twelve-inch shells—shrapnel and high explosive—and thirty-five thousand charges of grapeshot; fifty-six thousand four-inch shells; a hundred and twelve thousand rounds of mortar ammunition; disassembled caissons and limbers for all the guns; and over twenty-five hundred draft horses and dragons for the artillery alone.

The contents of that convoy effectively cleaned out the arsenals and warehouses of Old Charis. The Delthak Works and the other foundries were laboring around the clock to produce still more weapons, and the coal and iron miners struggling to feed those foundries' voracious appetite were taking too many chances as they wrestled the sinews of war from the earth. Fifty miners had been killed in a gallery collapse just three five days ago . . . and the shaft was already being reopened. Howsmyn had twelve of the steam-powered river barges in service now—well, eight, after subtracting the almost completed gunboat conversions—with thirty more under construction. But the new steam engines were only just beginning to come into operation at the Delthak Works, and although most of the other foundries had engines of their own on order, none had been delivered yet. The mines and ore boats had a higher priority, and output was climbing quickly, but it remained far short of actual needs.

Given the size of the armies the Temple Loyalists were prepared to hurl against Siddarmark, even that massive load of weapons was entirely too little for anyone's peace of mind. Merlin felt certain any Charisian army would demolish any opponent, at least the first time they met. Given time to digest the lessons, though, the Army of God and its secular allies would learn to use their own weapons more effectively, and it wouldn't be long before they acquired specimens of the Mahndrayn. They might be unable to match its percussion cap ignition, but even a flintlock breech-loader would be far more dangerous than a muzzle-loader. And enough smoothbore artillery would be able to inflict far worse casualties than Merlin wanted to think about.

And the bastards will probably improve faster than we will, he thought grimly. *It's always that way, unless you're up against idiots. The side with the weaker doctrine and the poorer weapons learns more from its mistakes than the other side learns from doing what it already knows how to do right. And the Republic's just too frigging big and there are too damned many armies coming at us for us to even daydream about winning a decision on the battlefield this year. Or even the next, probably. We're simply not going to have a high enough ratio of force to space, and the best we're going to manage will be to keep from losing any more ground . . . if that.*

He decided that thought was sufficiently depressing to keep to himself.

"At least Ruhsail and Kynt are on their way," he said instead, and Rock Point grunted far more cheerfully.

Eastshare and Green Valley had embarked the first three infantry brigades of the Charisian Expeditionary Force from Ramsgate Bay. The brigades—twenty-six thousand infantry, with their attached artillery and engineering support—had made the march in even better shape than Merlin had hoped, although their uniforms were already rather the worse for wear. The men and, just as importantly, the draft animals were well fed and generally healthy, however, and Eastshare had been careful to allocate space aboard ship for the draft dragons and horses he'd need when he landed. He hadn't required any SNARCs to know the Republic's supply of draft animals of all sorts must have been devastated, and he'd also arranged, on his own authority, for massive shipments of Chisholmian grain and potatoes to follow him to Siddarmark. Chisholm had been too far away to contribute significantly to the emergency food lift over the winter, which meant Sharleyan's kingdom still had at least some surplus to provide to the war effort, and he was bringing as much of it with him as he could.

"They should reach North Bay by the last five-day in June," the high admiral said. "And we'll be picking up the rest of the Expeditionary Force about the same time. As soon as I can turn the shipping around, I'll be sending it off to Cherayth and Port Royal to pick up the next two corps, but they're going to be a lot slower arriving."

"All we can do is all we can do," Merlin replied philosophically. "And eighty thousand men's nothing to sneer at, either. Especially not eighty thousand men Eastshare and Kynt have trained."

"Not to mention your having had a little something to do with that yourself, eh?" Rock Point shot back with a grin.

"We also serve who stand and train. And it's probably just as well it's going to take longer to get the rest of the troops loaded on shipboard. There's a limit to how much food we can ship in. Hopefully, by the time the second wave reaches the Republic, this year's crops're going to be coming in."

"Hopefully," Rock Point agreed.

The eastern half of the Republic hadn't truly realized just how dependent it had become on the western provinces' productivity until that food supply was abruptly chopped off. Now eastern second-growth woodlot was being cleared; land that had lain fallow, in some cases for decades or even longer, was back under the plow; and carefully hoarded seed was going into the ground. By the standards of any mechanized society, Safeholdian agriculture was hideously labor-intensive; by the standards of most muscle-powered societies, it was incredibly productive, and Shan-wei's genetically boosted food crops bore early and bountifully.

In the Harchong Empire, farming truly was as primitive as it had been on preindustrial Old Earth. Seed was sown broadcast, by hand; single-blade plows were the order of the day, despite the drawing power of the Safeholdian dragon; and human labor was so cheap landowners (despite their ostentatious orthodoxy and the books of Sondheim and Truscott) saw little need to invest in expensive draft animals when there were human backs to bear the load. Wheat, for example, was harvested by men with scythes and then threshed by more men with flails, with the result that it took four men a full day simply to reap a single acre. The greater productivity of Shan-wei's modified crops, the better use of fertilizers, and an understanding of crop rotation still produced a substantially higher productivity per man-hour than, say, seventeenth-century Old Earth, despite such medieval methods, but the number of farmers required to support a single craftsman remained punishingly high. That was one of the primary contributing factors to the continued existence of not just serfdom but outright slavery in Harchong, where any overseer from an Imperial Roman latifundium would have felt right at home.

The Republic's farmers were—or had been—more efficient. Without Harchong's repressive social system workers were far more expensive, so landowners had always substituted horse and dragon power for human muscle power wherever possible. In a way, however, that meant the Sword of Schueler had hurt them even more badly. Because so many of those draft animals had been slaughtered for food—or simply starved—the new farms were badly handicapped by lack of animals to pull the multiblade plows and disk harrows. And Siddarmarkian agricultural equipment wasn't as efficient as the latest Charisian designs, to begin with. Two men and a two-horse or one-dragon mechanical reaper could cut, rake, and bind about fifteen acres of wheat a day in the Republic, as compared to the sixty serfs who would have been required in Harchong. But the latest Charisian dragon-drawn combine let those same two men and a dragon harvest over twenty-five acres in a day . . . and simultaneously thresh the grain *and* bale the hay. That was, perhaps, the most dramatic single example of Charisian innovation in agriculture, but in the last forty years Old Charis had also begun to introduce animal-drawn machines to harvest potatoes, sugar cane, corn, and—especially since Merlin had introduced the cotton gin—cotton and cotton silk.

Siddarmark's farmers were no fools, and some of them had begun importing the new Charisian designs as soon as they became available. Even so, they'd been twenty years behind Charis because the new equipment had been so expensive, even from Charisian manufactories, before the spate of innovations Ehdwyrd Howsmyn had spearheaded. They'd replaced their existing equipment only on an incremental basis as the old designs wore out and required replacement anyway . . . and then the Church's embargo had put a serious crimp in the process. Worse, well over half the imported equipment had been purchased by farmers in the western provinces. The Sword of Schueler had deliberately targeted and destroyed large quantities of that equipment—after all, it had been produced by the hated, heretical, Shan-wei-worshiping *Charisians*, hadn't it?—and virtually all of what hadn't been destroyed was unavailable to the new eastern farms, anyway.

With so much of Charis' productivity diverted to military ends, it was impossible for the Empire to provide the Republic with all it needed for its new farmland, but Cayleb and Sharleyan had sent what they could. And Ehdwyrd Howsmyn and several other ironmasters had sent teams of experts and plans for harrows, seed drills, plows, cultivators, and harvesters to Sid-darmarkian foundries, while the tide of refugees had concentrated vast amounts of human muscle power in the east. The Republic would be short on the skilled farmers it needed—too many of them had gone over to the Temple Loyalists, been trapped behind rebel lines, or simply died—but if they got through this year, by the next, the eastern provinces would be ca-pable of feeding not simply themselves but the armies fighting their enemies as well.

"Do you really think we'll be able to free up enough manpower?" Rock Point asked, and Merlin, standing atop the Charisian embassy in Siddar City, shrugged.

"Pre-technic societies back on Old Earth had all they could do to put about three percent, maximum, of their population into military service. Actually, the numbers were even lower than that until they were into at least the early stages of industrialization. One of my Academy instructors told me the real reason Rome was able to conquer the entire ancient world was that it could support a surplus, a standing military force of eighty thou-sand men . . . and no one else could. An industrialized society, especially with mechanized agriculture, could get that up to about ten percent, even twelve. After the development of advanced technology, the percentage started dropping again, because the limiting factor was the cost of the weapons themselves and the training your troops had to have to use them properly. You just couldn't afford to buy enough of them to put that much of your population in uniform . . . and they were so lethal you didn't need that many warm bodies, anyway.

"We're not going to manage anything like ten percent, even with all our new toys, but I wouldn't be surprised if we could get as high as, say, *six* percent. For that matter, we might crack seven sometime in the next few years, if Ehdwyrd's able to make his more optimistic deadlines on the other foundries and we get even more equipment into production. The other side's not going to do anywhere near that well, Domynyk."

"Maybe not, but the other side has eight hundred million warm bod-ies, give or take, and even with Siddarmark—*all* of Siddarmark on our side, which it *isn't*—we'd have *two* hundred million. And that, I might point out, counts everybody in Zebediah and Corisande as being on 'our' side, which is another one of those questionable calculations. So, let me see here. If we can put six percent of two hundred million into uniform, we get— I'm not Rahzhyr, you understand, but I *can* do simple math—we get twelve million, which, admittedly, is an absolutely stupendous number. But if they get, say, four percent of eight hundred million, they end up with *thirty-two* million." The high admiral smiled mirthlessly. "I think we're going to need an even bigger technological edge than we've already got, Merlin."

"By the time the numbers get anything like that, the Group of Four's going to be history," Merlin replied calmly. "And two hundred million of their total is from Harchong. How many of those serfs can they put into uniform without gutting that miserable excuse for an agricultural sector? For that matter, how many serfs can they give guns before they start ending up with a lot of dead Harchongian aristocrats? Which wouldn't exactly break my mollycirc heart."

"Mine, either," Rock Point agreed. "Something to look forward to, isn't it?"

"Despite what I just said, I'd really prefer to take down the Church without its going that far," Merlin said much more somberly. "Peasant rebellions can be even uglier than religious wars, especially when the peasantry in question's been as systematically abused for as long as the Harchongian serfs have. When you add *that* to a religious war, we could see the kind of carnage that turns an entire empire into a wasteland. Watching the Republic last winter was bad enough, Domynyk. I'd really rather not see thirty or forty percent of the most populous nation on Safehold murdered, starved, and dead from disease."

"Point taken." Rock Point grimaced. "Damn. I *hate* not being able to look forward to seeing those bigoted, holier-than-thou, decadent bastards get what they deserve. Thank you very much, Merlin. You've just wrecked my entire afternoon."

"You're welcome." Merlin smiled out across the roofs of Siddar City.

"And speaking about people getting what they deserve," Rock Point said, "what's this business about assassinated vicars? I thought Bynzhamyn was supposed to be monitoring the take from the Temple Lands."

"Just a fragment that caught my attention." Merlin shrugged, wondering how Rock Point would have reacted if he'd told the high admiral whose attention that fragment had *actually* caught. "I know Bynzhamyn's had his hands full since we lost Nahrmahn, so I've sort of been . . . skimming, I suppose. Especially in the areas Nahrmahn used to have primary responsibility for. It's not really confirmed, either, you know—only a couple of sentences between two men getting into a carriage."

"A couple of sentences from a conversation between a general officer of the Temple Guard and one of Clyntahn's senior inquisitors, however," Rock

Point pointed out. "That may not be 'confirmation' as far as you're concerned, *Seijin* Merlin, but it's close enough to it for me to be going on with."

"Agreed. And if someone *has* managed to assassinate 'several' vicars, it's exactly the sort of thing Clyntahn would clamp an iron lid on. He wouldn't want that sort of news getting out."

"Then maybe we should make sure it *does* get out."

"Not until we can confirm it actually happened. One of the things that's made our propaganda effective is that we haven't told any lies in the broadsheets Owl's remotes keep tacking up. We haven't had to—Clyntahn's provided us with all of the real live atrocities we could ever need, damn him to hell."

Merlin paused as he heard the raw, ugly hatred which had flowed into his own voice. He stood silent for a moment, then gave himself a shake.

"As I say," he continued in a more normal tone, grateful to Rock Point for not mentioning the pause, "we haven't had to invent anything to give our propaganda teeth. By this time, a lot of people even in the Temple Lands are beginning to figure that out, too. So the last thing we need to do is report vicars are being assassinated right and left and then have Clyntahn produce the supposedly dead vicars alive and well."

"You know he's going to *claim* they're alive and well even if they're deader than last five-day's fish."

"Yes, but I think that trick's beginning to wear thin, at least among the more sophisticated. And let's face it, psychological warfare on this kind of scale, when the other side has such an overpowering advantage at the outset, is going to take a while."

"Umph."

Rock Point glowered across the waters of Tellesberg harbor. He much preferred problems he could solve with a sword or a broadside, he admitted. Reeducation and the conversion of the enemy was more his older brother's forte.

"All right. So we have to sit on that one a while longer. I'll tell you, though, Merlin—if those two Owl overheard had it right and these mysterious deaths aren't accidents—I know who could confirm it for you."

"You're thinking about Aivah?"

"Of course I am! Nobody has better contacts than her in the Temple Lands. Hell, at least a quarter of the time she hears things even Owl hasn't snooped on! For that matter, if there really are bodies in the streets of Zion, I'll bet you a hundred marks she's the one who put them there."

"I don't think I'd take that bet on a bet." Merlin grinned. "Clyntahn surprised her with the Sword of Schueler, and I'm pretty sure the Reformist groups she was nurturing back home have gone to ground. I *hope* they have, anyway, because she didn't have anything like enough time to get them properly armed and organized. But that lady believes in as many strings to her bow as she can manage."

"Damned right she does." Rock Point smiled suddenly. "You know, it's just occurred to me that unlike Maikel, I've never married. I never thought a sea officer had the time or the opportunity to raise a family properly, not to mention the chance he'd get himself killed at some absurd young age. But now that I've attained a certain degree of maturity and made a place for myself in the world, perhaps it's time I rectified that oversight. Do you think Madam Pahrsahn might be open to a respectfully phrased proposal of marriage?"

"I think if she did marry you, you'd get exactly what you deserve," Merlin said repressively.

"Really?" Rock Point cocked his head. "Surely someone of her sophistication and worldly knowledge would appreciate the wonderful matrimonial prize I'd make."

"I have to go meet with Cayleb and Stohnar now," Merlin told him, heading for the roof stair, "so I'll just leave you with one final thought where this entire notion of yours is concerned."

"And that thought is?" the high admiral inquired when he paused.

"And that thought," Merlin said, starting down the stairs, "is that you might want to remember that the woman you're talking about has had at least eleven would-be assassins *that I know of* dropped into North Bay with large rocks tied to their ankles." He smiled sweetly. "Sailor or not, I don't think you'd float any better than they did."

.XI.
The Delthak Works,
Barony of High Rock,
Kingdom of Old Charis,
Empire of Charis

Excuse me, Master Howsmyn. Might I have a few minutes of your time?"

Ehdwyrd Howsmyn glanced up from his clicking abacus and tried not to look irritated. It wasn't easy, under the circumstances. Iron output in his mines was climbing, but not rapidly enough, and one of his major coke ovens had to be torn down and completely rebuilt, which was going to put yet another kink in his production. He was quite possibly the wealthiest single man in the entire Charisian Empire, which meant his was almost certainly the biggest single secular fortune in the world, and money was running like water as he tried to juggle one emergency against another.

It was fortunate, he sometimes thought, that his wife Zhain was willing to put up with being married to the fastest-running hamster in that self-same world.

As usual, the thought made him smile, and he looked across at the hamster cage in one corner of his office. The exercise wheel was squeaking busily, and he shook his head at the sight. He'd never been especially interested in hamsters, although his sister had had dozens of the little critters as a child, until he'd discovered every single one of the fuzz balls was descended from a half dozen who'd come all the way from Old Earth in the personal baggage allotment of none other than Pei Shan-wei herself. That had been more than enough to move them to a place of honor in his personal pantheon.

The thought restored some of his habitual good humor, and he drew a deep breath and looked at the man standing somewhat anxiously in his office doorway. Nahrmahn Tidewater knew better than to waste his time, he reminded himself, and if his work schedule had been interrupted it was his own fault. He'd made it a practice, for very good reasons, to adopt what Merlin called an "open-door policy" where his artisans, mechanics, and workmen were concerned.

"Yes, Nahrmahn. What is it?" he asked pleasantly.

"I know you're busy, Sir, but I've a fellow here I think you'd better talk to. He's a notion I think might just work out very well indeed, and I'm none too sure in my own mind why it's never occurred to anyone else."

"Ah?" Howsmyn tipped back in his chair, and Tidewater shrugged.

"Not to put too fine a point on it, Sir, but I'm thinking you may just be calling on Father Paityr after you've had this little talk."

"I see."

The ironmaster felt the last of his irritation flicker away. One of the reasons he'd instituted his open-door policy was to encourage the flow of innovation. Quite a few addled notions had walked through that door over the last few years, but so had some very good ideas, and the pace was picking up in satisfying fashion. Tidewater himself, for example, had been instrumental in the development of the sewing machines which were in the process of more than quadrupling the output of Raiyhan Mychail's clothing manufactories.

"Well, in that case, bring him in!"

"Aye, Sir." Tidewater leaned back and looked down the hall. "Taigys! Master Howsmyn's ready to see you."

There was a moment of silence, and then a small, wiry fellow with graying brown hair stepped just a bit awkwardly into the office. Howsmyn recognized the face and the shrewd dark eyes, but he couldn't quite put a name to them. Then he saw the left hand, stiff and awkward, its little finger and ring finger missing, and he remembered.

"Taigys . . . Mahldyn?" he said, standing behind his desk, and the man in front of him beamed.

"Indeed I am, Sir!" He shook his head. "And to think you remember after so long!"

"I try to remember people who get hurt in my employ, Master Mahldyn. Especially when it happens because of my mistake."

"Ahhh!" Mahldyn waved his good hand in a dismissing gesture. "You'd warned us all about the shafting, Master Howsmyn. 'Twas my own fault I didn't listen hard enough. And the trade you had me taught, it's paid well." He beamed again. "My youngest, Fhranklyn, he's been accepted to the Royal College, you know!"

"No, I didn't. That's good—that's *very* good!" Howsmyn smiled back at him and offered his right hand. Mahldyn hesitated for a moment, then clasped forearms with him. "And your wife . . . Mathylda?"

"Oh, she's fine, Sir. The patience of a saint! She's survived three boys—and me—after all!"

"I'm glad to hear it." Howsmyn released the other man's arm and stepped back, sitting on the edge of his desk and looking back and forth between Mahldyn and Tidewater. "But I understand from Master Tidewater you have something you wanted to talk to me about?"

"Aye, Sir, that I do."

Mahldyn seemed to hesitate, then he squared his shoulders and looked Howsmyn straight in the eye.

"The thing is, Sir, the last three years I've been one of the barrel makers in the pistol shop. I only need the one hand to turn the barrel under the drop hammer, you know. And then, in November, Master Tidewater promoted me to shop supervisor. And a little after that, you sent round that new pistol—that 'revolver'—of *Seijin* Merlin's, and we started the new tooling."

Howsmyn nodded.

"I hadn't realized you were the supervisor, Master Mahldyn, but Master Tidewater obviously made a good choice. Production is up to—what? Forty a day?"

"Almost. It's a wonderful, clever design, Sir, but we've had a few problems with the trigger spring. They're solved now, and I think we may get up to as many as fifty a day, though we'll not do better than that without expanding further."

"I'd love to, Master Mahldyn," Howsmyn sighed. "But the truth is, revolvers we can live without. It's rifles we need more than anything else, so when it comes to prioritizing—"

He shrugged, and Mahldyn nodded.

"Oh, I know that, Sir! That's not what I wanted to talk to you about, although if it should turn out you think there's anything in this notion that's occurred to me, we'll probably have to retool quite a bit."

"Oh?" Howsmyn cocked his head again, invitingly.

"You see, Sir, when I first saw what the *seijin* had made, I thought what a clear, wonderful notion it was. It was like having six barrels, not just the two, and each one available as fast as you could cock the hammer and squeeze the trigger. And what a sweet, sweet action it had! But the more I've looked at it, the more it's struck me to wonder if we couldn't make it even better."

"Better?"

"It's clear as Langhorne's sunlight it's the most deadly handgun in all the world as it stands," Mahldyn said soberly. "And with extra cylinders, you've Shan-wei's own firepower for as long as they last. But then it's a matter of quite some time to reload—longer to reload the cylinder then to reload an old-style pistol, in fact. But what if we were to take the idea behind the cylinder, the extension of the barrel that's already loaded before ever you cock the hammer, and drill it all the way through?"

"Drill what all the way through, Master Mahldyn?" Howsmyn was careful about his tone, letting it show perplexity and not the sudden sparkle of hope he felt deep inside. If Mahldyn was headed . . . .

"The cylinder, Sir."

Mahldyn reached into the pocket of his leather apron and pulled out a folded piece of paper. He waved it in the direction of Howsmyn's desk, his eyebrows raised, and Howsmyn nodded and stepped aside so the artificer could unfold his sketch on the desk. It was very rough—whatever else he might be, Taigys Mahldyn was no draftsman—but the basic idea was clear enough.

"What I was thinking, Sir, was we've gone to the new breech-loading cartridge and percussion caps in the Mahndrayns, and it's worked well enough. But it struck me to wonder if we couldn't do the same thing with the *seijin*'s revolvers? Oh, we couldn't open and close the back of the cylinder the way the Mahndrayn does, so we couldn't use the kind of paper cartridge the rifle uses, but you know, Sir, the thing that really makes the Mahndrayn work is that felt wad on the end of the cartridge. The one that crushes up against the breech face and seals the flash. It's no strength at all, really, when you come down to it. It's the metal all about it holds it against the pressure when the cartridge fires. All the felt does is seal the crack. And if you can do it with felt, why not another way? And once I was thinking about that, I got to thinking about the crush gauges, and it occurred to me felt's not the only thing deforms under pressure. So, the long and the short of it is that I found myself wondering why we couldn't make the cartridge out of *metal* instead of paper? It wouldn't have to be all that fearsomely strong or heavy with the cylinder wall to hold it. And if it was made out of copper—or bronze, maybe—why shouldn't it expand the same way the base of the bullet does when the cartridge fires? If the bullet seals the bore on the way out the *front*, why couldn't a metal cartridge seal the flash on the way out the *back*?"

He was looking at Howsmyn as if he half-expected his employer to decide he was a gibbering idiot, but Howsmyn's eyes were narrow, intent, and he nodded slowly.

"It just might work," he said, equally slowly. "It really might. But how do you get the powder inside this . . . metal cartridge of yours to explode?"

"I've two or three thoughts on that, Sir," Mahldyn said eagerly, the words coming faster, almost tripping over one another, at the evidence of Howsmyn's interest. "We'd be needing some kind of a ledge or rim on the end of the cartridge to keep it from sliding too far into the cylinder when it was loaded. So if we made the rim hollow, and we put the fulminated mercury into the rim, then hit it with the hammer, that should work. I'm a mite concerned about the possible weakness that could create, though, so I've another sketch . . . here." He tapped one of the detail sketches on his big sheet of paper. "You see there's a pin sticking out the side of the cartridge, and the hammer comes down on it from the side. It's charged with the fulminated mercury, and it flashes over into the cartridge the same as a percussion cap in a Mahndrayn. I've done a little experimenting, and it works well enough, but the pins are fragile. There's precious few things a soldier can't break, and I'd as soon not give him anything easier to break than needs must. So I think it comes down to putting it into the rim—a 'rimfire,' I suppose you'd call it—or figuring a way to crimp something like a regular cap into the base, where it could flash up into the powder. A 'centerfire' cartridge, so to speak. I've not actually experimented with that yet, you understand, but if you look here, at this sketch—"

"Enough, Master Mahldyn!" Howsmyn broke in on the torrential explanation, and Mahldyn skidded to a halt. He looked at his employer apologetically, but Howsmyn only shook his head with a grin.

"So you think there's something in it, Master Howsmyn?" Tidewater said, recognizing that grin of old, and Howsmyn nodded.

"Master Mahldyn," he said, "I think you've just become a rich man."

"Beg pardon, Sir?" Mahldyn looked at him uncertainly.

"Surely you know my policy, Master Mahldyn!" Howsmyn shook his head again at the artificer's expression. "*You* thought of it, not me. So as the fellow who came up with the idea, the patent application will list your name as the primary applicant."

"But—!"

"Master Tidewater, I thought we'd explained this to everyone," Howsmyn said.

"That we have, Sir. In fact, I've personally explained it twice in Taigys' presence. You may have noticed, though, that there's a deal going on inside that head of his. Sometimes the latest notion chasing itself through it causes him to . . . lose touch with the world about him for a while. As he says," Tidewater smiled broadly, "Mistress Mathylda really does have the patience of a saint!"

"I see." Howsmyn turned back to Mahldyn. "The way it works, Master Mahldyn, is that while you did come up with the notion in my employ, the idea was *yours*, not mine. So the patent application will be filed jointly in your name and in mine. I'll see to the licensing and to the manufacturing, although I've no doubt you'll want to be what a friend of mine calls 'hands-on' with that end of things as well. The income from the licensing fees and sales will be accounted, and after production costs have been covered, the net profit will be divided equally between you and me."

Mahldyn was staring at him now, and Howsmyn smiled. The artificer knew perfectly well that quite a few of Howsmyn's competitors took a very different view of who owned what if one of their workers devised a new idea while working in their manufactory. And that was fine with Ehdwyrd Howsmyn. If they were stupid enough to rob their own workers of the fruit of their labors rather than making those same workers partners in developing the idea in question, more and more of those workers would be finding themselves in *his* employ.

"Don't think you're done yet, though, Master Mahldyn!" he continued briskly. "I think this 'centerfire' notion of yours is definitely the way to go, and I'll want to be involved in the process, myself. I can think of a couple of other refinements we might want to consider, including finding the fastest way we can come up with to clear the expended cartridges and reload. Then there's the question of how to manufacture the cartridges—it's going to have to be a drawing process, I think, but we can handle that. The alloy, though. *That's* going to be tricky—too soft and it's going to jam, too hard and we may split the case after all. And I'll want to see sketches and ideas about how we go about seating the primer in the base of the cartridge without weakening it."

His smile grew broader.

"I'm sure you'll be equal to the task, Master Mahldyn! And as Master Tidewater can tell you, I'm a fair hand at suggesting possible approaches once someone's aimed me in the right direction. So I've no doubt at all you'll be able to make this work, and if you can make it work for revolvers, then I've no doubt you can make it work for a modified *Mahndrayn*, as well. And if you can do that, Master Mahldyn, with all of the ammunition we're going to need to deal with those bastards in Zion, you'll retire a very wealthy man indeed . . . and no one in this world will deserve it more."

. XII.
The Temple,
City of Zion,
The Temple Lands

Archbishop Wyllym Rayno moved quickly across the Plaza of Martyrs towards the Temple's soaring colonnade.

The Plaza bore little resemblance to the spacious, celebratory garden it had been before the serpent of heresy reared its head in far-off Charis. The majestic sculptures of the archangels continued to look out upon the court-yard from their places around its perimeter, but somehow their expressions were no longer benign and sternly approving. Instead, they seemed harsh, angry—the faces of holy beings who had looked upon the heart of evil and judged it deserving of punishment. Perhaps that was because the reverent statues of the heroic martyrs who'd stood with them against Shan-wei's deluded adherents after the arch-traitor Kau-yung struck at Langhorne's own fellowship no longer formed the center of the plaza. Instead, they'd been removed, for fresh evil and corruption had fallen upon Safehold. This was no longer a time for reverent deference; it was a time once more for the hard duty and unflinching, obedient dedication which had inspired those first martyrs in the War Against the Fallen, and in place of their statues stood the grim, blackened reminders of the punishment awaiting Shan-wei's and Kau-yung's current servants.

As a general thing, Rayno had little problem with the change. He was no more enamored of the loss of what had been a pleasant, breeze-filled garden than the next man, and he admitted that the fountains the vanished statues had once surrounded looked naked and . . . forlorn, somehow, de-spite their dancing, ever-changing lace-work of spray. But he found the mes-sage behind the change, the readiness of Mother Church to show her stern, unyielding devotion as the shepherd of men reassuring. It was the evidence that, come what may, God's Church would never allow herself to be dic-tated to by the changeable, unpredictable, ephemeral currents of merely mortal prejudices or the transitory enthusiasms of the day. And if Mother Church must make occasional accommodations with the letter of the *Writ* in order to preserve its spirit and keep herself and her doctrine inviolate, then those accommodations—however regrettable at that moment—must simply be made.

This morning, however, even he felt a shiver as he hurried past those scorched, heat-cracked portions of paving. His superior, the man most responsible for creating that change in the Plaza of Martyrs, was not going to be happy with his report.

▼   ▼   ▼

"Not acceptable, Wyllym." Zhaspahr Clyntahn's eyes were hard, almost glittering, as he looked across his desk at the adjutant of the Order of Schueler. "*Somebody* was responsible for these acts of murder." His index finger tapped ominously on his blotter. "I *want* whoever it was. I want them captured, interrogated, and punished as their crimes deserve!"

"Your Grace, we've tried," Rayno replied in an unusually humble tone. "Our best investigators have examined every scrap of evidence. Our inquisitors have pursued every hint of a lead. We've doubled the agents of inquisition inserted into potentially heretical groups. And we've found nothing more than I've already reported to you."

"Which is that *five* vicars of Mother Church, all loyal servants of the Jihad and strong supporters of the Inquisition, have been most foully murdered in the last seven months, and that you're no closer to discovering who was responsible than you were when they first occurred. *That's* what you've already reported to me, Wyllym!"

"I realize that, Your Grace." Rayno bowed, commanding his face to remain politely attentive—merely deferential and humbly contrite—for he'd seen what had happened to others who'd shown fear at a moment like this. "And I certainly haven't abandoned the investigation. But I'd be remiss in my duties as the adjutant of your Order if I didn't tell you the truth, as frankly and fully as I can." His eyes showed no awareness of the many times he'd actually . . . tailored that truth rather carefully. "And the truth is that whoever was behind those murders must have been very tightly organized and, I suspect, sent from outside Zion itself."

"Oh?" Clyntahn leaned back, his expression dangerous. "And what about your *theory* that the first two murders were simply outbursts of spontaneous, irrational rage—'crimes of passion and opportunity,' I believe you called them at the time."

"That was only one of several possible scenarios I sketched in my initial reports, Your Grace," Rayno reminded him respectfully. "And it fitted the evidence then available to us. Vicar Suchung and Vicar Vyncnai were set upon on their way home from . . . an evening's entertainment." They had, in fact, been on their way home from a brothel, and knowing the vicars in question, Rayno was confident both had been thoroughly drunk at the time. "They had only two Guardsmen each in attendance, and that simply wasn't enough security when they encountered the food riot. Or that's what it looked like at the time, at any rate."

"And now?" Clyntahn asked unpleasantly.

"And now, it doesn't appear the food riot in question was, in fact, as spontaneous as we believed." Rayno met his superior's irate glare unflinchingly. "There was no pattern of violence against the vicarate to suggest anything to the contrary then, but what's happened since has placed rather a different complexion on that first incident. As a result, I instructed our investigators to go back and thoroughly re-interrogate every original witness to what happened. That's been completed now, and allowing for the fact that every person sees and remembers things slightly differently, their stories all confirm that the riot began when two women and three men all of them can describe but *none* of them can identify began to quarrel with two of the local vendors over food prices. It seems apparent—now—that those five individuals deliberately instigated the riot to cover the attack on the vicars. And I find the fact that none of the witnesses had ever seen them before in their lives—a point upon which they were all consistent, even under rigorous questioning—and that none of them were swept up in the arrests after the riot, suggestive evidence they were outsiders. Certainly that they were from outside the neighborhood in which the attack took place, at any rate.

"At the same time, Your Grace, honesty requires me to tell you that if not for the additional attacks, neither I nor any of my investigators would have returned to that original incident and re-sifted the evidence and the testimony as closely as we have."

"*That* I can believe," Clyntahn growled.

"The other murders," Rayno continued, still meeting his master's gaze, "were more clearly that—planned and carefully executed murders, I mean—although how the killers gained access to Vicar Hyrmyn's apartment is still a bit unclear."

It wouldn't do, he thought, to bring up the fact that the only reason Vicar Hyrmyn had acquired his luxurious "hideaway" off the Temple's own grounds had been to provide the privacy for his esoteric tastes. Those tastes had become a particularly sensitive issue after several members of the Wylsynns' circle had been condemned for pederasty. The Grand Inquisitor wouldn't want to hear about *that* . . . especially since the closest thing they had to a suspect was the still unidentified child Hyrmyn's personal Guardsman had admitted to the apartment.

Whoever's behind this, he thought, not for the first time, *clearly knows a lot about his targets, and he isn't picking them at random. And not just because they're the Grand Inquisitor's allies, either. No, he's targeting them on the basis of . . . personal habits no one outside the Inquisition's supposed to know a thing about. And he's using the nature of those habits to help get to them.*

He grimaced mentally at the irony of the thought, since it was those very habits which had helped Zhaspahr Clyntahn assure himself of their loyalty. The problem was trying to figure out who *else* might have had access to the records and evidence Clyntahn had very quietly tucked away among his insurance policies.

"In the cases of Vicar Erwyn and Vicar Tairy the methods of access are relatively clear," he continued out loud, "and we have good descriptions of the men responsible for Vicar Erwyn's death. Unfortunately, I've come to the conclusion that the witnesses were *supposed* to see the killers. They'd deliberately dressed in distinctive garments and successfully induced what I believe were completely honest eyewitnesses to send the Guardsmen—who responded immediately and effectively to the attack—off on a wild wyvern chase after vividly described assailants while they themselves, having discarded the disguise which made them so describable, simply disappeared into the crowd.

"It's that sort of touch that convinces me we're dealing with an organized, well-trained, imaginative group, Your Grace." The archbishop shook his head. "These aren't amateurs or fanatics who come straight at their targets in a burst of rage, and our usual methods for identifying enemies of Mother Church aren't going to work in this case.

"I've searched the records of the Inquisition diligently without uncovering any other situation quite like this one, and whoever orchestrated it is definitely not a typical, crazed heretic. Baffling all our agents and investigators this way shows intelligence, skill, and determination, however foul and blasphemous the purpose to which they've set themselves, and their actual assassins are as skillful as any of our own agents inquisitor." He drew a deep breath. "In fact, I've found myself forced to wonder if the hand behind these killings wasn't also the one behind the . . . disappearance of the traitor Dynnys' family and so many others."

As Rayno had expected, Clyntahn's already thunderous expression darkened still further at the reminder of the family members who'd escaped the Punishment he'd meted out to his enemies almost exactly two years earlier. The Grand Inquisitor opened his mouth, his eyes flashing . . . but then he stopped. He sat glaring at the archbishop for endless nerve-racking seconds. Then he braced both hands on his desk, pushing himself even farther back in his chair, and sucked in a deep, angry breath.

"What you're saying," he said flatly, "is that there is, right here in Zion, an organization—a conspiracy—which has proven itself capable of striking even members of the vicarate with impunity and of which not *one* of our agents has ever caught so much as a sniff. Is that what you're telling me, Wyllym?"

"I'm afraid so, Your Grace." Rayno folded his hands before him in the sleeves of his cassock and bowed. "I believe it must've been put into place years ago, and if I'm correct about that, it amply demonstrates your own argument that what we face in the Jihad is no mere consequence of a secular

rivalry between realms gone awry but the result of a long-building conspiracy against Mother Church's rightful primacy. I can't point to any proven
connection between the traitor Staynair and whoever this group in Zion
might be, or between him and the Wylsynns, but it must have existed. It's
possible Samyl's son Paityr was that connection—it would certainly explain
the eagerness with which he accepted the posting to Charis, and also the
way in which he's so effortlessly turned his coat to support Staynair and this
'Church of Charis' abomination."

Of course, he thought, *the fact that we had his father, his uncle, all of their
friends, and a dozen of his cousins killed might also explain it. Best not mention that
just now, either.*

"The fact that it existed, perhaps for years, before we became aware of
it probably also explains its success in orchestrating the escape of so many of
the traitors' families two years ago," he went on. "Since we knew nothing
of its existence, we were unprepared to respond to its activities, and its willingness to resort to the cold-blooded murder of consecrated vicars certainly
suggests what happened to the inquisitors we'd assigned to keep watch on
individuals like Samyl Wylsynn's wife and family." He shook his head
again. "I never believed so many of our brethren might have been suborned
or induced to actively abet their flight, and the fact that none of the missing
inquisitors have appeared in Charis proclaiming their change of allegiance
seems to confirm that they were murdered, taken unaware by the agents of
a conspiracy they didn't realize even existed."

"All of which suggests a massive failure on the Inquisition's part," Clyntahn growled, glaring at the man responsible for the Inquisition's day-to-
day operations, especially here in Zion.

"If I'm correct in my analysis, Your Grace, then the foundations of this
conspiracy must predate your own elevation to Grand Inquisitor," Rayno
responded, and Clyntahn's nostrils flared ever so slightly at the reminder of
who was ultimately responsible for *all* of the Inquisition's operations.

"Assuming this . . . adventure novel of an explanation bears any resemblance at all to reality," he said after a moment, "what do you intend to do
about it?"

"I think we have to approach it as if it were an entirely new and fresh
problem, Your Grace." Rayno's calm, deliberative manner disguised his
powerful surge of relief at the implication that he'd be around to have the
opportunity to do anything about it. "We have to discard all our assumptions,
realize that none of our existing agents and information sources know anything at all about this conspiracy. Or, even worse, that some of them may
know about it because they're actually *part* of it."

Fresh lava smoked in Clyntahn's eyes, but the archbishop continued
unhurriedly.

"Clearly these traitors weren't able to gain enough penetration into the Inquisition to corrupt the agents inquisitor we'd assigned to watch the traitors' families two years ago, Your Grace. On that basis, I doubt they could've penetrated our inquisitors as a whole sufficiently to compromise our basic ability to gather intelligence and information. But it would be foolish to assume we haven't been penetrated at all. And I think it would be wise to remember how effective the heretics' spies have demonstrated themselves to be, even here in Zion and the Temple Lands, when it comes to such things as Bishop Kornylys' sailing orders. They obviously have agents in places we haven't looked yet, and I think we have to operate on the assumption that at least some of them *could* be"—he stressed the verb delicately but—"hidden among our own, trusted ranks."

Clyntahn subsided again, slightly, and Rayno thanked Langhorne and Schueler the Grand Inquisitor hadn't brought up Phylyp Ahzgood and Rhobair Seablanket. His reaction when he realized the Earl of Coris and his valet had successfully played the entire Inquisition and all its agents for fools had been terrifying. Only the fact that Seablanket had been recruited as an agent decades before Clyntahn rose to the Grand Inquisitor's chair (and that he'd personally interviewed Coris and been reassured of the man's suitability) had prevented widespread reprisals against everyone—including Wyllym Rayno—involved in the abortive plan to assassinate Daivyn and Irys Daikyn.

"At the same time," the archbishop went on, "it would be counterproductive to begin suspecting everyone and searching under every bed in Zion for traitors within our own ranks. I believe it's very probable—indeed, almost certain—these conspirators stayed largely away from the Temple Guard and the Inquisition when recruiting. They've obviously managed to successfully evade our attention, and the odds would've been high that they would eventually have betrayed themselves attempting to suborn or corrupt our most faithful and highly motivated brethren and servants. All it would have taken was for one of our people to play along with the approach and inform us of it for us to have penetrated the conspiracy early on. So I think we may assume the fundamental loyalty of our own people, yet at the same time we must proceed carefully, restricting the truth about our suspicions to those we *know* we can trust. Proceeding in that way will require us to go slowly and cautiously, which means there will be no quick answers, Your Grace. But I believe we can gradually spread our net wider and wider, possibly without explaining even to our investigators and agents exactly what it is we're looking for, while maintaining security about the broader threat we believe exists."

Clyntahn looked disgusted, but after a moment, he nodded. It was a grudging, furious, unwilling nod, but a nod nonetheless.

"Very well," he growled. "But I want reports every five-day, Wyllym! No pushing this one onto a back burner while you deal with more pressing problems. Is that understood?"

"Of course, Your Grace." Rayno bowed again.

"And in the meantime, we need to keep this out of those Shan-wei-damned broadsheets."

Clyntahn's jowls darkened dangerously once more as they always did at the thought of the anti-Church—and, especially, anti-Clyntahn—posters that continued to appear throughout the mainland's major cities. Every so often, Rayno's agents inquisitor ran down some Reformist fool trying to print broadsheets in his cellar or attic, but it always seemed that whoever they'd arrested had distributed only a handful of his traitorous tracts. They never seemed to find any of the dozens of other agitators operating across the width and breadth of Hauwerd and both Havens.

I wonder, the vicar thought through the red haze of anger with which those taunting, elusive traitors always filled him. *I wonder. If Wyllym's even remotely correct about all this, could the sons of bitches behind these murders be connected to all these invisible printing presses as well?*

Probably not, he decided, or else those broadsheets would already be proclaiming the successful, impious murder of no less than five princes of God's own Church.

Rayno, he noted resentfully, had kept his own mouth prudently shut about *that* possibility.

"So far, the news that any of the vicars may have died by violence—aside from Vicar Suchung and Vicar Vyncnai—has been kept quiet successfully, Your Grace," the archbishop said instead. "There's no evidence knowledge of the other murders has become public, although, of course, the people responsible obviously know about them. In the case of Vicar Suchung and Vicar Vyncnai, the original account—that they were on their way back to the temple, encountered the riot, and lost their lives in the confusion when they attempted to reason with the rioters and quell the violence—seems an adequate explanation. As for the others, I'd advise releasing the fact of their deaths gradually and individually over a reasonable period of time as a consequence of appropriate natural causes."

"Do you really expect that to fool anyone else in the vicarate?"

"No, Your Grace, but my concern isn't *with* the vicarate." Rayno permitted himself his first smile—a cold, thin one—since entering Clyntahn's office. "The vicarate understands the reality of the Jihad, Your Grace." His tone was flat. "They know the Inquisition and the Order stand behind you and that, just as you, we will neither flinch nor quail from anything our duty to God and Mother Church require. If anything, I would expect this outside threat to push some of your . . . less devoted supporters into renewed and strengthened commitment in return for the Inquisition's protection."

"You may be right about that," Clyntahn mused in a much more thoughtful tone, pursing his lips. He considered it for a few seconds, then brushed the thought aside.

"In the meantime, we need to tighten that protection you've mentioned," he said. "Apparently these killers, whoever they are, still hesitate to strike in the precincts of the Temple itself. Perhaps they fear to come too close to the presence of the archangels here on earth. I don't think we can afford to take it for granted that they never will attempt to strike here, but I do think we can consider the Temple and its grounds a relative bastion of safety. I believe we should encourage those of the vicarate who retain quarters beyond the Temple to abandon them until we deal with this threat. And we should also insist that all vicars—and probably our senior archbishops as well—be accompanied by much stronger bodyguards in the future." He grimaced. "I'd really prefer to use additional trained inquisitors, but we still don't have enough of them for that."

"As you say, Your Grace," Rayno murmured, bending his head in acknowledgment.

His program to radically increase the Inquisition's strength was gaining speed steadily, but it wasn't something that could be rushed too hastily. As the murders of five vicars had just demonstrated, there were forces in the world as dedicated to the overthrow of Mother Church as the Inquisition was to her protection. Finding the right material for inquisitors, training it properly, and—above all, and especially in light of those murders—being certain of its reliability, put a bottleneck on expansion which couldn't simply be waved away. As the Inquisition's numbers grew, it became easier to train still more inquisitors, because the cadre available to do the training increased, but he'd come to the conclusion that there simply would never— *could* never—truly be a sufficient supply of them.

"Ah, one question, Your Grace," he said in a rather delicate tone as he raised his head once more.

"Which is?" Clyntahn growled.

"I believe most of the vicars will gladly accept the additional security of enlarged bodyguards, Your Grace. Vicar Allayn may not, but since as Mother Church's Captain General, he's continuously accompanied by members of the Temple Guard or the Army of God, I'm not unduly concerned over his safety." *Besides,* he thought, *how big a loss could* Maigwair *be?* "There is, however, the matter of Vicar Rhobair. He's already quite unhappy about the size of the bodyguard we've insisted he accept. I think it's probable he'll refuse a still larger bodyguard when he leaves the Temple to visit the hospices and hospitals."

"Um."

Clyntahn sat back again, rubbing his upper lip with an index finger while he thought.

"Still bitching about Major Phandys, is he?"

"I wouldn't put it quite that way, Your Grace," Rayno said with another small smile. "I do get a routine request to 'release Major Phandys' valuable services to more pressing duties' about every other five-day, however."

"Really?" Clyntahn chuckled harshly. "I'm glad to see dear sanctimonious, holier-than-thou Rhobair properly appreciates Major Phandys' 'valuable services,' but I think we'll just leave him where he is for now. As for your other point . . . ." He rubbed his lip again, then shrugged. "Tell Rhobair I think he ought to accept the reinforcement of his bodyguards but I won't attempt to dictate to his conscience on this matter." He chuckled again, the sound harder and even harsher. "If some lunatic does get through to him in the street and cut his throat, it won't break my heart. And if at some future time we should . . . require such a lunatic, I'm sure that, with Major Phandys' assistance, one could be provided."

.XIII.
Royal Palace,
City of Cherayth,
Kingdom of Chisholm,
Empire of Charis

So what do you think of Archbishop Ulys?" Mahrak Sahndyrs asked. "Now that you've had time to watch him and Archbishop Maikel together, I mean?"

Empress Sharleyan cocked her head to give the Baron of Green Mountain a moderately exasperated look.

"I've been home in Cherayth less than twenty-six hours, Mother's visiting with her granddaughter for the first time in months, and you're retired. Don't you think we could spend, oh, twenty or thirty whole minutes just visiting with one another?"

"And it's very good to see you, too, Sharleyan," he said with a flicker of a familiar smile. "Did you have a nice voyage? Was Alahnah less seasick this time? And what do you think of Archbishop Ulys?"

Sharleyan made a face and struck him—very gently—on top of his head with a small fist. He winced theatrically, and she laughed.

"There were times I wanted to do that *so* badly—and a *lot* harder!—when

I was a little girl. You have no idea how lucky you were to have Mairah around to protect you!"

"Why do you think I gave in and let you have her as your lady-in-waiting? I knew I'd need a friend at court eventually."

She laughed again and bent beside his chair to put her arm around him. She hugged him a bit more tightly than she'd really intended to, trying to stifle a fresh pang as she felt how frail his robust frame had become. She'd known how badly wounded he'd been in the terrorist attack which had almost killed him, but there was a difference between intellectual knowledge, even backed up by the direct visual evidence through Owl's remotes, and actually hugging her second father. He'd lost his right arm between elbow and shoulder and his right leg below the knee, and if he wore the black eye patch over what had been his left eye with a certain debonair style, his face was still badly scarred . . . and far, far thinner than she remembered.

Well, of course he feels frail. It's been barely six months since the attack! It takes time to come back from something like that—if you ever do—and he's not a young man anymore.

"You," she told him, straightening and trying to hide her concern, "are incorrigible."

"Agreed. And my question?"

"All right, I surrender!" She threw up both hands dramatically. Then her expression sobered. "Actually, I think I like him a lot. I miss Archbishop Pawal, and I hate the way he was killed." Her eyes turned bleak as she remembered watching the imagery of Pawal Braynair's death when the archbishop personally tackled the grenade-armed assassin in his own cathedral and smothered the explosion with his body. "He seems to be smart," she went on, "and I have to say he seems to have . . . I don't know, maybe what Cayleb would call more 'fire in his belly' than Archbishop Pawal did."

"I think you're right," Green Mountain agreed. "Pawal was a good man, and no one on the face of this world was ever more determined to do the right things, but I always thought of him as a man who'd been driven by principle to do something his heart found almost too hard to bear. Young Ulys is a Reformist to his toenails, though." He shook his head with a smile that held more than a trace of regret. "He hates the Group of Four with a passion and fire I think he sometimes finds hard to reconcile with his priestly calling. And I think—maybe I'm even afraid—he's going to be much more . . . apt to your needs then Pawal was."

"Afraid, Mahrak?"

She looked down at him, eyes questioning, and he shrugged.

"Pawal was like me, Sharley. He was *driven* into resisting Mother Church because she'd fallen into the grasp of men like Clyntahn, but in his heart of hearts, he was still her son. He was never comfortable as a rebel;

he'd simply been left no choice but to become one. Ulys is younger than Pawal was—and considerably younger than I am now—and his opposition to Mother Church stems from outrage over her failings, not grief at the failings of men who captured her and caused her to fail. He's embraced that opposition in a way Pawal and I never could. And that means that when the schism is finally formalized, he'll be one of the Church of Charis' strongest pillars. You'll need that."

"And you, Mahrak?" she asked softly, finally willing to ask the question out loud now that he was free of the crushing responsibilities of his office.

"And I was never a willing rebel, either," he told her with a twisted smile. "But, like Pawal, Mother Church left me no choice." He reached up and touched her cheek with his remaining hand. "And neither did you. So young, so *fiery*! So determined . . . and so right. In the end, I cared too much about you and too little about God, perhaps. You left me no choice but to *look* at what men like Clyntahn had made of the Church I loved. I couldn't do anything but support you after my eyes had been opened, Sharley, but there were always tears in them."

"Oh, Mahrak."

The words were barely a sigh as she bent once more, this time putting her cheek against his, and wrapped both arms around him. He returned her embrace, and they stayed that way for several seconds before she straightened once more.

"I always suspected you felt that way," she said, realizing there were tears in her own eyes, "and I felt guilty for dragging you behind me."

"Don't be silly!" he scolded her. "Didn't I always teach you a queen does what she must in the service of her people and of God?" He held her gaze until she nodded. "Well, that's exactly what you did. Because the truth, however hard I found it, is that there really is a difference between God and any mortal edifice, even one ordained by His own archangels. God would never—*could* never—condone the acts of a Zhaspahr Clyntahn or the rest of his murderous clique. That much I *know*, without question. And because you had the courage to face that squarely, and do it before I did, you proved you were worthy of your crown. I was never prouder of you, Sharley, however much I regretted what you'd been forced to do."

She looked down at him for a moment, and then nodded again. This time it was a nod of acceptance.

"I wish you'd never had to be put into that position," she told him, resting her hand on his shoulder. "But, you know, if I turned out 'worthy' of my crown, it was because I had such good teachers. Like you. Always like you, Mahrak."

"You were your father's daughter, and your mother's," he replied, looking up and smiling as he put his hand over hers. "And you were my Queen, with the courage to do what you knew was *right* and damn the consequences before you were tall enough to see over the council table. It was easy to give you my love with all of that going for you."

▼　▼　▼

"—why I'm concerned, Your Majesty. *Concerned*, not worried. Not yet, at any rate."

"I understand, My Lord," Sharleyan said, looking across the council chamber table at Sir Dynzayl Hyntyn, the Earl of Saint Howan and the Kingdom of Chisholm's Chancellor of the Treasury.

Saint Howan was young for his position, only in his midforties. Fair-haired and gray-eyed, he was also smart, and his earldom's coastal position made him a strong supporter of the Imperial Navy, with a keen appreciation for the possibilities of maritime trade. At the moment, those gray eyes showed the concern he'd just mentioned, and she understood his position.

"We here in Chisholm were never as devoted to manufactories as Charis," she said. "And Charis had to begin preparing for war sooner than we did. That meant they had to expand their foundries, their shipyards, their textile mills and sail lofts—all the things that go into supporting a war—which is why so much of the Empire's manufactories are concentrated in Old Charis now. It is, however, Emperor Cayleb's and my policy to encourage and sustain such enterprises here in Chisholm, as well, to the very best of our ability. It was my impression that policy was clearly understood."

"The policy *is* clearly understood, Your Majesty," Saint Howan replied. "It's its implementation that concerns me."

"My Lord?" Sharleyan turned to Braisyn Byrns, Earl White Crag, the former lord justice who'd replaced Mahrak Sahndyrs as her first councilor.

"Dynzail's talking about certain of our fellow peers, I'm afraid, Your Majesty."

White Crag was twenty years older than Saint Howan, with white hair and shoulders which were a bit stooped. He looked rather frail, but he had an underlying toughness, like well-cured leather, and he was possibly even smarter than the chancellor. His blue eyes were beginning to turn cloudy with cataracts, and his vision was so bad he had most of his correspondence read to him by his secretaries rather than reading it himself. Sharleyan always felt vaguely guilty over her inability to do anything about that without revealing far too many difficult truths, but he was far more cheerful about it than she was, claiming that his present duties actually required less reading than those of the kingdom's highest jurist had imposed.

"I'm afraid we've been facing some obstruction," he continued. "I don't think it's that anyone actively wants to oppose the introduction of Charisian manufactories, but some of the nobility want to make certain they get their share of the profits from them. And, frankly, their idea of a fair share isn't mine."

"Oh, go ahead and be honest, Braisyn!" Sylvyst Mhardyr snapped.

The Baron of Stoneheart, who'd replaced White Crag as lord justice, was as bald as Bynzhamyn Raice, but scrubbed, scented, and manicured, without the Charisian's air of weathered toughness. His brain was no flabbier than Wave Thunder's, however, and he waved one elegant hand when White Crag looked at him.

"There is so 'active opposition,' and you know it! And the *real* reason the ones doing the opposing are such pains in the—" He paused and glanced at Sharleyan. "The real reason they're being so difficult," he continued, "is that they're worried that bringing in Charisian techniques is going to bring in Charisian *attitudes*! They already think commoners're too uppity, and half of them are afraid they'll get even more uppity, especially when they start having employment opportunities the nobles can't control." He snorted. "They were pis—*angry* enough when we adopted Old Charis' new child labor laws. They resent the Shan-wei out of that, and they're smart enough—barely, I admit, but smart enough—to realize that's only the tip of an iceberg." His expression was as disgusted as his tone. "If you think for one moment they haven't heard all the horror stories about how Howsmyn treats *his* workers, you're not nearly so clever as I always thought you were!"

Sharleyan raised one hand to hide a smile as the lord justice gave the first councilor something remarkably like a glare. She wasn't a bit surprised a Chisholmian noble would find the notion of a crew of common-born rabble actually being permitted to send representatives to sit down and discuss labor conditions and wages with the owner of the manufactory which employed them . . . distasteful. And the notion of paying them bonuses keyed to exceeding production quotas rather than docking their pay if they didn't *meet* those quotas would be equally alien to them.

Her smile faded as she considered the rest of what Stoneheart had just said, however, because it cut to the heart of the difference between Chisholm and Old Charis. The majority of Cayleb's nobles had been infected with the same drive to expand and explore new possibilities as the rest of their society, which meant accepting the legitimacy of trade and joining forces with the less nobly born in pursuit of their common goal. The *Chisholmian* nobility still cherished a landowner's contempt for mere tradesmen and wasn't prepared to give up its economic primacy without a fight, especially since her father, King Sailys, had used the commons' support to break the great nobles' political stranglehold. They were afraid of what would happen to their power and positions when the sinews of wealth slipped irrevocably towards the Charisian model, in which men of no blood—like, say, Ehdwyrd Howsmyn—could rise to the most dizzying heights. And it wasn't simply blind reactionism, either. Oh, it *was* reactionism, but it wasn't *blind*, for they were right about what would happen.

It would also happen to the guilds, which were far more powerful in Chisholm than in Old Charis, although the guild masters didn't seem to have scented the change in the wind quite as quickly as the nobility. The guilds had operated in large part as a mutual-protection society for master craftsmen for centuries; the discovery that their treasured apprenticeship structure was about to be overturned might well bring them into opposition as well, once it penetrated. That could prove even more of a problem than the aristocracy, especially if they decided to ally with the nobles.

"Don't mistake me, Your Majesty," Saint Howan said now. "The Charisians you and His Majesty have sent are finding places to locate manufactories. The problem is that they aren't finding them quickly and that too many of them aren't in the best places from the perspective of efficiency and *are* concentrated in . . . certain areas. For example, there's plenty of coal and some rich iron deposits in Lantern Walk, and the Lantern River's navigable most of the way to Saint Howan's Bay. We'd have to put in locks in two or three places, but that's not an insurmountable problem, and I assure you that I personally would love to see Sherytyn turn into a major seaport! But Duke Lantern Walk wants ten percent of any coal or iron mined in his duchy. And the Earl of Swayle"—his eyes met Sharleyan's—"has thrown up every conceivable roadblock to improving the Lantern where it flows through his lands. Under the circumstances," he raised his hands, palms uppermost, "I can't really blame any Charisian investors for . . . hesitating to even try to develop those possibilities."

Sharleyan didn't allow herself to grimace, but she was tempted. Barkah Rahskail, the previous Earl of Swayle, had been executed for plotting with the previous Grand Duke Zebediah and the Northern Conspiracy in Corisande. Once a confidant of her own uncle, the Duke of Halbrook Hollow, he'd followed Halbrook Hollow into treason against the Crown out of loyalty to the Church. His widow Rebkah's religious convictions were at least as strong as his had been, to which she'd added bitter hatred for her husband's execution, and the situation wasn't helped by her choice of chaplains. Father Zhordyn Rydach was Temple Loyalist to the bone. He was also charismatic, physically striking, and preached a potent sermon. Officially he was an under-priest of the Order of Chihiro; actually, he was an upper-priest of that order—almost certainly affiliated with the Order of the Sword, not the Quill, as he claimed—and one of the Inquisition's more energetic apologists. Wave Thunder and the rest of the inner circle suspected he'd also been the conduit through which Barkah had initially reached out to the Corisandian conspirators. Unfortunately, not even Owl's remotes had been able to catch him in any overtly treasonous act, which meant they couldn't arrest him without violating their own policy of religious tolerance.

Wahlys Rahskail, the new Earl of Swayle, was only seventeen and thoroughly under his mother's thumb. He was also even more thoroughly cowed by Rydach than by Rebkah, for the priest had convinced him his soul hovered on the lip of hell, ready to slip over the brink the moment he gave his allegiance to the Church of Charis.

Sir Ahlber Zhustyn, Sharleyan's own spymaster, was watching the situation closely—aided, though he wasn't aware of it, by Wave Thunder via Owl's remotes—because in addition to her own enmity, Rebkah was related by blood to a great many of western Chisholm's nobles. In particular, to Zhasyn Seafarer, the Duke of Rock Coast; Payt Stywyrt, the Duke of Black Horse; and Edwyrd Ahlbair, the Earl of Dragon Hill. The three of them were firm allies, all with seats in the Imperial Parliament as well as the Chisholmian House of Lords, and all of them were mulishly opposed to anything which might further enhance the Crown's authority. They formed a potentially potent bloc of opposition in the west, and Sharleyan was uncomfortably aware that Duke Eastshare's Expeditionary Force had been forced to pull troops out of the garrisons and bases usually maintained in and around the Western Crown Demesne. There was no sign so far that Rock Coast and the others might contemplate taking advantage of those troops' absence, but he and Black Horse were stupid enough to try something like that if they thought they saw an opportunity. Rebkah Rahskail probably *wasn't*, and neither was her cousin, Dragon Hill, but they might find themselves pulled into an adventure if the others got the bit between their teeth.

And then there was the other part of what Saint Howan had just said. The handful of spots where Old Charisian investors had so far found places to put manufactories were in places already firmly behind the Crown, like Eastshare, her own Duchy of Tayt, and the eastern territories between Maikelsberg and Port Royal. It was good to see her and Cayleb's core supporters embracing prosperity, but if that created affluence in those areas and poverty in others, the Crown's opponents might find themselves with a potent economic weapon to rally disaffection behind them.

And one thing they won't *do is admit they're the reason for the poverty, either! They'll just point to the way we're unjustly favoring our toadies*— obviously *the only reason for their prosperity!*—*and scream that all they* want is *"fairness" and "justice"!*

The thought made her want to spit, but she couldn't do that, so instead, she smiled.

"I wish I could say I was surprised to hear about the Earl of Swayle's position. Unfortunately, I'm not." She looked at White Crag. "I imagine you've tried . . . reasoning with him, My Lord?"

"I've tried reasoning with him with everything short of a baseball bat, Your Majesty," White Crag said tartly. "I've even gotten him to agree—twice!—to lease that stretch of river to the consortium and let *them* pay for the improvements. But that was when I had him here in Cherayth. And, unfortunately, he refuses to actually *sign* anything without discussing it with his mother." He rolled his eyes ever so slightly. "Somehow, whenever he goes home to discuss it with her, he goes back to his original position. We might have more success with him if we could, ah . . . adjust his household slightly."

" 'Get thee behind me, Shan-wei,' " Sharleyan quoted dryly, shaking her head at him. "I'm not particularly pleased by the reports of Father Zhor-dyn, either, but if the Crown started trying to remove a peer of the realm's chaplain just because we don't like him, it would only justify even greater opposition. And"—she added grudgingly—"rightly so, unless we have overt proof of treason."

"We're looking, Your Majesty," Zhustyn said. "Unfortunately, he's either very, very careful, very, very lucky, or very, very disinclined to act on his own advice about opposing the 'heretical tyranny' of the 'monstrous' Church of Charis." He shook his head in exasperation. "We haven't been able to find a single piece of hard evidence."

"All you can do is keep looking, Sir Ahlber," Sharleyan commiserated, and looked back at Saint Howan.

"I believe it would be possible for us to . . . lean on Lantern Walk a bit about that demand of his," she said. "Perhaps the thought of seeing someone next door making the profit instead of him would induce him to lower his demands. Duke Lake Land's proven surprisingly reasonable, for example. In fact, he's emerged as one of the leaders of the Crown party in the Imperial House of Lords. Unless I'm mistaken, his duchy also has extensive iron deposits, doesn't it?"

"Yes, it does," the chancellor agreed. "But they'd have to be shipped through Mountain Heart, and I'm pretty sure the Grand Duke would want a hefty toll. Not only that, but the Shelakyl River's shallower than the Lantern, and if memory serves it has at least three sets of cataracts. That would require a lot more improvement than the Lantern before we could ship large quantities of ore down it. And Lake Land doesn't have coal to go with it."

"I think I could bring Grand Duke Mountain Heart to see reason," Sharleyan said with a thin smile. "He and I have crossed swords in the past, and I don't think he wants to lose any more blood. Besides, what if we were to sweeten the pot by offering to subsidize the improvement of the Shelakyl out of Crown funds? We offer to save him the cost of making the improvements in return for his charging a minimal toll on the rest of the river once the improvements are in."

"That might work, Your Majesty, but with all due respect, the Treasury isn't brimming over with marks at the moment. I've gone over Baron Ironhill's numbers since your arrival, and to meet our share of the imperial expenses for next year, especially after what Duke Eastshare's already committed us to pay to support the Expeditionary Force, we're going to have to dip deep into our reserves. Frankly, part of the problem is that more and more of our own revenues are flowing into Old Charis."

Sharleyan sensed the internal tightening of several of the other councilors. It didn't come as much of a surprise, and she understood it fully. Not only that, she knew the situation was likely to get worse over the next few years. Unless they did something about it, that was.

"I understand what you're saying, Sir Dynzail. But I also understand why it's happening, and I think there's only one solution to it. The problem, put most simply, is that Charis—*Old* Charis—had the most efficient manufactories in the world even prior to the Group of Four's attack on it. Since then, the Old Charisians've done nothing but improve their efficiency and output, and the result is that the cost of their goods has actually dropped steadily, despite the war. As the cost went down, they sold more and more of those goods, both here in Chisholm and, despite Clyntahn's embargo, on the mainland. What's happening in Siddarmark is going to disrupt that cash flow from the mainland, of course, but they're compensating for that to a large extent by opening additional markets here, in Emerald, in Tarot, and even in Corisande. Which means, equally of course, that money's flowing from customers in Chisholm to manufactories in Charis in ever greater amounts."

Heads nodded. Chisholmians were less accustomed than Old Charisians to thinking in mercantile terms, but they could understand simple mathematics. What they might not yet grasp, Sharleyan reflected, was the extent to which the availability of cheap, manufactured goods was going to get behind the entire Charisian Empire's economy and push. Just the output of Rhaiyan Mychail's textile mills was already having a huge effect as the price of clothing plummeted. It meant a Chisholmian workman could afford to buy an imported Old Charisian shirt, for example, for less than a quarter of what the same shirt would have cost from a Chisholmian tailor, and the price was still falling. In fact, it was dropping so rapidly it would soon be almost as cheap to buy a far better sewing machine-produced shirt from Old Charis than to have his wife make it for him out of homespun. And that was only one area in which the expanding flood of Old Charisian goods was hammering traditional economic arrangements. Had it not been for the absolute need to focus on military requirements—had not so much of Old Charis' output, especially its heavy industry, been required for the navy and the army rather than available for release to the civilian economy— the situation would have been even worse, and it was only a matter of time before it *got* worse.

"We can't blame our people for buying goods as cheaply as possible," she went on somberly. "We not only can't, but we *shouldn't*. Anything that improves their lives should be encouraged, not *dis*couraged. At the same time, we're looking at a significant imbalance in trade between us and Old Charis, and it's going to get worse if we don't do something about it."

"Your Majesty," one of the councilors sitting well down the table from her began, "in that regard—"

"A moment, My Lord," she said. "I wasn't quite finished."

Her tone was courteous but firm, and Vyrgyl Fahstyr, the Earl of Gold Wyvern, closed his mouth. He sat back in his chair, his expression one of patience, but there was a stubborn look in his eyes.

"I know some members of this Council"—Sharleyan said, meeting that stubborn look squarely as she grasped the dilemma by the horns—"favor the imposition of duties on Old Charisian imports to 'level the playing field.' The idea is tempting from several perspectives, including the boost to tax revenues. It would, however, hurt the Empire's economy as a whole, it would drive up the prices our own people here in Chisholm must pay just to live, and it would arouse great resentment in Old Charis. Not only that, the Crown's position is that internal trade barriers within the Empire would constitute a dangerous precedent We"—the entire Council sat just a bit straighter as it heard the *royal* we in that unwavering voice—"have no intention of allowing to arise. Understand Us, My Lords," she let her eyes sweep around the table, "We and Emperor Cayleb are as one in Our understanding that Our Empire's very survival—and that of every member of it—depends upon Our ability to build and pay for the weapons of war We require. And building those weapons, and raising and paying the men to wield them, will require money, and that money can come only from encouraging the growth of Our own economy in every way possible. The Group of Four is finding it progressively more difficult to pay for their own armies and navies, yet at this time their absolute resources remain far greater than Ours. We can change that only by increasing those available to Us, and internal imposts that discourage free trade and the most vibrant economy We can sustain are not the way to do that."

Gold Wyvern's face had gone completely expressionless as her measured words flowed around the table. Most of the men in that room had heard that tone from her before. They knew what it meant, and they hadn't forgotten during her absence in Old Charis.

"So," she continued, still firmly yet speaking once more in the voice of a young woman and not the avatar of an empire, "the official policy of the Crown is not to impose duties upon commerce, but to deliberately encourage the expansion of manufactories to other portions of our combined realm. That's the reason Master Howsmyn and other Old Charisian manufactory owners are seeking investment opportunities and partners here in Chisholm. It's our intention to offer not increased protective duties, but a *reduction* in duties, with the understanding that Old Charisian suppliers will build additional manufactories in Chisholm, financed in no small part by the profit they show on their Chisholmian trade. And"—she looked at Saint Howan again—"the Crown will also grant a reduction of taxation on new manufactories here in Chisholm, for a period of fifteen years, equal to the proportion of Chisholmian ownership in the enterprise. That is, if fifty percent of the cost of a new manufactory is borne by a Chisholmian partner or partnership, the taxes paid by that manufactory for the first fifteen years of its operation will be fifty percent of what they would otherwise have been."

Saint Howan winced visibly, but her voice continued levelly.

"If our noble landowners are wise, they'll find partnerships with Old Charisian investors. I feel certain that if they're willing to contribute land, resources, and labor to the construction of new manufactories, they'll readily find Old Charisians prepared to provide the marks, and both they and their Old Charisian partners will profit thereby. At the same time, we'll provide employ for those in the guilds who find manufactured goods depriving them of customers, and that same opportunity will keep a higher percentage of our own people's money at home, buying from their fellow Chisholmians. It will, admittedly, mean that for a period of fifteen or twenty years, the Crown's tax revenues from the manufactories themselves will be lower than they might otherwise have been. However, the revenues we'll receive off the greater flow of goods will more than compensate, and it will help to prevent Chisholm from becoming an economic appendage of Old Charis. In the long run, that will be in the interest of both kingdoms, whereas a battle of protectionism within the Empire will serve only our enemies."

Saint Howan's expression changed, becoming much more thoughtful. He gazed at her for several seconds, then nodded slowly, and she nodded back.

"As for the need to improve navigation on our rivers," she said, "while I agree it's something we need to look at accomplishing, there may be an alternative."

A stir went through the councilors, and she suppressed a smile. Some of them were still moderately in shock from her previous proposal, given how it flew in the face of their own economic models. What she'd just said, however, was clearly nonsense. Chisholm and Charis had canal networks, but nothing to compare with the mainland's centuries-long development of inland water transportation. They'd been settled later, their populations were sparser, and—in Charis' case, at least—Howell Bay had been an even broader highway than any canal. Given its existing infrastructure and economy, the lack of water transport in Chisholm hadn't been a crippling disadvantage, but no one could possibly supply the quantities of iron ore, limestone, and coal a complex on the order of Howsmyn's Delthak Works required without it.

"I'm sure all of you have read the attestation by Father Paityr, as Intendant of Charis, approving the 'steam engine' devised by Master Howsmyn's artisans," she said. "I suspect, however, that you haven't had the attestation long enough to fully grasp its implications."

She saw White Crag raise one hand to cover the smile her tactful choice of words had evoked, given that the attestation in question had arrived in Chisholm long before she had.

"One of those implications, My Lords," she continued serenely, ignoring her first councilor's unseemly mirth, "is that waterwheels will no longer be necessary to power manufactories, which means, of course, that they can be located anywhere, not simply where a river or waterfall makes it convenient. Still, the problem of transport, especially of raw materials, remains. However, allow me to tell you about a new mechanism one of Master Howsmyn's artisans is in the process of developing and which is likely to bring about a very significant change in our transportation system. He calls it a 'steam automotive,' since it moves under its own power, and—"

.XIV.
Charisian Embassy,
Siddar City,
Republic of Siddarmark,
and,
Royal Palace,
Eraystor,
Princedom of Emerald,
Empire of Charis

The Charisian standard atop the embassy's roof snapped briskly on the evening breeze. The city was calmer, although there was a sense of unease stemming from the departure of so much of the army strength which had been concentrated in and around it. Confident of the arrival of Duke Eastshare, Lord Protector Greyghor and Lord Daryus had sent almost half the forty-six thousand regulars in Old Province off to help defend the loyal portion of Shiloh. It wasn't that the citizens of Siddar City distrusted their leaders' judgment; it was simply that so many terrible things had happened since the previous fall that they were waiting to see what new disaster was headed their way.

Cayleb Ahrmahk could understand that as he stood on the rooftop balcony which had become his favorite vantage point and gazed out across the city. The sun was settling steadily in the west, and he'd just finished a late-night conversation with Sharleyan in distant Cherayth.

"You do realize," a deep voice said musingly from behind him, "that there *are* rifles in Temple Loyalist hands now, don't you?"

"And your point is?" he asked without turning.

"That it wouldn't be so very difficult, with you standing up here like a target in a gallery, for one of those rifles in the hands of some ill-intentioned soul to hit you from any one of several firing points I can think of right offhand."

"At which point my 'antiballistic undies,' as Sharley's taken to calling them, will save my no doubt reckless life, right?"

"As long as you're not unfortunate enough to get hit in, oh, the *head*, for instance. Not beyond the realm of possibility, I'd think. And you might remember just how battered and bruised Sharley got from a *pistol* ball. Don't you think it's remotely possible a rifle bullet might be even more painful? For that matter, a bit of splintered rib driven into a lung or, say, an aorta would probably come under the heading of A Really Bad Thing, too, now that I think about it."

"My, you *are* in a pessimistic mood." Cayleb turned. "Is there a partic-ular reason you're so intent on raining on my parade?"

"I just worry sometimes," Merlin Athrawes said in a much more serious tone. "I don't want to try to wrap you up in cotton wool and protect you from every bump and bruise, Cayleb. But . . . all you flesh-and-bloods are so damned *fragile*. I just . . . don't want to lose any more of you."

The *seijin's* sapphire eyes were darker than the evening light could ac-count for, and Cayleb reached out and rested his hands on the taller man's shoulders.

"What brought that on?" he asked more gently. "Watching Sharley and Mahrak?"

"Partly, I suppose." Merlin twitched a shrug. "That and watching her with Archbishop Ulys and thinking about Archbishop Pawal and everybody else Clyntahn's butchers killed. It shouldn't bother me that much, I suppose. I mean, all the deaths of all the 'Rakurai' combined are such a tiny, insignifi-cant number compared to the people he's killed by proxy here in the Repub-lic. But it *does* bother me, damn it!" His face tightened. "I *knew* too many of those people, Cayleb. I *cared* about them. And now they're gone."

"It happens." The words might have been flip; the tone was not, and Cayleb smiled sadly. "And it doesn't happen just to you theoretically im-mortal *seijin* PICAs, either. But with the embassy so crowded, this is the only place I can be sure of the privacy to talk to Sharleyan out loud, and that's worth a little risk. It really is."

He shook Merlin gently, and the *seijin* chuckled.

"Well, I don't suppose I can argue with that. But since the only reason you can be sure of that privacy, even up here, is that the deadly, mysterious *Seijin* Merlin is standing menacingly at the bottom of the stairs to keep anyone from disturbing you, I hope you've already enjoyed a satisfactory conversation."

"Why?" Cayleb cocked his head. "Did you have an appointment somewhere?"

"As a matter of fact, I do."

Cayleb's eyes narrowed. He looked at Merlin very intently for a moment.

"Is this more of whatever took you off so mysteriously last month?"

"In a manner of speaking."

Merlin met the emperor's gaze with level eyes. He offered no further explanation, however, and Cayleb held his gaze for another second or two, then drew a deep breath.

"All right," he said simply. "Do you know when we should expect you back? I only ask because Paityr, Ahndrai, and the rest of the detachment have to cover for you if anyone asks any questions. They'd probably appreciate any little hint I might be able to give them about just how long that will be."

"I should be back well before dawn," Merlin assured him.

"In that case," Cayleb released his shoulders, "go. I'll see you in the morning."

"Of course, Your Majesty."

Merlin bowed with rather more formality than usual when the two of them were alone. Then he turned, headed down the stairs, and disappeared.

▼ ▼ ▼

Ohlyvya Baytz sat on the balcony above her garden, gazing down onto its lantern-lit paths and listening to the night wyverns' soft whistles, and smiled gently. She doubted Prince Zhan had realized she was up here—he was a very . . . direct young man, rather like his older brother—but she knew her daughter had. It was probably just as well. Young Zhan would be fifteen in another few months, and Princess Mahrya was a very attractive twenty-one. She was also betrothed to him, and in the three and a half years since that marriage had been arranged he'd gone from a somewhat bemused little boy not at all certain about this entire marrying business to a very nice-looking and well-grown young man with all a young man's curiosity about the opposite sex. True, it was a marriage of state, arranged for the most cold-blooded of political reasons. The two of them had spent much of the time since in one another's company, however, and it was obvious more than hormones were involved in their attitudes.

Not that Zhan's hormones aren't roaring along quite nicely. It's a good thing he's basically such a nice young man. And that Haarahld and Cayleb both had such strong views on the subject of proper restraint. At least he's thankfully free of the notion that just because he's a prince, the rules don't apply to him! And, of course, having said that, it probably was a good thing Mahrya knew I was up here. Not that anything remotely improper would've happened if I hadn't been, of course. Oh, of course not!

She snorted in amusement. The truth was that betrothals were serious things on Safehold. Mother Church had seen to that. They were legal contracts as binding in many ways as the marriage itself, although it had always been possible for the wealthy and powerful to acquire the proper indulgence to slip out of one or have it annulled if that seemed desirable. It wasn't all that unusual for a bride to appear at the altar pregnant, or even accompanied by a young child, without anyone looking particularly askance, however, as long as the betrothal period had been long enough to account for it. It wasn't considered the very best form, but no scandal usually attached to it. Princes and princesses, however, were just a bit more visible than most young couples, and she rather hoped the two of them would bear that in mind for the next couple of years. She wasn't foolish enough to think such an intelligent and resourceful pair hadn't managed to evade their various keepers and bodyguards long enough for at least a little discreet experimentation, but she was philosophical about it. Far better for them to come to know and care for one another, complete with the aforesaid discreet experimentation, than for Mahrya to never even have met her proposed husband before her wedding.

Yes, it is, she thought, *but it didn't work out that badly for you, did it?* Her lips curved in a tender smile. *He was already plump, poor thing. But there was something so . . .* endearing *about him. Like a gawky puppy. I wonder how many times he'd been told he* had *to marry me to legitimize the dynasty? I know how many times they told* me *I had to marry* him *to make sure the legitimate dynasty's blood still sat on the throne! But he was so eager, so* earnest, *about trying to put me at ease. And I think he probably thought the only reason an attractive young lady would have looked at him—if she hadn't had to marry him for reasons of state, of course—was because he was a prince. But he never was really fair to himself. He always thought of himself as a clever little man, not simply as a* man *. . . when he was all the man anyone could ever have needed.*

A single tear brimmed at the corner of her eye, but it wasn't a tear of sorrow. Not anymore. Regret, perhaps, for all the years they'd lost, but the memory of all the years they'd *had*—that defeated the sorrow. And she only hoped Mahrya and Zhan would find the same happiness she and Nahrmahn had.

And at least they probably won't have to worry about figuring out where the various parts go, the way we did, she told herself with a suddenly impish grin. *That's something. Besides—*

"Excuse me, Ohlyvya," a deep, familiar voice said behind her, and she turned quickly.

"Merlin!" Her eyes widened in surprise—at seeing him here, not that he'd managed to get to her balcony without anyone spotting him along the way. "I didn't expect you. Why didn't you com?"

"Because this is something best done personally," he told her with a bow which was deeper than usual and oddly formal. "It's not the sort of conversation we should have over the com."

"Really?" She regarded him more narrowly. "That sounds faintly ominous, as Nahrmahn would have said."

"Interesting you should mention Nahrmahn," Merlin said with a strange smile. "He has quite a lot to do with this visit, as a matter of fact."

"What?" Her brow furrowed in confusion, and he waved one hand at the balcony's marble bench.

"Why don't you sit down? I have a story to tell you."

▼   ▼   ▼

"And that's how it happened," Merlin said, twenty minutes later. "I know I had no right to make a decision like that without consulting him—and you. But there wasn't time, I didn't know if it was going to work, and you had enough grief without hoping for something that might never come to pass."

Ohlyvya stared at him, her face pale and streaked with tears in the balcony's lamplight. She pressed her hand to her quivering lips, and he could almost physically feel the tension trembling through her muscles. At that moment, he thought, what she'd learned from him and Owl in the last two years must be at war with everything she'd ever learned before that.

"I can't—" She broke off and swallowed hard. "I can't . . . take it in," she said then, her voice hoarse. "He's *dead*, Merlin. I *buried* him!"

"So is Nimue Alban, Ohlyvya," he said gently, his blue eyes dark and bottomless.

"But . . . but I never *knew* Nimue." She lowered her hand and managed a tight, strained smile. It was fleeting. "Intellectually—here—" she touched her temple, "I know the man I see in front of me is really a machine with someone else's memories. But that isn't *real* to me, Merlin. Nimue isn't—*you* are. It's . . . different."

"Is it really? Or is it just that you feel like you'd be cheating?"

"Cheating?" She looked at him. "Cheating *who*?"

"That would be my own attitude," he told her. "On the other hand, I haven't committed myself to a rebellion against the only Church, the only faith, I've ever known. The Church of God Awaiting is nothing to me but an enormous con game, a scam perpetrated upon the entire human race by a batch of megalomaniacs who were loony as bedbugs, whatever their intentions may've been. It's not hard for me to kick over that anthill, Ohlyvya, but I think it could be harder for you than your intellect's ready to admit."

She opened her mouth, but he held up one hand, stopping her.

"I'm not saying your rebellion isn't absolutely one hundred percent genuine. In fact, it's probably even more genuine—if that's an allowable term—than my own, because it *did* require you to think about and reject the lies you'd been taught all your life. But human minds are funny things. Sometimes, they punish themselves for doing what they know was the right thing because someone they loved and trusted once told them it was the *wrong* thing. So are you punishing yourself for having dared to defy the archangels by feeling as if you'd be cheating to accept that Nahrmahn isn't really gone?"

"I—" She began, then paused suddenly and looked around. "Is he watching us right now?"

"No." Merlin shook his head. "He's had Owl take his VR offline until you or I tell him to put it back online. He wanted you to be able to think or say anything you wanted to—or needed to—without worrying about how it might affect his feelings. This decision is up to you, Ohlyvya. He doesn't want to put any more pressure on you than he can help, because—as he put it—God knows just sending me to tell you about him has to be pressure enough for any long-suffering wife to put up with."

She gurgled a strained laugh.

"Oh, that does sound like him! *Just* like him."

"I know." Merlin rose, crossed to the balcony railing, and looked out across the garden. "I can't tell you for certain that this is *really* Nahrmahn, Ohlyvya." His voice came back across his shoulder. "That's because I can't tell you for certain that I'm really Nimue Alban. I *think* I am . . . usually, but I suspect I'll never know for certain until the day this PICA finally powers down for the last time. Maybe when that happens I'll find out all I ever really was was an electronic echo of someone who died a thousand years before I ever opened my eyes on this planet."

He turned to face her once more, his eyes dark.

"Maikel doesn't think that's going to happen, and as a general rule, I'm prepared to accept his expertise where souls are concerned. If that man doesn't have it right, no one I've ever known did. So all I can tell you is that I *think* this really is Nahrmahn, the man who loves you. That's what I believe. And he asked me to tell you one more thing."

"What?" she asked very softly.

"He asked me to tell you *he* thinks he's Nahrmahn, and that he loves you. That there are still things the two of you have never told each other—that he always meant, or at least wanted, to tell you. That he wants to tell them to you now. And that he's pretty sure that if he isn't the 'real' Nahrmahn, the original couldn't possibly object to your taking what comfort you can out of at least talking to him. After all, *he* wouldn't."

She laughed again, a much less strained sound this time, and shook her head.

"And that sounds even *more* like him! I can even see his smile when he said it! He always was an unscrupulous devil when it came to getting what he wanted."

"I see you're an excellent judge of character," Merlin said with a chuckle, and she laughed yet again. The laugh segued into a smile, pensive and still more than a little strained, but definitely a smile.

"He hasn't told me this, Ohlyvya," Merlin said after a moment, "but I think he plans on having his VR terminated on the day you die."

Her smile disappeared and her eyes widened, one hand rising to her throat, and Merlin shook his head quickly.

"I don't mean he's going to terminate tonight if you don't feel you can talk to him! I just mean that when the time comes for you to die, he intends to follow you to wherever it is you go. I think . . . I think he doesn't want either of you to be left behind. And I think he believes that if he isn't really Nahrmahn, if despite everything he thinks and feels neither he nor I are truly 'real,' it won't matter one way or the other when he shuts down. But if he *is* Nahrmahn, he's not going to hang on to an existence here when it might cost him the opportunity to follow you, or whatever of both of you survives."

Her eyes softened, and she drew a deep, tremulous breath.

"Do I have to decide tonight?"

"No. And it's not like you're going to leave him on tenterhooks while you think about it, either." Merlin grinned suddenly. "Now that I think about it, that might be another reason he had Owl take him offline. It would be like him to combine selflessness with self-interest, wouldn't it?"

"Yes, it certainly would," she said in a rather more entertained voice, a trace of amusement glinting in her eye. "*Just* like him!"

"That's the second time you've said that—'just like him,' I mean," Merlin pointed out gently.

"I know. It's just . . . hard." Her expression was calmer, her eyes deep and thoughtful. "I've been through losing him. I think part of it is that I'm afraid of finding out it isn't really *him* after all—that I'll have to go through losing him all over again."

"I guess it's like Maikel's always telling us." She looked at him and he shrugged. "There comes a time when we just have to *decide*, Ohlyvya. Sometimes all we can consult is our heart, because the mind doesn't supply the answers we need. So what it comes down to, I think, is whether or not you're willing to risk that. Do you have the courage to open yourself to that sort of possible hurt in the hope of finding that sort of possible joy?"

She looked at him oddly for a moment, then rose and crossed to stand directly in front of him. She reached out, laying both palms flat against his armored breastplate, and looked up into those dark blue eyes.

"Merlin," she asked quietly, "was Nimue ever in love?"

He froze for a long, quivering heartbeat, then very gently covered the hands on his breastplate with his own.

"No," he said, his deep voice soft. "Nimue loved many people in her life, Ohlyvya. Her parents, Commodore Pei, Shan-wei, the people who fought and, in the end, died with her. But she was never brave enough to love someone the way you loved Nahrmahn, the way Cayleb and Sharleyan love each other. She knew they were all going to die, that they could never have a future together, and she wasn't willing to open her heart to the pain of loving someone when she knew what the end had to be."

She stared up at him, hearing the stark regret, tasting the honesty it had taken for him to admit that. And then she bent forward, laying her cheek atop the long-fingered, sinewy swordsman's hands which had covered hers.

"Poor Nimue," she whispered. "Trust me in this, Merlin. If she ever had opened that heart of hers, if she'd found the right man, it wouldn't have mattered to him how little time they had. And"—she drew a deep breath—"I think I see now another reason why you love so deeply here, on Safehold."

"I don't know about that. Maybe I never will. But I do know the people I've met here, on this world, are worth everything. They're worth what Commodore Pei and Pei Shan-wei and all the others of the Alexandria Enclave gave, and they're worth everything Nimue Alban gave."

"No, we aren't," she told him, head never moving from where it lay against his chest, "but because you *believe* we are, we have to be worth it anyway. You don't leave a choice."

They stood there for at least two full minutes, and then she drew a deep, lung-cleansing breath and straightened. She leaned back, looking up at his face once more, and cupped his cheeks in her hands.

"Damn you, Merlin Athrawes," she said softly. "Damn you for making all of us pretend we're characters in some legend somewhere! It's a lot more comfortable being one of those people who just tries to get along in the world, but you couldn't let us do that, could you?"

"That's me," he told her with a crooked smile. "Just a natural-born troublemaker who never could leave well enough alone."

"Which sounds a lot like someone else I once knew, now that you mention it." She drew another breath. "And since it does, I suppose I'd better talk to him about all this, hadn't I? Did you say *I* could ask Owl to . . . wake him up?"

"I think he'd like that," Merlin told her, touching her cheek in return. "I think he'd like that a lot."

.XV.
Royal Palace,
City of Cherayth,
Kingdom of Chisholm,
Empire of Charis

Irys Daykyn tried to still the flutter deep in the pit of her stomach as she followed Edwyrd Seahamper down the passageway to the suite reserved for Sharleyan and Cayleb whenever they were in Cherayth. She hadn't spent much time in the royal palace—as Archbishop Maikel's charges, she and Daivyn had been housed with him in a guest suite in Archbishop Ulys' palace adjoining the cathedral—but she knew very few people were admitted to this wing, and even fewer of them to Whiterock Tower. The second oldest part of the entire palace, the tower had been thoroughly renovated at least twice during its lengthy lifespan. It also happened to be the most secure, heavily fortified portion of the entire complex, a grim reminder of a time when this palace had been, in very fact, a fortress . . . and one which had been needed, more than once.

Seahamper was only a sergeant, but she'd noticed lieutenants, captains, and even majors—with one exception—tended to defer to him. She supposed that when someone had been Empress Sharleyan's personal armsman since she was a little girl, and when that someone was also the only survivor of the guards who'd died to protect her at Saint Agtha's, he acquired a little extra authority.

She suspected Tobys Raimair was going to find himself in a similar position where Daivyn was concerned, one day.

Assuming Daivyn survived.

My, aren't you the gloomy one? she thought. *Anything else you'd care to be depressed about today? It's sunny out, but I'm sure clouds could come up and a tornado could sweep through. Or we could have a nice roaring fire that burns the entire city. Or . . . I know—a tidal wave! That would be just about perfect, wouldn't it?*

She snorted at her own perversity, then felt herself unconsciously straightening her shoulders as Seahamper paused, glanced over his shoulder, and knocked gently on a polished wooden door.

"Your Majesty?"

"Yes, Edwyrd," a voice came back through the door. "Show them in, please."

"Of course, Your Majesty." He tugged on the bright brass handle, opening the heavy slab of wood—it was at least two inches thick, Irys saw; probably a leftover from the old fortress days—and bowed to her and her companions.

Irys' eyebrows tried to rise as she realized she, Coris, and Daivyn were to be admitted to Sharleyan's presence without a single Imperial Guardsman present. Not only that, but Coris wore a belt dagger, and Seahamper didn't even ask for it. From the look in his eyes, the sergeant wasn't what anyone would have called overjoyed by that minor fact, but he only held the door patiently, waiting.

"A moment, Sergeant," Coris said, and drew his dagger. He flipped it in his hand, extending the hilt to Seahamper. "I promise it would have stayed in its sheath," he said with a whimsical smile, "but I think we'll probably both feel better if it stays here with you, instead."

Seahamper looked at him for a moment, then bowed again, more deeply, and took the weapon. He smiled—not so much at Coris, Irys thought, as at some memory—and closed the door quietly behind them.

The Corisandians crossed a vestibule into a chamber, fitted as a sitting room, which was surprisingly large, given the Tower's dimensions. It must take up most of this floor, she realized, and there was another stair in the corner, leading to the floor above.

Sharleyan sat alone in a comfortable chair beside a cavernous fireplace in which someone had installed one of Ehdwyrd Howsmyn's iron stoves. Afternoon sunlight streamed in through the window behind her, touching her black hair with hints of fire, lighting stray wisps like coppery wire, and Crown Princess Alahnah was in her lap. Irys felt an even stronger flicker of surprise and—she admitted to herself—satisfaction at the thought that Sharleyan was prepared not simply to meet them herself without a bodyguard but to do the same thing with her daughter and the heir to the imperial throne. She couldn't imagine another crowned head of state doing that.

Except for Cayleb, she thought then. *Except for Cayleb.*

"Please, be seated," Sharleyan invited, and Irys and Daivyn sat in the two chairs facing hers. Actually, Irys sat and Daivyn perched, balancing on the front of the chair seat, his wiry young frame tense. She doubted he fully understood what this meeting was all about, really, but he understood enough to be acutely nervous. Despite which, and despite all the uncertainty and fear which had touched his life, he'd trusted Coris and her without question, and she suppressed an almost overpowering urge to reach out and smooth that unruly hair back from his forehead.

Coris didn't sit. Instead, he positioned himself behind them, with Daivyn to his left and Irys to his right. He stood with one hand on the back of each chair, and Irys saw Sharleyan smile slightly as she noticed the empty dagger sheath.

"I see history has a tendency to repeat," she murmured. Irys cocked her head questioningly, but Sharleyan only shook her own head and waved one hand. "Never mind. It was just an old memory. Maybe it will turn out to be a good omen as well."

Irys nodded, although she had no idea what the empress was talking about, and folded her hands in her lap. For some reason she felt even younger than her age at that moment.

"Daivyn, Irys, Earl Coris," Sharleyan said, nodding gravely to each of them in turn. "I know you're all more than a little nervous about this meeting. In your places, I would be, too. However, I've been thinking a great deal about what you said to me aboard *Destiny*, Irys, and I can't quite shake the conviction that the name of that ship may have been more appropriate than her builders realized when they bestowed it."

She paused, and Irys glanced up and to her left, looking at Coris' profile, then back at the empress.

"I think I'd like to believe that, Your Majesty," she said finally. "Daivyn and I have been buffeted about enough. I'd like to think we do have a destiny somewhere we can find. On that doesn't leave us drifting at the mercy of the storm forever."

"I remember something *Seijin* Merlin said to me once," Sharleyan told her, looking levelly into her hazel eyes. "He said destiny is what we make it. That it's our own choices, our own decisions, that lead us through life. There are other factors, sometimes—often—elements we can't control. But we can *always* control our own decisions. Sometimes they're good, sometimes they're bad, but they're always *ours*, and no one can take them away from us . . . unless we let them."

"That's undoubtedly true, Your Majesty," Coris said. "But sometimes all the decisions in the world can't change what happens to us."

"No, they can't, My Lord." Sharleyan's eyes rose to his. "But they can change why we do what *we* do, and in the end, on the most basic level, isn't that really all that matters?"

Coris looked back at her for several seconds. Then he inclined his head silently, and she looked back to Irys and Daivyn.

"Daivyn, I know you're young, and I know you're worried, and I know you're wondering what this is all about. Well, I'm going to tell you, and then you'll have a decision to make. Irys and Earl Coris can advise you, they can try to help you, but in the end the decision will be yours."

Daivyn's brown eyes went huge, and Sharleyan smiled slightly.

"It's okay to be nervous," she told him. "I was only about a year older than you are now when I became Queen, you know." His eyes went even rounder as he tried to digest the preposterous proposition that someone as obviously aged as the empress had ever been *that* young. "No, it's true," she assured him. "I was. And for the first few months?" He nodded. "I threw up before every council meeting."

His jaw dropped, and she dimpled as she smiled much more broadly.

"It's true," she repeated in an almost conspiratorial tone. "I promise. So if you're feeling nervous right now, I understand entirely. But please, if you think you're going to need to throw up, warn us ahead of time, all right? I'd like to ring the bell and get Sairaih to bring us a basin, first."

Daivyn goggled at her for a moment, then surprised himself with a bright little spurt of laughter.

"I promise, Your Majesty," he said, and she winked at him. Then she looked back at Irys and Coris, and her expression turned serious once more.

"My Lord, I haven't spoken directly with you about this, but I know you and Irys have talked about it at length. I know she's also discussed it with Archbishop Maikel, and he's discussed with me the portions of their conversations she authorized him to share with me. I assure both of you that he did not, and would not, violate her confidence by discussing anything more than that with me or with anyone else."

She paused until Irys nodded, then continued.

"First, let me say I won't pretend for an instant that I wasn't delighted by what Irys said to me. Frankly, it was more than I'd allowed myself to hope I might ever hear from her or, to be honest, any other member of her family. Given all the anger and hatred—and blood—that lies between our houses, it took someone with one of what Maikel calls 'the great souls' to reach out that far.

"Second, let me acknowledge that I'm fully aware of the implications of this situation—of all the ways in which it could contribute to the safety and the security of the Charisian Empire, and of all the advantages which could stem from it for all of us.

"And third, let me make it clear that where this could lead in the end could be disastrous for all three of you."

She let that last sentence lay between them, cold and heavy, stinking of danger, before she sat back, wrapped her arms around her daughter, and spoke again.

"Irys, you told me you can no longer support Mother Church. That you believe you have no choice but to fight against Clyntahn and the rest of the Group of Four in any way you can. I think there's a way for you—for all of us—to do that, but if you do—if Daivyn does—you make yourselves the declared enemy of the Inquisition, of the Group of Four, of every Temple Loyalist in the world, and of Mother Church herself. I think you understand that, but before I go any further, I need to *know* you do."

Irys fought down an almost overpowering need to look up at Coris. This was a question she had to answer herself—not just for Sharleyan, but for *herself,* as well. And so she looked levelly into the eyes of the most powerful woman in the world and nodded.

"I do, Your Majesty."

She was a bit surprised by how clearly those four words came out. Like Sharleyan's statement, it lay between them, yet this was clean, with the cold, sharp taste of ice and an edge of polished steel.

"But the Inquisition and Mother Church have already declared themselves *our* enemies," she went on. "I know the official story is that *Seijin* Merlin kidnapped us on your orders and Phylyp sold us to you. It could hardly be anything else, with Clyntahn in the Grand Inquisitor's chair. And I'm not so foolish as to believe for a moment that Daivyn or I would ever be allowed the opportunity to tell anyone the truth." She smiled without humor. "Under the circumstances, whether we openly fight the Church and lose or simply wait for his inquisitors to dig us out of our final burrow, the outcome will be very much the same, don't you think?"

"I suppose so." Sharleyan rocked Alahnah gently. "Another thing *Seijin* Merlin once said to me—I'm sure he was quoting someone else; he's very wise and well-informed, but not really the fount of *all* knowledge—'If we do not hang together, we will all surely hang separately.' It does rather cut to the heart of the matter, doesn't it?"

"Yes, it does."

"Very well, here's what I propose."

Sharleyan stopped rocking the little girl in her lap and her expression had become deadly serious.

"Understand that I'm speaking now not just for myself but for Cayleb. We've told the world we're co-rulers, and we are. If I pledge the faith of the Empire of Charis to you, Cayleb will honor that pledge, even if the whole world goes to ruin in the process."

She looked at all three of them, and Irys felt a strange shiver run through her bones. What must it be like, she wondered, to have that kind of faith in another human being? For two people, be they ever so close, trust one another however deeply, to bind themselves to each accept the other's decision, even in a choice that was life or death for an entire empire? No wonder people spoke of them not as Cayleb or Sharleyan but as Cayleb-and-Sharleyan, as one being with two hearts, two minds . . . and one soul.

And no wonder they'd already entered the realms of legend.

"I propose to allow the three of you to return to Corisande aboard a Charisian warship—I think *Destiny* would serve quite well for the purpose. You'll travel with Archbishop Maikel as he continues his pastoral journey. His will be the only official Charisian presence in your party, and you'll be under his protection until you touch Corisandian soil. At that time, Daivyn, you'll meet with your Regency Council for the first time, and the members of that council will become your protectors."

She looked up over the suddenly very still prince's head to meet Coris' eyes.

"Messages will be sent ahead to General Zhanstyn. They will inform him that no Charisian military forces are to be present at the time you land in Manchyr. That Prince Daivyn's Regency Council is to have full freedom to determine where he will be housed, who will be assigned to protect him, and where and when he will travel within his own princedom. Should the Regency Council or General Gahrvai desire assistance from General Zhanstyn or any other Charisian soldier, Marine, or seaman, it will be provided. If he does not desire it, that will be his decision and the Regency Council's, and—if the Regency Council is guided by my advice, My Lord— yours as the legal guardian designated for Prince Daivyn by his father, and Princess Irys as his sister.

"The terms of the armistice arranged between Cayleb and Earl Anvil Rock and Earl Tartarian on behalf of the Regency Council will stand. I cannot compromise on that point. For Daivyn to be recognized by us as the legitimate, *reigning* Prince of Corisande, he must accept those terms. If he chooses not to, and the Regency Council crowns him Prince anyway, the Empire of Charis will feel justified in using military force to compel obedience to those terms . . . and it will. That decision, however, will be made by Corisandians. I hope it will be the right decision, but for better or worse, it must be *yours*, and it must be seen by your people to be yours. There will be those in Zion and elsewhere who will denounce any decision you make if it isn't to resume open warfare against Charis. Our only defense against that can be, must be—and *will* be—the truth, and that truth must be as widely known in Corisande as possible.

"For reasons I'm sure you and Earl Coris, at least, understand fully, Irys, it simply isn't possible at this time for Corisande to be independent of Charisian control. We've tried—at the cost of Charisian blood, on occasion—to control the violence in Corisande with a minimum of Corisandian bloodshed, to promote peace and tolerance, and to obey the rule of law rather than govern with an iron rod. I hope you'll see for yourself when you reach Manchyr that that's the plain, unvarnished truth. Yet I can think of no circumstances under which we could possibly agree at this time to Corisandian independence. That's why the terms of the armistice—at a minimum—must stand."

Irys swallowed. Sharleyan's tone was measured, deliberate, almost harsh. Irys wasn't certain what she'd expected to hear, but if the terms of the armistice—the armistice which subjected Corisande to military occupation, to disarmament, to control by Charis—were the *minimum* Charis could accept, what more must Sharleyan be about to propose?!

"There is an alternative to occupation and foreign control, however," Sharleyan said, almost as if she'd read Irys' mind. "That alternative is the same one Cayleb and I offered to Nahrmahn of Emerald and Gorjah of Tarot. Membership in the Empire of Charis—not as an occupied territory, but as an integral unit, with internal autonomy under the constitution which governs the existing Empire. With representation in the Imperial Parliament. With Daivyn on the throne of Corisande as his father's heir, sustained and supported by the Imperial Charisian Navy and the Imperial Charisian Army. With Corisandian troops and seamen raised, trained, armed, and integrated into the imperial military at all levels. With full Corisandian participation in imperial markets, trading routes, and banking houses—with full access to Charisian manufactories and innovations. The full integration of the Corisandian Church into the Church of Charis. And with Daivyn as the third-ranking noble of the Charisian Empire after the heir to the throne herself, second only to Nahrmahn Gareyt of Emerald and Gorjah of Tarot."

Irys' eyes had gone as huge as Daivyn's, and Daivyn himself sat almost paralyzed on the edge of his chair. Behind her, she heard Coris inhale sharply.

"Our policy, our desire, from the very beginning has been to expand the Empire not by conquest but by covenant," Sharleyan said softly. "What's conquered by the sword is owned only so long as the sword stays sharp. What's brought together in amity, in recognition of common needs and purpose—of common enemies—has the strength to stand even after swords are no longer required. As Cayleb said to me in his proposal letter, what we need isn't an alliance which can and does change as the tides of chance dictate, but a union. A common identity. An empire strong enough to survive the hurricane sweeping over our world—one in which prosperity and freedom are the common property of all, and where the corruption of those evil men in Zion can never triumph. We conquered Corisande because we had no other choice; now, perhaps, we have one after all, and if we do, we choose to take it. We choose to risk what you may do in Corisande outside our custody because we believe the prize we offer both to you and to ourselves is amply worth that risk."

She sat back in her chair, cradling her daughter, and looked at them levelly. For what seemed an eternity, Irys could only look back at her, stunned by the offer. Then Daivyn reached out and touched her on the knee.

"Irys?" His voice sounded very small, and she saw the wonder and confusion—and the trust—in his brown eyes. "Irys?" he repeated. "What should I say?"

"Oh, Daivy," she said, and reached out both hands to him, gathering him up, holding him on her lap as she had when he was much younger and she herself had been only a girl. She laid her cheek against the top of his head, hugging him tightly. "Oh, Daivy, I don't know. I know what I *want* to say, but I just don't know. This . . . this is more than I expected." She looked over her shoulder. "Phylyp?"

"I can't say it's . . . totally unexpected," Coris said slowly, meeting her eyes and then looking over her head at Sharleyan. "The scope of it, yes. And the degree of autonomy Her Majesty's offering. But something like this, the inclusion of Corisande in the Empire, is inevitable, Irys. As Her Majesty says, Charis has no choice. And the truth is that Daivyn doesn't, either. The men in Zion who ordered him killed can't—they literally *cannot*—allow him or you to live. It's that simple. I suppose a good, devious spymaster really ought to recommend that you *pretend* to accept Her Majesty's terms. Let Daivyn swear whatever oaths they require, because an oath sworn under duress—and how could it not be under duress, under the circumstances?—can't be binding. As far as that goes, Her Majesty and His Majesty have both been excommunicated by the Grand Vicar himself, so any oath sworn to them is automatically void in Mother Church's eyes. So, by all means, accept her terms and prepare to be bound by them only so long as it's convenient.

"But this isn't the time for good, devious spymasters." His voice was soft, his eyes level as they met Sharleyan's over the head of the prince and princess he loved. "This is a time for truth, and for me to speak not as your father's spymaster, but as his friend, who's been allowed to see things he . . . couldn't. As the friend he asked to protect you and Daivyn. And what that friend has to say to you tonight is that, despite a lifetime of cynicism and calculation, I really can recognize truth when I hear it and generosity of heart when I see it. I'm not blind to how advantageous it would be for Charis to have Corisande willingly become part of its empire. I'm not blind to the way in which this diminishes Daivyn's authority as a sovereign prince, free to make his own policy as he pleases, to make war when he chooses. But what it offers him—what it offers all of Corisande—is a chance to live the way God meant men and women to live. Not as the slaves of some petty secular tyrant, and not at the whim of some psychotic in an orange cassock in Zion, but following their own consciences in peace and security."

He drew a deep breath and looked down at Irys once more, meeting those hazel eyes of her dead mother, and he smiled.

"My advice is to accept Her Majesty's terms, Your Highness," he said simply.

There was silence for a long, still moment, and then Sharleyan cleared her throat.

"There is one other small, minor point," she said, and Irys felt herself stiffen, wondering if this was the velvet-draped dagger all the rest of Sharleyan's offer had been designed to hide. She didn't want to think that, but she was her father's daughter, and so she made herself face the possibility.

"Yes, Your Majesty?"

She was pleased her voice sounded so level.

"Corisande and Emerald have in common that they were both the avowed enemies of Charis—Old Charis, I mean—well before the Group of Four sponsored the attack upon King Haarahld. Since that's indisputably the case, I'm afraid we're inclined to require one additional surety from you."

"And that surety is . . . what?" Irys asked.

"No more than we asked of Prince Nahrmahn," Sharleyan told her. "We believe it's particularly important to bind our house to its allies in a case such as this one. I considered proposing a marriage between Daivyn and Alahnah, but upon contemplating it more fully, I decided the age differential was simply too great. And that, unfortunately, left me with really only one option, I'm afraid."

She looked at Irys with a regretful expression.

"The only alternative I can see, Irys, is to require *you* to marry my stepson Hektor."

Irys felt a sudden, bright bubble—one whose strength astonished her—welling up within her, and Sharleyan shook her head, her expression sad but her eyes twinkling.

"I realize it's a great sacrifice to ask of you, but I'm afraid I'm really going to have to insist."

JUNE

YEAR OF GOD 896

It looks like not everybody got the word, Sir," Lieutenant Pawal Blahdysnberg said dryly as yet another schooner put her helm hard over and
sheared off wildly. He shook his head, his expression a mixture of amusement and resignation. "I wonder if this one thinks we're demon spawn or
just hopelessly on fire?"

"Judging by how hard he jibed, my money's on demon spawn." Captain Halcom Bahrns' tone carried more disgust than amusement, and he
shook his head. "He almost had the mast out of her. And that's a *coaster*, not
somebody who's been off in Siddarmark or Chisholm for the last six months.
Haven't the idiots spent *any* time getting drunk ashore and listening to the
sea stories about us?"

Blahdysnberg suppressed a chuckle. He didn't *think* the captain would
take his head off if he laughed, but he wasn't positive. Still . . . .

"Actually, you know, Sir, at least at first, this"—he jutted his chin at the
thick plumes of smoke rising from HMS *Delthak*'s twin, tall funnels—"is
probably going to work for us the first time the Temple Loyalists see us
coming."

"And they *will* see us coming," Bahrns replied. He, too, looked up at
the smoke. "That's got to be visible from twenty miles in good weather."

"Well, Sir, they didn't exactly design these for sneaking up on people,"
Blahdysnberg said cheerfully. "And to tell the truth, seeing us coming won't
help the sorry bastards much, when you come down to it. They won't be
able to *outrun* us, that's for sure, and when we catch up with them . . . . "

He let his voice trail off, then rapped his knuckles on the steel armor
and shrugged.

"Once we've got some damned guns on board, anyway," Bahrns growled,
but he was forced to nod. And the truth was, he was nowhere near as affronted by the uninformed's reaction to his smoking, snorting command as he
might choose to sound. There were, however, appearances to be maintained.

He turned forward and found himself looking directly over the ship's
bow, which was just plain wrong. And that was only one of the . . . uncon-
ventional things about his new vessel. Ships were supposed to be conned from
aft, from the quarterdeck, where the officer of the deck and the helmsman

could see the sails and know what the ship was doing. But not in HMS *Del-thak* or any of the other river-class gunboats. No, he and Blahdysnberg were standing on a narrow, bridgelike platform wrapped around an armored wheelhouse—what Sir Dustyn Olyvyr called a "conning tower"—located at the *front* of the ship's slab-sided casemate. It was a profoundly unnatural place from which to command a vessel at sea, much less to locate the ship's helm, but that was where they were. And the truth was, it actually made sense, however bizarre it felt.

His new command had no sails, so there was no need for anyone to be stationed where he could keep an eye on them. In fact, it had only a single mast—one spar, standing on end, supporting a single fat pod ninety feet above the casemate for the ship's lookout. And locating the wheel and "conning tower" so far forward and at such a height above deck level at least gave him excellent visibility ahead. Considering the speed of which *Delthak* was capable, that was scarcely a minor consideration.

She was squat, unlovely, and had all the grace of an old barn, he thought, and yet she also had an undeniable presence. A hundred and forty feet overall, she would have displaced just over twelve hundred tons (according to Sir Dustyn's new way of calculating) with her weapons and normal load of coal and feed water on board. At the moment, she displaced rather more than that, and with her hundred-and-twenty-foot casemate—angling inwards at a sixty-degree angle, each side broken by eight gunports, and painted solid black, without the customary white strake—she seemed to sit heavily in the water, her shoulders hunched. She lacked the graceful bow of a galleon, with no cutwater and no flare, her stem rising straight and uncompromising out of the water, butting its way through waves in stubborn clouds of spray. They were scarcely thirty minutes out of The Throat into the Charis Sea, and the wind was barely a moderate breeze, raising waves no higher than four feet. They happened to be steaming directly into that wind, however, and water was already breaking white over *Delthak*'s short foredeck. When they met anything resembling a real wind, that water was going break white and *green* across the curved face of the casemate, and he hoped to hell those three forward gunports were as solidly built—and securely fastened—as Olyvyr and the Delthak Works foreman had assured him they were.

The truth was, he'd expected her to be an absolute pig in any sort of seaway, but it didn't look like she was going to be anywhere near as bad as he'd feared. For one thing, she had a very low freeboard compared to any true oceangoing vessel. She didn't look that way, given her angular profile, but the reality was that she sat much lower in the water than any galleon her size. That was going to make her wet, as her current behavior already demonstrated, but combined with her lack of masts, it also meant she exposed less area to the wind, which meant, in turn, that she was far more weatherly than he'd feared from her shallow draft. There simply wasn't much for the wind to push against, compared to a galleon's higher sides and lofty rig, when it tried to force her to leeward. For another thing, she answered the wheel with remarkable speed—far more rapidly than any galleon he'd ever served aboard. Indeed, she answered more quickly than most *galleys* had, when the Charisian Navy had still possessed galleys. She was still going to heave her guts out if the weather blew up, but for all her squattiness, she was actually remarkably maneuverable.

And she was fast. *Langhorne*, she was fast! In smooth water, at least. The resistance of those bluntly rounded bows was going to slow her down in any sort of heavy weather, but they were making well over twelve knots, and the engines weren't even straining.

I suppose putting in the extra engine has a little something to do with that, he reflected. *God knows I never would've expected "propellers" to be able to drive a ship this size this way, though, even with two of them.*

He reflected on how many oar blades it had taken to drive a considerably smaller and far more lightly built galley—or the sail area it took to drive a galleon—and shook his head. Admittedly, the three-bladed propellers on *Delthak*'s shafts were almost eight feet across, and they turned remarkably quickly—as many as two hundred and twenty revolutions in a single minute. He didn't even want to think about the amount of water they were moving at that speed, but he'd had her up to seventeen knots over a timed distance on Ithmyn's Lake. In fact, he'd *exceeded* seventeen knots according to the "pitometer" Ehdwyrd Howsmyn and Sir Dustyn Olyvyr had devised. He might even have been able to force her higher (at risk of overstraining her machinery) and that was just insane. He'd never heard of any other ship coming *remotely* close to that kind of speed, even with the most favorable possible combination of wind and wave.

She might be ugly, she might smoke like an out-of-control furnace, and her stokehold might reach temperatures that would make Shan-wei sweat, but the sheer exhilaration of speeding across the lake that quickly, watching the great white waves rolling away on either side of her blunt bow, the wake trailing away behind her. . . . that was something he'd never experienced before. Yet even at its most thrilling, there was something subtly wrong about the whole thing. Ships were supposed to have masts and sails—even galleys had them. That was the real reason *Delthak* and her sisters looked so unfinished—so incomplete—and where was the seamanship in simply standing on this "conning tower" bridge and telling the helmsman to come to starboard or to larboard?

Oh, stop it! Pawal's right, and you know it! Once you get the guns mounted, you'll command one of the four most powerful—and fastest—warships in the history of the world, and all you can do is moan about how it doesn't have masts?

His lips twitched in an unwilling grin at the thought. He was pretty sure High Admiral Rock Point hadn't picked the captains for his first four ironclads at random, which made his assignment a huge professional compliment, as well. And he was young for his rank. That might have something to do with the high admiral's choice, actually; he might have figured a younger officer, less set in his ways, might be more adaptable to the novel requirements of this entirely new sort of warship.

And be reasonable, Halcom. It was only five or six years ago the Navy didn't even have galleons. I don't suppose anyone's really had a lot of time to get "set in his ways," given how things keep changing.

He thought about that as the wind hummed around his ears with the speed of *Delthak*'s thumping, thrashing progress. Looked at from that sort of perspective, maybe the skipper of that schooner could be forgiven—or at least excused—for his panicky reaction. To suddenly find four iron monsters steaming at impossible speed almost directly into the wind had to come as a shock to anyone who'd never seen them before. Perhaps that schooner's master had seen *Mule* working in King's Harbor or off the Tellesberg waterfront, but the tug had only a single funnel, never moved at more than five or ten knots, and—aside from the smoke—was a remarkably tame introduction to the new generation of ships Ehdwyrd Howsmyn and Sir Dustyn were about to introduce.

He stepped around to the protruding wing of the bridge and looked aft, past the banner of smoke trailing from *Delthak*'s funnels, to where HMS *Saygin* followed in her wake. HMS *Tellesberg* and HMS *Hador* brought up the rear, visible more as additional smoke clouds than ships, but he knew exactly where they were. One thing they'd already discovered was that steam-powered vessels could maintain far tighter formation than sailing ships. Indeed, in some ways they could keep better formation than galleys, and that was going to have tactical implications of its own when the time came.

At the moment, however, what he felt most at knowing those other three ships were back there was relief. They'd just set out on a six-thousand-mile voyage, and they didn't have a single sail amongst them. He *did* have Shan-wei's own piles of bagged coal stacked all over his gundeck as well as crammed into the official bunker space, however. The absence of guns made that practical, but getting the coal dust out of the ship after they'd expended all the fuel wasn't going to be enjoyable. In fact, the worst aspect of this newfangled teapot was the need to feed it regularly with fresh heaps of coal. It was going to be a backbreaking job, he could already see that, although Master Huntyr and Sir Dustyn had worked hard to come up with clever ways to ease the task. Worse, it was going to be filthy, with clouds of coal dust everywhere.

He did feel naked without a single gun mounted, although he couldn't really think of anything any hypothetical opponent could do to them, given their preposterous speed. And the haste with which this whole project had been completed had required more than a little improvisation. The ships were intended, ultimately, to mount the new "recoil-system" guns Admiral Seamount and Captain Rahzwail were muttering about. Bahrns didn't know much about them—just that they were supposed to be a lot more powerful than the existing thirty-pounder kraken yet required much smaller crews—but it didn't matter, since they didn't exist yet. Instead, *Delthak* and her sisters would each be armed with twenty-two thirty-pounders once they reached their destination, although no one had explained exactly where the guns in question would be coming from.

In the meantime, aside from that mountain of coal, *Delthak* carried very little except replacement parts for her engines, boilers, and all of what Lieutenant Zhak Bairystyr, her engineer—a brand-new position, filled by an officer who had very little seagoing experience and looked as if he were about fifteen—called "the fiddly bits." Bahrns was accustomed to thinking in terms of ships being completely dependent upon their own resources while at sea, but thinking in terms of replacement parts to repair broken machinery was something else entirely. The notion that a ship's carpenter and blacksmith couldn't find or fabricate anything they'd need if they did have a failure was a sobering reflection on the fragility at the heart of this hulking, armored monster. In theory, a pair of galleons fitted out as repair ships and tenders would be following along behind them with complete crews of artificers from the Delthak Works, although they'd make a much slower passage, so the repair problem *shouldn't* be insurmountable in the long run, but it was all very bothersome at the moment.

So was the fact that at this particular moment, his entire ship's company consisted of only fifty-three men: him; Blahdysnberg and two other watch-keeping lieutenants; Bairystyr and his assistant engineer; eleven deck hands; twelve "oilers" to tend the two engines and their complex pistons, crank-shafts, and bearings; and twenty-four stokers to keep the four boilers fed. That was a tiny complement compared to the four hundred men serving aboard his last ship, and even after they'd added gun crews and the ship's surgeon, they'd have only a hundred and ninety-seven. That was only enough manpower to work the ship and man half the thirty-pounders she'd be receiving, and he had no idea what the rest of the crew would look like, since it was going to be made up out of drafts from warships operating out of Bedard Bay. That meant it was going to be catch-as-catch-can, with the three other ironclads in competition with *Delthak* and every galleon skipper doing his damnedest to hang on to his best men. Bahrns had a very unhappy suspicion that they were going to end up drafting landsman, probably from the army, to make up the necessary warm bodies.

In which case, not having sails to worry about will turn out to be a very good thing, he thought grimly. *Even a soldier can swing a shovel, and with our armor, we ought to be able to get too close to an enemy for even an* Army *gunner to miss.*

He thought about that for a moment, reflecting on the shots he'd seen trained *naval* gunners miss, even at point-blank range, and shuddered. Then he reached out and rapped the conning tower bridge's wooden planking for luck.

After all, he thought, raising his spyglass and sweeping it around the horizon, *it couldn't* hurt, *could it?*

.II.
Royal Palace,
City of Cherayth,
Kingdom of Chisholm,
Empire of Charis

Sharleyan Ahrmahk stifled a smile she knew would have turned into something entirely too much like a grin as she watched Irys and Daivyn Daykyn walk solemnly into the long receiving room that overlooked the palace garden's cherry trees. It was one of her favorite rooms, but for the moment she'd loaned it to Archbishop Ulys Lynkyn, who was here, officially, for a simple dinner with his empress and her family. Actually, there was rather more to it, and she watched Lynkyn's expression as the two young people approached him.

She'd gotten to know her new archbishop better over the last few five-days, although she still didn't know him as well as she'd known Pawal Braynair. She was of the opinion, however, that as Mahrak Sahndyrs had said, she and Cayleb would find him even more apt to their needs than Braynair had been. Except for one small, possible problem, the thought of which erased her temptation to smile.

Lynkyn was a stocky, gray-eyed man, three inches or so shorter than Cayleb, with dark, bushy, brick red hair and an even bushier mustache of which he seemed inordinately proud. He was also young for an archbishop—very young, in fact, only forty years old—and a Chihirite who'd come up as one of the Church's bureaucrats. That pedigree had concerned Sharleyan, since the Church's bureaucracy had been the path of self-aggrandizement for so many prelates over the years. She'd worried that Lynkyn might be one of those, someone more concerned with seizing a chance for power and wealth when it came rather than someone driven by conviction. She'd wronged him in that regard, however, for Mahrak Sahndyrs had read the new archbishop's character with all his usual acuity. Lynkyn's outrage burned hot and fierce, with a clear, terrible flame, just below the surface of those thoughtful gray eyes.

And he shared something with Maikel Staynair, as well. He, too, was one of the clergy the Church hadn't moved when his priest's cap received the white cockade of a bishop. His superiors had left him in the kingdom of his birth, rather than reassigning him beyond reach of the potential temptations of patriotism, and, as with Staynair, that had been a serious mistake. He was fiercely loyal to Sharleyan herself, not simply as his empress but as his queen, and by extension to Cayleb and the Charisian Empire, which was good. But one of the factors which explained much of his loyalty to Sharleyan's ferocity was the fact that his father, his elder brother, and one of his uncles had been killed in the same "piratical attack" which had killed King Sailys.

Her new archbishop, Sharleyan had discovered, was a man who did nothing by halves. In many ways, his personality was diametrically opposed to Maikel Staynair, driven by an energy and a need to grapple with anything that stood in the path of what he believed to be right that were almost frightening to behold. Those beliefs of his included loyalty, compassion, and commitment, all of which made him such a tower of strength for the Church of Charis. But they *also* included a burning sense of justice—one whose power had only fanned the heat of his personal hatred for Hektor of Corisande, the murderer of the father and the brother he'd loved . . . and his king.

And now he was about to come face-to-face with Hektor's only surviving children.

Irys, at least, knew what had happened to Lynkyn's family, and Sharleyan knew how little the princess looked forward to this interview. Irys also knew how important the political, as well as the religious, support of someone like Lynkyn was likely to prove, however. It wasn't that the archbishop could prevent Sharleyan—or Irys—from making whatever decisions they chose, but there was an enormous difference between "couldn't prevent" and throwing his weight behind a decision. And given the Church's centrality to every aspect of Safeholdian life, having the backing—the *active* backing—of the Empire's senior prelates could well prove critical. All of which was more than enough to explain why Irys might approach this meeting with trepidation.

If she was nervous, however, there was little sign of it. She moved withall of her usual graceful carriage, resting her right hand lightly on Daivyn's shoulder. She looked magnificent, Sharleyan thought. A very attractive young lady at any time, this afternoon she looked positively regal, her head high, the formal coronet of a princess glittering on her dark hair. Her hazel eyes were no more than calmly attentive, and yet . . . .

That temptation to grin returned, almost overpowering this time, as Sharleyan watched the one absolute giveaway of Irys' internal tension. She never so much as glanced at Phylyp Ahzgood, her mentor, where the Earl of

Coris stood to one side, resplendent in formal attire. Nor did she look in Sharleyan's direction, or to where Queen Mother Alahnah stood beside Mahrak Sahndyrs' wheeled chair.

Oh, no, not at any of *them*. And yet, for all her discipline, all her awareness of this meeting's importance, those eyes of hers strayed repeatedly to the left. She pulled them back resolutely whenever they did, and yet as soon as she'd recalled them to order, they began wandering ever so slightly yet again, returning once more to the wiry young man who looked almost drab in that audience chamber in the gold-laced dress uniform of a lieutenant in the Imperial Charisian Navy.

His Grace the Duke of Darcos, on the other hand, had no need to command his eyes into obedience. After all, no one was looking at *him*, so he could gaze unbrokenly at Irys.

Which was precisely what he was doing.

Sharleyan was fairly certain it had genuinely never occurred to Hektor Aplyn-Ahrmahk that anything remotely like a betrothal between Irys Daykyn and him could ever happen. One of the most charming things about him, in Sharleyan's opinion, was that despite his elevation to the pinnacle of the Empire's nobility, deep inside he remained the same young man he'd always been. He genuinely didn't think of himself as important, as privileged, and even now, he thought of himself as Hektor Aplyn first, and the Duke of Darcos only second. It would never in a thousand years have occurred to him that Irys Daykyn—daughter, granddaughter, and great-granddaughter of reigning princes—could see him as anything other than the young man whose barely middle-class parents had sent him off to sea in his King's uniform when he was ten years old.

Personally, Sharleyan suspected that was largely why he'd been so comfortable with Irys. He'd been deeply attracted to her, but he'd "known" anyone had to recognize his complete ineligibility as a serious contender for her hand. He'd been confident enough of his own noble rank to be perfectly willing to lean on it to allow him to spend time talking with her, but at the same time he'd known she couldn't possibly see him as any sort of marital prospect. If it had crossed his mind even once—or perhaps it might have been more accurate to say if he'd *allowed* it to cross his mind even once—that anyone might see him as anything of the sort, he probably would have bolted in confusion. And if anyone had suggested Irys might be *compelled* to marry him, the notion would have filled him with dismay.

In fact, Sharleyan had been afraid it might do just that even now. Fortunately, she was a seasoned, cunning, and unscrupulous monarch. As such, she'd known better than to announce the decision to him. Instead, she'd let *Irys* inform him of it, which the princess had done in a fashion which had made it quite clear, even to Hektor Aplyn-Ahrmahk, that *she* was anything but dismayed by the prospect.

One of our better notions, my love, she thought at the absent Cayleb. *I don't know if they'll be as good a match as you and I turned out to be, but the early indications seem favorable. Of course, there is something just a little disturbing about the absolute mindlessness I'm surprising in Hektor's eyes every so often when he looks at her now. I've got a feeling I know what's behind it, though. He is a sailor, after all.*

This time she really did have to raise her hand to hide a smile as she thought about another sailor whose last name was Ahrmahk and the look she'd seen in *his* eyes upon more than one occasion.

And a very satisfying look it was, too, she admitted cheerfully. She strongly suspected Irys would find herself in agreement on that point in the fullness of time.

While she'd been thinking, Irys had reached the end of the receiving line and curtsied to the archbishop. Beside her, Daivyn bowed, and then both of them kissed Lynkyn's ring when he extended it. The archbishop was taller than Irys, and those gray eyes were dark, unreadable, as he gazed at her. Then he looked down at Daivyn, immaculately dressed in court clothes, unruly hair momentarily tamed, scrubbed face shining . . . and sporting an absolutely magnificent black eye.

The archbishop's mustache seemed to twitch ever so slightly and he put a hand under Daivyn's chin, tilting his head back and to the side gently, the better to appreciate the splendor of that purple, black, and delicately yellow work of art. It covered his eye, reached up over the arch of his eyebrow, and spilled out over his right cheekbone as well. It was obviously a couple of days old, but time had only broadened its palette.

"Your Highness had a quarrel with someone?"

"No, Your Eminence." Daivyn was clearly more nervous—or, at least, more visibly nervous—than Irys, and he had to pause to clear his throat, but he never looked away from Lynkyn. "I was playing baseball with Lady Mairah's sons and some of the other kids here in the Palace. Haarahld hit a fly ball to right off Zhaky's best pitch—a really good fastball—and Tym caught it. But it was deep enough for Alyk to tag from first, and I was playing second, waiting for the throw from Tym, when Alyk came down the line. I was sort of blocking the baseline, really." His eyes gleamed in memory for a moment; then he shrugged. "Alyk didn't stop . . . and I didn't duck in time."

"I see." Lynkyn took his hand from under the youngster's chin and brushed it lightly across the boy's hair. "Did you have it seen to immediately, Your Highness?"

"Well. . . ." Daivyn seemed to wiggle slightly and glanced up at his sister's profile. "It was tied, with two out in the ninth, Your Eminence," he explained, "and after Alyk got to second, they had the winning run in scoring position. And we didn't have anyone else who could've played second. So, you understand I couldn't *possibly*'ve gone to the healers just then."

His voice ended on a slightly rising note, turning his final statement into a question, and this time Sharleyan was certain she saw Lynkyn's mustache quiver. The archbishop glanced sideways at Irys, and his gray eyes narrowed in amusement as they saw the martyred older-sister's resignation in her hazel ones. Then he looked back down at the son of the man he'd most hated in all the world and ruffled his hair again.

"I understand entirely, Your Highness," he assured the boy. Then he held out his hand. Daivyn took it, and the archbishop smiled a bit crookedly at him. "Why don't you—and your sister, of course—" he looked back at Irys for a moment, "take a little walk with me while we get to know one another better?"

"Of course, Your Eminence," Daivyn said obediently, and the three of them moved towards the open glass doors looking out over the blossom-laden cherry trees.

Sharleyan watched them go, and then glanced at the other archbishop in the room, standing at her elbow.

"That went better than I was afraid it might, Maikel," she said quietly, and he smiled.

"I, on the other hand, was quite certain it would go splendidly," he assured her. "By the time they leave for Corisande with me at the end of the month, he's going to be heartbroken at seeing them leave. Mark my words."

"And you were absolutely positive that was what was going to happen, were you? That's what you want me to believe?"

There was an undeniable, if perhaps unbecoming, edge of skepticism in her tone as she looked at the supreme religious leader of the Church of Charis.

"I am a man of great faith, Sharleyan," he replied serenely.

"And God *told* you this was going to work out, is that it?" she inquired even more skeptically, and he shook his head.

"Oh, I never had to consult *God* about this one, my dear," he told her, smiling even more broadly as he captured her right hand and tucked it into the crook of his left elbow. "I would, of course, have trusted Him to get it right if I'd had to, but, fortunately, I didn't."

"But you just said—" she began.

"I *said* I'm a man of great faith," he interrupted her, "which is true. It's simply that in this case, my faith was placed in something rather more earthly—a certain scamp of a prince." His smile faded gently, and he shook his head. "My dear, that boy, despite everything that's happened in his life, could melt an iceberg with a smile. A mere archbishop's heart never had a chance."

.III.
Lake City,
Tarikah Province,
and
Siddar City,
Republic of Siddarmark

Drums rattled, fifes and bugles sang, and the thunder of thousands of massed voices rose in hymn as the long column of marching infantry, interspersed with blocks of cavalry, moved out along the Traymos High Road. The sky was a deep, perfect cerulean, burnished with a thin, high scatter of cloud, and the sun poured down warmth, as if seeking to make amends for the winter past. There was still the tiniest edge of chill in the air sweeping across the city from the twin lakes from which it took its name, for spring and summer came late in these high northern latitudes, and the seasonal trees were only beginning to clothe themselves in green. High-flying wyverns and birds swept down the wind or hovered motionless, like God's own thoughts, high above, and the crash of boots, the clatter of hooves, the rattle and bang of wheels, the whistles of dragons, stretched a thick line of energy, color, and vitality across the land.

Arthyn Zagyrsk, Archbishop of Tarikah, stood at his window, watching the Army of God's departure and tried to feel glad, or at least confident, as became one of Mother Church's archbishops.

It was hard.

He'd stood here for two hours, and the endless snake of men, weapons, guns, and wagons didn't seem to have become any smaller. He supposed that made sense—a hundred and forty-six thousand men, with all their draft horses and dragons, would take a while to pass through any city. Not all of them were headed down the Traymos High Road, but enough of them were. It was Bishop Militant Bahrnabai's main column, and the men in it were overwhelmingly confident of their ability to deal with anything they might meet.

Zagyrsk was, too, if not for exactly the same reasons they were.

He heaved a deep sigh and turned from the window. Father Avry Pygain, his senior aide and secretary, stood waiting just inside the office door, hands folded in the sleeves of his cassock and expression patient. Pygain had been with Zagyrsk for almost five years, since shortly after this madness with Charis had begun, and they'd come to know one another well. The upper-priest was a Chihirite, of the Order of the Quill, and as bright and efficient as one might have expected from that background. His social skills were, unfortunately, rather less well developed, and all too often he had what Zagyrsk's mother had always called a "deaf ear" all too often when it came to dealing with other human beings instead of reports and tabulations. Still, he couldn't help being a likable sort, in his occasionally cross-grained fashion, and he provided the clerical skills Zagyrsk knew were not his own strong suit. Unlike the majority of serving archbishops, he was a Pasqualate, and he still wasn't quite certain how he'd ended up in an archbishop's palace instead of teaching in one of the healers' colleges.

And there are times—altogether too many of them, lately—when I pray to Pasquale to send me back to a quiet, peaceful college somewhere far, far away from here, he thought dismally.

"Well, they're on their way," he said, and Pygain nodded as if the silence-breaking sentence hid some deep significance, hovering just beyond his mental grasp. Zagyrsk's lips twitched, and he felt a sudden powerful surge of affection for his aide.

"It's all right, Avry," he said, reaching out and patting the younger man on the shoulder. "I suppose we'll get used to the quiet eventually."

"Yes, Your Eminence." Pygain nodded again, then cleared his throat. "I'm afraid Father Ignaz has asked for a little of your time this afternoon, Your Eminence."

Zagyrsk managed not to sigh. It wasn't that he disliked Father Ignaz Aimaiyr, his intendant. In fact, he liked him quite a lot and knew he was luckier than many to have him. It was just that—

"Very well," he said, turning and walking back to the window to gaze out it once more. "Ask Father Ignaz to join me here."

"Of course, Your Eminence." Pygain bowed, and Zagyrsk heard the office door closed behind him.

The archbishop's gray-blue eyes rested sadly on the marching column. He knew the *Writ* as well as any, and it offered only one prescription for the disease devouring Safehold. But he was a healer, that was all he'd ever really wanted to be, and the thought of where that army was headed, what it was going to do when it got there, filled his heart with grief.

Even the most hardened, heretical heart in the entire world belongs to someone who was once a child of God. To see it come to this, to know it can only get worse before it becomes better—surely that grief is enough to break the soul of even an archangel.

A throat cleared itself behind him, and he turned to see Aimaiyr. The intendant bent to kiss Zagyrsk's extended ring, then straightened.

"Thank you for seeing me, Your Eminence. I know you have a lot on your mind."

Actually, the intendant thought, studying his archbishop, the weight rested far more heavily on Zagyrsk's heart and soul than on his mind. The archbishop felt too deeply, Aimaiyr often thought. It showed in the eyes behind the lenses of the wire-frame glasses, in the thinning silver hair and the lined face with its somehow appealing beak of a nose.

"I imagine we all do, my son," Zagyrsk responded, and waved for Aimaiyr to seat himself in the chair to the right of the archbishop's desk. Zagyrsk waited until he'd sat, then settled into his own chair, tipped it back, and folded his hands across his midsection.

"Father Avry said you needed to speak to me, but I neglected to ask him what your subject might be, Father."

"I have a few . . . concerns," Aimaiyr replied. "Obviously our situation here in Lake City and in Tarikah generally has been . . . stressed by the presence of so many soldiers. Now that the army's begun its march, I expect much of that stress to ease, although the need to supply so many men and animals in the field is bound to have a significant impact, especially here in the city. But I think we'd all do well to attempt to return to something as close to normal as we can in these disturbed and disturbing days." He shook his head, his eyes—a deeper, darker blue than Zagyrsk's—worried. "I realize we can't possibly return to 'normal' until the heresy and schism have been dealt with, Your Eminence. Still, the closer we can come, the more a sense of the familiar—of the right and proper—will help all God's children marshal their inner strength in this time of need."

Zagyrsk nodded slowly, although he deeply doubted it would be possible for anyone to pretend things were remotely near "normal" for a long time to come. Nonetheless, he understood what Aimaiyr was saying, and he realized again how fortunate he was in his intendant. The fair-haired Schuelerite was an intense, passionate priest, a quarter-century younger than Zagyrsk's own seventy years. He was also compassionate—more so, to be honest, then Zagyrsk would have expected out of any Schuelerite.

And despite his position as Tarikah's intendant, he clearly had reservations of his own about the Grand Inquisitor's policies. In fact, despite how careful he was about what he said, and even more careful about anything he committed to writing, he'd made Zagyrsk nervous more than once, for Zhaspahr Clyntahn had been a dangerous, dangerous man even before the Jihad. The archbishop was far from certain how a priest of Aimaiyr's independence of thought had risen so high in Clyntahn's Inquisition, and he knew the intendant was deeply concerned by the severity of that Inquisition's current policies, the frequency with which it had imposed the full Punishment of Schueler.

Yet for all his compassion, Father Ignaz burned with an ardent fire against the heresy. He saw only too clearly how the "Church of Charis'" insistence upon independence of thought—the primacy of the individual's direct, personal relationship with God, even when his understanding of it clashed with Mother Church's definition of it—must undermine the unity and centrality of Mother Church. That doctrine *must* splinter once that core direction was broken, allowing error to contaminate the teachings the archangels themselves had entrusted to her care. And in the welter of new devices, techniques, and infernal mechanisms produced by the Empire of Charis, he saw Shan-wei's talon reaching into the world of men once more. Indeed, much as the Grand Inquisitor's willingness to use the iron rod of discipline distressed him, he was even more distressed by Clyntahn's willingness to grant dispensations for the soldiers of God to adopt so many of those innovations.

"I agree that the closer we can come to normalcy, the better, Father," the archbishop said. "Unfortunately, I question how close we can come at this time." He shook his head sadly. "While the army was quartered in and around the city, it was possible to forget how empty that city is. Now, even with all the extra stevedores and canal boats, that emptiness is going to become apparent to all."

Aimaiyr bent his head in acknowledgment of the archbishop's point. The population of the province and archbishopric of Tarikah had been catastrophically reduced over the previous winter—possibly by as much as two-thirds, or even more. With fewer than a million inhabitants even before the Sword of Schueler, it had never been remotely as densely populated as, say, Old Province, and the privation and starvation of the winter had cost its people dear. Many had fled as refugees, despite the bitter winter weather, making their way into the Border States and even into the Temple Lands beyond; others had simply died, either in their own homes or struggling to reach some hopefully safe haven. Desolate farmland stretched for miles around Tarikah's towns and villages, with no hand to till the soil or plant the seed. No one had been able to take any sort of a census yet, although Father Avry had that on his to-do list, but Aimaiyr knew as well as Zagyrsk that the numbers were going to be heartbreaking when they were finally available.

"I'm sure you're right about that, Your Eminence," he said. "In fact, one of the things I've been wondering about—the reason I asked to speak to you this morning—is whether or not it might be better to bring as many as possible of our surviving people together here in Lake City or in some of the other larger towns. I realize I may be stepping beyond my own sphere of authority to make such a suggestion, but it struck me that perhaps Mother Church should . . . encourage that movement. Under the circumstances, with so many homes and farms and businesses simply abandoned, surely Mother Church would be justified in extending her hand over them, seeing to it that they're protected for their rightful owners, in hopes those owners will someday return, but also put to good use in our present emergency. It would bring together the hands we need to plow, plant, and reap, and surely there are many craftsmen still among us. Yet as dispersed and scattered as our people have become, how can a craftsman find his customers? Or how can someone who needs the craftsman's work find *him*?"

Zagyrsk's eyes narrowed. After a moment, he took off his spectacles and closed his eyes completely, pinching the bridge of his prominent nose as he considered what the intendant had just said very carefully.

"You're right that it steps considerably beyond your normal sphere, Father," the archbishop said finally, not yet opening his eyes. "But that doesn't mean it's a bad idea. I hate the thought of abandoning villages and farms, some of which have been in their owners' families for hundreds of years. But our people have been devastated by this past winter. If nothing else, the sight of other faces and the sound of other voices would have to gladden their hearts."

He lowered his hand, replaced his spectacles, and looked at Aimaiyr intently.

"May I ask how this idea came to you?"

"It's the Inquisition's duty to safeguard the minds and souls of God's children, Your Eminence." Aimaiyr touched his pectoral scepter. "But our schools and village priests have been as decimated as anyone else, as I'm sure you realize even better than I, and without those teachers, without those priests, Mother Church can't protect her children against the poisons sweeping in from the outer world. I must confess that my first thought was the conservation and preservation of souls, Your Eminence. It was only after that that it occurred to me it might also preserve lives and help fight off the sense of grief and hopelessness too many of our people must feel at a time like this."

Zagyrsk nodded again, thoughtfully, his mind still running through the implications of the intendant's suggestion. It wouldn't be as simple as Aimaiyr might think. Quite a lot of the stubborn villagers and farmers of Tarikah would resist abandoning all they owned, no matter how firmly Mother Church promised to record their ownership and guarantee their eventual return. And then there was the question of how moving that many people would affect the military movements and chains of supply needed to support the Army of God's campaign. It was already late to be getting crops into the ground, too. That was going to be a factor as well. They were going to need all the food they could harvest, and that meant they'd have to find out where the land had been planted and move people to those locations, first. But still . . . .

"I think this idea may have a great deal of promise, Father Ignaz," he said. "I'm going to have to consider the implications, and if we do it, we'll have to move quickly on it, before we lose the planting season entirely. But I do think it's definitely worth considering. Thank you for bringing it to my attention."

"You're most welcome, Your Eminence." Aimaiyr smiled. "If it proves practical and useful, I'll be delighted. And"—his tone softened—"if it eases your heart in any way, I'll be even more delighted."

Zagyrsk's eyes widened, and he felt a spurt of wonder at the intendant's admission. But most of all, he felt touched.

"It may be that it will do both, Father," he said with a smile. "It may do both."

▼   ▼   ▼

Merlin Athrawes stood at his chamber window, gazing down at the busy street outside the Charisian embassy. That street bustled with activity, and a sense of energy and purpose hung over the Republic's capital, a far cry from the grim, gray fear and despair—even apathy—which had gripped it over the winter. Food continued to flow in from the Charisian Empire, but something close enough to normalcy had returned for that food to be distributed through the vendors and the greengrocers who normally served Siddar City. Free distribution to those who couldn't afford to buy continued, but the majority of it was actually being purchased now, which had at least eased the hemorrhaging from Baron Ironhill's accounts, although the war's ever escalating costs meant the reduction in strain was purely relative. Trade with eastern Siddarmark was beginning to pick up again, as well, although it remained enormously below what it had been with the loss of all the goods which had previously flowed through the Republic to the Border States and the Temple Lands themselves. Even if all of that trade hadn't been lost, the Republic had been so hammered over the past few months that its internal demand—or, rather, the wherewithal to purchase the goods to satisfy that demand—remained far, far lower than it had been. Still, there was an undeniable air of optimism and hope in the capital's air.

He wondered if there would have been if any of those bustling people had been able to see what he'd just seen through Owl's SNARCs.

The reason Zhaspahr Clyntahn had concentrated his Sword of Schueler's activities so heavily in northwestern Siddarmark was obvious from the most cursory glance at a map of East Haven's canals. The primary connections between East Haven and West Haven passed through the Border States' Earldom of Usher, Sardahn, Duchy of Ernhart, and Barony of Charlz into Tarikah. From Tarikah's Lake City, the route extended south into Westmarch via the Hildermoss and Sair rivers and the Sair-Selkyr Canal, and east, all the way to Siddar City, via the Hildermoss and the Guarnak-Sylmahn Canal. Safehold's climate meant rivers that far north froze every winter, but when they *weren't* frozen, the canals, rivers, and the network of high roads which accompanied them were the arteries that knitted the two Havens together. They were the route along which all those illicit Charisian goods had flowed in defiance of Clyntahn's will to buyers in the Border States . . . and the Temple Lands.

That would have been enough to draw the Grand Inquisitor's ire and attention to it, but for all his megalomania, Clyntahn was smart. Anger and his thirst for vengeance upon anyone who thwarted him in any way might betray him into colossal blunders, but even when he blundered, there was usually a dangerous core of rationality within the blunder. And in fairness to the Grand Inquisitor, little though Merlin liked being fair to him even in the privacy of his own thoughts, quite a few of his errors had stemmed from fundamental changes of which he'd been unaware when he made them. He could hardly be blamed, for example, for failing to realize reconnaissance satellites were spying on the movements of his armies and fleets, and his failure to make allowance for things he didn't know about didn't prevent him from planning intelligently where things he *did* know about were concerned. Nor did what he didn't know about SNARCs prevent him from making allowance for the merely mortal spies he *assumed* were responsible for his enemies' uncanny anticipation of those armies' and fleets' movements.

His emphasis on seizing Tarikah, Westmarch, New Northland, and Mountaincross was a case in point; it had snatched control of the roads and canals leading from the Temple Lands into the heart of the Republic of Siddarmark into his hands. True, some of those canals had been significantly damaged by agents of the Sword of Schueler bent on following their instructions to prevent the shipment of food east, although not even Clyntahn had dreamed of fully setting aside the *Book of Langhorne*'s injunction to maintain them. The sabotage he'd ordered had been intended to disable them only temporarily, but some of his agents—more enthusiastic than skilled—had exceeded his intentions in several instances. That had inflicted even more suffering on the people of Siddarmark and—far more significantly, as far as Clyntahn was concerned—delayed his own troop movements. The New Northland Canal, for example, still hadn't been fully returned to service, although the labor gangs the Church had sent to see to its repairs were close to completing their task.

But the canals that were operable—like the eighteen hundred miles of the Holy Langhorne Canal—provided a logistics pipeline all the way from the Temple Lands to Lake City. And that was why Allayn Maigwair had been able to move close to half a million men of the Army of God into Tarikah and Westmarch despite those provinces' devastated state. With the local Temple Loyalists already in arms against the Republic, the Church had over six hundred thousand armed and organized men on Siddarmarkian soil, which didn't even count the Dohlaran forces already operating in the South March and the Desnairian forces moving steadily across Silkiah. If those were added to the tally, Maigwair—and Zhaspahr Clyntahn—had over a million men poised to crush the life out Greyghor Stohnar's Republic. But almost worse, they'd repeated their tactics before the Battle of the Gulf of Tarot.

They lied to their own field commanders to be sure they could lie to us when our "spies" found out about their orders, Merlin thought grimly. *We thought they were all coming east, because that's what Maigwair told them they'd be doing. But Kaitswyrth's going south out of Westmarch, instead.*

The rest of the inner circle had responded to the knowledge that Nahrmahn Baytz wasn't actually dead—or no deader than Nimue Alban, at any rate—with far less incredulity (and far more joy) than Merlin had allowed himself to hope. The outpouring of happiness was ample indication of how much they'd all come to care for the rotund little Emeraldian, yet from a purely pragmatic perspective, the discovery that they not only had their best analyst back, but that he and the now fully self-aware Owl could actually spend the equivalent of five-days or even months considering intelligence data yet get back to them within no more than ten or fifteen minutes, was an even greater godsend. Yet even Nahrmahn and Owl, with all the advantages the SNARCs bestowed, had given them less than a five-day's warning, specifically because they'd been able to read every word of Bishop Militant Cahnyr Kaitswyrth's original orders.

But those orders had been changed with breathtaking suddenness, and the canal system—and the Church's wartime administration of it—meant Kaitswyrth had been able to shift his planned line of march and still make his originally scheduled departure date. Now the entire Army of God was in motion, half of it in a totally unexpected direction . . . and all of it moving at a terrifying rate of speed.

No, he thought, looking down at the people scurrying along the street below him. *No, if they knew what I knew,* optimism would be a scarce commodity in Siddar City.

.IV.
Fort Sheldyn,
The South March,
Republic of Siddarmark

S hit."
     As a reaction to a scout's report, it left a little to be desired, Colonel Phylyp Mahldyn reflected, but it did sum up the situation well. And it seemed so damned unfair.

He sat for a long, still moment, eyes focused on something only he could see, as he digested the news. Lieutenant Zherald Ahtkyn stood waiting patiently, his prematurely aged face worried.

But not worried enough, Mahldyn thought grimly. *The boy thinks I'm go-*

ing to produce another miracle, but it would take an archangel to get us out of this one.

He winced inwardly at his own thought. It was hard sometimes, even for him, not to wonder if the fiery sermons of the "Sword of Scheuler's" Schuelerite priests—and the even more inflammatory rhetoric of the rabble-rousing lay preachers—might not be right about the calamities to be visited upon the Republic if it failed to throw off its heretical leadership. There were times he'd actually *wanted* to believe that, wanted to absolve himself of the thankless task of somehow holding the Republic's authority together. The thought of abandoning the struggle, and of knowing it was what God wanted him to do, was almost more seductive than he could stand at times. Unfortunately, he was a man who took his duty and his sworn oath seriously, and he'd seen the measure of the men who called themselves "God's warriors" in the destruction of the small towns which had once been strung along the St. Alyk and the Seridahn. Cheraltyn, Traigair, Evyrtyn . . . he was sick unto death of all the evidence of "God's warriors'" *holiness.*

The South March population had never been dense. The entire vast province had boasted barely a third of the inhabitants of Old Province, alone. Even now, much of the land between the Branath and Shingle Mountains and the Dohlaran frontier had yet to be prepared for human occupation as the *Book of Sondheim* and *Book of Truscott* required, although the unconsecrated areas had been shrinking steadily before the current madness. Except for the Sheryl-Seridahn Canal, there'd been little to attract human settlement inland from the Gulf of Mathyas, anyway, until the Desnairians had invaded Shiloh—then the Republic's frontier province—the better part of two centuries ago. That had touched off the succession of bitter wars with the Desnairian Empire which had been brought to a close only by the Church's creation of the Grand Duchy of Silkiah as a buffer zone.

The Dohlarans had been wise enough to stay out of that conflict, although they seemed to be making up for it now. But the fighting between the Republic and Desnair had discouraged settlement in the area until it finally guttered out. More and more Siddarmarkians had been pouring into the South March since the Church had imposed peace, yet even today there were—or had been—no true cities and few towns. The South March had been a place of villages and peaceful, isolated farms, trying to forget the bloodshed which had swept across this very ground. Its citizens had been far more concerned with Sondheim's Law and Truscott's Law than with tensions within the Church or worries over the long-quiescent border. They'd traded across the Dohlaran frontier into Reskar and Thorast, intermarried with Dohlaran and Silkiahan families, and done their best to raise their own families in accordance with the *Writ*.

And then the world had gone mad, and not even the peaceful, sleepy South March had been spared.

Mahldyn's jaw clenched as he remembered the stomach-churning ruins of Cheraltyn and the mutilated bodies not just of fellow soldiers but of two-thirds of the town's civilians, as well. That had been the worst, he thought. But only because it had also been the first—*his* first. Because it was where he'd inherited responsibility for the entire area, and because it had been the army's job to protect the citizens of Cheraltyn, and they'd failed.

I couldn't have stopped it even if I'd been in command and known it was coming, he thought dismally. *And it wasn't Colonel Suwail's fault, either. We were both too busy dealing with the mutineers in our own commands, trying to figure out what the hell was going on and who we were supposed to be taking orders from to think about ambushes. And that was* before *the winter . . . and before the semaphore stations went down. No wonder it's gotten only worse since!*

He'd lost over half his own 110th Regiment in the mutiny's savage internal fighting. A third of his casualties had been among the troopers who'd stayed loyal to their oaths, another ten percent had been simple desertions . . . and the rest had been killed by their loyal comrades in arms in the fighting. At that, he'd been more fortunate than a lot of officers. His current regiment was at almost full strength, all of them regulars, although it had been patched together from the remnants of three pre-revolt regiments, including the survivors of Suwail's 93rd Pikes. Between the 110th, Colonel Vyktyr Mahzyngail's 14th South March Militia, and the Provisional Company he'd formed out of various odds and sods, he actually had a bit more than two regiments' paper strength, but he was over strength in pikes and badly under strength in arbalesters . . . and he had less than a hundred musketeers, all of them with matchlock smoothbores.

That wasn't much in the face of so much madness.

What happened? he wondered for no more than the ten-thousandth time. *How could people who were neighbors, friends—family—turn on each other this way? Where did all the* hatred *come from?*

Perhaps he should be asking other questions. Like why he himself and the men who'd somehow hung together under his command hadn't renounced their oaths to the Republic when the Grand Inquisitor proclaimed the Lord Protector's excommunication? Like what stubborn, stupid, idealistic concept of duty had kept him and his men on their feet, in uniform, trying to protect the civilians around them from those following the proclaimed orders of God's own priests?

He couldn't answer those questions, either, but whatever the answers might have been, they weren't going to matter much longer.

"All right," he said finally, his eyes refocusing on young Ahtkyn's hunger-gaunt face. "It would've been nice to have a little more warning, but what we have is what we have. Pass the word to Colonel Mahzyngail and Major Fairstock. I want everyone we've got ready to march within thirty minutes. Tell Colonel Mahzyngail that if that's not enough time to set all the charges, we'll just have to leave them." He smiled thinly. "I don't suppose letting them have the shell's going to make all that much difference in the end."

"Yes, Sir!" Lieutenant Ahtkyn slapped his chest and turned to hurry from the office.

Mahldyn sat looking around it for a few more moments. Then he sighed, climbed out of his chair, and took his breastplate from the armor tree.

At least we got Syrk and the settlements between here and St. Alyk's evacuated . . . mostly. There shouldn't be too many refugees to slow us down. That's something.

He started buckling the breastplate's straps and wondered if he'd be alive to unbuckle them that evening.

.V.
Near Evyrtyn,
The South March,
Republic of Siddarmark

The cadence of steadily marching boots pounded the morning quiet as the column slogged through the burned-out ruins of the town of Evyrtyn. A few three-quarters-starved dogs and a feral-looking cat lizard crept through the shells of houses, watching the intruders warily, as if they recognized invaders when they saw them. Or perhaps they'd realized that it didn't take *foreign* invaders to burn a town and slaughter its inhabitants, Sir Fahstyr Rychtyr thought glumly. It was his army, but he wasn't immune to the dreariness of the desolation stretching out around the damaged Evyrtyn locks. The damage to those locks was less severe than he'd feared—the pumps had been broken up, but the locks themselves were intact; they could be fixed fairly rapidly now that they were here—but it was the reason he'd had to march overland for the last two hundred and fifty miles, instead of using the Sheryl-Seridahn Canal. His engineers would have them back in service within the five-day, but until then feet, hooves, and wheels remained the only things that were going to move his command and all the supplies upon which it depended.

He was a long, long way from home, and no one would be coming to watch his back until the canal was back in operation and Sir Rainos Ahlverez moved the main body up behind him. But the desert into which the South

March seemed to have been turned was almost reassuring in its promise that no major enemy force could operate against him here, and they'd been restoring the semaphore stations as they came. He could pass messages back and forth—all the way back to Gorath and Duke Salthar himself, if he had to—although that didn't keep him from feeling acutely lonely.

He heard the sound of approaching hooves and looked up from the map on the folding table under the nearoak's shade as the horseman cantered up, drew rein, and dismounted.

"Colonel," he said, and Sir Naythyn Byrgair, the commander of his lead cavalry regiment, touched his breastplate in salute.

"General," he replied. "I understand you wanted to see me, Sir Fahstyr?"

"Yes, I did." Rychtyr tapped the map. "According to the locals, there's still a heretic garrison at Fort Sheldyn. They say it's a couple of Siddarmarkian pike regiments. Sir Rainos doesn't want them moving south to reinforce Fyguera in Thesmar, but I don't think that's the direction they're likely to go anyway. I'm more inclined to think they'd retreat north." He tapped the map again. "Up towards St. Alyk's and Cliff Peak. It's where I'd go if I had an army this size coming at me. They have to know the damned Charisians can support Thesmar through Sandfish Bay and Thesmar Bay. Hell, they can pull the whole damned garrison out by sea, if they have to! Even if that weren't true, they've got a lot more depth to the east before we could get to Shiloh or Trokhanos, and they have to know Cliff Peak's hanging, so if I wanted my men where they'd do some good, that's where I'd head."

"Yes, Sir." Byrgair looked down at the map and nodded.

He didn't much care for Siddarmarkians, and especially not those who'd chosen to side with blasphemers, heretics, and excommunicates, but he wasn't about to underestimate the guts and determination it must have taken to remain loyal to Stohnar over the winter just past. It made sense that a garrison commander who'd managed to pull that off would be thinking along exactly those lines. And while the Royal Dohlaran Army had no combat experience against Siddarmarkian pike blocks, he wasn't about to discount their lethality. The First Desnair-Siddarmark War had been a disaster for the Republic, costing them over half of Shiloh, a nasty chunk of Trokhanos, and twice as many casualties as the Desnairians had suffered. The Second Desnair-Siddarmark War, ten years later, had been almost as bad in terms of casualties, although at least they hadn't lost any territory that time. But by the *Third* Desnair-Siddarmark War, the Republic had reinvented infantry tactics, after which they'd proceeded to kick the Desnairians' arse up one side and down the other for the next fifty years, until Mother Church finally stepped in. And that was a sobering thought for the commanding officer of a cavalry regiment, since Desnairian cavalry was widely regarded—especially by Desnairians—as the finest in the world.

"If getting themselves into Cliff Peak *is* what they have in mind," Rychtyr said grimly, "I don't want them pulling it off. If we've got the opportunity to punch out four or five thousand of their infantry, hopefully in the open, I intend to take it."

"Yes, Sir."

"The high road isn't going to help us." The general's finger traced the line of the road from Evyrtyn through Trevyr and on to Cheryk. "And I realize we're the better part of a hundred miles from Fort Sheldyn. That doesn't mean it's not worth trying to intercept them before they can get away from us, especially since they're on foot."

"I understand, Sir."

Byrgair nodded again, although he hoped to Chihiro that Rychtyr wasn't about to suggest *he* was supposed to do the intercepting. The Dohlaran army was light on cavalry by Desnairian standards, with no more than half its total manpower mounted, and while that cavalry was good, in his own modest opinion, it wasn't up to Desnarian standards. Which, given *Desnair's* record against Siddarmarkian pikes, suggested all sorts of unpleasant outcomes to him, even though he'd done all he could to improve the odds.

The aristocracy and landed gentry were heavily represented in the cavalry regiments. That meant most of them had money, and Byrgair had seen to it that all his own men acquired at least one pair of the new flintlock pistols out of their own resources. A handful had grumbled—less at the not inconsiderable expense than at the "ignobility" of such weapons compared to the proper, knightly combat of cold steel—but they hadn't grumbled very loudly or very long. Especially not after they'd watched their own riflemen practicing their marksmanship. Yet their pistols certainly didn't have the range to confront Siddarmarkian arbalesters or musketeers, which left only one real tactical option, and charging pike blocks with lances and sabers was a good way to get the cavalry doing the charging gutted.

"I want you to take your regiment and cut across country," Rychtyr said, tracing a line on the map that cut the angle of a triangle with Evyrtyn at one corner and Fort Sheldyn and Syrk at the other two. "There are supposed to be farm roads running through along this line. If there are, and if they're as good as I've been told they are, you should be able to get ahead of them. I doubt like hell you can catch them before they reach Syrk, no matter how good the going is. If you can, good, but don't founder your horses trying. And if you can't, don't go in after them. Try to keep them from realizing you're in the area and wait till they clear the town, then hit them north of it, between Syrk and St. Alyk's."

Byrgair nodded as the general looked up at him, and Rychtyr's lips twitched in a small smile below his bushy mustache as he saw the colonel's expression.

"I'm not sending you alone, Sir Naythyn," he said reassuringly. I'll be sending Colonel Bahcher's regiment with you. And I've got two batteries of horse guns—Captain Fowail's and Captain Syrahlla's—close enough to the head of the column to attach to you. What I don't have is any ammunition wagons that could keep up with you, so you'll be limited to whatever they have on their limbers. You're senior, so the command will be yours. I don't anticipate any problems in that respect."

Byrgair nodded again, with considerably more enthusiasm. Sir Zhory Bahcher was unusual in having earned his knighthood the hard way. He was several years Byrgair's elder, although his lack of noble connections meant he'd been only a captain two years ago, and he was also a hard-bitten professional who'd spent twenty years dealing with brigands and the occasional small-scale battle with raiders out of Sodar. He wasn't terribly popular with his officers, some of whom resented serving under someone of such ignoble birth, but his troopers loved him, and he was as tough-minded and pragmatic as Byrgair could have asked for. He didn't know Captain Fowail as well as he knew Bahcher, and he didn't know Syrahlla at all. But Fowail, at least, had been transferred from the navy, given the desperate need for artillerists, and he seemed thankfully immune to—or perhaps simply unaware of—the romantic cavalry tradition Byrgair had been working to exterminate in his own command.

"I don't expect you to wade straight into four or five times your own number of pikemen," Rychtyr continued. "What I do expect you to do is to force them into a defensive posture. Slow them down. If you can get them to form square against you by threatening charges and then hit them with the guns, do it. Otherwise, hang on their flanks, get ahead of them and drop trees across the road, do whatever you can to slow them up. I'll be coming along behind you with all the infantry and artillery I can dig up in the next couple of hours. General Traylmyn can take the rest of the column on towards Trevyr until we either deal with this or I get a dispatch from you that our information was bad or that the garrison left too early for you to catch up with them. That should let him intercept them if they do break south for Thesmar. If they don't and we manage to catch up and deal with them, we can march down the high road through Fort Sheldyn and link back up with Baron Traylmyn at Cheryk. Is all that understood?"

"Yes, Sir!" Byrgair slapped his breastplate again, far more cheerfully.

"Then be on your way, Colonel."

▼ ▼ ▼

Sir Naythyn Byrgair felt much more optimistic as he went about assembling his force. It wasn't as difficult as it might have been, given that the real reason he and Bahcher had been chosen was that they happened to command two of the three cavalry regiments closest to the head of the column. It would have been nice if the detailed artillery had been equally easy to extract, but that would have been asking too much. The army formed a column that stretched literally for miles from its vanguard units to the supply wagons rumbling along in its rear. Two-thirds of it consisted of cavalry, although—predictably, in Byrgair's opinion—less than a quarter of its artillery was horse artillery that could hope to keep up with horsemen cross-country. Each of its ten infantry regiments formed a column one platoon across and seventy-five yards deep. A cavalry regiment had less than half as many men as an infantry regiment, but horses were much bigger, so each of them formed a road column sixty-five yards long, and there were forty of them. Allow a sixty-yard interval between regiments, and the column stretched for over a mile and a half. But that, of course, didn't allow for the artillery, ammunition wagons, or supply wagons, which added almost three and a half miles all by themselves.

The high road allowed that enormous column to move relatively rapidly, but only as long as it *stayed* in column. Each regiment was accompanied by its own dragon-drawn supply wagon, which was one reason for the extended interval between regiments that helped lengthen the column. But it also meant they could bivouac in their march order, strung along the road like beads. In turn, that meant the army could resume its march much more quickly each morning, and woe betide the colonel whose regiment wasn't ready on time.

So far, it had worked amazingly well. Of course, so far they had yet to meet any opposition, either, so that satisfactory state was undoubtedly subject to change. The instant anyone started pulling units out of that column, chaos would quickly ensue, which meant General Rychtyr had been forced to give very careful thought to the order of march before they ever set out. He'd formed his army in the order in which he intended to deploy it when the enemy was encountered, but he'd also had to compromise by spacing cavalry along its length to give him a quick reaction force if the enemy should be inconsiderate enough to turn up somewhere other than where he'd been expected.

Frankly, Byrgair would be glad to get away from the column for a while. Despite the hard marching and ruthless discipline Rychtyr and Father Pairaik Metzlyr, the general's special intendant, had imposed, it didn't actually move that fast, thanks to its infantry. An average speed of two miles an hour, allowing for periodic rest breaks, equated to over twenty-five miles a day, but keeping pace with infantry as it trudged endlessly down the road hour after hour was almost as boring for cavalry as it was exhausting for the infantry in question.

Of course, when it came to wars, boredom was good in Naythyn

Byrgair's opinion. That didn't mean he had to like it, though, and he felt a lot better about this particular break in it than he'd expected to.

He should have known Rychtyr wasn't going to give him the kind of orders he'd been afraid of. Unlike Sir Rainos Ahlverez, Rychtyr had been actively involved in the Royal Dohlaran Army's reorganization of its infantry ever since the Charisian conquest of Corisande. Ahlverez, like the majority of the army's senior officers, remained a cavalryman of the old school—the sort who might just have given Byrgair exactly the orders he'd dreaded. But he might not have, at that. After all, Ahlverez had been smart enough to assign Rychtyr to command his advanced guard, and that said something hopeful about the army's command structure.

Now, as his thirteen hundred cavalry and twelve guns left the column, heading rapidly and purposefully down the country lanes their local guide assured them struck the Thesmar–St. Alyk's high road somewhere north of Syrk, he drew a deep breath of relief and—he finally admitted to himself—anticipation.

.VI.
North of Syrk,
The South March,
Republic of Siddarmark

Phylyp Mahldyn didn't bother to curse.

First, because it wouldn't do any good. Secondly, because he was too damned tired. And third, because, deep in his bones, he'd known it was going to happen from the moment he'd read the report about the oncoming Dohlaran invasion force.

"At least it's only cavalry," Major Fairstock said as he stood beside Mahldyn on the crest of the small hill.

The foothills of the Snake Mountains were clearly visible to the north, with higher peaks rising blue and misty beyond them, crowned with the white of permanent snowpack. Another thirty miles and they'd have been into those foothills, in the heavy timber growth and steep hillsides where infantry would be far better able to deal with cavalry. In fact, Mahldyn had to wonder if it was a coincidence the enemy had encountered them here.

Syrk had been all but empty as they marched through it, watched only by the hollow, hating eyes of fellow Siddarmarkians who'd given their allegiance to the Temple. Everyone still loyal to the Lord Protector had fled, obedient to his warning, or at least he certainly hoped they had. More than a few Temple Loyalists had fled as well, having no desire to find themselves trapped between warring armies, whatever their loyalties might be. He hadn't even slowed down as he passed his column through the town, although he'd been aware even then that Syrk's buildings would be more defensible than someplace in the open in the middle of nowhere.

Well, if you'd been thinking about defensible positions, you should've stayed put in Fort Sheldyn, he thought. *Of course, there was the little problem that you knew it would be a death trap, given the numbers headed towards you and the fact that you had less than a month's worth of food. So let's not be kicking ourselves too hard over not holding up in Syrk, shall we?*

At least Fort Sheldyn wasn't going to be particularly defensible for anyone else, either, he reflected with a grimace, remembering the roar of flames as they consumed every wooden structure in the fort. He hadn't had much gunpowder, and all of it had been old-style "meal powder," but then, he hadn't had many musketeers left, either, so he'd used a bit of it in strategic places along the curtain wall. He had no idea whether or not the Dohlarans would have been interested in occupying Fort Sheldyn, but at least he'd make sure that if they did, they'd have to do quite a bit of rebuilding first.

Which is all very well, and doesn't say squat about what's likely to happen here.

"They're ahead of us, Sir," Colonel Mahzyngail said grimly.

"Yes, they are," Mahldyn agreed. "And if they're ahead of us, one has to wonder who's coming along *behind* us."

The militia colonel's face tightened and he nodded choppily. Mahldyn sighed and raised his spyglass, considering what he could see.

"So far, it's just scouts, it looks like," he said, never lowering the glass. "But those aren't local Temple Loyalists—not in that armor, and not with horses that good. I can't see any standards yet, but it looks like they're wearing red tunics and—"

He broke off as a much larger, solid block of horsemen appeared behind the scouts he'd already spotted. These did have a banner, and his eyes went bleak as he saw the green wyvern on the red field of Dohlar.

"Dohlaran regulars," he said flatly.

"Wonderful," Mahzyngail muttered, and Mahldyn snorted in harsh agreement.

"At least Klymynt's right about their being cavalry," he said. "I know the lads are tired, but there's no way in hell Dohlaran infantry got around ahead of us through cow pastures and lizard trails the way these fellows must have. And cavalry aren't so very fond of pikes."

"No, they aren't, Sir," Major Fairstock agreed.

His voice was hard, with an actual edge of anticipation, and Mahldyn wondered whether or not he envied the major's youthful sense of immortality. Or perhaps he was wronging Fairstock. Langhorne knew the boy had seen more than enough wreckage and ruin over the past half year. Maybe he had no more illusions than Mahldyn himself and simply figured he at least had the opportunity to send a few Dohlarans to hell before it was his turn.

"All right." He lowered the spyglass and turned to his two subordinates. "We know they're ahead of us on the road, and once we got into the woods and the briars and brambles, we'd never be able to hold formation. So as I see it, our only real option is to go *through* them, since we can't go around."

Mahzyngail and Fairstock nodded, and he tapped the major's breastplate.

"Klymynt, the Hundred and Tenth and I'll take the lead. We don't have enough room to deploy with both regiments up, so we'll go up the road first to clear the way. You'll take the middle of the formation with the Provisional Company as our reserve, and Vyktyr and the Fourteenth will watch the back door. Vyktyr, I think I'm going to borrow your arbalesters. I don't know whether or not these bastards have pistols, but if they do, I don't want them thinking about riding close enough to shoot us in the face."

"Makes sense to me, Sir," Mahzyngail agreed. "But what if they get around you and Klymynt and come at my boys?"

"I don't think that's going to happen." Mahldyn waved his arm in the direction of the watching Dohlaran cavalry on the next ridgeline to the north. "The terrain's too close and tangled to either side of the roadbed. Neither one of us is going to have a flank to maneuver around, so if cavalry wants to come at pikes head on in ground like this, let them try it."

He decided not to mention his fear that the Dohlarans *wouldn't* come at them, that they'd fall back, staying in visual contact but out of fighting range. Assuming they were willing to do that for the next five or ten miles, his men were going to enter a valley which would be almost perfect cavalry terrain. But they couldn't turn around and go back the way they'd come, so there was no point worrying about that yet.

"One thing," he said after a moment, his voice harsh. "Remember what's waiting for anyone who surrenders. Remind the boys." He met his officers' eyes levelly, his own cold. "If anyone doesn't think that's the case, remind them of what happened to Colonel Suwail."

Mahzyngail's jaw tightened, and Fairstock's eyes turned as cold as Mahldyn's own.

Colonel Zhordyn Suwail and one company of the 93rd had marched to the relief of Cheraltyn. Suwail hadn't realized the frantic message begging for help was a trap until he actually reached the town, at which point his four hundred men had been swarmed by an entire regiment of rebel militia and at least two hundred "irregulars." They'd managed to form ranks before the attackers actually hit them, but they'd never had a chance against that sort of numbers. None of them had survived, and Mahldyn felt a renewed surge of hatred as he remembered the flayed and mutilated bodies he'd found when he'd led the rest of Suwail's regiment and his own to what he'd hoped desperately might be the rescue.

The men who'd died fighting had been the lucky ones, and the rebels had reserved the most inventive punishment for the officers and noncoms who'd led their subordinates into heresy and blasphemy. He didn't know whether or not they'd had an inquisitor along for guidance, but they'd certainly done their best to apply the full rigor of the Punishment of Schueler.

He'd caught about half of the rebel militia three five-days later. He hadn't allowed his men to repay their prisoners in kind, however; he'd been willing to settle for ropes, and they'd hung every single one of the murderous bastards.

It was that sort of war.

▼   ▼   ▼

"I see you were right, Master Navyz," Colonel Byrgair said, gazing south towards the infantry-crowned hilltop.

"Told you I'd get you 'round the motherless, Shan-wei-damned heretics, Colonel." Hatred thickened Wylfryd Navyz' Siddarmarkian accent. "Bastards thought they could hang three of my brothers and just walk away home, did they?" He leaned from the saddle and spat noisily. "*That* for the lot of 'em!"

"Well, I don't think they'll be walking away home after all, Master Navyz." Byrgair tried to hide his distaste. He supposed the man's corrosive hatred was inevitable, but Navyz—and quite a few others he'd encountered since crossing the Republic's frontier—radiated a sick, burning rage that seemed to poison the very air around them. "And thanks to you, I think they're in an even worse predicament than they realize."

Drums began to rattle, and he looked at his company commanders.

"Gentlemen, you know what to do. Don't screw it up!"

He glowered ferociously and waited until they'd answered him with salutes and confident grins. Then he reined his horse around and headed north, up the road.

He felt a vague sense of pity for those Siddarmarkian pikemen, although it wasn't going to deflect him from his own duty. He hadn't seen a single horse among them, which wasn't surprising after the last winter. The Republic boasted very little cavalry, but usually even an infantry regiment had an attached section or two of mounted scouts. This infantry didn't, and because it didn't, it couldn't have any idea what was happening beyond eyeshot of the road itself. And unless it was more intimately familiar with the territory than Wylfryd Navyz, it wouldn't know about the narrow trail which paralleled the high road to the west, beyond the thick growth of pre-consecration trees and vines which shaded the main roadbed. He'd had to take the teams from

Captain Syrahlla's guns to drag Captain Fowail's artillery through that miserable slot of a so-called road. Syrahlla hadn't cared for that at all, and he'd tried to argue, but Byrgair had needed those big, strong draft horses. Syrahlla, coming up the high road with Bahcher after the Siddarmarkians had passed, could make do with borrowed cavalry horses on the main roadbed's much better going. Even with the double teams, getting Fowail's guns through had been a nightmare, but they'd managed, and in about another thirty or forty minutes, those Siddarmarkians were going to get a most unpleasant surprise.

▼   ▼   ▼

Phylyp Mahldyn marched with his drawn sword in his hand, the spine of the blade across his shoulder like an abbreviated pike, as his solid block of infantry moved up the road in the meticulously dressed formation of Siddarmarkian regulars.

He'd taken the lead because his men were more experienced at maintaining the tight formation essential to infantry who planned on taking battle to a mounted adversary. Mahzyngail's militiamen were damned near as good, and after the last bitter months, he trusted them the way he trusted the steel of his breastplate. But there was no denying the 110th was better suited to take the lead, with Fairstock's Provisional Company to back them up. Besides, there was no telling when someone was going to turn up behind them, as well.

He'd managed to get a couple of hundred arbalesters deployed to either flank of the pike block, and their bolts seemed sufficient to keep the Dohlarans at bay. Some of his men were looking away briefly from the men in front of them, exchanging brief, stolen sidelong glances with their companions, and he saw smiles on some of those faces as the cavalry continued to back away. It was easy to understand why nervous men in a situation like this one would take what comfort they could from the enemy's refusal to close with them, but his own heart sank steadily with every stride towards the north.

These people hadn't ridden like Shan-wei herself just to avoid contact. And they weren't backing away in anything remotely like panic or fear, either. They were maintaining formation, drifting northward, careful not to stack up and clog the roadway.

They're not taking any chances on getting stuck long enough for us to try an actual charge, he thought grimly. *They're keeping their distance, and they're going exactly where they want to go.*

He thought again about that valley. This was outside his own area of responsibility and he wasn't familiar with the maps very far north of Syrk, but he'd passed this way on his original journey from St. Alyk's to Fort Sheldyn, and if he remembered correctly, some sort of country road or track joined the high road from the west about a mile and a half before they'd reach the valley. It wasn't much better than a trail—he'd do well to get four men abreast along it—but someone had cleared the trees back where it met the high road. There might just be room in the resulting clearing for the 110th to advance far enough to block the cavalry while Fairstock's and Mahzyngail's men moved west along the side road. He might even be able to back his own men—or most of them—into that same narrow slot, where all the cavalry in the world would be useless against a couple of dozen steady men with pikes.

It would be the counsel of desperation, perhaps. He had no idea where that narrow, rutted dirt road might lead, only that it *didn't* lead directly into the cavalry in front of him and what might be waiting beyond them. But if they continued forward into the valley's open terrain, he'd become increasingly vulnerable, especially if it turned out the bastards had brought along a couple of regiments of their dragoons. Eleven or twelve hundred arbalests—or, even worse, horse bows—would be disastrous in that sort of terrain. He hadn't seen any sign of them yet, but that didn't mean they didn't have them.

He listened to the steady, measured rattle of the drums, pacing the pike block's steady advance, and wondered if there might be a way out of the trap he sensed after all.

▼   ▼   ▼

Sir Naythyn Byrgair watched his last company drift back out of the woods into the broader space of the clearing, withdrawing smoothly to either side, and listened to the grim, steady, determined beat of the Siddarmarkian drums.

Not much longer, he thought, glancing to where Captain Fowail had emplaced his six-pounders.

They'd gotten here with time to spare, and they'd used that time properly emplacing the guns. Fowail had dug in the two-gun sections, throwing up the spoil from the gun pits to form low breastworks, so that the pieces' long, slim muzzles just cleared the dirt when they were run forward into battery. He'd taken time to seed the ground directly in front of each pit with caltrops, as well. Traditionally regarded as an anti-cavalry weapon, a caltrop's wickedly sharp, vertical spur could be equally effective against infantry . . . especially infantry whose effectiveness depended upon the tightness of its formation. And as an added security measure, Byrgair had dismounted one of his companies, spreading its hundred and fifty men in blocks between the three well-separated gun pits. Their lances were considerably shorter than the Siddarmarkians' eighteen-foot pikes, but they were more than long enough to be dangerous, especially given his troopers' heavier armor.

The one thing that did worry him were the arbalesters his advanced platoons had reported. On the other hand, they'd have to get into range, and Fowail's six-pounders had a fire zone four hundred yards deep.

▼   ▼   ▼

The afternoon sun was warm on Colonel Mahldyn's back, and his left hand reached up under the brim of his helmet, swiping sweat from his forehead. The trees were beginning to thin ahead of them. Not much longer before he discovered if the bolt hole he thought he remembered really existed. He hoped it did, because—

▼   ▼   ▼

"Fire!"

Six six-pounder guns fired as one. The savage concussion was like a physical fist, punching at every ear, and each gun spewed twenty-seven four-ounce canister balls into the stunned Siddarmarkians' front rank.

The range was four hundred yards, and at that range, twenty percent of the balls found targets. And not just a single target—the quarter-pound projectiles exploded through human tissue and bone with great, flat, *wet* slapping sounds, then slammed into the men directly behind their original targets. Mahldyn's pike block was sixty men across, and the canister tore great, gaping holes all across that frontage. Men screamed—almost as much in shock as in agony—as that totally unexpected blast of fury ripped through them.

They'd never experienced anything like it—never even *seen* field artillery before. Nothing could have prepared them for that apocalyptic moment, Siddarmarkian regulars or not, and their formation wavered, stumbled to a halt in a welter of blood and bodies, of fallen pikes and screaming, mutilated companions.

Fowail's crews sprang into action as the guns recoiled, their muzzles streaming smoke. Swabs went down the fuming barrels, canister charges—the projectiles wired to the powder charge so both could be rammed home together—followed, rammers tamped, priming quills stabbed into touchholes, locks were cocked, and then the gunners heaved the pieces back into firing position and they bellowed fresh thunder.

It took twenty seconds to reload and fire again. Twenty seconds in which the men of the 110th Infantry fought to understand what had happened, while sergeants and lieutenants in the forward companies struggled to fill the holes in the forward ranks. It was an impossible task, but Mahldyn's men were veterans. They'd already made their tour of hell under their officers, and they responded. They closed up their ranks, faces like iron as they marched directly across the bodies of dead and wounded companions, and the pikes steadied as the drums snarled fiercely, ordering the charge.

And as they started forward, those dreadful guns fired again.

▼　▼　▼

The brisk wind rolled the choking, rotten-smelling clouds of powder smoke to the east, clearing the range, and Byrgair watched the front of the Siddarmarkian pike block disintegrate. It was like watching an ocean wave sweep into a child's sand castle as the tide came in, but no sand castle ever bled and screamed and died. He'd had his doubts about the effectiveness of six-pounders, especially since no one had figured out how to produce any of the exploding "shells" for guns that small. Indeed, even as he watched the carnage, a small voice in the depths of his brain told him that at greater ranges, against rifle-armed opponents, it might be different. But he wasn't *at* long range, and his opponents *weren't* armed with rifles.

The second salvo of canister struck the pikemen in terrible sprays of red, and Fowail's men flung themselves on the recoiling pieces again.

▼　▼　▼

Phylyp Mahldyn swore savagely as he realized what had happened.

He didn't know how many guns the Dohlarans had managed to concentrate, and he couldn't begin to imagine how they'd gotten them here in the first place. He'd never actually seen a fieldpiece, but he'd seen naval guns on clumsy, old-style, wheelless carriages. Because of that, the true implications of Charis' introduction of mobile artillery to the battlefield had been impossible for him to conceptualize, but he recognized the sounds and sights of disaster when they were all around him.

He grabbed one of his runners, a wide-eyed young corporal, and shook him savagely by the shoulder.

"Get to the rear! Tell Major Fairstock and Colonel Mahzyngail to fall back—they're to get clear! Understand me? *They're to get clear!*"

"Yes, Sir!"

Somehow, the youngster even remembered to salute, then he went tearing towards the rear, right arm raised to show the red brassard that marked him as one of Mahldyn's couriers rather than a deserter fleeing from danger.

The colonel spared him one glance, hoping the boy would have the good sense to stay with Mahzyngail, if he got that far, rather than heading back into these slaughter-pen woods. In the meantime, he had an appointment of his own.

He jerked his head at his white-faced standard-bearer, and the two of them started fighting their way towards the mangled front of his regiment.

▼   ▼   ▼

Byrgair's mouth tightened as somehow, in that inferno of smoke and blood, the Siddarmarkian drums continued to roll, beating the attack. And despite the carnage and the shock, the men of the 110th Infantry responded. That rent and ruined column ground forward, driving into the teeth of Fowail's canister, but it had four hundred yards to come. Even at a hundred and twenty paces a minute, the fastest a pike block could move, that would take them over three minutes to cover, and Fowail's gunners hammered them with fists of fire and blood.

▼   ▼   ▼

"*Forward*, boys!" Mahldyn screamed, even as his heart broke. "Forward! Come on, damn it! *Forward the Hundred and Tenth!*"

He heard the screams, the curses and prayers, and between them he heard a few deep, hoarse voices responding to him, shouting their defiance and hatred, fighting their way into that hurricane of canister shot and flame with their heads down, like men wading into a heavy wind.

But this was a wind of iron, and the thunder behind it reeked of Shanwei's own brimstone, and they stumbled and fell over the heaped and twisted bodies of men they'd known and fought beside, in some cases for years.

"*Come on, Hundred and Tenth!*" Mahldyn cried, hardly able to see through his tears as he watched and heard his regiment dying around him. "Come on, boys! For me! *Follow me!*"

And follow they did, to the very ramparts of hell. They were no saints, no heroes out of legend. They were only men, loyal to their oaths, to their Republic, to each other . . . and to him. Men for whom surrender was not an option, who knew they were going to die and whose only remaining desire was to kill one more enemy before they did.

"*Follow me! Follow—*"

Phylyp Mahldyn flew backwards as the canister ball struck him squarely in the throat and half decapitated him.

He died almost instantly, but other voices took up the cry. Not in words—there *were* no words any longer. There was only a primal bellow, a snarling, furious sound of rage, and the men of the 110th Infantry broke ranks at last—not to run away, but to hurl themselves bodily upon their enemies.

▼   ▼   ▼

Sir Naythyn Byrgair stiffened incredulously in his saddle as shrieking wildmen erupted out of the smoke and carnage. He'd never heard of a Siddarmarkian pike block breaking formation to charge, but this one had taken too much, been hammered too hard, to do anything else. They threw themselves into the teeth of the six-pounders, fanning out, lunging forward as if eighteen-foot pikes were bayoneted muskets, and yet another withering blast of canister erupted into their faces.

Men were blown back off their feet by threes and by half-dozens, yet other men charged right across them, and they were too close now for the guns to reload again.

They were a spent force, with no hope in the world of breaking through their enemies, and they didn't care. Not one of them threw away his weapon and tried to surrender. Not one turned and ran. And before they died, ninety-three of Byrgair's cavalrymen and twenty-six of Captain Maikel Fowail's artillerists died with them.

▼　▼　▼

Byrgair dismounted slowly, aware there was blood on his saber but not really remembering how it had gotten there. He stood there, his shoulder leaning against his nervous horse, smelling the blood and sewer stench of the battlefield, the reek of powder smoke, listening to the chorus of moans and shrieks.

Langhorne, he thought, wiping his blade. He sheathed it, then wiped his face with a hand he was vaguely surprised wasn't trembling. *Sweet Langhorne. I didn't really think . . . didn't expect . . . .*

The truth, he realized numbly, was that nothing could have prepared him for this. For all his years of service, the quick cut-and-thrust encounters with Sodaran brigands or horse thieves, this was his first true battlefield, and the sheer, concentrated carnage surpassed anything he'd ever dreamed of.

These new weapons are Shan-wei's own get. Langhorne, what have we loosed on the world?!

Father Zhon Bhlakyt, his regiment's senior surgeon, headed forward with his assistant surgeons and their lay brother helpers. Half of them moved towards his own wounded, but the other half started into the wilderness of torn and twisted Siddarmarkian bodies.

"Waste of good time," a voice rasped beside him, and he turned his head, looking at the speaker. "They're for the Punishment if they live, the bastards." Wylfryd Navyz's jaw worked on a thick plug of chewleaf, and there was an ugly glint in his eye. He spat a thick stream of brown juice. "Better'n they *deserve*, if you ask me!"

Byrgair regarded the Siddarmarkian for a moment, then inhaled deeply. He crossed to where Bhlakyt knelt beside a wounded pikeman and touched the priest's shoulder.

"Colonel?" Bhlakyt looked up quickly. "What is it? Are *you* wounded?"

Byrgair looked down at him for a long, still moment. Then he shook his head.

"No, Father," he said quietly.

For a moment, Bhlakyt only looked at him. But then he understood what that "no" truly meant. His eyes widened and his face tightened in a Pasqualate's automatic protest, but Byrgair shook his head again.

"Saving these men will do them no favor, Father," he said even more quietly, squeezing the priest's shoulder. "I think it's time for Pasquale's Grace." He held Bhlakyt's eyes steadily. "For *all* of them, Father."

For a moment, he saw a different kind of protest in the healer's eye. And not, the colonel thought, because Pasquale's Grace was supposed to be granted only to those a healer could not save. And neither was that protest born because Pasquale's Grace would deprive the Inquisition of heretics whose only hope of salvation lay in the mortification of their bodies in the Punishment.

No, it was a protest born of the possible consequences for Sir Naythyn Byrgair if the Inquisition discovered he'd ordered it.

But the protest died. The priest bent his head in acknowledgment, rose from where he'd knelt, and gathered the other surgeons and their assistants with a gesture. Byrgair watched them react to the instructions, saw them glance quickly in his own direction, yet none of them protested, and they spread out once more among the Siddarmarkians, the green cassocks of Pasquale moving more slowly and purposefully. He saw some of the dying pikemen looking up at them, saw the gratitude in their eyes as they recognized the consecrated daggers, heard some of those priests murmuring the last rites of Mother Church, which were denied by law to any excommunicate or servant of excommunicates. And he saw dozens of those dying men signing Langhorne's Scepter before razor-edged steel set them free.

He turned away, unable to watch, wondering if he would, indeed, face the consequences of his decision. At the moment, he almost didn't care. He was no martyr, cherished no death wish, but those men had suffered and bled at his orders, and they had, by God, been *men*! They would *die* like men, not screaming under the Punishment to please the hollow shells of other men as filled with hate as Wylfryd Navyz.

The day might come when Sir Naythyn Byrgair would be just as filled with hate, just as eager to see the heretic and servant of heretics pay the full price for his crimes against man and God. But that day was not yet, and that place was not here, and he hoped that when it was his own turn to face the archangels, they would remember this day and set it to his credit.

▼   ▼   ▼

Thirty minutes later, and two miles to the south, Colonel Vyktyr Mahzyn-gail's 14th South March Militia emerged from the woods which choked and clogged the high road . . . directly into the deployed and waiting guns of Captain Marshyl Syrahlla.

.VII.
Malphyra Bay,
Raven's Land

W ell, that's a sight for sore eyes," Ahlyn Symkyn said, watching the long line of Charisian galleons beat into Malphyra Bay.

"Yes, Sir," the young man standing a respectful half pace behind him and to his right on the waterfront replied. It wasn't the sort of automatic, polite agreement one might have expected out of a general officer's youthful aide. Instead, it carried a certain note of *heartfelt* agreement, Symkyn thought.

"Feet tired, Bynzhamyn?" he inquired without taking his eyes from those tan and gray, weathered sails.

"Not so much my feet as another portion of my anatomy, Sir," Captain Wytykair replied in a serious tone. "While I'm fully appreciative of the fact that I didn't have to walk the whole way, I have to admit that the thought of sitting down for a while on something that doesn't move under me has a certain appeal."

"Ever been to sea before?"

"Well, no, Sir. Actually I haven't."

"I see. Well, in that case I hope you've brought along a supply of golden berry."

The general didn't have to glance at his aide to picture the golden-haired young man's suddenly worried expression. Golden berry was a sovereign specific for nausea, motion sickness . . . and seasickness.

"Do you expect a very rough crossing, Sir?" Wytykair asked after a moment, and the general shaded his eyes with one hand, studying the galleons even more attentively.

"This time of year? Crossing the Passage of Storms and the Markovian Sea?" He shook his head, voice grim. "Half the lads'll be puking their guts up by the time we're five leagues from shore."

"I see."

Symkyn's lips twitched at the youthful captain's tone. He was very fond of young Wytykair, despite the fact that the captain was considerably better born than Symkyn himself. Like many of the old Royal Chisholmian Army's senior officers, Symkyn had come up through the ranks, earning his general's golden-sword collar insignia the hard way. In the course of a quarter century's service, he'd dealt with more nobly bred young snots that he could count, and Wytykair was vastly different from any of them. But the youngster also didn't have quite as much worldly experience as he might wish people to believe, and there were times . . . .

"I think they'll be ready for us to begin boarding the men first thing in the morning," he continued in a more serious tone. "I hope so, anyway. I hate to think of His Grace stuck in the middle of Siddarmark with only three brigades."

"He'll kick their arse, Sir," Wytykair said, and this time the assurance in his voice was the product of the hard experience of two solid years worth of training and drill.

And the boy had a point, Symkyn told himself. No one else in the entire world understood the new weaponry the way the Imperial Charisian Army did. Not only had the Royal Chisholmian Army which had shaped it already been a professional, standing force with a pre-existing tradition of critical thinking, but it had profited significantly from General Green Valley's experience.

There'd been a time when Symkyn would have pooh-poohed the possibility that a Marine might have anything to teach professional soldiers. Marines, after all, were basically brawlers—even *Charisian* Marines. Oh, for the purposes for which they'd been raised and required in *naval* service, Charisian Marines had been superb, beyond compare. But for a sustained campaign on land? For managing the logistics of an entire army? Organizing supply trains? Coordinating cavalry and infantry? Recognizing the reason for field formations and how to combine arbalest fire, pikes, and swords to lend one another their strengths and offset one another's weaknesses? That wasn't what Marines understood.

Kynt Clareyk had forced Symkyn to reconsider that view. He'd had a few lessons of his own still to learn, and he'd worked hard to master everything officers like Symkyn could teach him, without the least sign that he resented their tutorship. But he'd had far more to teach *them*, and his ability to conceptualize what the new firearms and artillery really represented had been nothing short of breathtaking. Under Duke Eastshare's firm leadership and Baron Green Valley's ability to describe the most radical concepts clearly and concisely, the Imperial Charisian Army had evolved a tactical doctrine such as the world had never imagined. And it was a doctrine that went right on growing and changing. That was something Green Valley and the other Charisian Marines who'd accompanied him had shared with the Chisholmian core of the army: the understanding that there was always a way even the best of doctrines could be improved upon.

The new breech-loading "Mahndrayns," for example. Symkyn had yet to get his hands on one of them personally, but a few thousand had made their way to Chisholm before the Expeditionary Force set out through Raven's Land. Even before the first of them had arrived, however, just from descriptions of them, Green Valley had recognized how radically a breech-loading capability was going to change even the tactics he'd formulated as recently as last year. And so the army had found yet another way to tweak itself, and that was why young Wytykair was right about what was going to happen to any mainlander army that ran into the ICA in anything like equal numbers.

But that's the problem, isn't it? Symkyn thought more grimly. *We're not going to be running into them in anything like "equal numbers" . . . not for a long time, at any rate. And they've got rifles and new-model artillery of their own. That's going to make them a hell of a lot more dangerous, even if they haven't figured things out as well as our Old Charisian wizard has.*

"I'm sure the Duke can look after himself, Bynzhamyn," the general said after a moment. "It never hurts to have somebody watching your back, though."

"No, Sir. It doesn't," Wytykair agreed.

"And on that note," Symkyn turned his back on the harbor and looked at his aide, "I've got some errands for you. First, find Colonel Khlunai. Tell him to get the rest of the staff busy. I want the first troops ready to go aboard ship as soon as there's enough daylight for them to see where they're putting their feet. And we're going to have to get a hard count on the galleons available as horse and dragon transports, too. I doubt we're going to be able to pack as many of them aboard as I'd like, but we can't even start thinking about that till we know how much space we've got. So, after you've found Colonel Khlunai, go find the harbor master. Tell him—"

.VIII.
Fort Darymahn
and
Sandfish Bay,
The South March,
Republic of Siddarmark

S hit!"

Private Paitryk Zohannsyn, recently of the militia of the Republic of Siddarmark and currently in the service of Mother Church, pressed his cheek even more firmly against the inner slope of the earthwork. He tried very hard, but it was impossible to get any closer to it. His buttons and belt buckle were in the way.

Fresh thunder rumbled in a long, slow crescendo out on the Taigyn River estuary's dark water, flashing in boiling light and smoke above the river's surface, and glowing streaks drew lines across the night, reflecting in the mirror-like water as they flashed towards the entrenchments around Fort Darymahn. They arced high, then descended with a terrifying, warbling whistle before they exploded.

Some of the incoming shells hit the ground and rolled and bounced, sputtering and spitting flame, trailing the stink of brimstone, before they erupted in bursts of Shan-wei's own fury. They shattered into what seemed like thousands of jagged-edged fragments that went scything out in all directions. Most of those fragments thudded into the earth or went whining off the fort's stonework, but some of them didn't, and Zohannsyn heard fresh screams as they found targets. Other shells seemed to drive into the earth, burying themselves deep before they exploded like hellish volcanoes. And other streaks of light—the ones that *didn't* hit the ground—were worse. *Far* worse. Their fragments scattered over a much wider area, slicing down from directly overhead where earthworks and walls offered no protection. And some of them seemed to rain down much smaller, much more numerous projectiles—as if some fiend had packed them with musket balls as well as gunpowder.

"Keep your heads down!" Corporal Stahnyzlahs Maigwair was shouting, his normally powerful voice sounding frail and a little shrill to ears stunned by the bombardment. "Keep your heads down!"

"*It's Shan-wei!*" another voice screamed. "They've brought Shan-wei herself to take our souls!"

"Stow that!" Maigwair snapped. "It's *not* Shan-wei, Parkair! And even if it were, what we'd need now is prayers, not panic!"

Sure it is, Zohannsyn thought, digging his fingers into the earthen slope. He was as religious and as dutiful a son of Mother Church as the next man, or he wouldn't have been here, but somehow he didn't think prayers were going to do a lot of good at the moment. If they were, those bastards wouldn't be here in the first place.

Another slow, methodical broadside rumbled out of the night. This time there were at least twice as many guns in it, and the streaks of light came in a flatter trajectory, without the high, looping flight of the ones before them. Zohannsyn heard them slamming into the face of the earthwork like some giant's angry fists. For a moment, nothing else happened, and then the earth itself quivered and twitched as, one by one, those flaming projectiles exploded. He wondered fearfully how many of them it would take to tear the thick wall of earth apart? To let the following thunderbolts right in among the frail men sheltering behind them?

Another plunging rain of fire whistled and wailed down out of the heavens, exploding viciously on the ground or in midair, and he heard fresh screams.

Please, Langhorne! he prayed. *Help us! We're* your *champions—don't let the heretics just* massacre *us this way!*

His only answer was another bellowing broadside.

▼   ▼   ▼

"How are they *doing* this?!" General Erayk Tympyltyn demanded, looking around the ashen faces gathered in the fort's great keep.

So far, that massive structure's five-foot-thick walls of solid stone seemed to be resisting the heretics' bombardment. Half the fort's buildings were heavily on fire, however, and none of the eyes looking back at him seemed confident the keep's immunity would last much longer. He saw their fear—he could almost *smell* it—and he knew they could see exactly the same thing when they looked at him.

"It's Shan-wei's doing," one of his officers said flatly. "They're heretics, demon-worshipers! Why shouldn't she help them?!"

"Don't be any stupider than you have to!" Colonel Ahdymsyn, Tympyltyn's second in command snapped, glaring at the speaker. "This is the same weapon they used at Iythria last year—that's all! And you know as well as I do what the Grand Inquisitor had to say about that!"

"He only said Mother Church could duplicate the *effect*," Major Kolyn Hamptyn responded stubbornly. "That Mother Church could figure out a way to make ammunition that would do the same thing—not that they did it the same *way*!"

"That's enough, both of you!" Tympyltyn barked.

Like himself, both of them had been militia officers prior to the Rising. None of the regular officers in Fort Darymahn's garrison who might have come over to Mother Church had survived, and Tympyltyn—only a colonel the year before—had found himself in command. His current rank was purely self-bestowed, although he had hopes it would be confirmed once Mother Church's regular forces relieved the fort, and he'd promoted Hamptyn from captain to major, as well. At the moment, he found himself wondering if that had been such a good idea after all.

Tympyltyn was as devout as a man could be, as his willingness to stand up for God and the archangels demonstrated, but Hamptyn's devotion sometimes substituted for thought. Ahdymsyn, on the other hand, seemed less devout and more . . . pragmatic than Tympyltyn could have preferred, and he and the major had come into conflict more than once before this. At the moment, however, the colonel's explanation was far more helpful than Hamptyn's.

"Whether it's Shan-wei doing this for them, or whether it's exactly the same kind of ammunition Mother Church's working on, what matters is that they're bombarding us," Tympyltyn grated, glaring around the table. "At this moment, that's the only thing I'm interested in! Is that understood?"

Heads nodded, and he allowed his expression to relent slightly.

"How bad is it, really?" he asked, the question punctuated by fresh peals of thunder while the midair explosions stabbed light through the arrow slits like lightning.

"We're losing a lot of men," Ahdymsyn replied, his tone flat. "We didn't provide them with enough overhead cover, and some of it's not heavy enough, anyway."

Tympyltyn jerked a nod at the colonel. Executive officer or not, he didn't much care for Tahlyvyr Ahdymsyn. But it was Ahdymsyn who'd suggested on the basis of reports about Iythria that it might be a good idea to bury Fort Darymahn's magazines under an additional layer of earth and stone. He'd also overseen the construction of shelters to offer whatever protection they could from exploding cannonballs that might come plunging out of the sky.

Tympyltyn himself had never so much as seen a cannon fired before he'd led the assault that stormed Fort Darymahn and slaughtered the mutiny-depleted garrison. He'd seen them fired in practice since then, but the guns on the fort's walls were the old-fashioned, massive, wheelless version, not the new-model weapons about which they'd all heard such tall tales. He'd thought Ahdymsyn was panicking unduly, but he hadn't argued. If nothing else, it had given the men something to do to help take their minds off of the short rations all of them had been on.

"A lot of barracks and storehouses are on fire, and I know their fire's dismounted at least some of our parapet guns, Sir," Ahdymsyn continued, remembering to add the military honorific this time. "I don't know how many—not yet. I think—"

He paused as a fresh cascade of explosions drowned his voice.

"I think they're actually doing more damage to personnel than to the fort itself," he continued after the thunder eased. "Enough of this is going to flatten everything *inside* the fort—except for the keep itself and the walls, I think—but it'll take them a long time to manage that, and I don't think their fire's really having that much effect on the entrenchments. Dirt does a pretty good job of absorbing explosions. Unfortunately, at the rate they're killing our men, that may not matter in the long run. Sir."

Tympyltyn glared at him, less for the afterthought of that "sir" than for the bitter taste of his conclusion, but nothing he'd seen or heard suggested Ahdymsyn was wrong.

"Whether it's Shan-wei or not, Sir," Hamptyn said, "they wouldn't be here just to bombard us. We're a hundred and fifty miles inland, and the semaphore stations told us how many galleons they've brought up the river with them. They're going to pound us until there's nothing left but rubble, or else until they kill enough of us they can send their Shan-wei-damned Marines ashore to kill the rest of us by hand." The major looked around the table. "They're trying to open the river, Sir. That has to be what this is about."

Much as Tympyltyn sometimes disliked Hamptyn, he couldn't argue with the major's conclusions. If the heretics could reopen the Taigyn River between Tabbard Reach and the Branath Mountains and retake Fort Tairys, they'd be able to use the river and the Branath Canal to move troops more rapidly between Glacierheart and the Gulf of Mathyas than the servants of Mother Church could possibly move overland. And the troops they were likely to be moving were the Godless, heretical Charisians with their demonically inspired weapons.

"You're right," he said, and drew a deep breath. "Send a runner, Colonel Ahdymsyn. We can't wait for daylight, and our semaphore tower may not be here by morning. Get the message out that we're under attack and the heretics are moving up the Taigyn in strength."

▼　▼　▼

"Think they're getting the message, Sir?!"

Lieutenant Allayn Trumyn had to lean close to his captain's ear to make himself heard over the thunder of the guns. HMS *Volcano*'s rifled angle-guns were reloading at the moment, but her sister ships *Thunderer* and *Whirlwind* were perfectly happy to fill the intervals of silence. And the four regular, smoothbore-armed galleons hammering the hulking fortifications fired far more rapidly than any of the bombardment ships. Their flatter fire and lighter, smoothbore shells had to be less effective than the angle-guns' far heavier, plunging projectiles, but it certainly looked impressive as the scores of thirty-pounder shells exploded all across the face of the earth works the Temple Loyalist rebels had thrown up to screen the approaches to the fort.

"Oh, I imagine so." Captain Zhorj Byrk had succeeded to *Volcano*'s command after Ahldahs Rahzwail's promotion to flag rank. "It's more spectacular than Iythria was, anyway," he continued, watching the flames and smoke spiral up above the battered fortifications. "I'm a little surprised we found that much to burn, actually. Must be more wooden buildings than I thought. Looks like they figured out it'd be a good idea to protect their magazines better, though." He shrugged. "Pity, that."

"I bet they're crapping themselves, though, Sir!" Trumyn shook his head. "*I* damned well would be!"

"That's the idea, Allayn," Byrk said. "That's the idea."

▼　▼　▼

"Well," Hauwerd Breygart said, "if things are going according to plan, that bastard Tympyltyn's probably crapping himself about now."

"Oh, I think we can take that pretty much as a given," Sir Paitryk Hywyt replied.

The admiral stood beside the Earl of Hanth on the quarterdeck of HMS *King Tymythy*, and the night was very quiet. The only sounds were those of wind, wave, and sailing ships moving steadily through the darkness.

"I hope one of Byrk's shells lands right on the bastard's head," Hanth said much more grimly.

In his previous career in the service of King Haarahld, Hauwerd Breygart had seldom hated any enemy personally. That wasn't the case in this war— not with the stories coming out of the occupied provinces. And Erayk Tympyltyn's men had distinguished themselves even among their fellow religious fanatics.

"It would be nice. I'll settle for him sending the message, though."

"So will I . . . but that doesn't mean I don't really wish it could come from his successor in command."

Hywyt turned his head and smiled thinly at the Marine general in the light of the binnacle. The admiral appreciated a sneaky mind when he encountered one, and the supply galleons anchored safely out into the Taigyn estuary beyond the bombardment ships, certainly *looked* like troop transports. And to help underscore that appearance, Hanth had sent along barges and fishing boats gathered up all around Eralth Bay to suggest they'd be ferrying Marines ashore—or upriver—shortly. Actually, however, the only land forces Hanth had anywhere close to Fort Darymahn where the few hundred cavalry he'd been able to scrape up among the local Siddarmarkian forces and put ashore on a nicely deserted piece of Shreve Bay's coastline a five-day and a half earlier. If all had gone according to plan, that cavalry had crossed the Taigyn River several days ago and was currently waiting near one of the towers in the chain connecting Fort Darymahn to the main semaphore network. They'd wait until Tympyltyn's frantic report that he was about to be assaulted had time to get out to Fort Tairys, and then, sometime around midmorning, they'd burn the semaphore station in question. If possible, they'd burn a couple of more before they rode back to Shreve Bay for extraction.

The message should concentrate Temple Loyalist attention on Fort Darymahn and the line of the Taigys for at least the next several days. Which was the entire point, since in about another two hours, Hywyt's flagship and the transports carrying seventy-five hundred Charisian Marines and armed seamen would pass through the sixteen-mile-wide channel into Thesmar Bay in complete darkness. The uninhabited marshes stretching for miles

on either side of the channel would probably have precluded anyone's noticing them, anyway, but there was no point taking chances. And with just a
little luck, nobody on the other side would realize General Fyguera in Thesmar was about to receive a very potent reinforcement.

Besides, Hywyt thought with a slow smile, *they're going to be too busy looking east, towards Fort Darymahn, to be thinking about us. Which could be just a* little
unfortunate for them.

▼　▼　▼

"God, that's a sight for sore eyes."

General Kydryc Fyguera's voice was deep, befitting his bull-necked and
bull-shouldered physique's massive chest, but there was something else in it,
Earl Hanth thought. Not quite a quaver, but *something.*

The two of them stood on a bastion of the entrenchments Fyguera had
thrown up around the city of Thesmar's landward side. Actually, calling
Thesmar a city might have been a bit of an overstatement, but it certainly
deserved the designation in South March terms. It had been a sleepy, provincial town before the Sword of Schueler, with relatively little commerce
outside harvest season, when the produce shipped down the Seridahn and
St. Alyk rivers to Thesmar Bay brought it to frenetic life.

Of course, that hadn't happened this harvest season. And even if there'd
been a harvest to ship, the Sword's planners had devoted special attention to
Thesmar as part of their efforts to cripple the food transportation system.
The fighting had been especially ugly here, but Fyguera had somehow managed to hold four entire regiments of regulars together. Their discipline and
training had been crucial in helping the loyal inhabitants of Thesmar and
the surrounding portion of the South March Lands resist the tidal wave of
rebels and mutineers.

In the end, the inhabitants of most of the small towns strung along the
Seridahn and the St. Alyk between Thesmar and Cliff Peak had still refu-
geed out. Many had gone no farther than Thesmar, where the extra mouths
had stretched rations even thinner, despite the normally abundant productivity of South March farms. Others had been lifted out by sea, carried as
far as Eralth and then sent overland to what they hoped would be places of
refuge in eastern Siddarmark. But Fyguera had held the critical posts between
Thesmar, Fort Sheldyn, and Cliff Peak, imposing a barrier against any efforts
to supply the Temple Loyalists east of the St. Alyk's by water out of Dohlar.

Until recently.

Now Fyguera turned from watching the column of Marines (and somewhat less orderly column of seamen) marching up the high road towards
Cheryk. The first of the naval thirty-pounders on improvised land carriages

creaked past, drawn by one of the draft dragons Hanth had brought from Eralth, along with the fodder to keep them fed, and the Siddarmarkian general watched them go by, then looked Hanth in the eye.

"If the reports about the number of Dohlarans headed this way are accurate, General Hanth," he said flatly, "they would've punched us out of Thesmar in a five-day. Especially since we have exactly eight old-style artillery pieces, and they're big bastards, designed to cover the waterfront, not deal with infantry. If you hadn't turned up . . . ."

He let his voice trail off, and Hanth nodded.

"I can't guarantee we can hold the city even with my people, General," he said, "but I'm willing to bet my artillery can kick their artillery's arse." He grinned suddenly. "I wouldn't normally pick sailors for a fight on land, to be honest. I've spent some time working with these boys, and I think they'll do well, but the sad truth is that they're not Marines and they're not soldiers. But what they *are* are the best damned *gunners* in the world, and I *am* willing to guarantee you the Dohlarans haven't brought along any thirty-pounders. We'll get a dozen or so of those dug into your entrenchments here before we do anything else."

"Good." Fyguera's satisfaction was clear, but then he glanced back at the marching column for a moment.

"I'm not sure the idea of marching out to meet the bastards is the best strategy, though, My Lord," he said, and that whatever-it-was in his voice was stronger. "There have to be at least thirty or forty thousand of them already up to the line of the Seridahn, and the last report I had says their second wave's lead regiments have to be almost to Evyrtyn. That's another fifty-five thousand, and you've got less than eight. Even if I stripped the entire garrison out of Thesmar and sent it with you, you wouldn't have more than twelve. And like you say, two-thirds of yours are sailors."

"True," Hanth looked unobtrusively past Fyguera to where Colonel Rahskho Gyllmyn, Fyguera's second-in-command, stood at the Siddarmarkian's shoulder, "but *these* sailors have rifles and they've been taught to shoot by *Marines.*" He smiled thinly. "I wouldn't like to say it where it might go to their heads, but I'll put them up against anything Dohlar's got. Besides," something cold and bleak replaced his smile, "a lot of these men served under Gwylym Manthyr. They're looking for a little payback."

"But—" Fyguera began, then stopped himself. "You're senior, according to the Lord Protector," he said, "and you know your men's capabilities better than I do. Just . . . be careful, My Lord. You say your men are looking for payback? Well, so are most of mine after last winter. But I've discovered that's not enough if there's too many of the bastards on the other side."

He held Hanth's eye for a moment, then inhaled deeply and gave himself a shake.

"I understand your Commander Parkyr's looking for the best places to put the guns you're leaving behind. I have a few ideas on that topic myself," his lips quirked in a smile that looked only slightly forced, "so I think I'll just go have a word with him. If you have any needs, Rahskho will see to them for you. I hope you'll at least have time for dinner before you head out? We've been on short rations for quite a while, and my cooks are looking forward to the supplies you've brought along. I did hear one of them asking what a 'yam' is, though, so I can't promise what kind of results we're going to get!"

"I look forward to it, General," Hanth said, and Fyguera nodded and headed back into the city.

Hanth watched him go in silence, then turned and cocked an eyebrow at Rahskho Gyllmyn. The colonel—a militia officer, but one who looked tough, competent, and smart—looked back at him in matching silence for several seconds. Finally, he shrugged ever so slightly.

"I can't say I disagree with the General entirely, General. About the numbers, I mean. But that's not really all he's thinking about."

"I had that impression," Hanth replied in a carefully neutral tone.

"Don't get me wrong, General Hanth! That man's been a giant when it came to holding this town. Drove us all like the wrath of God, too, while he was about it. Never rested, didn't eat until everyone else had, and he was up before dawn every day. Not a man in this garrison wouldn't die in his tracks for General Fyguera, and that's a fact."

"Colonel, nobody could've done what General Fyguera's accomplished here without being something extraordinary. Trust me, I realize that. But even extraordinary people have limits."

"Aye, they do," Gyllmyn acknowledged after a moment. He looked away, watching the marching Marines and seamen. "I'll not say he's reached his, because I don't think he has. But the strain's showing. Three months ago, he'd've been trying to figure out how he could squeeze at least a few men out of the garrison to go with you. Now—?"

The colonel shrugged, and Hanth reached out to lay one hand on his forearm.

"Colonel Gyllmyn," he said quietly, "you don't have to defend him to me. You don't have to think for a moment I don't deeply respect what he—and you—have accomplished here in Thesmar. And you don't have to think I'm worried over how much fire he has in his belly, either. The truth is, Thesmar's his responsibility, and he's entirely right to worry about its security first and foremost. And, to be honest, given the kind of battle I'm planning to fight, trying to figure out how to coordinate Siddarmarkian and Charisian tactics on the fly wouldn't be a very good idea." He smiled briefly. "But as for the rest of that, if what I just saw is all the 'strain' he's showing, then that man is made out of steel, and he'll do for me."

Gyllmyn regarded him for a moment, and then he smiled back, slowly.

"Aye, he is that," he said. "And I'll tell you this, General. Don't you worry about your rear while you're out there. Thesmar'll still be here when you come back, because 'that man' will hold it in the teeth of Shan-wei herself."

.IX.
Siddar City,
Republic of Siddarmark

Greyghor Stohnar's face was more deeply lined than ever.

The relief he'd felt when the Charisian food shipments arrived, the knowledge that the Charisian Expeditionary Force, as everyone had begun calling it, was en route from Chisholm, the enormous convoy loaded with weapons and munitions which would be arriving soon—all of it had helped ease the crushing burden of the winter just past. But the information coming in from the western provinces over the past three five-days seemed to mock the false hope those earlier reprieves had offered.

The army moving out of Lake City had swung one hook up into Icewind, clearly bent on crushing resistance in that lightly inhabited province, and the Icewinders who'd remained so stubbornly loyal to the Republic were fleeing for their lives. The province's Temple Loyalists were openly celebrating the Army of God's advance . . . and all too frequently ambushing their fleeing neighbors, or burning their houses behind them. The refugees were headed for Salyk, the province's one real town, on Spinefish Bay, and at least transport galleons and warships of the Charisian Navy were available to lift them out by the thousand. Charisian seamen, the Icewind militia, and the handful of Marines remaining to the ICN galleons were going ashore in Salyk as well, and many of the fittest locals were assisting in the construction of the entrenchments going up around the town. It was possible they'd be able to hold Salyk—at least until the winter ice drove the navy out of Spinefish Bay—but all of the rest of the province would be in enemy hands by the end of July at the latest.

Nor was that all the bad news coming out of Tarikah. The second, and far more powerful, column from Lake City was driving hard down the Hildermoss River in barges, traveling at almost fifty miles a day along the river even against the current and obviously heading for the city of Guarnak and the Sylmahn Gap. According to their reports, Bishop Militant Bahrnabai was personally leading that column, and he should reach Guarnak before the end of the month.

Yet Bishop Militant Cahnyr Kaitswyrth's equally powerful army was almost worse. It was driving south along the Sair-Selkyr Canal towards the Daivyn River to link up with the Temple Loyalists who'd seized control of Westmarch over the winter, and none of their spies had predicted that. It clearly intended to hammer its way across the border into Cliff Peak from the north while the Dohlarans hooked up from the south to meet them and then—almost certainly—turn east and drive into Glacierheart, as well. Kaitswyrth was headed for the East Glacierheart mountains; if he took them, Glacierheart would be gone and there'd be no way in the world to save the loyal portions of Shiloh, either. And within only a few more days, Desnairian troops out of Silkiah would cross the Somyr River, moving between the Salthar Mountains and Lake Somyr into the South March, while an even vaster Harchong army, over a million strong, was marshaling in harbors and embarkation points all around the Gulf of Dohlar.

It was small wonder, Merlin thought, that a man who'd been a lifelong military professional should look at those odds and quail. Nimue Alban had seen even worse odds as the Gbaba tightened their noose around humanity's home star system, but that was very little comfort, given how that campaign had turned out in the end.

"The arms convoy from Charis will be entering North Bay sometime day after tomorrow," Daryus Parkair said, glancing through the notes he'd prepared for the daily briefing. "And according to the dispatch boat that arrived last night, Duke Eastshare should reach us a day or so after that." He looked up from his notes. "That's going to be a *major* increase in our combat power."

"I know, Daryus," Stohnar said. "And don't think for in instant that I didn't spend quite a while on my knees thanking Langhorne for it, but compared to the threat . . . . ." He waved his hand at the huge map table and the tokens advancing ominously across the Republic. "And glad as I'll be to see the Duke and his troops, they'll be here, in Siddar City, a hell of a long way from Cliff Peak or even the Sylmahn Gap."

"True," Parkair agreed. "But at least the damage those idiots did to the canals in their own rear delayed them for almost a full month. Anybody who could pull a stunt like that is probably capable of fucking up in any number of other ways, as well."

"Now *there*, Daryus, you have a point," Stohnar acknowledged with a poison-dry smile. He looked down at the map for several more seconds, then raised his eyes to where Cayleb stood on the other side of the table.

"I hope you realize I meant every word about my gratitude, Your Majesty," he said quietly, and Cayleb nodded.

"I do. And I also realize why eighty thousand men doesn't seem anywhere near enough. After all," the emperor snorted harshly, "they aren't. Unfortunately, they're all we're going to have for at least another several months." He shook his head. "I'm sorry to say it, but it's going to take us at least that long to get the transports we need to eastern Chisholm and then to the mainland. And I'm even sorrier to say that once we lift the rest of the troops from Maikelsberg and Port Royal, we'll have scraped the bottom of the barrel. Building an army big enough for mainland campaigns had to take second place to building a navy that could keep mainland armies out of the islands, I'm afraid."

"I understand." Stohnar looked back down at the map. "And from what Brigadier Taisyn said—and what I saw with my own eyes, for that matter—eighty thousand Charisians will be a hell of a handful for the Army of God. We just can't get them to enough places fast enough. Not without Shanwei's own luck, at any rate."

"I'm not sure there *is* a way, My Lord, however lucky we are," Merlin said quietly from where he stood at Cayleb's shoulder. "I think we can probably get a column to the Sylmahn Gap in time, and the rifles in the weapons convoy will let you put eighty thousand riflemen of your own into the field as soon as you can get the new regiments stood up and trained. But even having said that—"

He paused, drew a deep breath, and shook his head.

"My Lord," he said even more quietly, looking up from the map and meeting Stohnar's eyes levelly, "Cliff Peak is gone. You're right. We simply can't get anyone there to stop it."

He didn't mention what had happened to Colonel Mahldyn's regiments, or what had already happened to a half-dozen other garrisons that hadn't been able to retreat fast enough. Stohnar didn't have to know about that; in fact, Merlin wished *he* didn't know, given what had happened to most of those "heretics and blasphemers" when they fell into the hands of Mother Church's loyal sons.

There was silence in the map room as the words were finally said. Then Stohnar straightened his back slowly, his mouth grim . . . and nodded.

"You're right, *Seijin* Merlin. And it's time we admitted it." That grim mouth smiled without becoming one bit less grim. "That's one of the hardest lessons for any soldier—to learn you can't waste resources reinforcing failure . . . no matter how desperately the men holding those positions are depending on you. God help them."

He closed his eyes for a moment and signed Langhorne's scepter. Merlin's mouth tightened as he saw the gesture, but he couldn't fault the sentiment behind it.

"If Cliff Peak's gone," Stohnar said, opening his eyes once more, "then reinforcing Archbishop Zhasyn and Brigadier Taisyn in Glacierheart becomes even more important. If Kaitswyrth punches through to the East Glacierhearts and the Clynmarh Hills, he's got a cakewalk into Shiloh. Or he could keep driving straight east, up the Siddar."

"I think even the Army of God is going to find it's bitten off a mouthful big enough to choke a dragon," Cayleb said. "And it's going to get worse for them the farther east they come. In the western provinces, they can count on having the majority of the population on their side, since the Temple Loyalists already have overall control. But as they come east, they're going to start running into civilians who didn't think the 'Sword of Schueler' was such a wonderful idea, and there are a *lot* of people in the Republic, My Lord." He swept one hand in an arc from Midhold to Trokhanos. "If they actually get this far east, they'll discover that even a million men aren't *nearly* enough to occupy that much territory."

"Maybe not," Stohnar said grimly. "That doesn't mean they won't try, and it doesn't mean they won't kill thousands or even hundreds of thousands of my citizens doing it. Shan-wei! They've already killed *millions* without even firing a shot of their own!"

Merlin nodded, although he knew Cayleb had a valid point. The Church in general—and Zhaspahr Clyntahn, in particular—had no real concept of what it would take to suppress a deep-seated resistance in a population the size of Siddarmark's. No Safeholdian realm had ever had to make the attempt, and the Church's "occupation" had never even been challenged before. Merlin, on the other hand, *did* realize what a challenge that entailed, and so did Cayleb, thanks to his access to Owl's history banks. Napoleon's experience in Spain came to mind . . . as did Adolf Hitler's in the Soviet Union. An army could bleed to death far more quickly than anyone might believe when stretched too far under those conditions. But Stohnar had an equally valid point. The cost to the civilians would be even higher than to the occupying force.

And, he admitted, looking down at the enormous sweep of territory Cayleb's gesture had taken in, *there's no point denying that Clyntahn has something Napoleon and Hitler didn't—a political program which could actually generate popular support . . . especially if the alternative is the Punishment of Schueler.*

That was the true Achilles' heel of a purely military occupation. Without some political or ideological or economic—or *religious*—basis for garnering the support of the occupied, the occupiers had to have a huge ratio of force to space. But *with* such a basis, all the military really had to do was keep a lid on the situation while the pressure to reach an accommodation worked. That, after all, had been *Charis'* policy in Corisande, where Reformist sentiment had worked for it, and overall, the policy had worked well. And for all Zhaspahr Clyntahn's twisted ambition, and all the rest of the vicarate's cupidity, the basic faith of Safehold was stronger than bedrock.

If Clyntahn could simply restrain his own need for vengeance, or even just slake it *once* and then back off, that faith could very well begin working for the Church once more.

And at the rate they're moving, they'll have lots of territory for it to start working for them in, too, he thought bitterly. *In fact—*

His brain paused in midsentence and his eyes narrowed suddenly as another thought hit him. He had no idea where it had come from, and it had to be one of the most insane thoughts even *he* had ever had. And yet, if it was even remotely possible—

"I didn't mean to suggest an occupation wouldn't be a disaster for your people, My Lord," Cayleb said. "I was simply observing that they're going to have to begin deploying garrisons and protecting their communications, and that's going to gradually erode the strength they can deploy forward."

"That's true enough," Stohnar acknowledged.

"I don't want to suggest making any definite troop commitments until we've had a chance to discuss it personally with Duke Eastshare," the emperor continued. "I do think, though, that we're going to have to think in terms of splitting the first wave of the Expeditionary Force. It's organized into three brigades, but I think we should split the third brigade and use it to reinforce the other two, Then we send one of the reinforced brigades to the Sylmahn Gap and the other to Glacierheart. As far west in Glacierheart as we can get them, at any rate. We'll have the second echelon coming in in a few more five-days to provide us with a reserve, so let's push everything we have now as far forward as we can."

Stohnar's mouth tightened again, but he nodded heavily.

"If Kaitswyrth keeps moving this fast, we'll be lucky to get troops as far west as Saint Maikel's of the Snows before they run into him," he acknowledged, his voice bitter.

"There's another point or two I'd like to bring up, if I may," Merlin said, and the others looked at him.

"Certainly, *Seijin*," Stohnar invited.

"Thank you, My Lord. My first point is that because of the way they were deployed, Duke Eastshare's troops were still equipped primarily with muzzle-loading flintlocks when he started them moving. The weapons convoy will provide enough Mahndrayns to reequip his entire force with breech-loading caplocks and also a significant increase in his artillery. It would take a day or so to mate them up with the new equipment, and I realize we need to get troops to both the Sylmahn Gap and Glacierheart as quickly as possible, as His Majesty says, but believe me, holding them here in Siddar City long enough to draw the Mahndrayns, much less the artillery, would at least double their effectiveness."

Stohnar looked a little dubious, but Cayleb nodded firmly.

"At least that much, My Lord," he said. "Merlin's right about that."

"I doubt waiting one more day would make that much difference in getting them to the front," Stohnar agreed. Then he snorted. "Not to mention that they're *your* troops, Your Majesty. I suppose that gives you at least a modest voice in where and when they're deployed." He looked at Merlin. "Consider your point accepted, *Seijin* Merlin. You said you had another?"

"Two more, actually, My Lord. The next one is that it's going to take at least several five-days to train your own troops to use the additional rifles from the convoy properly, and there are other weapons they're going to have to master as well. I don't think we're going to be able to get even your existing regiments rearmed, retrained, and into combat before the end of August. The new ones will take even longer."

Stohnar's expression was bleak, but not because he could dispute what Marlin had just said. The Republican Army was sticking with its existing unit structure, rather than try to adopt some new and foreign organizational basis in midcampaign. And Stohnar and Parkair were raising dozens of new regiments, built around whatever cadre of regulars and experienced militia they could spare. The rifles being shipped to Safehold would permit them to field thirty pure-rifle regiments, unburdened by pikes, but as Merlin had just said, raising them and *training* them were two different things. Both the lord protector and his seneschal were too experienced to send men into combat before they were ready. Unfortunately . . . .

"I agree with your analysis, *Seijin*," Stohnar said somberly, "and I know the kind of casualties half-trained troops take. But I don't think we have a choice. I have every faith in the combat power of your Army, but even if they can annihilate ten times their own number of the enemy, they simply can't cover enough *space*. We're going to need every man we can throw at them if just to slow them down. And we need to slow them down. If we can, we need to *stop* them, hold them no more than a couple of hundred miles farther east than the area they already control until winter sets in, but if we can't do that, we *have* to at least slow them. If that means committing the new regiments before they're fully trained, then we'll just have to do that, too."

"I agree about the need to slow them down, My Lord," Merlin said. "But that brings me to my final point. One that only occurred to me a minute or so ago, actually."

"Really?" Cayleb regarded him intently.

"Really, Your Majesty," Merlin assured him with a slight smile. "It *should* have occurred to me earlier. For that matter, with all due respect, it should've occurred to *you*, too."

"Well, if I should've thought of it, I suppose I'm grateful you've admitted that *you* should have, too," Cayleb said dryly. "Could you, by any chance, share this new thought of yours with us?"

Something suspiciously like a chuckle came from the general direction of Daryus Parkair, despite the grimness of the mood, and Merlin half bowed to Cayleb.

"Certainly, Your Majesty. I was just thinking about the very point the Lord Protector's raised—that we have to slow them down. And that reminded me that once upon a time, a very wise man told me that amateurs study tactics but *professionals* study logistics. I think we've been guilty of focusing on tactics to an extent that's blinded us to other possibilities for slowing them down."

"What sort of possibilities, *Seijin*?" Stohnar asked, his eyes intent, and Merlin smiled. It was a cold, sharp, somehow *hungry* smile, and his sapphire eyes gleamed.

"I'm glad you asked me that, My Lord," he said.

. X .
Thesmar-Cheryk High Road,
The South March,
Republic of Siddarmark

What do those idiots think they're doing?" Sir Zhadwail Brynygair muttered irritably. "Besides being a pain in the arse, that is."

The scout made no reply, possibly because he recognized a rhetorical question when he heard it, but more probably because of Brynygair's tone. Sir Zhadwail had a well-deserved reputation for bellicosity which did not limit itself solely to the battlefield.

The colonel glanced at his executive officer. At thirty-five, Major Ahrnahld Suvyryv was twelve years younger than Brynygair, and unlike the colonel, he was of commoner stock, the son of a wealthy Gorath merchant. He had a sharp brain and a good eye for terrain, however, and despite a certain initial disparagement of his plebeian birth, Brynygair had learned to rely on his judgment. They'd even become friends . . . after a fashion, at any rate. And the ferocity of young Suvyryv's devotion to Mother Church made up for quite a lot in the colonel's book.

"What do *you* think they're doing, Major?" he growled.

"I don't know, Sir," Suvyryv replied with the frankness which was one of his great virtues in Brynygair's opinion. And one, unfortunately, shared by altogether too few other cavalry officers he could have named.

"From what the sergeant here has to say, it's a fairly good position as far as flank security's concerned," the major continued. He scowled. "The maps are even worse than usual once you get off the high road or away from the river, but from the looks of this"—he waved the sketch the scout had brought back with him—"we'd break the legs of every horse in the regiment trying to get through that ravine on the east. We won't get formed infantry through there, either—it looks like some of the rocks in it are bigger than damned houses! But no more than a single regiment of pikes? Standing around in the middle of nowhere all by itself? On a crest line where even a blind man, much less one of our scouts, is bound to see it?" He shook his head. "Beats the Shan-wei out of me, Sir!"

"Could you make out uniforms, Sergeant?" Brynygair asked.

"No, Sir Zhadwail," the scout replied. "Didn't look like they were wearing any, to be honest. I didn't see any breastplates, though."

Brynygair and Suvyryv exchanged glances. Regulars wore breastplates; if the sergeant hadn't seen any, the lunatics standing out in the open had to be militia. Of course, any surviving militia in the South March had been through a brutal period of polishing, and Siddarmarkian militia had been far better than their Dohlaran counterparts to begin with. And then there was the fact that *these* militia, according to the scout, had a light company armed entirely with muskets. That was an unusual and unhappy circumstance.

"All right, Sergeant." Brynygair nodded brusquely. "A good job. Find the Sergeant Major and keep yourself handy in case we have any more questions."

"Yes, Sir!"

The sergeant slapped his breastplate, turned his horse, and trotted off towards the regiment's color party. Brynygair watched him go, then turned back to Suvyryv with a scowl.

"I don't like those damned muskets," he growled. "Not when we can't get at them in a charge without hitting the pikes."

"Bring up the artillery, Sir?" Suvyryv asked, and Brynygair's scowl deepened.

"That would take hours. We're too far out in front."

Suvyryv nodded. Sir Ohtys Godwyl, Baron Traylmyn, commanding the column which had taken the ruins of the town of Cheryk three days ago, was the very point of the Dohlaran spear at the moment. General Rychtyr had taken two more cavalry regiments, two of the vanguard's infantry regiments, and all of the vanguard's horse artillery north after Colonel Byrgair to make sure of the destruction of the Fort Sheldyn garrison. From the dispatches they'd received, it had been far more firepower than could possibly have been needed, but no one had known that at the time. And by the time Byrgair's message detailing the total obliteration of his target had reached Rychtyr, the general had been so far along the miserable cow paths he'd been following that it made more sense for him to continue to the high road, then march south along it to rejoin Baron Traylmyn.

Unfortunately, that meant ten percent of the vanguard's cavalry and twenty percent of its infantry wouldn't reach Cheryk for at least another two days. And it also meant the only artillery available to Baron Traylmyn was foot artillery, most of it drawn by dragons, who had a lively distaste for the sounds of artillery and musketry, rather than by horses. Worse, the nearest batteries, from Major Shanyn's regiment, were at least an hour and more probably two from Brynygair's current position. And that was a great pity, given what the far lighter horses guns Byrgair had taken with him had apparently done to the Siddarmarkian *regulars* he'd faced.

"Beggars can't be choosers," the colonel said after a moment's intense thought. "We'd play hell trying to pass guns through the column in this terrain, anyway." He waved one hand at the fifteen- or twenty-mile-deep belt of second-growth trees through which the road ran at the moment. "On the other hand, according to the Sergeant, the idiots in that clearing are over two thousand yards back from where the road comes out of the trees." He shook his head in disgust. "They've given us two thousand yards of depth and at least a four- or five-thousand-yard frontage between the ravine and where the trees close back in to the east."

He stared at the scout's sketch for a moment, as if disgusted to see even an enemy choose such a foolish position. Even spread out the way the sergeant had reported, the Siddarmarkians could cover no more than about two hundred yards, barely a tenth of the frontage available to deploy against them. And with the woods squeezing in on the high road less than two thousand more yards behind them, they'd be in a virtual sack if they tried to retreat. Small as their force was, it would clog that narrow slot of a road solid. In the face of a determined mounted pursuit, they were looking at a massacre.

"All right," he said, still gazing at the sketch map and thinking aloud. "We've got room for it, so we bring up Barwail's and Tohmpsyn's infantry and form them on both sides of the roadbed. Then we put our regiment on the east flank and Tahlmydg's on the west. And let's go ahead and close up Zherdain's and Klymynt's cavalry behind us. See if we can get another infantry regiment and at least a couple of batteries of twelve-pounders moved up, too. If they want to stand and fight outnumbered five to one in rifles and muskets, that's fine with me. If they decide to turn and run—which is what they'll *probably* do once they realize we're serious—we've got the cavalry to ride them down from behind, and I want enough weight behind us to keep right on hammering them once they break. I don't want them pulling themselves back together and actually finding a *smart* place to bog us down in these woods closer to Thesmar."

Suvyryv narrowed his eyes, considering what the colonel had said, then nodded.

"Might be a bit of using a sledgehammer to crack a slabnut, Sir, but that's fine with me." He grinned. "And, frankly, the thought of hitting them from behind after they break is a lot more appealing than charging pikes head-on!"

Brynygair snorted, trying to imagine one of his more nobly born company commanders saying anything of the sort. The fact that he couldn't was one reason he'd come to value Suvyryv so highly.

"All right, then," he said. "Let's get moving. Oh, and be sure to send a dispatch back to General Traylmyn!"

▼   ▼   ▼

The line of pikemen blocking the high road where it crossed the east-west ridgeline looked even more ragged than Brynygair had anticipated from the scout's report. The pikes were still in their vertical, marching positions, which made the irregularity of their ranks even more evident, and he wondered what was going through that motley formation's minds as it watched his own efficiently trained infantry filing out of the woods and spreading across the road to face it.

The new Dohlaran infantry regiments consisted of six companies, each of two hundred and thirty men. They still didn't have anywhere near the number of rifles they would have preferred, and until they'd had a chance to actually test the proposition in battle, no one had been willing to rely solely on the ability of bayoneted rifles to hold cavalry at bay, anyway. So each regiment contained one company of pikemen and five companies of riflemen or musketeers. The majority of the regiments—and both Sir Sahlmyn Tohmpsyn's and Haarahld Barwail's in particular—had three companies armed with the new rifles, but the other two non-pike companies carried old-fashioned matchlocks. Those matchlocks weren't going to be effective at anywhere near the range rifles were, they fired far more slowly, and they needed almost twice as much frontage per man as flintlocks, since no one wanted to get too close to the other fellow's lit match while he was loading his own weapon. But at least he wasn't dealing with the handful of regiments where the proportions of rifles and matchlocks were reversed.

He saw a shiver go through those raised pikes as his infantry deployed into the clearing. Despite the ravine to the east and the trees to the west, the slope up to the Siddarmarkian position was clear of any real obstacle—good terrain for cavalry, and equally good for an infantry advance. Grass rose high enough to drag at their stirrups, but it was sparse enough, clustered in knots and patches, for his troopers and their mounts to be confident no hidden obstacles were going to break any legs or scatter his formation.

His own pikes stayed to the rear, prepared to form a reserve position the other infantry companies could retreat on if it turned out that by some miracle there was actually cavalry somewhere behind that crest line. The rifle companies formed a three-deep line across the high road in the knee- and waist-high grass, a thousand yards short of the Siddarmarkian position, with the matchlocks behind them in a fourth line, and his cavalry formed a solid block at either end of the infantry, anchoring its line and poised to sweep forward if the Siddarmarkians broke.

There were even fewer pikemen than he'd thought there were, he realized as he raised his spyglass and considered the mass of ragged, obviously nervous farmers along the crest line. A Siddarmarkian regiment normally consisted of eighteen hundred pikes and four hundred and fifty arbalesters or musketeers, but he'd be astonished if there were actually as many as a thousand men in that line. He couldn't blame the scouts for their misesti- mate, given the way those raised pikes and extended formation confused the eye, but he wished he'd realized how weak they actually were. He probably *could* have driven them into headlong retreat with no more than a cavalry regiment or two, and saved the hour and a half he'd spent organiz- ing this more elaborate attack.

Well, Suvyryv had a point, he told himself. *Better to find out you're using a sledgehammer to crack a slabnut than find out the hard way that the slabnut was actu- ally a shellhorn* pretending *to be a slabnut until you walked into the stinger*.

He grimaced sourly, remembering the time a far younger Zhadwail Brynygair had reached out to pick a slabnut only to discover it was one of the venomous insects, folded up inside its segmented shell. His hand had swelled to almost twice its normal size after that episode, and it had been days before the nausea fully passed. In this case, though, it not only looked like a slabnut, it *was* a slabnut.

And it was time to crack that shell.

"Sound advance," he said, and the bugle notes rose clear and clean from his color party. Nothing happened for a moment, and then the infantry line started forward through the grass at a measured seventy-five paces per min- ute with the cavalry advancing steadily on either flank.

For one minute, then two, there was no motion out of the Siddarmarki- ans at all. The pikes didn't even come down into fighting position. Then a fresh, more violent shiver ran through those upright weapons, and Brynygair's eyes widened in surprise as that entire, ragged line simply disintegrated. They didn't even try to take their pikes with them; they simply dropped them, turned, and bolted back across the crest line in a formless, panic-stricken mob.

For a moment, even though he'd anticipated that they'd probably break, the sheer suddenness and totality of the rout was more than he could pro- cess. Then he grinned savagely.

"Sound the charge!" he snapped, and the bugle notes rose, strident and insistent as the cavalry moved from the walk up to the trot.

The grass made things more awkward, and it took longer than usual for the horses to begin building speed. By the time they were halfway up the slope, though, they were up to a maneuvering gallop, the horses devouring over three hundred yards every minute. It took a total of just over five minutes to cover the total distance to the crest of the ridge, and they went over it in a compact, deadly bristle of lowered lances.

The universe blew apart around them.

The "routed, panic-stricken" Siddarmarkians who'd actually been Imperial Charisian Navy seamen in borrowed farmers' smocks stood up in the waist-deep trenches to either side of the high road at the bottom of the reverse slope. The spoil from the trenches had been thrown up on the northern side, forming a parapet that covered them to the shoulder, and the breech-loading Mahndrayns they'd left in the trench were leveled across the parapet.

So were the Mahndrayns of the other fifteen hundred seamen who'd been waiting for them.

Brynygair's stomach clenched as he saw the barrier in front of his men. It didn't have time to register—not really, not with his cavalry racing down the slope towards it—and even if there'd been more time, he couldn't wrap his mind around that many firearms. Not the matchlocks he'd expected, but bayoneted rifles in the hands of steady, unshaken, entrenched infantry. Infantry who were seamen of the Imperial Charisian Navy . . . and who had a score to settle with the kingdom which had surrendered over four hundred of their fellows to the Inquisition's butchery.

There was no mercy behind those rifles, and the surprise was total, with far too little time for anyone to even think about stopping that headlong charge.

Twenty-five hundred rifles fired almost as one against a mere nine hundred cavalry. The astonishing thing was that almost three hundred of that cavalry survived the crashing volley.

Sir Zhadwail Brynygair was among the survivors. He found himself on the ground, half-stunned by the impact, only vaguely aware he'd managed to kick free of the stirrups when his horse went down. His right shoulder felt as if he'd been shot as well, but it was "only" broken, and he shoved himself to his knees with his good arm.

The afternoon was a bedlam of screaming men and shrieking horses, and a solid wall of smoke rose above the entrenchments in front of him. Some of the horses who hadn't been hit had gone down, breaking legs, spilling their riders, as they crashed into other horses who'd been killed or wounded. But horses were bigger targets than men; they'd absorbed a much higher percentage of the Charisian bullets, and he saw other troopers pushing themselves back to their feet. Some of them drew pistols from their saddle holsters to shoot screaming horses, others reached for dropped lances or drew their swords, but some just stood there, looking around, dazed by the sudden, total shock of surprise. Perhaps a hundred of his men were still mounted, but their horses had stopped dead, blocked by the barricade of dead and wounded men and animals. At least twenty or thirty others had turned and bolted back the way they'd come, and Brynygair didn't blame them. It was time to—

The second volley crashed on the heels of the first, equally large and impossibly quickly, and a half-inch rifle bullet slammed through Sir Zhadwail Brynygair's breastplate like the sledgehammer he'd thought he was about to apply to a slabnut.

▼ ▼ ▼

The Earl of Hanth raised the short, handy (and fiendishly expensive) double-spyglass—"binoculars" the Royal College called them—and his mouth was a grim line of satisfaction. He'd hoped he might entice either more cavalry or a couple more infantry regiments to come across the crest, but he'd settle for what he'd gotten. Especially since his trap was only beginning to close.

Bugles sounded, and the seamen of his naval "battalions" climbed out of their earthworks, formed into a skirmish line, and headed back towards the crest they'd "abandoned in panic." From Hanth's position in the trees west of them, he could see along the front slope of the ridge. Not all the way, but far enough to know the Dohlaran infantry had halted in consternation at the sudden roar of rifle fire and the tumultuous retreat of the handful of surviving horsemen.

More rifle fire crackled suddenly—this time from *behind* them, from the thousand Marines he'd hidden in the woods on either side of the high road. Those Marines had camouflaged their positions with care, but it hadn't really mattered. The Dohlaran scouts had been cavalry troopers, not infantry, and it had never occurred to them to search the woods, especially after they'd spotted the "Siddarmarkians" formed up along the crest with the pikes Breygart had borrowed from General Fyguera precisely so that they could be abandoned at the critical moment. Now those Marines, responding to the seamen's fire and scattered through the woods that were effectively impassable for cavalry, opened fire in turn, using trees, fallen logs, rocks, even folds in the ground for cover. They fired from prone positions, using the Mahndrayn's breech-loading capability with ruthless efficiency, and panic ripped through the regiments Brynygair had brought up behind his spearhead to exploit his anticipated victory.

The men and horses packed together on the high road and pinned between the encroaching banks of forest, couldn't even *see* their attackers. All they saw were muzzle flashes in the deep, green gloom—muzzle flashes *everywhere*—as a fog bank of gun smoke rolled through the trees. Bullets slammed into them like fists of flame, shattering flesh and bone, sending men, horses—even draft dragons—down in sodden death or screaming agony. The carnage, coupled with the sheer astonishment of the totally unexpected attack, was too much. They turned to flee back the way they'd come, but they were packed too tightly. The rifle fire continued to rip into them mercilessly, and the press of bodies turned them into a motionless mass that couldn't escape.

A wounded seven-ton dragon shrieked in pain and fury. It heaved up on its four rearmost limbs, its front limbs hammering at everyone around it. Then it turned, heading north, and unlike infantrymen or a mere horse, it had the size and strength of Juggernaut. It trampled men and horses alike underfoot, raging back up the high road, the limbered field gun behind it crushing bone and flesh under iron-rimmed wheels.

And even as the butchery exploded in the woods, Hanth's seamen came back across the crest line.

Colonel Tohmpsyn and Colonel Barwail had managed to hold their men together, and their front ranks had knelt, bringing their rifles to bear on the crest of the ridge while the rank behind them leveled their weapons over their heads. They were shaken, touched with more than an edge of panic, but they were also disciplined, well-trained men whose officers had earned their trust. They knew what their rifles could do, and they waited for the order to fire.

But Hanth had anticipated that, and when his "infantry" reached the crest, the seamen went across it on their bellies, prone, exposing only their heads and shoulders and scattered along the full width of the ridge. The deep grass screened even the small targets they presented, making them all but invisible, and they opened fire from that position, without ever rising even to their knees.

The bullets slammed into the tightly formed infantry who stood fully exposed to their attack. They didn't fire in volleys; they fired as individuals, picking their own targets as rapidly as they could find them, using the doctrine Sir Kynt Clareyk had devised around the new breech-loading rifles. The Dohlarans could hardly even *see* their enemies, and they were packed together in the classic, close-order formation of musketeers, not the dispersal of *riflemen*, so dense any Charisian who missed his intended victim was almost certain to hit another one. There was no comparison between the targets the adversaries presented to one another.

Nor was there any comparison between the rates of fire they could maintain. The Dohlarans were well trained, able to load and fire their flintlock rifles in as little as fifteen seconds. But they had to stand upright to do that, and the Charisians who outnumbered them three to two could fire once every *five* seconds . . . from a prone position.

It was a massacre. That storm of fire was more than the most disciplined men imaginable, even men who *knew* they fought for God Himself, could endure. Blood, screams, and the Shan-wei reek of gun smoke enveloped them, and it was more than they could stand. They fired a single volley, and then chaos, confusion, and death marched through them in iron boots.

Less than a quarter of them lived long enough to run.

▼   ▼   ▼

The holocaust Earl Hanth supposed would probably be called the Battle of Thesmar lasted twenty minutes. It took less than five to shatter the Dohlaran attack; the other fifteen minutes were an unmitigated slaughter as his Marines poured fire into the column trapped on the high road. His own losses were less than forty men.

Well, he thought harshly, looking out over the writhing, moaning, sobbing carpet of wounded and dying Dohlarans, *you bastards know the cakewalk's over now, don't you?* He bared his teeth. *Now let's just see if we can't encourage you to turn around and go home while you're still more or less in one piece.*

.XI.
North Bedard Bay,
City of Siddar,
Republic of Siddarmark

It was cool on the waterfront. The cloudy day promised rain by afternoon, and the wind was brisk and muscular as it swept across the broad blue waters. The tide was coming in, the white-crested waves breaking higher on the pilings of massive piers, washing against the seawall with ageless, timeless patience. The piers and wharfs were crowded with Charisian transport galleons, and from where he stood at quayside, Merlin Athrawes watched long lines of imperial Charisian soldiers filing across dozens of gangplanks under the weight of heavy knapsacks and slung rifles.

Hundreds of Siddarmarkians had come out to welcome the Charisians, and he heard them cheering, waving small Charisian flags which had appeared mysteriously all over the city. The soldiers were too disciplined to break ranks, but their step turned a little jauntier, their regimental bands struck up a more lively marching note, and more than one of them managed to make eye contact with the more attractive—and younger—female members of the crowd. They'd taken pains to refurbish their worn-out gear after the long, weary march from The Fence to Ramsgate Bay, and their boot heels struck the cobblestones with a fierce, strong rhythm.

Those infantry regiments would be changing those slung rifles for new ones before evening, Merlin thought, watching them march past him without ever realizing he was there. And after that, they'd be off on yet another voyage, this time aboard canal boats with double teams of dragons, priority-cleared through every lock between them and the fighting. They'd make the trip at an average of fifty miles or more per day . . . and the odds were they wouldn't get there in time anyway.

He folded his arms across his chest, standing in the little pocket of clear space his *seijin's* reputation always seemed to create. No one wanted to crowd the fearsome *Seijin* Merlin, which he'd found quite useful on occasion. At the moment, he wasn't sure he liked it very much, however; it gave him too much privacy for his thoughts.

Dark thoughts.

The one real bright spot was Hauwerd Breygart, and even that one was purely conditional. The Earl of Hanth's mixed bag of Marines and sailors had decisively halted the Dohlaran vanguard's advance towards Thesmar. The Battle of Thesmar—although it had been fought miles from the city, Merlin was certain the name Hanth had used in his dispatches was going to stick—had come as a catastrophic shock to the Dohlarans. It had cost them almost eight thousand men, more than two-thirds dead and wounded, as well as eighteen twelve-pounder field guns. That was twenty percent of Sir Fahstyr Rychtyr's initial order of battle, and the blow to the Dohlarans' confidence had been even worse.

Unfortunately, it hadn't been *decisive*. Baron Traylmyn hadn't panicked, although several of his regimental commanders had come close when the initial reports—and the fleeing survivors on their lathered horses—reached his main body. Unlike his colonels, the baron had proven much more flexible than Merlin could have wished, however. He wasn't certain what had happened, but he'd reacted quickly, and with a firm grasp of operational and strategic realities. He'd fallen back towards Trevyr on the Seridahn, leaving two artillery batteries, one of his remaining infantry regiments, and four cavalry regiments to delay Hanth's advance while he threw up earthworks around the eastern side of the town.

His rearguard, unfortunately, had been given time to recover its morale and dig in because the Battle of Thesmar's wreckage had delayed Hanth more than the Marine had counted upon. The high road through the woods was completely choked with dead men, horses, and dragons, not to mention abandoned artillery pieces, limbers, and ammunition wagons. He'd had to clear that ghastly roadblock before he could follow his fleeing enemy, and his healers' need to separate the merely wounded from the dead and see to their proper treatment had slowed the process still further.

The surviving Dohlarans were fortunate they'd been defeated by Charisians, not Siddarmarkians. Because they had, they'd been permitted to go *on* surviving, but the delay had cost Hanth a full day, and by the time he'd reached Traylmyn's rearguard, the artillery and its single supporting regiment of infantry had dug in directly across the high road. The enemy cavalry had been more of a nuisance, albeit a serious one, than a genuine threat, but those guns and that infantry had to be dealt with. Hanth *needed* the road if he was going to support his own forces that far from Thesmar, and so he'd deployed his guns and gone to work.

To their credit, the outnumbered Dohlaran infantry and artillerists had stood their ground with stubborn, dogged courage. Traylmyn's fragmentary reports had given him no idea the Charisians' rifles were breech-loaders, but he had a very firm idea of the advantages which accrued to infantry behind thick earthen parapets, and his uncompromising instructions to dig in deeply had blunted most of the Mahndrayns' tactical advantages. The Charisians could still fire much more rapidly—and suffered virtually no misfires, which the more poorly designed Dohlaran flintlocks did more than fifteen percent of the time—but the protection of the entrenchments offset their more dispersed formations and ability to fire from a prone position, and there'd been no handy tree trunks or boulders for their skirmishers to use. It had turned into an old-fashioned artillery duel, with the Marines watching the flanks to keep the cavalry at bay, and the larger number— and greater caliber—of the Charisian pieces had been decisive, despite the Dohlarans' entrenched position.

Hanth's naval gunners hadn't had it all their own way. He'd lost over sixty of them, but the thirty-pounders' shells were more than three times as heavy as those of the Dohlarans' twelve-pounders, and even though the *design* of the Dohlaran shells was virtually identical, Charisian quality control was much better. Charisian shells had a far greater tendency to explode where they were supposed to, whereas variations in the Dohlaran fuses made them substantially less reliable. The thirty-pounders had fired much more slowly, but each shell had been far more effective.

The Dohlarans had stood their ground until all but two of their guns had been silenced. Then they'd spiked the two survivors—they'd no longer had the draft animals to withdraw them—and pulled back, with the cavalry screening the infantry's withdrawal. The rearguard's stand had cost half the infantry committed to it—another six hundred dead and wounded, ten times Hanth's casualties—in addition to the artillery, but it had served its purpose. By the time the earl was able to close up to Trevyr, Traylmyn was firmly dug in, with all of his remaining field guns emplaced. Not only that, but his dispatches to Rychtyr had hastened his superior's approach, and the rest of the vanguard's remaining strength had reached Trevyr before Hanth had.

Since he was now outnumbered by better than four-to-one by an opponent dug in behind thick, well laid out earthworks, and since he had no cavalry of his own, Hanth had declined to assault the town. Instead, he'd stopped just outside artillery range and dug in his own forces. He had to be careful, since his thirty-pounders were heavy and cumbersome, even with their field carriages. Getting them limbered up and on the road back to Thesmar would take time that was unlikely to be available if the Dohlarans surprised him with a sudden assault. But if Rychtyr and Traylmyn were content to sit in Trevyr and be besieged, Hauwerd Breygart was perfectly prepared to sit *outside* Trevyr and do the besieging. He'd posted pickets on the Cheryk-Cheraltyn high road to make sure nobody snuck up on him from the north, and he'd entrenched four of his thirty-pounders north of Trevyr, covered by two hundred of his Marines, where they could sweep the surface of the St. Alyk River. No one was going to use that river to support any advances into Cliff Peak unless they first pushed him out of position, and as long as he sat where he was, he held almost five times as many Dohlarans in place.

Actually, the total number was higher than that. Sir Rainos Ahlverez had reached Evyrtyn, farther north on the Seridahn, with the leading elements of the fifty-thousand-strong Dohlaran main body. If he'd chosen to move south with his entire strength, he could undoubtedly have brushed Hanth out of his path, no matter how good the earl and his men were. He'd chosen otherwise, however, partly because of persistent reports that the Charisians who'd bloodied Traylmyn's nose had also sent troops up the Taigyn, past Fort Darymahn, to hold that river line against him, too. He had no desire to face any more of those Charisian weapons than he had to, and so he'd sent an additional four infantry regiments to reinforce Rychtyr, but the remainder of his men were moving not south, but *north*. They were headed up the Seridahn to Alyksberg, the fortress guarding the pass where the East Seridahn flowed out of the Snake Mountains.

The fall of Alyksberg would divert him from his secondary objectives in the eastern South March, but he was perfectly willing to leave that little chore to Desnair. And the change would give *him* access to Cliff Peak . . . without needing to operate up the St. Alyk or force a crossing of the Taigyn. Perhaps even more important, from his perspective, Alyksberg was manned by only five badly understrength Siddarmarkian regiments, composed mainly of militia, and without a single rifle or new-model artillery piece. And according to his spies, the garrison was virtually out of food and its ranks were riddled by illness.

From his perspective, it was a much more inviting target, and Merlin couldn't disagree with him. Hanth had done a superb job, but as Greyghor

Stohnar had pointed out, they simply couldn't be in enough places at once. Merlin had no doubt Alyksberg would fall, and quickly, when fifty thousand men moved to assault it, and as soon as Alyksberg fell, the door into Cliff Peak Province would be wide open for the Royal Dohlaran Army.

Nor would the Dohlarans be alone. Kaitswyrth's advance out of Westmarch had crossed the Cliff Peak border two days ago, and the city of Aivahnstyn on the Daivyn River had fallen without a fight, because General Charlz Stahntyn, commanding the fifteen-thousand-man garrison, had been wise enough to realize what would have happened to the city if he'd tried to defend it. He'd also realized what would have happened if he'd taken his fifteen thousand men out to face a hundred and ten thousand in the field, however, and so he'd fallen back south, towards the city of Sangyr.

Unfortunately, Stahntyn had possessed virtually no cavalry, and the bishop militant had used his own cavalry to get around the weary, ill-nourished Siddarmarkian infantry. The Church's horsemen had caught them within twenty miles of Aivahnstyn and held them in play until Kaitswyrth's infantry came up. Stahntyn had formed his men for battle even though he'd known it was hopeless, but Kaitswyrth had seen no reason to suffer avoidable casualties. He'd simply brought up his guns and done to the defenders of Aivahnstyn what Sir Naythyn Byrgair had done to Colonel Mahldyn's regiments on the Syrk high road.

Except, of course, Merlin thought, his mouth tightening, that no one in the Army of God had been prepared to give Stahntyn's survivors Pasquale's Grace. Father Sedryk Zavyr, Kaitswyrth's Schuelerite special intendant, was far more concerned with punishing sinners for their offense against God than with attempting to save their souls, and the inquisitors attached to Kaitswyrth's army took their cue from him. Not that Merlin had ever seen any practical difference between those like Zavyr and those who claimed they sought to reclaim Shan-wei's victims from the lip of hell. Whatever their motives, the butchery was the same.

Bishop Militant Bahrnabai Wyrshym, whose army was headed towards Guarnak, was a very different man from Kaitswyrth. He was older, and while both were Chihirite members of the Order of the Sword and experienced ex-Temple Guardsmen, that was the end of the similarities between them. Muscular and tough, with gray hair and eyes, Wyrshym gave the impression of a man made of iron, yet unlike Kaitswyrth, he clearly didn't agree with Clyntahn's extremism. He'd also served in the same unit as Hauwerd Wylsynn many years ago, and Merlin suspected that was the main reason he'd been sent to secure New Northland and the Sylmahn Gap while Clyntahn had selected Kaitswyrth to deal with Cliff Peak.

He wasn't sure what to make of Wyrshym's special intendant, Auxiliary

Bishop Ernyst Abernethy, though. Abernethy was very young for his position, having risen rapidly in his order as Clyntahn and Rayno expanded their pool of inquisitors, and he seemed to be prepared to be however severe his duties required, yet Merlin suspected he regretted all the violence and ugliness. He didn't go out of his way to be vicious, the way Zavyr did, at any rate.

But then there was Bishop Wylbyr Edwyrds, Clyntahn's handpicked choice for the newly created post of Inquisitor General to head the Inquisition in the territories occupied by the Army of God. He wasn't technically part of that army at all, although he had authority to call upon it whenever he felt that was necessary. In fact, despite the fact that both Wyrshym and Kaitswyrth were senior to him in the Church's hierarchy, he could actually give *them* orders in anything that pertained to his own responsibilities . . . and he was the one who determined when it was appropriate for him to do that. He and his administration reminded Merlin irresistibly of the SS following the Wehrmacht into occupied territory in Old Earth's World War Two, and Owl's remotes had snooped on enough of Edwyrds' correspondence for Merlin to know Clyntahn had personally charged him to crush Siddarmarkian heresy—which included opposition to Clyntahn's policies on *any* basis, secular or temporal—with blood and terror.

He clearly intended to do just that.

The denunciation of neighbor by neighbor had already begun . . . and so had the autos-da-fé. The hatred the previous winter's bitter fighting had created and stoked fed those fires with a steady flow of victims, and the bitterness between the informers and the informed upon only fed the hatred, in turn. The body count, already high in the fighting of the Sword of Schueler, was rising steadily, and it wasn't going to get any better any time soon.

The only good news—and even it posed fresh problems for the Republic's overwhelmed defenders—was how many thousands of additional refugees had managed to escape. The Army of God was advancing on its designated targets with disciplined efficiency, not allowing itself to be diverted. That gave those it had bypassed the opportunity to flee, and the weather was far better than it had been during the bitter winter months, so none of those refugees were dying from hypothermia. But food was still scarce, and the refugee columns' paths were marked by the bodies of all too many victims of starvation. Somehow, the Siddarmarkian army and government had to find housing, food, and medical care for all of them, even as they tried desperately to defend what remained of their country against the invaders.

And that's the good *news*, Merlin thought bitterly. *God, I knew it was going to be ugly, but this—! It's like one enormous ongoing atrocity, and even if my brainstorm actually works, there's not a single solitary* damned *thing we can do about what's*

*going to happen to anyone trapped behind Church lines. Not a thing, before next sum-
mer at the earliest, and even for that, we have to hang on through the rest of this campaigning season!*

A longshoreman hurrying past almost ran into the stationary *seijin*. He
slid to a stop and turned his head to apologize for the near collision. But his
expression congealed and he scurried away without a word as he saw those
grim, dark eyes.

Merlin watched him go with a certain bitter amusement.

Didn't realize I looked quite that bad, he thought. *I suppose I ought to try to
cultivate a more confident expression in public. It's just not my cup of tea, though. I'm
more the mayhem and massacre sort myself, I suppose. Or that's the way I'm feeling
right this minute, anyway. Maybe—*

His thoughts broke off as he saw what he'd been waiting to see. A cloud
of smoke forged steadily across North Bedard Bay towards the city, and
there were three more plumes behind it.

He watched them for a few more moments, then started down the stone
steps to the launch waiting for him at their feet.

▼ ▼ ▼

"Sir, *please* tell me you're joking," Pawal Blahdysnberg said, looking across
the chart table in HMS *Delthak*'s conning tower at his captain.

"Is this my 'I'm telling a funny story' face?" Halcom Bahrns demanded
testily. "We've got three days."

"But, Sir—!"

Blahdysnberg broke off, staring at his CO. His expression was a mix of
consternation and something very like desperation, and Bahrns didn't blame
him one bit. His own reaction to the orders *Seijin* Merlin had delivered had
been . . . less than calm.

"The men are exhausted, Sir," the lieutenant continued after a moment. "I'll admit we've arrived in one hell of a better shape than I expected
when we left, but the stokers, especially, are worn out. And Zhak thought
we'd have time to do maintenance on the engines. Sir, we've just steamed
six thousand miles! I don't have any *idea* what that means about these engines'
reliability. Do you?"

"No, I don't. But we don't have any choice, Pawal," Bahrns said now, his
voice flatter. "They've been waiting for us, and this comes direct from the
Emperor. The barge conversions are almost done. Commodore Shailtyn's
already picked the drafts from his galleons' crews—and if you think *you're*
upset, you should hear what his captains had to say about this. We're stripping almost six hundred seamen and gunners right out from under them! Not
only that, they've had to give up the *artillery* we're going to need, as well—

it's already been swayed ashore; it's waiting for us at Saint Angyloh's Quay, along with our coal. More galleons left two days ago to ferry additional coal to Ranshair and Salyk, too. Assuming all of this works, it'll be waiting for us when we get there. Oh, and in addition to the seamen and gunners Commodore Shailtyn's giving up, we're also taking along two hundred of his Marines and six companies of Siddarmarkian riflemen. Riflemen, I hasten to add, who received their rifles for the first time day before yesterday. But don't worry. *Seijin* Merlin assures me they'll be spending all the time before we depart learning how to load and fire without blowing off their own heads—or anyone else's—in the process."

Blahdysnberg's consternation had segued into shock as he listened to Bahrns' "explanation." He looked as if he'd just been hit over the head, and the captain gave him a minute or two to absorb it before he reached out and squeezed his shoulder.

"You know the old Navy saying, Pawal—'If you can't take a joke, you shouldn't have joined,'" he said in a gentler voice. "I'll admit I'm finding the humor just a bit hard to see at the moment myself, but that doesn't change what we have to do. And it's important." He looked into Blahdysnberg's eyes. "It's more important than you could possibly guess."

Blahdysnberg looked back at him. Then his nostrils flared as he inhaled deeply, and he gave himself a shake.

"In that case, Sir," he said with a crooked smile, "I suppose I'd better get started working on it."

.XII.
Alyksberg,
Cliff Peak Province,
and
Lake City,
Tarikah Province,
Republic of Siddarmark

Alyksberg was dying.

Sir Rainos Ahlverez stood at the fly of his command tent, watching the clouds turn the color of blood above the burning roofs of the fortress city his guns had set afire, and listened to the sounds of musketry. His tent was five thousand yards from the walls, and he couldn't hear the screams from here, but he knew they were there, and he bared his teeth.

The city had held out for five days and, frankly, he'd expected it to hold far longer. But that had been true only until the spy reached him with the news that the garrison commander had deserted his post before Ahlverez' army ever reached it.

Fury snarled inside him at the thought of the four entire days he'd wasted preparing a formal siege of the fortress. And wasted was exactly the right word, he thought grimly. Clyftyn Sumyrs, the apostate Siddarmarkian general who'd held the city for the excommunicate Stohnar, was a man of no birth, and he'd proven it by abandoning his command. He'd run for his own life, like the cur he was, but before he had, he'd asked for volunteers to man the walls and the artillery to deceive Ahlverez into believing the city was still garrisoned and cover his own craven flight. According to the spy's report, almost a quarter of his entire force actually *had* volunteered, too, despite the welcome they knew the Inquisition held in store for them.

Ahlverez took that particular part of the report with a large grain of salt, but true or not, Sumyrs had been forced to choose who stayed, and— once more according to the spy—he'd chosen primarily the sick and the weak, men who couldn't have kept up with his retreating column anyway. And then he'd slipped away, like a thief creeping away in the night, leaving them to delay Ahlverez until the remainder of his force was safely beyond pursuit . . . which was exactly what the bastards had done.

And much joy may they have of it, he thought venomously, watching the flash of matchlocks and slow-firing, old-style artillery on the parapets, listening to the sounds as his assaulting troops swarmed forward, going up the scaling ladders in scores of places simultaneously. Whole stretches of the wall were falling silent as his men swarmed over the defenders who'd manned them, and he smiled grimly.

I knew they couldn't have the men to hold the wall against a general assault! Now that we're over it, we'll swamp the bastards, and Father Sulyvyn will see to it they answer for their heresy. And Sumyrs wouldn't have cut and run in the first place if he'd thought there was anywhere else he could hold short of St. Alyk's Abbey. He may have slowed us up long enough to save his own worthless arse—for now, at least—but he did it by handing over the key to Cliff Peak's front door! Once Alyskberg goes down, we'll march straight through and—

The night turned suddenly to day, and Sir Rainos Ahlverez staggered backwards, hands rising instinctively to cover his head despite his distance from the city, as the fortress' main magazine erupted. More explosions rumbled, rolling along the walls, flashing and bellowing as if Shan-wei had stolen Langhorne's own Rakurai, as the burning fuses reached the waiting charges. The sound was an echoing, deafening roar as the waves of overpressure beat on him like the fury of some unseen, storm-lashed sea, and he saw flaming chunks of wreckage—all too many of which, he knew, must be the bodies of his own assaulting infantry—arcing across the fire-sick night.

His jaw tightened as he realized what had happened, and then he swore savagely. He didn't know whose hand had lit the fuse, and he never would, but the son of a whore had timed it with Kau-yung's own cunning! And that rolling avalanche of smaller explosions told him it had been no hastily improvised act. The motherless bastards had *planned* it this way—planned it from the very beginning! They'd known they couldn't hold, so they'd found a way to escape the Punishment and simultaneously cost him more men than they could ever have killed in a conventional defense!

He watched the blazing debris reach the top of its trajectory, come plunging back to earth, and knowing the heretics who'd set those explosions had just hastened their own journeys to hell failed to make him feel one bit better. He had the key to Cliff Peak, all right . . . and Langhorne only knew how many men he'd just paid to gain it.

▼ ▼ ▼

"I assume this . . . request is necessary, Father?" Arthyn Zagyrsk said in a careful tone.

"I'm afraid so, Your Eminence." Ignaz Aimaiyr, Zagyrsk noticed with a sense of bitter satisfaction, didn't sound any happier than his archbishop. "The *instruction*"—he emphasized the noun very slightly, not that he seemed to want to—"carries Bishop Wylbyr's personal signature."

"I see."

Zagyrsk remained where he was, hands folded behind him, gazing out his office window across Lake City's roofs until he was confident he had his expression back under control. Aimaiyr was right, he thought; it wasn't a request, it was an *order*. It took him a moment, but then he nodded, without turning back to face the intendant. It wasn't Aimaiyr's fault, yet just at that moment, he really didn't want to look at anyone in a Schuelerite's purple cassock.

"Very well, Father. Tell Father Avry I've approved the Inquisitor General's 'instructions.'"

He heard the quotation marks in his own voice and knew they were dangerous, but he couldn't help it.

"Thank you, Your Eminence."

Aimaiyr's quiet voice was no happier than it had been, and Zagyrsk heard his office door close as the younger man silently departed without kissing his ring. Technically, that was a serious violation of Mother Church's etiquette; at the moment, Zagyrsk was simply grateful the Schuelerite had been wise enough to spare them both.

And that Father Ignaz was too good a man to comment on those dangerous quotation marks.

He felt his shoulders sag now that he was alone, and he leaned forward, hanging his head and bracing himself on the windowsill with both hands as he tried not to feel like a coward.

I should have the courage to protest. At the very least to protest using my *people for this, even if I dared not protest anything else,* he thought wretchedly. *I should. But . . . I don't.*

Not that it would have done any good. If he'd thought it might, if he'd believed it could, he might have protested anyway. But Wylbyr Edwyrds was the Grand Inquisitor's own choice. No argument from a mere archbishop was going to lead Zhaspahr Clyntahn to rein him in—not when he was doing exactly what he'd been ordered to do.

And maybe they're actually right *to do it,* the archbishop told himself. *The Book of Schueler's plain enough, and the Grand Inquisitor's right when he points out that Schueler himself said misplaced mercy to the heretic only robs him of his opportunity to expiate his sin and return to God even on the lip of hell itself. But—*

He thought about that "request" from Edwyrds, the order to find another thousand laborers to send forward to help construct the camps in which the accused were to be held until the Inquisition got around to sifting them and sending them to the Punishment as they deserved, and closed his eyes in pain. Bad enough that those camps were being built in such numbers; even worse that *his* people had to be a part of it.

At least he'd saved his own archbishopric from that poisonous stew of denunciation, condemnation, and savage, punitive bloodshed . . . for now, at any rate. He'd managed that much, if nothing more, and he tried not to think about the cold, biting tone of Clyntahn's grudging agreement to exempt Tarikah from Edwyrds' sphere of authority.

If I had protested *what Edwyrds is doing in Hildermoss and New Northland, Clyntahn would have removed me by now, and he'd be doing exactly the same thing right here in Tarikah,* Zagyrsk thought, and even the knowledge that it was nothing but the truth couldn't make him feel one bit less unclean.

He looked out the window, but his eyes were unseeing, and his lips moved in silent prayer as he raised one hand to grip his pectoral scepter.

.XIII.
Siddar City,
Republic of Siddarmark

I can't believe we actually did it," Lieutenant Blahdysnberg said, shaking his head as HMS *Delthak* demonstrated yet another of her remarkable capabilities by backing smoothly away from Saint Angyloh's Quay.

At least part of her new ship's company seemed to find that smooth, gliding sternward motion as profoundly unnatural as many of the spectators did, but it was an undeniably useful ability.

"Neither can I," Halcom Bahrns said absently, watching the water gap between his ship and quayside widen. He waited a moment longer, then looked at the petty officer standing by the big, brass-handled "engine room telegraph."

"Ahead slow starboard," he said.

"Ahead slow starboard, aye, Sir," the petty officer replied, reaching for the right-hand handle. Bells jangled, and after a minute or two, *Delthak* began pivoting sharply.

Bahrns wished he'd had longer to experiment with handling her in confined quarters, but he wasn't going to complain about the maneuverability her twin screws bestowed. Just as long as he didn't get carried away and smash her into something, at any rate!

Despite the fact that her guns had been mounted and she had her full complement on board, she was far lighter than she'd been when she departed Old Charis with six times her normal fuel supply stuffed into every corner. She was also far more crowded, however, and far too many of "his" people were still learning their duties aboard her. Fortunately, Lieutenant Bairystyr's stokers and oilers had been given ample time to learn *their* duties on the voyage to Siddarmark, and his gunners already knew their business, as well.

Which suggests you're probably worrying about whether or not they *know what to do to keep from worrying about what it is* you're *supposed to be doing,* he reflected.

"Stop engines," he ordered.

"Stop engines, aye, Sir."

Bells jangled again, and he glanced at the helmsman waiting another minute or two while the ship continued gliding astern, until he could see the barges lying to their buoys almost dead ahead.

"Rudder amidships."

"Rudder amidships, aye, Sir."

Delthak's course straightened, and he looked at the telegraphsman again

"Slow ahead, both," he said.

"Slow ahead, both, aye, Sir."

▼　　▼　　▼

"I'm with Blahdysnberg," Cayleb Ahrmahk said quietly. "I never really believed they could do it, either."

He stood beside Merlin on his favored balcony on the Siddarmarkian Embassy's roof, watching through Owl's sensors as the ironclads prepared to pick up their tows before leaving harbor. They would be towing a total of six canal barges when they left North Bay, and it had taken almost as long to prepare the barges as it had to prepare the ironclads themselves. They'd been "armored" with thick wooden bulwarks and sandbags, and two of the barges each ironclad would tow had been fitted with four fifty-seven-pounder carronades apiece. Nobody had felt that mounting cannon on barges loaded almost exclusively with gunpowder and coal would have been a very good idea, but the ones carrying the Marines and fledgling Siddarmarkian riflemen needed to be able to look after themselves.

"I can understand that," Merlin replied. "But that was the *easy* part, you know."

"Nothing about this inspiration of yours is going to be remotely 'easy,' Merlin." Cayleb looked at him levelly. "The only thing it's going to be is absolutely necessary . . . assuming Bahrns can pull it off." The emperor shook his head. "I can hardly believe you came up with it even now."

Merlin shrugged, his own eyes still distant as he watched *Delthak* and the other ships easing alongside their tows.

"At least the weather looks good for the run to Ranshair," he said. "That's something. But Wyrshym's going to reach Guarnak tomorrow. Even if everything works perfectly, Bahrns isn't going to be in time to keep him from hammering the Sylmahn Gap before Kynt can get there. It's all going to be up to General Stohnar's people."

"That would've been the case even without this," Cayleb replied, waving one hand in a gesture that took in the maneuvering ironclads he, unlike Merlin, could barely have seen with his own merely human eyes from where they stood. "You couldn't have changed it any more than I could. And even if he manages to push all the way through and take Serabor, he may have to pull back if this works."

"And he may not, too." Merlin's voice was flat. "He's a determined man, Cayleb, and he knows exactly how critical Serabor is. If he gets his hands on it before we can stop him, he's not going to let go even if he has to starve half the rest of his army to hold onto it."

"Then Stohnar's just going to have to hold." Cayleb reached up to lay a hand on Merlin's shoulder. "We've done everything we can, Merlin. As Maikel says, at some point we simply have to trust God to do His part, too."

"Then I just hope He's listening," Merlin said softly. "I just hope He's listening."

JULY
YEAR OF GOD AWAITING
896

✦

.I.
The Sylmahn Gap,
Mountaincross Province,
Republic of Siddarmark

G et your head down, Sir!" Grovair Zhaksyn snapped.

Zhorj Styvynsyn flung himself flat as the shell whizzed overhead. It slammed into the trees behind him, crashing from trunk to trunk, then exploded in a whirlwind of iron shards, shrapnel balls, and shredded greenery.

"What the *fuck* do you think you're *doing*, Sir?!" the sergeant demanded harshly as Styvynsyn raised his dripping face once more.

"I don't think they're targeting individuals—even one as important as me—with *cannon*, Sergeant," the major replied, spitting out a mouthful that was too thin to be called mud but too thick to call water.

"I wasn't talking about the frigging cannon . . . Sir. I was talking about the *rifles!*"

As if to punctuate the sergeant's acid rejoinder, a fresh fusillade of bullets slapped into the muddy earthwork like the hooves of a galloping horse. More sliced across the parapet—about where his superior's head would have been if he hadn't ducked—and more leaves came fluttering down as they severed branches and splintered limbs.

"Oh, you were talking about the *rifles!*" Styvynsyn said, and grinned tightly.

Zhaksyn shook his head, and the major crawled back up onto the earthwork's firing step and raised his head much more cautiously than before.

Bullets whistled overhead like leaden sleet, and fresh white clouds of smoke blossomed, rolling up to meet the gray overcast pressing down from above as the cannon fired steadily. The people on the other ends of those rifles and artillery pieces were a far cry from the late, unlamented Major Cahrtair, he thought grimly.

The 37th Infantry had used its time well since it had mouse-trapped Cahrtair's company. The spring floodwaters had abated, but the dams at the Serabor end of the Gap had been further improved. The inundation was even wider than it had been (and home to Shan-wei's own plague of insects, he thought glumly), with only the roadbed of the high road and occasional raised hummocks of land standing above the sheet of water like islands. The

37th had worked hard to throw up earthworks in front of the belt of woods just south of the section of high road they'd blown up, and Colonel Wyllys had seen to it that they'd fortified fallback positions in the woods themselves. The front of the earthworks was covered with a fifty-yard-deep abatis of tangled tree limbs hacked away to clear killing zones in front of those fortified positions, and Styvynsyn was confident that if his regiment could only have been brought back up to strength, it could have held their position indefinitely against Pawal Baikyr's rebellious militia.

Unfortunately, the 37th was down to little more than two-thirds strength . . . and it no longer faced Baikyr's militia. The Army of God was quite a different proposition, and his mouth tightened in a thin, hard line as he studied the rafts Bishop Gorthyk Nybar's men had brought with them.

It wouldn't have occurred to Baikyr to try something like that . . . and it wouldn't have done him much good if he had. But Nybar and his men were far better organized and disciplined than Baikyr's rebels, they had far better weapons, and it was obvious they also had a far better idea of what to *do* with those weapons. Styvynsyn was grateful General Stohnar's men had been thoroughly briefed on the new-model artillery before they came under fire from it, which had at least kept them from panicking when it happened, but they hadn't managed to get any of their own dragged forward to the 37th's entrenchments. They had barely a dozen pieces altogether, all heavy guns on naval carriages supplied by the Charisian Navy and barged forward from Siddar City, and they were too precious—and immobile—to risk in such an exposed, forward position.

That had been General Stohnar's opinion, at any rate, and Styvynsyn wasn't prepared to second-guess his commanding officer, yet at this moment he wished desperately that he had just one or two of those cannon, preferably with naval gunners, ready to hand. After all, they'd been designed to sink boats, hadn't they?

Fresh artillery fire boomed from the closest of the "gun rafts" Bishop Gorthyk's men had floated into position. Getting them into place must have been a royal pain in the arse, but the Temple Loyalists had managed it, Styvynsyn reflected, giving credit where it was due. At least the current had been in their favor, however; that had to have helped. And he found it bitterly ironic that it was only the defenders' own inundations which had made it possible to get artillery that close without losing gunners in droves to his dug-in riflemen.

Each raft was big enough to carry four of the Army of God's twelve-pounder field guns, protected by a stout, bullet-proof bulwark. They fired through what amounted to naval gunports, their crews shielded from the fire of Styvynsyn's riflemen, and they were gradually creeping ever closer. The nearest raft was barely five hundred yards clear now, close enough to sweep his parapet with canister from its protected position while those farther back tossed what the Charisians called "shrapnel shells" over the earthworks top. It was fortunate the timing on the Church's fuses was so unreliable. Many—possibly even most—of the shells overshot their marks before exploding, but that didn't keep 2nd Company from losing men in a steady trickle, and the enemy's infantry had worked its way forward under cover of the bombardment, as well.

By now, Nybar's riflemen had waded across the gap where Captain Klairynce's explosion had sent Cahrtair's infantry to discuss their rebellion personally with God. They'd carried their rifles and ammunition over their heads as they slogged through the waist-deep and chest-deep water, and they were using the lip of the breach in the high road for protection. Styvynsyn felt confident that, scattered as they were, a quick bayonet charge, covered by his own entrenched riflemen, could have driven them back . . . if not for the damned artillery. As soon as his men came out from behind their earthwork, the guns would slaughter them.

But if we don't *come out, we can't keep the bastards from filling in the gap,* he thought grimly, watching the engineers and working parties systematically filling in the hole he'd blown in the roadbed.

He knew what was going to happen once that gap was filled, and there wasn't one damned thing he could do about it. Not as long as those Shanwei-damned gun rafts were out there.

He dropped back down, sitting with his back to the parapet, and looked up at the lowering sky. Then he glanced in either direction along the firing step and tried not to show his pain as he saw the scattering of bodies sprawled down its length. The best earthwork in the world couldn't provide perfect protection if you meant to shoot back at the enemy, but at least the 37th had four times the rifles they'd had the last time he'd fought here. The Gap's defenders had been given priority on the production from the single Siddarmarkian foundry which had been producing them before the rebellion, and Colonel Wyllys had reequipped three of his four pike companies—including Styvynsyn's—with them. That was going to give the bastards pause when they came up the high road into the 37th's teeth, but he didn't think it was going to be enough.

"Get a runner back to Colonel Wyllys," he told Zhaksyn. "They're going to have that gap filled by sundown, and it's going to be pouring by Langhorne's Watch. If I were them, I'd come at us in the dark, when we don't have the light to pick targets and the rain soaks our priming."

▼   ▼   ▼

Bishop Gorthyk Nybar, commanding officer, Langhorne Division, Army of God, clamped his jaws on the stem of his pipe, his expression grimly satisfied as he listened to the steady thudding of his guns and the crackle of rifles. It wouldn't be long now.

He looked up at the clouds, then down at the map on the table, green eyes hard, and stroked his heavy cavalryman's mustache thoughtfully. Langhorne was Bishop Militant Bahrnabai's favorite division, and Nybar knew it. He also knew his men had *earned* that regard. They'd been the lead element of Wyrshym's advance all the way down the Hildermoss River and the Guarnak-Sylmahn Canal. And it had been Nybar's suggestion to build the rafts and tow them along with the barge loads of infantry and cavalry in order to turn the heretics' strategy of flooding the Gap against them.

He was pleased, overall, with how well the Army of God in general and the Langhorne Division in particular had done, but that didn't mean he was blind to some of the problems they'd turned up. Nor had he been surprised when they did turn up. The entire Army of God was less than two years old, and not even the archangels could have gotten *everything* right with so many new and radical weapons being introduced in such a short period of time.

The artillery organization seemed workable, although he wished the damned fuses were more reliable, but Vicar Allayn and his advisors had been unsure of how to balance the relative effectiveness of pikes and the newfangled rifles. In Nybar's opinion, they'd gotten it wrong. Indeed, from what he'd heard, it sounded as if the Dohlarans, of all people, had come closest to getting it *right*, although that was at least partly because they'd been willing to settle for a much smaller total force while the Army of God had been determined to get as many men as possible under arms.

And it hadn't hurt that the Dohlarans had possessed at least the core of an army, much of its infantry armed with matchlocks to begin with, while Mother Church hadn't. The Temple Guard had provided her with *some* secular might, but it had been tiny compared to the needs of the Jihad—more of a police force than what anyone might have called an army, really—which had required her to massively expand her forces. Dohlar had increased its army by a much smaller amount, which meant a lower absolute number of rifles had sufficed to arm a far higher percentage of King Rahnyld's total infantry.

Mother Church hadn't enjoyed that luxury, and even though she'd been able to produce a far higher absolute number of rifles, she had a much lower *percentage* of them. Worse, the Temple Guard had been forced to split the limited number of experienced officers it did possess between the Army of God and the *Navy* of God . . . and until very recently, the navy had taken precedence. And even if that hadn't been true, none of the officers who hadn't been sent to sea (and largely lost when Bishop Kornlys' fleet surrendered) had possessed the least experience in raising or officering a true army.

So Mother Church had begun more or less from scratch, and the truth was that Vicar Allayn and his advisors had done a much better job than Nybar had been afraid they might. It wasn't perfect, not by a long chalk, but it worked, and experience was already suggesting ways in which it could be improved.

In Nybar's opinion, the unit organization they'd adopted had the potential to be more flexible than the Dohlaran model and a *lot* more flexible than the Siddarmarkian model, once they could fix the problems with its armament. One of Mother Church's divisions was about half again the size of a Dohlaran regiment, which gave it—or should have given it—considerably more punch. Unfortunately, half the men in each of the division's sixteen companies were armed with pikes, not rifles and not matchlocks. He understood why Captain General Maigwair hadn't wanted to co-mingle matchlocks, with their much shorter range, miserable rate of fire, and wretched accuracy, with the new rifles, but he'd come to the conclusion that combining pikes and firearms in the same companies had been a mistake. Pure companies—or even regiments—in which every man was equipped with the same weapon would have been more efficient than having a little bit of each piled together. Rifles were better than smoothbores, and flintlocks were better than matchlocks, but he personally would rather have seen entire four hundred and eighty-man regiments armed solely with matchlocks than to have half the platoons in each company carrying pikes. He knew the high percentage of pikemen was at least partly the result of the Army of God's uncertainty about the ability of men armed with bayoneted rifles to hold off cavalry or opposing pikes. Until they'd had an opportunity to actually try the new weapons in the field, he'd entirely agreed that it was best to be cautious in that regard; now he realized they'd all been wrong, himself included, but it was too late to do anything about it . . . this year, at least.

And pikemen are just fine for dealing with the militia rabble we've been running into so far, he reminded himself. *If we'd tried to equip everyone with a firearm, we'd've had no more than two-thirds our current manpower—probably less!—even if we'd used every matchlock we had, and that would leave us spread even thinner when it comes to securing our rear areas. So I can't really argue with the decision to bring the pikes along; they just aren't what we need for dealing with regulars— especially regulars with rifles of their own.*

On the other hand, there were circumstances under which pikes could be decidedly useful, as he intended to demonstrate tonight.

He took the pipe from his mouth and blew a smoke ring, watching it drift away on the breeze, then bent back over the map. Hastings' maps gave an infallibly accurate picture of the world on the Day of Creation, but fallen man and the forces of nature had been making changes ever since, and the inaccuracy of maps produced by mere mortals often hid all sorts of unpleasant surprises. The tree-dotted terrain here in the Sylmahn Gap offered more examples of that than Nybar could have wished, but his scouts had been correcting and amending his original maps throughout the army's long advance from Lake City. He knew what the terrain immediately in front of them looked like, at any rate, and assuming Colonel Baikyr's militiamen could be relied upon, his picture of the rest of the Gap south to Serabor ought to be more than adequate for his needs.

What mattered most was that once he got past Harystn there were no more belts of trees like the one the heretics had dug themselves into here. The Gap widened for the next forty miles or so, too, until it pinched back down to no more than five and a half or six miles twenty-five miles north of Serabor. If he were the heretics, that would be where he'd put his next strongpoint, and digging them out of there would be Shan-wei's own bitch. But he'd deal with that when he got there. What mattered now was clearing the woods directly in front of him, and he had Bishop Adulfo Vynair's Holy Martyrs Division, Bishop Edwyrd Tailyr's Jwo-jeng Division, and Bishop Harys Bahrkly's Rakurai Division to help with that little task.

And if that's *not enough, I've got all the rest of the army*, he told himself.

"Tell the guns to start concentrating on the woods now," he said, glancing up at his aide. "Then get a runner to Colonel Mairyai and ask him for his best estimate on when the engineers will have that gap in the road filled."

"Yes, Sir!"

The aide sketched Langhorne's scepter in salute, turned, and hastened off on his mission, and Nybar sniffed at the damp, freshening breeze, then looked back down at the map.

▼   ▼   ▼

"Zhorj is right; they'll be coming tonight," Colonel Stahn Wyllys said quietly, looking at his company commanders' faces in the fading light. He wondered if his own looked as grim as theirs did. "That's why they've been tearing up the trees. They're trying to kill—or at least disorder—as many of our reserves as possible."

They looked back at him silently while the Church's artillery boomed steadily behind his words and the first few drops of rain sifted down through the branches. Most of them were at least ten years younger than he was, but those silent eyes looked far older than they'd been a year ago, he thought.

"If I were them," he continued, "I'd put the pikes in front. In the dark, at close quarters, rifles would lose a lot of their effectiveness even without rain, and, frankly, they can afford to lose pikemen more than they can afford to lose riflemen. They'll probably go on pounding the parapet with their guns until the pikes are right on top of us, and then it's going to get ugly. *Very* ugly."

He drew a deep breath.

"Ahbnair," he looked at Major Ahbnair Dynnys, commanding 1st Company, the only pure-pike company he had left, "I'm putting you in with Zhorj. It's going to be the best opportunity for you to make effective use of your pikes. I want you in the center, right on the roadbed. Zhorj," he turned to Major Styvynsyn, "I want three of your platoons on either of Ahbnair's flanks. Keep the Seventh and your HQ section behind him in the middle to reinforce as needed. Hainree," he turned to the absurdly youthful Captain Klairynce, "Third Company's the reserve for First and Second. I'll be with you, trying to keep an eye on things and hopefully lending you the seasoned counsel of an older and wiser head."

His last sentence got the chuckle he'd hoped for. It might have been more than a little dutiful, but there was at least some genuine humor in it. He let them enjoy it for a moment before he looked at Ahrnahld Mahkynty and Gahvyn Sahlys, the commanders of his 4th and 5th Companies.

"You two will stay right where you are," he said, his voice much more serious. "You're our backstop. If it comes apart for us, you're who we're going to rally behind . . . and you're also the last position between us and the Forty-Third."

Mahkynty and Sahlys nodded, their faces grimmer than ever. Colonel Paityr Chansayl's 43rd Infantry, dug in almost forty miles behind them, was the linchpin of the last defense before Serabor itself. He had Colonel Fraihman Hyldyr's 123rd Infantry and Colonel Frahnklyn Pruait's 76th Infantry under his command, as well, and General Stohnar had given him half the Charisian thirty-pounders to bolster his forces, but all of his regiments were understrength. He ought to have had sixty-seven hundred infantry; what he actually had was barely five thousand men and six guns to hold over ten thousand yards of frontage. The backed-up canal and river cut that total by perhaps a third, but it was still an unenviable position.

"We're going to *hold*," Wyllys said looking around their faces again. "But if we don't, if they manage to push our arses out of here, we rally on Colonel Chansayl's line. He'll need every rifle and pike he can get when it's his turn, and we'd going to give them to him. Understand me on that, and make sure all the rest of our people do, too. That's as far as we go. I don't care if they bring Shan-wei herself with them, *that's as far as we go*."

▼   ▼   ▼

Colonel Spyncyr Mairyai, CO, 2nd Regiment, Langhorne Division, tilted his head back and smiled as he looked up into the rain. In some ways, it was a bit like gilding the spike-thorn. The heretics had already turned the entire Gap into a mucky, squelching quagmire. Anywhere off the roadbed itself, a man was likely to step into a submerged pothole deeper than he was tall, and he'd seen dragons get so thoroughly mired that at least one of them had had to be put down where it was because they simply couldn't get it back out of the mud. So they hardly needed more rain to make the going even more wretched.

But it was a lovely, beautiful, Langhorne-sent rain, in Mairyai's considered opinion. A rain that was turning steadily heavier, pelting out of a sky blacker than Shan-wei's riding boots and promising to soak the priming of any rifle ever made.

Of course, finding his way to his objective was going to be an interesting challenge, but the gun rafts still blazing away out on the flooded canal gave his lead companies a reference point, and the engineers had lined the edges of the road in the same sort of lime they used for baselines on a baseball diamond. The broad, white stripes gleamed wetly, picked out of the blackness in sporadic spits of lightning by the muzzle flashes of the artillery. With the rain picking up, it was questionable how long the guide stripes would last, but they'd last long enough.

He drew rein and climbed down from his horse, handing the bridle to his orderly. Colonels weren't supposed to get involved in the confusion and carnage of desperate nighttime assaults, but the 2nd wasn't going in without him, and the last thing he needed was to be trying to control a spooked horse in the middle of a pitch black melee.

He half-drew his sword, checking to make sure it would come out of the scabbard cleanly when he needed it, and touched the grips of the two pistols thrust through his sash. Chihiro only knew if the pans were closed tightly enough to protect the priming, and he had no intention of relying on them unless he had absolutely no choice, but it was still good to know they were there.

He turned his head, looking at the bugler beside him. The whites of the youngster's eyes gleamed starkly, picked out of the darkness as two or three twelve-pounders went off as one, and his shoulder quivered with tension when Mairyai gripped it encouragingly.

"Anxious, lad?"

"N—" the bugler began, then stopped. "Yes, Sir," he confessed instead.

"Well, so am I." Mairyai squeezed his shoulder. "So is every other man in that column." He twitched his head at the endless ranks of pikemen moving soddenly down the high road between the stripes of lime. "So you're hardly alone, now, are you?"

He chuckled, and after a moment, the boy chuckled back a bit nervously.

"Better!" The colonel smiled. "We're in God's hands now, son—His and the archangels'—and when you think about it, that's not such a bad place to be, now, is it?"

"No, Sir. It isn't," the bugler said with more assurance, and Mairyai gave his shoulder a little shake.

"Good lad! And now, I think it's time we put you to work. Sound reveille."

"Yes, Sir!"

The boy took just long enough to sign Langhorne's scepter in salute, then raised the bugle to his lips.

▼　▼　▼

"Stand to! *Stand to!*" Ahbnair Dynnys bawled as the bugle notes flared sweet and golden through the rainy dark. Reveille was the last thing he'd expected to hear in the middle of the night, but he was confident it didn't mean anything good.

More bugles sounded, taking up the same call, and eight of the Church twelve-pounders thudded as one.

They'd clearly been waiting for the bugles. The shells' sputtering fuses drew lines of fire across the night, and six of them carried across the parapet to slam into the trees beyond, but this time they didn't explode. Instead of gunpowder and musket balls, they were filled with a mixture of saltpeter, sulfur, and meal powder, with three extra holes bored around the fuse. They hit the trees, dropped to the ground, and suddenly those holes were volcanoes, spewing smoke and fountains of brilliant, blinding light that simultaneously dazzled the defenders and silhouetted them against their glaring intensity.

As if the flares had been a signal, all of the other artillery stopped firing instantly . . . and a great, deep-throated roar came out of the dark.

"God wills it!"

The pikeheads came on the wings of that shout.

▼　▼　▼

There were four thousand pikemen in that column; there were three understrength companies, with just under *one* thousand men behind the parapet.

"Fire!" Sergeant Zhaksyn shouted from the western end of the line, and a hundred and sixty riflemen squeezed their triggers.

Ninety-seven of the rifles actually fired in the driving rain, and long, lurid fingers of flame reached across the parapet. Perhaps another hundred rifles fired from the eastern flank, ripping through the half-seen, half-guessed column of pikes. Men screamed and went down, and others tripped over them in the dark, but the bugles were sounding the charge now, not reveille, and another shout went up from the Army of God.

"Holy Schueler and no quarter!"

▼   ▼   ▼

"Stand your ground, boys!" Dynnys bellowed. *"Stand your ground!* Send these bastards to hell!"

The front of the pike column reached the abatis and tried to drive bodily through it. But the branches were too thick, and at least some of Styvynsyn's riflemen were managing to reload, despite the rain, sending fresh fire into the tangle of limbs and enemies. More pikemen screamed, folding up, writhing in agony, yet others dropped their pikes. They grabbed the interwoven branches, heaving, wrenching at them, tearing holes in the obstacle. More of them fell, but for every man who went down, two more seemed to take his place, and some of them had brought axes that flashed in the glare of flares and the blaze of rifles. The axe blades rose and fell, hewing at the abatis, and the barricade began to leak.

The men of the Langhorne Division roared in triumph as they forced a path through the barrier. Every yard of that path was draped with a dead or wounded body as the Siddarmarkian rifles continued to sputter and bark through the rain, but only a small percentage of those rifles were managing to fire reliably, and pikeheads crossed as the charging Temple Loyalists drove up the face of the entrenchment.

▼   ▼   ▼

"Siddarmark! *Siddarmark!*"

The battle cry went up as the men of Ahbnair Dynnys' 1st Company lunged over their parapet. This was the kind of combat for which they had trained, and no one in the world was better at it than they were. They stood shoulder-to-shoulder, pikes raised two-handed and almost head-high, slamming them forward with shoulders and backs, ramming the keen-edged, leaf-shaped steel into their enemies. They had every advantage of height and position, and they used those advantages ruthlessly, reaping a gory harvest as they ruptured chests and bodies. They slaughtered the first men up that wet, soft, treacherous slope, and the Temple Loyalists following behind stumbled and slid across the writhing bodies of their dead and dying fellows.

But there were four hundred and thirty pikemen defending the line; there were ten times that many assaulting it, and the weight of all those charging ranks drove the column forward.

Zhorj Styvynsyn drew his sword as the first of the Temple Loyalist pikeheads reached across the parapet and found a victim. More of the abatis was being pulled apart, and all too many of his riflemen found themselves face-to-face with pikes. A bayoneted rifle was a lethal close-quarters melee weapon, but it was far shorter than an eighteen-foot pike, and his men found themselves at a deadly disadvantage, despite the parapet. They started going down, and he felt the pain of their loss as if those pikeheads had been driving into his own flesh. But there was no time to let himself acknowledge that pain, and he bared his teeth as he dropped his sword and snatched up a fallen rifleman's bayoneted weapon in its place..

"Reinforce right!" he shouted to the youthful platoon commander standing beside him, and the youngster slapped his chest in salute, shouted to his platoon sergeant, and vanished into the glare-slashed darkness. Somehow Styvynsyn knew he would never see the lieutenant again.

"The rest of you, follow me!" he snapped, and his headquarters section moved left on his heels.

▼   ▼   ▼

Men shouted their hate, boots slipping and sliding in the mud, rain pounding down, fresh thunderbolt flares arriving from the guns on the rafts. Screams, grunts of effort, and the horrible wet, rending sound of steel cleaving flesh was all the universe, and there was very little to choose between the discipline, the fury and determination—and the courage—of either side. Men who had remained loyal to their lord protector and their constitution through every privation of that horrible winter stood their ground against men who had given their allegiance to no mortal power or piece of paper but to God Himself, and there was no give in them. They bared their teeth, the spray of blood hot on their faces in the icy rain, the stink of death rising over the smell of mud and water . . . and they died.

In the end, when courage met courage and determination trumped fury, it was numbers that counted. The men of the Army of God were not—quite—the equal in training and experience of the 37th Infantry, but they were close. And there were many, many more of them.

▼   ▼   ▼

Regulations said the proper sidearm for a Siddarmarkian officer was a sword, but Zhorj Styvynsyn didn't much care about that. He'd discovered that a bayoneted rifle was a far more lethal weapon, even if the Republican Army hadn't yet devised the bayonet drill Merlin Athrawes had originated for the Royal Charisian Marines and the Marines, in turn, had bequeathed to the Imperial Charisian Army. The twelve men of his headquarters section—there'd once been fifteen of them, but that had been an eternity ago—followed on his heels as he slammed into the wedge of Temple Loyalist pikemen beginning to penetrate the left end of the fraying Siddarmarkian line.

The flash and crack of occasional rifle muzzles and the glaring glitter of the Church's flares lit the scene in a nightmare of midnight black shadow and blinding light, picking individual raindrops out of the night like fleeting jewels in a madman's crown. Men cursed and screamed and died in that maelstrom, and Styvynsyn saw Grovair Zhaksyn fighting madly at the heart of an isolated knot of defenders. The pikemen of Langhorne Division were intermingled with those of the Holy Martyrs Division, their own cohesion vanished in the chaos, but they closed in on the major's company sergeant like a ravening beast with pikes for fangs.

"Hang on, Grovair!" he shrieked, though the sergeant couldn't possibly have heard him in the clamor and roar of battle. *"Hang on!"*

He and his twelve men hit the Temple Loyalists like a hammer. He lunged, feeling the horrible, twitching softness as his bayonet sank into an unwary pikeman's back. He withdrew, kicking the writhing body aside, and slammed into the next enemy. He blocked the thrust of a shortened pike with his rifle, slammed a muddy boot into the man's belly, smashed his skull with the rifle butt as he went down, and whirled back to yet another Temple Loyalist. He heard screams from every side, knew the men of his section were fighting desperately to cover his back, and spared another glance for his sergeant . . . just in time to see Grovair Zhaksyn go down as a pikehead drove into him just below his breastplate.

A moment later, it was Styvynsyn's turn.

▼　　▼　　▼

"Stand! *Stand!*" Major Dynnys shouted.

His men were going down, turning from a tight, disciplined line into knots and clusters of individual, desperately fighting men. He'd picked up a dead man's pike, and he stood shoulder-to-shoulder with his company sergeant, thrusting again and again.

"Stand, boys! *Stand with me!*"

They heard the boom of that deep, familiar voice, the men of 1st Company, and they obeyed it. They stood with their major, falling around him, ranks thinning with every second, but they *stood*.

"Stand, First! *Stand!* Don't let—"

The pikehead hit Dynnys' breastplate and skidded up the rain-soaked steel. The razor point went into his throat, just under his chin, and he went down, the voice which had held his company like iron stilled forever.

Yet even without that voice, 1st Company never broke. It simply died around its major's body.

▼　　▼　　▼

"Fall back!" Stahn Wyllys shouted as the center of the defensive line collapsed. "Third Company, stand where you are! Second Company, fall back!"

Zhorj Styvynsyn's surviving men heard the colonel's voice. They backed away from the parapet, still snarling defiance, and their bayonets ran red as the Temple Loyalists scrambled across the entire front of the earthwork, close enough now that a man with a rifle could get inside the points of their pikes and claim his vengeance.

But there was no holding that tide of roaring fury, and the men of 2nd Company obeyed Colonel Wyllys. Less burdened than someone carrying a pike three times his own height in length, far more familiar with the terrain behind the earthwork, they managed to break contact in the darkness and chaos, falling back behind the thin double line of young Hainree Klairynce's depleted company.

"Take your aim!" Klairynce's tenor voice cut through the confusion and cacophony with impossible clarity. "Ready! *Fire!*"

Despite the rain, despite everything, three hundred rifles fired as one. The shocking sheet of flame stabbed out like an old-fashioned musket volley at a range of under twenty yards, and Temple Loyalists went down like grass before a Charisian reaper. Third Company blew a hole in the Army of God's advance—a moment of sheer slaughter not even the Langhorne Division could bring itself to cross.

It didn't last long, but it lasted long enough for the 37th's survivors to break contact and fall back on its last two companies' entrenched positions in the belt of woods they'd defended for so long. They fell back in that brief window of time before the thirty-two hundred surviving Temple Loyalists recovered from the shock and came charging after them.

Of the thousand Siddarmarkians who'd held that muddy wall of earth, less than three hundred survived to retreat.

.II.
Daivyn River,
Cliff Peak Province,
Republic of Siddarmark

C rap."
Once upon a time, Howail Brahdlai would have used a somewhat stronger term. That, however, had been when he had been Howail Brahdlai, apprentice brick mason, and not Corporal Howail Brahdlai, 191st Cavalry Regiment, Army of God. Most of the clergy attached to the army were

remarkably tolerant where soldier-style language was concerned. Unfortunately, the 191st's chaplain wasn't among them, and he'd been "counseling" Brahdlai ever since the day he'd heard the corporal pointing out the shortcomings of his section in pungent, pithy style.

Personally, Brahdlai thought God and the archangels probably had better things to do than listen in on their servants' language, but Father Zhames held a different view, and Colonel Mardhar had a tendency to support his chaplain . . . who'd been his *personal* chaplain before both of them had joined the Army of God. Brahdlai respected the Colonel, and the Father was a good and godly man, even if he did tend to be what Brahdlai's mother had always called a "fussbudget," so the corporal was genuinely trying to amend his language.

"What?" Svynsyn Ahrbukyl asked. He was the senior trooper in Brahdlai's scouting detail—a good, solid man, like all of them.

"WW's disappeared again," Brahdlai growled. "Damn it," he appended a mental apology to Father Zhames, "I *told* him to stay in sight!"

"Hard not to get *out* of sight sometimes," Ahrbukyl pointed out philosophically. He liked Brahdlai, and the corporal was a good leader and hardworking. Like altogether too many of the Army of God's cavalry, he'd been only an indifferent rider when he was "volunteered" for the cavalry, but he'd buckled down to master that skill the same way he had the rest of his duties. He was a bit prone to fuss and worry, though, in Ahrbukyl's opinion.

"Sergeant Karstayrs doesn't see it that way," Brahdlai pointed out in reply. He liked Ahrbukyl, but the man could be so phlegmatic that sometimes the corporal wanted to choke him. "Do *you* want to explain to him that it's 'hard not to get out of sight sometimes' after the new asshole he ripped Hyndryk last five-day?"

Perhaps, Ahrbukyl reflected, the corporal wasn't *quite* that prone to worry too much, after all.

"Not especially," he admitted, but he also shrugged. "Still, Corp, it's WW we're talking about."

Brahdlai grunted in sour agreement. Wyltahn Waignair was one of their company's characters. He was smart, he was always cheerful, and unlike Corporal Howail Brahdlai, he rode as if he were a part of his horse, all of which was fortunate, since he was constantly in trouble for one practical joke or another. He was also the best scout in the entire 191st, and Ahrbukyl was right—one of the things that made him the regiment's best scout was a tendency to follow his nose wherever it led him. On the other hand . . . .

"All right, you've got a point. But even if it *is* WW, I don't want the Sergeant 'discussing' my shortcomings with me. So let's get a move on"— the corporal looked over his shoulder at the other four men of his section— "and catch up with him."

"Suits me," Ahrbukyl agreed, and the small group of horsemen moved up to a hard trot along the westbound tow road.

They'd been trotting for about three or four minutes when Brahdlai realized someone had been logging off the slope north of the road. They'd seen plenty of signs of that during their advance out of Westmarch, given how bitter the winter had been and how little coal had come west out of Glacierheart last year. But this was more recent than the fuel-cutting they'd seen earlier—the stumps were still green—and he frowned thoughtfully, wondering who'd been cutting up here. The Daivyn River snaked its way through a line of low hills and steep bluffs here, about a hundred and fifty miles west of Ice Lake, and aside from the abandoned inn they'd passed a few miles back, where the high road from Sangyr crossed the river, there didn't seem to have been very many people in the area even before the Rising.

He was still scratching at that mental itch when he and his troopers trotted up and over a riverside hill and suddenly saw a cavalry horse standing by the side of the road cropping grass. The gelding's reins had been tied to a sapling, and its rider, in the same uniform Brahdlai wore, sat facing away from them with his back to a tree, his arms crossed against his chest, and his head down, obviously catching up on his sleep on a pleasant summer afternoon.

Brahdlai drew rein, his eyes widening with too much astonishment for immediate outrage.

The insulation of surprise didn't last long, and the eyes which had widened narrowed, crackling with a dangerous light. This was a serious business, damn it! The Siddarmarkians this close to the Glacierheart border had almost all embraced the heresy. Rather than greeting the Army of God as liberators, they'd fled before it, like the owners of the inn they'd passed, which meant there were precious few—if any—local guides available. That made scouting parties like this one the eyes and cat lizard whiskers of Bishop Militant Cahnyr's entire army! Waignair *damnned* well knew better than to be taking a frigging *nap* at a time like this!

The corporal swung down from the saddle, his expression thunderous. Father Zhames was just going to have to set him a penance for what he was about to say, he thought as he strode angrily towards the trooper who hadn't even bothered to wake up at the noise of his arriving companions. Well, he'd just see—

Howail Brahdlai paused in midstride as he rounded the trooper's position and suddenly saw the bloodstain those folded arms had concealed.

An arbalest bolt protruded from the left side of Waignair's rib cage, an isolated corner of his brain observed. The rest of his mind was still trying to catch up with what that might mean when a dozen more arbalest bolts came sizzling out of the underbrush.

▼ ▼ ▼

"Told you it'd work," Private Zhedryk Lycahn said, watching as the Marines who'd been hiding farther back along the tow road emerged from concealment to make sure none of the cavalry horses got away. He nodded in satisfaction as the last of them eased up just a bit skittishly to one of the Marines and allowed its bridle to be grasped. "Don't think we should set them all up to be having a tea party, though," he said then, looking over his shoulder at Corporal Wahlys Hahndail.

"Probably not," Hahndail agreed dryly.

The corporal had always suspected that Private Lycahn hadn't always been respectably—or even legally—employed before his enlistment. That hadn't bothered the corporal much before, but he was beginning to wonder exactly *how* illegally Lycahn might have earned his living. The private hadn't simply picked the spot for their ambush; he'd also been the one who dragged their first . . . customer over and arranged him so artfully to suck in the rest of his patrol. And he'd been remarkably cool about going through the first trooper's pockets for any potentially useful information.

"I suppose that since we've got their horses, we might as well use them to carry the bodies back," he continued, waving his hand to catch another Marine's attention. He pointed at the bodies, then waved at the empty saddles, and the Marine nodded back.

"Makes sense to me," Lycahn replied agreeably. "Can I keep the first one, though?" He showed two missing teeth when he grinned. "Makes fine bait, Wahlys!"

"Yes, Zhedryk," Hahndail sighed, shaking his head as he watched the other Marines heaving the dead cavalry troopers up across their saddles. "You can keep the first one. Just make damned sure anyone else who stops by to visit with him gets the same treatment this batch did."

"Oh," the private said, his voice suddenly much less amused, "you can *count* on that."

▼ ▼ ▼

Private Styv Walkyr, Zion Division, Army of God, sat on the barge's abbreviated foredeck, his legs hanging over the side, and watched the trio of dragons leaning against their collars. Walkyr was a farm boy, a man who appreciated fine draft animals when he saw them, and two of these—one of them might go as high as eight tons—were clearly well above average. They ought to be, he thought. The Church was used to getting first quality when it bought, and the dragons had come all the way from the Temple Lands—most of the trip by water themselves—and been grain-fed the entire way. It was a scandalously expensive way to feed something the size of a dragon, but he'd long since come to the conclusion that the Church (and her army) didn't worry about the kind of mark-pinching a farmer had to keep in mind.

And, he thought grimly, remembering all of the abandoned farms they'd passed on their way through, *it makes more sense to feed them grain than hay. Easier to transport and gives them more energy . . . and no one around here was cutting that much hay last fall, anyway.*

He sighed, leaning forward and stretching one leg down until he could just dip a toe into the river water. They'd passed through some wonderful farmland on their way south into Cliff Peak, and the farmer in him hated to see it going to wrack and ruin this way. And, he admitted to himself, he hadn't found as much satisfaction in chastising the heretics as he'd expected to. They seemed to be people much like any other people, except that their faces were gaunt and thin with hunger from the winter just past.

The Faithful who'd greeted the Zion Division along the way were no better fed, but he'd seen the fire in their eyes, heard the fierce baying of their welcoming cheers as they beheld Mother Church's green and gold standards. That filled the army with a sense of pride, of having come to the relief of God's loyal children, but there'd been an ugly side to that fire, as well. Walkyr was just as glad the Zion Division's place at the head of the advance had kept it moving, prevented it from getting involved in rounding up heretics for the Inquisition's attention. Even so, he'd seen some things he wished he hadn't, heard the shrill edge of hatred in the voices denouncing neighbors for heresy . . . and the panicky edge in voices frantically protesting their innocence and orthodoxy.

He was still more than a bit bemused by how rapidly Bishop Militant Cahnyr had moved once they crossed the border, especially after such an abrupt change in plans. Aside from the brief overland march from Aivahnstyn towards Sangyr to deal with the fleeing heretical garrison—Zion had missed that one; they'd been detailed to watch the Daivyn east of the city—they'd stuck to the canals and rivers, and the lack of other traffic had let them advance even more rapidly than anyone—even the Church officials overseeing their transport, he suspected—had anticipated. There'd been only three locks between Aivahnstyn and today, and with the army in charge and civilian traffic banned, they'd used both sets of locks, eastbound and west, each time. They'd been averaging close to fifty miles a day for the entire five-day since the rest of the army had returned to Aivahnstyn. At that rate, they should reach Ice Lake and the Glacierheart border in another three or four days.

He watched the drovers slowing the dragons slightly while the barge crew veered more tow cable. They were coming up on another bend in the river as it wound its way through the hills, and the clear channel was farther from the bank than it had been. The current was with them, though, and the helmsman was swinging to the north, obedient to the buoys and channel markings, while the drovers started their dragons up a steeper than usual section of the tow road. The extra cable let them make the ascent at their own best pace, and the long, six-legged dragons whistled cheerfully as they climbed.

Walkyr leaned to one side, craning his neck to see around the bend. The trees had been cut back on either bank to clear the tow road, but the hills farther back from the stream looked green and cool. He wondered what the local hunting was like? They hadn't seen—

The thirty-pounder shell slammed into the foredeck beside him before he heard the sound of the shot. The impact transmitted to him through the barge's planking was enough to stun anyone, and Styv Walkyr was still trying to figure out what in Langhorne's name had happened when the shell's two pounds of gunpowder exploded almost directly under him.

▼   ▼   ▼

"*That's* the way you do it!" Petty Officer Laisl Mhattsyn shouted, capering in glee as the lead barge spewed smoking fragments, like white-edged feathers, from the red-and-white-cored explosion. "*That's* the way to hit the bastards!"

"A little less dancing and a little more shooting, Mhattsyn!" Lieutenant Yerek Sahbrahan snapped. The lieutenant was fifteen years younger than the petty officer, and he used his sword like a pointer, indicating the other barges on the river below the battery's high, bluff-top perch. "They're not going to sit there fat, dumb, and happy for long, so let's get back on the guns, shall we?!"

"Aye, aye, Sir!" Mhattsyn agreed, still grinning. Then he glared at the rest of his gun crew. "Come on, you buggers! You *heard* the Lieutenant!"

The gunners swarmed over the piece, swabbing the barrel and reloading, and Sahbrahan nodded in satisfaction and stepped up to the parapet. Building the thick earthen berm had been a backbreaking task—almost as bad as dragging the guns themselves into position, although the tow road had helped a lot in that respect. He'd thought Brigadier Taisyn's notion of camouflaging the entrenchments' raw earth had been ridiculous, however . . . until he'd taken a hike upstream and realized the cut greenery made it extremely difficult to realize the guns were there until one came within two or three hundred yards. The bends in the river helped, of course, but the brigadier and Commander Watyrs had chosen their spot with care.

The guns commanded almost two thousand yards of the river, sweeping across it at an angle, although some of the men in the redoubts closer to river level and nearer to the bend had expressed doubts about having fused shells fired over their heads. Even Charisian fuses malfunctioned occasionally, but at least they weren't firing shrapnel . . . yet, at any rate.

Mhattsyn's thirty-pounder roared again. The fourteen-pounders in the river-level redoubts were firing as well, although they weren't provided with explosive rounds, and he heard the dull thuds of the fifty-seven-pounder carronades . . . and the much louder explosions of *their* massive shells. Two of the barges, including Mhattsyn's target, were already sinking. Three more were heavily on fire, and as he shaded his eyes with one hand, he saw men leaping frantically over the sides into the river. Some of them, obviously, swam almost as well as rocks.

The wind was out of the east, sweeping the smoke upriver, and he couldn't hear the shrieks and screams—not from here. The Marines and Siddarmarkian infantry in the redoubts could undoubtedly hear them just fine, though, and young Sahbrahan's mouth was a bleak, hard line as he thought about that. He'd never been a vengeful man, but he'd seen what Archbishop Zhasyn and his people had been through over this past winter. He'd seen the way the citizens of Glacierheart had cheered as their column came up the Siddarmark River from the capital. And he'd seen their desperation as reports of the juggernaut grinding down through Cliff Peak—and what was happening to the people behind it—came to them with each fresh waves of fugitives.

And Brigadier Taisyn had made sure they'd *all* heard what the "Army of God" had done to General Stahntyn's men after the Battle of Sangyr.

He could live with a few screams from *those* bastards, he thought.

▼   ▼   ▼

"Shan-wei take them!" Bishop Khalryn Waimyan snarled. "Where the hell were our scouts?! How the *fuck* did we walk into something like this!?"

His regimental commanders looked at one another. There were times Bishop Khalryn reverted to the Temple Guard officer he'd been and forgot the decorum expected out of a consecrated bishop of Mother Church. At moments like that, it was best not to draw attention to oneself.

"*Well*, Stywyrt?" Waimyan demanded, turning on Colonel Stywyrt Sahndhaim, the CO of Zion Division's 1st Regiment, whose men had been in the lead barges.

"I don't know, Sir," Sahndhaim said flatly. He was normally a calm, courteously spoken officer, but today his voice was flat and hard. His reports were still preliminary, but the casualty totals he'd already heard were ugly. "The scouts were out, and I don't see how anyone who wasn't deaf and blind as *well* as stupid could've missed something like *that*!"

He jabbed an angry fist in the direction of the heretic entrenchments on either side of the river.

"Excuse me, My Lord," Colonel Tymythy Dowain, Waimyan's executive officer, said. Waimyan turned a choleric eye upon him, goaded by the clerical address. It was technically correct, but he knew Dowain had used it at least partly to calm him down.

"What?" he said shortly.

"My Lord," Dowain said, "Colonel Mardhar was responsible for the scouting today. As you know, the Hundred and Ninety-First has done an excellent job in that regard ever since we entered Westmarch. One of the first things I did was to ask *him* what had gone wrong, and he couldn't answer me. *But*, My Lord, at least three of his scouting sections haven't reported in." The colonel shrugged. "I think we know now why they haven't."

"Why the hell didn't anyone *miss* them?" Sahndhaim demanded harshly.

"Because they weren't due to report back in yet, Stywyrt." Dowain spoke patiently, clearly aware of what was goading his fellow colonel's temper. "They're supposed to send back word if they spot anything; otherwise the assumption is that if they haven't sent back word, they *haven't* spotted anything. Mardhar's as angry and as upset as you could wish—some of those men have been with him from the very beginning, and he doesn't pick his advanced scouts because they're incompetent. He asked me to tell you he feels terrible about what's happened."

Sahndhaim's mouth twisted, but he made himself inhale deeply and nodded. There was no point venting his fury on someone who'd clearly been doing his job . . . and wasn't even present, anyway.

"All right," Waimyan said, after a moment, following Sahndhaim's example and forcing himself to step back from his own temper, "the Bishop Militant's going to want to know what we're up against. What do I tell him?"

"I'm working on that, Sir," Dowain said, reverting to the military address he knew Waimyan preferred. "So far, it looks like they have redoubts on both sides of the river." He laid a rough sketch on the table. "As you can see, they're about ten miles east of where the high road crosses the river. The Daivyn gets a little narrower and deeper at that point, and it bends around these hills, here." He tapped the sketch. "It looks like the bulk of their guns are here, on the north bank. That lets them fire up past the bend, and from the weight and accuracy of the fire, they have to be heavier than anything we've got." He looked up to meet his general's gaze. "If I had to guess, they're naval guns."

Waimyan's jaw muscles clamped, but he nodded. It made sense. Siddarmark didn't have any mobile artillery—Vicar Zhaspahr and Vicar Allayn had made certain of *that*, thank Langhorne!—and there probably hadn't been time for any Charisian field guns to reach the Republic. Or to get this far forward, at any rate. One of the reasons for how rapidly they were advancing was to beat the Imperial Charisian Army into Glacierheart. But the bastards certainly *did* have artillery aboard their galleons, and after what had happened to Bishop Kornylys' fleet, they could afford to spare some of it. But that meant—

"So we're looking at *thirty-pounders*?" one of his other regimental commanders demanded, and Dowain shrugged.

"Probably. In fact, I think they may have some *fifty-seven*-pounders in their forward redoubts." He showed his teeth in a thin smile. "They'd only be carronades, but with the bend in the river leading up to them, they don't need a lot of range."

"Shit," someone muttered, and Waimyan smiled even more thinly than his executive officer had.

"Whoever decided where to put these people knew what he was about," the bishop said. "He's doing exactly what he needs to do: slow us down until they can get someone up to help him try to stop us." He glowered at the map. "The bastard's got the river locked up tighter than a drum—we're going to have to raise the barges he's already sunk just to clear the channel— and we're damned well not going to be able to march right down the river and punch him out of our way. And I'll bet you that whoever it was kept an eye on his flanks, as well. We need to find out just how well entrenched they are. I don't want any lives thrown away in the process, but until we know that, we can't know anything else about how to deal with them. And we *will* deal with them, Gentlemen." His eyes were hard. "Trust me on that one."

▼　▼　▼

"Well, we damned well bloodied their noses," Colonel Hauwerd Zhansyn observed with bitter, heartfelt satisfaction. "The bodies're still floating down-river." He smiled fiercely at Commander Watyrs. "Makes at least a nice little down payment for General Stahntyn. Tell your gunners my boys appreciate it."

"You're welcome," Hainz Watyrs said. If a naval officer was out of place seventeen hundred miles from the nearest salt water, the Old Charisian seemed unaware of it. "It helped that they walked right into it, though." He shook his head. "I really didn't think we'd be able to get away with that, Brigadier."

"Never know until you try," Mahrtyn Taisyn said, and shrugged. "Major Tyrnyr's suggestion that we issue arbalests to the security forces probably helped a lot. At least there weren't any shots for anyone on the other side to hear. Not until your guns opened up, at any rate, Hainz."

Watyrs nodded, and the three of them looked down at the river. They stood outside the log-and-earth-roofed dugout which had been built as Taisyn's headquarters, and normally there wouldn't have been a lot to see. The moon was only a pale sliver, and even that wan illumination was half obscured by high, thin cloud, but there were still a few smears of fire out on the river where some of the beached barges had smoldered for hours. And the lookouts had orders to ignite the massive bonfires laid ready to illuminate the water if the Temple Loyalists should be feeling adventurous enough to try forcing the river under cover of darkness.

Wish they would, the Marine brigadier told himself grimly, thinking about the barricade they'd laid across the main barge channel.

It would take work parties at least two or three days to clear the river of the logs, sunken river barges full of rock, and other obstacles his men had emplaced, and Watyrs had arranged nine of his fifty-seven-pounder carronades to cover the barricade. If the bastards would be kind enough to send men down to clear it, he'd be delighted to use them for target practice. Nobody was coming down that river alive as long as Taisyn's batteries and redoubts commanded its channel.

"What do you think they're going to do next, Sir?" Zhahnsyn asked.

The colonel commanded the two thousand Siddarmarkians who provided half of Taisyn's infantry. Taisyn's remaining five hundred Marines and Zhahnsyn's other three thousand pikemen and arbalesters had taken over security from young Byrk Raimahn's volunteers on the Green Cove Trace and the Hanymar Gap. Especially the Gap. If Cahnyr Kaitswyrth decided to send a flanking column overland . . . .

He'd hated detaching that much of his manpower, but Raimahn's people were ready to drop. Even if he'd been willing to ask it of them, they were simply too exhausted to stop a fresh, determined push. Taisyn only hoped his professional soldiers could do half as well as those "civilian volunteers" had in holding their ground until Duke Eastshare could reach Glacierheart.

In the meantime, it was *his* job to slow Bishop Militant Cahnyr down, and he'd tried not to think about the enormous risk he was running. Unfortunately, Zhahnsyn's question didn't give him a lot of choice *but* to think about it.

"Everything we've seen or heard indicates that unlike their Navy, their Army *can* find its arse, as long as it gets to use both hands," he said, eyes still fixed on the guttering flames. "According to the reports, they did for General Stahntyn's regiments in jig time, too. I think we have to assume they aren't going to do anything stupid . . . unfortunately. What I'd really like them to do is to try to assault straight down the river, but they aren't dumb enough to do that. So I expect the first thing they'll do is probe to see exactly where we are and try to get a feel for how strong we are. After that?"

He shrugged.

"I wish we had some cavalry to operate against their rear, Sir," Zhahnsyn said. "Something to keep them looking over their shoulders instead of concentrating on what's—or *who's*—in front of them!"

"It'd be nice," Taisyn agreed. "Unfortunately, neither Marines nor Siddarmarkian pikemen make very good cavalry . . . and you don't even want to *think* about what one of Hainz' sailors would look like in a saddle!"

"What worries me, Sir—aside from the fact that we're outnumbered about thirty-five to one or so—is that they *do* have cavalry. A lot of it,"

Commander Watyrs pointed out. "We've got a strong position here, but outside the entrenchments, we're not very mobile. As long as we've got the river in our rear, the obstacles in the channel mean we can pull out faster in boats than they can march downstream or even send cavalry after us. But if they manage to cut the river between here and Ice Lake . . . ."

It was his turn to shrug, and Taisyn nodded.

"That's the biggest danger," he agreed. "And their guns don't have to be anywhere near as good as ours if they get them to the riverbank. But like you say, it's a strong position, and Hauwerd and I made sure we could defend from the rear or the flank, as well as frontally. If they do get around behind us, then we stay right here where we are, stuck in their throat like a frigging fishbone." He bared his teeth in the darkness. "Trust me, if the Duke gets to Ice Lake while we're still here, he'll have a *damned* good chance of clearing the river behind us long enough to pull us out. As long as we can keep their barges and their heavy stuff west of here, at least."

The other two nodded, their faces as grim as his own, for all of them understood the unspoken corollary. If Eastshare *didn't* get here in time, and the Army of God, with its hundred thousand-plus regulars and the forty or fifty thousand Temple Loyalist militia it had added to itself, got around behind their positions, it didn't matter how deeply and well dug in their *four* thousand men were. Not in the end.

But if we don't stop them here, we lose all of western Glacierheart—probably the whole damned province, Taisyn thought. *And we can't possibly fight them in an open field battle, not when they've got that big a numerical advantage and even a half-ass idea of what to do with it. Give me a full army brigade, and I'd take my chances, even without cavalry, but with only two thousand Marines and sailors and Zhansyn's pikemen? In the open? We'd hurt them—maybe—but we'd never have a prayer of stopping them . . . and we'd all be just as dead at the end of it.*

He stood between his artillery commander and the Siddarmarkian colonel, watching the beached barges burn and prayed for the duke to hurry.

.III.
Serabor, The Sylmahn Gap,
Old Province,
Republic of Siddarmark

The distant rumble wasn't thunder, and the flashes reflecting from the low-lying cloud to the north weren't lightning, either. General Kynt Clareyk, Baron Green Valley and commanding officer, 2nd Brigade (reinforced), Charisian Expeditionary Force, knew exactly what both of them actually were as he watched the flickering illumination while the lead barge of his brigade glided towards the improvised landing below the dam at Serabor.

He didn't know how Trumyn Stohnar's men had managed to stop Bahrnabai Wyrshym's army. Over half of them were dead. Colonel Wyllys was still on his feet, somehow, but he was one of only two of Stohnar's original regimental commanders who hadn't been killed or wounded, and his regiment hadn't been as fortunate as him. Of the twenty-two hundred men he'd led to the Sylmahn Gap last winter, two hundred and sixty-five were still alive, and ninety of them were wounded. Of his company commanders only young Hainree Klairynce had survived, commanding the single quarter-strength company which was all that remained of the 37th.

Yet that company was still up there, where those guns were flashing, hunkered down as part of the tattered reserve General Stohnar had managed to constitute out of the broken bits and pieces of his regulars and the more brutally winnowed militia. Wyllys commanded that reserve—all eight hundred men of it—while Colonel Fhranklyn Pruait of the 76th held the entrenchments.

Well, him and Commander Tyrwait, Green Valley amended, and shook his head. He hadn't really thought he was going to get here in time. And he wouldn't have, if not for Lieutenant Commander Shain Tyrwait and his naval artillerists.

He looked down through one of Owl's SNARCs as the big barge squeaked against the fenders. The stabbing flashes of rifles and the bigger, fiercer eruptions of cannon and the shrapnel shells streaking in both directions showed clearly to the SNARC's sensors, despite the overcast. A lot more shells were being fired south than north, he thought grimly, and reliable fuses or not, the solid wall of guns Nybar, Vynair, and Bahrkly had assembled almost hub-to-hub were steadily killing Stohnar's men and ripping his earthworks apart. But they weren't having it all their own way, either, and Green Valley's eyes glittered with approval as one of Tyrwait's thirty-pounder shells found an Army of God ammunition wagon. The spectacular explosion killed half the crews of a Temple Loyalist twelve-pounder section . . . and fresh gunners advanced grimly to the pieces, stepping over the dead and writhing bodies of their predecessors.

The reasonably dry ground in front of Stohnar's entrenchments was heaped with the bodies of men who'd died assaulting the earthworks. There were a lot of bodies out there, Green Valley thought with bleak, grim satisfaction. More than there should have been, although it was hard to fault Wyrshym or his divisional commanders.

They're still making it up as they go along, and it's not their fault they're making mistakes. They're not making as many of them as I'd wish, for that matter. And one of those mistakes they're not making is how important Serabor is to them. They don't like losing men any more than anyone else, even if they do believe every one of them's going straight to Heaven, but they know they have to have the Sylmahn Gap if they want Old Province this year. They're willing to pay the price to get it, too, and unless something—like Second Brigade, perhaps—changes the equation, they've got more than enough manpower to grind Stohnar away and take it. They're in the same position Grant was at Petersburg, and the fact that they don't like it hasn't kept them from doing it anyway. But at the same time, they're determined not to lose any more men than they have to, and their learning curve's a hell of a lot steeper than Europe's was in 1914. The only question is whether or not it's steep enough because the truth is, both sides still have a lot to learn. Which shouldn't surprise anyone, when you think about it.

Neither Siddarmark nor the Army of God had been given any yardstick by which to measure the lethality of rifles and combat until they actually used them for the first time. So it was hardly surprising they'd extrapolated from their experience with smoothbore matchlocks, treated the rifles as simply more rapidly firing, more reliable versions of the weapons they already knew and understood. But rifles *weren't* smoothbore matchlocks, and both sides' doctrine of standing in the open in close formation, pouring volleys at the other, had resulted in enormous casualties.

Faster learners than their officers (since personal survival tended to be the fastest teacher known to man), the infantrymen on both sides had discovered the wonderful virtues of the shovel, although neither the Army of God nor the Republican Army had yet evolved anything like the Imperial Charisian Army's policy of digging in every single night in the field. In the final analysis, though, a man armed with a muzzle-loader had little choice but to stand upright if he was going to fire at the enemy, and officers on both sides had been trying to figure out how to do that and survive.

Well, we'll just have to show them, won't we? Green Valley thought. *It'll be interesting to see how willing they are to learn the lesson, though. Our tactical doctrine puts an awful lot of the responsibility on noncoms and junior officers, and senior officers have a problem when it comes to giving up tactical control of their own units and trusting some nineteen- or twenty-year-old lieutenant to make the right call. Hard to blame them, really, and there were enough Chisholmians Ruhsyl had to boot before we got it right, for that matter!*

Up until a few five-days ago, he'd have given odds Siddarmark would accept the new reality more quickly than the Army of God, but he'd acquired a very healthy respect for the Temple Loyalists' adaptability after watching through the SNARCs as they forged across western and northern Siddarmark in a tide of fire. They were tough-minded, those division-commanding bishops, and a lot more willing to think critically about their own doctrine than he'd expected. Probably because so many of them had played major roles in evolving that doctrine in the first place in conjunction with Allayn Maigwair.

And Maigwair's *been an unpleasant surprise, too,* Green Valley admitted. *Everything I ever heard about him suggested he should still be trying to figure out how to shoot pikes out of twelve-pounders, but he's put a lot of thought into equipping and organizing this Army of God of his. And given the fact that he doesn't have Merlin and Owl as advisors, he's done one hell of a job, too. He made mistakes, but they were* smart *mistakes, more often than not.*

In fact, the baron admitted grimly as the mooring lines were made fast and he stepped across onto the rickety dock, if not for Charis, the Army of God would have swept across Siddarmark like the *scourge* of God before first snowfall. There was no question in his mind of that . . . or that something like it might still happen.

They'd play hell holding the Siddarmarkians down, especially with all the hate-fodder the Inquisition's generating, but Merlin's right. Left to their own devices, with no one interfering on either side, they'd reach Siddar City by the end of September.

Except, he told himself harshly, that that wasn't going to happen.

"General Green Valley?" an exhausted-looking lieutenant greeted him with a salute.

"Yes." Green Valley touched his own chest, acknowledging the salute, and the lieutenant seemed to sway for a moment.

"Lieutenant Dahglys Sahlavahn," he said. "I'm General Stohnar's senior—well, I guess I'm his only aide, now." He smiled mirthlessly. "He sent me ahead to greet you. He asked me to tell you he'll be here in about another hour and a half. He should be on his way back from consulting with Colonel Pruait by now."

"I understand."

Green Valley looked back over his shoulder to where the second and third barges in the convoy were gliding towards shore. Then he looked back at Sahlavahn.

"I've got the better part of thirteen thousand infantry and eighty guns coming ashore in the next two or three hours, Lieutenant. I need someplace to put them."

"Yes, Sir!" Lieutenant Sahlavahn's exhausted face was transfigured. "I don't know how we'll be able to get all of those guns to the front, Sir—we've only got about six or seven thousand yards of frontage—but by *God,* they'll give those bastards a headache when we do! And I've got someplace you can park them and mate them up with their draft animals in the meantime. Uh . . . you *did* bring draft animals, didn't you, Sir?"

"Yes, Lieutenant, we did," Green Valley assured him with a faint smile.

"I figured you had, Sir, but—"

The young man shrugged, and Green Valley nodded.

"Always better to make certain," he agreed. "Now, there's one other thing I'm going to need, as well as to meet with General Stohnar."

"Yes, Sir?"

"I need someone who knows the lizard paths above the Gap. I'm going to have to get some of my men up there to make this work the way I have in mind."

"Up in the mountains, Sir?" Sahlavahn looked dubious, and Green Valley nodded again, more firmly.

"Trust me, Lieutenant." He showed his teeth, a white gleam reflecting the artillery muzzle flashes bouncing off the clouds. "If it sounds crazy to you, it'll sound crazy to them. But I think you and General Stohnar are going to like the way it works out a hell of a lot more than *they* will."

.IV.
North of Serabor,
The Sylmahn Gap,
Old Province,
Republic of Siddarmark

Gorthyk Nybar scowled as he considered the morning casualty report. Langhorne Division was at two-thirds strength, but that was only because Bishop Militant Bahrnabai had drawn heavily on the replacements who'd been brought along in the Army of God's advance. Vicar Allayn had known they were going to take casualties, so each army had been assigned a pool of unassigned but trained replacements equal to twenty percent of its paper strength.

They hadn't had sufficient rifles and pikes to give each of those men *weapons*, but there'd been more than enough of those from men who no longer needed the ones they'd been issued, Nybar thought bitterly. And there weren't as many of those unassigned men as there had been, either. In fact, if he simply looked at the number of replacement bodies, Langhorne had taken one hundred percent casualties. Almost half his original men were still with him; the other half had been replaced not just once, but twice.

It's these frigging frontal assaults, he told himself, looking up from his paperwork to listen to the continually pounding guns. *Our artillery ammunition expenditure's three times what we figured, and we still have to hammer straight ahead into these bastards' teeth. And by now, everybody they've got left has a Shan-wei-damned rifle of his own!*

Unfortunately, understanding why his division was bleeding to death didn't change the situation. Their spy reports about troop movements behind the heretics' front were a lot less detailed than he would have preferred, but according to the information he *did* have, the first Charisians couldn't be more than another couple of five-days from Serabor. The Army of God had to punch through and take that town's ruins—and blow up those *damned* dams to drain the Gap once and for all—before that happened. He didn't even want to think about what would happen once the Charisians got here. Servants of Shan-wei or not, they'd had longer to think about these new weapons than anyone else in the world, and what their navy had accomplished was enough to make him acutely nervous about what their *army* might be able to do.

He scowled again and checked his watch as the bombarding artillery began to build towards a crescendo once more. Another ninety minutes, he thought, and then he got to send his men into the meat grinder all over again. His eyes went bleak and hard at the thought of the losses to come, but the frigging Siddarmarkians had to run out of ammunition—and men— sooner or later. If he had to run them out of bullets by giving them bodies to shoot, then he'd by God do it . . . and afterwards, when Siddar City lay in flames, the bastards would pay in spades for every man he lost in the process.

▼   ▼   ▼

The skies were clearing, Kynt Clareyk observed. That was a pity. He'd have preferred rain, since his men's caplock Mahndrayns fired just as reliably in a thunderstorm as in clear, dry weather.

Don't want much, do you? he asked himself sardonically. *You've already got a big enough advantage. Except, of course, that there's no such thing as an advantage that's "big enough" when you're talking about things that can get men under your command killed, is there?*

Perhaps not. But it was about time to find out how well the doctrine he and Ruhsyl Thairis had put together worked out in practice.

He drew a deep breath and looked at the young lieutenant—but they were *all* young, weren't they?—standing next to him.

"All right, Bryahn. It's show time," he said simply.

"Yes, Sir!"

Bryahn Slokym saluted, reached into a belt pouch, withdrew a Shan-wei's candle, and rasped it across the buckle of his sword baldric. The strike-anywhere match burst into sulfurous, stinking life, and he touched it to the length of quick match.

The quick match flared almost instantly, the flame racing away from them at three hundred feet per second, and the signal rocket fifteen yards away from Green Valley's command post hissed into the heavens on a rushing, gushing tail of flame. It rose high into the clearing morning sky, and then it burst in brilliant splendor.

▼ ▼ ▼

"What the—?"

Gorthyk Nybar's eyes narrowed as the . . . whatever it was climbed into the heavens above the heretic entrenchments. He felt a brief flicker of something entirely too much like fear for his comfort, but it fled as quickly as it had come, and his nostrils flared. Of course. The heretics had used . . . "signal rockets," that was the term, in the past. He simply hadn't seen one yet, and he watched it soaring higher and higher. Then it burst, shooting out dozens of tendrils of light that were pale in the morning sunlight but would undoubtedly have been spectacular in the dark.

"What is it, Sir?" one of the division runners asked in a sharp-edged voice, and Nybar snorted.

"They call it a 'rocket,' I think, Private," he said. "Pretty, I suppose, but nothing to worry about—just a way to send signals."

"Oh. Uh, I mean, thank you, My Lord!" the runner said hastily, his face turning red as he realized he'd just interrupted the commanding bishop's thoughts. Nybar saw his expression and chuckled, but then his chuckle faded as he thought about his own words.

A signal, he thought. *Now who in Shan-wei's name could Stohnar be sending signals to . . . and why?*

A moment later, he found out.

▼ ▼ ▼

Lieutenant Hairym Clyntahn, Imperial Charisian Army, had been hazed unmercifully over his last name from the first day he'd enlisted.

He didn't suppose he could blame anyone for it, not that understanding had made the experience any more enjoyable. And he'd been deeply disappointed when he was turned down as a cavalry officer for no better reason than that he looked like a particularly untidy sack of potatoes in the saddle. Then he'd discovered he wasn't even being assigned an infantry platoon. Instead, they'd told him he was going to command something called a "support platoon" and tried to make it sound like it was going to be something special. He'd known better, of course, but he was a Chisholmian. He loved his Empress—and now his Emperor—and he loved the Church. Not the Church *Zhaspahr* Clyntahn represented, but the Church of Maikel Staynair. And because he did, he'd been prepared to serve in whatever capacity the army could find for him.

And boy, was I wrong! he thought now, turning to his platoon sergeant as the rocket burst overhead. *Cavalry?!* Hah! *You can* keep *it!*

"Two thousand yards, fused for airburst!" he snapped.

"Two thousand yards, airburst, yes, Sir!" the platoon sergeant responded, and turned to glower at the closest squad. The order came back, repeated by each of the platoon's squads in turn, and Clyntahn nodded.

"*Fire!*"

Support Platoon, 1st Battalion, 3rd Regiment, consisted of four squads, each armed with three three-inch mortars. They were unlovely weapons, with a four-foot barrel mounted on a steel plate, supported by a bipod fitted with a wheel to control the tube's elevation. Each projectile weighed ten pounds and terminated in a short rod. It was fitted with studs which engaged in the tube's rifling grooves as the mortar bomb was muzzle-loaded into the tube, and a felt "donut" of gunpowder was wrapped around the rod. A side-lock at the base of the tube was fitted with a percussion cap, and when the hammer fell and the cap detonated, the bomb left the weapon at approximately six hundred and fifty feet per second. That gave it a minimum range of three hundred yards . . . and a maximum of *twenty-five* hundred, depending on the tube's elevation.

At the moment, Clyntahn's platoon was high on a mountainside on the western side of the Gap and well behind the Army of God's front line. The total weight of each of their weapons was two hundred and thirty-four pounds, and it broke down into six separate pieces, the heaviest of which was the base plate, at a hundred and fifteen pounds. That made it man-portable—although Pasquale pity the poor bastard with the base plate!—but the platoon had been assisted in this instance by the pack mules it had brought along all the way from Chisholm. Sure-footed and smart, the mules had followed Clyntahn's men and their guide along the narrow, serpentine, treacherous trails to their present positions before dawn, carrying not simply the mortars but the crated ammunition, as well.

Twenty-five hundred yards was only a mile and a quarter, and the Sylmahn Gap was over five miles wide at this point. But the high road down which every bit of traffic must travel, thanks to the flooding, passed within *less* than a mile of Clyntahn's mortars, and he watched through his spyglass as the explosions began to blossom below him.

"Too much fuse!" he announced. "Either that, or they're burning long. Elevation's on, but cut the fuse for eighteen hundred yards!"

Responses came back, and the next covey of mortar bombs went booming into the air, shrilling towards the enemy with the peculiar, warbling whistle the rifling studs imposed.

The projectiles fell almost vertically, and this time the fuses were the right length. The bombs detonated perhaps forty feet up, spraying canister in a lethal cone. The balls hit the high road, and the water, and the mud—and half a hundred soldiers of the Army of God—in a pattern that looked like pelting hail where it pounded into the ground. But this "hail" was made of lead, and it was traveling at over six hundred feet per second.

The consequences when it met flesh instead were ghastly.

▼   ▼   ▼

Each battalion in 2nd Brigade had its own support platoon, and there were twelve battalions—each one three-quarters the size of an Army of God division—in the reinforced brigade's three regiments. Only one other platoon had been sent forward to support Clyntahn; the others were still available to accompany their parent battalions in the advance. But if all those other mortars weren't available at the moment, the two "angle-gun" batteries Green Valley had brought from Chisholm *were*.

The angle-guns—or just plain "angles"—of the Imperial Charisian Army were a lighter, land-going version of the navy's weapons. They fired rifled, six-inch, sixty-eight-pound shells at high elevations to a range of almost eight thousand yards, and there were eight of them in each of Green Valley's batteries.

Sixteen six-inch shells came warbling down out of the heavens, and they were equipped not with time fuses, but with *impact* fuses. It was a very simple, rudimentary design, and it had a failure rate of almost twelve percent . . . but that meant it worked perfectly *eighty-eight* percent of the time, and the shells driving into the ground each carried almost twelve pounds of gunpowder.

A pattern of volcanoes erupted across the Army of God's position, hurling mud, water, and bits and pieces of bodies into the air. The angles couldn't fire as rapidly as a standard field gun, but they could still manage a peak rate of fire of three rounds every two minutes and one round a minute thereafter as their barrels heated, and the concussion of their shells marched across the Temple Loyalists' artillery positions in flaming, hobnailed boots.

And they did it without ever actually seeing their targets.

It took them five or six rounds to range in, even with the heliograph on the cliffs on the *eastern* side of the Gap, opposite Clyntahn's mortars, signaling them corrections. The angles were, after all, a very crude version of a proper howitzer, without a reliable recoil system, which required them to be repositioned for each shot. They were, however, dug into gun pits fitted with ranging and bearing stakes so that their crews could be certain they'd repositioned them *correctly*, and the Army of God's artillerists had never imagined a cannon that could shoot them from an invisible, protected position four miles away, on the far side of the entrenchments they'd been trying to batter their way through for almost six days. Nor had they ever imagined a gun that could hit them with shells half again as big and twice as heavy as their own.

Their steady, pounding fire began to falter as those volcanoes erupted—scattered, at first, but growing more concentrated, moving towards them. By the sixth salvo, the angles had the range, and six-inch shells came smashing down on the tight-packed target of Temple Loyalist fieldpieces. Men and horses shrieked as shell splinters ripped and whined through them, but it was worse when the limbers started exploding. Still more of the whistling shells came slicing down, pounding the Church's gun positions, and battery officers began shouting frantic orders to limber up.

It said an enormous amount for the Army of God's discipline that despite the terrifying effectiveness of an attack they'd never seen coming, Bishop Militant Bahrnabai's gunners stuck to their pieces. They'd already begun to evolve the artillerist's tradition—the gun was the battery's standard, its colors, and it could not be abandoned to the enemy. Men would die to avoid that dishonor . . . and they died this day to save their guns.

But many of them died in vain.

▼   ▼   ▼

Kynt Clareyk watched through his binoculars—and through the far more capable, all-seeing sensors of an artificial intelligence named Owl—as the Army of God recoiled from the sudden, unexpected flail of his artillery.

The Gap was a miserable place to fight, even without the inundations the defenders had arranged. There was little room to maneuver, no flanks to work around, and only a single, predictable axis of advance for anything heavier than his nimble-footed mortars. It wasn't a place for finesse . . . but that didn't mean it had no possibilities, he thought, watching explosions rip along the Church gun line. Half the guns had managed to limber up and race towards the rear, but the rest had already been disabled—or simply lost so many crewmen no one remained to work them—and he nodded in satisfaction. Those guns had worried him more than the Temple Loyalists' rifles, and he was delighted to have them silenced.

Not all of the guns which had fled were going to escape, either. They still had to run the gauntlet of Clyntahn's mortars, and horses and men went down—dead, dying, or wounded—as that merciless rain of shrapnel marched up and down the high road.

"Stage two, Bryahn," he said, never lowering his binoculars.

Another rocket raced into the heavens, and the angle-guns retargeted obediently. Their shells left the silenced gun line and began crashing down on the Army of God's infantry redoubts with a fury which filled him with vengeful satisfaction.

No point pretending I don't want to pay these bastards back, he thought coldly. *I admire their discipline, I respect their guts, I understand they're sincere in their be-*

liefs . . . and I'll strangle every last motherless one of them with my bare hands for what they've done. Or settle for this.

He would have liked to get some of the four-inch muzzle-loading rifles he'd brought along from Siddar City into action, as well, but there was only so much space and he refused to crowd his troops. There'd be time to get the field guns into action once he'd broken the Army of God's current position.

Of course, there's the little problem that even after I start driving them, I won't be able to push them forever, he reflected. *There's just too many of them, and once they get over the shock, they've got the unit cohesion—and the courage, damn their black hearts to hell—not to panic and break again. For that matter, Wyrshym already covered his bets with those frigging entrenchments around Saiknyr. If they pull back across the bridge and blow it, getting across Wyvern Lake'll be an unmitigated—and painful—pain in the arse.*

For that matter, he reminded himself, a hundred thousand men were still a hundred thousand men, however he sliced it . . . and he had only thirteen thousand. As Merlin was fond of saying, quoting someone from Old Earth, after a certain point, quantity took on a quality all its own.

I'll settle for driving them back across the lake. Hell, for that matter, I'll settle for pushing them back as far as Jairth! In fact, I'd rather stop there than somewhere between Jairth and Malkyr, where the Gap gets too frigging wide to cover even with fire, much less infantry! It's not my job to kick them all the way back to Tarikah, and I'll be damned *if I push too far too fast and let them chew up the brigade that's hopefully putting the fear of Shan-wei into them right this minute. Besides*—he smiled thinly, binoculars still to his eyes—*unless Merlin's brainstorm turns into a total disaster, I won't* have *to push them any farther . . . this year, anyway.*

The angle-guns had been pounding the redoubts for almost fifteen minutes now, and he saw the first confused signs of a withdrawal. Sensible of them. Those redoubts had been built to include overhead protection against shrapnel shells bursting in midair; they'd never been intended to resist six-inch explosive shells plunging straight down onto them. With their own artillery silenced and driven from the field, it made no sense for those men to simply hunker down in the abattoirs their fortifications had become, and their officers had the good sense—and the moral courage—to pull them out.

You've got to love good officers, Kynt, even when they're on that *side,* he told himself. *It would* be *nice if they'd just sit there and let you kill them with artillery, but they're not going to. So . . . .*

He lowered the binoculars and looked at Colonel Allayn Powairs, his chief of staff.

"Pass the word to Colonel Tompsyn," he said. "Tell him to give them another ten minutes or so to come out into the open, then go get them.

And"—he held Powairs' eyes for just a moment—"remind him we *are* taking prisoners."

"Yes, Sir," Powairs agreed.

Zhon Tompsyn was an excellent officer, but he was also a man of firm Reformist principles . . . and he'd lost a brother with Gwylym Manthyr. He was unlikely to go out of his way to encourage surrenders, yet his 3rd Regiment was the best trained, best choice for his current mission; that was one reason *his* support platoon had been deployed so far forward.

"See to it, then," Green Valley said, and turned back to the carnage, raising his binoculars once more.

▼   ▼   ▼

Gorthyk Nybar wiped blood from his face and looked at his red palm, wondering when his forehead had acquired that cut.

He listened to the shouts of command, the screams of pain, and the thunder of the heretics' terrible artillery and wondered how the situation could have gone so disastrously wrong so quickly.

Obviously the Charisians were a little closer than we knew, he thought bitterly. *Langhorne! How the hell many of them* are *there?*

He'd already realized there weren't actually that many of those dreadful cannon on the other side. No more than fifteen or twenty, he estimated, although that had been more than enough to break the back of their own artillery. The Army of God had lost at least half its guns, he estimated, and that was going to hurt. But there wasn't anything he could do about that now. The best he could hope for was to pull back, get out of range of whatever they were using to hammer his men, and reorganize.

We're going to have to dig in deeper and better. And we have to figure out how the hell they can do this! It's got to be more of what they used at Iythria.

He wished now that he'd paid more attention to the rumors about the bombardment of the Iythrian forts, but that whole report had been . . . heavily edited by the Inquisition after Baron Jahras and Duke Kholman deserted to the heretics. Still, there'd been something about firing *over* the forts' walls instead of through them. He'd assumed the Charisians had simply cut their fuses so that standard shells exploded as they crossed the forts, but that wasn't what had happened here! No, these shells were coming down *vertically*. They were plunging fire, and unless he was badly mistaken, the damned things were detonating on *impact*, not with time fuses. So how—?

Time enough to be thinking about that later, Gorthyk! For now, let's get your arse—and as many of your men as you can—out of this bitched-up mess.

His forward regiments were disengaging, filing out of the redoubts in remarkably good order, given the unanticipated carnage which had enveloped them so abruptly, and he felt a surge of pride. It wasn't every army that

could go from a planned assault into a hasty, *unplanned* retreat without losing its cohesion, but his men were doing it.

Then he realized the shelling had begun to taper off. It would have
been nice if he'd believed that meant they were running out of ammunition, but—

No, they aren't, he thought coldly, looking over the parapet as infantry
in strange, mottled-looking uniforms, came forward at last.

His eyes narrowed as he watched them. Those uniforms . . . they looked
ridiculous, at first glance, but as he gazed at them, he realized that the mottled green and brown pattern would blend into most terrain far better than
the Temple's Schuelerite purple tunics and dark red trousers.

But that realization was a small and distant thing, for the Charisians
were advancing like no infantry he'd ever heard of. They came forward not
in a line, or in a column, but in a . . . swarm. At first, it looked like there was
no order to it at all, but then he realized there was. It was just the . . . the
wrong sort of order. Groups of perhaps a dozen men worked together, trotting warily forward in a loose, open formation without any immediately
apparent coordination with any other group. There were hundreds of men
in those groups—possibly even thousands—and he couldn't imagine how
anyone could possibly control them when they were scattered so broadly.

There *was* a column behind them, he saw. It was just beginning to come
out of the Siddarmarkians' entrenchments, but it was well back. Not to lend
its solid, close-ordered weight to combat, he realized, but merely to simplify
movement while it kept up close enough to augment the infantry already
advancing towards his own positions if that should become necessary.

Rifle fire sputtered from one of the Holy Martyrs Division's redoubts,
and he saw the Charisians stop and drop. At first he thought they'd been hit,
but then he realized it was a preplanned maneuver. They went prone, turning themselves into all but impossible targets . . . and then they began to fire
back!

Impossible! he thought. *Nobody can load a musket or a rifle lying on his* belly!

But the Charisians could—and far more rapidly than the Army of God,
to boot. He felt an icy chill as he considered the implications of a man who
could lie flat—or take shelter behind a rock or a tree—shooting at another
man who had to stand out in the open to reload between shots.

*That's why they're so scattered out. They're not going to stand up and shoot it
out with us; they're going to hide behind every scrap of cover they can find while they
blow our infantry lines away!*

He forced himself to remain calm. There was no weapon whose effects
couldn't be mitigated, whether it could be duplicated or not. And so far, at
least, nothing else the heretics had come up with had been impossible to
duplicate, he reminded himself.

We've got to capture some of those rifles, figure out how they work.

Even as he thought that, a fresh pattern of explosions erupted in the Holy Martyrs redoubt. They were smaller, and he couldn't see where they were coming from. And they weren't exploding on contact, either—they were exploding in midair, showering the redoubt's interior with shrapnel balls.

The defending fire from the parapet died, and the Charisian infantry who'd gone to ground rose again. They went forward once more, in short, sharp rushes, while those explosions kept the defenders' heads down, and his jaw clenched at the fresh evidence of just how sophisticated the Charisians' tactics were.

Well, he thought grimly, watching the heretics flow towards the redoubt as remorselessly as the sea, *they may be more "sophisticated" than we are* now, *but I'm not too proud to learn from example.*

"Sir—My Lord—you have to fall back now!"

He looked over his shoulder. Colonel Mairyai's uniform was splattered with mud and there was blood on his right cheek. He'd lost his helmet, and his black hair was clotted with still more mud.

"I'll get the rest of the division out of here, Sir. We need you back there getting us reorganized before these bastards come right up our backside!"

"That's probably true, Spyncyr." His own voice sounded preposterously calm to him. "Unfortunately, if I'm going to reorganize, I've got to have some idea what I'm reorganizing *against,* don't I?"

Mairyai stared at him, obviously wanting to protest, and Nybar gripped his shoulder.

"Go ahead and organize the withdrawal. Assign one platoon to keep an eye on me, if you like. I promise I'll withdraw before the heretics get here. But I have to *see,* Spyncyr. I have to watch as long as I can, try to understand what we're up against."

The colonel held his superior's eyes for a long, taut moment. Then he exhaled noisily and shook his head.

"I'm going to take you at your word, Sir . . . but I *will* assign a platoon to you, too. And its orders are going to be very explicit. When the enemy gets within five hundred yards of this redoubt, you *are* heading to the rear, even if I have to have you knocked on the head and dragged! Is that clear?"

"Clear, Spyncyr," Nybar said quietly while Charisian rifle fire rattled and snarled behind his voice. "Very clear."

. V .
Guarnak–Ice Ash Canal,
New Northland Province,
and
Ice Ash River,
Northland Province,
Republic of Siddarmark

Merlin Athrawes' recon skimmer floated silently above the Guarnak–Ice Ash Canal, three hundred and forty miles inland from the city of Ranshir, where the Ice Ash emptied into the bay of the same name, while he watched the SNARCs imagery of two ironclads preparing to get underway. No one would have guessed from looking at him, as he reclined in the comfortable flight couch, that he was at least as anxious as Captain Halcom Bahrns himself. Probably more, he reflected with a humorless smile. It was his idea, after all.

He checked his instruments, not that he had any need to. He had plenty of time for what he had to do, and he was pretty sure he was trying to find reasons to delay. He caught himself wishing yet again that there were some way to avoid his self-assigned task. Unfortunately, there wasn't.

His plan's one enormous drawback was that there was a very simple way to thwart it. Not just thwart it, but turn it into hideous disaster.

HMS *Delthak* and her sisters had been intended to work on inland waterways, but he'd had *rivers* in mind when he came up with that idea. And he hadn't been thinking only of rivers—he'd been thinking of the model of *Old Earth's* rivers in the American Civil War. Although they were sixty feet shorter than the *Passaic*-class monitors from that war and had considerably thinner (though far tougher) armor, they came within two hundred tons of the monitor's displacement. Small as they were by oceanic standards, that made them *big* ships by riverine standards . . . and it had never occurred to him to think of their using *canals* except as a means of getting from one river to another. He'd certainly never thought of their fighting their way along canals whose locks were controlled by someone else!

Yet as Ehdwyrd Howsmyn had told him on that seemingly long-ago night when the River-class gunboats were born, the newer mainland canals—like the ones in northeastern Siddarmark—had been built with bigger locks than the older ones, and the same was true for improvements to the rivers they served, as well. That meant *Delthak* and her sister could use those locks, which was precisely what Merlin intended for them to do now. But it also meant that *without* those locks—or with the canals simply blocked ahead and behind them—the ironclads would be trapped inland, far from the sea, with no possible way to withdraw or escape, and there were over thirty critical locks along Bahrns' course. Obstacles might achieve the same purpose in unimproved stretches of the river, much as Brigadier Taisyn had managed on the Daivyn, but it would take time—and quite a lot of it—for anyone to erect an obstacle a thousand tons of armored gunboat couldn't ram out of the way. And the three thousand infantry riding the barges behind the ironclads ought to be enough to clear any obstacle which could be quickly dumped into a canal while the ironclads' guns discouraged any interference with the task.

No, it was the locks which were his plan's Achilles' heel. Without them, it was doomed, and despite his own arguments, despite the persuasive logic based on the *Book of Langhorne*'s injunctions and Safehold's nine hundred years of history, he couldn't be positive some senior commander wouldn't realize that and order the locks upon which everything depended destroyed. No Temple Loyalist would consider that lightly—it had taken direct orders from the Inquisition, the keeper of doctrinal orthodoxy, to authorize the Sword of Schueler to disable canals even temporarily—but what if someone with the moral courage to risk condemnation recognized what needed to be done and acted *without* that authorization? Or what if some senior inquisitor, alerted by the semaphore, saw the answer and sent the order back down the chain? In daylight, the semaphore transmitted messages at up to six hundred miles in an hour, and it was only five hundred and ninety miles by the semaphore chain from Fairkyn on the Guarnak–Ice Ash Canal to Bishop Militant Barnabai's headquarters in Guarnak itself. He could learn of the ironclads' intrusion within less than one hour of their passage of Fairkyn, and his intendant could send back a special injunction to destroy the locks just as quickly.

It was highly unlikely he would, given the *Writ*'s injunctions and the importance of the canal system to every aspect of the mainland's economic life, not to mention how essential it was to the Army of God's own operations. But it wasn't remotely *impossible* that he would, and that made maintaining the element of surprise as long as possible absolutely essential to the ironclads' success.

And that was why Merlin Athrawes was in a recon skimmer, floating like the silent angel of death above the semaphore station he'd marked on his mental chart as "Target Alpha." There were four more targets on that chart—isolated targets, far from any town or village, which had to be . . . neutralized before word of what Cayleb had dubbed the Great Canal Raid reached them. With them destroyed, the first, critical six hundred miles of the semaphore chain would be broken, depriving the Temple Loyalists of the warning they'd need to trap the ironclads. And there was only one person in all of Safehold who could do that destroying.

Merlin's mouth tightened. It would have been simpler—or at least easier for his conscience, perhaps—if he could have used the skimmer's onboard weapons to destroy his targets through the impersonal detachment of a high-tech gunsight. But he dared not use those weapons, and so he was going to have to do it the hard way—by hand and in person. And if he didn't want any tales about the "Demon Merlin" floating around, he had to do it in a way which left no living witnesses.

Quit stalling, he told himself harshly. *Yes, they're civilians, and you're going to kill them all. A hell of a lot of other "civilians"—including children who never got a vote—have already died since Clyntahn kicked off this nightmare. And the people manning those semaphore stations aren't children . . . and are just as essential to the Church's war as the people in the Army of God's uniform. And at least when you take your downtime to satisfy Cayleb, you don't dream, so maybe you won't even have nightmares about it.*

He squared his shoulders and reached for the controls.

▼   ▼   ▼

"Both ahead slow."

"Both ahead slow, aye, Sir," the telegraphsman replied, rocking the big handles, and as the bells jangled, Halcom Bahrns felt *Delthak* quiver underfoot, coming back to life once more.

It felt . . . good. She still wasn't a *proper* warship, he supposed, but she was actually far more responsive than any sail-powered ship he'd ever commanded, and there was a lot to be said for not needing to wait for the wind. That was an advantage the Charisian Navy had given up when it embraced the galleon so enthusiastically. He knew why that had happened, and he approved wholeheartedly, and yet . . . .

He shrugged. They had a way to go yet, but the two of them were coming to know one another's ways, and whatever else she might be, *Delthak* was as willing as the day was long. And while it had taken her almost three fivedays to make the voyage from Siddar City to Ranshir Bay, she could have made the same voyage in only twelve days if not for the pair of barges towing behind her. There'd been more than one moment when Bahrns had longed to cast them off and just get *on* with it, but those barges—and the other four now linked together behind *Delthak* and *Hador*—were integral to his orders.

Saygin and *Tellesberg* had helped with the towing, but they'd barely paused to drop off their barges and refill their bunkers before they'd been off again, steaming on around the promontory where the northern end of the Samuel Mountains thrust out into the beginning of Hsing-wu's Passage.

They were bound for Salyk, to help hold the city, clear the lower three hundred miles of the Hildermoss River . . . and, just possibly, be available for a rescue effort, although that wasn't going to be required, assuming the emperor's mad plan actually worked.

Well, Seijin *Merlin's mad plan, actually, I suspect,* he thought as *Delthak* began to creep slowly forward. *But the Emperor certainly scooped it up and ran with it once the* seijin *suggested it!*

He started to speak to the helmsman, but Crahmynd Fyrgyrsyn, the gray-haired petty officer on the wheel, already had his instructions, and *Delthak*'s blunt bow aimed itself at the glow of the lantern on the river galley's stern. She began pushing a mustache of water in front of her, following the galley across the estuary towards the channel, and the canal pilot standing at Bahrns' elbow nodded unconsciously in approval.

No point talking just to hear myself proving to everyone else how nervous I am, the captain thought wryly. *Everything's under control so far, and we're—what? five whole minutes?—into the operation?*

His lips twitched in amusement, but then he thought of the other ironclad astern of him, and of the barges each was towing—of the three thousand infantry and the four hundred sailors under his command, and of all the things that could still go wrong—and the temptation to smile disappeared as swiftly as it had come.

▼   ▼   ▼

The flames roared into a night less empty than his own soul.

Assuming he had one of those, of course. At the moment, he almost hoped Maikel Staynair was wrong about that. It would be so much more comforting to believe that beyond his current existence there was only blackness, blankness and oblivion, no need to remember.

You'll probably feel differently about it . . . in time, he told himself drearily, wiping blood from his katana before he sheathed it. *Of course that's the thing that scares you the most, isn't it? You* will *feel differently about it. It won't bother you anymore. And when that happens, how will you be any different from Zhaspahr Clyntahn and his* butchers?

He knew he was being unfair to himself, harder than he would have been on anyone else. One of the reasons he hadn't discussed this part of the Great Canal Raid with Cayleb was that he knew Cayleb would have told him exactly that. He would have pointed out that it *had* to be done, and that it wasn't Merlin Athrawes who'd launched the Army of God at the Republic's throat like a ravening beast. And Cayleb would have been right . . . which wouldn't have changed the fact that he would have been arguing the morality of expediency.

And it wouldn't change the fact that I'm a killing machine.

He threw the last two words at himself harshly, viciously, his mind flickering with the perfect recall of a PICA . . . and the memory of all the men who'd died at his hands. None of them had ever had a chance, not really, no matter what they might have thought in those final seconds of their lives. Not one of them had had any chance at all of defeating a PICA's strength and speed and invulnerability.

It's too easy. It shouldn't be easy to kill human beings. To turn it into some kind of virtual reality combat game because that's how much chance you have of actually being stopped yourself.

It wasn't the first time he'd had such thoughts, but they were darker these days. Dark with the knowledge of how many millions of Siddarmarkians had perished over the past winter, how many thousands more were being herded into the Inquisition's holding camps even now. Of what was about to happen to Mahrtyn Taisyn's command, despite his men's courage and determination and skill, because none of *them* were PICAs. It was even uglier than he'd feared it could be, and the number of innocent people—civilians, women and children, not just soldiers or sailors—sliding down the monster's maw was more hideous than he could have imagined.

And Owl's SNARCs let him see every horrible moment of it.

He stood looking at the strengthening inferno which had been a semaphore station—"Target Delta," the name he'd given it in some vain hope that it might make what he had to do a proper military operation, not simply murder—and watched the smoke lifting into the night.

Thank you, God, he said silently. *Thank you that at least there was no one at any of them except the duty crews.*

He didn't know if he had the right any longer to thank God, but that made him no less grateful.

He looked at the blazing pyre of his latest victims for a moment longer. Then he turned on his heel and walked away from that place of death to his waiting recon skimmer.

▼　　▼　　▼

"Captain Tailahr's cleared the lock, Sir."

Bahrns nodded at the signalman's report that Tailahr's *Hador* and her trio of barges had just been passed through the final set of locks in the Ice Ash River before the Guarnak–Ice Ash Canal split off to the west. They were still two hours steaming from the canal at the bare ten knots they could manage burdened with barges and breasting the current, but *Delthak* had crossed the invisible line between the still loyal territory of Northland Province and into the hostile territory of New Northland over ten hours ago, and the sun was well above the horizon. The Canal Service staff on the locks they'd just used had been reduced to a skeleton since the rebellion, and most of them had been asleep when Colonel Wyntahn Harys' Marines rowed silently ashore and knocked on their bedroom doors. The Temple Loyalists' astonishment at seeing any enemies, and especially Charisian *Marines*, three hundred and fifty straight-line miles from the nearest salt water had been . . . profound. Their reaction when the Canal Service personnel attached to Bahrns' command smoothly locked through two twelve-hundred-ton, smoke-spewing ironclads and six "timber-clad" barges had been far worse. They'd been in such a state of shock after that that they'd made only token protests when they were bundled aboard one of those barges as prisoners.

The ironclads had seen very little barge traffic so far, and what little they had seen had been tied up along the riverbank until they'd passed. The cavalry patrols sweeping the tow roads on either side of the Ice Ash had seen to that, as long as they'd been in friendly territory, and for over fifty miles into New Northland, for that matter. From here on, there would be no convenient cavalry, and Bahrns put his hands into the pockets of his tunic as an alternative to wiping them nervously on his trousers.

"Very well, Ahbukyra," he said to the signalman. "Acknowledge his signal and then hoist the signal to proceed."

"Aye, aye, Sir."

"Ahead thirteen knots, both engines."

"Ahead thirteen knots, aye, Sir." The telegraphs rang again, and Bahrns heard the telegraphman bending over the bronze tube—the "voice pipe," Master Howsmyn had called it—to the engine room to confirm the actual speed through the water. Given the three-knot current, their true speed would be only ten knots, but by now Lieutenant Bairystyr and his oilers had a very good idea of how many revolutions per minute equated to a given speed, and Bharns could count on the telegraphsman to coach him through any fine adjustments.

It was so *convenient* to have a permanent speed indicator here on the conning tower, connected to the spinner in the pitometer's shrouded tunnel beneath *Delthak*'s keel.

Face it, he thought wryly. *All your concerns about "proper warships" are fighting a dying rearguard action against just how much you love what this ship can do, Halcom!*

"And now, Master Myklayn," he turned to the canal pilot, "I believe it's up to you."

"Aye, Captain, I believe it is."

Zhaimys Myklayn had never been to sea in his life, but he'd sailed more miles than most professional naval officers, all of it on freshwater. His entire career had been spent on the rivers and canals of East Haven in the Canal Service administered by the Order of Langhorne, and no man alive knew them better than he did. Even towed barges needed helmsmen, but Myklayn was more than that. He was one of the master canal pilots, the men charged with keeping charts updated not just for the canals but for the rivers they linked, reporting when and where repairs were needed, and suggesting possible improvements to the routes.

Now the square-shouldered, gray-haired pilot in his shabby, well-worn Canal Service tunic, stuck his pipe into his mouth and stepped out onto the starboard wing of the bridge outside *Delthak*'s conning tower.

Bahrns followed him through the heavily armored conning tower door, which had been latched open so he could call helm instructions to PO Fyrgyrsyn. He took a Shan-wei's candle from his pocket, struck it on the wooden-planked bridge's iron railing, and cupped his left hand to shield the flame as he offered it to Myklayn's pipe.

The pilot hesitated for just a moment, then leaned forward—a bit cautiously—and puffed the tobacco alight. Fragrant smoke curled around his ears as he straightened, and he grinned crookedly at Bahrns around the pipe stem.

"First time I've actually seen one of those, Captain. A mite on the . . . surprising side, I suppose is the best way to put it. Handy, though."

"I've found them so," Bahrns agreed, dropping the spent candle into the spittoon set aside for the watchkeepers who used chewleaf, and Myklayn chuckled.

"I imagine the Grand Inquisitor might take a tad of offense, though," he observed, and Bahrns showed his teeth.

"Master Myklayn, we've given Zhaspahr Clyntahn so many things to take offense over that I don't think a few Shan-wei's candles are going to make a whole lot of difference, do you?"

"Probably not." Myklayn drew on his pipe and blew out a streamer of smoke, watching it move rapidly astern as *Delthak* gathered speed. "Come to that, what we're about to do's bound to get all of us into his black books, isn't it?" He shook his head. "Part of me hates to do it, Captain. I've spent my entire life maintaining the canals as the *Writ* commands, and I know better'n most how important they are."

He paused, gazing forward into the wind of *Delthak*'s motion, his pipe trailing smoke for a long, silent moment before he looked back at Bahrns, and if his eyes were sad when he did, his expression was determined.

"Even with Archbishop Dahnyld's injunction in my pocket, that part of me's more'n half afraid the Rakurai's going to come crashing down on my head just for thinking of it. But when I think 'bout how that bastard in Zion's going to react when *he* hears about it—well, let's just say I don't expect my regrets to keep me awake nights, after all."

He looked back up the river again, scratching the side of his jaw gently, then nodded like a man recognizing a familiar spot in his neighborhood.

"You'll want to keep closer to midstream along here, Captain. There's a nasty sandbank with an unfriendly habit of extending itself along the in-side of this bend in the spring."

"Will another . . . thirty yards be enough?"

"Best make it forty to be on the safe side. This lady"—Myklayn tapped the planks below the railing with his knuckles—"draws a bit more water'n most of the barges through here."

"Very good." Bahrns leaned in through the open conning tower door. "Bring her a quarter point larboard, Crahmynd."

"Quarter-point to larboard, aye, Sir."

▼   ▼   ▼

The office door burst open with a bang loud enough to make Captain Dy-gry Verryn jump in his chair. Hot tea flew everywhere, inundating his late-morning breakfast, splashing the correspondence on his desk, and soaking his tunic, and he whipped around with a glare.

"What the *hell*— ?!"

"Sorry, Sir!" Sergeant Zhermo Taigyn interrupted. "Know you didn't want to be disturbed, but you'd better hear this. Quick."

Verryn's eyes narrowed. Zhermo Taigyn wasn't the sharpest blade he'd ever met, but then Dygry Verryn had scarcely been Chihiro's own gift to the militia. That was how he'd ended up in command of the forty-man "garrison" of Fairkyn. It made him more of a glorified policeman than any-thing else, which was probably just as well, given his total lack of combat experience. Of course, the regular police didn't much care for having him breathing over their shoulders, but the previous police chief had tried to or-ganize a counterattack against the Faithful who'd seized control of Fairkyn in the first five-day of the Rising. Fortunately for him, he'd died in the fighting, but Father Ahnsylmo, the Sword of Schueler's representative in Fairkyn, had decided someone whose first loyalty was clearly to Mother Church should take over supervision of the remaining city Guardsmen.

It was remotely possible, Verryn acknowledged, that the under-priest had also seen it as a way of keeping his own questionable talents away from a field of battle. If it was, the same was probably true of Sergeant Taigyn. For that matter, none of his detachment were what he would have called steely-eyed warriors.

"Hear *what*?" the captain snapped after a fulminating moment, reaching for his napkin and beginning to mop.

"This, Sir."

Taigyn reached behind him and half-dragged Paidryg Tybyt and his son Gyffry into Verryn's office. The Tybyts looked pale and agitated, and Verryn's eyes narrowed at the sight. Gyffry was about as excitable as a thirteen-year-old usually came, but Paidryg was a stolid, dependable sort, not prone to excitement and agitation. The two of them worked the barges during harvest season; during the off-season, Paidryg farmed a stretch of canal bank east of town.

"What's this all about?" Verryn asked, looking back between father and son, and Paidryg shook his head.

"I don't know," he said, his voice hoarse. "But whatever it is, it's a-coming up the canal from the Ice Ash, and it's a-spewing smoke like Shanwei herself!"

"What?" Verryn blinked and dropped the napkin on his blotter. "Smoking? What're you *talking* about, Paidryg?!"

"I don't *know*, I'm telling you!" The older man shook his head, his expression a combination of fear, ignorance, and frustration. "It's . . . it's some kind of big, black . . . *barge*, I guess. Only it looks like . . . like . . . well, like the roof of my *barn*, damn it! And it's a-moving twicet as fast as any barge I ever saw, with nothin' towing it! Shan-wei, Captain—*it's* a-towing at least *three* barges its ownself, and there's another one of it a-coming on behind! Gyffry here saw 'em first, and he called me, and I flung saddles on our two best plow horses soon as *I* saw it. But even with us cutting cross-country, it can't be more'n five, ten minutes behind us, and I'm a-telling you—!"

Something screamed in the distance. Something unearthly and horrible, ripping across Tybyt's efforts to describe a thing he'd never seen before. The shrieking sound went on and on until it finally died in a horrible, wailing sob, and it jerked Verryn out of his chair, the tea soaking his tunic forgotten.

"Sound the alarm, Zhermo! Get the duty section turned to—*now*!"

▼　　▼　　▼

"That's enough, I think," Halcom Bahrns said as Ahbukyra Matthysahn reached for the hanging lanyard again. The signalman looked at him almost imploringly, but the captain shook his head with a tight grin. "I'm sure you've gotten their attention, Ahbukyra. Now it's only polite to give them time to respond."

"Yes, Sir."

The disappointment in the young man's tone was palpable, but he stepped back and Bahrns turned away from him, looking back through the vision slit in the front of *Delthak*'s conning tower. He hadn't actually realized until this moment how addicted he'd become to the visibility which had seemed so unnatural when he first took command. Now, as he looked through the slit's restricted field of view, he found himself longing for the bridge wing on the other side of the closed armored door.

I ought to be out there, anyway, he thought. *Can't see a thing from in here*—that wasn't really true, but he was in no mood to admit anything of the sort—*and I ought to be out there where Harys' Marines and General Tylmahn's people could see me. They're all going to be out there, anyway. If anybody's going to get shot at—*

"Larboard a half-point," he said tautly. "We want a clear line of fire to the quay, Crahmynd."

"Half-point larboard, aye, Sir," PO Fyrgyrsyn repeated unflappably, and Bahrns' mouth twitched. The petty officer's tone was a gentle reprimand, reminding him they'd discussed this maneuver with painstaking care long before they reached Fairkyn.

The captain moved to the starboard side of the conning tower, looking through the vision slit on that side, and his nostrils flared with satisfaction as he watched the confusion boiling along the waterfront. Fairkyn wasn't an enormous town, but it had a sizable complex of canal-front warehouses and docks, and he was delighted to see so many people running in the opposite direction just as fast as they could.

Smoke probably would've done that all by itself, he reflected, *but young Ahbukyra and his whistle made sure.*

He shook his head, remembering his own first reaction to the unbelievable, shrill sound of a steam whistle fed by hundreds of pounds per square inch of pressure. No wonder the townsfolk were running in every direction!

Movement caught the corner of his eye, and he leaned forward, his forehead almost in contact with the steel, to look as far aft as he could, then grunted in satisfaction. The first of the launches had cast off from the troop barge towing behind *Delthak*, filled with men in the dark blue tunics and light blue trousers of Charisian Marines. It pulled strongly for its objective—the lock master's office—and other boats followed it.

"Stop engines," he ordered.

▼   ▼   ▼

Captain Verryn decided he perfectly understood Paidryg Tybyt's inability to describe what he'd seen. It did look like some kind of floating house, but he'd never seen a house with chimneys that tall or pouring out so much thick, dark smoke.

And you've never seen one of them moving along a canal without one damned thing to make *it move, either!*

The terror of that smooth, unnatural movement, the memory of its shrieking cry, filled him with dread.

The heretics serve Shan-wei, he thought. *Langhorne and Schueler only know what kind of deviltry she's able to get up to! And if she's giving it to* them —*!*

"Why are you just *standing* here? The heretics are landing *troops*, Captain! *Do* something about it!"

Verryn wheeled and found himself confronting Owain Kyrst, Fairkyn's mayor.

"What in Schueler's name d'you *want* me to do, Master Mayor?" he demanded. "I've got forty men, and only fifteen of them are here right now. *Look* at that!"

He jabbed an index finger down the street where more of the blue-uniformed men were appearing every moment. And there were men in Siddarmarkian uniform—but armed with muskets, not pikes—moving with them now. Lots of them. And beyond that, he saw the leading black monster open *gunports* all along its side. The black, blunt muzzles of cannon snouted out of them as he watched, and while Dygry Verryn might not have been a battlefield hero out of legend, he *did* have a working brain.

"There's nothing I can do, Master Mayor," he said flatly. "Nothing but get a lot of people killed. If you want somebody to do something, then I suggest *you* go out there and have a word with them. You're the mayor, aren't you?"

▼　▼　▼

"What the—?"

Wyllym Bohlyr was Fairkyn's Canal Service lockmaster, the man charged with overseeing the daily operation and maintenance of the two-step locks that allowed the Guarnak–Ice Ash Canal's water to find the level of the river. Those locks were the real reason Fairkyn existed, and Bohlyr took his responsibilities seriously, although it was scarcely what anyone could have called an onerous task. Things got lively during harvest season, when traffic on the canal and the river peaked; the rest of the time, his office was a calm, even slightly sleepy place while the pumpmaster and master gatekeeper saw to the locks' actual operation.

Not today.

The hubbub along the canal front had already disturbed his concentration on his usual morning paperwork, but oddly enough, no one had thought to run and tell him what was happening. Not until the door of his office opened abruptly to admit Rhobair Kulmyn, the day pumpmaster, and Zhoel Wahrlyw, the master gatekeeper on the day shift. Nor were they alone. Half a dozen men in a uniform he'd never seen before—armed with some sort of long, slender musket—followed them. And so did one person he *had* seen before.

"Master Myklayn!" he snapped. "What in Langhorne's name is going on here?"

"Actually, that's what we're here to explain." It wasn't Myklayn, but one of the men in uniform, speaking with a strange accent. "Lieutenant Byrnhar Raismyn, Imperial Charisian Marines," he continued with a slight, ironic bow, "I'm afraid your locks are under new management just for the moment, Master Bohlyr."

"Here, now!" Bohlyr spluttered. "You can't—I mean, there's ways—"

"I realize it's . . . inconvenient, Master Bohlyr," the stranger—Raismyn—

said in a slightly cooler tone. "Nevertheless," his hand brushed ever so lightly across the sword sheathed at his side, "I'm really going to have to insist."

▼　▼　▼

"All right," Zhaimys Myklayn said ninety minutes later. "That'll do."

"Yes, Sir."

The Marine who'd overseen the placement of the charges under Myklayn's direction while the ironclads and barges locked through the town nodded, then waved for the men of his detachment to scamper for the waiting boats.

"You sure this'll do the job, Sir?" he asked. Myklayn looked at him, and the Charisian shook his head. "Oh, I'm not questioning your judgment, Sir. Probably sounded like I was, and I apologize for that. It's just . . . We've come a far piece to do this, and I'd like to be sure it's done right."

"Believe me, Sergeant, it's done right."

Myklayn's tone was grim, but as he'd told Halcom Bahrns, given the options, he wouldn't lose a bit of sleep over his part in all this.

"When this lot goes up," he waved at the charges which had been placed around the massive pipes, "it's going to leave one huge damned hole in the ground. With the charges on the other side, it should also cave in both sides of both of the downstream locks, take out the valves, *and* wreck both sets of gates." He bared his teeth. "It'll be faster and simpler for them to start all over again than to try to fix what we're going to leave them." He shook his head. "I'll be surprised if they can have it back up and operating before this time next year . . . if then."

"Really?" The Marine looked down at the charges, then chuckled harshly. "Good enough for me, Sir. Now why don't you get your much more important backside into the lead boat while *I*"—he pulled his hand out of his belt pouch with a Shan-wei's candle and grinned—"do my bit to piss off Zhaspahr Clyntahn?"

.VI.
Daivyn River,
Cliff Peak Province,
Republic of Siddarmark

N o good, Sir."

Sergeant Dahltyn Sumyrs shook his head, shoulders drooping with exhaustion.

"Can't get through," he continued. "Lost five good men trying, but the bastards're thicker'n fleas on a Sodaran sheep-stealer. Those as don't have rifles have pistols, and the trees're too thick for us to see them before we're right on top of 'em."

"Thank you, Sergeant." Mahrtyn Taisyn was clean-shaven, his uniform still neatly arranged, but there were shadows in his eyes in the candlelight. "I can't say that's not what I expected to hear, but we had to try."

"'Course we did, Sir." Sumyrs sounded almost affronted by the suggestion that he might not have tried. "They don't seem to be short on gunpowder, either, do they, Sir?"

"That's one of the beauties of having a secure supply connection all the way back to Westmarch, Sergeant," Taisyn said dryly. "I wish we had the same."

"Aye, Sir. And so do I."

"Very well, Sergeant. I think that's everything."

The sergeant drew himself to attention, touched his chest, and started to turn away, but the brigadier's voice stopped him.

"Look after yourself, Dahltyn," he said quietly.

"And you, Sir," Sumyrs said gruffly, never turning. Then he continued out the dugout door into the dark, and Taisyn sank into the folding canvas chair at the upturned barrel that served him as a desk.

Sumyrs was a good man. He'd been with the brigadier for over four years, and if anyone could have found a path through the Temple Loyalists surrounding their position, it would have been Sumyrs.

Not that it would've done a lot of good if he had *gotten through*, Taisyn admitted grimly. *You took a chance, and it doesn't look like it's going to turn out so well, after all, does it?*

He leaned back in the chair, scrubbing his face with the heels of both hands, shoulders slumping with a despair he would never have allowed anyone else to see.

He and his four thousand men were still in place—sticking in the throat of Cahnyr Kaitswyrth's advance like a fishbone, just as he'd promised Zhansyn and Watyrs. But it was a fishbone Kaitswyrth was determined to dislodge, and the bishop militant was equally determined to destroy the last organized resistance to his invasion of Glacierheart in the process.

We came too far forward with too few men, Taisyn told himself. *I couldn't possibly have held the river all the way to the lake, prevented them from getting around us* somewhere, *and I damned well knew it. But I had to stop them* here —*it was the last place a force this size could block the river. I needed the bluffs, needed someplace to put guns with a clear field of fire and let me entrench to protect them. If I'd had more men, maybe I'd have been able to dig in farther east, closer to the lake, instead of needing the hills. But* . . . .

There was no point arguing about it with himself yet again. Besides, he knew he'd made the right decision. Or the best one available to him, at least; sometimes there wasn't a "right" decision, only the best choice among wrong ones. And he and his people had bled the bastards. They'd blocked them, locked the river solid and kept it that way for two entire five-days. Ten full days in which Kaitswyrth's army hadn't moved a single foot deeper into Glacierheart . . . and had lost hundreds of men in failed probing assaults on their position.

I wish there were some way for me to know where the Duke is. I don't see any way he could've reached Ice Lake yet, but maybe. Maybe there's even still a chance he can fight his way forward to us, get us out of this crack. Not bloody likely, though.

He lowered his hands and drew a deep breath.

He'd never had the numbers to keep Kaitswyrth from swinging around his position, and the bishop militant had done just that. He had both infantry and cavalry on the river between Taisyn's positions and Ice Lake, and they'd taken guns with them, as well, to do to Taisyn exactly what *he'd* done to *them*. Neither side could get river traffic by the other's guns, but Kaitswyrth's supply chain was intact *behind* his position; Taisyn's wasn't, which meant he could no longer count on supplies of food or ammunition while Kaitswyrth could.

It's not the food or the ammunition, really, he told himself. *It's the fact that you can't retreat. And because you can't, they've been working their way forward all around your positions for two five-days. They've got you completely surrounded now, and they've got too many men.*

A throat cleared itself, and he looked up to see Hauwerd Zhansyn in his doorway.

"Come in," he invited, and the Siddarmarkian colonel seated himself in the other folding chair.

"I saw Sumyrs," he said. "From his expression—and the fact that he's still *here*—I assume his mission failed?"

"You could put it that way," Taisyn replied with a humorless smile. "'Thick as fleas on a Sodaran sheep-stealer' is how he put it, I believe."

"A way with words, the Sergeant." Zhahnsyn chuckled, but then his expression sobered. "I can't say I'm surprised to hear it, though. These people don't want to let go."

"These people aren't *going* to let go," Taisyn corrected. "And we're running out of rifle ammunition. I think they know it, too."

"We never did have as much as we would've liked," Zhahnsyn observed, and shrugged.

"No, we didn't," Taisyn agreed. He looked at Zhansyn for a moment. "I really expected—hoped, at least—that we'd be able to get out of this one."

"You did?" Zhahnsyn's smile was lopsided. "I didn't—not really. I suppose I should've said something at the time, actually. But I always figured we were pushing too far. Always thought that's what *you* really thought, deep down inside, as a matter of fact."

He arched an eyebrow, and Taisyn exhaled noisily.

"Probably," he acknowledged. "I guess I just didn't want to say so, even to myself."

"That's what I thought." Zhahnsyn leaned back, propping one heel on Taisyn's upturned barrel. "The thing is, Mhartyn, I never thanked you for it."

"*Thanked* me?" Taisyn waved one hand around the dimly lit dugout. "It doesn't look to me like you've got anything to thank me for, Hauwerd!"

"Of course I do." Zhahnsyn looked him in the eye. "I am a Siddar-markian; you're not. These aren't your people you've stuck your neck out for—they're *mine*. And if you hadn't made your stand here, Kaitswyrth would already be within striking distance of the East Glacierhearts and the Tyrnyr Gap, and all of Glacierheart Province would be burning behind him. I don't know where Duke Eastshare is by now any more than you do, but because of you, he's going to be four or five hundred miles farther west when Kaitswyrth runs into him than he would have been otherwise. God alone knows how many Siddarmarkian lives you've saved. I just think some-body should tell you thank you for saving them."

Taisyn looked back at him, feeling his sincerity, and then, finally, he nodded.

"Consider me thanked," he said. Then he cleared his throat. "I'll be sending out the last message wyvern before dawn," he continued in a harder, brisker voice. "If you want to send a final report of your own, let Lieutenant Hahskans have it in the next two or three hours."

▼　　▼　　▼

"Are we ready?"

Bishop Militant Cahnyr Kaitswyrth had brown hair, brown eyes, and a pleasant, easy-going exterior that had fooled more than one unwary soul into missing the zealot who lived behind it. A Chihirite of the Order of the Sword, his experience as a Temple Guardsman showed in the way he cut his hair, the way he walked—even the way he stood—and his brown eyes were hard as he looked around the circle of senior officers.

"This crap has wasted too much time already," he continued in a voice of iron. "And it's going to waste more. If those heretic bastards were as thor-ough as I expect, it'll take us days just to clear the river, even after we kill every last one of them, and every one of those days is a day Stohnar and that son of a bitch Cayleb can move something farther west. Their Shan-wei-damned Marines've been bad enough; I want to be on the line of the East Glacierhearts before we see the first fucking Charisian *soldier*. Is that clear?"

A murmur of acknowledgment came back to him, and he made himself draw a deep breath.

"What's happened here is no one's fault," he said in a tone which was closer to normal. "We walked into them and got hit by surprise. All right, maybe—*maybe*—that much could've been avoided if our scouts had been more thorough . . . or more lucky. But they'd've been there, waiting for us, anyway. They picked the best damned spot in a hundred miles of river, maybe more, to drive in their cork, and we don't have any choice but to dig it back out again. It's going to cost us, too. This isn't going to be another case of overrunning a bunch of pikemen in the open. We've already lost better than thirteen hundred men, not counting the barge crews, and the count's going to get worse, because we're going to have to walk straight into their guns, and they're going to kill a lot more of our men in the process. We can't change that, unless we want to sit here and starve their asses out, and if we do that, we can be absolutely positive that anything Stohnar and Cayleb can dig up will be waiting for us when we're done."

He looked around at the faces again.

"I don't know what—if anything—they've got behind this position. Our spies are having trouble getting information out, and none of the local Faithful have a clue what might be headed this way. Rumors? *Those* we've got, including one that says Cayleb Ahrmahk himself is headed this way at the head of half a million men." He snorted. "Somehow, I find that one a *bit* hard to believe."

Several people chuckled, and he tapped the sketch map on the camp table.

"They don't have any damned half-million men," he said flatly. "In fact, the best estimate we had before we began marching was that it would be at least the end of July or the beginning of August before the Charisians could get significant forces into the field. All their army was in Chisholm, and that's Shan-wei's own distance from Siddarmark. But our intelligence reports have been wrong more than once since the Jihad began, and I'm not going to count on them now. I'm assuming there are Charisian troops on their way to Glacierheart right this moment. And that's why, tomorrow morning, we're *taking* this position."

His hand curled into a fist, and he thumped it on the map.

"We're taking it even if it costs us two or three divisions. They can't retreat, we've gotten our jump-off positions to within five hundred yards of their redoubts, and they can't shift troops *between* redoubts because we're in a position to assault all of them simultaneously. Nobody wants to throw away the lives of his men, but we'll lose more of them later if we let these bastards hold us here too long. So I don't want any hesitation. The columns will go in on signal, and they'll keep right on going in unless I personally order differently."

He looked around the circle of faces one last time. No one was smiling now, but he saw no hesitation, no doubt.

"Good." He straightened. "Return to your commands. I'll make the signal a half-hour before dawn."

.VII.
Ohlarn,
New Northland Province,
Republic of Siddarmark

Halcom Bahrns was more than a little bemused by the Temple Loyalists' lack of reaction to his inland invasion. The terrain leading up to the Ohlarn Gap was remarkably flat and level, and they'd passed only one more set of locks in the eleven hours since leaving Fairkyn behind. The Canal Service personnel manning those locks had been just as surprised as Fairkyn had, though, which seemed ridiculous. The captain hadn't been impressed by Mayor Kyrst when he'd come aboard *Delthak*—not entirely willingly—to protest the blasphemous destruction of the city's locks. Lockmaster Bohlyr, though, had struck him as having a working brain. Surely *he'd* had the wit to send a semaphore message up the canal ahead of them!

Bahrns wasn't about to question a gift from the archangels, however. Colonel Harys' Marines had swept up the astounded lock tenders in a pounce which seemed to have gotten all of them, and General Tylmahn's Siddarmarkians had established a perimeter around the position while the ironclads and barges were locked through.

The average time for a canal lock to fill—or drain—in order to pass a vessel through was fifteen minutes, which meant it took about an hour to pass *Delthak* and each of her barges individually through each lock they encountered. Fortunately, he didn't particularly care if he inconvenienced any barge traffic they might meet, which meant he could use both the eastbound and westbound locks at each stop, passing *Hador* and *her* barges through at the same time *Delthak* made the trip. He hated the feeling of immobility while they moved through, but he'd also taken advantage of it to top off *Delthak*'s bunkers from her coal and explosives barge, and he knew Tailahr had done the same.

That, however, had been two and a half hours ago, and they'd passed at least a dozen barges since. All of them had taken one look at the oncoming behemoths and headed for the side of the canal, and aside from one brushing collision, Bahrns and his command had passed them without incident.

Somebody must have gotten ashore and found a horse, though, he thought. Which could make what was about to happen more interesting than he might have preferred.

▼   ▼   ▼

"It's coming!" a voice hissed.

It took Major Edmynd Maib a moment to identify it as Bynno Leskyr, Mayor of Ohlarn. The mayor—who'd held office for barely two five-days, since his predecessor had fallen afoul of Father Ghatfryd's inquiries—was usually a blustery, confident, booming-voiced sort. That strained, frightened whisper didn't sound a bit like him, and an ignoble part of Major Maib took a certain pleasure in it.

Stop that! he scolded himself. *Yes, Leskyr's a pain in the arse. And, yes, he probably* was *the one who started the rumors about Mayor Bekatyro. But Father Ghatfryd's no fool. He'll realize soon enough there's nothing to them, and then it'll be* Leskyr's *turn to answer some pointed questions. And even if he is an unmitigated bastard, he* is *the mayor and you don't have any better idea what the hell is headed this way than he does!*

The major—the commanding officer of the 20th Artillery Regiment, Army of God—couldn't understand why there hadn't been more warning. The exhausted runner had panted his way into Ohlarn less than two hours ago, and all he'd been able to provide was some kind of garbled account of barges moving up the canal packed full of heretic soldiers. And about some kind of massive explosion which *might* have come from the direction of the Harysmyn Llocks thirty miles east of town. Oh, and at least one of the "barges" had been on *fire*, according to him!

That was the sum total of his knowledge, and no one was more aware than he of how completely inadequate it was. But if something was coming along the canal, why hadn't the semaphore stations sent word ahead? Damn it, they should have had at least *some* warning! That was what the semaphore was *for!*

He glowered, wishing he'd had more of his regiment anywhere in the vicinity. Or, for that matter, that there was anything other than the local militia to back up the single battery he did have here in Ohlarn.

If the semaphore had given me another four or five hours, I might've had another battery here, he thought resentfully. *On the other hand, six twelve-pounders should be able to deal with any barge ever built! And it's always possible the yokel who saw them coming didn't really see anything of the sort. Half these bumpkins still—*

His thoughts broke off as he saw what Leskyr had seen. A shower of what looked like . . . sparks? No, not that exactly. More like . . . like . . . .

He couldn't think of anything exactly like it, but whatever it was, there were two of it, side by side, and they were coming closer.

Major Maib swallowed hard, much more nervous suddenly than he cared to admit, and looked over his shoulder.

"The Mayor's right," he grated. "Stand to!"

"Yes, Sir!" Lieutenant Orlynoh Praieto replied sharply. "Sergeant Wyldyng—stand to the guns!"

Responses came back from the six gun crews of Battery B, and Maib peered into the darkness, shading his eyes with his hand, even though he knew it was useless and probably made him look ridiculous. That burst of sparks—or whatever—had disappeared, yet there was something like a faint glow, almost like smoke lit from below . . . .

▼   ▼   ▼

Halcom Bahrns sighed in resignation as the shower of sparks abated. That wouldn't have mattered in daylight, when the smoke would have precluded *Delthak* from sneaking up on anyone, anyway. He could have wished, however, that the stokers hadn't been forced to throw fresh coal into the fireboxes just as the dim lights of Ohlarn were becoming visible.

Nothing we could've done about it, he thought. *On the other hand—*

"Master Myklayn, I'd be grateful if you'd step inside the conning tower."

"Captain, I need to be able to see." The reply came back from the bridge wing. "There's a bridge across the canal in the middle of Ohlarn, and I need to be sure we're high enough to take it on the casemate instead of the conning tower, so—"

"So you'll see that from in here," Bahrns said flatly. "I don't know if they've heard we're coming or not, but if anyone was looking this way, they probably just saw those sparks. So get in here under armor, *now*." He showed his teeth in a thin smile. "We can't afford for anything to happen to you this early into the operation."

For a moment, he thought the pilot was going to argue. But then Myklayn stepped into the conning tower, swung the armored door shut, and dogged it firmly.

"Might be you've a point, Captain," he acknowledged, smiling in the dim, red light of the lantern above the chart table. "Besides, it's only a *wooden* bridge, when all's said."

▼   ▼   ▼

"Sweet Langhorne!" someone shouted, and Edmynd Maib took an involuntary step backwards as the monster lumbering up the canal finally entered the spill of light from the canalfront's lanterns.

It was enormous! A vast, slab-sided creature of the night snorting out of the darkness at preposterous speed, pushing a wide horseshoe bow wave in front of it. It was black as the darkness which had spawned it, and two tall smokestacks belched smoke. The militia companies lining the docks opened fire with arbalests and matchlocks, and the musket flashes shredded the darkness. They showed him the oncoming nightmare more clearly, and he saw arbalest bolts and musket balls alike skipping and sparking, bouncing as if their target were made of iron. And there were open—

"Fire!" he screamed. *"Fire as you bear!"*

▼ ▼ ▼

"Glad you made that suggestion, Captain!" Zhaimys Myklayn had to speak loudly, even inside the conning tower, to make himself heard over the sudden rattle of musketry. "It'd be a mite lively out there just now!"

Bahrns nodded, but he had other things on his mind at the moment. He leaned closer to the bulkhead, peering through the starboard view slit as the darkness came alive with hundreds of muzzle flashes. He heard at least two or three musket balls slam into the armor next to the view slit, and it was entirely possible some of those other bullets were going to find their way inside the ship through the open gunports. He hoped not, but what concerned him more were what looked like several fieldpieces lined up along the canal embankment.

He strained his eyes for a moment longer, then grabbed the voice tube to the gundeck in both hands and leaned over it.

"Action starboard!" he shouted. "Field guns!"

He put his ear close to the bell-shaped mouth of the tube, and Pawal Blahdysnberg's voice came back up it.

"Action starboard, aye, Sir! Targets are field guns!"

Bahrns nodded in satisfaction and straightened to look back out the slit.

▼ ▼ ▼

Major Maib's frantic warning allowed two-thirds of Lieutenant Praieto's guns to get their shots off before the cannon poking out of those open gunports could come to bear upon them. He smiled in vicious satisfaction as the long, lurid tongues of flame erupted. He hadn't known what was coming up the river, so he'd had Praieto load half his pieces with round shot and half with shells, and he watched with anticipation as the artillery fire ripped into the oncoming . . . whatever it was.

That anticipation disappeared abruptly when *cannonballs* skipped off it as easily as *musket* balls had. His jaw dropped as Praieto's guns left it completely unmarked, and then he was flinging himself to the ground as eight thirty-pounder guns came to bear.

▼ ▼ ▼

"*Fire!*" Pawal Blahdysnberg shouted, and *Delthak*'s guns went off for the very first time, like the hammer of Shan-wei itself.

Blahdysnberg had wondered what it was going to sound like inside the armored box. Now he knew, and he was glad he'd stuffed the cotton earplugs into place before he'd given the order to fire. The guns recoiled, squealing as the friction of the new Mahndrayn slide carriages absorbed the recoil. The muzzles came inboard, streaming smoke that turned the entire spacious gundeck into a fog-shrouded, foul-smelling cavern. The powerful blowers built into the rear of the casemate sucked the smoke out as rapidly as possible, but it still took time, and he heard his gun crews coughing and spluttering.

It didn't keep them from reloading, though. They'd loaded with grapeshot, on the theory that anything they had to fire on in the dark would be close at hand, and that was what they reloaded with, as well. Blahdysnberg left them to it, leaning cautiously out of the starboard bow gunport to see what their first broadside had accomplished.

▼   ▼   ▼

Screams were all around him.

Major Maib levered himself up on his hands, looking around wildly, and realized Mayor Leskyr wouldn't be answering any questions from Father Ghatfryd after all. At least half Praieto's gun crews—including the lieutenant, it looked like—were also dead, and others were wounded. The storm of grapeshot which could be thrown by ten thirty-pounders at a range of eighty yards was simply indescribable, and what truly astounded Maib was that *anyone* was still alive on the battery's position.

"*Reload!*" Sergeant Wyldyng was shouting. "Reload ball! *Move*, damn your souls!"

The major admired the sergeant's spirit, but it wasn't going to do any good.

There were barges behind the lead ship, he realized, yet even they looked unlike anything he'd ever seen before. They might have started life as standard canal craft, but they'd been fitted with some sort of heavy timber upper works and what looked like sandbags. He could just make out a line of militia musketeers, frantically reloading their matchlocks, and then the barge directly behind the lead ship suddenly sprouted riflemen all along that wooden-armored side.

.   Most of the musketeers probably never realized what was happening. They were still reloading when a hurricane of rifle fire ripped through them like the wrath of God.

▼   ▼   ▼

"There's your drawbridge, Master Myklayn," Halcom Bahrns observed as Blahdysnberg's guns belched another terrible broadside into the night.

The captain wasn't concerned about those field guns any longer. First, because their shot had bounced off *Delthak*'s armor as if they'd been so many baseballs. Second, because very few—if any—of those gunners could still be alive after the ironclad's second broadside.

What he was rather more concerned about was the drawbridge directly in front of *Delthak*. It was a heavy affair, designed for freight traffic, and, as usual, it had been lowered for the night, when the barges moored and the canals shut down until there was light for movement once more. It was also right at water level, and he shook his head.

"I think about the top three feet of the casemate's going to hit it," he remarked, rather more calmly than he felt. The conning tower's solid tube of armor extended down through the roof of the casemate to gundeck level. *It* would probably survive impact with the drawbridge, but he very much doubted that its navigating wings would. And even if it did—

"Pass the word to brace for collision," he said.

▼ ▼ ▼

Edmynd Maib was still alive. He was one of only three of the 20th Artillery Regiment's personnel in Ohlarn who could make that statement, although it was going to take him a while to learn to walk again with no left leg.

He sat up, leaning back against the shattered wheel of a twelve-pounder while someone—a civilian he didn't recognize—finished tightening the tourniquet on his splintered leg. He wondered why it didn't hurt more, and a corner of his brain suggested that it had to be shock. That the pain would be along soon enough. For now, though, his attention was locked on the huge ship forging through the center of Ohlarn, spouting fire from either side while more rifle fire raked the night from the barge behind it.

There was another one coming in the first's wake, and another corner of his mind wondered how many *more* might be out there? But even that was a distant, purely academic consideration as the first ship rammed the Ohlarn drawbridge.

It didn't even slow down.

The bridge ripped loose with a shriek of riven wood. It folded like a jackknife, crashing down onto the terrible ship's short foredeck, and then the ship bellowed its triumph in a high, terrible shriek of sound that went on and on and on.

Maib covered his ears, his mind a whirlpool of confusion, terror, and beginning pain, and wondered what demon had escaped from Shan-wei's pit to loose such a horror upon men.

Are you certain, Master Zhevons?" Ruhsyl Thairis looked at the brown-haired man in front of him, his eyes dark in the twilight. "Positive?" he pressed.

"I'm afraid so, Your Grace," Ahbraim Zhevons said sadly.

He'd turned up alongside Duke Eastshare's moored command barge an hour ago, without anyone having spotted him on his way there. Not the cavalry patrols, not the sentries . . . no one. Eastshare would have found that disturbing if he hadn't become intimately familiar with someone else who could have done the same thing. In fact, this Zhevons reminded him strongly of Merlin Athrawes. There was little *physical* resemblance between them, and Zhevons' tenor was quite unlike Merlin's bass, yet there was something . . . , Something about the way they stood, perhaps. Or the way their eyes met his without any sense of deference to his noble rank.

Or maybe it's just the fact that you know they're both seijins, he told himself, and shook his head mentally. *After so many centuries without a single verified* seijin-*sighting, they seem to be coming out of the damned woodwork now. Not* a good *sign, considering how busy they were in the War Against the Fallen. But at least the* Testimonies *all insist they were on the side of Light then. And so far, I haven't seen anything to suggest they aren't this time, as well.*

Of course, Zhevons hadn't outright *said* he was a *seijin*, which was the reason Eastshare hadn't addressed him by that title . . . yet. Not that such niceties really concerned him at the moment.

"When?" he asked now, his own voice heavy.

"Day before yesterday, Your Grace." Zhevons exhaled. "It took me a while to find you."

"I see."

Eastshare looked down at the map. Seventy miles. That was how close he'd come . . . and it might as well have been seven thousand.

"How bad was it?"

He looked up from the map, and there was more than a shadow of dread in his eyes. He was a soldier, and soldiers dealt with hard truths, but this was the same army which had slaughtered Charlz Stahntyn's men.

"They weren't taking prisoners, Your Grace," Zhevons said quietly. He shook his head. "It doesn't look to me like many of our people were trying to surrender, anyway, but it wouldn't have done them any good. The handful they did take alive, the wounded—" He shrugged. "The one good thing, I suppose, is that none of them got handed over to the Inquisition for the Punishment. I'm pretty sure Kaitswyrth gave orders Brigadier Taisyn and his senior officers were to be taken alive for that specific purpose"—in fact, he knew Kaitswyrth had; he'd listened in on the conversation through Owl's remotes—"but all of them died fighting."

"And the Army of God?" Eastshare asked harshly, his face tight.

"It cost them close to ten thousand casualties." Zhevons' voice was flat now—hard. "They came over the redoubts in the end, Your Grace, but they paid in blood for every inch of that ground. Taisyn and his men gutted six of their divisions before they went down."

"The river?" Eastshare did his best to make his voice equally flat, armored with professionalism, but it was hard.

"Still obstructed. I estimate it's going to take them at least another two days, probably three, to clear it."

Eastshare nodded slowly, his eyes back on the map. Zhevons might use the verb "estimate," but if his estimates were anything like Merlin Athrawes' . . . .

"Are they pushing troops beyond it?"

"Not yet. In another day or so, perhaps." Zhevons showed his teeth. "They're too busy reorganizing around the casualties, Your Grace. They're bringing fresh infantry divisions to the head of the column, and that's taking longer than Kaitswyrth expected thanks to the way their barges got packed together with the river blocked. They've got a few cavalry patrols probing down the high road toward Haidyrberg, but they're not more than twenty-five or thirty miles beyond Brigadier Taisyn's positions. I think it'll be a few days before they're feeling any more adventurous than that."

"Good."

Eastshare studied the map for a few more moments, then tapped a spot with his finger.

"Here, do you think, Master Zhevons?"

Zhevons craned his neck, looking at the map. Unlike the Army of God's, Eastshare's maps had been updated by the Republican Army before he set out. They gave a much more accurate idea of the actual terrain, including the changes which had occurred in it since the Day of Creation. The Temple Loyalists were still in the process of finding out just how far off *their* maps were, although they'd managed to avoid the worst consequences so far, thanks to the fact that they'd been advancing through territory where they could expect to find local guides.

Of course, Kaitswyrth didn't have *"local guides" when he ran into Taisyn's posi-*

tion, the *seijin* thought with grim satisfaction. *I wonder if he's starting to get some idea of just how much bad maps can cost him in the end?*

"If I might suggest, Your Grace, I think this might be the better position." He laid his index finger on a spot ten miles farther west than the one Eastshare had indicated, where the high road came closest to the canal. "There was a forest fire through here six or seven years ago," he said, tapping the spot gently. "The fire scar's almost twenty miles long, north to south, with man-height saplings scattered through it and a few old-growth nearoak and even two or three titan oaks that survived the fire. It's mostly brush and undergrowth, with a lot of wire vine in places. The titan oaks will provide natural lookout posts and OPs for your mortars and artillery; it's wide enough east to west to give your guns as much as five- or six-thousand-yard fields of fire, especially between the river and the high road; and that undergrowth's God's own abatis." He looked up to meet Eastshare's eyes and smiled coldly. "They'll play hell getting lines of infantry through *that,* Your Grace."

Eastshare rubbed his chin thoughtfully, contemplating the map. It was closer to the Army of God's current position than he might have wished, but assuming Zhevons was right about how long Kaitswyrth was going to take getting himself reorganized, that might not be as dangerous as he'd feared. And that kind of terrain would make miserable going for the cavalry he didn't have, while the sort of fire lanes Zhevons was describing would go a long way towards letting his superior weapons equalize the numerical odds . . . .

For a moment, he wondered why Taisyn hadn't chosen the same position, but then he shook his head. Taisyn had had only four thousand men, only two thousand of them with rifles, and he'd been forced to rely on borrowed naval artillery— powerful, but cumbersome and slower-firing than proper field guns. He'd needed that hilly terrain if he was going to hold against such an enormous numerical disparity.

"I think you're right, Master Zhevons," he said finally. "Our lead battalions can be there by tomorrow evening, using the river. I can have the engineers up to support them by morning, and the rest of the infantry and the field artillery by this time day after tomorrow."

He let his hand lie flat on the map, his palm over the designated spot, and looked up at Zhevons.

"I don't think they'll be getting by me anytime soon." The words were ordinary enough, but they came out in the tone of a man swearing a vow to the ghosts of Mahrtyn Taisyn's slaughtered command, and Zhevons nodded.

"I don't think so, either, Your Grace," he said softly.

Well, Captain Bahrns, I'd say they know we're here now," Zhaimys Myklayn observed as another volley of rifle fire whined and bounced from HMS *Delthak's* casemate.

"You might have a point about that, Master Myklayn," Bahrns agreed judiciously as he peered out the vision slit.

He was more cautious about that than he had been. Young Ahbukyra Matthysahn wouldn't be using his right hand to sound any more shrieks on *Delthak's* whistle. Not after the flattened rifle bullet screamed in through the slit and turned his elbow into shattered bits and pieces. They'd suffered a dozen casualties on the gundeck, as well, from the same source, and more among his infantry, but his gunners and the troop barges' riflemen—and carronades—had repaid the Temple Loyalists at a usurious rate.

Which'll be damned small comfort to their survivors, he thought grimly. *But at least I won't be losing any more infantry in this next bit, thank God.*

He was feeling the exhaustion now, and he knew that was true of all the rest of his people, as well. It certainly ought to be, given that they'd been sailing across the interior of the Republic of Siddarmark for almost an entire five-day.

And as Myklayn had just pointed out, whatever had paralyzed the semaphore stations was clearly no longer a factor. Not at their current position, at least.

"How much farther d'you think we can get, Captain?" Myklayn asked in a lower voice, and Bahrns shrugged.

"I'd love to go all the way to Saiknyr. That's not what the orders call for, though . . . and probably just as well." Bahrns grimaced. "We're running more risk than a sane person would going as far south as Guarnak."

"Had the same thought m'self," Myklayn acknowledged, and grinned. "Guess it's just as well there's not so many sane people aboard your ship, then, isn't it?"

"I don't know what you mean, Master Myklayn!" Bahrns said virtuously, then ducked reflexively as another volley of rifle fire spanged off the conning tower's armor.

"Master Blahdysnberg!" he called down the voice tube. "Those . . . people on the north bank are beginning to irritate me!"

"I'll deal with them for you in just a minute, Sir!" Blahdysnberg's voice came back, and two guns in the forward section of *Delthak*'s larboard broadside bellowed almost before he finished speaking.

The rifle fire slackened immediately, and when Bahrns looked back out, the Church infantry who'd been drawn up in a two-deep line to blaze away at the invaders had been turned into so much ripped and torn flesh.

"Very good, Master Blahdysnberg!" he said.

"Thank you, Sir!"

Delthak's black paint had acquired any number of scrapes, scratches, and scars during the course of her thousand-mile voyage to her present position, but her armor had sneered at the worst the Army of God could do, and speed had kept her ahead of any effective response.

So far, at any rate.

He coughed as gun smoke drifted up the access ladder from the gundeck. That gundeck was a close enough approximation to hell when the guns were firing, he thought; his stokers, laboring over the boiler furnaces, opening the iron doors and shoveling in the coal, raking out the ash and clinker, cleaning the grates even as they continued steaming, had it worse. He'd seen to it they had all the fresh water they could drink and used extra hands to spell them whenever he could, and when the Delthak Works had designed the conversion, they'd provided the fire and engine rooms with blowers, sucking in air through mushroom-headed ventilators spaced across the hull between the funnels. That helped a lot, as well, but he knew exhaustion was even more of a factor for them than for the rest of his crew.

Not that much longer, boys. We're more than halfway home—assuming we ever get home, of course.

He moved to the forward view slit, and his lips drew back as he saw what he'd come for. The city of Guarnak was a major transshipment point on the Republic's northern canal system; at this moment, it was also the forward staging base for Bishop Militant Bahrnabai Wyrshym's entire army. With no word from anyone since they'd set out, Bahrns had no idea how the campaign in the Sylmahn Gap was proceeding. For all he knew, Wyrshym's men had blown their way through the Gap and were advancing on the capital at this very instant. But from the huge raft of barges, moored two- and three-deep along the curving canal front, and the mountains of crates, bags, and casks piled along the wharves—

It looks like Baron Green Valley got here in time, after all, Halcom, he thought with savage glee. *And, oh my, what a lovely target he's given you!*

"Both engines slow astern! Helm, come a half-point to starboard!"

Confirmations came back, and *Delthak* slowed, turning to her right in the bend of the canal, bringing the three guns of her forward battery—and all eight of the guns in her larboard battery—to bear on that sprawling cluster of barges and supplies.

"Master Blahdysnberg!"

He didn't use the voice tube, this time. Instead, he leaned over the edge of the access trunk, and Pawal Blahdysnberg appeared at the base of the ladder, looking up.

"Yes, Sir?"

"This is what we came for, Pawal," Bahrns said simply. "Make it count."

▼   ▼   ▼

Bishop Militant Bahrnabai stood on the second story of one of the canal-front warehouses, staring through his spyglass at the ugly, black monster turning to bring its guns to bear on his helpless barges, and tried not to curse.

It was hard.

Langhorne! How in Shan-wei's name did they get within two days—two days!—of Guarnak without anyone so much as telling me they were coming?! Did they just fly across everything between here and the coast?! Where the hell was the sema-phore?! Hell, for that matter, hasn't anyone but me ever heard of horseback couriers?!

There was going to be Shan-wei to pay for this, and he wondered where the *other* one of them was. There were supposed to be two of them, according to the fragmentary reports he'd finally gotten, but only one was anywhere to be seen.

Maybe somebody actually managed to sink the other bastard, he thought venomously. *That would be nice. But now—*

He'd done what he could, especially after what the heretics had done to his gun line outside Serabor. That debacle still left a sour taste in his mouth, but Gorthyk Nybar had been absolutely right to pull back. Some of Wyr-shym's other officers had argued for digging in farther forward—at Terykyr, perhaps—but Gorthyk had been right yet again. With the high road bridge across the Wyvern Lake narrows destroyed, the heretics couldn't follow up their advantage before the Army of God figured out how to respond to their *newest* weapons. And they weren't leaving the cliff-top lizard paths to the enemy any longer, either. The vicious fighting among the clouds was costing him more men than the heretics—he was certain of that, given their Langhorne-forsaken ability to load and fire while prone—but he *had* more men, and the back-and-forth, bickering action at least kept them from getting those . . . those portable cannon of theirs around behind his main positions. And no matter what the heretics at the other end of the Gap might do, his army had tightened Mother Church's grasp on everything north of the Moon Thorns and west of Ranshir Bay. He was perfectly willing to sit here and keep the cork in the bottle while the Grand Inquisitor's agents figured out how the heretics had accomplished their latest surprise.

And once we know that, once we're able to do the same thing, we'll head right back down the Gap and kick their asses up between their ears!

The thought was a distant voice in the back of his brain as he looked down at the thirty-one twelve-pounders—most of his army's surviving field guns—emplaced along the canal side behind hasty breastworks of sandbags and paving stones. The range was absurdly short as he watched them take their aim, and he felt his lips tighten in anticipation. The tiny bit of information he'd received suggested shells, at least, had no effect on the thing's armored sides, so he'd ordered them to load with round shot . . . and to fire with double powder charges.

His artillerists understood the threat that black monster represented, and they hadn't even blinked at his dangerous command.

Now that long row of cannon exploded in a thunderous, rolling blast, and the brown water around the Charisian ship was suddenly lashed into white, tormented foam by plunging masses of iron.

▼　　▼　　▼

Delthak's hull rang like an enormous bell—or perhaps more like an even more enormous set of wind chimes, Bahrns thought, listening to the rapid-fire impacts of iron round shot on his ship's steel armor. One punched through the starboard funnel, sending smoke streaming out both sides of the new vent. More hit the navigating bridge punching ripping holes through its wooden planking. At least three hit the conning tower itself, with a clanger like the world's biggest sledgehammer. But for all the noise, all the fury of muzzle flash and smoke boiling above the enormous battery of field guns, not a single man aboard *Delthak* was injured.

Halcom Bahrns looked through the view slit as his ship came almost to a halt under the pull of her reversed engines.

"Stop engines!"

"Stop engines, aye, Sir!" the telegraphsman responded, and the bells jangled as the last of *Delthak*'s forward momentum dissipated.

"Any time now, Master Blahdysnberg!" he called down the access way.

"Cover your ears, Sir!"

The response was scarcely proper, Bahrns thought with a grin, but it was good advice, and he took it . . . just as *Delthak* fired back at last.

▼　　▼　　▼

Wyrshym's eyes went wide in astonishment as eleven thirty-pounders fired almost as one. Their shells slammed into the tight-packed barges, completely ignoring his thundering fieldpieces, and explosions answered. Huge flashes, clouds of splinters, pillars of smoke—they spewed up like loathsome, hell-born mushrooms, and as he watched those cataclysmic explosions, the bishop militant was enormously grateful he'd ordered the barge crews ashore.

He looked back at the iron ship and saw his field artillery's round shot bounce like so many spitballs. Some of them went spinning high into the heavens, but others continued across the canal, crashing into buildings on the far side.

And they were accomplishing exactly nothing.

"Message to the artillery," he grated, never turning away from the window or lowering his spyglass.

"Yes, Sir?"

Wyrshym heard the quaver in the white-faced lieutenant's voice, but he was hardly in any position to rebuke the youngster for that! And at least the lieutenant, like those artillerists along the canal, was standing his ground in the face of yet another hell-spawned heretic invention.

"They don't even *care* about our guns right now," he said. "They're too busy concentrating on the barges and our supplies. But once they've finished with that, they'll get around to the guns. Tell them to pull back. There's no point getting them destroyed for nothing."

▼　▼　▼

The Guarnak canal front was an inferno, roaring like a Delthak Works blast furnace.

The barges were a burning, smoking sea of flame, and more shells ripped into the warehouses beyond, setting fresh blazes with every shot. Three stupendous blasts had answered direct hits on barges loaded with gunpowder, and Bahrns was just as happy they'd been as far away as they had. A sixty-foot chunk of wreckage from one of them had been blown straight into the air and crashed back into the canal barely fifty yards from *Delthak*'s prow. He didn't like to think about what that could have done if it had hit the top of the casemate. At the very least, it would have carried away the funnels, and probably the ventilator intakes, as well.

And there was enough wreckage floating in the canal now to make him nervous about his propellers, too. Especially since it was too narrow for him to turn around.

He looked back at the Church artillery and discovered it was gone.

Wrong move, Halcom. Idiot! *The barges and the warehouses weren't going anywhere, so why didn't you deal with the artillery first and then take your time with the* immobile *targets, genius?*

Well, no one was perfect, he supposed, returning his attention to the river of fire which had once been a line of wharves piled with supplies for the Army of God. He probably hadn't destroyed anywhere near as much of Wyrshym's supply depot as it seemed, but every little bit helped.

Besides, destroying these *supplies isn't really what the operation's about, is it?*

"Dead slow astern both," he said.

"Dead slow astern both, aye, Sir."

"And now we're going to be very careful, Crahmynd," he said quietly to the helmsman. He'd deliberately rested Fyrgyrsyn, changing the watch schedule to do it, to be sure he had his best man on the wheel at the critical moment, and the gray-haired petty officer looked at him and nodded.

"Just you give the orders, Sir," he said calmly.

"I'll do that thing."

Bahrns patted the helmsman's shoulder, then moved to the aftermost vision slit, peering back across the casemate. The smoke from the pierced funnel didn't help, and neither did all the other smoke from the raging fires *Delthak*'s guns had set. At least the wind was out of the northwest, pushing the worst of it to one side. And at least he had a good ten feet of overhang aft of the propellers. *That* ought to find the canal bank and stop him before he rammed the screws into it, though the rudder was another matter.

Just as long as we don't find something hidden in the water *that strips a shaft,* he thought almost absently.

"A quarter-point of starboard helm," he said.

"Quarter-point of starboard helm, aye, Sir."

▼　　▼　　▼

Bahrnabai Wyrshym's eyes burned with futile rage as the monster which had savaged Guarnak backed impossibly away.

How does that damned thing work? *Schueler seize them all! What kind of deviltry are they dabbling in* now?

He didn't know. He couldn't imagine how that ship moved without mast or sail or oar. It was impossible according to everything he knew, and yet it was happening before his very eyes. It was moving stern-first through the water, just as smoothly, if not as rapidly, as it had moved when it came charging to the attack.

And there wasn't one damned thing he could do about it.

▼　　▼　　▼

"Tow secured, Sir."

"Very good, Master Cahnyrs."

Halcom Bahrns acknowledged his second lieutenant's report and stepped back into the smoke-reeking conning tower once more. The navigating bridge's port wing had been smashed, and he wasn't going to trust it to bear anyone's weight until he'd had it thoroughly repaired. They'd lost a couple of ventilator intakes, as well, and there were actually *three* holes in the funnels, now that they'd had an opportunity to take stock properly. But that was it, the extent of their damages, and he turned to Myklayn.

"The helm is yours, Master Myklayn."

"Thank you, Captain." The canal pilot resettled his pipe between his teeth and looked at the telegraphsman. "Ahead slow both while we see how the tow holds."

The bells jangled, and *Delthak* began moving once more.

They'd steamed back north to the confluence of the Guarnak–Ice Ash and Guarnak-Sylmahn Canals to pick up the fifteen hundred Marines and infantry they'd left to hold the critical locks in their rear. Bahrns was a little surprised that someone as offense-minded as Wyrshym was reported to be hadn't thought about wrecking the lock behind them to prevent them from retreating. *Writ* or no *Writ*. It seemed like the logical counter to him, but to be fair, he'd had a lot longer to think about it than the bishop militant had almost certainly been granted.

And a lot more already smashed locks behind him.

Not that it really mattered. Any effort on Wyrshym's part to do anything of the sort would have run into fifteen hundred rifles, two dozen mortars, and the flanking fire of eight fifty-seven-pounders, and there was no way the Army of God could have fought its way through *that* before *Delthak* returned to deal with it.

The canal builders had provided a sizable mooring basin where the canals came together. They'd intended it primarily to allow barges to run alongside one another and transship cargo without continuing all the way to Guarnak, but it had provided a handy layover point for *Delthak*'s barges, which would have fared considerably worse than she had under the fire of all those fieldpieces. It also, thank Langhorne, gave the ironclad plenty of room to turn, especially with her ability to back on one engine while going forward on the other. Unlike any other vessel Bahrns had ever commanded, she could literally turn in place, which was one more reason he was coming to love her unlovely, reeking self.

Now she headed up the Guarnak-Sylmahn Canal towards the Hildermoss River. *Hador* had gone ahead, securing control of the first three locks along the four hundred miles of canal between Guarnak and the river. Captain Tailahr had dropped off parties of Siddarmarkian infantry to hold each of them, after planting his charges, and *Delthak* would pick them up on the way through to rejoin her sister. In the meantime—

Halcom Bahrns stood on the sound starboard wing of his navigating bridge, looking astern, and bared his teeth in a wild, triumphant snarl as the complicated set of locks where the canals met erupted in thunder and flame, adding a fresh, gushing pillar of smoke to the pall rising above Guarnak.

And now we go home, he thought. *Six more days . . . assuming nobody thinks to blow the locks in front of us after all, of course.*

The semaphore chain followed the line of the canal, and his ironclads had been systematically destroying the towers as they went. A few thirty-pounder shells made marvelous wrecking crews. No doubt word of their invasion had run ahead of them, but the authorities farther up the line would have very little information to act upon before *Delthak* and *Hador* came calling. It was entirely possible they wouldn't even realize the ironclads had been destroying every lock they passed through, and in Bahrns' opinion, *Seijin* Merlin had been right. Whatever might have been the case with a military commander like Wyrshym, Langhorne's injunction to maintain the canals and high roads was deeply ingrained in mainlander minds. That duty had never been as deeply impressed on Bahrns and his men, since Charis and Chisholm had so few canals, but it was an integral part of the lives of the men who serviced the canals and realized how much of the mainland's economic life depended upon them. He'd seen evidence enough of that in Myklayn's ambivalence where their task was concerned.

Merlin had argued that even though destroying the locks would have trapped the ironclads, it simply wouldn't occur to most mainlanders. For one thing, with no inkling of the ironclads' existence, or of the speed the new steam engines bestowed, their reactions were likely to lag well behind the threat, because they simply wouldn't believe *Delthak* and *Hador* could move that quickly. But that solemn duty to *maintain* the canals and the locks would be an even greater factor.

So far, it looked as if the *seijin* had read the situation correctly, Bahrns thought, and reached out to rap his knuckles on a splintered section of the bridge's planking.

Now to find out if he truly had.

.X.

The Temple,
City of Zion,
The Temple Lands

I t was very quiet in the council chamber.

The proverbial lull before the storm, Rhobair Duchairn thought, gazing across the table at Zhaspahr Clyntahn. *I can't believe he's not already ranting and raving.*

The Grand Inquisitor had been positively genial for the last several months as the Army of God moved up to the Siddarmarkian frontier and

then went crunching across it with fire and the sword. He hadn't even complained too much about Duchairn's diversion of a full quarter of Mother
Church's logistic capability to feed the starving . . . and evacuate as many as
possible of her children to safety in the Temple Lands.

There'd been a few setbacks, of course. The blunting of the Dohlaran
thrust towards Thesmar, for example. But even that had been only temporary, since it had merely diverted Ahlverez into Cliff Peak to assist
Kaitswyrth's campaign—which obviously *had* caught the heretics completely
by surprise—while the Desnairian army, coming up through Silkiah, could
deal with any problems in the South March.

But for the most part, there'd been only triumph. Tarikah, Westmarch,
Icewind, New Northland, Mountaincross, Hildermoss, two-thirds of the
South March, and now Cliff Peak had been secured for Mother Church,
and Clyntahn's inquisitors had fanned out behind the advancing army to
ferret out any sniff of heresy. All the criticism of his Sword of Schueler and
his decision to settle the "Siddarmarkian problem" once and for all had
been proven wrong as Mother Church's armies ripped away more than a
third of the Republic's territory in mere months. And the vaunted Siddarmarkian army—the Army of the Republic, which had loomed like a titan
across the mainland realms for so long—had shattered like glass. Torn by
mutiny and desertion, hammered by starvation, and then confronted by
hundreds of thousands of men armed with the rifles Clyntahn had insisted
Siddarmark not be allowed to produce, it had died or fled at the Army of
God's approach.

Of course, the Inquisition's reign of terror in western Siddarmark could
only further enrage the heretics, and Duchairn wondered if Clyntahn had
really considered the Charisians' declared policy to hang or shoot all inquisitors on the spot. Did Zhaspahr think the acts of men like Wylbyr Edwyrds were likely to *soften* Charis' policies? Or prevent Greyghor Stohnar
from adopting exactly the same ones? And if Stohnar did, would Clyntahn
even care?

*Probably not. He can't conceive of the possibility of the "heretics" penetrating all
the way to Zion, and since he's here, safe behind the Temple's walls, no one's going to
be hanging him anytime soon. So if he has to lose a few hundred—or a few thousand—
fellow Schuelerites stamping out all resistance to his will, that doesn't bother him at all.*

"Well, Allayn," Clyntahn said finally, his voice cold. "Suppose you explain how something you told us was going so well has now been so completely fucked up?"

Allayn Maigwair looked at the Grand Inquisitor, and there was something different about him, Duchairn thought. He met Clyntahn's glare
levelly, without the nervousness of days gone by, and the treasurer's eyes
narrowed. Had little Allayn—?

"I can explain exactly how it happened, Zhaspahr," the captain general said coolly. "The heretics realized they couldn't stand up to us in the field. They were being driven back at every point, suffering extremely heavy casualties. Oh, Wyrshym and Nybar have a point about what the Charisians did in the Sylmahn Gap, although Kaitswyrth hasn't encountered the same sorts of weapons yet in Cliff Peak. That doesn't mean they're not there; it only means that until he pushes forward where the heretics have dug in on the Glacierheart border he won't know whether or not Eastshare has them as well. My personal opinion is that Eastshare almost certainly does, and that Nybar and Wyrshym are perfectly correct that we have to figure out how they're doing what they're doing. For that matter, the rifles Kaitswyrth captured on the Daivyn are already on their way back here, and from his dispatches, it shouldn't be difficult to duplicate them for our own men.

"But the plain truth is that even with every new weapon the Charisians brought to bear, we'd have driven all the way across Siddarmark in a single campaign—*two thousand miles* in one campaigning season, Zhaspahr!—if they hadn't sent their damned ships up the rivers and blown the hell out of the canal system."

Clyntahn sat back in his chair, eyes narrowing, face suddenly masklike, and Duchairn hid a smile as Maigwair's assertive tone registered on the Grand Inquisitor. Little Allayn *had* grown up, the treasurer thought. The Army of God had been *his* brainchild, the product of his thought and his imagination, and while it hadn't performed perfectly, he was right about how well it *had* performed. He'd been on the brink of the most crushing military triumph in the history of the world, and even now his forces controlled close to half of the Republic.

"And why weren't the canals protected against them?" Clyntahn demanded, this time splitting his glower between Maigwair and Duchairn.

"Because no one knew anyone could *attack* them!" Maigwair snapped before Duchairn could reply. His eyes bored into the Grand Inquisitor. "Men can only respond to threats they know about, Zhaspahr, and not a single spy's report—or a single *inquisitor's* report—even hinted that something like these . . . armored ships existed! I passed along Earl Thirsk's suggestion about armored ships, and if I remember correctly, you suggested no one would be able to produce enough iron plate to build a significant number of them. It may be you're right about that . . . except that just *four* of them turned out to be a *very* significant number in this instance."

The captain general opened the folder in front of him and pulled out a copy of the report Duchairn had prepared.

"Twenty-seven hundred miles of canal and river, Zhaspahr. *Twenty-seven hundred*, from the point where they entered the Guarnak–Ice Ash clear to Spinefish Bay. And fifty-one major locks, all destroyed. Not sabotaged, *destroyed.* Taken completely out of service for a *minimum* of six months—probably a lot longer!" He dropped the report on the table. "It's all very well to say the canals should have been protected, Zhaspahr, but Wyrshym couldn't stop *one* of them with *thirty* heavy field guns firing at less than a hundred yards range with double charges. Three of his guns *burst* trying! How in Langhorne's name was anyone supposed to 'protect' the canals against an attack like that?!"

"By destroying the locks ourselves, in front of them and behind them!" Clyntahn shot back. "Much good their armor would've done them sitting in a dry canal bed!"

"I'm afraid there was never a real possibility of that, Zhaspahr," Duchairn said in a carefully neutral voice. Clyntahn turned his glare upon him, and the treasurer shrugged. "First, someone—probably local heretics in New Northland—apparently attacked several semaphore stations before the Charisians headed inland. My administrators didn't even know they were coming until they were three-quarters of the way to Guarnak, and they sent two more of their ships up the Hildermoss from Salyk to Cat Lizard Lake. Icewind's got so few people it's never been connected to the chain, so there wasn't any semaphore to report them on the way, and they arrived in the middle of the night and took out the semaphore junction at Traymos, which cut off any warnings along the northern chain.

"Even after we finally began to learn what was happening, they moved too quickly for anyone to organize effective action against them. Our best estimate is that they were moving at an average speed of ten knots, even with the need to pass through all those locks, Zhaspahr. *Ten miles an hour!* They made the entire trip in barely thirteen days. Nobody ever dreamed of a ship that could move that fast, and they were destroying more semaphore stations as they advanced. By the time anyone in their path could have been thinking about trying to find anything to stop them with—and God knows every militia unit that ran into them got chewed to pieces—the heretics were already on top of them, with enough infantry to seize each lock as they came to it. And you may recall that the *Book of Langhorne* enjoins us to *preserve* canals, not blow them up! It would've taken direct orders from Mother Church—from *your* inquisitors, Zhaspahr!—to set that commandment aside, and there was no way to get those orders to them in time."

He shrugged and sat back in his chair.

"You're absolutely right that wrecking the canal locks would've stopped them," he said. "And, to be honest, this looks to me like the sort of thing you can only get away with once. The next time it happens, we'll *know* what they're doing and how quickly they can move. If you'll join me in issuing the necessary instructions ahead of time to permit Mother Church's loyal sons to destroy locks, if that's the only way to stop them, I think we can ensure this never happens again. But the first time? Coming at everyone involved with absolutely no warning?" He shook his head. "It just wasn't going to happen, Zhaspahr. And it's not anyone's fault, either."

Except, of course, he very carefully did not add aloud, *the fault of your idiot agents inquisitor who never gave us a single breath of warning ahead of time. And just how* did *the heretics manage it, Zhaspahr? I don't think they just set their own ships on fire, so how* are *they doing it? And how long will it take you to figure this one out so you can grant the proper dispensations and indulgences to bend the Proscriptions even further and do the same thing ourselves?*

Clyntahn seemed to hunch down in his chair. Duchairn and Maigwair's joint defiance appeared to have at least temporarily blunted his normal bellicosity, although the treasurer didn't expect that to last. Soon enough, Clyntahn would be reminding himself of the brilliance of his own strategic concept . . . and blaming its failure on the poor execution of others.

"So how bad is it?" he demanded, looking back and forth between the treasurer and the captain general again. "How soon can we resume the offensive?"

"Zhaspahr, we *can't,*" Duchairn said, almost gently. "Not until we get the canals repaired." He tapped the report Maigwair had dropped on the table. "They destroyed every major lock, and most of the secondary ones, for the entire length of the Guarnak–Ice Ash Canal, the Guarnak-Sylmahn Canal, and the Hildermoss River between the Guarnak-Sylmahn Canal and Spinefish Bay. They made a side excursion far enough up the Sair to cripple the northern end of the Sair-Selkyr Canal, as well, and they destroyed every lock on the Tarikah River between East Wing Lake and the Hildermoss." He shook his head. "The entire northern lobe of our logistic system's been severed. Everything we were sending up the Holy Langhorne can't go any farther than Lake City by water until we get the locks repaired, and that means we have two hundred thousand men we can no longer properly supply, most of them in territory where the crops either weren't planted at all this year or went in late. And that's not counting the loyal militia who've joined up with them, which adds about fifty percent to their own troop strength . . . and the mouths we have to feed. Without those supply lines, the best they're going to be able to do is hold their positions. Even the Dohlarans will find themselves in the same situation, because we're going to have to commandeer their supply route up the Fairmyn River and the Charayan Canal just to keep Kaitswyrth's troops fed."

"But we've got them on the *run!*" Clyntahn snarled. "If we let up *now*—!"

"I imagine that's exactly what they had in mind," Duchairn said in that same calm voice. "And it's worked. We can probably get our waterborne communications at least as far as the Hildermoss restored by sometime late next spring or next summer. Until then, Allayn's just going to have to hold what he's already got." The treasurer shrugged. "The only good news, if it can be called that, is that Siddarmark's economy had already been so hammered that this isn't going to cost us any revenue we would've had otherwise. *Fixing* it's going to make Shan-wei's own hole in the Treasury, though—don't think it won't! We haven't had a chance to put the new revenue measures into place, and they're going to help, so I can't say for certain how bad the hole's going to be, but I'm sure it's going to be ugly. On the other hand, we don't have any choice but to figure out how to plug it, so I imagine that's what my clerks and I will be doing for the next few months while you and Allayn find out how the heretics did this to us."

Clyntahn's eyes smoldered dangerously, but he had his temper under control, for a change. There wasn't much way he could have argued with Duchairn's conclusions, after all.

"It's no one's fault, Zhaspahr," Duchairn repeated. "And despite everything, we're in a much better position than last winter. Allayn has far more depth between the Temple Lands and the heretics than we had before, and once we get the farms in western Siddarmark back into production—and repair enough of the canal system to transport their produce—the Army's logistic problems will be enormously reduced. And for the immediate future, I don't see any way the heretics can press the attack against *us* any more than we can press the attack against *them*. Our supplies are hamstrung; they're still enormously outnumbered, and Stohnar is going to have to recreate *his* army from scratch.

"Neither side's going to be able to mount a campaign before next summer. I think we need to spend the intervening time learning all we can about the heretics' new weapons and these smoking iron ships of theirs. If our spies and the Inquisition can do that, I think Allayn and I can promise to have an army ready to use that information, next May or June."

.XI.
Charisian Embassy,
Siddar City,
Republic of Siddarmark

The thunderstorm rolled across Siddar City, sweeping in from the west across Old Province. Wind roared over the rooftops, roiling the massive black clouds, and lightning whickered and flashed, lighting those heavy-bellied clouds from within, etching them purple and white against its own jagged forks.

One of those forks of fury struck the ornate lightning rod atop Lord Protector's Palace. The brilliance of the strike bleached the night into day, stunning any unwary eye, and the re-echoing peal of thunder pounded the city like Shan-wei's hammer. More than one of the capital's people—especially those who hewed to the Temple—quailed, shrinking in on themselves, in some cases actually hiding under blankets or even beds, as Langhorne stalked the heavens in the terrible blaze of his Rakurai, venting his fury at the people who had betrayed Mother Church.

Merlin Athrawes didn't.

He sat in his darkened chamber, the window open, smelling the storm's ozone, watching the lightning, listening to the rain. He let the storm's fury wash through him, let it crackle and seethe around him, churning with energy, and deep at the heart of him were the images of that other, greater storm sweeping out of the west. A storm not of impersonal, uncaring nature, but built out of steel and gunpowder, out of fire and the sword and the rope, and fueled by hatred.

"Merlin?"

The voice spoke in his ear, quietly, and he closed his eyes. Perhaps, he thought, if he sat very still, he could hide from it.

"Merlin," the voice repeated, firmer, refusing to be ignored, and he sighed wearily.

"Yes, Nahrmahn?"

"Cayleb's worried about you," Nahrmahn Baytz said, and an image appeared in Merlin's vision. The plump little prince sat on his favorite balcony in Eraystor . . . and a storm very like the one churning across Siddar City came bellowing and roaring in off Eraystor Bay.

"He shouldn't be." Merlin looked past the projected storm into the reality of his own. Rain blew in the window, hitting his face like ocean spray, and he tasted it cold and fresh on his lips. "I'm fine."

"No, you aren't," Nahrmahn disagreed.

"Of course I am." Merlin closed his eyes, his profile etched against the window as fresh lightning plowed the clouds. "I'm immortal, Nahrmahn. I'm a machine, even if I do think I'm also Nimue Alban. What could possibly harm *me*?"

Nahrmahn winced at the pain in that tireless yet bone-deep exhausted voice.

"You can't do this," he said softly. "You just can't, Merlin."

"Do what?" Merlin's voice was harder, almost angry. "What *is* it all of you want me to stop doing, Nahrmahn?!"

"You know," Nahrmahn said thoughtfully, "if there's a single person on Safehold better placed to understand what's happening to you than I am, I can't imagine who it might be. You think you're a machine that thinks it's a person?" The Emeraldian chuckled harshly. "What does that make *me*? I'm not even a machine, Merlin—just a thought in the mind of God . . . and a computer you built!"

It was Merlin's turn to wince without ever opening his eyes.

"I'm not complaining," Nahrmahn went on, as if he'd read Merlin's mind. "I've lost a lot, but I've gained even more—especially considering the alternative!" He laughed more easily. "But it does give me a different perspective from the others . . . and it gives me more time to think than anyone else. Isn't that why you've all handed so much more of the intelligence analysis over to me? But SNARC reports aren't the only things I think about, you know. I think about friends, too. About people I love. And I've been thinking a lot about you lately."

"Nahrmahn, don't—" Merlin began, then cut himself off.

He climbed out of his chair and strode to the window, gripping the frame shoulder-high in each hand, standing in the full power of the storm. The pounding rain blew almost horizontally on ever stronger blasts of wind, soaking him, but he only stood there, letting it batter him.

"Merlin," Nahrmahn said softly, "you can't take this entire world on your shoulders. You just *can't*—it's as simple as that. For all the wonders of your technology, all the things that 'machine' you live in can do, you're still *one* person. There's only so much you can do. And what's even more important, there's only so much you can bear."

"We bear what we have to," Merlin said drearily, his eyes empty but for the reflected lightning.

"And sometimes what we try to bear *breaks* us, Merlin. Sometimes we try to bear loads that aren't ours, either because we think they *are*, or because we're so desperate to take them off the shoulders of people we care about. You're doing *both* those things, Merlin Athrawes, and you can't . . . go . . . on . . . doing . . . it."

There was silence, made only more perfect by the crackling, roaring thunderstorm. It seemed to last a long time, that silence, and then Merlin bowed his head.

"I can't hand it to anyone else, Nahrmahn. Even if I wanted to. I'm the one who started this war, and I knew—I *knew*, Nahrmahn, unlike anyone else on this planet—*exactly* what a religious war on this scale was going to entail. I knew about the atrocities, the cruelty, the hatred, the starvation, the bloodshed—*all* of it, Nahrmahn. *I knew what I was doing!*"

The final sentence was a cry of agony, and the PICA's shoulders shook as the human being who lived inside it wept.

"Don't be absurd," Nahrmahn said harshly. Merlin's head rose again—quickly, as if startled—and the little prince stood on the virtual reality balcony, in the heart of his own thunderstorm, and glared at him. "If you hadn't come along, hadn't done what you did, Charis would be an even worse nightmare than Siddarmark by now, and you damned well know it! You brought things to a head, but Haarahld and the Brethren of Saint Zherneau were *already committed* to breaking the Church, revealing the lie, and the Group of Four was already committed to breaking Charis! The only thing you've done is give them a chance to survive rather than die at Zhaspahr Clyntahn's whim!"

"No, it isn't!" Merlin said fiercely. "God only knows how many people I've personally killed in the last five years, Nahrmahn—*I* sure as hell don't! I can tell myself lots of them deserved to die if anyone ever did. The fanatics who tried to kill Sharley, the inquisitors who were going to murder Daivyn and Irys. But what about all the men who were only serving their own country, their own prince? What about all the good and decent men doing their duty? Doing what they've been taught all their lives that God Himself *wants* them to do? And what about the staffs of those semaphore stations? The men who'd never personally hurt anyone in their entire lives until I slaughtered them in order to make my wonderful plan work?! I can't pretend I haven't done those things."

"No, you can't," Nahrmahn agreed more gently. "But don't pretend you had any other option."

"There's *always* a choice, Nahrmahn." Merlin's voice was hard, flat. "Always. Don't think for a moment that I didn't *choose* to do them, because I damned well *did*."

"That wasn't what I said. I said you didn't have any other *option*, Merlin. If you hadn't come up with your 'wonderful plan' and made it work, the Army of God would've rolled right over Siddarmark. So, yes, you could've chosen not to do that—or all the *other* things you've done—but only by choosing to betray not just Nimue Alban's sacrifice—or Pei Shan-wei's, or Pei Kau-yung's, or that of every man and woman in the Federation Navy who died so this world could live—but the future of the entire human race. So tell me, Merlin Athrawes—Nimue Alban—what gives you the *right* to place your guilt above the human race's survival? Are you so *arrogant* you think this is about *you*?"

Merlin's eyes opened wide, glittering like flame-cored sapphires in the lightning's glare.

"The Gbaba are still out there," Nahrmahn said flatly. "I know what that means now, more than anyone else in the universe . . . except you. I've had time now to read the records, view the history. I've seen the same ruin Nimue Alban saw, and I know what will happen if the human race runs into them a second time without knowing what I know. What *you* know, because unlike me, you didn't just study it, you saw it. You *lived* it. You watched it happen to everything and everyone Nimue Alban ever loved. So tell me you had the *option* to choose not to do the things you've done here on Safehold! *Tell* me you could've walked away, let what happened to the Terran Federation happen to mankind all over again!"

Merlin was silent, and after a moment, Nahrmahn's expression softened.

"There's a term I've found in my research, Merlin: 'combat fatigue.' It's a valuable concept. So is 'survivor's guilt' . . . and I can't think of anyone in the world—in the *universe*—with a better right to feel both those things than Nimue Alban . . . and you. You don't have just Merlin Athrawes' guilt and pain riding in your soul; you have all of *hers*, too. And you can't keep punishing her—and you—for still being here while everyone she ever knew is dead, just as you can't keep punishing yourself for what you've had no *option* but to do here on Safehold."

"I can't write myself a blank check, Nahrmahn," Merlin whispered, closing his eyes once more, letting the rain wash over him. "I can't be some omniscient, godlike being who goes around choosing the slain. *This* one lives—*that* one dies! I can't just strike people down and tell myself it's okay, that I didn't have any 'option,' and that that absolves me of guilt or washes away the blood. Nimue Alban swore an oath to protect and defend humanity, Nahrmahn—*protect and defend*. She probably killed or helped to kill thousands, even hundreds of thousands, of Gbaba doing just that. And, yes, she was sick to her soul with all the killing and all the death and knowing that in the end it was all for nothing. But I'm still *her*, and I'm supposed to keep human beings *alive*, not kill them myself! If I decide my 'mission imperative' empowers me to kill anyone I think needs to die, I'm no different from one of Zhaspahr Clyntahn's inquisitors. Maybe I'm better than *he* is, but I'm still doing what I do because I believe—genuinely believe—it *has* to be done. Isn't that the perfect description of a Schuelerite?"

"Actually, it *is* a pretty good description of a Schuelerite like—oh, Paityr Wylsynn," Nahrmahn said. "I don't recall *his* ever doing a single capricious, selfish, or needlessly cruel thing in his life . . . which pretty well describes you, too."

"Oh, sure!" Merlin said bitterly. "A real candidate for *sainthood*—that's me."

"I've always thought most saints were probably pains in the arse," Nahrmahn said thoughtfully. "Of course, the people Mother Church has chosen to canonize didn't have quite the worldview I've discovered *I* have."

It was Merlin's turn to surprise himself with a chuckle.

"Merlin," Nahrmahn's voice had turned gentle again, "I'm not asking you not to feel responsible, even guilty, for your own actions. I'm only telling you you can't lock yourself in a prison cell for being who you are and doing what you know, without question, needs to be done. In my life, while I was playing the 'Great Game,' I did terrible, even despicable things for far more selfish reasons and with far less justification than anything you've ever done, and assuming Nahrmahn Baytz isn't really already completely dead, my accounting for those things has only been deferred. I'll still have to face it in the end, and the only thing I can hope is that some of the good I've done—most of it after meeting *you*—will stand to my credit when the account's rendered. You, at least, don't have that baggage, and I'll tell you this right now, Merlin Athrawes—when the time comes for you to stand before God, I will be *honored* to stand at your side, and I'm not alone in feeling that way. There are people who love you—not the mysterious, deadly, mystic warrior *Seijin* Merlin, but simply *you*. We know what you've done for us, and we know what it's cost you—what it's still *going* to cost you— and we would do anything we could to take that burden from you. But we can't. All we can do is help you bear it . . . and that's what I'm asking you to let us do."

Silence hovered once more, endlessly, still and quiet at the heart of the thunder, until at last, slowly, Merlin straightened.

"I still have to be responsible for my own acts and decisions, no matter what my justification for them, Nahrmahn," he said softly. "But you're right about love. When you come down to it, at the bottom of everything, that's the basis, the place we stand while we try to find some decency in the world around us."

"Yes, it is," Nahrmahn agreed. "And love doesn't always mean sacrificing yourself for someone else. Sometimes it means letting them sacrifice themselves for *you,* because it's that important to them. And that's who you are, who you've become—the person who's so important to us, who we need so much, we can't let you sit here in this dark room with the ghosts of your dead while you let them devour you. I'm sorry, Merlin, we just can't do it."

"Stubborn, you Safeholdians," Merlin said with a crooked smile.

"Yes, we are. Sneaky, too. I usually get what I want, you know."

"I've heard that about you."

"Well, I *do* have a reputation to uphold."

"And you really are going to pester me into going downstairs and joining Cayleb for dinner?"

"Oh, definitely. And after that, I'm going to pester you until you have a long—and, frankly, given your current state, a long *overdue*—conversation with him, Sharleyan, and Maikel. Possibly even with your own humble servant and Ohlyvya in attendance, as well. *Cayleb* made the mistake of respecting your privacy, which gave you entirely too much time to brood and take all of the ills of the world upon your shoulders, but I'm far too unscrupulous to make that sort of mistake."

"Yes, you are," Merlin said with a theatrical sigh. "So I suppose I might as well give up and surrender now. Save us both a lot of energy and time."

"Very wise of you."

"I thought you'd see it that way."

Merlin smiled again, sapphire eyes still dark but infinitely softer while the thunder rolled behind him.

"Can I at least change into a dry uniform, first?"

Characters

ABERNETHY, AUXILIARY BISHOP ERNYST—Schuelerite upper-priest; Bishop Militant Bahrnabai Wyrshym's assigned intendant.

ABYLYN, CHARLZ—a senior leader of the Temple Loyalists in Charis.

AHBAHT, CAPTAIN RUHSAIL, IMPERIAL DESNAIRIAN NAVY—commanding officer HMS *Archangel Chihiro*, 40; Commodore Wailahr's flag captain.

AHBAHT, LYWYS—Edmynd Walkyr's brother-in-law; XO, merchant galleon *Wind*.

AHBAHT, ZHEFRY—Earl Gray Harbor's personal secretary. He fulfills many of the functions of an undersecretary of state for foreign affairs.

AHDYMS, COLONEL TAHLYVYR—Temple Loyalist ex-militia officer; "General" Erayk Tympyltyn's executive officer, Fort Darymahn, South March Lands, Republic of Siddarmark.

AHDYMSYN, BISHOP ZHERALD—previously Erayk Dynnys' bishop executor for Charis, now one of Archbishop Maikel's senior auxiliary bishops.

AHLAIXSYN, RAIF—well-to-do Siddarmarkian poet and dilettante; a Reformist.

AHLBAIR, EDWYRD—Earl of Dragon Hill.

AHLBAIR, LIEUTENANT ZHEROHM, ROYAL CHARISIAN NAVY—first lieutenant, HMS *Typhoon*.

AHLDARM, MAHRYS OHLARN—Mahrys IV, Emperor of Desnair.

AHLVAI, CAPTAIN MAHLYK, IMPERIAL DESNAIRIAN NAVY—CO, HMS *Emperor Zhorj*, 48. Baron Jahras' flag captain.

AHLVEREZ, ADMIRAL-GENERAL FAIDEL, ROYAL DOHLARAN NAVY—Duke of Malikai; King Rahnyld IV of Dohlar's senior admiral.

AHLVEREZ, SIR RAINOS, ROYAL DESNARIAN ARMY—CO of the Dohlaran army assigned to invade the Republic of Siddarmark.

AHLWAIL, BRAIHD—Father Paityr Wylsynn's valet.

AHNDAIRS, TAILAHR—a Charisian-born Temple Loyalist living in the Temple Lands; recruited for Operation Rakurai.

AHRBUKYL, TROOPER SVYNSYN, ARMY OF GOD—one of Corporal Howail Brahdlai's scouts, 191st Cavalry regiment.

AHRDYN—Archbishop Maikel's cat lizard.

AHRMAHK, CAYLEB ZHAN HAARAHLD BRYAHN—Duke of Ahrmahk, Prince of Tellesberg, Prince Protector of the Realm, King Cayleb II of Charis, Emperor Cayleb I of Charis. Husband of Sharleyan Ahrmahk.

AHRMAHK, CROWN PRINCESS ALAHNAH ZHANAYT NAIMU—infant daughter of Cayleb and Sharleyan Ahrmahk; heir to the imperial Charisian crown.

AHRMAHK, HAARAHLD VII—King of Charis.

AHRMAHK, KAHLVYN—Duke of Tirian (deceased), Constable of Hairatha; King Haarahld VII's first cousin.

AHRMAHK, KAHLVYN CAYLEB—younger son of Kahlvyn Ahrmahk, deceased Duke Tirian, King Cayleb's first cousin once removed.

AHRMAHK, RAYJHIS—Duke of Tirian; Kahlvyn Ahrmahk's elder son and heir.

AHRMAHK, SHARLEYAN ALAHNAH ZHENYFYR AHLYSSA TAYT—Duchess of Cherayth, Lady Protector of Chisholm, Queen of Chisholm, Empress of Charis. Wife of Cayleb Ahrmahk; *see also* Sharleyan Tayt.

AHRMAHK, ZHAN—Crown Prince Zhan; King Cayleb's younger brother.

AHRMAHK, ZHANAYT—Princess Zhanayt; Cayleb Ahrmahk's younger sister; second eldest child of King Haarahld VII.

AHRMAHK, ZHENYFYR—Dowager Duchess of Tirian; mother of Kahlvyn Cayleb Ahrmahk; daughter of Rayjhis Yowance, Earl Gray Harbor.

AHRNAHLD, SPYNSAIR—Empress Sharleyan's personal clerk and secretary.

AHRTHYR, SIR ALYK—Earl of Windshare, CO of Sir Koryn Gahrvai's cavalry.

AHSTYN, LIEUTENANT FRANZ, CHARISIAN ROYAL GUARD—the second-in-command of King Cayleb II's personal bodyguard.

AHTKYN, LIEUTENANT ZHERALD, REPUBLIC OF SIDDARMARK ARMY—Colonel Phylyp Mahldyn's aide.

AHUBRAI, FATHER AHNSYLMO—Schuelerite under-priest; senior Temple Loyalist clergyman, Fairkyn, New Northland Province, Republic of Siddarmark.

AHZGOOD, PHYLYP—Earl of Coris; previously spymaster for Prince Hektor of Corisande; Irys and Daivyn Daykyn's legal guardian, chief advisor, and minister in exile.

AIMAIYR, FATHER IGNAZ—Archbishop Arthyn's upper-priest Schuelerite intendant in Tarikah Province.

AIMAYL, RAHN—a member of the anti-Charis resistance in Manchyr, Corisande; an ex-apprentice of Paitryk Hainree's.

AIRNHART, FATHER SAIMYN—Father Zohannes Pahtkovair's immediate subordinate; a Schuelerite.

AIRYTH, EARL OF—*see* Trumyn Sowthmyn.

AIWAIN, CAPTAIN HARYS, IMPERIAL CHARISIAN NAVY—CO, HMS *Shield*, 54.

ALBAN, LIEUTENANT COMMANDER NIMUE, TFN—Admiral Pei Kau-zhi's tactical officer.

ANVIL ROCK, EARL OF—*see* Sir Rysel Gahrvai.

APLYN, CHESTYR—one of Hektor Aplyn-Ahrmahk's younger brothers; newly admitted student at the Royal College of Charis.

APLYN, SAILMAH—Hektor Aplyn-Ahrmahk's biological mother.

APLYN-AHRMAHK, LIEUTENANT HEKTOR, IMPERIAL CHARISIAN NAVY—Duke of Darcos; flag lieutenant to Sir Dunkyn Yairley, Baron Sarmouth; Cayleb Ahrmahk's adoptive son.

ARCHBISHOP MAIKEL—*see* Archbishop Maikel Staynair.

ARCHBISHOP PAWAL—*see* Archbishop Pawal Braynair.

ARTHMYN, FATHER OHMAHR—senior healer, Imperial Palace, Tellesberg.

ASHWAIL, COMMANDER SAHLAVAHN, IMPERIAL CHARISIAN NAVY—CO of one of Hauwerd Breygart's Navy "battalions" at Thesmar.

ATHRAWES, CAPTAIN MERLIN, CHARISIAN IMPERIAL GUARD—King Cayleb II's personal armsman; the cybernetic avatar of Commander Nimue Alban; promoted to Major in 896.

AYMEZ, MIDSHIPMAN BARDULF, ROYAL CHARISIAN NAVY—a midshipman, HMS *Typhoon*.

BAHCHER, COLONEL SIR ZHORY, ROYAL DESNARIAN ARMY—CO, "Bahcher's Regiment," cavalry regiment assigned to Sir Fahstyr Rychtyr's invasion column.

BAHLTYN, ZHEEVYS—Baron White Ford's valet.

BAHNYR, HEKTOR—Earl of Mancora; one of Sir Koryn Gahrvai's senior officers; commander of the right wing at Haryl's Crossing.

BAHR, DAHNNAH—senior chef, Imperial Palace, Cherayth.

BAHRDAHN, CAPTAIN PHYLYP, IMPERIAL CHARISIAN NAVY—CO, HMS *Undaunted*, 56.

BAHRDAILAHN, LIEUTENANT SIR AHBAIL, ROYAL DOHLARAN NAVY—the Earl of Thirsk's flag lieutenant.

BAHRKLY, BISHOP HARYS, ARMY OF GOD—CO, Rakurai Division.

BAHRMYN, ARCHBISHOP BORYS—Archbishop of Corisande for the Church of God Awaiting.

BAHRMYN, TOHMYS—Baron White Castle; Prince Hektor's ambassador to Prince Nahrmahn.

BAHRNS, CAPTAIN HALCOM, IMPERIAL CHARISIAN NAVY—CO, HMS *Delthak*, 22.

BAHRNS, KING RAHNYLD IV—King of Dohlar.

BAHZKAI, LAIYAN—a Leveler and printer in Siddar City; a leader of the Sword of Schueler.

BAIKET, CAPTAIN STYWYRT, ROYAL DOHLARAN NAVY—Earl of Thirsk's flag captain; CO, HMS *Chihiro*, 50.

BAIKYR, CAPTAIN SYLMAHN, IMPERIAL CHARISIAN NAVY—CO, HMS *Ahrmahk*, 58. High Admiral Lock Island's flag captain at Battle of Gulf of Tarot.

BAIKYR, COLONEL PAWAL—a regular officer of the Republic of Siddarmark Army who went over to the Temple Loyalists; commander of Temple Loyalist rebels in the Sylmahn Gap.

BAILAHND, SISTER AHMAI—Abbess of the Abbey of Saint Evehlain.

BAIRAHT, DAIVYN—Duke of Kholman; Emperor Mahrys IV of Desnair's Navy minister; Sir Urwyn Hahltar's brother-in-law.

BAIRYSTYR, LIEUTENANT ZHAK, IMPERIAL CHARISIAN NAVY—senior engineer, HMS *Delthak*, 22.

BAIRZHAIR, BROTHER TAIRAINCE—treasurer of the Monastery of Saint Zherneau.

BANAHR, FATHER AHZWALD—head of the priory of Saint Hamlyn, city of Sarayn, Kingdom of Charis.

BARCOR, BARON OF—*see* Sir Zher Sumyrs.

BARHNKASTYR, MAJOR PAITRYK, IMPERIAL CHARISIAN ARMY—XO, 2nd Regiment, Imperial Charisian Army.

BAYTZ, FELAYZ—Prince Nahrmahn of Emerald's youngest child and second daughter.

BAYTZ, HANBYL—Duke of Solomon; Prince Nahrmahn of Emerald's uncle and the commander of the Emeraldian Army.

BAYTZ, MAHRYA—Princess Mahrya; oldest child and older daughter of Nahrmahn and Ohlyvya Baytz; betrothed to Prince Zhan of Old Charis.

BAYTZ, NAHRMAHN—Prince Nahrmahn II of Emerald; deceased Prince of Emerald and councilor for intelligence, Empire of Charis.

BAYTZ, NAHRMAHN GAREYT—Prince Nahrmahn Gareyt of Emerald; elder son and second child of Prince Nahrmahn and Princess Ohlyvya Baytz.

BAYTZ, NAHRMAHN HANBYL GRAIM—*see* Prince Nahrmahn Baytz.

BAYTZ, OHLYVYA—Dowager Princess of Emerald; widow of Prince Nahrmahn; mother of Prince Nahrmahn Gareyt.

BAYTZ, PRINCE NAHRMAHN II—ruler of the Princedom of Emerald; Cayleb and Sharleyan Ahrmahk's Imperial Councilor for Intelligence.

BAYTZ, PRINCESS OHLYVYA—wife of Prince Nahrmahn of Emerald.

BAYTZ, TRAHVYS—Prince Trahvys; third child and younger son of Nahrmahn and Ohlyvya Baytz.

BÉDARD, DR. ADORÉE, PH.D.—chief psychiatrist, Operation Ark.

BEKATYRO, ELAIYS—previous Temple Loyalist mayor of Ohlarn, New Northland Province, Republic of Siddarmark; unjustly denounced to the Inquisition by Bynno Leskyr, who wanted his position.

BISHOP EXECUTOR WYLLYS—*see* Bishop Executor Wyllys Graisyn.

BISHOP ZHERALD—*see* Bishop Zherald Ahdymsyn.

BLACK HORSE, DUKE OF—*see* Payt Stywyrt.

BLACK WATER, DUKE OF—*see* Sir Adulfo Lynkyn.

BLACK WATER, DUKE OF—*see* Admiral Ernyst Lynkyn.

BLAHNDAI, CHANTAHAL—an alias of Lysbet Wylsynn in Zion.

BLAHDYSNBERG, LIEUTENANT PAWAL, IMPERIAL CHARISIAN NAVY—XO, HMS *Delthak*, 22.

BLAIDYN, LIEUTENANT ROZHYR, ROYAL DOHLARAN NAVY—second lieutenant, galley *Royal Bédard*.

BOHLYR, WYLLYM, CANAL SERVICE—lockmaster, Fairkyn, New Northland Province, Republic of Siddarmark.

BORYS, ARCHBISHOP—*see* Archbishop Borys Bahrmyn.

BOWAVE, DAIRAK—Dr. Rahzhyr Mahklyn's senior assistant, Royal College, Tellesberg.

BOWSHAM, CAPTAIN KHANAIR, ROYAL CHARISIAN NAVY—CO, HMS *Gale*.

BRADLAI, LIEUTENANT ROBYRT, ROYAL CORISANDIAN NAVY—true name of Captain Styvyn Whaite.

BRAHDLAI, LIEUTENANT HAARAHLD, ROYAL DOHLARAN NAVY—third lieutenant, HMS *Chihiro*, 50.

BRAHDLAI, CORPORAL HOWAIL, ARMY OF GOD—scout patrol commander, 191st Cavalry regiment.

BRAHNAHR, CAPTAIN STYVYN, IMPERIAL CHARISIAN NAVY—CO, Bureau of Navigation, Imperial Charisian Navy.

BRAHNSYN, DOCTOR FYL—member of the Royal College of Charis, specializing in botany.

BRAIDAIL, BROTHER ZHILBYRT—under-priest of the Order of Schueler; a junior Inquisitor in Talkyra.

BRAISHAIR, CAPTAIN HORYS, IMPERIAL CHARISIAN NAVY—CO, HMS *Rock Point*, 38; POW of Earl Thirsk, surrendered to the Inquisition.

BRAISYN, AHRNAHLD, IMPERIAL CHARISIAN NAVY—a seaman aboard HMS *Destiny*, 54; a member of Stywyrt Mahlyk's boat crew.

BRAISYN, CAPTAIN DYNNYS, IMPERIAL CHARISIAN NAVY—CO, Bureau of Supply, Imperial Charisian Navy.

BRAYNAIR, ARCHBISHOP PAWAL—first Archbishop of Chisholm for the Church of Charis.

BREYGART, FHRANCYS—younger daughter of Hauwerd and Fhrancys Breygart; Lady Mairah Breygart's stepdaughter.

BREYGART, FRAIDARECK—fourteenth Earl of Hanth; Hauwerd Breygart's great-grandfather.

BREYGART, HAARAHLD—second oldest son of Hauwerd and Fhrancys Breygart; Lady Mairah Breygart's stepdaughter.

BREYGART, LADY MAIRAH LYWKYS—Countess of Hanth; Empress Sharleyan's former chief lady-in-waiting; second wife of Sir Hauwerd Breygart, Earl of Hanth.

BREYGART, GENERAL SIR HAUWERD, IMPERIAL CHARISIAN MARINE CORPS—the rightful heir to the Earldom of Hanth; becomes earl 893; Marine officer recalled for service in Siddarmark.

BREYGART, STYVYN—elder son of Hauwerd and Fhrancys Breygart; Lady Mairah Breygart's stepson.

BREYGART, TRUMYN—youngest son of Hauwerd and Fhrancys Breygart; Lady Mairah Breygart's stepson.

BREYGART, ZHERLDYN—elder daughter of Hauwerd and Fhrancys Breygart; Lady Mairah Breygart's stepdaughter.

BROUN, FATHER MAHTAIO—Archbishop Erayk Dynnys' senior secretary and aide; Archbishop Erayk's confidant and protégé.

BROWNYNG, CAPTAIN ELLYS—CO, Temple galleon *Blessed Langhorne*.

BRYNDYN, MAJOR DAHRYN—the senior artillery officer attached to Brigadier Clareyk's column at Haryl's Priory.

BRYNYGAIR, COLONEL SIR ZHADWAIL, ROYAL DESNARIAN ARMY—CO, "Brynygair's Regiment," cavalry regiment assigned to Sir Fahstyr Rychtyr's invasion column.

BYRGAIR, COLONEL SIR NAYTHYN, ROYAL DESNARIAN ARMY—CO, "Byrgair's Regiment," cavalry regiment assigned to Sir Fahstyr Rychtyr's invasion column.

BYRK, MAJOR BREKYN, ROYAL CHARISIAN MARINES—CO, Marine detachment, HMS *Royal Charis*.

BYRK, FATHER MYRTAN—upper-priest of the Order of Schueler; Father Vyktyr Tahrlsahn's second-in-command.

BYRK, CAPTAIN ZHORJ, IMPERIAL CHARISIAN NAVY—CO, HMS *Volcano*, 24, one of the Imperial Charisian Navy's "bombardment ships."

BYRKYT, FATHER ZHON—librarian and ex-Abbot of the Monastery of Saint Zherneau.

BYRNS, BRAISYN—Earl of White Crag; former Lord Justice of Chisholm, currently first councilor, replacing Mahrak Sahndyrs.

CAHKRAYN, SAMYL—Duke of Fern, King Rahnyld IV of Dohlar's first councilor.

CAHMMYNG, AHLBAIR—a professional assassin working for Father Aidryn Waimyn.

CAHNYR, ARCHBISHOP ZHASYN—fugitive Archbishop of Glacierheart; a Reformist member of Samyl Wylsynn's Circle; a major spiritual leader of the Reformists in Siddar City.

CAHNYRS, LIEUTENANT ZHERALD, IMPERIAL CHARISIAN NAVY—second lieutenant, HMS *Delthak*, 22.

CAHRTAIR, MAJOR HAHLYS—rebel Temple Loyalist CO, 3rd Company, 3rd Saiknyr Militia Regiment.

CHAHLMAIR, SIR BAIRMON—Duke of Margo; a member of Prince Daivyn's

Regency Council in Corisande who does not fully trust Earl Anvil Rock and Earl Tartarian.

CHAIMBYRS, LIEUTENANT ZHUSTYN, IMPERIAL DESNAIRIAN NAVY—second lieutenant, HMS *Archangel Chihiro*, 40.

CHALMYR, LIEUTENANT MAILVYN, ROYAL CHARISIAN NAVY—first lieutenant, HMS *Tellesberg*.

CHALMYRZ, FATHER KARLOS—Archbishop Borys Bahrmyn's aide and secretary.

CHANSAYL, COLONEL PAITYR, REPUBLIC OF SIDDARMARK ARMY—CO, 43rd Infantry Regiment, Republic of Siddarmark Army, a part of General Trumyn Stohnar's Sylmahn Gap command.

CHARLZ, CAPTAIN MARIK—CO, Charisian merchant ship *Wave Daughter*.

CHARLZ, MASTER YEREK, ROYAL CHARISIAN NAVY—gunner, HMS *Wave*, 14.

CHERMYN, MAJOR DAHNEL—rebel Temple Loyalist CO, 1st Company 3rd Saiknyr Militia Regiment.

CHERMYN, VICEROY GENERAL HAUWYL, IMPERIAL CHARISIAN MARINES—CO, Charisian occupation forces in Corisande. Cayleb and Sharleyan Ahrmahk's regent in Corisande; later Grand Duke of Zebediah.

CHERMYN, MATHYLD—Hauwyl Chermyn's wife.

CHERMYN, RHAZ—Hauwyl Chermyn's oldest son.

CHERMYN, LIEUTENANT ZHOEL, IMPERIAL CHARISIAN NAVY—senior engineer, HMS *Hador*, 22.

CHERYNG, LIEUTENANT TAIWYL—a junior officer on Sir Vyk Lakyr's staff; he is in charge of Lakyr's clerks and message traffic.

CLAREYK, GENERAL KYNT, IMPERIAL CHARISIAN ARMY—Baron Green Valley; Old Charisian ex-Marine; senior advisor to Duke of Eastshare; effectively second-in-command of the Imperial Charisian Army; CO, 2nd Brigade (reinforced), Charisian Expeditionary Force.

CLYNTAHN, LIEUTENANT HAIRYM, IMPERIAL CHARISIAN ARMY—CO, Support Platoon, 1st Battalion, 2nd Regiment, Imperial Charisian Army.

CLYNTAHN, VICAR ZHASPAHR—Grand Inquisitor of the Church of God Awaiting; one of the so-called Group of Four.

COHLMYN, ADMIRAL SIR LEWK, IMPERIAL CHARISIAN NAVY—Earl Sharpfield, second-ranking officer, Imperial Charisian Navy; ex-Royal Chisholmian Navy.

CORIS, EARL OF—*see* Phylyp Ahzgood.

CRAGGY HILL, EARL OF—*see* Wahlys Hillkeeper.

CROSS CREEK, EARL OF—*see* Ahdem Zhefry.

DAHGLYS, CAPTAIN LAINYR, IMPERIAL CHARISIAN NAVY—CO, HMS *Tellesberg*, 22.

DAHNSYN, LIEUTENANT CHARLZ, REPUBLIC OF SIDDARMARK ARMY—Colonel Stahn Wyllys' senior aide.

DAHNVAHR, AINSAIL—Charisian-born Temple Loyalist living in the Temple Lands recruited for Operation Rakurai.

DAHNVAHR, RAHZHYR—Ainsail Dahnvahr's father.

DAHNVAIR, CAPTAIN LAIZAHNDO, IMPERIAL CHARISIAN NAVY—CO, HMS *Royal Kraken*, 58.

DAHNZAI, LYZBYT—Father Zhaif Laityr's housekeeper at the Church of the Holy Archangels Triumphant.

DAHRYUS, MASTER EDVARHD—an alias of Bishop Mylz Halcom.

DAIKHAR, LIEUTENANT MOHTOHKAI, IMPERIAL CHARISIAN NAVY—XO, HMS *Dart*, 54.

DAIKYN, GAHLVYN—King Cayleb's valet.

DAIVYN, PRINCE—*see* Daivyn Daykyn.

DAIVYS, MYTRAHN—a Charisian Temple Loyalist.

DARCOS, DUKE OF—*see* Hektor Aplyn-Ahrmahk.

DARYS, CAPTAIN TYMYTHY, IMPERIAL CHARISIAN NAVY—CO, HMS *Destroyer*, 54; Sir Domynyk Staynair's flag captain.

DAYKYN, DAIVYN DAHNYLD MAHRAK ZOSHYA—Prince Daivyn of Corisande; only surviving son of Prince Hektor of Corisande; rightful Prince of Corisande.

DAYKYN, HEKTOR (THE YOUNGER)—Prince Hektor of Corisande's second oldest child and heir apparent; assassinated 893.

DAYKYN, HEKTOR—Prince of Corisande, leader of the League of Corisande; assassinated 893.

DAYKYN, IRYS ZHORZHET MAHRA—Princess Irys of Corisande; only daughter of Prince Hektor of Corisande; older sister of Daivyn Dahnyld Mharak Zoshya Daykyn, Prince of Corisande.

DAYKYN, RAICHYNDA—Prince Hektor of Corisande's deceased wife; born in Earldom of Domair, Kingdom of Hoth.

DEEP HOLLOW, EARL OF—*see* Bryahn Selkyr.

DEKYN, SERGEANT ALLAYN—one of Kairmyn's noncoms, Delferahkan Army.

DOBYNS, CHARLZ—son of Lyzbyt Dobyns; an adolescent Corisandian convicted of treason as part of the Northern Conspiracy and pardoned by Empress Sharleyan.

DOBYNS, EZMELDA—Father Tymahn Hahskans' housekeeper at Saint Kathryn's church.

DOWAIN, COLONEL TYMYTHY, ARMY OF GOD—XO, Zion Division.

DOYAL, SIR CHARLZ—Sir Koryn Gahrvai's chief of staff and intelligence chief; also serves as the Regency Council's chief of intelligence.

DRAGON HILL, EARL OF—*see* Edwyrd Ahlbair.

DRAGONER, SIR RAYJHIS—Charisian ambassador to the Republic of Siddarmark.

DRAGONER, CORPORAL ZHAK, ROYAL CHARISIAN MARINES—a member of Crown Prince Cayleb's bodyguard.

DRAGONMASTER, BRIGADE SERGEANT MAJOR MAHKYNTY ("MAHK"), ROYAL CHARISIAN MARINES—Brigadier Clareyk's senior noncom during Corisande Campaign.

DUCHAIRN, VICAR RHOBAIR—Minister of Treasury, Council of Vicars; one of the so-called Group of Four.

DYMYTREE, FRONZ, ROYAL CHARISIAN MARINES—a member of Crown Prince Cayleb's bodyguard.

DYNNYS, ADORAI—Archbishop Erayk Dynnys' wife.

DYNNYS, MAJOR AHBNAIR, REPUBLIC OF SIDDARMARK ARMY—CO, 1st Company, 37th Infantry Regiment, Republic of Siddarmark Army.

DYNNYS, ARCHBISHOP ERAYK—Archbishop of Charis. Executed for heresy.

DYNNYS, STYVYN—Archbishop Erayk Dynnys' younger son, age eleven in 892.

DYNNYS, TYMYTHY ERAYK—Archbishop Erayk Dynnys' older son, age fourteen in 892.

EASTSHARE, DUKE OF—*see* Ruhsyl Thairis.

EDWAIR, FATHER SHAINSAIL—Schuelerite upper-priest; senior inquisitor attached to the Sylmahn Gap Temple Loyalists in Mountaincross.

EDWYRDS, KEVYN—XO, privateer galleon *Kraken*.

EDWYRDS, BISHOP WYLBYR—Schuelerite bishop; Zhaspahr Clyntahn's personal choice as Inquisitor General to head the Inquisition in territories occupied by the Army of God.

EKYRD, CAPTAIN HAYRYS, ROYAL DOHLARAN NAVY—CO, galley *King Rahnyld*.

EMPEROR CAYLEB—*see* Cayleb Ahrmahk.

EMPEROR MAHRYS IV—*see* Mahrys Ohlarn Ahldarm.

EMPEROR WAISU VI—*see* Waisu Hantai.

EMPRESS SHARLEYAN—*see* Sharleyan Ahrmahk.

ERAYK, ARCHBISHOP—*see* Erayk Dynnys.

ERAYKSYN, LIEUTENANT STYVYN, IMPERIAL CHARISIAN NAVY—Sir Domynyk Staynair's flag lieutenant.

ERAYKSYN, WYLLYM—a Charisian textiles manufacturer.

FAHRMAHN, PRIVATE LUHYS, ROYAL CHARISIAN MARINES—a member of Crown Prince Cayleb's bodyguard.

FAHSTYR, VYRGYL—Earl of Gold Wyvern.

FAIRCASTER, SERGEANT PAYTER, CHARISIAN ROYAL GUARD—one of Emperor Cayleb's personal guardsmen; a transferee from Crown Prince Cayleb's Marine detachment.

FAIRSTOCK, MAJOR KLYMYNT, REPUBLIC OF SIDDARMARK ARMY—CO,

Provisional Company, Republic of Siddarmark Army, Fort Sheldyn, South March Lands.

FAIRYS, COLONEL AHLVYN, IMPERIAL CHARISIAN MARINES—CO, 1st Regiment, 3rd Brigade, ICMC.

FALKHAN, CAPTAIN AHRNAHLD, ROYAL CHARISIAN MARINES—CO, Crown Prince Cayleb's personal bodyguard as lieutenant; later promoted to captain and CO, Prince Zhan Ahrmahk's bodyguard.

FARDHYM, ARCHBISHOP DAHNYLD—Bishop of Siddar City, elevated to Archbishop of Siddarmark by Greyghor Stohnar after the rebellion of the Sword of Schueler ordered by Vicar Zhaspahr Clyntahn.

FATHER MICHAEL—parish priest of Lakeview.

FAUYAIR, BROTHER BAHRTALAM—almoner at the Monastery of Saint Zherneau.

FERN, DUKE OF—*see* Samyl Cahkrayn.

FHAIRLY, MAJOR AHDYM, IMPERIAL DESNARIAN ARMY—the senior battery commander on East Island, Ferayd Sound, Kingdom of Delferahk.

FHARMYN, SIR RYK—a foundry owner and ironmaster in the Kingdom of Tarot.

FAHRMYN, FATHER TAIRYN—the priest assigned to Saint Chihiro's Church, a village church near the Convent of Saint Agtha.

FAHRNO, MAHRLYS—one of Madam Ahnzhelyk Phonda's courtesans.

FAHRYA, CAPTAIN BYRNAHRDO, IMPERIAL DESNAIRIAN NAVY—CO, HMS *Holy Langhorne*, 42.

FOFÃO, CAPTAIN MATEUS,TFN—CO, TFNS *Swiftsure*.

FOHRDYM, MAJOR KARMAIKEL, IMPERIAL CHARISIAN ARMY—CO, 2nd Battalion, 2nd Regiment, Imperial Charisian Army.

FORYST,VICAR ERAYK—a member of Samyl Wylsynn's Zionist circle of Reformists.

FOWAIL, CAPTAIN MAIKEL ROYAL DESNARIAN ARMY—CO, "Fowail's Battery," six-pounder horse artillery assigned to Sir Fahstyr Rychtyr's invasion column.

FRAIDMYN, SERGEANT VYK, CHARISIAN ROYAL GUARD—one of King Cayleb II's armsmen and bodyguards.

FUHLLYR, FATHER RAIMAHND—chaplain, HMS *Dreadnought*.

FURKHAL, RAFAYL—second baseman and leadoff hitter, Tellesberg Krakens.

FYSHYR, HARYS—CO, privateer galleon *Kraken*.

FYGUERA, GENERAL KYDRYC, REPUBLIC OF SIDDARMARK ARMY—CO, Thesmar, South March Lands.

FYRGYRSYN, PETTY OFFICER CRAHMYND, IMPERIAL CHARISIAN NAVY—senior helmsman, HMS *Delthak*, 22.

FYRLOH, FATHER BAHN—a Langhornite Temple Loyalist under-priest in

Tellesberg nominated by Father Davys Tyrnyr as Irys and Daivyn Daykyn's chaplain and confessor on their voyage to Chisholm.

FYRMAHN, ZHAN—a mountain clansman and feudist from the Gray Wall Mountains; becomes the leader of the Temple Loyalist guerrillas attacking Glacierheart.

FYRMYN, FATHER SULYVYN—a Schuelerite upper-priest assigned as Sir Rainos Ahlverez special intendant.

GAHDARHD, LORD SAMYL—keeper of the seal, Republic of Siddarmark.

GAHLVYN, CAPTAIN CAHNYR, IMPERIAL CHARISIAN NAVY—CO, HMS *Saygin*, 22.

GAHRBOR, ARCHBISHOP FAILYX—Archbishop of Tarot for the Church of God Awaiting.

GAHRDANER, SERGEANT CHARLZ, CHARISIAN ROYAL GUARD—one of King Haarahld VII's bodyguards.

GAHRMYN, LIEUTENANT RAHNYLD—XO, galley *Arrowhead*, Delferahkan Navy.

GAHRNAHT, BISHOP AMILAIN—deposed Bishop of Larchros.

GAHRVAI, GENERAL SIR KORYN, CORISANDIAN GUARD—Prince Hektor's army field commander; now CO, Corisandian Guard, in the service of the Regency Council; son of Earl Anvil Rock.

GAHRVAI, SIR RYSEL—Earl of Anvil Rock; Prince Daivyn Daykyn's cousin and official regent; head of Daivyn's Regency Council in Corisande.

GAHZTAHN, HIRAIM—Ainsail Dahnvahr's alias in Tellesberg.

GAIMLYN, BROTHER BAHLDWYN—under-priest of the Order of Schueler; assigned to King Zhames of Delferahk's household as an agent of the Inquisition.

GAIRAHT, CAPTAIN WYLLYS, CHISHOLMIAN ROYAL GUARD—CO of Queen Sharleyan's Royal Guard detachment in Charis.

GAIRLYNG, ARCHBISHOP KLAIRMANT—Archbishop of Corisande for the Church of Charis.

GALVAHN, MAJOR SIR NAITHYN—the Earl of Windshare's senior staff officer; Corisande Campaign.

GAHRDANER, SERGEANT CHARLZ, CHARISIAN ROYAL GUARD—one of King Haarahld VII's bodyguards.

GAHRMYN, LIEUTENANT RAHNYLD, ROYAL DELFERAKHAN NAVY—XO, galley *Arrowhead*.

GARDYNYR, ADMIRAL LYWYS, ROYAL DOHLARAN NAVY—Earl of Thirsk and King Rahnyld IV's best admiral and fleet commander.

GARDYNYR, COLONEL THOMYS, ROYAL DESNAIRIAN ARMY—one of Sir Rainos Ahlverez' senior regimental commanders.

GARTHIN, EDWAIR—Earl of North Coast; one of Prince Hektor of Corisande's councilors serving on Prince Daivyn's Regency Council in Corisande; an ally of Earl Anvil Rock and Earl Tartarian.

GHADWYN, SAMYL—a Temple Loyalist mountain clansman from the Gray Wall Mountains; one of Zhan Fyrmahn's cousins.

GHATFRYD, SANDARIA—Ahnzhelyk Phonda's/Nynian Rychtair's personal maid.

GODWYL, GENERAL SIR OHTYS, ROYAL DESNAIRIAN ARMY—Baron Traylmyn; General Sir Fahstyr Rychtyr's second-in-command.

GOLD WYVERN, EARL OF—*see* Vyrgyl Fahstyr.

GORJAH, FATHER GHARTH—Archbishop Zhasyn Cahnyr's personal secretary; a Chihirite of the Order of the Quill.

GORJAH, SAHMANTHA—Father Gharth Gorjah's wife; a trained healer; daughter of Archbishop Zhasyn Cahnyr's previous housekeeper.

GORJAH, ZHASYN—firstborn child of Gharth and Sahmantha Gorjah.

GOWAIN, LIEUTENANT FAIRGHAS, IMPERIAL CHARISIAN NAVY—XO, HMS *Victorious*, 56.

GRAHSMAHN, SYLVAYN—employee in city engineer's office, Manchyr, Corisande; Paitryk Hainree's immediate superior.

GRAHZAIAL, LIEUTENANT COMMANDER MAHSHAL, IMPERIAL CHARISIAN NAVY—CO, schooner HMS *Messenger*, 6.

GRAISYN, BISHOP EXECUTOR WYLLYS—Archbishop Lyam Tyrn's chief administrator for the Archbishopric of Emerald.

GRAIVYR, FATHER STYVYN—Bishop Ernyst's intendant, Ferayd, Delferahk.

GRAND VICAR EREK XVII—secular and temporal head of the Church of God Awaiting.

GRAY HARBOR, EARL OF—*see* Rayjhis Yowance.

GRAY HILL, BARON OF—*see* Byrtrym Mahldyn.

GREEN MOUNTAIN, BARON OF—*see* Mahrak Sandyrs.

GREEN VALLEY, BARON OF—*see* General Kynt Clareyk.

GREENHILL, TYMAHN—King Haarahld VII's senior huntsman.

GUYSHAIN, FATHER BAHRNAI—Vicar Zahmsyn Trynair's senior aide.

GYLLMYN, COLONEL RAHSKHO, REPUBLIC OF SIDDARMARK ARMY—General Kydryc Fyguera's second-in-command, Thesmar, the South March Lands.

GYRARD, CAPTAIN ANDRAI, ROYAL CHARISIAN NAVY—CO, HMS *Empress of Charis*.

HAARPAR, SERGEANT GORJ, CHARISIAN ROYAL GUARD—one of King Haarahld VII's bodyguards.

HAHL, LIEUTENANT PAWAL, ROYAL DOHLARAN NAVY—second lieutenant, HMS *Chihiro*, 50.

HAHLCAHM, DOCTOR ZHER—member of the Royal College of Charis, specializing in biology and food preparation.

HAHLEK, FATHER SYMYN—Archbishop Klairmant's personal aide.

HAHLMAHN, PAWAL—King Haarahld VII's senior chamberlain.

HAHLMYN, FATHER MAHRAK—an upper-priest of the Church of God Awaiting; Bishop Executor Thomys Shylair's personal aide.

HAHLMYN, SAIRAIH—Sharleyan Ahrmahk's personal maid.

HAHLMYN, MIDSHIPMAN ZHORJ, IMPERIAL CHARISIAN NAVY—a signals midshipman aboard HMS *Darcos Sound*, 54.

HAHLTAR, ADMIRAL GENERAL SIR URWYN, IMPERIAL DESNAIRIAN NAVY—Baron Jahras; commanding officer, Imperial Desnairian Navy; Daivyn Bairaht's brother-in-law.

HAHLYND, FATHER MAHRAK—Bishop Executor Thomys Shylair's personal aide.

HAHLYND, ADMIRAL PAWAL, ROYAL DOHLARAN NAVY—Earl Thirsk's senior subordinate admiral and one of his most trusted officers.

HAHLYS, BISHOP GAHRMYN, ARMY OF GOD—CO, Chihiro Division (Bishop Militant Cahnyr Kaitswyrth's favored division).

HAHNDAIL, CORPORAL WAHLYS, IMPERIAL CHARISIAN MARINE CORPS—Marine section commander attached to Brigadier Taisyn's forces in Glacierheart.

HAHRAIMAHN, ZHAK—a Siddarmarkian industrialist and foundry owner.

HAHSKANS, DAILOHRS—Father Tymahn Hahskans' wife.

HAHSKANS, FATHER TYMAHN—a Reformist upper-priest of the Order of Bédard in Manchyr; senior priest, Saint Kathryn's Church.

HAHSKYN, LIEUTENANT AHNDRAI, CHARISIAN IMPERIAL GUARD—a Charisian officer assigned to Empress Sharleyan's initial guard detachment. Captain Gairaht's second-in-command.

HAHVAIR, COMMANDER FRANZ, IMPERIAL CHARISIAN NAVY—CO, schooner HMS *Mace*, 12.

HAIMLTAHN, BISHOP EXECUTOR WYLLYS—Archbishop Zhasyn Cahnyr's executive assistant in the Archbishopric of Glacierheart.

HAIMYN, BRIGADIER MAHRYS, ROYAL CHARISIAN MARINES—CO, 5th Brigade, RCMC.

HAINAI, COMMANDER FRAHNKLYN, IMPERIAL CHARISIAN NAVY—one of Sir Ahlfryd Hyndryk's senior assistants; Bureau of Ordnance's chief liaison with Ehdwyrd Howsmyn's and his artificers.

HAINE, FATHER FHRANKLYN—upper-priest of the order of Pasquale; the senior healer attached to Archbishop Zhasyn Cahnyr's relief expedition to Glacierheart province.

HAINREE, PAITRYK—a silversmith and Temple Loyalist agitator in Manchyr, Princedom of Corisande.

HALBROOK HOLLOW, DUCHESS OF—*see* Elahnah Waistyn.

HALBROOK HOLLOW, DUKE OF—*see* Byrtrym Waistyn and Sailys Waistyn.

HALCOM, BISHOP MYLZ—Temple Loyalist, Bishop of Margaret Bay.

HALMYN, ARCHBISHOP—*see* Halmyn Zahmsyn.

HAMPTYN, MAJOR KOLYN—Temple Loyalist ex-militia officer, Fort Darymahn, the South March Lands, Republic of Siddarmark.

HANTAI, WAISU—Waisu VI, Emperor of Harchong.

HANTH, COUNTESS OF—*see* Lady Mairah Lywkys Breygart.

HANTH, EARL OF—*see* Sir Hauwerd Breygart; *see also* Tahdayo Mahntayl.

HARMYN, MAJOR BAHRKLY, EMERALD ARMY—an Emeraldian Army officer assigned to North Bay.

HARPAHR, BISHOP KORNYLYS—Bishop of the Order of Chihiro; Admiral General of the Navy of God.

HARRISON, MATTHEW PAUL—Timothy and Sarah Harrison's great-grandson.

HARRISON, ROBERT—Timothy and Sarah Harrison's grandson; Matthew Paul Harrison's father.

HARRISON, SARAH—wife of Timothy Harrison and an Eve.

HARRISON, TIMOTHY—Mayor of Lakeview and an Adam.

HARYS, FATHER AHLBYRT—Vicar Zahmsyn Trynair's special representative to Dohlar.

HARYS, COLONEL WYNTAHN, IMPERIAL CHARISIAN MARINE CORPS—senior officer in command, Marines detailed to support Captain Halcom Bahrns' operation.

HARYS, CAPTAIN ZHOEL, ROYAL CORISANDIAN NAVY—CO, galleon *Wing*; responsible for transporting Princess Irys and Prince Daivyn to safety from Corisande.

HASKYN, MIDSHIPMAN YAHNCEE, ROYAL DOHLARAN NAVY—a midshipman aboard *Gorath Bay*.

HAUWYL, SHAIN—Duke of Salthar; CO, Royal Dohlaran Army.

HAUWYRD, ZHORZH—Earl Gray Harbor's personal guardsman.

HENDERSON, LIEUTENANT GABRIELA ("GABBY"), TFN—tactical officer, TFNS *Swiftsure*.

HILLKEEPER, WAHLYS—Earl of Craggy Hill; a member of Prince Daivyn's Regency Council; also a senior member of the Northern Conspiracy.

HOLDYN, VICAR LYWYS—a member of Samyl Wylsynn's Zionist circle of Reformists.

HOTCHKYS, CAPTAIN SIR OHWYN, ROYAL CHARISIAN NAVY—CO, HMS *Tellesberg*.

HOWSMYN, EHDWYRD—"the Ironmaster of Charis"; the wealthiest and most innovative Old Charisian industrialist.

HOWSMYN, ZHAIN—Ehdwyrd Howsmyn's wife.

HUNTYR, LIEUTENANT KLEMYNT, CHARISIAN ROYAL GUARD—an officer of the Charisian Royal Guard in Tellesberg.

HUNTYR, ZOSH—Ehdwyrd Howsmyn's master artificer.

HWYSTYN, SIR VYRNYN—a member of the Charisian Parliament elected from Tellesberg.

HYLDYR, COLONEL FRAIHMAN, REPUBLIC OF SIDDARMARK ARMY—CO, 123rd Infantry Regiment, Republic of Siddarmark Army, a part of General Trumyn Stohnar's Sylmahn Gap command.

HYLLAIR, SIR FARAHK—Baron of Dairwyn.

HYLMAHN, RAHZHYR—Earl of Thairnos, a relatively new addition to Prince Daivyn's Regency Council in Corisande.

HYLMYN, LIEUTENANT MAINYRD, IMPERIAL CHARISIAN NAVY—senior engineer, HMS *Saygin*, 22.

HYNDRYK, ADMIRAL SIR AHLFRYD, IMPERIAL CHARISIAN NAVY—Baron Seamount, CO, Bureau of Ordnance.

HYNDYRS, DUNKYN—purser, privateer galleon *Raptor*.

HYNTYN, SIR DYNZAYL—Earl of Saint Howan; chancellor of the treasury, Kingdom of Chisholm.

HYRST, ADMIRAL ZOHZEF, CHISHOLMIAN NAVY—Earl Sharpfield's second-in-command.

HYSIN, VICAR CHIYAN—a member of Samyl Wylsynn's Zionist circle of Reformists.

HYWSTYN, LORD AVRAHM—a cousin of Greyghor Stohnar, and a midranking official assigned to the Siddarmarkian foreign ministry.

HYWYT, ADMIRAL PAITRYK, ROYAL CHARISIAN NAVY—CO, HMS *Wave*, 14 (schooner); later promoted to captain as CO, HMS *Dancer*, 56; later promoted to commodore; CO of squadron escorting Empress Sharleyan to Zebediah and Corisande; later promoted admiral as CO, Charisian naval forces, Gulf of Mathyas; he is specifically assigned to support Sir Hauwerd Breygart's operations ashore.

IBBET, AHSTELL—a blacksmith convicted of treason as part of the Northern Conspiracy in Corisande.

ILLIAN, CAPTAIN AHNTAHN—one of Sir Phylyp Myllyr's company commanders.

IRONHILL, BARON OF—*see* Ahlvyno Pawalsyn.

IRYS, PRINCESS—*see* Irys Daykyn.

JAHRAS, BARON OF—*see* Admiral General Sir Urwyn Hahltar.

JYNKYN, COLONEL HAUWYRD, ROYAL CHARISIAN MARINES—Admiral Staynair's senior Marine commander.

JYNKYNS, BISHOP ERNYST—Bishop of Ferayd.

KAHBRYLLO, CAPTAIN AHNTAHN, IMPERIAL CHARISIAN NAVY—CO, HMS *Dawn Star*, 58, Empress Sharleyan's transport to Zebediah and Corisande.

KAHMPTMYN, MAJOR HAHLYND, IMPERIAL CHARISIAN ARMY—XO, 4th Regiment, Imperial Charisian Army.

KAHNKLYN, AIDRYN—Tairys Kahnklyn's older daughter. Rahzhyr Mahklyn's older granddaughter and oldest grandchild.

KAHNKLYN, AIZAK—Rahzhyr Mahklyn's son-in-law; senior librarian, Royal College of Charis.

KAHNKLYN, ERAYK—Tairys Kahnklyn's oldest son; Rahzhyr Mahklyn's older grandson.

KAHNKLYN, EYDYTH—Tairys Kahnklyn's younger daughter; Rahzhyr Mahklyn's younger granddaughter; twin sister of Zhoel Kahnklyn.

KAHNKLYN, HAARAHLD—Tairys Kahnklyn's middle son. Rahzhyr Mahklyn's middle grandson.

KAHNKLYN, TAIRYS—Rahzhyr Mahklyn's married daughter; a senior librarian with the Royal College of Charis.

KAHNKLYN, ZHOEL—Tairys Kahnklyn's youngest son. Rahzhyr Mahklyn's youngest grandson; twin brother of Eydyth Mahklyn.

KAHRNAIKYS, MAJOR ZHAPHAR, TEMPLE GUARD—an officer of the Temple Guard and a Schuelerite.

KAILLEE, CAPTAIN ZHILBERT, TAROTISIAN NAVY—CO, galley *King Gorjah II.*

KAILLYT, KAIL—Major Borys Sahdlyr's second-in-command in Siddar City.

KAIREE, TRAIVYR—a wealthy merchant and landowner in the Earldom of Styvyn, Kingdom of Charis.

KAIRMYN, CAPTAIN TOMHYS, ROYAL DELFERAHKAN ARMY—one of Sir Vyk Lakyr's officers.

KAITS, CAPTAIN BAHRNABAI, IMPERIAL CHARISIAN MARINES—CO, Marine detachment, HMS *Squall*, 36.

KAITSWYRTH, BISHOP MILITANT CAHNYR, ARMY OF GOD—a Chihirite of the Order of the Sword and ex-Temple Guard officer; CO, western column of the Army of God, invading the Republic of Siddarmark through Westmarch Province.

KARMAIKEL, COMMANDER WAHLTAYR, IMPERIAL CHARISIAN NAVY—CO of one of Hauwerd Breygart's Navy "battalions" at Thesmar.

KARSTAYRS, SERGEANT THOMYS, ARMY OF GOD—regiment command sergeant, 191st Cavalry regiment.

KEELHAUL—High Admiral Lock Island's rottweiler; later Baron Seamount's.

KESTAIR, AHRDYN—Archbishop Maikel's married daughter.

KESTAIR, SIR LAIRYNC—Archbishop Maikel's son-in-law.

KHAILEE, MASTER ROLF—a pseudonym used by Lord Avrahm Hywstyn.

KHALRYN, FATHER FAILYX—Schuelerite upper-priest and inquisitor sent by

Zhaspahr Clyntahn and Wyllym Rayno to support and lead the insurrection in Hildermoss Province.

KHAPAHR, COMMANDER AHLVYN, ROYAL DOHLARAN NAVY—effectively, the Earl of Thirsk's chief of staff.

KHARMYCH, FATHER AHBSAHLAHN—an upper-priest of the Order of Schueler and Archbishop Trumahn Rowzvel's intendant.

KHATTYR, CAPTAIN PAYT, EMERALD NAVY—CO, galley *Black Prince*.

KHLUNAI, COLONEL RHANDYL, IMPERIAL CHARISIAN ARMY—General Ahlyn Symkyn's chief of staff.

KHOLMAN, DUKE OF—*see* Daivyn Bairaht.

KHOWSAN, CAPTAIN OF WINDS SHOUKHAN, IMPERIAL HARCHONGESE NAVY—Count of Wind Mountain, CO, IHNS *Flower of Waters*, 50; flag captain to the Duke of Sun Rising.

KING GORJAH III—*see* Gorjah Nyou.

KING HAARAHLD VII—*see* Haarahld Ahrmahk.

KING RAHNYLD IV—*see* Rahnyld Bahrns.

KING ZHAMES II—*see* Zhames Olyvyr Rayno

KLAHRKSAIN, CAPTAIN TYMAHN, IMPERIAL CHARISIAN NAVY—CO, HMS *Talisman*, 54.

KLAIRYNCE, CAPTAIN HAINREE, REPUBLIC OF SIDDARMARK ARMY—acting CO, 3rd Company, 37th Infantry Regiment, Republic of Siddarmark Army.

KNOWLES, EVELYN—an Eve who escaped the destruction of the Alexandria Enclave by being sent by Shan-wei to Tellesberg.

KNOWLES, JEREMIAH—an Adam who escaped the destruction of the Alexandria Enclave by being sent by Shan-wei to Tellesberg, where he became the patron saint of the Brethren of Saint Zherneau.

KOHRBY, MIDSHIPMAN LYNAIL, ROYAL CHARISIAN NAVY—senior midshipman, HMS *Dreadnought*.

KRAHL, CAPTAIN AHNDAIR, ROYAL DOHLARAN NAVY—CO, HMS *Bédard*, 42.

KRUGAIR, CAPTAIN MAIKEL, IMPERIAL CHARISIAN NAVY—CO, HMS *Avalanche*, 36; POW of Earl Thirsk, surrendered to the Inquisition.

KRUGHAIR, LIEUTENANT ZHASYN, IMPERIAL CHARISIAN NAVY—second lieutenant, HMS *Dancer*, 56.

KULMYN, RHOBAIR, CANAL SERVICE—pump master, Fairkyn, New Northland Province, Republic of Siddarmark.

KWAYLE, TYMYTHY, IMPERIAL CHARISIAN NAVY—chief petty officer and boatswain's mate, HMS *Destiny*, 54.

KWILL, FATHER ZYTAN—upper-priest of the Order of Bédard; abbot of the Hospice of the Holy Bédard, the main homeless shelter in the city of Zion.

KYRST, OWAIN—Temple Loyalist mayor of Fairkyn, New Northland Province, Republic of Siddarmark.

LACHLYN, COLONEL TAYLAR, ARMY OF GOD—upper-priest of the Order of Langhorne; Bishop Gahrmyn's senior regimental commander, Chihiro Division.

LAHANG, BRAIDEE—Prince Nahrmahn of Emerald's chief agent in Charis before Merlin Athrawes' arrival there.

LAHFAT, CAPTAIN MYRGYN—piratical ruler of Claw Keep on Claw Island.

LAHFTYN, MAJOR BRYAHN—Brigadier Clareyk's chief of staff.

LAHMBAIR, PARSAIVAHL—a prominent Corisandian greengrocer convicted of treason as part of the Northern Conspiracy and pardoned by Empress Sharleyan.

LAHRAK, NAILYS—a senior leader of the Temple Loyalists in Charis.

LAHSAHL, LIEUTENANT SHAIRMYN, IMPERIAL CHARISIAN NAVY—XO, HMS *Destroyer*, 54.

LAICHARN, ARCHBISHOP PRAIDWYN—ex-Archbishop of Siddar; the ranking prelate of the Republic of Siddarmark; a Langhornite and Temple Loyalist.

LAIMHYN, FATHER CLYFYRD—Emperor Cayleb's personal secretary, assigned to him by Archbishop Maikel.

LAINYR, BISHOP EXECUTOR WYLSYNN—Bishop Executor of Gorath; a Langhornite.

LAIRAYS, FATHER AWBRAI—under-priest of the Order of Schueler; HMS *Archangel Chihiro*'s ship's chaplain.

LAIRMAHN, FAHSTAIR—Baron of Lakeland; first councilor of the Kingdom of Delferahk.

LAITEE, FATHER ZHAMES—priest of the Order of Schueler; assistant to Father Gaisbyrt Vandaik in Talkyra.

LAITYR, FATHER ZHAIF—a Reformist upper-priest of the Order of Pasquale; senior priest, Church of the Holy Archangels Triumphant; a close personal friend of Father Tymahn Hahskans.

LAKE LAND, DUKE OF—*see* Paitryk Mahknee.

LAKYR, SIR VYK—SO, Ferayd garrison, Kingdom of Delferahk.

LANGHORNE, ERIC—chief administrator, Operation Ark.

LARCHROS, BARON OF—*see* Rahzhyr Mairwyn.

LARCHROS, BARONESS OF—*see* Raichenda Mairwyn.

LATHYK, CAPTAIN RHOBAIR, IMPERIAL CHARISIAN NAVY—CO, HMS *Destiny*, 54; Sir Dunkyn Yairley's flag captain.

LAYBRAHN, BAHRYND—Paitryk Hainree's alias.

LAYN, MAJOR ZHIM, ROYAL CHARISIAN MARINES—Brigadier Kynt's subordinate for original syllabus development; now the senior training officer, Helen Island Marine Base.

LEKTOR, ADMIRAL SIR TARYL—Earl of Tartarian; CO, Royal Corisandian Navy under Prince Hektor during Corisande Campaign; Earl Anvil Rock's main ally since Hektor's death, another member of Prince Daivyn's Regency Council.

LESKYR, BYNNO—Temple Loyalist Mayor of Ohlarn, New Northland Province, Republic of Siddarmark.

LOCK ISLAND, EARL OF—*see* High Admiral Bryahn Lock Island.

LOCK ISLAND, HIGH ADMIRAL BRYAHN, IMPERIAL CHARISIAN NAVY—Earl of Lock Island; CO, Imperial Charisian Navy. Cayleb Ahrmahk's cousin.

LOHGYN, MAHRAK—a Temple Loyalist mountain clansman from the Gray Wall Mountains; one of Zhan Fyrmahn's cousins.

LORD PROTECTOR GREYGHOR—*see* Lord Protector Greyghor Stohnar.

LYAM, ARCHBISHOP—*see* Archbishop Lyam Tyrn.

LYBYRN, FATHER GHATFRYD—Schuelerite under-priest; senior clergyman, Ohlarn, New Northland Province, Republic of Siddarmark.

LYCAHN, PRIVATE ZHEDRYK, IMPERIAL CHARISIAN MARINE CORPS—a Marine private in Brigadier Taisyn's forces in Glacierheart; ex-poacher and thief.

LYNDAHR, SIR RAIMYND—Prince Hektor of Corisande's keeper of the purse; he serves Prince Daivyn's Regency Council in the same capacity; an ally of Earl Anvil Rock and Earl Tartarian.

LYNKYN, SIR ADULFO—Duke of Black Water; son of Sir Ernyst Lynkyn, killed at the Battle of Darcos Sound.

LYNKYN, ADMIRAL ERNYST, CORISANDIAN NAVY—Duke of Black Water; CO, Corisandian Navy; KIA, Battle of Darcos Sound.

LYNKYN, ARCHBISHOP ULYS—second Archbishop of Chisholm for the Church of Charis, replacing the murdered Archbishop Pawal Braynair.

LYWKYS, LADY MAIRAH—Maiden name of Empress Sharleyan's chief lady-in-waiting; Baron Green Mountain's cousin; later marries Sir Hauwerd Breygart, Earl of Hanth.

LYWSHAI, SHAINTAI—Trumyn Lywshai's Harchong-born father.

LYWSHAI, TRUMYN—Sir Dunkyn Yairley's secretary and clerk.

LYWYS, DR. SAHNDRAH—faculty member, Royal College, Tellesberg, specializing in chemistry.

MAHGAIL, LIEUTENANT BRYNDYN, IMPERIAL CHARISIAN MARINES—senior Marine officer assigned to Sarm River operation.

MAHGAIL, CAPTAIN BYRT, DELFERAHKAN ROYAL GUARD—a company commander in King Zhames' palace detachment.

MAHGAIL, MASTER GARAM, IMPERIAL CHARISIAN NAVY—carpenter, HMS *Destiny*, 54.

MAHGAIL, CAPTAIN RAIF, IMPERIAL CHARISIAN NAVY—CO, HMS *Dancer*, 56. Sir Gwylym Manthyr's flag captain.

MAHGENTEE, MIDSHIPMAN MAHRAK, ROYAL CHARISIAN NAVY—senior midshipman, HMS *Typhoon*.

MAHGYRS, COLONEL ALLAYN, REPUBLIC OF SIDDARMARK ARMY—General Fronz Tylmahn's senior Siddarmarkian subordinate in support of Captain Halcom Bahrns' operation.

MAHKELYN, LIEUTENANT RHOBAIR, ROYAL CHARISIAN NAVY—fourth lieutenant, HMS *Destiny*, 54.

MAHKHOM, WAHLYS—Glacierheart trapper turned guerrilla; leader of the Reformist forces in the Gray Wall Mountains.

MAHKHYNROH, BISHOP KAISI—Bishop of Manchyr for the Church of Charis; an Old Charisian sent out by Archbishop Maikel to fill that see.

MAHKLYN, AHNGAZ—Sir Domynyk Staynair's valet.

MAHKLYN, DR. RAHZHYR—Chancellor of the Royal College of Charis, Chairman, Imperial Council of Inquiry, and a senior member of the inner circle.

MAHKLYN, TOHMYS—Rahzhyr Mahklyn's unmarried son; a merchant marine captain.

MAHKLYN, YSBET—Rahzhyr Mahklyn's deceased wife.

MAHKNASH, SERGEANT BRAICE, ROYAL DELFERAHKAN ARMY—one of Colonel Aiphraim Tahlyvyr's squad leaders.

MAHKNEE, PAITRYK—Duke of Lake Land.

MAHKNEE, SYMYN—Paitryk Mahknee's uncle.

MAHKNEEL, CAPTAIN HAUWYRD, ROYAL DELFERAHKAN NAVY—CO, galley *Arrowhead*.

MAHKYNTY, MAJOR AHRNAHLD, REPUBLIC OF SIDDARMARK ARMY—CO, 4th Company, 37th Infantry Regiment, Republic of Siddarmark Army.

MAHLDAN, BROTHER STAHN—a Reformist sexton in Siddar City; Order of the Quill.

MAHLDYN, BYRTRYM—Baron Gray Hill; replacement on Prince Daivyn's Regency Council in Corisande for the Earl of Craggy Hill after Craggy Hill's execution for treason for his part in the northern conspiracy.

MAHLDYN, COLONEL PHYLYP, REPUBLIC OF SIDDARMARK ARMY—CO, 110th Infantry Regiment, Republic of Siddarmark Army; acting CO, Fort Sheldyn, South March Lands.

MAHLDYN, LIEUTENANT ZHAMES, IMPERIAL CHARISIAN NAVY—XO, HMS *Squall*, 36.

MAHLRY, LIEUTENANT RHOLYND, EMERALD NAVY—a lieutenant aboard galley *Black Prince*.

MAHLYK, STYWYRT, IMPERIAL CHARISIAN NAVY—Sir Dunkyn Yairley's personal coxswain.

MAHNDRAYN, COMMANDER URVYN, IMPERIAL CHARISIAN NAVY—CO, Experimental Board; Commodore Seamount's senior assistant.

MAHNDYR, EARL—*see* Gharth Rahlstahn.

MAHNTAIN, CAPTAIN TOHMYS, IMPERIAL DESNAIRIAN NAVY—CO, HMS *Blessed Warrior*, 40.

MAHNTAYL, TAHDAYO—usurper Earl of Hanth.

MAHNTEE, LIEUTENANT CHARLZ, ROYAL DOHLARAN NAVY—XO, HMS *Rakurai*, 46.

MAHNTYN, CORPORAL AILAS—a scout-sniper assigned to Sergeant Edvarhd Wystahn's platoon.

MAHRAK, LIEUTENANT RAHNALD, ROYAL CHARISIAN NAVY—first lieutenant, HMS *Royal Charis*.

MAHRLOW, BISHOP EXECUTOR AHRAIN—Archbishop Halmyn Zahmsyn's assistant, Archbishopric of Gorath, Kingdom of Dohlar.

MAHRLOW, FATHER ARTHYR—priest of the Order of Schueler; assistant to Father Gaisbyrt Vandaik in Talkyra.

MAHRTYN, ADMIRAL GAHVYN, ROYAL TAROTISIAN NAVY—Baron of White Ford; senior officer, Royal Tarotisian Navy.

MAHRTYNSYN, LIEUTENANT LAIZAIR, IMPERIAL DESNAIRIAN NAVY—XO, HMS *Archangel Chihiro*, 40.

MAHRYS, ZHAK "ZHAKKY"—a member of Prince Daivyn Daykyn's royal guard in exile; Tobys Raimair's junior noncom.

MAHRYS, ZHERYLD—Sir Rayjhis Dragoner's senior secretary and aide.

MAHZYNGAIL, LIEUTENANT HAARLAHM, IMPERIAL CHARISIAN NAVY—Sir Domynyk Staynair's new flag lieutenant (896).

MAHZYNGAIL, COLONEL VYKTYR—CO, 14th South March Militia Regiment, Fort Sheldyn, South March Lands.

MAIB, MAJOR EDMYND, ARMY OF GOD—CO, Twentieth Artillery Regiment, senior officer present, Ohlarn, New Northland Province, Republic of Siddarmark.

MAIDYN, LORD HENRAI—Chancellor of the Exchequer, Republic of Siddarmark.

MAIGEE, CAPTAIN GRAYGAIR, ROYAL DOHLARAN NAVY—CO, galleon *Guardian*.

MAIGEE, PLATOON SERGEANT ZHAK, IMPERIAL CHARISIAN MARINES—senior noncom, 2nd Platoon, Alpha Company, 1st/3rd Marines, ICMC.

MAIGOWHYN, LIEUTENANT BRAHNDYN, ROYAL DELFERAHKAN ARMY—Colonel Aiphraim Tahlyvyr's aide.

MAIGWAIR, VICAR ALLAYN—Captain General of the Church of God Awaiting; one of the so-called Group of Four.

MAIGWAIR, CORPORAL STAHNYZLAHAS—Temple Loyalist rebel, garrison of Fort Darymahn, the South March Lands, Republic of Siddarmark.

MAIK, BISHOP STAIPHAN—Schuelerite auxiliary bishop of the Church of God Awaiting; Earl Thirsk's special intendant; effectively intendant for the Royal Dohlaran Navy in the Church's name.

MAIKEL, CAPTAIN QWENTYN, ROYAL DOHLARAN NAVY—CO, galley *Gorath Bay*.

MAIKELSYN, LIEUTENANT LEEAHM, ROYAL TAROTISIAN NAVY—first lieutenant, *King Gorjah II*.

MAIKSYN, COLONEL LYWYS—rebel Temple Loyalist CO, 3rd Saiknyr Militia Regiment.

MAIRNAIR, LIEUTENANT TOBYS, IMPERIAL CHARISIAN NAVY—XO, HMS *Hador*, 22.

MAIRWYN, RAHZHYR—Baron of Larchros; a member of the Northern Conspiracy in Corisande.

MAIRWYN, RAICHENDA—Baroness of Larchros; wife of Rahzhyr Mairwyn.

MAIRYAI, COLONEL SPYNCYR, ARMY OF GOD—CO, 2nd Regiment, Langhorne Division.

MAIRYDYTH, LIEUTENANT NEVYL, ROYAL DOHLARAN NAVY—first lieutenant, galley *Royal Bédard*.

MAITLYND, CAPTAIN ZHORJ, IMPERIAL CHARISIAN NAVY—CO, HMS *Victorious*, 56.

MAITZLYR, CAPTAIN FAIDOHRAV, IMPERIAL DESNAIRIAN NAVY—CO, HMS *Loyal Defender*, 48.

MAIYR, CAPTAIN ZHAKSYN—one of Colonel Sir Wahlys Zhorj's troop commanders in Tahdayo Mahntayl's service.

MAIZUR, KHANSTANC—Archbishop Maikel Staynair's cook.

MAKAIVYR, BRIGADIER ZHOSH, ROYAL CHARISIAN MARINES—CO, 1st Brigade, RCMC.

MAKFERZAHN, ZHAMES—one of Prince Hektor's agents in Charis.

MAKGREGAIR, FATHER ZHOSHUA—Vicar Zahmsyn Trynair's special representative to Tarot.

MALIKAI, DUKE OF—*see* Faidel Ahlverez.

MALKAIHY, COMMANDER DAHRAIL, IMPERIAL CHARISIAN NAVY—Captain Ahldahs Rahzwail's senior assistant; senior liaison between the Bureau of Ordnance and Sir Dustyn Olyvyr; slated to officially command Bureau of Engineering when it is formally organized.

MANTHYR, ADMIRAL SIR GWYLYM, IMPERIAL CHARISIAN NAVY—Cayleb Ahrmahk's flag captain at battles of Crag Hook, Rock Point, and Darcos Sound; later admiral; CO, Charisian expedition to Gulf of Dohlar; senior Charisian POW surrendered to Inquisition by Kingdom of Dohlar.

MARDHAR, COLONEL ZHANDRU, ARMY OF GOD—CO, 191st Cavalry Regiment.

MARGO, DUKE OF—*see* Sir Bairmon Chahlmair.

MARSHYL, MIDSHIPMAN ADYM, ROYAL CHARISIAN NAVY—senior midshipman, HMS *Royal Charis*.

MATHYSYN, LIEUTENANT ZHAIKEB, ROYAL DOHLARAN NAVY—first lieutenant, galley *Gorath Bay.*

MATTHYSAHN, PETTY OFFICER AHBUKYRA, IMPERIAL CHARISIAN NAVY—signalman, HMS *Delthak*, 22.

MAYLYR, CAPTAIN DUNKYN, ROYAL CHARISIAN NAVY—CO, HMS *Halberd.*

MAYSAHN, ZHASPAHR—Prince Hektor's senior agent in Charis.

MAYTHIS, LIEUTENANT FRAIZHER, ROYAL CORISANDIAN NAVY—true name of Captain Wahltayr Seatown.

METZLYR, FATHER PAIRAIK—an upper-priest of Schueler; General Sir Fahstyr Rychtyr's special intendant.

MHARDYR, SYLVYST—Baron Stoneheart; current Lord Justice of Chisholm, replacing Braisyn Byrns.

MHARTYN, MAJOR ABSHAIR, IMPERIAL CHARISIAN ARMY—CO, 3rd Battalion, 4th Regiment, Imperial Charisian Army.

MHARTYN, MAJOR LAIRAYS, IMPERIAL CHARISIAN MARINE CORPS—Hauwerd Breygart's junior Marine battalion commander at Thesmar.

MHATTSYN, PETTY OFFICER LAISL, IMPERIAL CHARISIAN NAVY—a gun captain in Lieutenant Yerek Sahbrahan's battery under Commander Hainz Watyrs in Glacierheart Province.

MHULVAYN, OSKAHR—one of Prince Hektor's agents in Charis.

MULLYGYN, RAHSKHO—a member of Prince Daivyn Daykyn's royal guard in exile; Tobys Raimair's second-ranking noncom.

MYCHAIL, ALYX—Rhaiyan Mychail's oldest grandson.

MYCHAIL, MYLDRYD—one of Rhaiyan Mychail's married granddaughters-in-law.

MYCHAIL, RHAIYAN—a business partner of Ehdwyrd Howsmyn and the Kingdom of Charis' primary textile producer.

MYCHAIL, STYVYN—Myldryd Mychail's youngest son.

MYKLAYN, ZHAIMYS, CANAL SERVICE—a senior canal pilot of the Siddarmarkian Canal Service assigned to assist Captain Halcom Bahrns.

MYLLYR, ARCHBISHOP URVYN—Archbishop of Sodar.

MYLLYR, SIR PHYLYP—one of Sir Koryn Gahrvai's regimental commanders, Corisande Campaign.

MYLS, BRIGADIER GWYAHN, IMPERIAL CHARISIAN MARINES—CO, 2nd Regiment, 3rd Brigade, ICMC.

MYRGYN, SIR KEHVYN, ROYAL CORISANDIAN NAVY—CO, galley *Corisande.* Duke Black Water's flag captain. KIA, Battle of Darcos Sound.

NAHRMAHN, LIEUTENANT FRONZ, IMPERIAL CHARISIAN NAVY—second lieutenant, HMS *Destiny*, 54.

NAIGAIL, SAMYL—son of a deceased Siddarmarkian sailmaker; Temple Loyalist and anti-Charisian bigot.

NAIKLOS, CAPTAIN FRAHNKLYN, CORISANDIAN GUARD—CO of Sir Koryn Gahrvai's headquarters company; later promoted to major.

NARTH, BISHOP EXECUTOR TYRNYR—Archbishop Failyx Gahrbor's executive assistant, Archbishopric of Tarot.

NAVYZ, WYLFRYD—Siddarmarkian Temple Loyalist guide attached to General Sir Fahstyr Rychtyr's Dohlaran invasion column.

NETHAUL, HAIRYM—XO, privateer schooner *Blade*.

NOHRCROSS, BISHOP MAILVYN—Bishop of Barcor for the Church of Charis; a member of the Northern Conspiracy in Corisande.

NORTH COAST, EARL OF—*see* Edwair Garthin.

NYBAR, BISHOP GORTHYK, ARMY OF GOD—CO, Langhorne Division; Bishop Militant Bahrnabai Wyrshym's senior division commander.

NYLZ, ADMIRAL KOHDY, IMPERIAL CHARISIAN NAVY—senior squadron commander, ICN; previously commodore, Royal Charisian Navy.

NYOU, GORJAH ALYKSAHNDAR—King Gorjah III, King of Tarot.

NYOU, MAIYL—Queen Consort of Tarot; wife of Gorjah Nyou.

NYOU, PRINCE RHOLYND—Crown Prince of Tarot; infant son of Gorjah and Maiyl Nyou; heir to the Tarotisian throne.

NYXYN, DAIVYN, ROYAL DELFERAHKAN ARMY—a dragoon assigned to Sergeant Braice Mahknash's squad.

OARMASTER, SYGMAHN, ROYAL CHARISIAN MARINES—a member of Crown Prince Cayleb's bodyguard.

OHLSYN, TRAHVYS—Earl Pine Hollow, Prince Nahrmahn Baytz' cousin; first councilor of Emerald; later first councilor of the Charisian Empire.

OLYVYR, AHNYET—Sir Dustyn Olyvyr's wife.

OLYVYR, SIR DUSTYN—a leading Tellesberg ship designer; chief constructor and designer, Imperial Charisian Navy.

OWL—Nimue Alban's AI, based on the manufacturer's acronym: Ordoñes-Westinghouse-Lytton RAPIER Tactical Computer, Mark 17a.

PAHLMAHN, ZHULYIS—a Corisandian banker convicted of treason as part of the Northern Conspiracy.

PAHLZAR, COLONEL AHKYLLYS—Sir Charlz Doyal's replacement as Sir Koryn Gahrvai's senior artillery commander.

PAHRAIHA, COLONEL VAHSAG, IMPERIAL CHARISIAN MARINES—CO, 14th Marine Regiment.

PAHRSAHN, AIVAH—Nynian Rychtair's public persona in the Republic of Siddarmark.

PAHSKAL, MASTER MIDSHIPMAN FAYDOHR, IMPERIAL CHARISIAN NAVY—a midshipman assigned to HMS *Dawn Star*, 58.

PAHTKOVAIR, FATHER ZOHANNES—Intendant of Siddar. A Schuelerite.

PARKAIR, ADYM—Weslai Parkair's eldest son and heir.

PARKAIR, LORD DARYUS—seneschal, Republic of Siddarmark.

PARKAIR, WESLAI—Lord Shairncross; Lord of Clan Shairncross and head of the Council of Clan Lords, Raven's Land.

PARKAIR, ZHAIN—Lady Shairncross, Weslai Parkair's wife.

PARKAIR, ZHANAIAH—Daryus Parkair's wife.

PARKYR, COMMANDER AHRTHYR, IMPERIAL CHARISIAN NAVY—Hauwerd Breygart's senior Navy artillerist at Thesmar.

PARKYR, FATHER EDWYRD—upper-priest of the Order of Bédard; named by Archbishop Klairmant to succeed Father Tymahn at Saint Kathryn's Church.

PARKYR, GLAHDYS—Crown Princess Alahnah's Chisholmian wet nurse and nanny.

PAWAL, CAPTAIN ZHON, IMPERIAL CHARISIAN NAVY—CO, HMS *Dart*, 54.

PAWALSYN, AHLVYNO—Baron Ironhill, keeper of the purse (treasurer) of the Kingdom of Old Charis and treasurer of the Charisian Empire.

PEI, KAU-YUNG, COMMODORE, TFN—CO, Operation Ark final escort; husband of Dr. Pei Shan-wei.

PEI, KAU-ZHI, ADMIRAL, TFN—CO, Operation Breakaway; older brother of Commodore Pei Kau-yung.

PEI, SHAN-WEI, PH.D.—Commodore Pei Kau-yung's wife; senior terraforming expert for Operation Ark.

PEZKYVYR, MAJOR AHNDRAI, ARMY OF GOD—XO, 191st Cavalry regiment.

PHALGRAIN, SIR HARVAI—majordomo, Imperial Palace, Cherayth.

PHANDYS, MAJOR KHANSTAHNZO—an officer of the Temple Guard; promoted to major; CO of Vicar Rhobair Duchairn's personal security detachment.

PHONDA, AHNZHELYK—an alias of Nynian Rychtair; one of the most successful courtesans in the city of Zion; an agent and ally of Samyl Wylsynn.

PINE HOLLOW, EARL OF— *see* Trahvys Ohlsyn.

PLYZYK, CAPTAIN EHRNYSTO, IMPERIAL DESNAIRIAN NAVY—CO, HMS *Saint Adulfo*, 40.

PORTYR, COMMANDER DAIVYN, IMPERIAL CHARISIAN NAVY—CO of one of Hauwerd Breygart's Navy "battalions" at Thesmar.

POTTYR, MAJOR HAINREE, IMPERIAL CHARISIAN ARMY—CO, 4th Battalion, 4th Regiment, Imperial Charisian Army.

POWAIRS, COLONEL ALLAYN, IMPERIAL CHARISIAN ARMY—chief of staff, 2nd Brigade (reinforced), Charisian Expeditionary Force.

PRAIETO, LIEUTENANT ORLYNOH, ARMY OF GOD—CO, Battery B, 20th Artillery Regiment, Ohlarn, New Northland Province, Republic of Siddarmark.

PRAIGYR, STAHLMAN—one of Ehdwyrd Howsmyn's senior artificers, particularly involved with the development of steam engines.

PRINCE CAYLEB—*see* Cayleb Ahrmahk.

PRINCE DAIVYN—*see* Daivyn Daykyn.

PRINCE HEKTOR—*see* Hektor Daykyn.

PRINCE NAHRMAHN II—*see* Nahrmahn Baytz.

PRINCE NAHRMAHN GAREYT—*see* Nahrmahn Gareyt Baytz.

PRINCE RHOLYND—*see* Rholynd Nyou.

PRINCESS IRYS—*see* Irys Daykyn.

PROCTOR, ELIAS, PH.D.—a member of Pei Shan-wei's staff and a noted cyberneticist.

PRUAIT, COLONEL FHRANKLYN, REPUBLIC OF SIDDARMARK ARMY—CO, 76th Infantry Regiment, Republic of Siddarmark Army, a part of General Trumyn Stohnar's Sylmahn Gap command.

PRUAIT, CAPTAIN TYMYTHY, IMPERIAL CHARISIAN NAVY—newly captain of prize ship *Sword of God.*

PYGAIN, FATHER AVRY—Chihirite upper-priest of the Order of the Quill; Archbishop Arthyn Zagyrsk's secretary and aide.

QUEEN CONSORT HAILYN—*see* Hailyn Rayno.

QUEEN MAIYL—*see* Maiyl Nyou.

QUEEN SHARLEYAN—*see* Sharleyan Tayt.

QUEEN YSBELL—an earlier reigning queen of Chisholm who was deposed (and murdered) in favor of a male ruler.

QWENTYN, COMMODORE DONYRT, ROYAL CORISANDIAN NAVY—Baron of Tanlyr Keep, one of Duke of Black Water's squadron commanders.

QWENTYN, OWAIN—Tymahn Qwentyn's grandson.

QWENTYN, TYMAHN—head of the House of Qwentyn, a powerful banking and investment cartel in the Republic of Siddarmark.

RAHLSTAHN, ADMIRAL GHARTH, IMPERIAL CHARISIAN NAVY—Earl of Mahndyr, third-ranking officer, Imperial Charisian Navy; ex-Royal Emeraldian Navy.

RAHLSTYN, COMMODORE ERAYK, ROYAL DOHLARAN NAVY—one of Duke Malikai's squadron commanders.

RAHLSTYN, LIEUTENANT MHARTYN, ROYAL DOHLARAN NAVY—XO, HMS *Chihiro,* 50.

RAHSKAIL, AHNDRYA—Barkah and Rebkah Rahskail's youngest child.

RAHSKAIL, COLONEL BARKAH, IMPERIAL CHARISIAN ARMY—deceased Earl of Swayle.

RAHSKAIL, REBKAH—Dowager Countess of Swayle; widow of Barkah, mother of Wahlys.

RAHSKAIL, SAMYL—Wahlys Rahskail's younger brother.

RAHSKAIL, WAHLYS—current Earl of Swayle.

RAHZMAHN, LIEUTENANT DAHNYLD, IMPERIAL CHARISIAN NAVY—Sir Gwylym Manthyr's flag lieutenant.

RAHZWAIL, CAPTAIN AHLDAHS, IMPERIAL CHARISIAN NAVY—XO, Bureau of Ordnance; Sir Ahlfryd Hyndryk's chief assistant following Commander Urvyn Mahndrayn's death.

RAICE, BYNZHAMYN—Baron Wave Thunder; spymaster for King Haarahld Ahrmahk and later royal councilor for intelligence for Emperor Cayleb Ahrmahk in the Kingdom of Old Charis.

RAICE, LEAHYN—Baroness Wave Thunder; Bynzhamyn Raice's wife.

RAIGLY, SYLVYST—Sir Dunkyn Yairley's valet and steward.

RAIMAHN, BYRK—Old Charisian from a wealthy family; Claitahn and Sahmantha Raimahn's grandson; CO of the riflemen Aivah Pahrsahn provides to Archbishop Zhasyn Cahnyr to assist the Reformists of Glacierheart Province.

RAIMAHN, CLAITAHN—wealthy Charisian expatriate and Temple Loyalist living in Siddar City.

RAIMAHN, SAHMANTHA—Claitahn Raimahn's wife and also a Temple Loyalist.

RAIMAIR, TOBYS—ex-sergeant, Royal Corisandian Army; commander of Prince Daivyn and Princess Irys' unofficial guardsmen in Delferahk.

RAIMYND, SIR LYNDAHR—Prince Hektor of Corisande's treasurer.

RAISAHNDO, CAPTAIN CAITAHNO, ROYAL DOHLARAN NAVY—CO, HMS *Rakurai*, 46.

RAISLAIR, BISHOP EXECUTOR MHARTYN—Archbishop Ahdym Taibyr's executive assistant, Archbishopric of Desnair.

RAISMYN, LIEUTENANT BYRNHAR, IMPERIAL CHARISIAN MARINE CORPS—a lieutenant attached to Colonel Wyntahn Harys' Marines in support of Captain Halcom Bahrns' operation.

RAIYZ, FATHER CARLSYN—Queen Sharleyan's confessor.

RAIZYNGYR, COLONEL ARTTU, ROYAL CHARISIAN MARINES—CO, 2nd/3rd Marines (2nd Battalion, 3rd Brigade).

RAYNAIR, CAPTAIN EKOHLS—CO, privateer schooner *Blade*.

RAYNO, HAILYN—Queen Consort of the Kingdom of Delferahk; wife of King Zhames II; a cousin of Prince Hektor of Corisande.

RAYNO, ARCHBISHOP WYLLYM—Archbishop of Chiang-wu; adjutant of the Order of Schueler.

RAYNO, ZHAMES OLYVYR—King Zhames II of Delferahk. A kinsman by marriage of Irys and Daivyn Daykyn.

RAZHAIL, FATHER DERAHK—senior healer, Imperial Palace, Cherayth; upper-priest of the Order of Pasquale.

RHOBAIR, VICAR—*see* Rhobair Duchairn.

ROCK COAST, DUKE OF—*see* Zhasyn Seafarer.

ROCK POINT, BARON OF—*see* High Admiral Sir Domynyk Staynair.

ROHSAIL, CAPTAIN SIR DAHRAND, ROYAL DOHLARAN NAVY—CO, HMS *Grand Vicar Mahrys*, 50.

ROHZHYR, COLONEL BAHRTOL, ROYAL CHARISIAN MARINES—a senior commissary officer.

ROPEWALK, COLONEL AHDAM, CHARISIAN ROYAL GUARD—CO, Charisian Royal Guard.

ROWYN, CAPTAIN HORAHS—CO, Sir Dustyn Olyvyr's yacht *Ahnyet*.

ROWZVEL, ARCHBISHOP TRUMAHN—Archbishop of Gorath and senior prelate of the Kingdom of Dohlar; Order of Langhorne.

RUSTMAYN, EDMYND—Baron Stonekeep; King Gorjah III of Tarot's first councilor and spymaster.

RYCHTAIR, NYNIAN—Ahnzhelyk Phonda's birth name; adopted sister of Adorai Dynnys.

RYCHTYR, GENERAL SIR FAHSTYR, ROYAL DESNAIRIAN ARMY—CO of the vanguard of the Dohlaran army invading the Republic of Siddarmark.

RYDACH, FATHER ZHORDYN—Rebkah Rahskail's Temple Loyalist confessor; officially an under-priest (actually an upper-priest) of the Order of Chihiro.

RYNDYL, FATHER AHLUN—General Trumyn Stohnar's chaplain.

SAHBRAHAN, LIEUTENANT YEREK, IMPERIAL CHARISIAN NAVY—a naval battery commander serving under Commander Hainz Watyrs in Glacierheart Province.

SAHBRAHAN, PAIAIR—the Earl of Thirsk's personal valet.

SAHDLYR, LIEUTENANT BYNZHAMYN, ROYAL CHARISIAN NAVY—second lieutenant, HMS *Dreadnought*.

SAHDLYR, MAJOR BORYS, TEMPLE GUARD—a guardsman of the Inquisition assigned to Siddar City as part of the Sword of Schueler.

SAHLAVAHN, CAPTAIN TRAI—cousin of Commander Urwyn Mahndrayn; CO, Hairatha Powder Mill.

SAHLMYN, SERGEANT MAJOR HAIN, ROYAL CHARISIAN MARINES—Colonel Zhanstyn's battalion sergeant major.

SAHLYS, MAJOR GAHVYN, REPUBLIC OF SIDDARMARK ARMY—CO, 5th Company, 37th Infantry Regiment, Republic of Siddarmark Army.

SAHLYVAHN, LIEUTENANT DAHGLYS, REPUBLIC OF SIDDARMARK ARMY—General Trumyn Stohnar's aide.

SAHNDAHL, COLONEL FRAIMAHN, DELFERAHKAN ROYAL GUARD—XO, Delferahkan Royal Guard.

SAHNDHAIM, COLONEL STYWYRT, ARMY OF GOD—CO, 1st Regiment, Zion Division.

SAHNDYRS, GENERAL SIR LAIMYN, ROYAL DESNAIRIAN ARMY—Sir Rainos Ahlverez' senior field commander in the main body of the Dohlaran army invading the Republic of Siddarmark; effectively, Ahlverez' second-in-command.

SAHNDYRS, MAHRAK—Baron Green Mountain; ex-first councilor of

Chisholm, badly wounded and incapacitated by Zhaspahr Clyntahn's Rakurai terrorists.

SAHNDYRS, BISHOP STYWYRT—Bishop of Solomon, Princedom of Emerald.

SAHRKHO, FATHER MOHRYS—under-priest of the Order of Langhorne; Empress Sharleyan's confessor.

SAIGAHN, CAPTAIN MAHRDAI, ROYAL CHARISIAN NAVY—CO, HMS *Guardsman*, 44.

SAIGYL, COMMANDER TOMPSYN, IMPERIAL CHARISIAN NAVY—one of Sir Ahlfryd Hyndryk's senior assistants; Bureau of Ordnance's chief liaison with Sir Dustyn Olyvyr; slated to officially command Bureau of Ships when it is formally organized.

SAIKOR, BISHOP EXECUTOR BAIKYR—Archbishop Praidwyn Laicharn's bishop executor; a Pasqualate.

SAINT HOWAN, EARL OF—*see* Sir Dynzayl Hyntyn.

SAITHWYK, ARCHBISHOP FAIRMYN—Archbishop of Emerald for the Church of Charis.

SALTAIR, HAIRYET—Crown Princess Alahnah's Old Charisian nanny.

SALTHAR, DUKE OF—*see* Shain Hauwyl.

SARFORTH, COMMANDER QWENTYN, IMPERIAL CHARISIAN NAVY—senior officer in command, Brankyr Bay, Kingdom of Tarot.

SARMAC, JENNIFER—an Eve who escaped the destruction of the Alexandria Enclave and fled to Tellesberg.

SARMAC, KALEB—an Adam who escaped the destruction of the Alexandria Enclave and fled to Tellesberg.

SARMOUTH, BARON OF—*see* Sir Dunkyn Yairley.

SAWAL, FATHER RAHSS—an under-priest of the Order of Chihiro; the skipper of one of the Temple's courier boats.

SAWYAIR, SISTER FRAHNCYS—senior nun of the Order of Pasquale, Convent of the Blessed Hand, Cherayth.

SAYLKYRK, MIDSHIPMAN TRAHVYS, IMPERIAL CHARISIAN NAVY—senior midshipman, HMS *Destiny*, 54; later fourth lieutenant.

SCHAHL, FATHER DAHNYVYN—upper-priest of the Order of Schueler working directly for Bishop Mytchail Zhessop; attached to Colonel Aiphraim Tahlyvyr's dragoon regiment.

SEABLANKET, RHOBAIR—the Earl of Coris' valet.

SEACATCHER, SIR RAHNLYD—Baron Mandolin, a member of King Cayleb's Council.

SEAFARER, ZHASYN—Duke of Rock Coast.

SEAFARMER, SIR RHYZHARD—Baron Wave Thunder's senior investigator.

SEAHAMPER, SERGEANT EDWYRD—Charisian Imperial Guardsman; Sharleyan Ahrmahk's personal armsman since age ten.

SEAMOUNT, BARON OF—*see* Sir Ahlfryd Hyndryk.

SEAROSE, FATHER GREYGHOR, NAVY OF GOD—CO, NGS *Saint Styvyn*, 52; senior surviving officer of Kornylys Harpahr's fleet to escape capture; a Chihirite of the Order of the Sword.

SEASMOKE, LIEUTENANT YAIRMAN, IMPERIAL CHARISIAN NAVY—XO, HMS *Dancer*, 56.

SEATOWN, CAPTAIN WAHLTAYR—CO of merchant ship *Fraynceen*, acting as a courier for Prince Hektor's spies in Charis; *see also* Lieutenant Fraizher Maythis.

SELKYR, AHNTAHN, IMPERIAL CHARISIAN NAVY—a boatswain's mate, HMS *Destiny*, 54.

SELKYR, BRYAHN—Earl of Deep Hollow; a member of the Northern Conspiracy in Corisande.

SELKYR, AHNTAHN, IMPERIAL CHARISIAN NAVY—a petty officer aboard HMS *Destiny*, 54.

SELLYRS, PAITYR—Baron White Church, Keeper of the Seal of the Kingdom of Charis; a member of King Cayleb's Council.

SHAIKYR, LARYS—CO, privateer galleon *Raptor*.

SHAILTYN, CAPTAIN DAIVYN, IMPERIAL CHARISIAN NAVY—CO, HMS *Thunderbolt*, 58; "frocked" to commodore to command the squadron escorting the Charisian Expeditionary Force to the Republic of Siddarmark.

SHAIN, CAPTAIN PAYTER, IMPERIAL CHARISIAN NAVY—CO, HMS *Dreadful*, 48; Admiral Nylz' flag captain; promoted to admiral; flag officer commanding ICN squadron based on Thol Bay, Kingdom of Tarot.

SHAIOW, ADMIRAL OF THE BROAD OCEANS CHYNTAI, IMPERIAL HARCHONGESE NAVY—Duke of Sun Rising, senior officer afloat, Imperial Harchongese Navy.

SHAIRNCROSS, LADY—*see* Zhain Parkair.

SHAIRNCROSS, LORD—*see* Weslai Parkair.

SHANDYR, HAHL—Baron of Shandyr, Prince Nahrmahn of Emerald's spymaster.

SHARGHATI, AHLYSSA—greatest soprano opera singer of the Republic of Siddarmark; friend of Aivah Pahrsahn's.

SHARPFIELD, EARL OF—*see* Sir Lewk Cohlmyn.

SHAUMAHN, BROTHER SYMYN—hosteler of the Monastery of Saint Zherneau.

SHOWAIL, LIEUTENANT COMMANDER STYV, IMPERIAL CHARISIAN NAVY—CO, schooner HMS *Flash*, 10.

SHOWAIL, STYWYRT—a Charisian foundry owner deliberately infringing several of Ehdwyrd Howsmyn's patents.

SHULMYN, BISHOP TRAHVYS—Bishop of Raven's Land.

SHUMAKYR, FATHER SYMYN—Archbishop Erayk Dynnys' secretary for his 891 pastoral visit; an agent of the Grand Inquisitor.

SHUMAY, FATHER AHLVYN—Bishop Mylz Halcom's personal aide.

SHYLAIR, BISHOP EXECUTOR THOMYS—Archbishop Borys' executive assistant in the Archbishopric of Corisande.

SKYNYR, LIEUTENANT MHARTYN, IMPERIAL CHARISIAN NAVY—third lieutenant, HMS *Destiny*, 54.

SLOKYM, LIEUTENANT BRYAHN, IMPERIAL CHARISIAN ARMY—Baron Green Valley's aide, 2nd Brigade (reinforced), Charisian Expeditionary Force.

SMOLTH, ZHAN—star pitcher for the Tellesberg Krakens.

SOLAYRAN, LIEUTENANT BRAHD, IMPERIAL CHARISIAN NAVY—XO, HMS *Tellesberg*, 22.

SOMERSET, CAPTAIN MARTIN LUTHER, TFN—CO, TFNS *Excalibur*.

SOWTHMYN, TRUMYN—Earl of Airyth; one of Prince Hektor of Corisande's councilors serving on Prince Daivyn's Regency Council; an ally of Earl Anvil Rock and Earl Tartarian.

STAHKAIL, GENERAL LOWRAI, IMPERIAL DESNAIRIAN ARMY—CO, Triangle Shoal Fort, Iythria.

STAHNTYN, GENERAL CHARLZ, REPUBLIC OF SIDDARMARK ARMY—CO, Aivahnstyn garrison, Cliff Peak Province, Republic of Siddarmark.

STANTYN, ARCHBISHOP NYKLAS—Archbishop of Hankey in the Desnairian Empire.

STAYNAIR, AHRDYN—Archbishop Maikel Staynair's deceased wife.

STAYNAIR, HIGH ADMIRAL SIR DOMYNYK, IMPERIAL CHARISIAN NAVY—Baron Rock Point; Maikel Staynair's younger brother; uniformed commanding officer, Imperial Charisian Navy.

STAYNAIR, ARCHBISHOP MAIKEL—head of the Church of Charis; was senior Charisian-born prelate of the Church of God Awaiting in Charis; named prelate of all Charis by then-King Cayleb.

STOHNAR, GENERAL TRUMYN, REPUBLIC OF SIDDARMARK ARMY—a first cousin of Lord Protector Greyghor Stohnar; commander of the reinforcements sent to hold the Sylmahn Gap.

STOHNAR, LORD PROTECTOR GREYGHOR—elected ruler of the Siddarmark Republic.

STONEHEART, BARON OF—*see* Sylvyst Mhardyr.

STONEKEEP, BARON OF—*see* Edmynd Rustmayn.

STORM KEEP, EARL OF—*see* Sahlahmn Traigair.

STOWAIL, COMMANDER AHBRAIM, IMPERIAL CHARISIAN NAVY—Sir Domynyk Staynair's chief of staff.

STYLMYN, BRAHD—Ehdwyrd Howsmyn's senior civil engineer.

STYVYNSYN, MAJOR ZHORJ, REPUBLIC OF SIDDARMARK ARMY—CO, 2nd Company, 37th Infantry Regiment, Republic of Siddarmark Army.

STYWYRT, CAPTAIN AHRNAHLD, IMPERIAL CHARISIAN NAVY—CO, HMS *Squall*, 36.

STYWYRT, CAPTAIN DAHRYL, ROYAL CHARISIAN NAVY—CO, HMS *Typhoon*.

STYWYRT, PAYT—Duke Black Horse.

STYWYRT, SERGEANT ZOHZEF—another of Captain Kairmyn's noncoms, Delferahkan Army.

SUMYR, FATHER FRAHNKLYN—Archbishop Failyx Gahrbor's intendant, Archbishopric of Tarot.

SUMYRS, GENERAL CLYFTYN, REPUBLIC OF SIDDARMARK ARMY—CO, Alyksberg, Cliff Peak Province, Republic of Siddarmark.

SUMYRS, SERGEANT DAHLTYN, IMPERIAL CHARISIAN MARINE CORPS—a senior Marine noncom attached to Brigadier Taisyn's forces in Glacierheart.

SUMYRS, SIR ZHER—Baron of Barcor; one of Sir Koryn Gahrvai's senior officers, Corisande Campaign; later member of Northern Conspiracy.

SUN RISING, DUKE OF—*see* Admiral of the Broad Oceans Chyntai Shaiow.

SUVYRYV, MAJOR AHRNAHLD, ROYAL DESNAIRIAN ARMY—Colonel Sir Zhadwail Brynygair's executive officer, assigned to Sir Fahstyr Rychtyr's invasion column.

SUWAIL, BARJWAIL—Lord Theralt; Lord of Clan Theralt, Raven's Land.

SUWAIL, COLONEL ZHORDYN, REPUBLIC OF SIDDARMARK ARMY—CO, 93rd Infantry Regiment, Republic of Siddarmark Army.

SUWYL, TOBYS—an expatriate Charisian banker and merchant living in Siddar City; a Temple Loyalist.

SUWYL, ZHANDRA—Tobys Suwyl's wife; a moderate Reformist.

SVAIRSMAHN, MIDSHIPMAN LAINSAIR, IMPERIAL CHARISIAN NAVY—a midshipman, HMS *Dancer*, 56; youngest of Charisian POWs surrendered to the Inquisition by Kingdom of Dohlar.

SWAYLE, DOWAGER COUNTESS OF—*see* Rebkah Rahskail.

SWAYLE, EARL OF—*see* Colonel Barkah Rahskail and Wahlys Rahskail.

SYGHAL, COLONEL TREVYR, IMPERIAL CHARISIAN ARMY—senior artillery officer, 2nd Brigade (reinforced), Charisian Expeditionary Force.

SYLZ, PAHRSAHN—a Charisian foundry owner.

SYMKEE, LIEUTENANT GARAITH, IMPERIAL CHARISIAN NAVY—second lieutenant and later XO, HMS *Destiny*, 54.

SYMKYN, GENERAL AHLYN, IMPERIAL CHARISIAN ARMY—second ranking general, Imperial Charisian Army; CO of the second wave of the Charisian Expeditionary Force.

SYMMYNS, MAIKEL, IMPERIAL CHARISIAN NAVY—senior chief petty officer and boatswain, HMS *Destiny*, 54.

SYMMYNS, TOHMYS—Grand Duke of Zebediah; senior nobleman of Zebediah; a member of the Northern Conspiracy in Corisande.

SYMYN, LIEUTENANT HAHL, ROYAL CHARISIAN NAVY—XO, HMS *Torrent*, 42.

SYMYN, SERGEANT ZHORJ, CHARISIAN IMPERIAL GUARD—a Charisian non-com assigned to Empress Sharleyan's guard detachment.

SYNKLAIR, AHDYM, IMPERIAL CHARISIAN NAVY—a member of Laisl Mhatt-syn's gun crew in Glacierheart Province.

SYNKLYR, LIEUTENANT AIRAH, ROYAL DOHLARAN NAVY—XO, galleon *Guardian*.

SYRAHLLA, CAPTAIN MARSHYL, ROYAL DESNAIRIAN ARMY—CO, "Syrahlla's Battery," a six-pounder horse artillery assigned to Sir Fahstyr Rychtyr's invasion column.

SYRKUS, MAJOR PAWAL, IMPERIAL CHARISIAN ARMY—CO, 2nd Battalion, 4th Regiment, Imperial Charisian Army.

TAHLAS, LIEUTENANT BRAHD, IMPERIAL CHARISIAN MARINES—CO, 2nd Platoon, Alpha Company, 1st/3rd Marines, ICMC.

TAHLBAHT, FRAHNCYN—a senior employee (and actual owner) of Bruhstair Freight Haulers; an alias of Nynian Rychtair.

TAHLMYDG, COLONEL GAHDARHD, ROYAL DESNAIRIAN ARMY—CO, "Tahlmydg's Regiment," infantry regiment assigned to Sir Fahstyr Rychtyr's invasion column.

TAHLYVYR, COLONEL AIPHRAIM, ROYAL DELFERAHKAN ARMY—CO, dragoon regiment assigned to "rescue" Princess Irys and Prince Daivyn.

TAHLYVYR, MAJOR FRAIDARECK, IMPERIAL CHARISIAN ARMY—CO, 1st Battalion, 2nd Regiment, Imperial Charisian Army.

TAHRLSAHN, FATHER VYKTYR—upper-priest of the Order of Schueler detailed to deliver Charisian POWs from Dohlar to the Temple.

TAIBAHLD, FATHER AHRNAHLD, NAVY OF GOD—upper-priest of the Order of Schueler; CO, NGS *Sword of God*; Bishop Kornylys Harpahr's flag captain.

TAIBOR, LYWYS, IMPERIAL CHARISIAN NAVY—a healer's mate aboard HMS *Destiny*, 54.

TAIBYR, ARCHBISHOP AHDYM—Archbishop of Desnair for the Church of God.

TAIDSWAYL, LIEUTENANT KORY, IMPERIAL CHARISIAN NAVY—XO, HMS *Saygin*, 22.

TAIGYN, SERGEANT ZHERMO—Temple Loyalist noncom, Fairkyn, New Northland Province, Republic of Siddarmark.

TAILAHR, CAPTAIN ZAIKYB, IMPERIAL CHARISIAN NAVY—CO, HMS *Hador*, 22.

TAILYR, BISHOP EDWYRD, ARMY OF GOD—CO, Jwo-jeng Division.

TAILYR, LIEUTENANT ZHAK—a Temple Guard officer sent to Hildermoss with Father Failyx Khalryn to command Khalryn's force of Temple Loyalist Border States "volunteers."

TAILYR, PRIVATE ZHAKE—a member of the Delferahkan Royal Guard.

TAIRWALD, LORD—*see* Phylyp Zhaksyn.

TAISYN, BRIGADIER MHARTYN, IMPERIAL CHARISIAN MARINE CORPS—senior Charisian Marine officer in Siddarmark prior to Emperor Cayleb's arrival in Siddar City; sent with scratch force to defend the province of Glacierheart.

TALLMYN, CAPTAIN GERVAYS, EMERALD NAVY—second-in-command of the Royal Dockyard in Tranjyr.

TANLYR KEEP, BARON OF—*see* Donyrt Qwentyn.

TANNYR, FATHER HAHLYS—under-priest of the Order of Chihiro; CO, Temple iceboat *Hornet*.

TANYR, VICAR GAIRYT—a member of Samyl Wylsynn's Zionist circle of Reformists.

TARTARIAN, EARL OF—*see* Admiral Sir Taryl Lektor.

TAYLAR, MAJOR PAIDRHO, IMPERIAL CHARISIAN ARMY—CO, 1st Battalion, 4th Regiment, Imperial Charisian Army.

TAYSO, PRIVATE DAISHYN, CHARISIAN IMPERIAL GUARD—a Charisian assigned to Empress Sharleyan's guard detachment.

TAYT, ALAHNAH—Dowager Queen of Chisholm; Queen Sharleyan of Chisholm's mother.

TAYT, MAJOR CHARLZ, IMPERIAL CHARISIAN ARMY—CO, 4th Battalion, 2nd Regiment, Imperial Charisian Army; a distant cousin of Empress Sharleyan.

TAYT, SAILYS—King of Chisholm; deceased father of Queen Sharleyan.

TAYT, SHARLEYAN—Empress of Charis and Queen of Chisholm. *See* Sharleyan Ahrmahk.

TEAGMAHN, FATHER BRYAHN—upper-priest of the Order of Schueler, intendant for the Archbishopric of Glacierheart.

THAIRIS, RUHSYL, IMPERIAL CHARISIAN ARMY—Duke of Eastshare; CO, Imperial Charisian Army; CO, 1st Brigade (reinforced), Charisian Expeditionary Force.

THAIRNOS, EARL OF—*see* Rahzhyr Hylmahn.

THERALT, LORD OF—*see* Barjwail Suwail.

THIESSEN, CAPTAIN JOSEPH, TFN—Admiral Pei Kau-zhi's chief of staff.

THIRSK, EARL OF—*see* Admiral Lywys Gardynyr.

THOMPKYN, HAUWERSTAT—Earl of White Crag; Chisholm's Lord Justice.

THOMYS, FRAIDMYN—Archbishop Zhasyn Cahnyr's valet of many years.

THORAST, DUKE OF—*see* Aibram Zaivyair.

THYRSTYN, SYMYN—a Siddarmarkian merchant; husband of Wynai Thyrstyn.

THYRSTYN, WYNAI—Trai Sahlavahn's married sister; secretary and stenographer in Charis' Siddar City embassy.

TIANG, BISHOP EXECUTOR WU-SHAI—Archbishop Zherohm Vyncyt's bishop executor.

TIDEWATER, NAHRMAHN—one of Ehdwyrd Howsmyn's senior artificers.

TILLYER, LIEUTENANT COMMANDER HENRAI, IMPERIAL CHARISIAN NAVY—High Admiral Lock Island's chief of staff; previously his flag lieutenant.

TIRIAN, DUKE OF—*see* Kahlvyn Ahrmahk.

TOBYS, WING FLAHN—Lord Tairwald's senior "wing" (blooded warrior).

TOHMPSYN, COLONEL SIR SAHLMYN, ROYAL DESNAIRIAN ARMY—CO, "Tohmpsyn's Regiment," infantry regiment assigned to Sir Fahstyr Rychtyr's invasion column.

TOHMYS, FRAHNKLYN—Crown Prince Cayleb's tutor.

TOHMYS, FRAIDMYN—Archbishop Zhasyn Cahnyr's valet of many years.

TOMPSYN, COLONEL ZHON, IMPERIAL CHARISIAN ARMY—CO, 2nd Regiment, Imperial Charisian Army, one of the regiments assigned to 2nd Brigade (reinforced), Charisian Expeditionary Force.

TRAHLMAHN, FATHER ZHON—Nahrmahn Baytz' palace confessor; priest of the Order of Bédard; retained in that post by Prince Nahrmahn Gareyt.

TRAHSKHAT, MAHRTYN—Sailys and Myrahm Trahskhat's older son.

TRAHSKHAT, MYRAHM—Sailys Trahskhat's wife and also a Temple Loyalist.

TRAHSKHAT, PAWAL—Sailys and Myrahm Trahskhat's younger son.

TRAHSKHAT, SAILYS—ex-star third baseman for the Tellesberg Krakens; was a Temple Loyalist; is now Byrk Raimahn's second-in-command defending the Reformists of Glacierheart Province.

TRAHSKHAT, SINDAI—Sailys and Myrahm's Trahskhat's daughter and youngest child.

TRAIGAIR, SAHLAHMN—Earl of Storm Keep; a member of the Northern Conspiracy in Corisande.

TRAIGHAIR, FATHER LHAREE—rector of Saint Bailair's Church, Siddar City; Order of Bédard; a Reformist.

TRAYLMYN, BARON OF—*see* General Sir Ohtys Godwyl.

TRYNAIR, VICAR ZAHMSYN—Chancellor of the Council of Vicars of the Church of God Awaiting; one of the so-called Group of Four.

TRYNTYN, CAPTAIN ZHAIRYMIAH, ROYAL CHARISIAN NAVY—CO, HMS *Torrent*, 42.

TRYVYTHYN, CAPTAIN SIR DYNZYL, ROYAL CHARISIAN NAVY—CO, HMS *Royal Charis*.

TYBYT, GYFFRY—Paidryg Tybyt's thirteen-year-old son.

TYBYT, PAIDRYG—Temple Loyalist barge crewman and farmer, Fairkyn, New Northland Province, Republic of Siddarmark.

TYDWAIL, FATHER ZHORJ—Schuelerite upper-priest; Zion Division's special intendant.

TYLMAHN, GENERAL FRONZ, REPUBLIC OF SIDDARMARK ARMY—senior officer in command, Siddarmarkian infantry detailed to support Captain Halcom Bahrns' operation.

TYLMAHN, FATHER VYKTYR—Pasqualate upper-priest; senior Reformist clergyman in Thesmar, South March Lands.

TYMKYN, LIEUTENANT TOHMYS, IMPERIAL CHARISIAN NAVY—fourth lieutenant and later third lieutenant HMS *Destiny*, 54.

TYMKYN, FATHER ZHAMES—Langhornite under-priest, chaplain, 191st Cavalry regiment.

TYMKYN, ZHASTROW—High Admiral Rock Point's secretary.

TYMPYLTYN, GENERAL ERAYK—Temple Loyalist ex-militia officer whose mutinous troops seized Fort Darymahn, the South March Lands, Republic of Siddarmark; the promotion to general is self-awarded.

TYOTAYN, BRIGADIER BAIRAHND, IMPERIAL CHARISIAN MARINES—CO, 5th Brigade, ICMC. Sir Gwylym Manthyr's senior Marine officer.

TYRN, ARCHBISHOP LYAM—Archbishop of Emerald.

TYRNYR, SERGEANT BRYNDYN, CHISHOLMIAN ROYAL GUARD—a member of Queen Sharleyan's normal guard detail.

TYRNYR, FATHER DAVYS—a Bédardist Temple Loyalist upper-priest in Tellesberg who serves as Irys and Daivyn Daykyn's chaplain and confessor during their time in the city.

TYRNYR, COMMODORE RUHSAIL, IMPERIAL CHARISIAN NAVY—CO, Howard Island base, charged with blockading the Gulf of Jahras.

TYRNYR, SIR SAMYL—Cayleb's special ambassador to Chisholm; was placed/ supplanted/reinforced by Gray Harbor's arrival.

TYRNYR, MAJOR SYMPSYN, IMPERIAL CHARISIAN MARINE CORPS—the ranking Marine officer sent to Glacierheart with Brigadier Taisyn.

TYRNYR, ADMIRAL ZHORJ, ROYAL DOHLARAN NAVY—shoreside officer in charge of developing and producing artillery for the Royal Dohlaran Navy.

TYRWAIT, LIEUTENANT COMMANDER SHAIN, IMPERIAL CHARISIAN NAVY—Charisian naval officer commanding the naval thirty-pounder guns assigned to General Trumyn Stohnar's defense of the Sylmahn Gap.

UHLSTYN, YAIRMAN—Sir Koryn Gahrvai's personal armsman.

URBAHN, HAHL—XO, privateer galleon *Raptor*.

URVYN, ARCHBISHOP—*see* Urvyn Myllyr.

URVYN, LIEUTENANT ZHAK, ROYAL CHARISIAN NAVY—XO, HMS *Wave*, 14.

URWYN, LUDOVYC—first Lord Protector of Siddarmark; founder of Republic of Siddarmark.

USHYR, FATHER BRYAHN—an under-priest, Archbishop Maikel's personal secretary and most trusted aide.

VAHLAIN, NAIKLOS—Sir Gwylym Manthyr's valet; one of the Charisian POWs surrendered to Inquisition by the Kingdom of Dohlar.

VAHNWYK, MAHRTYN—the Earl of Thirsk's personal secretary and senior clerk.

VAHSPHAR, BISHOP EXECUTOR DYNZAIL—Bishop Executor of Delferahk. An Andropovite.

VANDAIK, FATHER GAISBYRT—upper-priest of the Order of Schueler; an inquisitor working directly for Bishop Mytchail Zhessop in Talkyra.

VELDAMAHN, BYRTRYM ("BYRT"), IMPERIAL CHARISIAN NAVY—Sir Domynyk Staynair's personal coxswain.

VERRYN, CAPTAIN DYGRY—senior Temple Loyalist officer, Fairkyn, New Northland Province, Republic of Siddarmark.

VRAIDAHN, ALYS—Archbishop Maikel Staynair's housekeeper.

VYKAIN, LIEUTENANT MAHRYAHNO, IMPERIAL CHARISIAN NAVY—XO, HMS *Ahrmahk*, 58.

VYNAIR, BISHOP ADULFO, ARMY OF GOD—CO, Holy Martyrs Division.

VYNAIR, SERGEANT AHDYM, CHARISIAN ROYAL GUARD—one of King Cayleb II's armsmen.

VYNCYT, ARCHBISHOP ZHEROHM—primate of Chisholm.

VYNTYNR, MAJOR FRAYDYK, IMPERIAL CHARISIAN MARINE CORPS—Colonel Wyntahn Harys' senior Charisian subordinate in support of Captain Halcom Bahrns' operation.

VYRNYR, DOCTOR DAHNEL—member of the Royal College of Charis, specializing in the study of pressures.

WAHLDAIR, LIEUTENANT LAHMBAIR, IMPERIAL CHARISIAN NAVY—third lieutenant, HMS *Dancer*, 56.

WAHLS, COLONEL STYVYN, ROYAL DELFERAHKAN ARMY—CO, Sarmouth Keep.

WAHLTAHRS, RAHZHYR—a member of Prince Daivyn Daykyn's royal guard in exile, Tobys Raimair's senior noncom.

WAHRLYW, ZHOEL, CANAL SERVICE—gatekeeper, Fairkyn, New Northland Province, Republic of Siddarmark.

WAIGAN, FRAHNKLYN, IMPERIAL CHARISIAN NAVY—chief petty officer and senior helmsman, HMS *Destiny*, 54.

WAIGNAIR, BISHOP HAINRYK—Bishop of Tellesberg; senior prelate (after Archbishop Maikel) of the Kingdom of Old Charis.

WAIGNAIR, TROOPER WYLTAHN, ARMY OF GOD—one of Corporal Howail Brahdlai's scouts, 191st Cavalry regiment.

WAILAHR, COMMODORE SIR HAIRAHM, IMPERIAL DESNAIRIAN NAVY—a squadron commander of the Imperial Desnairian Navy.

WAIMYN, FATHER AIDRYN—intendant for Church of God Awaiting, Archbishopric of Corisande.

WAIMYAN, BISHOP KHALRYN, ARMY OF GOD—Chihirite of the Order of the Sword; CO, Zion Division.

WAIMYS, ZHOSHUA, ROYAL DELFERAHKAN ARMY—a dragoon assigned to Sergeant Braice Mahknash's squad.

WAISTYN, AHLYS—Byrtrym and Elahnah Waistyn's younger daughter.

WAISTYN, BYRTRYM—deceased Duke of Halbrook Hollow; Empress Sharleyan's uncle; ex-commander of Chisholmian Royal Army.

WAISTYN, ELAHNAH—Dowager Duchess of Halbrook Hollow; widow of Byrtrym Waistyn; mother of Sailys Waistyn.

WAISTYN, SAILYS—Duke of Halbrook Hollow; Empress Sharleyan's cousin; only son and heir of Byrtrym Waistyn.

WAISTYN, SHARYL—Byrtrym and Elahnah Waistyn's older daughter.

WALKYR, EDMYND—CO, merchant galleon *Wave*.

WALKYR, MIDSHIPMAN FRAID, IMPERIAL CHARISIAN NAVY—midshipman in HMS *Shield*, 54.

WALKYR, GREYGHOR—Edmynd Walkyr's son.

WALKYR, LYZBET—Edmynd Walkyr's wife.

WALKYR, MYCHAIL—Edmynd Walkyr's youngest brother; CO, merchant galleon *Wind*.

WALKYR, PRIVATE STYV, ARMY OF GOD—a private assigned to 1st Regiment, Zion Division.

WALKYR, STYV—Tahdayo Mahntayl's chief advisor.

WALKYR, ZHORJ—XO, galleon *Wave*; Edmynd Walkyr's younger brother.

WALLYCE, LORD FRAHNKLYN—Chancellor of the Siddarmark Republic.

WATYRS, COMMANDER HAINZ, IMPERIAL CHARISIAN NAVY—naval officer commanding Brigadier Taisyn's attached naval artillery in Glacierheart.

WAVE THUNDER, BARON OF—*see* Bynzhamyn Raice.

WAVE THUNDER, BARONESS OF—*see* Leahyn Raice.

WAYST, CAPTAIN ZAKRAI, IMPERIAL CHARISIAN NAVY—CO, HMS *Darcos Sound*, 54.

WHAITE, CAPTAIN STYVYN—CO, merchant ship *Sea Cloud*, a courier for Prince Hektor's spies in Charis; *see also* Robyrt Bradlai.

WHITE CASTLE, BARON—*see* Tohmys Bahrmyn.

WHITE CRAG, EARL OF—*see* Hauwerstat Thompkyn.

WHITE FORD, BARON OF—*see* Gahvyn Mahrtyn.

WIND MOUNTAIN, COUNT OF—*see* Captain of Winds Shoukhan Khowsan.

WINDSHARE, EARL OF—*see* Sir Alyk Ahrthyr.

WYKMYN, COLONEL ROHDERYK, ROYAL DESNAIRIAN ARMY—one of Sir Rainos Ahlverez' senior regimental commanders.

WYLDYNG, SERGEANT MAHDYC, ARMY OF GOD—senior noncom, Battery B, 20th Artillery Regiment, Ohlarn, New Northland Province, Republic of Siddarmark.

WYLLYM, ARCHBISHOP—*see* Wyllym Rayno.

WYLLYMS, MARHYS—the Duke of Tirian's majordomo.

WYLLYMS, LIEUTENANT PRAISKHAT, ROYAL DELFERAHKAN ARMY—one of Colonel Aiphraim Tahlyvyr's junior platoon commanders.

WYLLYS, COLONEL STAHN, REPUBLIC OF SIDDARMARK ARMY—CO, 37th Infantry Regiment, Republic of Siddarmark Army, a part of General Trumyn Stohnar's Sylmahn Gap command.

WYLLYS, STYVYN—Doctor Zhansyn Wyllys' estranged father.

WYLLYS, DOCTOR ZHANSYN—member of the Royal College of Charis with an interest in chemistry and distillation.

WYLSYNN, ARCHBAHLD—younger son of Vicar Samyl and Lysbet Wylsynn; Father Paityr Wylsynn's half brother.

WYLSYNN, HAUWERD—Paityr Wylsynn's uncle; a Reformist member of the vicarate; ex Temple Guardsman; a priest of the Order of Langhorne.

WYLSYNN, LYSBET—Samyl Wylsynn's second wife; mother of Tohmys, Zhanayt, and Archbahld Wylsynn.

WYLSYNN, FATHER PAITYR—upper-priest of the Order of Schueler; Intendant of Charis; head of the Office of Patents; member of Charisian inner circle; son of Samyl Wylsynn.

WYLSYNN, SAMYL—Father Paityr Wylsynn's father; the leader of the Reformists within the Council of Vicars and a priest of the Order of Schueler.

WYLSYNN, TANNIERE—Samyl Wylsynn's deceased wife; mother of Erais and Paityr Wylsynn.

WYLSYNN, TOHMYS—older son of Vicar Samyl and Lysbet Wylsynn; Father Paityr Wylsynn's half-brother.

WYLSYNN, SERGEANT THOMYS—Temple Loyalist rebel, garrison of Fort Darymahn, the South March Lands, Republic of Siddarmark.

WYLSYNN, ZHANAYT—daughter of Vicar Samyl and Lysbet Wylsynn; Father Paityr Wylsynn's half-sister.

WYNDAYL, MAJOR BRAINAHK, IMPERIAL CHARISIAN MARINES—CO, 1st Battalion, 14th Marine Regiment.

WYNKASTAIR, MASTER PAYTER, IMPERIAL CHARISIAN NAVY—gunner, HMS *Destiny*, 54.

WYNSTYN, LIEUTENANT KYNYTH, ROYAL CORISANDIAN NAVY—first lieutenant, galley *Corisande*.

WYRKMYN, COLONEL MALIKAI, IMPERIAL CHARISIAN ARMY—commanding officer, 4th Regiment, Imperial Charisian Army; one of the three regiments assigned to 2nd Brigade (reinforced), Charisian Expeditionary Force.

WYRSHYM, BISHOP MILITANT BAHRNABAI, ARMY OF GOD—a Chihirite of the Order of the Sword and ex-Temple Guard officer; CO, eastern column of the Army of God, invading the Republic of Siddarmark through Tarikah Province.

WYSTAHN, AHNAINAH—Edvarhd Wystahn's wife.

WYSTAHN, SERGEANT EDVARHD, ROYAL CHARISIAN MARINES—a scout-sniper assigned to 1st/3rd Marines.

WYTYKAIR, CAPTAIN BYNZHAMYN, IMPERIAL CHARISIAN ARMY—General Ahlyn Symkyn's aide.

YAIR, FATHER AIRWAIN—chaplain and confessor to Rahzhyr Mairwyn, Baron Larchros.

YAIRLEY, CAPTAIN ALLAYN, IMPERIAL CHARISIAN NAVY—older brother of Captain Sir Dunkyn Yairley.

YAIRLEY, REAR ADMIRAL SIR DUNKYN, IMPERIAL CHARISIAN NAVY—Baron Sarmouth, CO, HMS *Destiny*, 54; later promoted to admiral; CO of the squadron escorting Empress Sharleyan to Chisholm in 896.

YOWANCE, EHRNAIST—Rayjhis Yowance's deceased elder brother.

YOWANCE, RAYJHIS—Earl Gray Harbor, First Councilor of Charis.

YUTHAIN, CAPTAIN GORJHA, IMPERIAL HARCHONG NAVY—CO, galley IHNS *Ice Lizard*.

ZAGYRSK, ARCHBISHOP ARTHYN—Pasqualate Temple Loyalist Archbishop of Tarikah Province, Republic of Siddarmark.

ZAHCHO, FATHER DAISHAN—an under-priest of the Order of Schueler; one of Father Aidryn Waimyn's inquisitors in Corisande.

ZAHMSYN, ARCHBISHOP HALMYN—Archbishop of Gorath; senior prelate of the Kingdom of Dohlar until replaced by Trumahn Rowzvel.

ZAHMSYN, VICAR—*see* Zahmsyn Trynair.

ZAVYAIR, AIBRAM—Duke of Thorast; effectively, King Rahnyld IV of Dohlar's Navy Minister; brother-in-law of (deceased) Admiral General Duke Malikai.

ZAVYR, FATHER SEDRYK—Schuelerite upper-priest; Bishop Militant Cahnyr Kaitswyrth's special intendant.

ZEBEDIAH, GRAND DUKE OF—*see* Tohmys Symmyns.

ZHADAHNG, SERGEANT WYNN, TEMPLE GUARD—Captain Walysh Zhu's senior noncom.

ZHADWAIL, MAJOR BRYWSTYR, IMPERIAL CHARISIAN ARMY—CO, 3rd Battalion, 2nd Regiment, Imperial Charisian Army.

ZHADWAIL, MAJOR WYLLYM, IMPERIAL CHARISIAN MARINE CORPS—Hauwerd Breygart's senior Marine battalion commander at Thesmar.

ZHADWAIL, TRAIVAHR—a member of Prince Daivyn Daykyn's royal guard in exile.

ZHAHNSYN, COLONEL HAUWERD, REPUBLIC OF SIDDARMARK ARMY—the senior Siddarmarkian officer sent to Glacierheart with Brigadier Taisyn.

ZHAKSYN, LIEUTENANT AHRNAHLD, IMPERIAL CHARISIAN NAVY—senior engineer, HMS *Tellesberg*, 22.

ZHAKSYN, LIEUTENANT TOHMYS, IMPERIAL CHARISIAN MARINES—General Chermyn's aide.

ZHAKSYN, SERGEANT GROVAIR, REPUBLIC OF SIDDARMARK ARMY—senior noncom, 2nd Company, 37th Infantry Regiment, Republic of Siddarmark Army.

ZHAKSYN, PHYLYP—Lord Tairwald; Lord of Clan Tairwald, Raven's Land.

ZHANDOR, FATHER NEYTHAN—a Langhornite lawgiver accredited for both secular and ecclesiastic law; assigned to Empress Sharleyan's staff in Corisande.

ZHANSAN, FRAHNK—the Duke of Tirian's senior guardsman.

ZHANSTYN, BRIGADIER ZHOEL, IMPERIAL CHARISIAN MARINES—CO, 3rd Brigade, ICMC. Brigadier Clareyk's senior battalion CO during Corisande Campaign.

ZHARDEAU, LADY ERAIS—Samyl and Tanniere Wylsynn's daughter; Father Paityr Wylsynn's younger full sister; wife of Sir Fraihman Zhardeau.

ZHARDEAU, SIR FRAIHMAN—minor Tansharan aristocrat; husband of Lady Erais Zhardeau; son-in-law of Vicar Samyl Wylsynn.

ZHARDEAU, SAMYL—son of Sir Fraihman and Lady Erais Zhardeau; grandson of Vicar Samyl Wylsynn; nephew of Father Paityr Wylsynn.

ZHASPAHR, VICAR—see Zhaspahr Clyntahn.

ZHASTROW, FATHER AHBEL—Father Zhon Byrkyt's successor as Abbot of the Monastery of Saint Zherneau.

ZHASYN, ARCHBISHOP—see Zhasyn Cahnyr.

ZHAZTRO, COMMODORE HAINZ, EMERALD NAVY—the senior Emeraldian naval officer afloat (technically) in Eraystor following Battle of Darcos Sound.

ZHEFFYRS, MAJOR WYLL, ROYAL CHARISIAN MARINES—CO, Marine detachment, HMS Destiny, 54.

ZHEFRY, AHDEM—Earl of Cross Creek.

ZHEPPSYN, CAPTAIN NYKLAS, EMERALD NAVY—CO, galley Triton.

ZHERMAIN, CAPTAIN MAHRTYN, ROYAL DOHLARAN NAVY—CO, HMS Prince of Dohlar, 38.

ZHESSOP, BISHOP MYTCHAIL—Intendant of Delferahk; a Schuelerite.

ZHESSYP, LACHLYN—King Haarahld VII's valet.

ZHEVONS, AHBRAIM—alias and alternate persona of Merlin Athrawes.

ZHOELSYN, LIEUTENANT PHYLYP, ROYAL TAROTISIAN NAVY—second lieutenant, King Gorjah II.

ZHONAIR, MAJOR GAHRMYN—a battery commander in Ferayd Harbor, Ferayd Sound, Kingdom of Delferahk.

ZHONES, MIDSHIPMAN AHRLEE, IMPERIAL CHARISIAN NAVY—a junior midshipman in HMS Destiny, 54.

ZHORJ, COLONEL SIR WAHLYS—Tahdayo Mahntayl's senior mercenary commander.

ZHU, CAPTAIN WALYSH, TEMPLE GUARD—senior officer of military escort delivering Charisian POWs from Dohlar to the Temple.

ZHUD, CORPORAL WALTHAR, ROYAL DELFERAHKAN ARMY—Sergeant Braice Mahknash's assistant squad leader.

ZHUSTYN, SIR AHLBER—senior minister for intelligence, Kingdom of Chisholm.

ZHWAIGAIR, LIEUTENANT DYNNYS, ROYAL DOHLARAN NAVY—third lieutenant, HMS *Wave Lord*, 54; previously attached to Admiral Zhorj Tyrnyr's Staff for Artillery Development.

ZHWAIGAIR, THOMYS—Lieutenant Dynnys Zhwaigair's uncle; an innovative Dohlaran ironmaster.

ZOHANNSYN, PRIVATE PAITRYK—Temple Loyalist rebel, garrison of Fort Darymahn, the South March Lands, Republic of Siddarmark.

Glossary

Abbey of Saint Evehlain—the sister abbey of the Monastery of Saint Zherneau.

Angora lizard—a Safeholdian "lizard" with a particularly luxuriant, cashmere-like coat. They are raised and sheared as sheep and form a significant part of the fine-textiles industry.

Anshinritsumei—"the little fire" from the *Holy Writ*; the lesser touch of God's spirit and the maximum enlightenment of which mortals are capable.

Ape lizard—ape lizards are much larger and more powerful versions of monkey lizards. Unlike monkey lizards, they are mostly ground dwellers, although they are capable of climbing trees suitable to bear their weight. The great mountain ape lizard weighs as much as nine hundred or a thousand pounds, whereas the plains ape lizard weighs no more than a hundred to a hundred and fifty pounds. Ape lizards live in families of up to twenty or thirty adults, and whereas monkey lizards will typically flee when confronted with a threat, ape lizards are much more likely to respond by attacking the threat. It is not unheard of for two or three ape lizard "families" to combine forces against particularly dangerous predators, and even a great dragon will generally avoid such a threat.

Archangels, The—central figures of the Church of God Awaiting. The archangels were senior members of the command crew of Operation Ark who assumed the status of divine messengers, guides, and guardians in order to control and shape the future of human civilization on Safehold.

Blink lizard—a small, bioluminescent winged lizard. Although it's about three times the size of a firefly, it fills much the same niche on Safehold.

Borer—a form of Safeholdian shellfish which attaches itself to the hulls of ships or the timbers of wharves by boring into them. There are several types of borer: the most destructive of which continually eat their way deeper into any wooden structure, whereas some less destructive varieties eat only enough of the structure to anchor themselves and actually form a protective outer layer which gradually builds up a coral-like surface. Borers and rot are the two most serious threats (aside, of course, from fire) to wooden hulls.

Briar berries—any of several varieties of native Safeholdian berries which grow on thorny bushes.

Cat lizard—a furry lizard about the size of a terrestrial cat. They are kept as pets and are very affectionate.

Catamount—a smaller version of the Safeholdian slash lizard. The catamount is very fast and smarter than its larger cousin, which means it tends to avoid humans. It is, however, a lethal and dangerous hunter in its own right.

Chewleaf—a mildly narcotic leaf from a native Safeholdian plant. It is used much as terrestrial chewing tobacco over much of the planet's surface.

Choke tree—a low-growing species of tree native to Safehold. It comes in many varieties and is found in most of the planet's climate zones. It is dense-growing, tough, and difficult to eradicate, but it requires quite a lot of sunlight to flourish, which means it is seldom found in mature old-growth forests.

Church of Charis—the schismatic church which split from the Church of God Awaiting following the Group of Four's effort to destroy the Kingdom of Charis.

Church of God Awaiting—the church and religion created by the command staff of Operation Ark to control the colonists and their descendants and prevent the reemergence of advanced technology.

Commentaries, The—the authorized interpretations and doctrinal expansions upon the *Holy Writ*. They represent the officially approved and Church-sanctioned interpretation of the original Scripture.

Cotton silk—a plant native to Safehold which shares many of the properties of silk and cotton. It is very lightweight and strong, but the raw fiber comes from a plant pod which is even more filled with seeds than Old Earth cotton. Because of the amount of hand labor required to harvest and process the pods and to remove the seeds from it, cotton silk is very expensive.

Council of Vicars—the Church of God Awaiting's equivalent of the College of Cardinals.

Dagger thorn—a native Charisian shrub, growing to a height of perhaps three feet at maturity, which possesses knife-edged thorns from three to seven inches long, depending upon the variety.

Deep-mouth wyvern—the Safeholdian equivalent of a pelican.

Doomwhale—the most dangerous predator of Safehold, although, fortunately, it seldom bothers with anything as small as humans. Doomwhales have been known to run to as much as one hundred feet in length, and they are pure carnivores. Each doomwhale requires a huge range, and encounters with them are rare, for which human beings are just as glad, thank you. Doomwhales will eat *anything* . . . including the largest krakens. They have been known, on *extremely* rare occasions, to attack merchant ships and war galleys.

Dragon—the largest native Safeholdian land life-form. Dragons come in two varieties: the common dragon (generally subdivided into jungle dragons and hill dragons) and the carnivorous great dragon. *See* Great dragon.

Fallen, The—the archangels, angels, and mortals who followed Shan-wei in her rebellion against God and the rightful authority of the Archangel Langhorne. The term applies to *all* of Shan-wei's adherents, but is most often used in reference to the angels and archangels who followed her willingly rather than the mortals who were duped into obeying her.

Fire vine—a large, hardy, fast-growing Safeholdian vine. Its runners can exceed two inches in diameter, and the plant is extremely rich in natural oils. It is considered a major hazard to human habitations, especially in areas which experience arid, dry summers, because of its very high natural flammability and because its oil is poisonous to humans and terrestrial species of animals. The crushed vine and its seed pods, however, are an important source of lubricating oils, and it is commercially cultivated in some areas for that reason.

Five-day—a Safeholdian "week," consisting of only five days, Monday through Friday.

Fleming moss—an absorbent moss native to Safehold which was genetically engineered by Shan-wei's terraforming crews to possess natural antibiotic properties. It is a staple of Safeholdian medical practice.

Forktail—one of several species of native Safeholdian fish which fill an ecological niche similar to that of the Old Earth herring.

Gbaba—a star-traveling, xenophobic species whose reaction to encounters with any possibly competing species is to exterminate it. The Gbaba completely destroyed the Terran Federation and, so far as is known, all human beings in the galaxy aside from the population of Safehold.

Golden berry—a tree growing to about ten feet in height which thrives in most Safeholdian climates. A tea brewed from its leaves is a sovereign specific for motion sickness and nausea.

Grasshopper—a Safeholdian insect analogue which grows to a length of as much as nine inches and is carnivorous. Fortunately, they do not occur in the same numbers as terrestrial grasshoppers.

Gray-horned wyvern—a nocturnal flying predator of Safehold. It is roughly analogous to a terrestrial owl.

Great dragon—the largest and most dangerous land carnivore of Safehold. The great dragon isn't actually related to hill dragons or jungle dragons at all, despite some superficial physical resemblances. In fact, it's more of a scaled-up slash lizard, with elongated jaws and sharp, serrated teeth. It has six limbs and, unlike the slash lizard, is covered in thick, well-insulated hide rather than fur.

Group of Four—the four vicars who dominate and effectively control the Council of Vicars of the Church of God Awaiting.

Hairatha Dragons—the Hairatha professional baseball team. The traditional rivals of the Tellesberg Krakens for the Kingdom Championship.

Hake—a Safeholdian fish. Like most "fish" native to Safehold, it has a very long, sinuous body but the head does resemble a terrestrial hake or cod, with a hooked jaw.

High-angle gun—a relatively short, stubby artillery piece with a carriage specially designed to allow higher angles of fire in order to lob gunpowder-filled shells in high, arcing trajectories. The name is generally shortened to "angle-gun" by the gun crews themselves.

Hill dragon—a roughly elephant-sized draft animal commonly used on Safehold. Despite their size, hill dragons are capable of rapid, sustained movement. They are herbivores.

Holy Writ, The—the seminal holy book of the Church of God Awaiting.

Ice wyvern—a flightless aquatic wyvern rather similar to a terrestrial penguin. Species of ice wyvern are native to both the northern and southern polar regions of Safehold.

Insights, The—the recorded pronouncements and observations of the Church of God Awaiting's Grand Vicars and canonized saints. They represent deeply significant spiritual and inspirational teachings, but as the work of fallible mortals do not have the same standing as the *Holy Writ* itself.

Intendant—the cleric assigned to a bishopric or archbishopric as the direct representative of the Office of Inquisition. The intendant is specifically charged with ensuring that the Proscriptions of Jwo-jeng are not violated.

Journal of Saint Zherneau—the journal left by Jeremy Knowles telling the truth about the destruction of the Alexandria Enclave and about Pei Shan-wei.

Jungle dragon—a somewhat generic term applied to lowland dragons larger than hill dragons. The gray jungle dragon is the largest herbivore on Safehold.

Kercheef—a traditional headdress worn in the Kingdom of Tarot which consists of a specially designed bandana tied across the hair.

Knights of the Temple Lands—the corporate title of the prelates who govern the Temple Lands. Technically, the Knights of the Temple Lands are *secular* rulers who simply happen to also hold high Church office. Under the letter of the Church's law, what they may do as the Knights of the Temple Lands is completely separate from any official action of the Church. This legal fiction has been of considerable value to the Church on more than one occasion.

Kraken—(1) generic term for an entire family of maritime predators. Kraken are rather like sharks crossed with octopi. They have powerful, fishlike bodies, strong jaws with inward-inclined, fanglike teeth, and a cluster of tentacles just behind the head which can be used to hold prey while they devour it. The smallest, coastal kraken can be as short as three or four feet; deepwater kraken up to fifty feet in length have been reliably reported, and there are legends of those still larger.

Kraken—(2) one of three pre-Merlin heavy-caliber naval artillery pieces. The great kraken weighed approximately 3.4 tons and fired a 42-pound round shot. The royal kraken weighed four tons. It also fired a 42-pound shot but was specially designed as a long-range weapon with less windage and higher bore pressures. The standard kraken was a 2.75-ton, medium-range weapon which fired a 35-pound round shot approximately 6.2 inches in diameter.

Kraken oil—originally, oil extracted from kraken and used as fuel, primarily for lamps, in coastal and seafaring realms. Most lamp oil currently comes from sea dragons (*see* below), rather than actually being extracted from kraken, and, in fact, the sea dragon oil actually burns much more brightly and with much less odor. Nonetheless, oils are still ranked in terms of "kraken oil" quality steps.

Kyousei hi—"great fire" or "magnificent fire," from the *Holy Writ*. The term used to describe the brilliant nimbus of light the Operation Ark command crew generated around their air cars and skimmers to "prove" their divinity to the original Safeholdians.

Langhorne's Watch—the 31-minute period which falls immediately after midnight. It was inserted by the original "archangels" to compensate for the extra length of Safehold's 26.5-hour day. It is supposed to be used for contemplation and giving thanks.

Marsh wyvern—one of several strains of Safeholdian wyverns found in saltwater and freshwater marsh habitats.

Master Traynyr—a character out of the Safeholdian entertainment tradition. Master Traynyr is a stock character in Safeholdian puppet theater, by turns a bumbling conspirator whose plans always miscarry and the puppeteer who controls all of the marionette "actors" in the play.

Messenger wyvern—any one of several strains of genetically modified Safeholdian wyverns adapted by Pei Shan-wei's terraforming teams to serve the colonists as homing pigeon equivalents. Some messenger wyverns are adapted for short-range, high-speed delivery of messages, whereas others are adapted for extremely long range (but slower) message deliveries.

Monastery of Saint Zherneau—the mother monastery and headquarters of the Brethren of Saint Zherneau, a relatively small and poor order in the Archbishopric of Charis.

Monkey lizard—a generic term for several species of arboreal, saurian-looking marsupials. Monkey lizards come in many different shapes and sizes, although none are much larger than an Old Earth chimpanzee and most are considerably smaller. They have two very human-looking hands, although each hand has only three fingers and an opposable thumb, and the "hand feet" of their other forelimbs have a limited grasping ability but no opposable thumb. Monkey lizards tend to be excitable, *very* energetic, and talented mimics of human behaviors.

Mountain ananas—a native Safeholdian fruit tree. Its spherical fruit averages about four inches in diameter with the firmness of an apple and a taste rather like a sweet grapefruit. It is very popular on the Safeholdian mainland.

Mountain spike-thorn—a particular subspecies of spike-thorn, found primarily in tropical mountains. The most common blossom color is a deep, rich red, but the white mountain spike-thorn is especially prized for its trumpet-shaped blossom, which has a deep, almost cobalt blue throat, fading to pure white as it approaches the outer edge of the blossom, which is, in turn, fringed in a deep golden yellow.

Narwhale—a species of Safeholdian sea life named for the Old Earth species of the same name. Safeholdian narwhales are about forty feet in length and equipped with twin hornlike tusks up to eight feet long. They live in large pods or schools and are not at all shy or retiring. The adults of narwhale pods have been known to fight off packs of kraken.

Nearoak—a rough-barked Safeholdian tree similar to an Old Earth oak tree. It is found in tropic and near tropic zones. Although it does resemble an Old Earth oak, it is an evergreen and seeds using "pine cones."

Nearpalm—a tropical Safeholdian tree which resembles a terrestrial royal palm except that a mature specimen stands well over sixty feet tall. It produces a tart, plumlike fruit about five inches in diameter.

Nearpalm fruit—the plumlike fruit produced by the nearpalm. It is used in cooking and eaten raw, but its greatest commercial value is as the basis for nearpalm wine.

Neartuna—one of several native Safeholdian fish species, ranging in length from approximately three feet to just over five.

NEAT—Neural Education and Training machine. The standard means of education in the Terran Federation.

New model—a generic term increasingly applied to the innovations in technology (especially war-fighting technology) introduced by Charis and its allies. *See* New model kraken.

New model kraken—the standardized artillery piece of the Imperial Charisian Navy. It weighs approximately 2.5 tons and fires a 30-pound round shot with a diameter of approximately 5.9 inches. Although it weighs slightly less than the old kraken (*see* above) and its round shot is twelve percent lighter, it is actually longer ranged and fires at a higher velocity because of reductions in windage, improvements in gunpowder, and slightly increased barrel length.

Nynian Rychtair—the Safeholdian equivalent of Helen of Troy, a woman of legendary beauty, born in Siddarmark, who eventually married the Emperor of Harchong.

Offal lizard—a carrion-eating scavenger which fills the niche of an undersized hyena crossed with a jackal. Offal lizards will take small living prey, but they are generally cowardly and are regarded with scorn and contempt by most Safeholdians.

Oil tree—a Safeholdian plant species which grows to an average height of approximately thirty feet. The oil tree produces large, hairy pods which contain many small seeds very rich in natural plant oils. Dr. Pei Shan-wei's terraforming teams genetically modified the plant to increase its oil productivity and to make it safely consumable by human beings. It is cultivated primarily as a food product, but it is also an important source of lubricants. In inland realms, it is also a major source of lamp oil.

Operation Ark—a last-ditch, desperate effort mounted by the Terran Federation to establish a hidden colony beyond the knowledge and reach of the xenophobic Gbaba. It created the human settlement on Safehold.

Pasquale's Basket—a voluntary collection of contributions for the support of the sick, homeless, and indigent. The difference between the amount contributed voluntarily and that required for the Basket's purpose is supposed to be contributed from Mother Church's coffers as a first charge upon tithes received.

Pasquale's Grace—euthanasia. Pasqualate healers are permitted by their vows to end the lives of the terminally ill, but only under tightly defined and stringently limited conditions.

Persimmon fig—a native Safeholdian fruit which is extremely tart and relatively thick-skinned.

Prong lizard—a roughly elk-sized lizard with a single horn which branches into four sharp points in the last third or so of its length. Prong lizards are herbivores and not particularly ferocious.

Proscriptions of Jwo-jeng—the definition of allowable technology under the doctrine of the Church of God Awaiting. Essentially, the Proscriptions limit allowable technology to that which is powered by wind, water, or muscle. The Proscriptions are subject to interpretation by the Order of Schueler, which generally errs on the side of conservatism, but it is not unheard of for corrupt intendants to rule for or against an innovation under the Proscriptions in return for financial compensation.

Rakurai—literally, "lightning bolt." The *Holy Writ*'s term for the kinetic weapons used to destroy the Alexandria Enclave.

Reformist—one associated with the Reformist movement. The majority of Reformists outside the Charisian Empire still regard themselves as Temple Loyalists.

Reformist movement—the movement within the Church of God Awaiting to reform the abuses and corruption which have become increasingly evident (and serious) over the last hundred to one hundred and fifty years. Largely underground and unfocused until the emergence of the Church of Charis, the movement is attracting increasing support throughout Safehold.

Round Theatre—the largest and most famous theater in the city of Tellesberg. Supported by the Crown but independent of it, and renowned not only for the quality of its productions but for its willingness to present works which satirize Charisian society, industry, the aristocracy, and even the Church.

Saint Evehlain—the patron saint of the Abbey of Saint Evehlain in Tellesberg; wife of Saint Zherneau.

Saint Zherneau—the patron saint of the Monastery of Saint Zherneau in Tellesberg; husband of Saint Evehlain.

Sand maggot—a loathsome carnivore, looking much like a six-legged slug, which haunts Safeholdian beaches just above the surf line. Sand maggots do not normally take living prey, although they have no objection to devouring the occasional small creature which strays into their reach. Their natural coloration blends well with their sandy habitat, and they normally conceal themselves by digging their bodies into the sand until they are completely covered, or only a small portion of their backs show.

Sea cow—a walrus-like Safeholdian sea mammal which grows to a body length of approximately ten feet when fully mature.

Sea dragon—the Safeholdian equivalent of a terrestrial whale. There are several species of sea dragon, the largest of which grow to a body length of approximately fifty feet. Like the whale, sea dragons are mammalian. They are insulated against deep oceanic temperatures by thick layers of blubber and are krill-eaters. They reproduce much more rapidly than whales, however, and are the principal food source for doomwhales and large, deepwater krakens. Most species of sea dragon produce the equivalent of sperm oil and spermaceti. A large sea dragon will yield as much as four hundred gallons of oil.

Seijin—sage, holy man, mystic. Legendary warriors and teachers, generally believed to have been touched by the *anshinritsumei*. Many educated Safeholdians consider *seijins* to be mythological, fictitious characters.

Shan-wei's War—the *Holy Writ's* term for the struggle between the supporters of Eric Langhorne and those of Pei Shan-wei over the future of humanity on Safehold. It is presented in terms very similar to those of the war between Lucifer and the angels loyal to God, with Shan-wei in the role of Lucifer. *See also* War Against the Fallen.

Shan-wei's candle—the deliberately challenging name assigned to strike-anywhere matches by Charisians. Later shortened to "Shan-weis."

Slabnut—a flat-sided, thick-hulled nut. Slabnut trees are deciduous, with large, four-lobed leaves, and grow to about thirty feet. Black slabnuts are genetically engineered to be edible by humans; red slabnuts are mildly poisonous. The black slabnut is very high in protein.

Slash lizard—a six-limbed, saurian-looking, furry oviparous mammal. One of the three top land predators of Safehold. Its mouth contains twin rows of fangs capable of punching through chain mail and its feet have four long toes, each tipped with claws up to five or six inches long.

Sleep root—a Safeholdian tree from whose roots an entire family of opiates and painkillers are produced. The term "sleep root" is often used generically for any of those pharmaceutical products.

Slime toad—an amphibious Safeholdian carrion eater with a body length of approximately seven inches. It takes its name from the thick mucus which covers its skin. Its bite is poisonous but seldom results in death.

SNARC—Self-Navigating Autonomous Reconnaissance and Communications platform.

Spider-crab—a native species of sea life, considerably larger than any terrestrial crab. The spider-crab is not a crustacean, but more of a segmented, tough-hided, many-legged seagoing slug. Despite that, its legs are considered a great delicacy and are actually very tasty.

Spider-rat—a native species of vermin which fills roughly the ecological niche of a terrestrial rat. Like all Safeholdian mammals, it is six-limbed, but it looks like a cross between a hairy gila monster and an insect, with long, multijointed legs which actually arch higher than its spine. It is nasty-tempered but basically cowardly. Fully adult male specimens of the larger varieties run to about two feet in body length, with another two feet of tail, for a total length of four feet, but the more common varieties average only between two or three feet of combined body and tail length.

Spike-thorn—a flowering shrub, various subspecies of which are found in most Safeholdian climate zones. Its blossoms come in many colors and hues, and the tropical versions tend to be taller-growing and to bear more delicate blossoms.

Steel thistle—a native Safeholdian plant which looks very much like branching bamboo. The plant bears seed pods filled with small, spiny seeds embedded in fine, straight fibers. The seeds are extremely difficult to remove by hand, but the fiber can be woven into a fabric which is even stronger than cotton silk. It can also be twisted into extremely strong, stretch-resistant rope. Moreover, the plant grows almost as rapidly as actual bamboo, and the yield of raw fiber per acre is 70 percent higher than for terrestrial cotton.

Stone wool—Safeholdian term for chrysotile (white asbestos).

Sugar apple—a tropical Safeholdian fruit tree. The sugar apple has a bright purple skin much like a terrestrial tangerine's, but its fruit has much the same consistency of a terrestrial apple. It has a higher natural sugar content than an apple, however; hence the name.

Surgoi kasai—"dreadful" or "great fire." The true spirit of God. The touch of His divine fire, which only an angel or archangel can endure.

Swivel wolf—a light, primarily anti-personnel artillery piece mounted on a swivel for easy traverse. *See* Wolf.

Teak tree—a native Safeholdian tree whose wood contains concentrations of silica and other minerals. Although it grows to a greater height than the Old Earth teak wood tree and bears a needle-like foliage, its timber is very similar in grain and coloration to the terrestrial tree and, like Old Earth teak, it is extremely resistant to weather, rot, and insects.

Tellesberg Krakens—the Tellesberg professional baseball club.

Temple Loyalist—one who renounces the schism created by the Church of Charis' defiance of the Grand Vicar and Council of Vicars of the Church of God Awaiting. Some Temple Loyalists are also Reformists (see above), but all are united in condemning the schism between Charis and the Temple.

Temple, The—the complex built by "the archangels" using Terran Federation technology to serve as the headquarters of the Church of God Awaiting. It contains many "mystic" capabilities which demonstrate the miraculous power of the archangels to anyone who sees them.

Testimonies, The—by far the most numerous of the Church of God Awaiting's sacred writings, these consist of the firsthand observations of the first few generations of humans on Safehold. They do not have the same status as the Christian gospels, because they do not reveal the central teachings and inspiration of God. Instead, collectively, they form an important substantiation of the *Writ*'s "historical accuracy" and conclusively attest to the fact that the events they describe did, in fact, transpire.

Titan oak—a very slow-growing, long-lived deciduous Safeholdian hardwood which grows to heights of as much as one hundred meters.

War Against the Fallen—the portion of Shan-wei's War falling between the destruction of the Alexandria Enclave and the final reconsolidation of the Church's authority.

Wing warrior—the traditional title of a blooded warrior of one of the Raven Lords clans. It is normally shortened to "wing" when used as a title or an honorific.

Wire vine—a kudzu-like vine native to Safehold. Wire vine isn't as fast-growing as kudzu, but it's equally tenacious, and unlike kudzu, several of its varieties have long, sharp thorns. Unlike many native Safeholdian plant species, it does quite well intermingled with terrestrial imports. It is often used as a sort of combination hedgerow and barbed-wire fence by Safehold farmers.

Wolf—(1) a Safeholdian predator which lives and hunts in packs and has many of the same social characteristics as the terrestrial species of the same name. It is warm-blooded but oviparous and larger than an Old Earth wolf, with adult males averaging betwen two hundred and two hundred and twenty-five pounds.

Wolf—(2) a generic term for shipboard artillery pieces with a bore of less than two inches and a shot weighing one pound or less. They are primarily anti-personnel weapons but can also be effective against boats and small craft.

Wyvern—the Safeholdian ecological analogue of terrestrial birds. There are as many varieties of wyverns as there are birds, including (but not limited to) the homing or messenger wyvern, hunting wyverns suitable for the equivalent of hawking for small prey, the crag wyvern (a flying predator with a wingspan of ten feet), various species of sea wyverns, and the king wyvern (a very large flying predator with a wingspan of up to twenty-five feet). All wyverns have two pairs of wings, and one pair of powerful, clawed legs. The king wyvern has been known to take children as prey when desperate or when the opportunity presents, but they are quite intelligent. They know that humans are a prey best left alone and generally avoid inhabited areas.

Wyvernry—a nesting place or breeding hatchery for domesticated wyverns.

The Archangels:

Archangel	Sphere of Authority	Symbol
Langhorne	law and life	scepter
Bédard	wisdom and knowledge	lamp
Pasquale	healing and medicine	caduceus
Sondheim	agronomy and farming	grain sheaf
Truscott	animal husbandry	horse
Schueler	justice	sword
Jwo-jeng	acceptable technology	flame
Chihiro (1)	history	quill pen
Chihiro (2)	guardian	sword
Andropov	good fortune	dice
Hastings	geography	draftman's compass

Fallen Archangel	Sphere of Authority
Shan-wei	mother of evil/evil ambition
Kau-yung	destruction
Proctor	temptation/forbidden knowledge
Sullivan	gluttony
Ascher	lies
Grimaldi	pestilence
Stavraki	avarice

The Church of God Awaiting's Hierarchy:

Ecclesiastic rank	Distinguishing color	Clerical ring/set
Grand Vicar	dark blue	sapphire with rubies
Vicar	orange	sapphire
Archbishop	white and orange	ruby
Bishop executor	white	ruby
Bishop	white	ruby
Auxiliary bishop	green and white	ruby
Upper-priest	green	plain gold (no stone)
Priest	brown	none
Under-priest	brown	none
Sexton	brown	none

Clergy who do not belong to a specific order wear cassocks entirely in the color of their rank. Auxiliary bishops' cassocks are green with narrow trim bands of white. Archbishops' cassocks are white, but trimmed in orange. Clergy who belong to one of the ecclesiastical orders (see below) wear habits (usually of patterns specific to each order) in the order's colors but with the symbol of their order on the right breast, badged in the color of their priestly rank. In formal vestments, the pattern is reversed; that is, their vestments are in the colors of their priestly ranks and the order's symbol is the color of their order. All members of the clergy habitually wear either cassocks or the habits of their orders. The headgear is a three-cornered "priest's cap" almost identical to the eighteenth century's tricornes. The cap is black for anyone under the rank of vicar. Under-priests' and priests' bear brown cockades. Auxiliary bishops' bear green cockades. Bishops' and bishop executors' bear white cockades. Archbishops' bear white cockades with a broad, dove-tailed orange ribbon at the back. Vicars' priests' caps are of orange with no cockade or ribbon, and the Grand Vicar's cap is white with an orange cockade.

All clergy of the Church of God Awaiting are affiliated with one or more of the great ecclesiastic orders, but not all are *members* of those orders. Or it might, perhaps, be more accurate to say that not all are *full* members of their orders. Every ordained priest is automatically affiliated with the order of the bishop who ordained him and (in theory, at least) owes primary obedience to that order. Only members of the clergy who have taken an order's vows are considered full members or brethren/sisters of that order, however. (Note: there are no female priests in the Church of God Awaiting, but women may attain high ecclesiastic rank in one of the orders.) Only full brethren or sisters of an order may attain to rank within that order, and only members of one of the great orders are eligible for elevation to the vicarate.

The great orders of the Church of God Awaiting, in order of precedence and power, are:

The Order of Schueler, which is primarily concerned with the enforcement of Church doctrine and theology. The Grand Inquisitor, who is automatically a member of the Council of Vicars, is always the head of the Order of Schueler. Schuelerite ascendency within the Church has been steadily increasing for over two hundred years, and the order is clearly the dominant power in the Church hierarchy today. The order's color is purple, and its symbol is a sword.

The Order of Langhorne is technically senior to the Order of Schueler, but has lost its primacy in every practical sense. The Order of Langhorne provides the Church's jurists, and since Church law supersedes secular law throughout Safehold that means all jurists and lawgivers (lawyers) are either members of the order or must be vetted and approved by the order. At one time, that gave the Langhornites unquestioned primacy, but the Schuelerites have relegated the order of Langhorne to a primarily administrative role, and the head of the order lost his mandatory seat on the Council of Vicars several generations back (in the Year of God 810). Needless to say, there's a certain tension between the Schuelerites and the Langhornites. The Order of Langhorne's color is black, and its symbol is a scepter.

The Order of Bédard has undergone the most change of any of the original great orders of the Church. Originally, the Inquisition came out of the Bédardists, but that function was effectively resigned to the Schuelerites by the Bédardists themselves when Saint Greyghor's reforms converted the order into the primary teaching order of the church. Today, the Bédardists are philosophers and educators, both at the university level and among the peasantry, although they also retain their function as Safehold's mental health experts and councilors. The order is also involved in caring for the poor and indigent. Ironically, perhaps, given the role of the "Archangel Bédard" in the creation of the Church of God Awaiting, a large percentage of Reformist clergy springs from this order. Like the Schuelerites, the head of the Order of Bédard always holds a seat on the Council of Vicars. The order's color is white, and its symbol is an oil lamp.

The Order of Chihiro is unique in that it has two separate functions and is divided into two separate orders. The Order of the Quill is responsible for training and overseeing the Church's scribes, historians, and bureaucrats. It is responsible for the archives of the Church and all of its official documents.

The Order of the Sword is a militant order which often cooperates closely with the Schuelerites and the Inquisition. It is the source of the officer corps for the Temple Guard and also for most officers of the Temple Lands' nominally secular army and navy. Its head is always a member of the Council of Vicars, as Captain General of the Church of God Awaiting, and generally fulfills the role of Secretary of War. The order's color is blue, and its symbol is a quill pen. The Order of the Sword shows the quill pen, but crossed with a sheathed sword.

The Order of Pasquale is another powerful and influential order of the Church. Like the Order of Bédard, the Pasqualates are a teaching order, but their area of specialization is healing and medicine. They turn out very well-trained surgeons, but they are blinkered against pursuing any germ theory of medicine because of their religious teachings. All licensed healers on Safehold must be examined and approved by the Order of Pasquale, and the order is deeply involved in public hygiene policies and (less deeply) in caring for the poor and indigent. The majority of Safeholdian hospitals are associated, to at least some degree, with the Order of Pasquale. The head of the Order of Pasquale is normally, but not always, a member of the Council of Vicars. The order's color is green, and its symbol is a caduceus.

The Order of Sondheim and the Order of Truscott are generally considered "brother orders" and are similar to the Order of Pasquale, but deal with agronomy and animal husbandry respectively. Both are teaching orders and they are jointly and deeply involved in Safehold's agriculture and food production. The teachings of the Archangel Sondheim and Archangel Truscott incorporated into the *Holy Writ* were key elements in the ongoing terraforming of Safehold following the general abandonment of advanced technology. Both of these orders lost their mandatory seats on the Council of Vicars over two hundred years ago, however. The Order of Sondheim's color is brown and its symbol is a sheaf of grain; the Order of Truscott's color is brown trimmed in *green*, and its symbol is a horse.

The Order of Hastings is the most junior (and least powerful) of the current great orders. The order is a teaching order, like the Orders of Sondheim and Truscott, and produces the vast majority of Safehold's cartographers and surveyors. Hastingites also provide most of Safehold's officially sanctioned astronomers, although they are firmly within what might be considered the Ptolemaic theory of the universe. The order's "color" is actually a checkered pattern of green, brown, and blue, representing vegetation, earth, and water. Its symbol is a compass.

The Order of Jwo-jeng, once one of the four greatest orders of the Church, was absorbed into the Order of Schueler in Year of God 650, at the same time the Grand Inquisitorship was vested in the Schuelerites. Since that time, the Order of Jwo-jeng has had no independent existence.

The Order of Andropov occupies a sort of middle ground or gray area between the great orders of the Church and the minor orders. According to the *Holy Writ*, Andropov was one of the leading archangels during the war against Shan-wei and the Fallen, but he was always more lighthearted (one hesitates to say frivolous) than his companions. His order has definite epicurean tendencies, which have traditionally been accepted by the Church because its raffles, casinos, horse and/or lizard races, etc., raise a great deal of money for charitable causes. Virtually every bookie on Safehold is either a member of Andropov's order or at least regards the Archangel as his patron. Needless to say, the Order of Andropov is not guaranteed a seat on the Council of Vicars. The order's color is red, and its symbol is a pair of dice.

▼ ▼ ▼

In addition to the above ecclesiastical orders, there are a great many minor orders: mendicant orders, nursing orders (usually but not always associated with the Order of Pasquale), charitable orders (usually but not always associated with the Order of Bédard or the Order of Pasquale), ascetic orders, etc. All of the great orders maintain numerous monasteries and convents, as do many of the lesser orders. Members of minor orders may not become vicars unless they are also members of one of the great orders.